ADVANCED ACCOUNTING

Prin. Dr. Kishor N. Jagtap

Dr. Sunil D. Zagade

Dr. Haribhau M. Jare

Prof. N. K. Aher

Diamond Publications

ADVANCED ACCOUNTING

Prin. Dr. Kishor N. Jagtap, Dr. Sunil D. Zagade
Dr. Haribhau M. Jare, Prof. N. K. Aher

First Edition : June 2015

ISBN : 978-81-8483-620-2

Type Setting :
Diamond Publications

Cover Page :
Sham Bhalekar

Published by :
Diamond Publications
264/3 Shaniwar Peth, 302 Anugrah Apartment
Near Omkareshwar Temple, Pune - 411 030
☎ 020-24452387, 24466642

info@diamondbookspune.com
www.diamondbookspune.com

Sole Distributor :
Diamond Book Depot
661 Narayan Peth
Appa Balwant Chowk
Pune 411 030
Tel. - 24480677, 66020282

PREFACE

It is a matter of great pleasure for us to present this book to our esteemed readers and students. This book has been designed as standard text on 'Advanced Accounting' for Third Year B. Com.

This book comprehensively covers the entire syllabus of T. Y. B. Com. Course of University of Pune w. e. f. June-2015. It has been written to meet the requirement of students. The special features of the book are :

- Full coverage of the revised syllabus.
- Chapter outline at the beginning of each chapter to give a bird's eye view of the topics covered in the chapter.
- Point wise explanation of each topic in the chapter.
- Topics are logically arranged in numbered paragraphs exactly according to the modified syllabus.
- Proposed questions at the end of each chapter.
- Extensive use of diagrams, tables and various forms to give visual view of key concepts and techniques.
- Conversional, lucid and simple language.

Every effort has been made to provide the readers with most up-to-date and authentic material on the subject.

We are very grateful to our publisher Mr. Dattatray Pashte of Diamond Publication, Pune who have rendered all possible assistance in bringing out this book. We wish to acknowledge our deep gratitude to staff who have assisted and helped us in preparing this book.

We will consider our efforts amply rewarded in case the book proves useful to the students and Faculty Members of the subject.

Suggestions of readers are welcome and shall be acknowledged with gratitude.

With best wishes.

Prin. Dr. Kishor N. Jagtap
Dr. Sunil D. Zagade
Dr. Haribhau M. Jare
Prof. N. K. Aher

1   Accounting Standards And Financial Reporting (IFRS)

Introduction :

Accounting standards constitute policy procedures and accounting rules focusing on valuation, disclosure and measurement. Accounting Standards are issued by the Accounting standards Board established by The Institute of Chartered Accountants of India (ICAI). Accounting standards acts as a conflict resolving device among different accounting practices and provides a sounds framework for ideal accounting methods suitable for various types of businesses.

1.1 Accounting Stardard on Cash Flow Statements - 3 (AS - 3) :

Following are the salient features of the Revised Accounting Standard 3 (AS 3 Revised) Cash Flow Statements, issued by the Council of the Institute of Chartered Accounts of India. This Standard supersedes AS 3, Changes in Financial Position, issued in June, 1981.

The standard has been made mandatory w.e.f. accounting periods commencing on or after 1 st April 2001, in respect of the following :

    (i)   Enterprises whose debt or equity securities are listed or to be listed on a recognised stock exchange in India, and

    (ii) All other commercial, business or industrial enterprises whose turnover for the accounting period exceeds Rs. 50 crores.

1. Objectives

Information about the cash flows of an enterprise is useful in providing users of financial statement with a basis to assess the ability of the enterprise to generate cash and cash equivalents and the needs of the enterprise to utilise those cash flows. The economic decisions that are taken by users require an evaluation of the ability of an enterprise to generate cash and cash equivalents and the timing and certainty of their generation.

The Statement deals with provision of information about the historical changes in cash and cash equivalents of an enterprise by means of a cash flow statement which classifies cash flows during the period from operating, investing and financial activities.

2. Scope

1. An enterprise should prepare a cash flow statement and should present it for each period for which financial statements are presented.

2. Users of an enterprise's financial statements are interested in how the enterprise generates and uses cash and equivalents. This is the case regardless of the nature of the enterprise's activities and irrespective of whether cash can be viewed as the product of the enterprise, as may be the case with a financial enterprise. Enterprises need cash for essentially the same reasons, however different their principal revenue-producing activities might be. They need cash to conduct their operations, to pay their obligations, and to provide returns to their investors.

3. Benefits of Cash Flow Information

1. A cash flow statement, when used in conjunction with the other financial statements, provides information that enables users to evaluate the changes in net assets of an enterprise, its financial structure (including its liquidity and solvency), and its ability to affect the amounts and timing of cash flows in order to adapt to changing circumstances and opportunities. Cash flow information is useful in assessing the ability of the enterprise to generate cash and cash equivalents and enables users to develop models to assess and compare the present value of the future cash flows of different enterprises.

2. It also enhances the comparability of the reporting of operating performance by different enterprises because it eliminates the effects of using different accounting

treatment for the same transactions and events.

3. Historical cash flow information is often used as an indicator of the amount, timing and certainty of future cash flows. It is also useful in checking the accuracy of past assessments of future cash flows and in examining the relationship between profitability and net cash flow and the impact of changing prices.

4. Definitions

The following terms are used in this Statement with the meanings specified: (1) Cash comprises cash on hand and demand deposits with banks. (2) Cash equivalents are short-term, highly liquid investments that are readily convertible into known amounts of cash and which are subject to an insignificant risk of changes in value. (3) Cash flows are inflows and outflows of cash and cash equivalents. (4) Operating activities are the principal revenue-producing activities of the enterprise and other activities that are not investing or financing activities. (5) Investing activities are the acquisition and disposal of long-term assets and other investments not included in cash equivalents. (6) Financing activities are activities that result in changes in the size and composition of the owner's capital (including preference share capital in the case of a company) and borrowings of the enterprise.

5. Presentation of a Cash Flow Statement

The cash flow statement should report cash flows during the period classified by operating, investing and financing activities.

(1) Operating Activities : Cash flows from operating activities are primarily derived from the principal revenue-producing activities of the enterprise. Therefore, they generally result from the transactions and other events that enter into the determination of net profit or loss. Examples of cash flows from operating activities are: (a) Cash receipts from the sale of goods and the rendering of services; (b) Cash receipt from royalties, fees, commissions and other revenue; (c) Cash payments to suppliers for goods and services; (d) Cash payments to and on behalf of employees;

(2) Investing Activities : Examples of cash flows arising from investing activities are:
(a) Cash payments to acquire fixed assets (including intangibles). These payments include those relating to capitalised research and development costs and self-constructed fixed assets;
(b) Cash receipts from disposal of fixed assets (including intangibles);
(c) Cash payments to instruments of other enterprises and interests in joint ventures (other than payments for those instruments considered to be cash equivalents and those held for dealing or trading purposes);
(d) Cash receipts from disposal of shares, warrants, or debt instruments of other enterprises and interests in joint venture (other than receipts from those instruments considered to be cash equivalents and those held for dealing or trading purposes);
(e) Cash advances and loans made to third parties (other than advances and loans made by a financial enterprise);
(f) Cash receipts from the repayment of advances and loans made to third parties (other than advances and loans of a financial enterprise);

(g) Cash payments for futures contracts, forward contracts, option contracts, and swap contracts except when the contracts are held for dealing or trading purpose, or the payments are classified as financing activities.

(3) Financing Activities : Examples of cash flows arising from financing activities are:

(a) Cash proceeds from issuing shares or other similar instruments;

(b) Cash proceeds from issuing debentures, loans, notes, bonds and other short or long-term borrowing; and

(c) Cash repayments of amounts borrowed.

(4) Reporting Cash Flows from Operating Activities

(1) An enterprise should report cash flows from operating activities using either.

    (a) The direct method, whereby major classes of gross cash receipts and gross cash payments are disclosed; or

    (b) The indirect method, whereby net profit or loss is adjusted for the effects of transactions of a non-cash nature, any deferrals or accruals of past or future operating cash receipts or payments, and items of income or expense associated with investing or financing cash flows.

(2) The direct method provides information which may be useful in estimating future cash flows and which is not available under the indirect method and is, therefore, considered more appropriate than the indirect method. Under the direct method, information about major classes of gross cash receipts and gross cash payments may be obtained either :

    (a) from adjusting sales, cost of sales (interest and similar income and interest expense and similar charges for a financial enterprise) and other items in the statement of profit and loss for:

        (i) changes during the period in inventories and operating receivables and payables;

        (ii) other non-cash items; and

        (iii) other items for which the cash effects are investing or financing cash flows.

(3) Under the indirect method, the net cash flow from operating activities is determined by adjusting net profit or loss for the effects of:

    (a) changes during the period in inventories and operating receivables and payables;

    (b) non-cash items such as depreciation, provisions, deferred taxes, and unrealised foreign exchange gains and losses; and

    (c) all other items for which the cash effects are investing or financing cash flows.

(4) Alternatively, the net cash flow operating activities may be presented under the indirect method by showing the operating revenues and expenses, excluding non-cash items disclosed in the statement of profit and loss and the changes during the period in inventories and operating receivables and payables.

(5) Reporting Cash flows from Investing and Financing Activities : An enterprise should report separately major classes of gross cash receipts and gross cash payments arising from investing and financing activities, except to the extent that cash flows described in Paragraph (6) are reported on a net basis.

(6) Reporting Cash Flows on a Net Basis

(1) Cash flows arising from the following operating, investing on financing activities may be reported on a net basis:

   (a) Cash receipts and payments on behalf of customers when the cash flows reflect activities of the customer rather than those of the enterprise,

   Example of cash receipts and payments referred to above are :

   (i)   the acceptance and repayment of demand deposits by a bank ;

   (ii) funds held for customers by an investment enterprise; and

   (iii) rents collected on behalf of, and paid over to, the owners of properties.

   (b) Cash receipts and payments for items in which the turnover is quick, the amounts are large, and the maturities are short.

   Examples of cash receipts and payments referred to above are advances made for, and the repayments of:

   (i)   principal amounts relating to credit card customers;

   (ii) the purchases and sales of investments; and

   (iii) other short-term borrowings, for example those which have a maturity period of three months or less.

(2) Cash flows arising from each of the following activities of a financial enterprise may be reported on a net basis :

   (a) cash receipts and payments for the acceptance and repayment of deposits with a fixed maturity date;

   (b) the placement of deposits with and withdrawal of deposits from other financial enterprises; and

   (c) cash advances and loans made to customers and the repayments of the those advances and loans.

(7) Foreign Currency Cash Flows : Cash flows arising from transactions in a foreign currency should be recorded in an enterprise's reporting currency by applying to the foreign currency amount the exchange rate between the reporting currency and the foreign currency at the date of the cash flow. A rate that approximates the actual rate may be used if the result is substantially the same as would arise if the rates at the dates of the cash flows were used. The effect of changes ia exchange rates on cash and cash equivalents held in a foreign currency should be reported as a separate part of the reconciliation of the changes in cash and cash equivalents during the period.

(8) Extraordinary Items : The cash flows associated with extraordinary items should be classified as arising from operating, investing or financing activities as appropriate and separately disclosed.

(9) Interest and Dividends : Cash flows from interest and dividends received and paid should each be disclosed separately. Cash flows arising from interest paid and interest and dividends received in the case of a financial enterprise should be classified as cash flows arising from operating activities. In the case of other enterprises, cash flows arising from interest paid should be classified as cash flows from financing activities while interest and dividends received should be classified as cash flows from investing activities. Dividends paid should be classified as cash flows from financing activities.

(10) Taxes on Income : Cash flows arising from taxes on income should be separately disclosed and should be classified as cash flows from operating activities unless they can be specifically identified with financing and investing activities.

(11) Investments in Subsidiaries, Associates, and Joint Ventures : When accounting for an investment in an associate or a subsidiary or a joint venture, an investor restricts its reporting in the cash flow statement to the cash flows between itself and the investee/joint venture, for example, cash flows relating to dividends and advances.

(12) Acquisitions and Disposals of Subsidiaries and other Business Units :
(1) The aggregate cash flows arising from acquisitions and from disposals of subsidiaries or other business units should be presented separately and classified as investing activities.
(2) An enterprise should disclose, in aggregate, in respect of both acquisition and disposal of subsidiaries or other business units during the period each of the following :
(a) the total purchase or disposal consideration ; and
(b) the portion of the purchase or disposal consideration discharged by means of cash and cash equivalents.

(13) Non-cash Transactions : Investing and financing transactions that do not require the use of cash or cash equivalents should be excluded from a cash flow statement. Such transactions should be disclosed elsewhere in the financial statements in a way that provides all the relevant information about these investing and financing activities.

(14) Disclosure

(1) Components of cash and cash equivalents : An enterprise should disclose the components of cash and cash equivalent and should present a reconciliation of the amounts in its cash flow statement with the equivalent items reported in the balance sheet.

(2) Other Disclosures : An enterprise should disclose, together with a commentary by management, the amount of significant cash and cash equivalent balances held by the enterprise that are not available for use by it.

1.2 Accounting Stardard - 7 (AS - 7)

Accounting for Construction Contracts

The salient features of AS: 7 are as follows:
1. In accounting for construction contracts in financial statements, either the percentage of completion method or the completed contract method may be used. When a contractor uses a particular method of accounting for a contract, then the same method

should be adopted for all other contracts which meet similar criteria.

2. The percentage of completion method can be used if the outcome of the contract can be reliably estimated.

   (a) In the case of fixed price contracts, this degree of reliability would be provided if the following conditions are satisfied:

      (i) total contract revenues to be received can be reliably estimated.

      (ii) both the costs to complete the contract and the stage of contract performance completed at the reporting date can be reasonably estimated; and

      (iii) the costs attributable to the contract can be clearly identified so that actual expenditure can be compared with prior estimates.

   (b) Profit in the case of fixed price contracts normally should not be recognised unless the work on a contract has progressed to a reasonable extent.

   (c) In the case of cost plus contracts, this degree of reliability would be provided only if both the following conditions are satisfied:

      (i) Costs attributable to the contract can be clearly identified; and

      (ii) costs other than those that are specifically reimbursable under the contract can be reliably estimated.

   (d) While recognising the profit under percentage of completion method, an appropriate allowance for future enforceable factors should be made on either a specific or a percentage basis.

3. The costs included in the amount at which construction contract work is stated should comprise those costs that relate directly to a specific contract and those that are attributable to the contract activity in general and can be allocated to specific contracts.

4. A foreseeable loss on the entire contract should be provided for in the financial statements irrespective of the amount of work done and the method of accounting followed.

5. There should be disclosure in the financial statements of:

   (i) the amount of construction work-in-progress;

   (ii) progress payments received and auvances and retentions on account of contracts included in construction work-in-progress; and

   (iii) the amount receivable in respect of income accrued under cost plus contracts not included in construction work-in-progress.

      If both the percentage of completion method and the completed contract method are simultaneously used by the contractor, the amount of contract work described in (i) above should be analysed to disclose separately, the amounts attributable to contracts accounted for under each method.

6. Disclosure of changes in an accounting policy used for construction contracts should be made in the financial statements giving the effect of the change and its amount. However, if a contractor changes from the percentage of completion method to the

completed contract method for contracts-in-progress at the beginning of the year, it may not be possible to quantify the effect of the changes. In such cases, disclosure should be made of the amount of attributable profits reported in prior years in respect of contracts-in-progress at the beginning of the accounting period..

The standard has become mandatory in respect of accounts for the period commencing on or after 1-4-1991.

1.3 Accounting Standard - 8 (AS - 8) (Withdrawn and Included in As 26)

Accounting for Research and Development

The salient features of AS: 8 are as follows:

1. Research and development costs should include:
   (i) salaries, wages and other related costs of personnel engaged in research and development;
   (ii) depreciation of building, equipment and facilities which have alternative economic use, to the extent they are used for research and development;
   (iii) an appropriate amortisation of the cost of building, equipment and facilities which have no alternative economic use, to the extent they are used for research and development;
   (iv) overhead costs related to research and development; and
   (v) payment to outside bodies for research and development projects related to the enterprise.

2. Amount of research and development cost described in paragraph 1 should be charged as an expense of the period in which they are incurred except where such costs may be deferred in accordance with paragraph 3.

3. Research and development costs of project may be deferred to future periods if the following criteria are satisfied :
   (i) The-product or process is clearly defined and the costs attributable to the product or process can be separately identified:
   (ii) the technical feasibility of the product or process has been demonstrated;
   (iii) the management of the enterprise has indicated its intention to produce and market, or use, the product or process;
   (iv) there is a reasonable indication that current and future research and development costs to be incurred on the project together with expected production, selling and administration costs are likely to be more than covered by related future revenues/benefits; and
   (v) adequate resources exist, or are reasonably expected to be available, to complete the project and market the product or process.

4. Wherever research and developments are deferred, the appropriate legal requirements should also be taken into account.

5. If an accounting policy of deferral of research and development costs is adopted, it should be applied to all such projects that meet the criteria in paragraph 1, given above.
6. If research and development costs of a project are deferred, they should be allocated on a systematic basis to future accounting periods by reference either to the sale or use of the product or process to the time period over which the product or process is expected to be sold or used.
7. The deferred research and development costs of a project should be reviewed at the end of each accounting period. When the criteria of paragraph 3, which previously justified the deferral of the costs, no longer apply, the unamortised balance should be charged as an expense immediately, When the criteria for deferral continue to be met but the amount of unamortised balance of the deferred research and development costs and other relevant costs exceed the expected future revenues/benefits related thereto, such expenses should be charged as an expense immediately.
8. Research and development costs once written off should not be reinstated even though the uncertainties which had led to their being written off no longer exist.
9. The total of research and development costs, including the amortised portion of deferred costs, charged as expense should be disclosed in the Profit and Loss Account for the period.
10. Deferred research and development expenditure should be separately disclosed in the balance sheet under the head "Miscellaneous Expenditure."
    This standard has become mandatory in respect of account for periods commencing on or after 1-4-1991.

1.4 Accounting Standard - 12 (AS - 12)

"Accounting for Government Grants"

The Council of the Institute of Chartered Accountants of India has issued .-AS 12: Accounting for Government Grants. The standard has come into effect in respect of accounting periods commencing on or after the 1st April 1992. It was recommendatory in nature for initial period of two years. The standard has become mandatory in respect of accounts for periods commencing on or after the 1st April, 1994.

The salient features of AS-12 are as follows:

1. Introduction : This standard deals with accounting for government grants. Government grants are sometimes, called by other names such as subsidies, cash incentives, duty drawbacks, etc.

2. Definitions : The following terms are used in this Standard with the meanings specified:
(i)   Government refers to government, government agencies and similar bodies whether local, national or international.
(ii) Government grants are assistance by government in cash or kind to an enterprise for past or future compliance with certain conditions. They exclude those forms of

government assistance which cannot reasonably have a value placed upon them and transactions with government which cannot be distinguished from the normal trading transactions of the enterprise.

3. Accounting Treatment : Two broad approaches may be followed for the accounting treatment of government grants: the 'capital approach', under which a grant is treated as part of shareholders' funds, and the 'income approach', under which a grant is taken to income over one or more periods.

It is generally considered appropriate that accounting for government grant would be based on the nature of the relevant grant. Grants which have the characteristics similar to those of promoter's contribution should be treated as part of shareholders' funds. Income approach may be more appropriate in the case of other grants.

4. Recognition of Government Grants : Government grants available to the enterprise are considered for inclusion in accounts only when the following conditions are satisfied:

(i)   Where there is reasonable assurance that the enterprise will comply with the conditions attached to them; and

(ii) Where such benefits have been earned by the enterprise and it is reasonably certain that the ultimate collection will be made.

Mere receipt of a grant is not necessarily a conclusive evidence that conditions attaching to the grant have been or will be fulfilled.

5. Presentation of Government Grants related to Specific Fixed Assets : Grants related to specific fixed assets are government grants whose primary condition is that an enterprise qualifying for them should purchase, construct or otherwise acquire such assets. Other conditions may also be attached restricting the type or location of the assets of the periods during which they are to be acquired or held.

Government grants related to specific fixed assets should be presented in the balance sheet by showing the grant as a deduction from the gross value of the assets concerned in arriving at their book value. Where the grant related to a specific fixed asset equals the whole, or virtually the whole, of the cost of the asset, the asset should be shown in the balance sheet at a nominal value. Alternatively, government grants related to depreciable fixed assets may be treated as deferred income which should be recognised in the profit and loss statement on a systematic and rational basis over the useful life of the asset, i.e., such grants should be allocated to income over the periods and in the proportions in which depreciation on those assets is charged. Grants related to nondepreciable assets should be credited to capital reserve under this method. However, if a grant related to a non-depreciable asset requires the fulfilment of certain obligations, the grants should be credited to income over the same period over which the cost of meeting such; obligations is charged to income. The deferred income balance should bf separately disclosed in the financial statements.

6. Presentation of Government Grants related to Revenue : Government grants related to revenue should be recognised on a systematic basis in the Profit & Loss Statement over the periods necessary to match them with the related costs which they are intended to compensate.

Such grants should either be shown separately under 'other income' or deducted in reporting the related expense.

7. Presentation of Government Grants of the nature of Promoter's Contribution : These are grants which are given with reference to the total investment in an undertaking or by way of contribution towards its total capital outlay (e.g. Central Investment Subsidy Scheme). No repayment is ordinarily expected in respect of such grants. Government grants of the nature of promoter's contribution should be credited to capital reserve and treated as a part of shareholders' funds.

8. Non-Monetary Government Grants : These are the grants which take the form of non-monetary assets such as land or other resources given at concessional rates. These grants should be accounted for by recording the assets so acquired at their acquisition costs. If a non-monetary asset is given free of cost, it should be recorded at a nominal value.

9. Government grants as Compensation for Expenses or Losses : Government grants that are receivable as compensation for expenses or losses incurred in a previous accounting period or for the purpose of giving immediate financial support to the enterprise with no further related costs, should be recognised and disclosed in the profit and loss statement of the period in which they are receivable, as an extraordinary item, if appropriate. [Accounting Standard (AS) 6: Prior Period and Extraordinary Items and Changes in Accounting Policies].

10. Contingency as to Government Grant : A contingency related to a government grant, arising after the grant has been recognised, should be treated in accordance with Accounting Standard (AS) 4: Contingencies and Events Occurring After the Balance Sheet Date.

11. Refund of Government Grants, (a) Government grants sometimes become refundable because certain conditions are not fulfilled. Such grants that become refundable should be accounted for as an extraordinary item.(Refer Accounting Standard (AS) 5: Prior Period and Extraordinary Items and Changes in Accounting Policies).

(b) The amount refundable in respect of a grant related to revenue should be applied first against any unamortised credit remaining in respect of the grant. To the extent that the amount refundable exceeds any such deferred credit, or where no deferred credit exists, the amount should be charged to Profit & Loss Statement. The amount refundable in respect of a grant related to a specific fixed asset should be recorded by increasing the book value of the asset or by reducing the capital reserve or the deferred income balance, as appropriate, by the amount refundable. In the first alternative, i.e., where the book value of the asset is increased, depreciation on the revised book value should be provided prospectively over the residual useful life of the asset. Government grants in the nature of promoters' contribution that becomes refundable should be reduced from the capital reserve.

12. Disclosure. The following disclosures are to be made:,
(i) This accounting policy adopted for government grants, including the methods of presentation in the financial statements: and

(ii) The nature and extent of government grant recognised in the financial statements, including grants of non-monetary assets given at a concessional rate or free of cost.

1.5 Accounting Standard - 15 (AS - 15)

Accounting for Retirement Benefits in the Financial Statement of Employers1

The following are the salient features of Accounting Standard 15 (AS: 15), "Accounting for Retirement Benefits in the Financial Statements of Employers", issued by the Council of the Institute of Chartered Accountants of India.

The Standard has come into effect in respect of accounting periods commencing on or after 1.4.1995 and is of mandatory nature.

1. Introduction : Retirement benefits usually consist of:
(a) Provident fund,
(b) Superannuation/pension,
(c) Gratuity,
(d) Leave encashment benefit on retirement,
(e) Post-retirement health and welfare schemes, and
(f) Other retirement benefits.

2. Definitions :
(i) Retirement benefit schemes are arrangements to provide provident fund, superannuation or pension, gratuity, or other benefits to employees on leaving service or retiring or, after an employee's death, to his or her dependants.
(ii) Defined contribution schemes are retirement benefit schemes under which amounts to be paid as retirement benefits are determined by contributions to a fund together with earnings thereon.
(iii) Defined benefit schemes are retirement benefit schemes under which amounts to be paid as retirement benefits are determinable usually by reference to employee's earnings and/or years of service.
(iv) Actuary means an actuary within the meaning of sub-section (1) of Section (2) of the Insurance Act, 1938.
(v) Actuarial valuation is the process used by an actuary to estimate the present value of benefits to be paid under a retirement benefit scheme and the present values of the scheme assets, land, sometimes, of future contributions.
(vi) Pay-as-you-go is a method of recognising the cost of retirement benefits only at the time payments are made to employees on, or after, their retirement.

3. Accounting Standard

(i) In respect of retirement benefits in the form of provident fund and other defined contribution schemes, the contributidn payable by the employer for a year should be charged to the statement of profit and loss for the year. Thus, besides the amount of contribution paid, a shortfall of the amount of contribution paid compared to the amount payable for the year should also be charged to the statement of profit and loss for the year. On the other hand, if contribution paid is in excess of the amount payable for the year, the excess should be treated as a pre-payment.

(ii) In respect of gratuity benefit and other defined benefit schemes, the accounting treatment will depend on the type of arrangement which the employer has chosen to make.

(a) If the employer has chosen to make payment for retirement benefits out of his own funds, an appropriate charge to the statement of profit and loss for the year should be made through a provision for the accruing liability. The accruing liability should be calculated according to actuarial valuation. However, those enterprises which employ only a few persons may calculate the accrued liability by reference to any other rational method, e.g., a method based on the assumption that such benefits are payable to all employees at the end of the accounting year.

(b) In case the liability for retirement benefits is funded through creation of a trust, the cost incurred for the year should be determined actuarially. Such actuarial valuation should normally be conducted at least once in every three years. However, where the actuarial valuations are not conducted annually, the actuarial report should specify the contributions to be made by the employer on annual basis during the inter-valuation period.

The annual contribution (which is in addition to the contribution that may be required to finance unfunded past service cost) reflects proper accrual of retirement benefit cost for each of the years during the inter-valuation period and should be charged to the statement of profit and loss for each such year. Where the contribution paid during a year is lower than the amount required to be contributed during the year to meet the accrued liability as certified by the actuary, the shortfall should be charged to the statement of profit and loss for the year. Where the contribution during a year is in excess of the amount required to be contributed during the year to meet the accrued liability as by the actuary, the excess should be treated as a pre-payment.

(c) In case the liability for retirement benefits is funded through a scheme administered by an insurer, an actuarial certificate or a confirmation from the insurer should be obtained that the contribution payable to the insurer is the appropriate accrual of the liability for the year. Where the contribution paid during a year is lower than the amount required to be contributed during the year to meet the accrued liability, as certified by the actuary or confirmed by the insurer, as the case may be, the shortfall should be charged to the statement of excess of the amount required to be contributed during the year to meet the accrued liability as certified by the actuary or confirmed by the insurer, as the case may be, the excess should be treated as a pre-payment.

(iii) Any alterations in the retirement benefit costs arising from -

(a) introduction of a retirement benefit scheme for existing employees or making of improvements to an existing scheme or

(b) changes in the actuarial method used or assumptions adopted, should be charged or credited to the statement of profit and loss as they arise in accordance with Accounting Standard-5 (AS-5), "Prior Period in Extraordinary Items and Changes in Accounting Policies".

Additionally, a change in the actuarial method used should be treated as a change in an accounting policy and disclosed in accordance with Accounting Standard (AS-5) "Prior Period and Extraordinary items and Changes in Accounting Policies."

(iv) When a retirement benefit scheme is amended with the result that additional benefits are provided to retired employees, the cost of the additional benefits should be accounted for in accordance with paragraph (iii) given above.

4. Disclosures : The financial statements should disclose the method by which retirement benefit costs for the period have been determined . In case the costs related to gratuity and other defined benefit schemes are based on an actuarial valuation, the financial statements should also disclose whether the actuarial valuation was made at the end of the period or at an earlier date. In the latter case, the date of the actuarial valuation should be specified and the method by which the accrual for the period has been determined should also be briefly described, if the same is not based on the report of the actuary.

1.6 Accounting Standard - 17 (AS - 17)

Segment Reporting

(In this Accounting Standard, the standard portions have been set in **bold italic** type. These should be read in the context of the background material which has been set in normal type, and in the context of the 'Preface to the Statements of Accounting Standards'.[1])

The following is the text of Accounting Standard 17, 'Segment Reporting', issued by the Council of the Institute of Chartered Accountants of India. This Standard comes into effect in respect of accounting periods commencing on or after 1.4.2001 and is mandatory in nature,[2] from that date, in respect of the following :

(i) Enterprises whose equity or debt securities are listed on a recognised stock exchange in India, and enterprises that are in the process of issuing equity or debt securities that will be listed on a recognised stock exchange in India as evidenced by the board of directors' resolution in this regard.

(ii) All other commercial, industrial and business reporting enterprises, whose turnover for the accounting period exceeds Rs. 50 crores.

Objective

The objective of this Statement is to establish principles for reporting financial information, about the different types of products and services an enterprise produces and the different geographical areas in which it operates. Such information helps users of financial statements :

---

1. Attention is specifically drawn to paragraph 4.3 of the Preface, according to which accounting standards are intended to apply only to material items.
2. This implies that, while discharging their attest function, it will be the duty of the members of the Institute to examine whether this Accounting Standard is complied with in the presentation of financial statements covered by their audit. In the event of any deviation from this Accounting Standard, it will be their duty to make adequate disclosures in their audit reports so that the users of financial statements may be aware of such deviations.

(a)   better understand the performance of the enterprise;

(b)   better assess the risks and returns of the enterprise; and

(c)   make more informed judgements about the enterprise as a whole.

Many enterprises provide groups of products and services or operate in geographical areas that are subject to differing rates of profitability, opportunities for growth, future prospects, and risks. Information about different types of products and services of an enterprise and its operations in different geographical areas — often called segment information — is relevant to assessing the risks and returns of a diversified or multi-locatipnal enterprise but may not be determinable from the aggregated data. Therefore, reporting of segment information is widely regarded as necessary for meeting the needs of users of financial statements.

Scope

1.   This Statement should be applied in presenting general purpose financial statements.

2.   The requirements of this Statement are also applicable in case of consolidated financial statements.[1]

3.   An enterprise should comply with the requirements of this Statement fully and not selectively.

4.   If a single financial report contains both consolidated financial statements and the separate financial statements of the parent company, segment information need be presented only on the basis of the consolidated financial statements. In the context of reporting of segment information in consolidated financial statements, the references in this Statement to any financial statement items should be construed to be the relevant item as appearing in the consolidated financial statements.

Definitions

5.   The following terms are used in this Statement with the meanings specified :

A business segment is a distinguishable component of an enterprise that is engaged in providing an individual product or service or a group of related products or services and that is subject to risks and returns that are different from those of other business segments. Factors that should be considered in determining whether products or services are related include :

(a)   the nature of the products or services;

(b)   the nature of the production processes;

(c)   the type or class of customers for the products or services;

(d)   the methods used to distribute the products or provide the services; and

(e)   if applicable, the nature of the regulatory environment, for example, banking, insurance, or public utilities.

A geographical segment is a distinguishable component of an enterprise that is engaged in providing products or services within a particular economic environment and that is subject

---

1.   A separate accounting standard on 'Consolidated Financial Statements', which is being formulated, will specify the requirements relating to consolidated financial statements.

to risks and returns that are different from those of components operating in other economic environments. Factors that should be considered in identifying geographical segments include :

(a) similarity of economic and political conditions;

(b) relationships between operations in different geographical areas;

(c) proximity of operations;

(d) special risks associated with operations in a particular area;

(e) exchange control regulations; and

(f) the underlying currency risks.

A reportable segment is a business segment or a geographical segment identified on the basis of foregoing definitions for which segment information is required to be disclosed by this Statement.

Enterprise revenue is revenue from sales to external customers as reported in the statement of profit and loss.

Segment revenue is the aggregate of

(i) the portion of enterprise revenue that is directly attributable to a segment,

(ii) the relevant portion of entrprise revenue that can be allocated on a reasonable basis to a segment, and

(iii) revenue from transactions with other segments of the enterprise.

Segment revenue does not include

(a) extraordinary items as defined in AS 5, Net Profit or Loss for the Period, Prior Period Items and Changes in Accounting Policies;

(b) interest or dividend income, including interest earned on advances or loans to other segments unless the operations of the segment are primarily of a financial nature; and

(c) gains on sales of investments or on extinguishment of debt unless the operations of the segment are primarily of a financial nature.

Segment expense is the aggregate of

(i) the expense resulting from the operating activities of a segment that is directly attributable to the segment, and

(ii) the relevant portion of entrprise expense that can be allocated on a reasonable basis to the segment, including expense relating to transactions with other segments of the enterprise.

Segment expense does not include

(a) extraordinary items as defined in AS 5, Net Profit or Loss for the Period, Prior Period Items and Changes in Accounting Policies;

(b) interest expense, including interest incurred on advances or loans from other segments, unless the operations of the segment are primarily of a financial nature;

(c) losses on sales of investments or losses on extinguishment of debt unless the operations of the segment are primarily of a financial nature;

(d) income tax expense; and

(e) general administrative expenses, head-office expenses, and other expenses that arise at the enterprise level and relate to the enterprise as a whole. However, costs are sometimes incurred at the enterprise level on behalf of a segment. Such costs are part of segment expense if they relate to the operating activities of the segment and if they can be directly attributed or allocated to the segment on a reasonable basis.

Segment result is segment revenue less segment expense

Segment assets are those operating assets that are employed by a segment in its operating activities and that either are directly attributable to the segment or can be allocated to the segment on a reasonable basis.

If the segment result of a segment includes interest or dividend income, its segment assets include the related receivable, loans, investments, or other interest or dividend generating assets.

Segment assets do not include income tax assets

Segment assets are determined after deducting related allowances/provisions that are reported as direct offsets in the balance sheet of the enterprise.

Segment liabilities are those operating liabilities that result from the operating activities of a segment and that either are directly attributable to the segment or can be allocated to the segment on a reasonable basis.

If the segment result of a segment includes interest expense, its segment liabilities include the related interest-bearing liabilities.

Segment liabilities do not include income tax liabilities.

1.7 Accounting Standard - 18 (A S - 18)

Related Party Disclosures

(In this Accounting Standard, the standard portions have been set in **bold italic** type. These should be read in the context of the background material which has been set in normal type, and in the context of the 'Preface to the Statements of Accounting Standards'.)[1]

The following is the text of Accounting Standard (AS) 18, 'Related Party Disclosures', issued by the Council of the Institute of Chartered Accountants of India. This Standard comes into effect in respect of accounting periods commencing on or after 1-4-2001 and is mandatory in nature.[2]

---

1. Attention is specifically drawn to paragraph 4.3 .of the Preface, according to which accounting standards are intended to apply only to material items.

2. This implies that, while discharging their attest function, it will be the duty of the members of the Institute to examine whether this Accounting Standard is complied with in the presentation of financial statements covered by their audit. In the event of any deviation from this Accounting Standard, it will be their duty to make adequate disclosures in their audit reports so that the users of financial statements may be aware of such deviations.

Objective

The objective of this Statement is to establish requirements for disclosure of:

(a) related party relationships; and

(b) transactions between a reporting enterprise and its related parties.

Definitions

10. For the purpose of this Statement, the following terms are used with the meanings specified :

Related party - parties are considered to be related if at any time during the reporting period one party has the ability to control the other party or exercise significant influence over the other party in making financial and/or operating decisions.

Related party transaction - a transfer of resources or obligations between related parties, regardless of whether or not a price is charged.

Control -

(a) ownership, directly or indirectly, of more than one half of the voting power of an enterprise, or

(b) control of the composition of the board of directors in the case of a company or of the composition of the corresponding governing body in case of any other enterprise, or

(c) a substantial interest in voting power and the power to direct, by statute or agreement, the financial and/or operating policies of the enterprise.

Significant influence — participation in the financial and or operating policy decisions of an enterprise, but not control of those policies.

An Associate — an enterprise in which an investing reporting party has significant influence and which is neither a subsidiary not a joint venture of that party.

Joint venture — a contractual arrangement whereby two or more parties undertake an economic activity which is subject to joint control.

Joint control — the contractually agreed sharing of power to govern the financial and operating policies of an economic activity so as to obtain benefits from it.

Key management personnel — those persons who have the authority and responsibility for planning, directing and controlling the activities of the reporting enterprise.

Relative — in relation to an individual, means the spouse, son, daughter, brother, sister, father and mother who may be expected to influence, or be influenced by, that individual in his/her dealings with the reporting enterprise.

Holding company — a company having one or more subsidiaries.

Subsidiary — a company :
(a) in which another company (the holding company) holds, either by itself and/or through one or more subsidiaries, more than one-half in nominal value of its equity share capital; or
(b) of which another company (the holding company) controls, either by itself and/or through one or more subsidiaries, the composition of its board of directors.

Fellow subsidiary — a company is considered to be a fellow subsidiary of another company if both are subsidiaries of the same holding company.

State-controlled enterprise — an enterprise which is under the control of the Central Government and/or any State Govemment(s).

11. For the purpose of this Statement, an enterprise is considered to control the composition of
(i) the board of directors of a company, if it has the power, without the consent or concurrence of any other person, to appoint or remove all or a majority of directors of that company. An enterprise is deemed to have the power to appoint a director if any of the following conditions is satisfied:
  (a) a person cannot be appointed as director without the exercise in his favour by that enterprise of such a power as aforesaid; or
  (b) a person's appointment as director follows necessarily from his appointment to a position held by him in that enterprise; or
  (c) the director is nominated by that enterprise; in case that enterprise is a company, the director is nominated by that company/subsidiary thereof.
(ii) the governing body of an enterprise that is not a company, if it has the power, without the consent or the concurrence of any other person, to appoint or remove all or a majority of members of the governing body of that other enterprise. An enterprise is deemed to have the power to appoint a member if any of the following conditions is satisfied :
  (a) a person cannot be appointed as memberof the governing body without the exercise in his favour by that other enterprise of such a power as aforesaid; or
  (b) a person's appointment as member of the governing body follows necessarily from his appointment to a position held by him in that other enterprise; or
  (c) the member of the governing body is nominated by that other enterprise.

12. An enterprise is considered to have a substantial interest in another enterprise if that enterprise owns, directly or indirectly, 20 percent or more interest in the voting power of the other enterprise. Similarly, an individual is considered to have a substantial interest in an enterprise, if that individual owns, directly or indirectly, 20 percent or more interest in the voting power of the enterprise.

13. Significant influence may be exercised in several ways, for example, by representation on the board of directors, participation in the policy making process, material inter-company

transactions, interchange of managerial personnel, or dependence on technical information. Significant influence may be gained by share ownership, statute or agreement. As regards share ownership, if an investing party holds, directly or indirectly through intermediaries, 20 percent or more of the voting power of the enterprise, it is presumed that the investing party does have significant influence, unless it can be clearly demonstrated that this is not the case. Conversely, if the investing party holds, directly or indirectly through intermediaries, less than 20 percent of the voting power of the enterprise, it is presumed that the investing party does not have significant influence, unless such influence can be clearly demonstrated. A substantial or majority ownership by another investing party does not necessarily preclude an investing party from having significant influence.

Summary : Disclosure

1. The statutes governing an enterprise often require disclosure in financial statements of transactions with certain categories of related parties. In particular, attention is focussed on transactions with the directors or similar key management personnel of an enterprise, especially their remuneration and borrowings, because of the fiduciary nature of their relationship with the enterprise.

2. Name of the related party and nature of the related party relationship where control exists should be disclosed irrespective of whether or not there have been transactions between the related parties.

3. Where the reporting enterprise controls, or is controlled by, another party, this information is relevant to the users of financial statements irrespective of whether or not transactions have taken place with that party. This is because the existence of control relationship may prevent the reporting enterprise from being independent in making its financial and/or operating decisions. The disclosure of the name of the related party and the nature of the related party relationship where control exists may sometimes be at least as relevant in appraising an enterprise's prospects as are the operating results and the financial position presented in its financial statements. Such a related party may establish the enterprise's credit standing, determine the source and price of its raw materials, and determine to whom and at what price the product is sold.

4. If there have been transactions between related parties, during the existence of a related party relationship, the reporting enterprise should disclose the following :

   (i)   the name of the transacting related party;

  (ii)   a description of the relationship between the parties;

 (iii)   a description of the nature of transactions;

 (iv)   volume of the transactions either as an amount or as an appropriate proportion;

  (v)   any other elements of the related party transactions necessary for an understanding of the financial statements;

 (vi)   the amounts or appropriate proportions of outstanding items pertaining to related parties at the balance sheet date and provisions for doubtful debts due from such parties at that date; and

(vii) amounts written-off or written-back in the period in respect of debts due from or to related parties.

5. The following are examples of the related party transactions in respect of which disclosures may be made by a reporting enterprise :

- purchases or sales of goods (finished or unfinished); .
- purchases or sales of fixed assets;
- rendering or receiving of services;
- agency arrangements;
- leasing or hire-purchase arrangement;
- transfer of research and development;
- licence agreements;
- finance (including loans and equity contributions in cash or in kind);
- guarantees and collaterals; and
- management contracts including for deputation of employees.

6. Paragraph 23(v) requires disclosure of any other elements of the related party transactions necessary for an understanding of the financial statements'. An example of such a disclosure would be an indication that the transfer of a major asset had taken place at an amount materially different from that obtainable on normal commercial terms.

7. Items of a similar nature may be disclosed in aggregate by type of related party.

1.8 Accounting Standard - 19 (AS - 19)

Leases

(In this Accounting Standard, the standard portions have been set in bold italic type. These should be read in the context of the background material which has been set in normal type, and in the context of the 'Preface to the Statements of Accounting Standards'.[1])

The following is the text of Accounting Standard (AS) 19, 'Leases', issued by the Council of the Institute of Chartered Accountants of India. This Standard comes into effect in respect of all assets leased during accounting periods commencing on or after 1.4.2001 and is mandatory in nature[2] from that date. Accordingly, the 'Guidance note on Accounting for Leases' issued by the Institute in 1995, is not applicable in respect of such assets. Earlier application of this Standard is, however, encouraged.

---

1. Attention is specifically drawn to paragraph 4.3 of the Preface, according to which accounting standards are intended to apply only to material items.
2. This implies that, while discharging their attest function, it will be the duty of the members of the Institute to examine whether this Accounting Standard is complied with in the presentation of financial statements covered by their audit. In the event of any deviation from this Accounting Standard, it will be their duty to make adequate disclosures in their audit reports so that the users of financial statements may be aware of such deviations.

Objective

The objective of this Statement is to prescribe, for lessees and lessors, the appropriate accounting policies and disclosures in relation to finance leases and operating leases.

Definitions

The following terms are used in this Statement with the meanings specified :

A lease is an agreement whereby the lessor conveys to the lessee in return for a payment or series of payments the right to use an asset for an agreed period of time.

A finance lease is a lease that transfers substantially all the risks and rewards incident to ownership of an asset.

An operating lease is a lease other than a finance lease.

A non-cancellable lease is a lease that is cancellable only :

(a)   upon the occurrence of some remote contingency; or

(b)   with the permission of the lessor; or

(c)   if the lessee enters into a new lease for the same or an equivalent asset with the same lessor; or

(d)   upon payment by the lessee of an additional amount such that, at inception, continuation of the lease is reasonably certain.

The inception of the lease is the earlier of the date of the lease agreement and the date of a commitment by the parties to the principal provisions of the lease.

The lease term is the non-cancellable period for which the lessee has agreed to take on lease the asset together with any further periods for which the lessee has the option to continue the lease of the asset, with or without further payment, which option at the inception of the lease it is reasonably certain that the lessee will exercise.

Minimum lease payments are the payments over the lease term that the lessee is, or can be required, to make excluding contingent rent, costs for services and taxes to be paid by and reimbursed to the lessor, together with :

(a)   in the case of the lessee, any residual value guaranteed by or on behalf of the lessee; or

(b)   in the case of the lessor, any residual value guaranteed to the lessor :

(i) by or on behalf of the lessee; or

(ii) by an independent third party financially capable of meeting this guarantee.

However, if the lessee has an option to purchase the asset at a price which is expected to be sufficiently lower than the fair value at the date the option becomes exercisable that, at the inception of the lease, is reasonably certain to be exercised, the minimum lease payments comprise minimum payments payable over the lease term and the payment required to exercise this purchase option.

Fair value is the amount for which an asset could be exchanged or a liability settled between knowledgeable, willing parties in an arm's length transaction.

Economic life is either :

(a) the period over which an asset is expected to be economically usable by one or more users; or

(b) the number of production or similar units expected to be obtained from the asset by one or more users.

Useful life of a leased asset is either :

(a) the period over which the leased asset is expected to be used by the lessee; or

(b) the number of production or similar units expected to be obtained from the use of the asset by the lessee.

Residual value of a leased asset is the estimated fair value of the asset at the end of the lease term.

Guaranteed Residual Value is

(a) in the case of the lessee, that part of the residual value which is guaranteed by the lessee or by a party on behalf of the lessee (the amount of the guarantee being the maximum amount that could, in any event, become payable); and

(b) in the case of the lessor, that part of the residual value which is guarantee by or on behalf of the lessee, or by an independent third party who is financially capable of discharging the obligations under the guarantee.

Unguaranteed residual value of a leased asset is the amount by which the residual value of the asset exceeds its guaranteed residual value.

Gross investment in the lease is the aggregate of the minimum lease payments under a finance lease from the standpoint of the lessor and any unguaranteed residual value accruing to the lessor.

Unearned finance income is the difference between :

(a) the gross investment in the lease; and

(b) the present value of

(i) the minimum lease payments under a finance lease from the standpoint of the lessor; and

(ii) any unguaranteed.residual value accruing to the lessor, at the interest rate implicit in the lease.

Net investment in the lease   is the gross investment in the lease less unearned finance income.

The interest rate implicit in the lease   is the discount rate that, at the inception of the lease, causes the aggregate present value of

(a) the minimum lease payments under a finance lease from the standpoint of the lessor; and

(b) any unguaranteed residual value accruing to the lessor, to be equal to the fair value of the leased asset.

The lessee's incremental borrowing rate of interest   is the rate of interest the lessee would have to pay on a similar lease or, if that is not determinable, the rate that, at the inception of the lease, the lessee would incur to borrow over a similar term, and with a similar security, the funds necessary to purchase the asset.

Contingent rent is that portion of the lease payments that is not fixed in amount but is based on a factor other than just the passage of time (e.g., percentage of sales, amount of usage, price indices, market rates of interest).

The definition of a lease includes agreements for the hire of an asset which contain a provision giving the hirer an option to acquire title to the asset upon the fulfillment of agreed conditions. These agreements are commonly known as hire-purchase agreements. Hire-purchase agreements include agreements under which the property in the asset is to pass to the hirer on the payment of the last instalment and the hirer has a right to terminate the agreement at any time before the property so passes.

Classification of Leases

The classification of leases adopted in this Statement is based on the extent to which risks and rewards incident to ownership of a leased asset lie with the lessor or the lessee. Risks include the possibilities of losses from idle capacity or technological obsolescence and of variations in return due to changing economic conditions. Rewards may be represented by the expectation of profitable operation over the economic life of the asset and of gain from appreciation in value or realisation of residual value.

A lease is classified as a finance lease if it transfers substantially all the risks and rewards incident to ownership. Title may or may not eventually be transferred. A lease is classified as an operating lease if it does not transfer substantially all the risks and rewards incident to ownership.

Since the transaction between a lessor and a lessee is based on a lease agreement common to both parties, it is appropriate to use consistent definitions. The application of these definitions to the differing circumstances of the two parties may sometimes result in the same lease being classified differently by the lessor and the lessee.

Whether a lease is a finance lease or an operating lease depends on the substance of the transaction rather than its form. Examples of situations which would normally lead to a lease being classified as a finance lease are :

(a) the lease transfers ownership of the asset to the lessee by the end of the lease term;

(b) the lessee has the option to purchase the asset at a price which is expected to be sufficiently lower than the fair value at the date the option becomes exercisable such that, at the inception of the lease, it is reasonably certain that the option will be exercised;

(c) the lease term is for the major part of the economic life of the a'sset even if title is not transferred;

(d) at the inception of the lease the present value of the minimum lease payments amounts to at least substantially all of the fair value of the leased asset; and

(e)   the leased asset is of a specialised nature such that only the lessee can use it without major modifications being made.

Indicators of situations which individually or in combination could also lead to.a lease being classified as a finance lease are :

(a)   if the lessee can cancel the lease, the lessor's losses associated with the cancellation are borne by the lessee;

(b)   gains or losses from the fluctuation in the fair value of the residual fall to the lessee (for example in the form of a rent rebate equalling most of the sales proceeds' at the end of the lease); and

(c)   the lessee can continue the lease for a secondary period at a rent which Is substantially lower than market rent.

Lease classification is made at the inception of the lease. If at any time the lessee and the lessor agree to change the provisions of the lease, other than by renewing the lease, in a manner that would have resulted in a different classification of the lease under the criteria in paragraphs 5 to 9 had the changed terms been in effect at the inception of the lease, the revised agreement is considered as a new agreement over its revised term. Changes in estimates (for example, changes in estimates of the economic life or of the residual value of the leased asset) or changes in circumstances (for example, default by the lessee), however, do not give rise to a new classification of a Jease for accounting purposes.

Disclosures for finance leases

(a)   assets acquired under finance lease as segregated from the assets owned;

(b)   for each class of assets, the net carrying amount at the balance sheet date;

(c)   a reconciliation between the total of minimum lease payments at the balance sheet date and their present value. In addition, an enterprise should disclose the total of minimum lease payments at the balance sheet date, and their present value, for each of the following periods :

(i)   not later than one year;

(ii)   later than one year and not later than five years;

(iii) later than five years;

(d)   contingent rents recognised as expense in the statement of profit and loss for the period;

(e)   the total of future minimum sublease payments expected to be received under non-cancellable subleases at the balance sheet date; and

(f)   a general description of the lessee's significant leasing arrangements including, but not limited to, the following;

(i)   the basis on which contingent rent payments are determined;

(ii)   the existence and terms of renewal or purchase options and escalation clauses; and

(iii) restrictions imposed by lease arrangements, such as those concerning dividends, additional debt, and further leasing.

Disclosures for operating leases

(a) the total of future minimum lease payments under non-cancellable operating leases for each of the following periods:

   (i) not later than one year;

   (ii) later than one year and not later than five years;

   (iii) later than five years;

(b) the total of future minimum sublease payments expected to be received under non-cancellable subleases at the balance sheet date;

(c) lease payments recognised in the statement of profit and loss for the period, with separate amounts for minimum lease payments and contingent rents;

(d) sub-lease payments received (or receivable) recognised in the statement of profit and loss for the period;

(e) a general description of the lessee's significant leasing arrangements including, but not limited to, the following:

   (i) the basis on which contingent rent payments are determined;

   (ii) the existence and terms of renewal or purchase options and escalation clauses; and

   (iii) restrictions imposed by lease arrangements, such as those concerning dividends, additional debt, and further leasing.

Sale and Leaseback Transactions

A sale and leaseback transaction involves the sale of an asset by the vendor and the leasing of the same asset back to the vendor. The lease payments and the sale price are usually interdependent as they are negotiated as a package. The accounting treatment of a sale and leaseback transaction depends upon the type of lease involved.

If a sale and leaseback transaction results in a finance lease, any excess or deficiency of sales proceeds over the carrying amount should not be immediately recognised as income or loss in the financial statements of a seller-lessee. Instead, it should be deferred and amortised over the lease term in proportion to the depreciation of the leased asset.

If the leaseback is a finance lease, it is not appropriate to regard an excess of sales proceeds over the carrying amount as income. Such excess is deferred and amortised over the lease term in proportion to the depreciation of the leased asset. Similarly, it is not appropriate to regard a deficiency as loss. Such deficiency is deferred and amortised over the lease term.

If a sale and leaseback transaction results in an operating lease, and it is clear that the transaction is established at fair value, any profit or loss should be recognised immediately. If the sale price is below fair value, any profit or loss should be recognised immediately except that, if the loss is compensated by future lease payments at below market price, it should be deferred and amortised in proportion to the lease payments over the period for which the asset is expected to be used. If the sale price is above fair value, the excess over fair value should be deferred and amortised over the period for which the asset is expected to be used.

If the leaseback is an operating lease, and the lease payments and the sale-price are established at fair value, there has in effect been a normal sale transaction and any profit or loss is recognised immediately.

For operating leases, if the fair value at the time of a sale and leaseback transaction is less than the carrying amount of the asset, a loss equal to the amount of the difference between the carrying amount and fair-value should be recognised immediately.

For finance leases, no such adjustment is necessary unless there has been an impairment in value, in which case the carrying amount is .reduced to recoverable amount in accordance with the Accounting Standard dealing with impairment of assets.

Disclosure requirements for lessees and lessors apply equally to sale and leaseback transactions. The required description of the significant leasing arrangements leads to disclosure of unique or unusual provisions of the agreement or terms of the sale and leaseback transactions.

Sale and leaseback transactions may meet the separate disclosure criteria set out in paragraph 12 of Accounting Standard (AS) 5, Net Profit or Loss for the Period, Prior Period Items and Changes in Accounting Policies.

1.9 Accounting Standard - 20 (AS - 20)

Earnings per Share

(In this Accounting Standard, the standard portions have been set in bold italic type. These should be read in the context of the background material which has been set in normal type, and in the context of the 'Preface to the Statements of Accounting Standards'.[1])

Accounting Standard (AS) 20, 'Earnings Per Share', issued by the Council of the Institute of Chartered Accountants of India, comes into effect in respect of accounting periods commencing on or after 1.4.2001 and is mandatory in nature[2], from that date, in respect of enterprises whose equity shares or potential equity shares are listed on a recognised stock exchange in India. An enterprise which has neither equity shares not potential equity shares which are so listed but which discloses earnings per share, should calculate and disclose earnings per share in accordance with this Standard from the aforesaid date. The following is the text of the Accounting Standard.

Objective

The objective of this Statement-is to prescribe principles for the determination and presentation of earnings per share which will improve comparison of performance among different enterprises for the same period and among different accounting periods for the same

---

1. Attention is specifically drawn to paragraph 4.3 of the Preface, according to which accounting standards are intended to apply only to material items.
2. This implies that, while discharging their attest'function, it will be the duty of the members of the Institute to examine whether this Accounting Standard is complied with in the presentation of financial statements covered by their audit. In the event of any deviation from this Accounting Standard, it will be their duty to make adequate disclosures in their audit reports so that the users of financial statements may be aware of such deviations.

enterprise. The focus of this Statement is on the denominator of the earnings per share calculation. Even though earnings per share data has limitations because of different accounting policies used for determining 'earnings', a consistently determined denominator enhances the quality of financial reporting.

Definitions

For the purpose of this Statement, the following terms are used with the meanings specified : An equity share is a share other than a preference share.

A preference share is a share carrying preferential rights to dividends and repayment of capital.

A financial instrument is any contract that gives rise to both a financial asset of one enterprise and a financial liability or equity shares of another enterprise.

A potential equity share is a financial instrument or other contract that entitles, or may entitle, its holder to equity share.

Share warrants or options are financial instruments that give the holder the right to acquire equity shares.

Fair value is the amount for which an asset could be exchanged, or a liability settled, between knowledgeable, willing parties in an arm's length transaction.

Presentation

An enterprise should present basic and diluted earnings per share on the face of the statement of profit and loss for each class of equity shares that has a different right to share in the net profit for the period. An enterprise should present basic and diluted earnings per share with equal prominence for all periods presented.

This Statement requires an enterprise to present basic and diluted earnings per share, even if the amounts disclosed are negative (a loss per share).

Measurement : Basic Earnings Per Share

Basic earnings per share should be calculated by dividing the net profit or loss for the period attributable to equity shareholders by the weighted average number of equity shares outstanding during the period.

Earnings - Basic

For the purpose of calculating basic earnings per share, the net profit or loss for the period attributable to equity shareholders should be the net profit or loss for the period after deducting preference dividends and any attributable tax thereto for the period.

All items of income and expense which are recognised in a period, including tax expense and extraordinary items, are included in the determination of the net profit or loss for the period unless an Accounting Standard requires or permits otherwise (see Accounting Standard (AS) 5, Net Profit or Loss for the Period, Prior Period Items and Changes in Accounting Policies). The amount of preference dividends and any attributable tax thereto for the period is deducted from the net profit for the period (or added to the net loss for the period) in order to calculate the net profit or loss for the period attributable to equity shareholders.

The amount of preference dividends for the period that is deducted from the net profit for the period is:

(a)   the amount of any preference dividends on non-cumulative preference shares provided for in respect of the period; and

(b)   the full amount of the required preference dividends for cumulative preference shares for the period, whether or not the dividends have been provided for. The amount of preference dividends for the period does not include the amount of any preference dividends for cumulative preference shares paid or declared during the current period in respect of previous periods.

If an enterprise has more than one class of equity shares, net profit or loss for the period is apportioned over the different classes of shares in accordance with their dividend rights.

Per Share - Basic

For the purpose of calculating basic earnings per share, the number of equity shares should be the weighted average number of equity shares outstanding during the period.

The weighted average number of equity shares outstanding during the period reflects the fact that the amount of shareholders' capital may have varied during the period as a result of a larger or lesser number of shares outstanding at any time. It is the number of equity shares outstanding at the beginning of the period, adjusted by the number of equity shares bought back or issued during the period multiplied by the time-weighting factor. The time-weighting factor is the number of days for which the specific shares are outstanding as a proportion of the total number of days in the period; a reasonable approximation of the weighted average is adequate in many circumstances.

Diluted Earnings Per Share

For the purpose of calculating diluted earnings per share, the net profit or loss for the period attributable to equity shareholders and the weighted average number of shares outstanding during the period should be adjusted for the effects of all dilative potential equity shares.

In calculating diluted earnings per share, effect is given to all dilutive potential equity shares that were outstanding during the period, that is :

(a)   the net profit for the period attributable to equity shares is :

(i)   increased by the amount of dividends recognised in the period in respect of the dilutive potential equity shares as adjusted for any attributable change in tax expense for the period;

(ii)   increased by the amount of interest recognised in.the period in respect of the dilutive potential equity shares as adjusted for any attributable change in tax expense for the period; and

(iii) adjusted for the after-tax amount of any other changes in expenses or income that would result from the conversion of the dilutive potential equity shares.

(b) the weighted average number of equity shares outstanding during the period is increased by the weighted average number of additional equity shares which would have been outstanding assuming the conversion of all dilutive potential equity shares.

For the purpose of this Statement, share application money pending allotment or any advance share application money as at the balance sheet date, which is not statutorily required to be kept separately and is being utilised in the business of the enterprise, is treated in the same manner as dilutive potential equity shares for the purpose of calculation of diluted earnings per share.

Dilutive Potential Equity Shares

Potential equity shares should be treated as dilutive when, and only when, their conversion to equity shares would decrease net profit per share from continuing ordinary operations.

An enterprise uses net profit from continuing ordinary activities as "the control figure" that is used to establish whether potential equity shares are dilutive or anti-dilutive. The net profit from continuing ordinary activities is the net profit from ordinary activities (as defined in AS 5) after deducting preference dividends and any attributable tax thereto and after excluding items relating to discontinued operations.[1]

Potential equity shares are anti-dilutive when their conversion to equity shares would increase earnings per share from continuing ordinary activities or decrease loss per share from continuing ordinary activities. The effects of anti-dilutive potential equity shares are ignored in calculating diluted earnings per share.

In considering whether potential equity shares are dilutive or antidilutive, each issue or series of potential equity shares is considered separately rather than in aggregate. The sequence in which potential equity shares are considered may affect whether or not they are dilutive. Therefore, in order to maximise the dilution of basic earnings per share, each issue or series of potential equity shares is considered in sequence from the most dilutive to the lest dilutive. For the purpose of determining the sequence from most dilutive to least dilutive potential equity shares, the earnings per incremental share is the least, the potential equity share is considered most dilutive and vice-versa.

Disclosure

In addition to disclosures as required by paragraphs 8, 9 and 44 of this Statement, an enterprise should disclose the following :
(a) the amounts used as the numerators in calculating basic and diluted earnings per share, and a reconciliation of those amounts to the net profit or loss for the period;
(b) the weighted average number of equity shares used as the denominator in calculating basic and diluted earnings per share, and a reconciliation of these denominators to each other; and
(c) the nominal value of shares along with the earnings per share figures.

---

1. A separate accounting standard on 'Discontinuing Operations', which is being formulated, will specify the requirements in respect of discontinued operations.

Contracts generating potential equity shares may incorporate terms and conditions which, affect the measurement of basic and diluted earnings per share. These terms and conditions may determine whether or not any potential equity shares are dilutive and, if so, the effect on the weighted average number of shares outstanding and any consequent adjustments to the net profit attributable to equity shareholders. Disclosure of the terms and conditions of such contracts is encouraged by this Statement.

If an enterprise discloses, in addition to basic and diluted earnings per share, per share amounts using a reported component of net profit other than net profit or loss for the period attributable to equity shareholders, such amounts should be calculated using the weighted average number of equity shares determined in accordance with this Statement. If a component of net profit is used which is not reported as a line item in the statement of profit and loss, a reconciliation should be provided between the component used and a line item which is reported in the statement of profit and loss. Basic and diluted per share amounts should be disclosed with equal prominence.

An enterprise may wish to disclose more information than -this Statement requires. Such information may help the users to evaluate the performance of the enterprise and may take the form of per share amounts for various components of net profit, e.g., profit from ordinary activities. Such disclosures are encouraged. However, when such amounts are disclosed, the denominators need to be calculated in accordance with this Statement in order to ensure the comparability of the per share amounts disclosed.

1.10 Accounting Standard - 21 (AS - 21)

Consolidated Financial Statements

(In this Accounting Standard, the standard portions have been set in bold italic type. These should be read in the context of the background material which has been set in normal type, and in the context of the 'Preface to the Statements of Accounting Standards'.[2])

Accounting Standard (AS) 21, 'Consolidated Financial Statements', issued by the Council of the Institute of Chartered Accountants of India, comes into effect in respect of accounting periods commencing on or after 1.4.2001.

An enterprise that presents consolidated financial statements should prepare and present these statements in accordance with this Standard. The following is the text of the Accounting Standard.

Objective

The objective of this Statement is to lay down principles and procedures for preparation and presentation of consolidated financial statements. Consolidated financial statements are presented by a parent (also known as holding enterprise) to provide financial information about the economic activities of its group. These statements are intended to present financial

---

2. Attention is specifically drawn to paragraph 4.3 of the Preface, according to which accounting standards are intended to apply only to material items.

information about a parent and its subsidiary(ies) as a single economic entity to show the economic resources controlled by the group, the obligations of the group and results the group achieves with its resources.

Definitions

For the purpose of this Statement, the following terms are used with the meanings specified Control :

(a) the ownership, directly or indirectly through subsidiary(ies), of more than one-half of the voting power of an enterprise; or

(b) control of the composition of the board of directors in the case of a company or of the composition of the corresponding governing body in case of any other enterprise so as to obtain economic benefits from its activities.

A subsidiary is an enterprise that is controlled by another enterprise (known as the parent).

A parent is an enterprise that has one or more subsidiaries.

A group is a parent and all its subsidiaries.

Consolidated financial statements are the financial statements of a group presented as those of a single enterprise.

Equity is the residual interest in the assets of an enterprise after deducting all its liabilities.

Minority interest   is that part of the net results of operations and of the net assets of a subsidiary attributable to interests which are not owned, directly or indirectly through subsidiary(ies), by the parent.

Consolidated financial statements normally include consolidated balance sheet, consolidated statement of profit and loss, and notes, other statements and explanatory material that form an integral part thereof. Consolidated cash flow statement is presented in case a parent presents its own cash flow statement. The consolidated financial statements are presented, to the extent possible, in the same format as that adopted by the parent for its separate financial statements.

Presentation of Consolidated. Financial Statements :

A parent which presents consolidated financial statements should present these statements in addition to its separate financial statements.

Users of the financial statements of a parent are usually concerned with, and need to be informed about, the financial position and results of operations of not only the enterprise itself but also of the group as a whole. This need is served by providing the users -

(a) separate financial statements of the parent; and

(b) consolidated financial statements, which present financial information about the group as that of a single enterprise without regard to the legal boundaries of the separate legal entitles.

Consolidation Procedures

In preparing consolidated financial statements, the financial statements of the parent and its subsidiaries should be combined on a line-by-line basis by adding together like items of assets, liabilities, income and expenses. In order that the consolidated financial statements present financial information about the group as that of a single enterprise, the following steps should be taken :

(a) the cost to the parent of its investment in each subsidiary and the parent's portion of equity of each subsidiary, at the date on which investment in each subsidiary is made, should be eliminated;

(b) any excess of the cost to the parent of its investment in a subsidiary over the parent's portion of equity of the subsidiary, at the date on which investment in the subsidiary is made, should be described as goodwill to be recognised as an asset in the consolidated financial statements;

(c) when the cost to the parent of its investment in a subsidiary is less than the parent's portion of equity of the subsidiary, at the date on which investment in the subsidiary is made, the difference should be treated as a capital reserve in the consolidated financial statements;

(d) minority interests in the net income of consolidated subsidiaries for the reporting period should be identified and adjusted against the income of the group in order to arrive at the net income attributable to the owners of the parent; and

(e) minority interests in the net assets of consolidated subsidiaries should be identified and presented in the consolidated balance sheet separately from liabilities and the equity of the parent's shareholders. Minority interests in the net assets consist of:

(i) the amount of equity attributable to minorities at the date on which investment in a subsidiary is made and

(ii) the minorities' share of movements in equity since the date the parent-subsidiary relationship came in existence.

Where the carrying amount of the investment in the subsidiary is different from its cost, the carrying amount is considered for the purpose of above computations.

The parent's portion of equity in a subsidiary, at the date on which investment is made, is determined on the basis of information contained in the financial statements of the subsidiary as on the date of investment. However, if the financial statements of a subsidiary, as on the date of investment, are not available and if it is impracticable to draw the financial statements of the subsidiary as on that date, financial statements of the subsidiary for the immediately preceding period are used as a basis for consolidation. Adjustments are made tp these financial statements for the effects of significant transactions or other events that occur between the date of such financial statements and the date of investment in the subsidiary.

If an enterprise makes two or more investments in another enterprise at different dates and eventually obtains control of the other enterprise, the consolidated financial statements are presented only from the date on which holding-subsidiary relationship comes in existence. If two or more investments are made over a period of time, the equity of the subsidiary at the date of investment, for the purposes of paragraph 13 above, is generally determined on a step.-by-step basis; however, if small investments are made over a period of time and then an investment is made that results in control, the date of the latest investment, as a practicable measure, may be considered as the date of investment.

Intragroup balances and intragroup transactions and resulting unrealised profits should be eliminated in full. Unrealised losses resulting from intragroup transactions should also be eliminated unless cost cannot be recovered.

Intragroup balances and intragroup transactions, including sales, expenses and dividends, are eliminated in full. Unrealised profits resulting from intragroup transactions that are included in the carrying amount of assets, such as inventory and fixed assets, are eliminated in full. Unrealised losses resulting from intragroup transactions that are deducted in arriving at the carrying amount of assets are also eliminated unless cost cannot be recovered.

The financial statements used in the consolidation should be drawn up to the same reporting date, fit is not practicable to draw up the financial statements of one or more subsidiaries to such date and, accordingly, those financial statements are drawn up to different reporting dates, adjustments should be made for the effects of significant transactions or other events that occur between those dates and the date of the parent's financial statements. In any case, the difference between reporting dates should not be more than six months.

The financial statements of the parent and its subsidiaries used in the preparation of the consolidated financial statements are usually drawn up to the same date. When the reporting dates are different, the subsidiary often prepares, for consolidation purposes, statements as at the same date as that of the parent. When it is impracticable to do this, financial statements drawn up to different reporting dates may be used provided the difference in reporting dates is not more than six months. The consistency principle requires that the length of the reporting periods and any difference in the reporting dates should be the same from period to period.

Consolidated financial statements should be prepared using uniform accounting policies for like transactions and other events in similar circumstances. If it is not practicable to use uniform accounting policies in preparing the consolidated financial statements, that fact should be disclosed together with the proportions of the items in the consolidated financial statements to which the different accounting policies have been applied.

If a member of the group uses accounting policies other than those adopted in the consolidated financial statements for like transactions and events in similar circumstances, appropriate adjustments are made to its financial statements when they are used in preparing the consolidated financial statements.

The results of operations of subsidiary are included in the consolidated financial statements as from the date on which parent-subsidiary relationship came in existence. The results of operations of a subsidiary with which parent-subsidiary relationship ceases to exist are included in the consolidated statement of profit and loss until the date of cessation of the relationship. The difference between the proceeds from the disposal of investment in a subsidiary and the carrying amount of its assets less liabilities as of the date of disposal is recognised in the consolidated statement of profit and loss as the profit or loss on the disposal of the' investment in the subsidiary. In order to ensure the comparability of the financial satements from one accounting period to the next, supplementary information is often provided about the effect of the acquisition and disposal of subsidiaries on the financial position at the reporting date and the results for the reporting period and on the corresponding amounts for the preceding period.

An investment in an enterprise should be accounted for in accordance with Accounting Standard (AS) 13, Accounting for Investments, from the date, that the enterprise ceases to be a subsidiary and does not become an associate .

The carrying amount of the investment at the date that it ceases to be a subsidiary is regarded as cost thereafter.

Minority interests should be presented in the consolidated balance sheet separately from liabilities and the equity of the parent's shareholders. Minority interests in the income of the group should also be separately presented.

The losses applicable to the minority in a consolidated subsidiary may exceed the minority interest in the equity of the subsidiary. The excess, and any further losses applicable to the minority, are adjusted against the majority interest except to the extent that the minority has a binding obligation to, and is able to, make good the losses. If the subsidiary subsequently reports profits, all such profits are allocated to the majority interest until the minority's share of losses previously absorbed by the majority has been recovered.

If a subsidiary has outstanding cumulative preference shares which are held outside the group, the parent computes its share of profits or losses after adjusting for the subsidiary's preference dividends, whether or not dividends have been declared.

Accounting for Investments in Subsidiaries in a Parent's Separate Financial Statements

In a parent's separate financial statements, investments in subsidiaries should be accounted for in accordance with Accounting Standard (AS) 13, Accounting for Investments.

Disclosure

In addition to disclosures required by paragraphs 11 and 20, following disclosures should be made :

(a) in consolidated financial statements a list of all subsidiaries including the name, country of incorporation or residence, proportion of ownership interest and, if different, proportion of voting power held:

(b) in consolidated financial statements, where applicable :

    (i) the nature of the relationship between the parent and a subsidiary, if the parent does not own, directly or indirectly through subsidiaries, more than one-half of the voting power of the subsidiary;

    (ii) the effect of the acquisition and disposal of subsidiaries on the-financial position at the reporting date, the results for the reporting period and on the corresponding amounts for the preceding period; and

    (iii) the names of the subsidiary(ies) of which exporting date(s) is/are different from that of the parent and the difference in reporting dates.

Transactional Provisions

On the first occasion that consolidated financial statements are presented, comparative figures for the previous period need not be presented. In all subsequent years full comparative figures for the previous period should be presented in the consolidated financial statements.

1.11 (AS - 22) (issued 2001) - Accounting for Taxes on Income :

Accounting Standard (AS) 22, 'Accounting for Taxes on Income', issued by the Council of the Institute of Chartered Accountants of India, comes into effect in respect of accounting periods commencing on or after 1-4-2001. It is mandatory in nature for:

(a) All the accounting periods commencing on or after 01.04.2001, in respect of the following:

  i) Enterprises whose equity or debt securities are listed on a recognised stock exchange in India and enterprises that are in the process of issuing equity or debt securities that will be listed on a recognised stock exchange in India as evidenced by the board of directors' resolution in this regard.

  ii) All the enterprises of a group, if the parent presents consolidated financial statements and the Accounting Standard is mandatory in nature in respect of any of the enterprises of that group in terms of (i) above.

(b) All the accounting periods commencing on or after 01.04.2002, in respect of companies not covered by (a) above.

(c) All the accounting periods commencing on or after 01.04.2003, in respect of all other enterprises.

The Guidance Note on Accounting for Taxes on Income, issued by the Institute of Chartered Accountants of India in 1991, stands withdrawn from 1.4.2001. The following is the text of the Accounting Standard.

Objective

The objective of this Statement is to prescribe accounting treatment for taxes on income. Taxes on income is one of the significant items in the statement of profit and loss of an enterprise. In accordance with the matching concept, taxes on income are accrued in the same period as the revenue and expenses to which they relate. Matching of such taxes against revenue for a period poses special problems arising from the fact that in a number of cases, taxable income may be significantly different from the accounting income. This divergence between taxable income and accounting income arises due to two main reasons. Firstly, there are differences between items of revenue and expenses as appearing in the statement of profit and loss and the items which are considered as revenue, expenses or deductions for tax purposes. Secondly, there are differences between the amount in respect of a particular item of revenue or expense as recognised in the statement of profit and loss and the corresponding amount which is recognised for the computation of taxable income.

Scope

1. This Statement should be applied in accounting for taxes on income. This includes the determination of the amount of the expense or saving.related to taxes on income in respect of an accounting period tyd the disclosure of such an amount in the financial statements.

2. For the purposes of this Statement, taxes on income include all domestic and foreign taxes which are based on taxable income.

3. This Statement does not specify when, or how, an enterprise should'account for taxes that are payable on distribution of dividends and other distributions made by the enterprise.

Definitions

4. For the purpose of this Statement, the following terms are used with the meanings specified: <u>Accounting income (loss)</u> is the net profit or loss for a period, as reported in the statement of profit and loss, before deducting income tax expense or adding income tax saving.

    <u>Taxable income (tax loss)</u> is the amount of the income (loss) for a period, determined in accordance with the tax laws, based upon which Income tax payable (recoverable) is determined.

    <u>Tax expense (tax saving)</u> is the aggregate of current tax and deferred tax charged or credited to (he statement of profit and toss for the period. Current tax is the amount of income tax determined to be payable (recoverable) in respect of the taxable income (tax loss) for a period.

    <u>Deferred tax</u> is the tax effect of timing differences.

    <u>Timing differences</u> are the defferences between taxable income and accounting income for a period that originate in one period and are capable of reversal in one or more subsequent periods, Permanent differences are the differences between taxable income and accounting income for a period that originate in one period and do not reverse subsequently.

5. Taxable income is calculated in accordance with tax laws. In some circumstances, the requirements of these laws to compute taxable income differ from the accounting policies applied to determine accounting income. The effect of this difference is that the taxable income and accounting income may not be the same.

6. The differences between taxable income and accounting income can be classified into permanent differences and timing differences. Permanent differences are those differences between taxable income and accounting income which originate in one period and do not reverse subsequently. For instance, if for the purpose of computing taxable income, the tax laws allow only a part of an item of expenditure, the disallowed amount would result in a permanent difference.

7. Timing differences are those differences between taxable income and accounting income'for a period that originate in one period and are capable of reversal in one or

more subsequent periods. Timing differences arise because the period in which some items of revenue and expenses are included in taxable income do not coincide with the period in which such items of revenue and expenses are included or considered in arriving at accounting income. For example, machinery purchased for scientific research related to business is fully allowed as deduction in the first year for tax purposes whereas the same would be charged to the statement of profit and loss as depreciation over its useful life. The total depreciation charged on the machinery for accounting purposes and the amount allowed as deduction for tax purposes will ultimately be the same, but periods over which the depreciation is charged and the deduction is allowed will differ. Another example of timing difference is a situation where, for the purpose of computing taxable income, tax laws allow depreciation on the basis of the written down value method, whereas for accounting purposes, straight line method is used. Some other examples of timing differences arising under the Indian tax laws are given in Appendix 1.

8. Unabsorbed depreciation and carry forward of losses which can be set-off against future taxable income are also considered as timing differences and result in deferred tax assets, subject to consideration of prudence (see paragraphs 15-18)

Recognition

9. Tax expense for the period, comprising current tax and deferred tax, should be included in the determination of the net profit or loss for the period.

10. Taxes on income are considered to be an expense incurred by the enterprise in earning income and are accrued in the same period as the revenue and expenses to which they relate. Such matching may result into timing differences. The tax effects of timing differences are included in the tax expense in the statement of profit and loss and as deferred tax assets (subject to the consideration of prudence as set out in paragraphs 15-18) or as deferred tax liabilities, in the balance sheet.

11. An example of tax effect of a timing difference that results in a deferred tax asset is an expense provided in the statement of profit and loss but not allowed as a deduction under Section 43B of the Income-tax Act, 1961. This timing difference will reverse when the deduction of that expense is allowed under Section 43B in subsequent year(s). An example of tax effect of a timing difference resulting in a deferred tax liability is the higher charge of depreciation allowable under the Income-tax Act, 1961, compared to the depreciation provided in the statement of profit and loss. In subsequent years, the differential will reverse when comparatively lower depreciation will be allowed for tax purposes.

12. Permanent differences do not result in deferred tax assets or deferred tax liabilities.

13. Deferred tax should be recognised for all the timing differences, subject to the consideration of prudence in respectof deferred tax assets as set out in paragraphs 15-18.

14. This Statement requires recognition of deferred tax for all the timing differences. This is based on the principle that the financial statements for a period should recognise the tax effect, whether current or deferred, of all the transactions occurring in that period.

15. Except in the situations stated in paragraph 17, deferred tax assets should be recognised and carried forward only to the extent that there is a reasonable certainty that sufficient future taxable income will be available against which such deferred tax assets can be realised.

16. While recognising the tax effect of timing differences, consideration of prudence cannot be ignored. Therefore, deferred tax assets are recognised and carried forward only to the extent that there is a reasonable certainty of their realisation. This reasonable level of certainty would normally be achieved by examining the past record of the enterprise and by making realistic estimates of profits for the future.

17. Where an enterprise has unabsorbed depreciation orcarry forward of losses under tax laws, deferred tax assets should be recognised only to the extent that there is virtual certainty supported by convincing evidence that sufficient future taxable income wiUbe available against which such deferred tax assets can be realised.

18. Theexistence of unabsorbed depreciation or carry forward of losses under tax laws is strong evidence, that future taxable income may not be available. Therefore, when an enterprise has a history of recent losses, the enterprise recognises deferred tax assets only to the extent that it has timing differences the reversal of which will result in sufficient income or there is other convincing evidence that sufficient taxable income will be available against which such deferred tax assets can be realised. In such circumstances, the nature of the evidence supporting its recognition is disclosed.

Re-assessment of Unrecognised Deferred Tax Assets

19. At each balance sheet date, an enterprise re-assesses unrecognised deferred tax assets. The enterprise recognises previously unrecognised deferred tax assets to the extent that it has become reasonably certain or virtually certain, as the case may be, that sufficient future taxable income will be available against which such deferred tax assets can be realised. For example, an improvement in trading conditions may make it reasonably certain that the enterprise will be able to generate sufficient taxable income in the future.

Measurement

20. Current tax should be measured at the amount expected to be paid to (recovered from) the taxation authorities, using the applicable tax rates and tax laws.

21. Deferred tax assets and liabilities should be measured using the tax rates and tax laws that have been enacted or substantively enacted by the balance sheet date.

22. Deferred tax assets and liabilities are usually measured using the tax rates and tax laws that have been enacted. However, certain announcements of tax rates and tax

laws by the government may have the substantive effect of actual enactment. In these circumstances, deferred tax assets and liabilities are measured using such announced tax rate and tax laws.

23. When different tax rates apply to different levels of taxable income, deferred tax assets and liabilities are measured using average rates.

24. Deferred tax assets and liabilities should not be discounted to their present value.

25. The reliable determination of deferred tax assets and liabilities on a discounted basis requires detailed scheduling of the timing of the reversal of each timing difference. In a number of cases such scheduling is impracticable or highly complex. Therefore, it is inappropriate to require discounting of deferred tax assets and liabilities. To permit, but not to require, discounting would result in deferred tax assets and liabilities which would not be comparable between enterprises. Therefore, this statement does not require or permit the discounting of deferred tax assets and liabilities.

Review of Deferred Tax Assets

26. The carrying amount of deferred tax assets should be reviewed at each balance sheet date. An enterprise should write-down the carrying amount of a deferred tax asset to the extent that it is no longer reasonably certain or virtually certain, as the case may be (see paragraphs 15 to 18), that sufficient future taxable income wittbe available against which deferred tax asset can be realised. Any such write-down may be reversed to the extent that it becomes reasonably certain or virtually certain, as the case may be, that sufficient future taxable income win be available.

Presentation and Disclosure

27. An enterprise should offset assets and liabilities representing current tax if the enterprise:
    (a) has a legally enforceable right to set off the recognised amounts; and
    (b) intends to settle the asset and the liability on a net basis.

28. An enterprise will normally have a legally enforceable right to set off an asset and liability representing current tax when they relate to income taxes levied under the same governing taxation laws and the taxation laws permit the enterprise to make or receive a single net payment.

29. An enterprise should offset deferred tax assets and deferred tax liabilities if :
    (a) the enterprise has a legally enforceable right to set off assets against liabilities representing currentax and
    (b) the deferred tax assets and the deferred tax liabilities relate to taxes on income levied by the same governing taxation laws.

30. Deferred tax assets and liabilities should be distinguished from assets and liabilities representing current tax for the period. Deferred tax assets and liabilities should be disclosed under a separate heading in the balance sheet of the enterprise, separately from current assets and current liabilities.

31. The break-up of deferred tax assets and deferred tax liabilities into major components of the respective balances should be disclosed in the notes to accounts.

32. The nature of the evidence supporting the recognition of deferred tax assets should be disclosed, if an enterprise has unabsorbed depreciation or carry forward of losses under tax laws.

Transitional Provisions

33. On the first occasion that the taxes on income are accounted for in accordance with this Statement, the enterprise should recognise, in the financial statements, the deferred tax balance that has accumulated prior to the adoption of this Statement as deferred tax asset/liability with a corresponding credit/charge to the revenue reserves, subject to the consideration of prudence in case of deferred tax assets (see paragraphs 15-18). The amount so credited/charged to the revenue reserves should be the same as that which would have resulted if this Statement had been in effect from the beginning.

34. For the purpose of determining accumulated deferred tax in the period in which this Statement is applied for the first time, the opening balances of assets and liabilities for accounting purposes and for tax purposes are compared and the differences, if any, are determined. The tax effects of these differences, if any, should be recognised as deferred tax assets or liabilities, if these differences are timing differences. For example, in the year in which an enterprise adopts this Statement, the opening balance of a fixed asset is Rs. 100 for accounting purposes and Rs. 60 for tax purposes. The difference is because the enterprise applies written down value method of depreciation for calmlatine taxable income whereas for accounting purposes straight line method is used. This difference will reverse in future when depreciation for tax purposes will be lower as compared to the depreciation for accounting purposes. In the above case, assuming that enacted tax rate for the year is 40% and that there are no other timing differences, deferred tax liability of Rs. 16 [(Rs. 100 - Rs. 60) x 40%] would be recognised. Another example is an expenditure that has already been written off for accounting purposes in the year of its incurrance but is allowable for tax purposes over a period of time. In this case, the asset representing that expenditure would have a balance only for tax purposes but not for accounting purposes. The difference between balance of the asset for tax purposes and the balance (which is nil) for accounting purposes would be a timing difference which will reverse in future when this expenditure would be allowed for tax purposes. Therefore, a deferred tax asset would be recognised in respect of this difference subject to the consideration of prudence (see paragraphs 15-18).

4.12 Accounting Standard (AS - 23) (issued in 2001)— Accounting for Investments in Associates in Consolidated Financial Statements :

(In this Accounting Standard, the standard portions have been set in bold italic type. These should be read in the context of the background material which has been set in normal type, and in the context of the 'Preface to the Statements of Accounting Standards'.1)

Accounting Standard (AS) 23, 'Accounting for Investments in Associates in Consolidated Financial Statements', issued by the Council of the Institute of Chartered Accountants of India, comes into effect in respect of accounting peridds commencing on or after 1 -4-2002. An enterprise that presents consolidated financial statements should account for investments in associates in the consolidated financial statements in accordance with this Standard.2 The following is the text of the Accounting Standard.

Objective

The objective of this Statement is to set out principles and procedures for recognising, in the consolidated financial statements, the effects of the investments in associates on the financial position and operating results of a group.

Scope

1. This Statement should be applied in accounting for investments in associates in the preparation and presentation of consolidated financial statements by an investor.
2. This Statement does not deal with accounting for investments in associates in the preparation and presentation of separate financial statements by an investor.3

Definitions

3. For the purpose of this Statement, the following terms are used with the meanings specified:

   An associate is an enterprise in which the investor has significant influence and which is neither a subsidiary nor a joint venture4 of the investor.

   Significant influence is the power to participate in the financial and/or operating policy decisions of the investee but not control over those policies.

Control :

(a) The ownership, directly or indirectly through subsidiary (ies), of more than one-half of the voting power of an enterprise; or

(b) control of the composition of the board of directors in the case of a company or of the composition of the corresponding governing body in case of any other enterprise so as to obtain economic benefits from its activities.

A subsidiary is an enterprise that is controlled by another enterprise (known as the parent). A parent is an enterprise that has one or more subsidiaries. A group is a parent and all its subsidiaries. Consolidated financial statements are the financial statements of a group presented as those of a single enterprise.

The equity method is a method of accounting whereby the investment is initially recorded at cost, identifying any goodwill/capital reserve arising at the time of acquisition. The carrying amount of the investment is adjusted thereafter for the post acquisition change in the investor's share of net assets of the investee. The consolidated statement of profit and loss reflects the investor's share of the results of operations of the investee.

Equity is the residual interest in the assets of an enterprise after deducting all its liabilities.

4. For the purpose of this Statement, significant influence does not extend to power to govern the financial and/or operating policies of an enterprise. Significant influence may be gained by share ownership, statute or agreement. As regards share ownership, if an investor holds, directly or indirectly through subsidiary(ies), 20% or more of the voting power of the investee, it is presumed that the investor has significant influence, unless it can be clearly demonstrated that this is not the case. Conversely, if the investor holds, directly or indirectly through subsidiary(ies), less than 20% of the voting power of the investee, it is presumed that the investor does not have significant influence, unless such influence can be clearly demonstrated.6 A substantial or majority ownership by another investor does not necessarily preclude an investor from having significant influence.

5. The existence of significant influence by an investor is usually evidenced in one or more of the following ways:
    (a) Representation on the board of directors or corresponding governing body of the investee;
    (b) participation in policy making processes;
    (c) material transactions between the investor and the investee;
    (d) interchange of managerial personnel; or
    (e) provision of essential technical information.

6. Under the equity method, the investment is initially recorded at cost, identifying any goodwill/capital reserve arising at the time of acquisition and the carrying amount is increased or decreased to recognise the investor's share of the profits or losses of the investee after the date of acquisition. Distributions received from an investee reduce the carrying amount of the investment. Adjustments to the carrying amount may also be necessary for alterations in the investor's proportionate interest in the investee arising from changes in the investee's equity that have not been included in the statement of profit and loss. Such changes include those arising from the revaluation of fixed assets and investments, from foreign exchange translation differences and from the adjustment of differences arising on amalgamations.

Accounting for Investments - Equity Method

7. An investment in an associate should be accounted for in consolidated financial statements under the equity method except when;
    (a) the investment is acquired and held exclusively with a view to Us subsequent disposal in the nearfuture; or

(b) the associate operates under severe long-term restrictions that significantly impair its ability to transfer funds to the investor. investments in such associates should be accounted for in accordance with Accounting Standard (AS) 13, Accounting for Investments. The reasons for not-applying the equity method in accounting for investments in an associate should be disclosed in the consolidated financial statements.

8. Recognition of income on the basis of distributions received may not be an adequate measure of the income earned by an investor on an investment in an associate because the distributions received may bear little relationship to the performance of the associate. As the investor has significant influence over the associate, the investor has a measure of responsibility for the associate's performance and, as a result, the return on its investment. The investor accounts for this stewardship by extending the scope of its consolidated financial statements to include its share of results of such an associate and so provides an analysis of earnings' and investment from which more useful ratios can be calculated. As a result, application of the equity method in consolidated financial statements provides more informative reporting of the net assets and net income of the investor.

9. An investor should discontinue the use of the equity method from the date that:
   (a) It ceases to have significant influence in an associate but retains-, either in whole or in part, its investment; or
   (b) the use of the equity method is no longer appropriate because the associateoperates under severe long-term restrictions that significantly impair its ability to transfer funds to the investor.

   From the date of discontinuing the use of the equity method, investments in such associates should be accounted for in accordance with Accounting Standard (AS) 13, Accounting for Investments. For this purpose, the carrying amount of the investment at that date should be regarded as cost thereafter.

Application of the Equity Method

10. Many of the procedures appropriate for the application of the equity method are similar to the consolidation procedures set out in Accounting Standard (AS) 21, Consolidated Financial Statements. Furthermore, the broad concepts underlying the consolidation procedures used in the acquisition of a subsidiary are adopted on the acquisition of an investment in an associate.

11. An investment in an associate is accounted for under the equity method from the date on-which it falls within the definition of an associate. On acquisition of the investment any difference between the cost of acquisition and the investor's share of the equity of the associate is described as goodwill or capital reserve, as the case may be.

12. Goodwill/capital reserve arising on the acquisition of an associate by an investor should be included in the carrying amount of investment in the associate but should

be disclosed separately.

13. In using equity method for accounting for investment in an associate, unrealised profits and losses resulting from transactions between the investor (or its consolidated subsidiaries) and the associate should be eliminated to the extent of the investor's interest in the associate. Unrealised losses should not be eliminated if and to the extent the cost of the transferred asset cannot be recovered.

14. The most recent available financial statements of the associate are used by the investor in applying the equity, method; they are usually drawn up to the same date as the financial statements of the investor. When the reporting dates of the investor and the associate are different, the associate often prepares, for the use of the investor, statements as at the same date as the financial, statements of the investor. When it is impracticable to do this, financial statements drawn up to a different reporting date may be used. The consistency principle requires that the length of the reporting periods, and any difference in the reporting dates, are consistent from period to period.

15. When financial statements with a different reporting date are used, adjustments are made for the effects of any significant events or transactions between the investor (or its consolidated subsidiaries) and the associate that occur between the date of the associate's financial statements and the date of the investor's consolidated financial statements.

16. The investor usually prepares consolidated financial statements using uniform accounting policies for the like transactions and events in similar circumstances. In case an associate uses accounting policies other than those adopted for the consolidated financial statements for like transactions and events in similar circumstances, appropriate adjustments are made to the associate's financial statements when they are used by the investor in applying the equity method. If it is not practicable to do so, that fact is disclosed along with a brief description of the differences between the accounting policies.

17. If an associate has outstanding cumulative preference shares held outside the group, the investor computes its share of profits or losses after adjusting for the preference dividends whether or not the dividends have been declared.

18. If, under the equity method, an investor's share of losses of an associate equals or exceeds the carrying amount of the investment, the investor ordinarily discontinues recognising its share of further losses and the investment is reported at nil value. Additional losses are provided for to the extent that the investor has incurred obligations or made payments on behalf of the associate to satisfy obligations of the associate that the investor has guaranteed or to which the investor is otherwise committed. If the associate subsequently reports profits, the investor resumes including its share of those profits only after its share of the profits equals the share of net losses that have not been recognised.

19. Where an associate presents consolidated financial statements, the results and net assets to be taken into account are those reported in that associate's consolidated financial statements.

20. The carrying amount of investment in an associate should be reduced to recognise a decline, other than temporary, in the value of the investment, such reduction being determined and made for each investment individually.

Contingencies

21. In accordance with Accounting Standard (AS) 4, Contingencies and Events Occurring After the Balance Sheet, Date, the investor discloses in the consolidated financial statements:

(a) its share of the contingencies and capital commitments of an associate for which it is also contingently liable; and

(b) those contingencies that arise because the investor is severally liable for the liabilities of the associate.

Disclosure

22. In addition to the-disclosures required by paragraph 7 and 12, an appropriate listing and description of associates including the proportion of ownership interest and, if different, the proportion of voting power held should be disclosed in the consolidated financial statements.

23. Investments in associates accounted for using the equity method should be classified as long-term investments and disclosed separately in the consolidated balance sheet. The investor's share of the profits or losses of such investments should be disclosed separately in the consolidated statement of profit and loss. The investor's share of any extraordinary or prior period items should also be separately disclosed.

24. The name(s) of the associate(s) of which reporting date(s) is/are different from that of the financial statements of an investor and the differences in reporting dates should be disclosed in the consolidated financial statements.

25. In case an associate uses accounting policies other than those adopted for the consolidated financial statements for like transactions and events in similar circumstances and it is not practicable to make appropriate adjustments to the associate's financial statements, the fact should be disclosed along with a brief description of the differences in the accounting policies.

Transitional Provisions

26. On the first occasion when investment in an associate is accounted for in consolidated financial statements in accordance with this Statement, the carrying amount of investment in the associate should be brought to the amount that would have resulted had the equity method of accounting been followed as per this Statement since the acquisition of the associate. The corresponding adjustment in this regard should be made in the retained earnings in the consolidated financial statements.

1.13 Accounting Standard (AS - 24) (issued 2002) - Discontinuing Operations :

(In this Accounting Standard, the standard portion have been set in bold italic type. These should be read in the context of the background material which has been set in normal type, and in the context of the 'Preface to the Statements of Accounting Standards'.[1])

Accounting Standard (AS) 24, 'Discontinuing Operations', issued by the Council of the Institute of Chartered Accountants of India, is recommendatory in nature2 at present. The following is the text of the Accounting Standard.

Objective

The objective of this Statement is to establish principles for reporting information about discontinuing operations, thereby enhancing the ability of users of financial statements to make projections of an enterprise's cash flows, earnings-generating capacity, and financial position by segregating information about discontinuing operations from information about continuing operations.

Scope

1.   This Statement applies to all discontinuing operations of an enterprise.

2.   The requirements related to cash flow statement contained in this Statement are applicable where an enterprise prepares and presents a cash flow statement.

Definitions

Discontinuing Operation

3.   A discontinuing operation is a component of an enterprise:
  (a)   that the enterprise, pursuant to a single plan, is:
  (i)   disposing of substantially in its entirety, such as by selling the component in a single transaction or by demerger or spin-off of ownership of the component to the enterprise's shareholders; or
  (ii)   disposing of piecemeal, such as by selling off the component's assets and settling its liabilities individually; or
  (iii)   terminating through abandonment; and
  (b)   that represents a separate major tine of business or geographical area of operations; and
  (c)   that can be distinguished operationally' and for financial reporting purposes.

4.   Under criterion (a) of the definition (paragraph 3 (a)), a discontinuing operation may be disposed of in its entirety or piecemeal, but always pursuant to an overall plan to discontinue the entire component.

5.   If an enterprise sells a component substantially in its entirety, the result can be a net gain or net loss. For such a discontinuance, a binding sale agreement is entered into on a specific date, although the actual transfer of possession and control of the discontinuing operation may occur at a later date. Also, payments to the seller may

occur at the time of the agreement, at the time of the transfer, or over an extended future period.

6. Instead of disposing of a component substantially in its entirety, an enterprise may discontinue and dispose of the component by selling its assets and settling its liabilities piecemeal (individually or in small groups). For piecemeal disposals, while the overall result may be a net gain or a net loss, the sale of an individual asset or settlement of an individual liability may have the opposite effect. Moreover, there is no specific date at which an overall binding sale agreement is entered into. Rather, the sales of assets and settlements of liabilities may occur over a period of months or perhaps even longer. Thus, disposal of a component may be in progress at the end of a financial reporting period. To qualify as a discontinuing operation, the disposal must be pursuant to a single co-ordinated plan.

7. An enterprise may terminate an operation by abandonment without substantial sales of assets. An abandoned operation would be a discontinuing operation if it satisfies the criteria in the definition. However, changing the scope of an operation or the manner in which it is conducted is not an abandonment because that operation, although changed, is continuing.

8. Business enterprises frequently close facilities, abandon products or even product lines, and change the size of their work force in response to market forces. While those kinds of terminations generally are not, in themselves, discontinuing operations as that term is defined in paragraph 3 of this statement, they can occur in connection with a discontinuing operation.

9. Examples of activities that do not necessarily satisfy criterion (a) of paragraph 3, but that might do so in combination with other circumstances, include:

    (a) gradual or evolutionary phasing out of a product line or class of service;

    (b) discontinuing, even if relatively abruptly, several products within an ongoing line of business;

    (c) shifting of some production or marketing activities for a particular line of business from one location to another; and

    (d) closing of a facility to achieve productivity improvements or other cost savings. An example in relation to consolidated financial statements is selling a subsidiary whose activities are similar to those of the parent or other subsidiaries.

10. A reportable business segment or geographical segment as defined in Accounting Standard (AS) 17, Segment Reporting, would normally satisfy criterion (b) of the definition of a discontinuing operation (paragraph 3) that is, it would represent a separate major line of business or geographical area of operations. A part of such a segment may also satisfy criterion (b) of the definition. For an enterprise that operates in a single business or geographical segment and therefore does not report segment information, a major product or service line may also satisfy the criteria of the definition.

11. A component can be distinguished operationally and for financial reporting purposes - criterion (c) of the definition of a discontinuing operation (paragraph 3) - if all the following conditions are met:
    (a) the operating assets and liabilities of the component can be directly attributed to it;
    (b) its revenue can be directly attributed to it;
    (c) at least a majority of its operating expenses can be directly attributed to it.
12. Assets, liabilities, revenue, and expenses are directly attributable to a component if they would be eliminated when the component is sold, abandoned or otherwise disposed of. If debt is attributable to a component, the related interest and other financing costs are similarly attributed to it.
13. Discontinuing operations, as defined in this Statement, are expected to occur relatively infrequently. All infrequently occurring events do not necessarily qualify as discontinuing operations. Infrequently occurring events that do not qualify as discontinuing operations may result in items of income or expense that require separate disclosure pursuant to Accounting Standard (AS) 5, Net Profit or Loss for the Period, Prior Period Items and Changes in Accounting Policies, because their size, nature, or incidence make them relevant to explain the performance of the enterprise for the period.
14. The fact that a disposal of a component of an enterprise is classified as a discontinuing operation under this Statement does not, in itself, bring into question the enterprise's ability to continue as a going concern.

Initial Disclosure Event

15. With respect to a discontinuing operation, the initial disclosure event is the occurrence of one of the following,

whichever occurs earlier :

    (a) the enterprise has entered into a binding sale agreement for substantially all of the assets attributable to the discontinuing operation; or
    (b) the enterprise's board of directors or similar governing body has both (i) approved a detailed, formal plan for the discontinuance and (ii) made an announcement of the plan.
16. Ajdetailed, formal plan for the discontinuance normally includes:
    (a) identification of the major assets to be disposed of;
    (b) the expected method of disposal;
    (c) the period expected to be required for completion of the disposal;
    (d) the principal locations affected;
    (e) the location, function, and approximate number of employees who will be compensated for terminating their services; and
    (f) the estimated proceeds or salvage to be realised by disposal.

17. An enterprise's board of directors or similar governing body is considered to have made the announcement of a detailed, formal plan for discontinuance, if it has announced the main features of the plan to those affected by it, such as, lenders, stock exchanges, creditors, trade unions, etc., in a sufficiently specific manner so as to make the enterprise demonstrably committed to the discontinuance.

Recognition and Measurement

18. An enterprise should apply the principles of recognition and measurement that are set out in other Accounting Standards for the purpose of deciding as to when and how to recognise and measure the changes in assets and liabilities and the revenue, expenses, gains, losses and cashflows relating to a discontinuing operation.

19. This Statement does not establish any recognition and measurement principles. Rather, it requires that an enterprise follow recognition and measurement current principles established in other Accounting Standards, e.g., Accounting Standard (AS) 4, Contingencies and Events Occurring After the Balance Sheet Date and Accounting Standard on Impairment of Assets[3].

Presentation and Disclosure

Initial Disclosure

20. An enterprise should include the following information relating to a discontinuing operation in its financial statements beginning with the financial statements for the period in which the initial disclosure event (as defined in paragraph 15) occurs:

    (a) a description of the discontinuing operation(s);

    (b) the business or geographical segments) in which it is reported as per AS 17, Segment Reporting;

    (c) the date and nature of the initial disclosure event;

    (d) the date or period in which the discontinuance is expected to be completed if known or determinable;

    (e) the carrying amounts, as of the balance sheet date, of the total assets to be disposed of and the total liabilities to be sealed;

    (f) the amounts of revenue and expenses in respect of the ordinary activities attributable to the discontinuing operation during the current financial reporting period;

    (g) the amount of pre-tax profit or loss from ordinary activities attributable to the discontinuing operation during the current financial reporting period, and the income tax expense4 related thereto; and

    (h) the amounts of net cashflows attributable to the operating, investing, and financing activities of the discontinuing operation during the current financial reporting period.

21. For the purpose of presentation and disclosures required by this Statement, the items of assets, liabilities, revenues, expenses, gains, losses, and cash flows can be attributed

to a discontinuing operation only if they will be disposed of, settled, reduced, or eliminated when the discontinuance is completed. To the extent that such items continue after completion of the discontinuance, they are not allocated to the discontinuing operation. For example, salary of the continuing staff of a discontinuing operation.

22. If an initial disclosure event occurs between the balance sheet date and the date on which the financial statements for that period are approved by the board of directors in the case of a company or by the corresponding approving authority in the case of any other enterprise, disclosures as required by Accounting Standard (AS) 4, Contingencies and Events Occurring After the Balance Sheet Date, are made.

Other Disclosures

23. When an enterprise disposes of assets or settles liabilities attributable to a discontinuing operation or enters into binding agreements for the sale of such assets or the settlement of such liabilities, it should include, in its financial statements, the following information when the events occur:

    (a) for any gain or loss that is recognised on the disposal of assets or settlement of liabilities attributable to the discontinuing operation, (i) the amount of the pre-tax gain or loss and (ii) income tax expense relating to the gain or loss; and

    (b) the net selling price or range of prices (which is after deducting expected disposal costs) of those net assets for which the enterprise has entered into one or more binding sale agreements, the expected timing of receipt of those cashflows and the carrying amount of those net assets on the balance sheet date.

24. The asset disposals, liability settlements, and binding sale agreements referred to in the preceding paragraph may occur concurrently with the initial disclosure event, or in the period in which the initial disclosure event occurs, or in a later period.

25. If some of the assets attributable to a discontinuing operation have actually been sold or are the subject of one or more binding sale agreements entered into between the balance sheet date and the date on which the financial statements are approved by the board of directors in case of a company or by the corresponding approving authority in the case of any other enterpris the disclosures required by Accounting Standard (AS) 4, Contingencies and Events Occurring After the Balance Sheet Date, are made.

Updating the Disclosures

26. In addition to the disclosures in paragraphs 20 and 23, an enterprise should include, in its financial statements, for periods subsequent to the one in which the initial disclosure event occurs, a description of any significant changes in the amount or timing of cashflows relating to the assets to be disposed or liabilities to be settled and the events causing those changes.

27. Examples of events and activities that would be disclosed include the nature and terms of binding sale agreements for the assets, a demerger or spin-off by issuing equity shares of the new company to the enterprise's shareholders, and legal or regulatory approvals.

28. The disclosures required by paragraphs 20,23 and 26 should continue in financial statements for periods up to and including the period in which the discontinuance is completed. A discontinuance is completed when the plan is substantially completed or abandoned, though full payments from the buyer(s) may not yet have been received.

29. If an enterprise abandons or withdraws from plan that was previously reported as a discontinuing operation, that fact, reasons therefor and its effect should be disclosed.

30. For the purpose of applying paragraph 29, disclosure of the effect includes reversal of any prior impairment loss5 or provision that was recognised with respect to the discontinuing operation.

Separate Disclosure for Each Discontinuing Operation

31. Any disclosures required by this Statement should be presented separately for each discontinuing operation.

Presentation of the Required Disclosures

32. The disclosures required by paragraphs 20, 23, 26, 28, 29 and 31 should be presented in the notes to the financial statements except the following which should be shown on the face of the statement of profit and loss:

    (a) the amount of pre-tax profit or loss from ordinary activities attributable to the discontinuing operation during the current financial reporting period, and the income tax expense related thereto (paragraph 20 (g)); and

    (b) the amount of the pre-tax gain or loss recognised on the disposal of assets or settlement of liabilities attributable to the discontinuing operation (paragraph 23 (a).

Illustrative Presentation and Disclosures

33. Appendix 1 provides examples of the presentation and disclosures required by this Statement.

Restatement of Prior Periods

34. Comparative information for prior periods that is presented in financial statements prepared after the initial disclosure event should be restated to segregate assets, liabilities, revenue, expenses, and cash flows of continuing and discontinuing operations in a manner similar to that required by paragraphs 20,23, 26,28,29, 31 and 32.

35. Appendix 2 illustrates application of paragraph 34.

Disclosure in Interim Financial Reports

36. Disclosures in an interim financial report in respect of a discontinuing operation should be made in accordance with AS 25, Interim Financial Reporting, including:

    (a) any significant activities or events since the end of the most recent annual reporting period relating to a discontinuing operation; and

    (b) any significant changes in the amount or timing of cash flows relating to the assets to be disposed or liabilities to be settled.

1.14 Accounting Standard 25 (AS - 25) Interim Financial Reporting :

(In this Accounting Standard, the standard portions have been set in bold italic type. These should be read in the context of the background material which has been set in normal type, and in the context of the 'Preface to the Statements of Accounting Standard'[1].)

Accounting Standard (AS) 25, 'Interim Financial Reporting', issued by the Council of the Institute of Chartered Accountants of India, comes into effect in respect of accounting periods commencing on or after 1-4-2002. If an enterprise is required or elects to prepare and present an interim financial report, it should comply with this Standard.[2]

The following is the test of the Accounting Standard.

Objective

The objective of this Statement is to prescribe the minimum content of an interim financial report and to prescribe the principles for recognition and measurement in a complete or condensed financial statements for an interim period. Timely and reliable interim financial reporting improves the ability of investors, creditors, and others to understand an enterprise's capacity to generate earnings and cash flows, its financial condition and liquidity.

Scope

1. This Statement does not mandate which enterprises should be required to present interim financial reports, how frequently, or how soon after the end of an interim period. If an enterprise is required or elects to prepare and present an interim financial report, it should comply with this Statement.

2. A statute governing an enterprise or a regulator may require an enterprise to prepare and present certain information at an interim date which may be different in form and/or content as required by this Statement. In such a case, the recognition and measurement principles as laid down in this Statement are applied in respect of such information, unless otherwise specified in the statute or by the regulator.

3. The requirements related to cash flow statement, complete or condensed, contained in this Statement are applicable where an enterprise prepares and presents a cash flow statement for the purpose of its annual financial report.

Definitions

4. The following terms are used in this Statement with the meanings specified :
   Interim period is a financial reporting period shorter than a full financial year.

Interim financial report means a financial report containing either a complete set of financial statements or a set of condensed financial statements (as described in this Statement) for an interim period.

5. During the first year of operations of an enterprise, its annual financial reporting period may be shorter than a financial year. In such a case, that shorter period is not considered as an interim period.

Content of an Interim Financial Report

6. A complete set of financial statements normally includes:

    (a) balance sheet;

    (b) statement of profit and loss;

    (c) cash flow statement; and

    (d) notes including those relating to accounting policies and other statements and explanatory material that are an integral part of the financial statements.

7. In the interest of timeliness and cost considerations and to avoid repetition of information previously reported, an enterprise may be required to or may elect to present less information at interim dates as compared with its annual financial statements. The benefit of timeliness of presentation may be partially offset by a reduction in detail in the information provided. Therefore, this Statement requires preparation and presentation of an interim financial report containing, as a minimum, a set of condensed financial statements. The interim financial report containing condensed financial statements is intended to provide an update on the attest annual financial statements. Accordingly, it focuses on new activities, events, and circumstances and does not duplicate information previously reported.

8. This Statement does not prohibit or discourage an enterprise from presenting a complete set of financial statements in its interim financial report, rather than a set of condensed financial statements. This Statement also does not prohibit or discourage an enterprise from including, in condensed interim financial statements, more than the minimum line items or selected explanatory notes as set out in this Statement. The recognition and measurement principles set out in this Statement apply also to complete financial statements for an interim period, and such statements would include all disclosures required by this Statement (particularly the selected disclosures in paragraph 16) as well as those required by other Accounting Standards.

Minimum Components of an Interim Financial Report

9. An interim financial report should include, at a minimum, the following components:

    (a) condensed balance sheet;

    (b) condensed statement of profit and loss;

    (c) condensed cash flow statement; and

    (d) selected explanatory notes.

Form and Content Interim Financial Statements

10. In an enterprise prepares and presents a complete set of financial statements in its interim financial report, the form and content of those statements should conform to the requirements as applicable to annual complete set of financial statements.

11. If an enterprise prepares and presents a set of condensed financial statements in its interim financial report, those condensed statements should include, at a minimum, each of the headings and sub-headings that were included in its most recent annual financial statements and the selected explanatory notes as required by this statement. Additional line items or notes should be included if their omission would make the condensed interim financial statements misleading.

12. If an enterprise presents basic and diluted earnings per share in its annual financial statements in accordance with Accounting Standard (AS) 20, Earnings Per Share, basic and diluted earnings per share should be presented in accordance with AS 20 on the face of the statement of profit and loss, complete or condensed, for an interim period.

13. If an enterprise's annual financial report included the consolidated financial statements in addition to the parent's separate financial statements, the interim financial report includes both the consolidated financial statements and separate financial statements, complete or condensed.

14. Appendix 1 provides illustrative formats of condensed financial statements,

Selected Explanatory Notes

15. A user of an enterprise's interim financial report will ordinarily have access to the most recent annual financial report of that enterprise. It is, therefore, not necessary for the notes to an interim financial report to provide relatively insignficant updates to the information that was already reported in the notes in the most recent annual financial report. At an interim date, an explanation of events-and transactions that are significant to an understanding of the changes in financial position and performance of the enterprise since the last annual reporting date is more useful.

16. An enterprise should include the following information, as a minimum, in the notes to its interim financial statements, if material and if not disclosed elsewhere in the interim financial report:

    (a) a statement that the same accounting policies are followed in the interim financial statements as those followed in the most recent annual financial statements or, if those policies have been changed, a description of the nature and effect of the change;

    (b) explanatory comments about the seasonally of interim operations;

    (c) the nature and amount of items affecting assets, liabilities, equity, net income, or cash flows that are unusual because of their nature, size, or incidence (see paragraphs 12 to 14 of Accounting Standard (AS) 5, Net Profit or Loss for the Period, Prior Period Items and Changes in Accounting Policies);

(d) the nature and amount of changes in estimates of amounts reported in prior interim periods of the current financial year or changes in estimates of amounts reported in prior financial years, if those changes have a material effect in the current interim period;

(e) issuances, buy-backs, repayments and restructuring of debt, equity and potential equity shares;

(f) dividends, aggregate or per share (in absolute or percentage terms), separately for equity shares and other shares;

(g) segment revenue, segment capital employed (segment assets minus segment liabilities) and segment result for business segments or geographical segments, whichever is the enterprise's primary basis of segment reporting (disclosure of segment information is required in an enterprise's interim financial report only if the enterprise is required, in terms of AS 17, Segment Reporting, to disclose segment information in its annual financial statements);

(h) the effect of changes in the composition of the enterprise during the interim period, such as .amalgamations, acquisition or disposal of subsidiaries and long-term investments, restructuring, and discontinuing operations; and

(i) material changes in contingent liabilities since the last annual balance sheet date. The above information should normally be reported on a financial year-to-date basis. However, the enterprise talso disclose any events or transactions that are material to an understanding of the current interim period.

17. Other Accounting Standards specify disclosures that should be made in financial statements. In that context, financial statements mean complete set of financial statements normally included in an annual financial report and sometimes included in other reports. The disclosures required by those other Accounting Standards are not required an enterprise's interim financial report includes only condensed financial statements and selected explanatory notes rather than a complete set of financial statements.

Periods for which Interim Financial Statements are required to be presented

18. Interim reports should include interim financial statements (condensed or complete) for periods as follows:

(a) balance sheet as of the end of the current interim period and a comparative balance sheet as of the end of the immediately preceding financial year;

(b) statements of profit and loss for the current interim period and cumulatively for the current financial year to date, with comparative statements of profit and loss for the comparable interim periods (current and year-to-date) of the immediately preceding financial year; cash flow statement cumulatively for the current financial year to date, with a comparative statement for the comparable year-to-date period of the immediately preceding financial year.

19. For an enterprise whose business is highly seasonal, financial information for the

twelve months ending on the interim reporting date and comparative information for the prior twelve-month period may be useful. Accordingly, enterprises whose business is highly seasonal are encouraged to consider reporting such information in addition to the information called for in the preceding paragraph.

20. Appendix 2 illustrates the periods required to be presented by an enterprise that reports half-yearly and an enterprise that reports quarterly.

Materiality

21. **In deciding how to recognise, measure, classify, or disclose an item for interim financial reporting purposes, materiality should be assessed in relation to the interim period financial data. In making assessments of materiality, it should be recognised that interim measurements may rely on estimates to a greater extent than measurements of annual financial data.**

22. The Preface to the Statements of Accounting Standards states that "The Accounting Standards are intended to apply only to items which are material." The Framework for the Preparation and Presentation of Financial Statements, issued by the Institute of Chartered Accountants of India, states that "information is material if its misstatement (i.e., omission or erroneous statement) could influence the economic decisions of users taken on the basis of the financial information."

23. Judgement its always required in assessing materiality for financial reporting purposes. For reasons of understandability of the interim figures, materiality for making recognition and disclosure decision is assessed in relation to the interim period financial data. Thus, for example, unusual or extraordinary items, changes in accounting policies or estimates, and prior period items are recognised and disclosed based on materiality in relation to interim period data. The over riding objective is to ensure that an interim financial report includes all information that is relevant to understanding an enterprise's financial position and performance during the interim period.

Disclosure in Annual Financial Statements

24. An enterprise may not prepare and present a separate financial report for the final interim period because the annual financial statements are presented. In such a case, paragraph 25 requires certain disclosures to be made in the annual financial statements for that financial year.

25. **If an estimate of an amount reported in an interim period is changed significantly during the final interim period of the financial year but a separate financial report is not prepared and presented for that final interim period, the nature and amount of that change in estimate should be disclosed in a note to the annual financial statements for that financial year.**

26. Accounting Standard (AS) 5, Net Profit or Loss for the Period, Prior Items and Changes in Accounting Policies, requires disclosure, in financial statements, of the

nature and (if practicable) the amount of a change in an accounting estimate which has a material effect in the current period, or which is expected to have a material effect in subsequent periods. Paragraph 16(d) of this Statement requires similar disclosure in an interim financial report. Examples include changes in estimate in the final interim period relating to inventory write-downs, restructuring, or impairment losses that were reported in an earlier interim period of the financial year. The disclosure required by the preceding paragraph is consistent with AS 5 requirements and is intended to be restricted in scope so as to relate only to the change in estimates. An enterprise is not required to include additional interim period financial information in its annual financial statements.

Recognition and Measurement

Same Accounting Policies as Annual

27. **An enterprise should apply the same accounting policies in its interim financial statements as are applied in its annual financial statements, except for accounting policy changes made after the date of the most recent annual financial statements that are to be reflected in the next annual financial statements. However, the frequency of an enterprise's reporting (annual, half-yearly, or quarterly) should not affect the measurement of its annual results. To achieve that objective, measurements for interim reporting purposes should be made on a year-to-date basis.**

28. Requiring that an enterprise apply the same accounting policies in its interim financial statements as in its annual financial statements may seem to suggest that interim period measurements are made as if each interim stands alone as an independent reporting period stands alone as an independent reporting period. However, by providing that the frequency of an enterprise's reporting should not affect the measurement of its annual results, paragraph 27 acknowledges that an interim period is a part of a financial year. Year-to-date measurements may involve changes in estimates of amounts reported in prior interim periods of the current financial year. But the principles for recognising assets, liabilities, income, and expenses for interim periods are the same as in annual financial statements.

29. To illustrate:

    (a) the principles for recognising and measuring losses from inventory write-downs, restructuring, or impairments in an interim period are the same as those that an enterprise would follow if it prepared only annual financial statements. However, if such items are recognised and measured in one interim period and the estimate changes in a subsequent interim period of that financial year, the original estimate is changed in the subsequent interim period either by accrual of an additional amount of loss or by. reversal of the previously recognised amount;

    (b) a cost that does not meet the definition of an asset at the end of an interim period is not deferred on the balance sheet date either to await future information as to whether it has met the definition of an asset or to smooth earnings over interim periods within a financial year; and

(c) income tax expense is recognised in each interim period based on the best estimate of the weighted average annual effective income tax rate expected for the full financial year. Amounts accrued for income tax expense in one interim period may have to be adjusted in a subsequent interim period of that financial year if the estimate of the annual effective income tax rate changes.

30. Under the Framework for the Preparation and Presentation of Financial Statements, recognition is the "process of incorporating in the balance sheet or statement of profit and loss an item that meets the definition of an element and satisfies the criteria for recognition". The definitions of assets, liabilities, income, and expenses are fundamental to recognition, both at annual and interim financial reporting dates.

31. For assets, the same tests of future economic benefits apply at interim dates as they apply at the end of an enterprise's financial year. Costs that, by their nature, would not qualify as assets at financial year end would not qualify at interim dates as well. Similarly, a liability at an interim reporting date must represent an existing obligation at that date, just as it must at an annual reporting date.

32. Income is recognised in the statement of profit and loss when an increase in future economic benefits related to an increase in an asset or a decrease of a liability has arisen that can be measured reliably. Expenses are recognised in the statement of profit and loss when a decrease in future economic benefits related to a decrease in an asset or an increase of a liability has arisen that can be measured reliably. The recognition of items in the balance sheet which do not meet the definition of assets or liabilities is not allowed.

33. In measuring assets, liabilities, income, expenses, and cash flows reported in its financial statements, an enterprise that reports only annually is able to take into account information that becomes available throughout the financial year. Its measurements are, in effect, one a year-to-date basis.

34. An enterprise that reports half-yearly, uses information available by mid-year or shortly thereafter in making the measurements in its financial statements for the first six-month period and information available by year-end or shortly thereafter for .the twelve-month period. The twelve-month measurements will reflect any changes in estimates of amounts reported for the first six-month period. The amounts reported in the interim financial report for the first six-month period are not retrospectively adjusted. Paragraphs 16(d) and 25 require, however, that the nature and amount of any significant changes in estimates be disclosed.

35. An enterprise that reports more frequently than half-yearly, measures income and expenses on a year-to-date basis for each interim period using information available when each set of financial statements is being prepared. Amounts of income and expenses reported in the current interim period will reflect any changes in estimates of amounts reported in prior interim periods of the financial year. The amounts

reported in prior interim periods are not retrospectively adjusted. Paragraphs 16(d) and 25 require, however, that the nature and amount of any significant changes in estimates be disclosed.

Revenues Received Seasonally or Occasionally

36. **Revenues that are received seasonally or occasionally within a financial year should not be anticipated or deferred as of an interim date if anticipation or deferral would not be appropriate at the end of the enterprise's financial year.**

37. Examples include dividend revenue, royalties, and government grants. Additionally, some enterprises consistently earn more revenues in certain interim periods of a financial year than in other interim periods, for example, seasonal revenues of retailers. Such revenues are recognised when they occur.

Costs Incurred Unevenly During the Financial Year

38. **Costs that are incurred unevenly during an enterprise's financial year should be anticipated or deferred for interim reporting purposes if, and only if, it is also appropriate to anticipate or defer that type of cost at the end of the financial year.**

Applying the Recognition and Measurement Principles

39. Appendix 3 provides examples of applying the general recognition and measurement principles set out in paragraph 27 to 38.

Use of Estimates

40. **The measurement procedures to be followed in an interim financial report should be designed to ensure that the resulting information is reliable and that all material financial information that is relevant to an understanding of the financial position or performance of the enterprise is appropriately disclosed. While measurements in both annual and interim financial reports are often based on reasonable estimates, the preparation of interim financial reports generally will require a greater use of estimation methods than annual financial reports.**

41. Appendix 4 provides examples of the use of estimates in interim periods.

Restatement of Previously Reported Interim Periods

42. A change in accounting policy, other than one for which the transition is specified by an Accounting Standard, should be reflected by restating the financial statements of prior interim periods of the current financial year.

43. One objective of the preceding principle is to ensure that a single accounting policy is applied to a particular class of transactions throughout an entire financial year. The effect of the principle in paragraph 42 is to require that within the current financial year any change in accounting policy be applied retrospectively to the beginning of the financial year.

Transitional Provision

44. On the first occassion that an interim financial report is presented in accordance with this statement the following need not be presented in respect of all the interim periods of the current financial year :
    (a) Comparative statements of profit & loss for the comparable interim periods (current and year to date) of the immediately preceeding financial year and
    (b) Comparative cash flow statement for the comparable year-to-date period of immediately precceding financial year.

AS - 26 : Intangible Assets [Effective Date : 1st April, 2003]

(Recently As - 8 Withdraw and included in AS 26)

Introduction

An intangible asset is a long-term asset without physical substance held for use in the business. Its value comes from the long-term rights or advantage that will flow to the owner. Examples are patents, copyrights, trademarks, licences, franchises, formulas and goodwill etc.

In the past, intangible assets have not been considered very significant for financial reporting. Recently, interest in intangible assets has grown because companies are paying huge amount for acquiring such assets. (For example, many new mobile telephone companies are ready to pay Rs 200-300 crores for obtaining licence from the government). In the past, the value of different intangible assets used to increase gradually as a company prospered. Nowadays, many intangible assets are purchased /developed for high prices. This includes not only traditional intangible assets, e.g., copyrights or trademarks, but also newer assets like mobile telephone licences, takeoff and landing rights at airports etc.

The growing financial significance of intangible assets has increased their importance as an accounting issue.

On the background of the above, the Council of Institute of Chartered Accounts of India issued AS - 26: 'Intangible Assets' in 2002. It is effective from 1st April, 2003 and mandatory in nature from that date for the following :
    (i) Enterprises whose equity or debt securities are listed on a recognised stock exchange in India;
    (ii) Enterprises that are in the process of issuing equity or debt securities that will be listed on a recognised stock exchange in India as evidenced by the board of directors' resolution in this regard;
    (iii) All other commercial, industrial and business reporting enterprises, whose turnover for the accounting period exceeds Rs. 50 crores;

Objectives

The objective of this Statement is to prescribe the accounting treatment for intangible assets that are not dealt with specifically in another Accounting Standard. This Statement requires an enterprise to recognise an intangible asset if, and only if, certain criteria are met. The Statement also specifies how to measure the carrying amount of intangible assets and requires certain disclosures about intangible assets.

Scope

This Statement should be applied by all enterprises in accounting for intangible assets, except :

(a) intangible assets that are covered by another Accounting Standard;

(b) financial assets;

(c) mineral rights and expenditure on the exploration for, or development and extraction of, minerals, oil, natural gas and similar non-regenerative resources; and

(d) intangible assets arising in insurance enterprises from contracts with policyholders.

If another Accounting Standard deals with a specific type of intangible asset, an enterprise applies that Accounting Standard instead of this Statement. For example, this Statement does not apply to:

(a) intangible assets held by an enterprise for sale in the ordinary course of business (see AS - 2, Valuation of Inventories, and AS - 7, Accounting for Construction Contracts);

(b) deferred tax assets (see AS - 22, Accounting for Taxes on Income) :

(c) leases that fall within the scope of AS - 19, Leases; and

(d) goodwill arising on an amalgamation (see AS - 14, Accounting for Amalgamations) and goodwill arising on consolidation (see AS - 2 1 , Consolidated Financial Statements).

Definitions

Intangible Asset

An intangible asset is an identifiable non-monetary asset, without physical substance, held for use in the production or supply of goods or services, for rental to others, or for administrative purposes.

Asset

An asset is a resource:

(a) controlled by an enterprise as a result of past events; and

(b) from which future economic benefits are expected to flow to the enterprise.

Monetary Asset

Monetary assets are money held and assets to be received in fixed or determinable amounts of money.

Non-monetary Asset

Non-monetary assets are assets other than monetary assets.

Research

Research is original and planned investigation undertaken with the prospect of gaining new scientific or technical knowledge and understanding.

Development

Development is the application of research findings or other knowledge to a plan or design for the production of new or substantially improved materials, devices, products, processes, systems or services prior to the commencement of commercial production or use.

Amortisation

Amortisation is the systematic allocation of the depreciable amount of an intangible asset over its useful life.

Depreciable Amount

Depreciable amount is the cast of an asset less its residual value.

Useful Life

Useful life is either:

(a) the period of time over which an asset is expected to be used by the enterprise: or

(b) the number of production or similar units expected to be obtained from the asset by the enterprise.

Residual Value

Residual value is the amount which an enterprise expects to obtain for an asset at the end of its useful life after deducting the expected costs of disposal.

Fair Value

Fair value of an asset is the amount for which that asset could be exchanged between knowledgeable, willing parties in an arm's length transaction.

Active Market

An active market is a market where all the following conditions exist:

(a) the items traded within the market are homogeneous;

(b) willing buyers and sellers can normally be found at any time; and

(c) prices are available to the public.

Impairment Loss

An impairment loss is the amount by which the carrying amount of an asset exceeds its recoverable amount.

Carrying Amount

Carrying amount is the amount at which an asset is recognised in the balance sheet, net of any accumulated amortisation and accumulated impairment losses thereon.

Intangible Assets

Enterprises frequently expend resources, or incur liabilities, on the acquisition, development, maintenance or enhancement of intangible resources such as

- scientific or technical knowledge;
- design and implementation of new processes or systems;
- licences;
- intellectual property;
- market knowledge and trademarks (including brand names and publishing titles).
  Common example of items encompassed by these broad headings are :
- Computer software
- Patents
- Copyrights
- Motion picture films
- Customer lists
- Mortgage servicing rights
- Fishing licences
- Import quotas
- Franchises
- Customer or supplier relationships
- Customer loyalty
- Market share and marketing rights

Not all the items described above will meet the definition of an intangible asset—(i) identifiability, (ii) control over a resource and (iii) expectation of future economic benefits flowing to the enterprise.

If an item covered by this Statement does not meet the definition of an intangible asset, expenditure to acquire it or generate it internally is recognised as an expense when it is incurred. However, if the item is acquired in an amalgamation in the nature of purchase, if forms part of the goodwill recognised at the date of the amalgamation.

Identifiability

The definition of an intangible asset requires that the asset be identified, to distinguish it from goodwill.

Goodwill arising on an amalgamation in the nature of purchase represents a payment made by the acquirer in anticipation of future economic benefits. The future economic benefits may result from synergy between the identifiable assets acquired or from assets which, individually, do not qualify for recognition in the financial statements but for which the acquirer is prepared to make a payment in the amalgamation.

An intangible asset can be clearly distinguished from goodwill if the asset is separable. An asset is separable if the enterprise could rent, sell, exchange or distribute the specific future economic benefits attributable to the asset without also disposing of future, economic benefits that flow from other assets used in the same revenue earning activity.

Separability is not a necessary condition for identifiability since an enterprise may be able to identify an asset in some other way. For example, if an intangible asset is acquired with a group of assets, the transaction may involve the transfer of legal rights that enable an enterprise to identify the intangible asset. Similarly, if an internal project aims to create legal rights for the enterprise, the nature of these rights may assist the enterprise in identifying an underlying internally generated intangible asset. Also, even if an asset generates future economic benefits only in combination with other assets, the asset is identifiable if the enterprise can identify the future economic benefits that will flow from the asset.

Control

An enterprise controls an asset if the enterprise has the power to obtain the future economic benefits flowing from the underlying resource and also can restrict the access of others to those benefits.

> **Example :** *Your company B Chini Ltd. wll be beniefitted from the construction of a road through its sugger cane fields, but the company do not control it, unless it can restrict the access of others to the road.*

The capacity of an enterprise to control these benefits would normally stem from legal rights, though an enterprise may be able to control the benefits in other way.

Market and technical knowledge may give rise to future economic benefits. An enterprise controls those benefits if. for example, the knowledge is protected by legal rights such as copyrights, a restraint of trade agreement (where permitted) or by a legal duty on employees to maintain confidentiality.

Personnel do not usually meet the definition of an intangible asset because an enterprise has insufficient control over (he expected future economic benefits arising from a team of skilled staff.

For a similar reason, specific management or technical talent is unlikely to meet the definition of an intangible asset, unless it is protected by legal rights to use it and to obtain the future economic benefits expected from it, and it also meets the other parts of the definition.

An enterprise may have a portfolio of customers or a market share and expect that, due to its efforts in building customer relationships and loyalty, the customers will continue to trade with the enterprise. However, in the absence of legal rights to protect, or other ways to control, the relationships with customers or the loyalty of the customers to the enterprise, the enterprise usually has insufficient control over the economic benefits from customer relationships and loyalty to consider that such items (portfolio of customers, market shares, customer relationships, customer loyalty) meet the definition of intangible assets.

Future Economic Benefits

The future economic benefits flowing from an intangible asset may include revenue from the sale of products or services, cost savings, or other benefits resulting from the use of the psset by the enterprise. For example, the use of intellectual property in a production process may reduce future production costs rather than increase future revenues.

Recognition and Initial Measurement

The recognition of an item as an intangible asset requires an enterprise to demonstrate that the item meets the:

(a) definition of an intangible asset

(b) recognition criteria

An intangible asset should be recognised if and only if

(a) it is probable that the future economic benefits that are attributable to the asset will flow to the enterprise; and

(b) the cost of the asset can be measured reliably.

Ar. enterprise should assess the probability of future economic benefits using reasonable and supportable assumptions that represent best estimate of the set of economic conditions that will exist over the useful life of the asset.

An enterprise uses judgement to assess the degree of certainty attached to the flow of future economic benefits that are attributable to the use of the asset on the basis of the evidence available at the time of initial recognition, giving greater weight to external evidence.

An intangible asset should be measured initially at cost.

Separate Acquisition

If an enterprise acquires intangible assets separately, or in amalgamation or through government grant, there is no restriction in recognising them. These should be recognised at cost.

The cost of an intangible asset comprises:

(i) purchase price

(ii) import duties

(iii) non-refundable other taxes

(iv) any directly attributable expenditure on making the assets ready for its intended use

(v) professional fees for legal services.

Any trade discounts and rebates are deducted in arriving at the cost.

If an intangible asset is acquired in exchange for shares or other securities of the reporting enterprise, the asset is recorded at its fair value, or the fair value of the securities issued, whichever is more clearly evident.

IFRS - Fair Value Accounting
International Financial Reporting Standards

Introduction

The IFRS Framework describes the basic concepts that underlie the preparation and presentation of financial statements for external users. The IFRS Framework serves as a guide to the Board in developing future IFRSs and as a guide to resolving accovn .ing issues that are not addressed directly in an International Accounting Standard or International Financial Reporting Standard or Interpretation. In the absence of a Standard or an Interpretation that specifically applies to a transaction, management must use its judgement in developing and applying an accounting policy that results in information that is relevant and reliable. In making that judgement, IAS 8.11 requires management to consider the definitions, recognition criteria, and measurement concepts for assets, liabilities, income, and expenses in the IFRS Framework.

The objective of general purpose financial reporting is to provide financial information about the reporting entity that is useful to existing and potential investors, lenders and other creditors in making decisions about providing resources to the entity. Those decisions involve buying, selling or holding equity and debt instruments, and providing or settling loans and other forms of credit. Many existing and potential investors, lenders and other creditors cannot require reporting entities to provide information directly to them and must rely on general purpose financial reports for much of the financial information they need. Consequently, they are the primary users to whom general purpose financial reports are directed.

General purpose financial reports do not and cannot provide all of the information that existing and potential investors, lenders and other creditors need. Therefore those users need to consider pertinent information from other sources. Other parties, such as regulators and members of the public other than investors, lenders and other creditors, may also find general purpose financial reports useful. However, those reports are not primarily directed to these other groups. In order to meet their objectives, financial statements are prepared on the accrual basis of accounting. Accrual accounting depicts the effects of transactions and other events and circumstances on a reporting entity's economic resources and claims in the periods in which those effects occur, even if the resulting cash receipts and payments occur in a different period. This is important because information about a reporting entity's economic resources and claims and changes in its economic resources and claims during a period provides a better basis for assessing the entity's past and future performance than information solely about cash receipts and payments during that period.

The financial statements are normally prepared on the assumption that an entity is a going concern and will continue in operation for the foreseeable future. Qualitative characteristics identify the types of information that are likely to be most useful to the existing and potential investors, lenders and other creditors for making decisions about the reporting entity on the basis of information in its financial report (financial information). If financial information is to be useful, it must be relevant (i.e. must have predictive value and confirmatory value, based on the nature or magnitude, or both, of the item to which the information relates in the context of an individual entity's financial report) and faithfully represents what it purports to represent (i.e. information must be complete, neutral and free from error). The usefulness of financial information is enhanced if it is comparable, verifiable timely and understandable. The LA SB acknowledges that cost may be a constrain on preparing useful financial information.

Scope of IFRS framework

The IFRS Framework addresses:

- the objective of financial reporting
- the qualitative characteristics of useful financial information

- the reporting entity
- the definition, recognition and measurement of the elements froln which financial statements are constructed
- concepts of capital and capital maintenance

The Objective of general purpose financial reporting

The primary users of general purpose financial reporting are present and potential investors, lenders and other creditors, who use that information to make decisions about buying, selling or holding equity or debt instruments and providing or settling loans or other forms of credit. The primary users need information about the resources of the entity not only to assess an entity's prospects for future net cash inflows but also how effectively and efficiently management has discharged their responsibilities to use the entity's existing resources (i.e., stewardsh't>). The IFRS Framework notes that general purpose financial reports cannot provide all the information that users may need to make economic decisions. They will need to consider pertinent information from other sources as well. The IFRS Framework notes that other parties, including prudential and market regulators, may find general purpose financial reports useful. However, the Board considered that the objectives of general purpose financial reporting and the objectives of financial regulation may not be consistent. Hence, regulators are not considered a primary user and general purpose financial reports are not primarily directed to regulators or other parties.

Information about a reporting entity's economic resources, claims, and changes in resources and claims

Economic resources and claims

Information about the nature and amounts of a reporting entity's economic resources and claims assists users to assess that entity's financial strengths and weaknesses; to assess liquidity and solvency, and its need and ability to obtain financing. Information about the claims and payment requirements assists users to predict how future cash flows will be distributed among those with a claim on the reporting entity. A reporting entity's economic resources and claims are reported in the statement of financial position.

Changes in economic resources and claims

Changes in a reporting entity's economic resources and claims result from that entity's performance and from other events or transactions such as issuing debt or equity instruments. Users need to b-?' able to distinguish between both of these changes.

Financial performance reflected by accrual accounting

Information about a reporting entity's financial performance during a period, representing changes in economic resources and claims other than those obtained directly from investors and creditors, is useful in assessing the entity's past and future ability to generate net cash inflows. Such information may also indicate the extent to.which general economic events have changed the entity's ability to generate future cash inflows. The changes in an entity's economic resources and claims are presented in the statement of comprehensive income.

Financial performance reflected by past cash flows

Information about a reporting entity's cash flows during the reporting period also assists users to assess the entity's ability to generate future net cash inflows. This information indicates how the entity obtains and spends cash, including information about its borrowing and repayment of debt, cash dividends to shareholders, etc. The changes in the entity's cash flows are presented in the statement of cash flows.

Changes in economic resources and claims not resulting from financial performance

Information about changes in an entity's economic resources and claims resulting from events and transactions other than financial performance, such as the issue of equity instruments or distributions of cash or other assets to shareholders is necessary to complete the picture of the total change in the entity's economic resources and claims.

The changes in an entity's economic resources and claims not resulting from financial performance is presented in the statement of changes in equity.

The Reporting entity

The Chapter on the Reporting Entity will be inserted once the f- IASB has completed its re-deliberations following the Exposure I Draft ED/2010/2 issued in March 2010.

Qualitative characteristics of useful financial information

The qualitative characteristics of useful financial reporting identify the types of information are likely to be most useful to users in making decisions about the reporting entity on the basis of information in its financial report. The qualitative characteristics apply equally to financial information in general purpose financial reports as well as to financial information provided in other ways. Financial information is useful when it is relevant and represents faithfully what it purports to represent. The usefulness of financial information is enhanced if it is comparable, verifiable, timely and understandable.

Fundamental qualitative characteristics

Relevance and faithful representation are the fundamental : qualitative characteristics of useful financial information.

Relevance

Relevant financial information is capable of making a difference in the decisions made by users. Financial information is capable of making a difference in decisions if it has predictive value, confirmatory value, or both. The predictive value and confirmatory value of financial information are interrelated.

Materiality is an entity-specific aspect of relevance based on t the nature or magnitude (or both) of the items to which the r information relates in the context of an individual entity's financial report.

Faithful representation

General purpose financial reports represent economic phenomena in words and numbers, To be useful, financial information must not only be relevant, it must also represent faithfully the phenomena it purports to represent. This fundamental characteristic seeks to maximise the underlying characteristics of completeness, neutrality and freedom from error. [FQC12] Information must be both relevant and faithfully represented if it is to be useful. [F QC17]

Enhancing qualitative characteristics

Comparability, verifiability, timeliness and understandabilhy are qualitative characteristics that enhance the usefulness of information that is relevant and faithfully represented.

Co mparability

Information about a reporting entity is more useful if it can be compared with a similar information about other entities and with similar information about the same entity for another period or another date. Comparability enables users to identify and understand similarities in, and differences among, items. [F QC20-QC21]

Verifiability

Verifiability helps to assure users that information represents faithfully the economic phenomena it purports to represent. Verifiability means that different knowledgeable and independent observers could reach consensus, although not necessarily complete agreement, that a particular depiction is a faithful representation. [F QC26]

Timeliness

Timeliness means that information is available to decision-makers in time to be capable of influencing their decisions. [F QC29]

Understandability

Classifying, characterising and presenting information clearly and concisely makes it understandable. While some phenomena are inherently complex and cannot be made easy to understand, to exclude such information would make financial reports incomplete and potentially misleading. Financial reports are prepared for users who have a reasonable knowledge of business and economic activities and who revie-.v and analyse the information with diligence. [F QC30-QC32]

Applying the enhancing qualitative characteristics

Enhancing qualitative characteristics should be maximised to the extent necessary. However, enhancing qualitative characteristics (either individually or collectively) render information useful if that information is irrelevant .or not represented faithfully. [F QC33]

The cost constraint on useful financial reporting

Cost is a pervasive constraint on the information that can be provided by general purpose financial reporting. Reporting such information imposes costs and those costs should be justified by the benefits of reporting that information. The IASB assesses costs and benefits in relation to financial reporting generally, and not solely in relation to individual reporting entities. The IASB will consider whether different sizes of entities and other factors justify different reporting requirements in certain situations. [F QC35-QC30]

Underlying assumption

The IFRS Framework states that the going concern assumption is an underlying assumption. Thus, the financial statements presume that an entity will continue in operation indefinitely or, if that presumption is not valid, disclosure and a different basis of reporting are required. [F 4.1]

The elements of financial statements

Financial statements portray the financial effects of transactions and other events by grouping them into broad classes according to their economic characteristics. These broad classes are termed the elements of financial statements.

The elements directly related to financial position (balance sheet) are: [F 4.4]

- Assets
- Liabilities
- Equity

The elements directly related to performance (income statement) are: [F 4.25]

- Income
- Expenses

The cash flow statement reflects both income statement elements and some changes in balance sheet elements.

Definitions of the elements relating to financial position

- **Asset -** An asset is a resource controlled by the entity as a result of past events arid from which future economic benefits are expected to flow to the entity. [F 4.4(a)]
- **Liability -** A liability is a present obligation of the entity arising from past events, the settlement of which is expected to result in an outflow from the entity of resources embodying economic benefits. [F 4.4(b)]
- **Equity -** Equity is the residual interest in the assets of the entity after deducting all its liabilities. [F 4.4(c)]

Definitions of the elements relating to performance

- **Income -** Income is increases in economic benefits during the accounting period in the form of inflows or enhancements of assets or decreases of liabilities that result in increases in equity, other than those relating to contributions from equity participants. [F 4.25(a)]
- **Expenses -** Expenses are decreases in economic benefits during the accounting period in the form of outflows or depletions of assets or incurrences of liabilities that result in decreases in equity, other than those relating to distributions to equity participants. [F 4.25(b)]

The definition of income encompasses both revenue and gains. Revenue arises in the course of the ordinary activities of an entity and is referred to by a variety of different names including sales, fees, interest, dividends, royalties and rent. Gains represent other items that meet the definition of income and may, or may not, arise in the course of the ordinary activities of an entity. Gains represent increases in economic benefits and as such are no different in nature from revenue. Hence, they are not regarded as constituting a separate element in the IFRS Framework. [F 4.29 and F 4.30]

The definition of expenses encompasses losses as well as those expenses that arise in the course of the ordinary activities of the entity. Expenses that arise in the course of the ordinary activities of the entity include, for example, cost of sales, wages and depreciation. They usually take the form of an outflow or depletion of assets such as cash and cash equivalents, inventory, property, plant and equipment. Losses represent other items that meet the definition of expenses and may, or may not, arise in the course of the ordinary activities of the entity. Losses represent decreases in economic benefits and as such they are no different in nature from other expenses. Hence, they are not regarded as a separate element in this Framework. [F 4.33 and F 4.34]

Recognition of the elements of financial statements

Recognition is the process of incorporating in the balance sheet or income statement an item that meets the definition of an element and satisfies the following criteria for recognition: [F 4.37 and F 4.38]

- It is probable that any future economic benefit associated with the item will flow to or from the entity; and
- The item's cost or value can be measured with reliability.

Based on these general criteria:

- **An asset** is recognised in the balance sheet when it is probable that the future economic benefits will flow to xhe entity and the asset has a cost or value that can be measured reliably. [F 4.44]
- **A liability** is recognised in the balance sheet when it is probable that an outflow of resources embodying economic benefits will result from the settlement of a present obligation and the amount at which the settlement will take pJa.ce can be measured reliably. [F 4.46]
- **Income** is recognised in the income statement when an increase in future economic benefits related to an increase in an asset or a decrease of a liability has arisen that can be measured reliably. This means, in effect, that recognition of income occurs simultaneously with the recognition of increases in assets or decreases in liabilities (for example, the net increase in assets arising on a sale of goods or services or the decrease in liabilities arising from the waiver cf a debt payable). [F 4.47]
- **Expenses** are recognised -when a decrease in future economic benefits related to a decrease in an asset or an increase of a liability has arisen that can be measured reliably. This means, in effect, that recognition of expenses occurs simultaneously with the

recognition of an increase in liabilities or a decrease in assets (for example, the accrual of employee entitlements or the depreciation of equipment). [F 4.49]

Measurement of the elements of financial statements

Measurement involves assigning monetary amounts at which the elements of the financial statements are to be recognised and reported.

The IFRS Framework acknowledges that a variety of measurement bases are used today to different degrees and in varying combinations in financial statements, including: [F 4.55]

- Historical cost
- Current cost
- Net realisable (settlement) value
- Present value (discounted)

Historical cost is the measurement basis -most commonly used today, but it is usually combined with other measurement basis. [F. 4.56] The IFRS Framework does not include concepts or principles for selecting which measurement basis should be used for particular elements of financial statements or in particular circumstances. Individual standards and interpretations do provide this guidance.

Impact of IFRS on Financial Statements

It is expected that once IFRS is implemented, it will have an impact on the financial statements of Indian companies ar, there are major differences between IFRS and Indian GAAP. There will be changes in accounting practices related to areas like Revenue Recognition,' Inventory Valuation-Service Sector, Accounting for taxes on Income, Current and non-current classification, Fixed Assets accounting, Business combination and useful life of Intangible Assets.

Once these standards are implemented, Indian companies will have to follow the following principles while preparing their Balance Sheet :
- Recognise all assets and liabilities whose recognition is required by IFRS,
- Derecognise assets or liabilities whose recognition is not permitted by IFRS,
- Classify all assets and liabilities in accordance with IFRS,
- Measure all recognised assets and liabilities in accordance with applicable IFRS.

Major Differences between Existing Indian Accounting Standards and IFRS

- AS 1 Disclosure of Accounting Policies: IFRS requires the classification of assets and Liabilities under the heading current Assets and current liabilities. Also extraordinary items are not shown separately as per IFRS.
- AS 2 Valuation on Inventory: IFRS provides guidelines for inventory of service providers.
- AS 3 Cash Flow Statement: As per IFRS, Bank Overdraft is specifically included in cash and cash equivalent and extraordinary items are not disclosed separately. v
- AS 4 Contingencies and Events occurring after Balance Sheet date: As per IFRS, Dividend proposed is not shown as Liability.

- AS 5 Net Profit or loss for the period, Prior Period Items and Changes in Accounting Policies: As per IFRS Adjustment for change in accounting policy anq^ correction of errors are made in opening balance of jetained earnings and not in current year P and L.
- AS 9 Revenue Recognition: In IFRS, service revenue is recognised only by percentage of completion method. Completed service contract method is not allowed. In case of exchange of goods of similar nature, no revenue is recognised.
- AS 14 Accounting for Amalgamation: As per IFRS, only purchase method is allowed for accounting of amalgamation. It requires acquired assets and liabilities to be recorded at fair value. Goodwill is not amortised but tested for impairment on annual basis. Profit on amalgamation is transferred to Profit and Loss A/c and not to capital reserve.

Research findings

Ruben Cordeiro, Gualter Couto and Francisco Silva (2007) measured the impact of the application of IFRS to the financial entities in IFRS 12 and IAS 27. Entities are required to apply the amendments for annual periods beginning on or after lst January 2014. Earlier applier application is permitted.

Mandatory Effective Date of IFRS 9 and Transition Disclosures (Amendments to IFRS 9 (2009), IFRS 9 (2010) and IFRS 7)

The International Accounting Standards Board (the Board has published these amendments to IFRS 9 [as issued in November 2009 (IFRS 9 (2009)) and in October 2010 (IFRS 9 (2010)); collectively referred to as IFRC 9]. These amendments require entities to apply IFRS 9 for annual periods beginning on or after 1st January 2015 instead of on or after 1st January 2013. Early application of both continues to be permitted.

The Board has also modified the relief from restating prior periods. The Board has made amendments to IFRS 7 Financial Instruments: Disclosures to require additional disclosures on transition from IAS 39 Financial Instruments: Recognition and Measurement to IFRS 9. Entities who initially apply IFRS 9 :

(a) before 1st January 2012 need not restate prior periods and are not required to provide the disclosures set out in paragraphs 44S - 44W of IFRS 7 ;

(b) on or after 1st January 2012 and before 1st January 2013 must elect either to provide the disclosures set out in paragraphs 44S - 44W of IFRS 7 or to restate prior periods; and

(c) on or after 1st January 2013 shall provide the disclosures set out in paragraphs 44S - 44W of IFRS 7. The entity need not restate prior periods.

The Board has undertaken the project to replace IAS 39 in several phases. The first phase of the project addressed the classification and measurement of financial instruments and resulted in the issue of IFRS 9 (2009) and IFRS 9 (2010). IFRS 9 (2009) addressed only financial assets. IFRS 9 (2010) added the requirements for - financial liabilities to those for financial assets. Entities that elect to apply IFRS 9 (2009) before its effective date are not subsequently required to apply IFRS 9 (2010) before its effective date also. Consequently, although IFRS

IFRS 1O - Consolidated Financial Statements

IFRS 10 on Consolidated Financial Statements provides a revised definition of control and related guidance. It replaces IAS 27 Consolidated and Separate Financial Statements and SIC 12 Consolidation - Special Purpose Entities and applies to all investees. Under IFRS 10, the investor, regardless of the nature of its involvement with an entity (the investee), whether it controls the investee. As per IFRS 10, an investor controls an investee when it is exposed, or has rights to variable returns from its involvement with the investee and has the ability to affect those returns through its power over the investee. An investor controls an investee if and only if the investor has all the following :

(a) power over the investee which is demonstrated -when the investor has existing rights that give it the current ability to direct the activities that significantly affect the investee's returns. Power can be the result of voting rights acquired from equity shares or from contractual arrangements;

(b) exposure, or rights, to variable returns from its involvement with the investee; and

(c) the ability to use its power over the investee to affect the amount of the investor's returns.

From the above, it is clear that IFRS 10 introduces a single control model for all entities, including Special Purpose Entities. It is likely to be a difficult standard to apply across many sectors. This is because the Standard pr n ides a series of indicators of control, without providing a hierarchy to be followed. One is required to understand the design and purpose of the investee and take into account evidence of power, which would entail application of significant judgment in making the control assessment.

IFRS 11 - Joint Arrangements

Under IFRS 11 Joint Arrangements, joint arrangements are essentially defined in the same way as under LAS 31 Interests in Joint Ventures - as an arrangement over which there is a joint, control. IFRS 11 sub-categorises joint arrangements into joint operations and joint ventures.

A joint arrangement is defined as an arrangement of which two or more parties have joint control. A joint arrangement has the folio-wing characteristics : -

(a) The parties are bound by a contractual arrangement.

(b) The contractual arrangement gives two or more of those parties joint control of the arrangement. A joint arrangement is either a joint operation or a joint venture.

IFRS 12 - Disclosure of Interest in Other Entities

IFRS 12 Disclosure of Interest in Other Entities is basically a disclosure standard. It requires an entity to disclose : -

(a) the significant judgments and assumptions it has made in determining the nature of its interest in another entity or arrangement, and in determining the type of joint arrangement in which it has an interest; and

(b) information about its interests in :

(i) subsidiaries

(ii) joint arrangements and associates; and

(iii) structured entities that are not controlled by the entity (unconsolidated structured entities).

A structured entity is an entity that has been designed so that voting or similar rights are not the dominant factor in deciding who controls the entity, such as when any voting rights relate to administrative tasks only and the relevant activities are directed by means of contractual arrangements.

IFRS 13 - Fair Value Measurement

IFRS 13 Fair Value Measurement replaces existing guidance in individual IFRSs. It provides a revised definition of fair value and related guidance as well as an extensive disclosure framework.

IFRS 13 establishes :

- a single definition of fair value (FV),
- a framework for measuring FV,
- disclosure requirements for FV measurements.

Such components as akin to separate assets. Such components are depreciated over the component's useful life and the replacement of such component is treated as akin to replacement of an asset (i.e. disposal and fresh purchase). These principles ure also included in the new Companies Bill.

The above are some important differences under IFRS which will need to be addressed by Indian companies on conversion to IFRS. Besides the impact on the financial results of companies across key sectors as covered above, one will also need to assess he impact of these on regulatory reporting (for example capital dequacy ratio etc), debt covenants from financial institutions, Inpact on dividend payout and impact on taxes as well.

Multiple Choice

Select the best choice to complete each sentence or each question below.

1) Which method of cash flow reporting starts with net profit for calculating cash flow from operatiing activities?

(A) Direct Method

(B) Indirect Method

(C) Neither

(D) Both

2) Cost - plus contract is a contract in which price is.

    (A) agreed upon in advance

    (B) Not agreed upon in advance

    (C) agreed upon in advance but subject to change in future

3) Government grant may be related to

    (A) Specific Fixed Assets

    (B) Revenue

    (C) Expenses

4) Lease liabilities are -

    (A) long term liability

    (B) current liability

    (C) Split between A and B

5) Lessors shall record assets, given under a finance lease.

    (A) as a leased asset

    (B) as held for - sale assets

    (C) as a receivable

6) An enterprise should present basic and diluted earnings per share

    (A) On the face of the balance of sheet

    (B) on the face of the profit and loss accounts

7) The cost of an intangible assets comprises.

    (A) purchase price

    (B) import duties

    (C) general office overheads.

8) Internally generated goodwill -

    (A) should be recognised as a fixed asset.

    (B) should be recognised as an intangible asset.

    (C) should not be recognised as an asset.

9) Expenditure on Research should be recognised as -

    (A) a deferred rexenue expenditure

    (B) a Capital expenditure

    (C) a revenue expenditure

Ans. : 1) B   2) B   3) B   4) C   5) C   6) B   7) B   8) C   9) C

Objective Type Questions

1. State whether the following statements are 'Ture' of 'False'.

1) The objective of AS - 3 is accounting for cash flow statements.

2) AS-7 deals with Accounting for research and devlopment.

3) AS-12 does not deal with Government participation in the ownership of the enterprise.

4) AS-12 deals with consolidated financial statments.

5) AS-25 deals with Interim Financial Report.

6) AS-23 deals with accounting for inverstments in associates in consolidated financial statment.

7) AS-19 deals with Related party disclosures.

8) AS-22 deals with Accounting for Taxes on Income.

Ans. : 1) True,   2) False   3) True   4) True   5) True

6) True   7) False   8) True.

2. Fill in the blanks by using suitable word from the following list :

1) .... Standard deals with the treatment of research and development in financial statments.

2) The objective of ...... is to prescribe the accounting and disclosure for employee benefits.

3) THe objective of ...... is to establish principles for reporting financial information.

4) The objective of AS - 18 is to establish requirement for disclosure of ....

5) Accounting Standard .... is to prescribe for lesses and lessors the appropriate accounting policies.

6) Accounting standard ..... deals with discontinuing operations.

7) Accounting standard .... deals with Accounting for Taxes on incomes.

Ans. : 1) AS - 8   2) AS - 15   3) AS - 17   4) related party relationship

5) AS - 19   6) AS - 24   7) AS - 22

International Accounting Standard Board (IASB) is now issuing International Financial Reporting Standards (IFRS), IASB has issued the following 13 IFRSs

IFRS No.	Title	Corresponding Converged Indian GAAP	Corresponding Converged Indian AS
IFRS -1	First time adoption of IFRS	Not relevant	IndAS 101
IFRS-2	Share Based Payments	Guidance Note	Ind AS 102
IFRS-3	Business Combination	AS- 14	Ind AS 103
IFRS-4	Insurance Contracts	—	Ind AS 104
IFRS-5	Non-current assets held for sale and discontinued operations	Partly covered by AS-24	Ind AS 105
IFRS-6	Exploration for and evaluation of mineral resources	—	Ind AS 106
IFRS-7	Financial Instrument: disclosure	AS-32	Ind AS 107
IFRS-8	Operating Segment	AS- 17	Ind AS 108
IFRS 9	Financial Instruments	—	Not yet issued
IFRS- 10	Consolidated Financial Statements	AS-21	Ind AS 27 (Exposure draft issued for IFRS 10)
IFRS 1 1	Joint Arrangement	AS-27	Ind AS 31(Exposure draft issued for IFRS 11)
IFR.S-12	Disclosure of interest in otner entities	—	Exposure draft issued
IFRS 13	Fair Valac Measurement	—	

Final Accounts of Banking Company

2.1 Introduction
2.2 Legal Provisions
2.3 Non Performing Assets (NPA)
2.4 Problems
2.5 Exercise

2.1 Introduction :

Prior to 1949, banks were governed by the Indian Companies Act. But to safeguard the interest of the depositors, Banking Regulation Act was passed in 1949 which regulates the banking companies in banking matters. For the remaining matters, Companies Act 1956 operates.

2.1.1. Definition of a Banking Company (Section 5) :

As per section 5(b) of the Banking Regulation Act, 1949. 'Banking' means the accepting, for the purpose of lending or investment, of deoposits of money from public, repayable on demand or otherwise and withdrawable by cheque, draft, order or therwise.

As per section 5(d) of the Banking Regulation Act, 1949, 'Company' means any company as definded in section 3 of the companies Act, 1956 and includes a foreign company within the meaning of section 591 of that Act.

As per section 5(c) of the Banking Regulation Act, 1949 a 'Banking Company' means any company which transacts the business of banking in India.

Thus if money is accepted for financing the business, the company cannot be treated as a banking company. To be a banking company, the following conditions should be satisfied :

1) Deposits from public must be accepted.

2) Bank should lend and invest the money so accepted.

3) The amount accepted from public is repayable on demand by cheque, draft or order.

2.2 Legal Provisions

Other Businesses Carried on by Banks (Section 6) :

The main business of the bank is accepting deposits from public and lend or invest these amounts in businesses or industries. Section 6 of the Banking Regulation Act, permits bank to carry on the following businesses in addition to its banking business :

1) acting as agent for any Government or Local Authority or any other person or persons; the carrying on of agency business of any description including the clearing or forwarding of goods, giving of receipts and discharges and otherwise acting as an attorney on behalf of customers but excluding the business of a Managing Agent or Secretary and Treasurer of a company;

2) contracting for public and private loan and negotiating and issuing the same;

3) The effecting, insuring, guaranteeing, underwriting, participating in managing and carrying out of any issue, public or private of State, municipal or other loans or of shares, Stock, debentures or debenture stock of any company, corporation or association and of lending of money, for the purpose of any such issue;

4) carrying on and transacting every kind of guarantee and indemnity business;

5) managing, selling and realising any property which may come into the possession of the company in satisfaction or part satisfaction of any of it's claims;

6) acquiring and holding and generally dealing with any property or any right, title or interest in any such property which may form the security or part of the security for any loans or advances or which may be connected with any such security;

7) undertaking and executing trusts;

8) undertaking the administration of estates as executor, trustees or otherwise;

9) establishing and supporting or aiding in the establishment and support of associations, institutions, funds, trusts and conviniences calculated to benefit employees and ex-employees of the company or the dependents or connections of such persons; granting pension and allowances and making payments towards insurance, subscribing to or guaranteeing moneys and for charitable or benevolent objects or for any exhibition or for any public, general or useful object;

10) acquiring, constructing, maintaining and altering any building or works necessary or convenient for the purposes of the banking company;

11) selling, improving, managing, developing, exchanging, leasing, mortgaging, disposing of or turning into accounts or otherwise dealing with all or any part of the property and rights of the company;

12) acquiring and undertaking the whole or any part of the business of any person or company, where such business is of the nature enumerated or described in section 6;

13) doing all such other things as are incidental or conducive to the promotion or advancement of the business such as acquisition, alteration etc. of any building or works, necessary or convinient for the purposes of the company;

14) any other form of business which the Central Government may notify in the Official Gazette.

Bank can not enter in any other business except mentioned above. Bank can not directly or indirectly deal in the buying or selling or bartering of goods except in connection with the realisation of securities given to or held by it. The bank can not engage in any trade or buy, sell and barter goods for others, otherwise than in connection with bills of exchange received. If the bank has immovable property (howsoever acquired) which is not required for its own use, then it must be disposed off within 7 years from the date of its acquisition.

Management :

At least 51% of the directors of a bank must be persons having specialised knowledge or practical experience in accountancy, agriculture and rural economy, banking, co-operation, economics, finance, law, small scale industry or any other matter useful to the bank in the opinion of the Reserve Bank. Directors must not have substantial interest in any trade, commerce or industry except a small scale industrial concern and they must not be employee or manager of any commercial company except a small scale industrial concern or a guarantee concern established as per section 25 of the Companies Act.

According to section 102 - A Notwithstanding anything to the contrary contained in the companies Act, 1956 (10 of 1956) or in any of law for the time being in force.

i)   no director of a banking company, other than, its chairman or whole time director, by what ever name called shall hold office continuously for a period exceeding eight years;

ii)   A chairman or other whole time director of a banking company who has been removed from office as such Chairman or whole time director as the case may be under the provisions of this Act, Shall also cease to be a director of the banking company and shall also not be eligible to be appointed as a director of such Banking company. whether by election or co - option or other wise for a period of four years from the date of ceasing to be the chairman or whole time director as the case may be.

Directors appoint a chiarman who will work as whole time chairman. He is appointed for 5 years at a time. In case of Nationalized Banks, the Central Government appoints the chairman. The chairman is expected to have special knowledge and practical experience of working of a bank or a financial institution or specialised in finance, economics or business administration. He can not accept any other job but he can be a director of a subsidiary company or company formed as per Section 25 of the Companies Act.

1) Accounting Year :

On account of the amended provisions of the Income Tax Act, 1961 requiring every company its accounts on 31st March every year, w.e.f . financial year ending 31st March 1989. A banking company also closes its accounts on 31st March each year.

2) Control :

The Reserve Bank of India is authorised to exercise general supervision and control over the working of banks and to conduct investigation into the affairs of any bank. The Reserve Bank issues guidelines from time to time about the working of the banks.

3) Non - Banking Assets :

A banking company may have to take possession of a certain asset charged in its favour on account of the failure of a debtor to repay the loan in time. Such an asset is termed as a non-banking asset. It must be disposed of by the banking company within 7 years and profit or loss on sale of such an asset has to be shown separately in the profit and loss account of the banking company.

4) Reserve Fund / Statutory Reserve (Section 17) :

Every Banking company incorporated in India shall create a reserve fund and transfer to it at least 20% of its annual profit as disclosed in the Profit and Loss Account prepared under Section 29 and before any dividend is declared.

Where a banking company appropriates any sum or sums from the reserve fund or the share Premium Account it shall report the fact to the Reserve Bank, explaining the circumstances relating to such appropriation within 21 days from the date of such appropriation.

5) Cash Reserve (Section 18) :

Every banking company, not being a scheduled bank, has to maintain a cash reserve of at least 3% of the total of its demand and time liabilities in India as on last Friday of the second preceding fortnight.

Cash reserve can be maintained with itself or by way of a balance in the Current Account with the Reserve Bank or by way of net balance in current accounts or in one or more of the aforesaid ways.

Every banking company is required to maintain in India in cash, gold and unenaumbered securities, an amount which shall not be less than 25 per cent of its time and demand liabilities in India. This is known as "Statutory Liquidity Ratio". The Reserve Bank has the power to increase this ratio up to 40 per cent. It now stands at 21.50%. w.e.f. 7-2-2015.

6) Bad Debts and Provision for Bad and Doubtful Debts :

The business of a banking company depends upon public confidence. In order to ensure that this confidence is not shaken, till recently the banks were given a special privilege permitting them not to show in their published accounts bad debts, provision for doubtful debts, etc. In the balance sheet, the amount of advances could be shown net remaining after providing for bad and doubtful debts. Similarly, in the Profit and Loss Account, the income from "interest and discount" was shown net after meeting such losses.

However, with effect from 1 st April, 1991, the above practice regarding bad debts and provision for bad debts has been discontinued. The amount for bad and doubtful debts has to be charged to the Profit and Loss Account under the heading 'Provision and Contingencies'. In the balance sheet, the amount advances is shown after deducting bad debts and provision for bad and doubtful debts. However, any excess provision is shown under the heading "Other Liabilities and Provisions."

7) Provision for Taxation :

Till recently in the financial statements of banking companies, the treatment of provision for taxation was similar as that of provision for bad and doubtful debts discussed above. In the Profit and Loss Account, the amount of provision for taxation was deducted from the income from Interest and Discount. As a matter of fact only the net amount of interest and discount was shown; and an outsider could not find out the amount of provision for taxation made by the banking company and also the amount of real profit earned by the banking company.

8) Rebate on Bills Discounted: Or Unexpired Discount

This refers to unexpired discount; A banking company charges discount in advance for the full period of the bill of exchange or promissory note discounted with it. The accounting entry made is as follows :

Bills Discounted and Purchased A/c.............Dr.
>   To Customer A/c
>   To Discount A/c

Customer account is credited with the net amount remaining after deducting the amount of discount. The amount credited to the discount account represents the earning of the bank. However, it may be possible that the bills discounted may mature after the closing of the financial year. It will not be appropriate to take to the credit of the profit and loss account that part of the discount charged which relates to the next year. An accounting entry is therefore, passed for unearned discount in the following manner:

>   Discount A/c .... Dr.

To Rebate on Bills Discounted A/c.

(With the amount of unearned discount relating to the next period) It appears in the balance sheet under 'Capital and Liabilities'. At the commencement of the next accounting year, it is transferred to Interest and Discount Account with reverse entry.

9) Branch Adjustment Account :

Bank has branches throughout the country and sometimes even outside the country. While preparing the balance sheet, the Head Office finds that some transactions remain unrecorded as the Head Office has not received an advice from the branch. The Head Office prepares Branch Account in its books and along with other transactions, enters these transactions in Branch Account. This Branch Account appears on the asset side of the balance sheet if it has a debit balance and on the liability side of the balance sheet if it has a credit balance.

10) Acceptances, Endorsements and Other Obligations :

The seller while selling the goods to the buyer may insist on some persons as surety or guarantor as the seller may not only depend on buyer's personal credit. The buyer may give a particular person's name as a surety or make arrangements with his bank so that the bank can accordance him in any one of the following three ways.

a)   Accepting a bill on behalf of the buyer, drawn by the seller, or
b)   Endorsing a promissory note drawn by the buyer and payable to the seller, or
c)   Giving a guarantee to make payments, if buyer fails to pay the amount.

These are shown in the Balance Sheet as a part of Contingent Liabilities.

11) Bills for Collection :

These bills are received by the bank from its clients to collect them on their due dates from the acceptors of the bills and credit the amount to the respective client's current account.

These bills are recorded in a special book viz. "Bills for Collection Register" and are not recorded in the books of accounts until they are realised. Hence, there does not arise the question of passing double entry in respect of these bills. They are shown as a separate item at the bottom of the balance sheet.

On collection of cash, the entry is passed.

CashA/c   Dr.
>   To Customer Current A/c (cash less commission)
>   To Commission A/c (Commission charged)

12) Provision and Contingencies:

This item includes all provisions made for bad and doubtful debts, provision for taxation, provision for diminution in the value of investments, transfer to contingencies and other similar items.

13) Preparation of Final Accounts in Vertical Form As per Banking Regulation Act, 1949:
Format

C, THE THIRD SCHEDULE
(See Section 29)
Form 'A'
Form of Balance Sheet

Balance Sheet of ....

(here enter name of the Banking company)

Balance Sheet as on 31st March (Year)

(000's omitted)

CAPITAL and LIABILITIES	SCHEDULE	AS ON 31 .3. ..... (CURRENT YEAR)	AS ON 31 .3..... (PREVIOUS YEAR)
Capital	1		
Reserve and Surplus	2		
Deposit	3		
Borrowings	4		
Other liabilities and provisions	5		
		....	....
Total		....	....
ASSETS			
Cash and Balance with Reserve Bank of India	6		
Balance with banks and money at call and short notice	7		
Investments	8		
Advances	9		
Fixed Assets	10		
Other Assets	11		
		....	....
Total		....	....
Contingent liabilities			
Bills for collection	12		

Form 'B'
Form of Profit and Loss Account
for the year ended 31 st March (year)

		SCHEDULE	AS ON 31 .3. .... (CURRENT YEAR)	AS ON 31 .3.... (PREVIOUS YEAR)
I	**INCOME**			
	Interest earned	13		
	Other Income	14		
		Total	....	....
II	**EXPENDITURE**			
	Interest expended	15		
	Operating expenses	16		
	Provisions and contingencies			
		Total	....	....
III	**PROFIT / LOSS**			
	Net Profit/ Loss(-) for the year			
	Profit / Loss (-) brought forward			
		Total	....	....
IV	**APPROPRIATIONS**			
	Tranter to statutory reserves			
	Transfer toother reserves			
	Transfer to / Government			
	Proposed dividend / Balance			
	Carried over to balance sheet			
		Total	....	....

SCHEDULE 1-CAPITAL

		As on 31.3.... (Current Year)	As on 31.3.... (Previous year)
I	**FOR NATIONALISED BANKS (Capital)**		
	(Fully owned by		
	Central Government)		
	Total	....	....
II.	**FOR BANKS INCORPORATED OUTSIDE INDIA (Capital)**		
	i) (The amount brought in by banks		
	by way of start-up capital as		
	prescribed by RBI should be		
	shown under this head)		

ii) Amount of deposit kept with the
RBI under Section 11 (2) of the
Banking Regulation Act, 1949.

Total ....

III FOR OTHER BANKS
Authorised Capital
(Shares of Rs. each)
Issued Capital
(Shares of Rs. each)
Subscribed Capital
(Shares of Rs. each)
Called-up capital
(Shares of Rs. each)
Less: Calls unpaid
Add: forfeited Shares

Total ....

SCHEDULE 2 - RESERVES and SURPLUS

	As on 31.3... (Current year)	As on 31.3... (Previous year)
I Statutory Reserves		
Opening Balance		
Additions during the year		
Deductions during the year		
II Capital Reserves		
Opening Balance		
Additions during the year		
Deductions during the year		
III Share Premium		
Opening Balance		
Additions during the year		
Deductions during the year		
IV Revenue and other Reserves		
Opening Balance		
Additions during the year		
Deductions during the year		
V Balance in Profit and Loss Account		
Total	....	....
(I, II, III, IV andV)	....	....

SCHEDULE 3 - DEPOSITS

		As On 31.3 ...... (Current year)	As on 31.3 ...... (Previous year)
A. I. Demand Deposits			
i) From banks			
ii) From others			
II Savings Bank Deposits			
III Term Deposits			
i) From banks			
ii) From others			
	Total	....	....
	(I, II and III)	....	....
B. I. i) Deposits of branches in India			
ii) Deposits of branches outside India	Total	....	....
		....	....

SCHEDULE 4-BORROWINGS

		As on 31.3 ...... (Current year)	As on 31.3 ...... (Previous year)
I. Borrowings in India			
i) Reserve Bank of India			
ii) Other Banks			
iii) Other Institutions and Agencies			
II. Borrowings outside India	Total	....	....
	(I and II)	....	....

Secured borrowings in included I and II above Rs.

SCHEDULE 5 - OTHER LIABILITIES AND PROVISIONS

		As on 31 .3 ...... (Current year)	As on 31 .3 ...... (Previous year)
I. Bills Payable			
II. Inter - Office adjustments (net)			
III. Interest accrued			
IV. Others (including provisions)	Total	....	....

SCHEDULE 6 - CASH AND BALANCE WITH RESERVE BANK OF INDIA

		As on 31.3... (Current year)	As on 31.3... (Previous year)
I.	Cash in hand (including foreign currency notes)		
II.	Balances with		
	Reserve Bank of India		
	i) In Current Account		
	ii) In other Accounts Total (I and II)	....	....

SCHEDULE 7 - BALANCES WITH BANKS and MONEY AT CALL and SHORT NOTICE

		As on 31.3 ... (Current year)	As on 31.3 ... (Previous year)
I.	**In India**		
	i) Balances with banks		
	a) In Current Accounts		
	b) In other Deposit Accounts		
	ii) Money at call and short notice		
	a) With banks		
	b) With other institutions		
	Total	....	....
	(i and ii)	....	....
II.	**Outside India**		
	i) In Current Accounts		
	ii) In other Deposits Accounts		
	iii) Money at call and short notice		
	(i, ii and iii)	....	....
	Grand Total (I and II)	....	....

SCHEDULE 8 - INVESTMENTS

		As on 31.3...... (Current year)	As on 31.3...... (Previous year)
I.	**Investments in India in**		
	i) Government Securities		
	ii) Other approved securities		
	iii) Shares		
	iv) Debentures and Bonds		
	v) Subsidiaries and / or joint ventures		
	vi) Others (to be specified)		
	Total	....	....

II. Investments outside India in

   i) Government securities
      (Including local authorities)

   ii) Subsidiaries and / or
      joint ventures abroad

   iii) Other investments (to be specified)

Total	....	....
Grand Total (1 and ll)	....	....

SCHEDULE 9 - ADVANCES

	As on 31.3 ... (Current year)	As on 31.3 ... (Previous year)
A. i) Bills purchased and discounted		
ii) Cash credits, Overdrafts and loans repayable on demand		
iii) Term loans		
Total	....	....
B. i) Secured by tangible assets		
ii) Covered by Bank / Government Guarantees		
iii) Unsecured		
Total	....	....
C.I. i) Priority Sectors		
ii) Public Sector		
iii) Banks		
iv) Others		
Total	....	....
C.II. Advances Outside India		
i) Due from banks		
ii) Due from others		
a) Bills purchased and discounted		
b) Syndicated loans		
c) Others		
Total	....	....
Grand Total : (C.I and II)	....	....

SCHEDULE 10 - FIXED ASSETS

	As on 31.3...... (Current year)	As on 31.3...... (Previous year)
I. Premises At cost as on 31 st March of the preceding year Additions during the year Deductions during the year Depreciation to date		
II. Other Fixed Assets (including Furniture and Fixture) At cost as on 31 st march of the preceding year Additions during the year Deductions during the year Depreciation to date		
Total (l and ll)	....	....

SCHEDULE 11 - OTHER ASSETS

	As on 31.3...... (Current year)	As on 31.3 ...... (Previous year)
i) Inter-Office adjustments (net)		
ii) Interest accrued		
iii) Tax paid in advance / tax deducted at source		
iv) Stationery and stamps		
v) Non-banking assets acquired in satisfaction of claims		
vi) Others *		
Total	....	....

* In case there is any unadjusted balance of loss the same may be shown under this item with appropriate foot - note

SCHEDULE 12-CONTINGENT LIABILITIES

	As on 31.3...... (Current year)	As on 31.3...... (Previous year)
I. Claims against the bank not acknowledged as debts		
II. Liability for partly paid investments		
III. Liability on account of outstanding forward exchange contracts		
IV. Guarantees given on behalf of constituents		
a) In India		
b) Outside India		
V. Acceptances, endorsements and other obligations		
VI. Other items for which the bank is contingently liable		
Total	....	....
	....	....

SCHEDULE 13 - INTEREST EARNED

	Year ended 31.3 ... (Current year)	Year ended 31.3 ... (Previous year)
I. Interest / discount on advances / bills		
II. Income on investments		
III. Interest on balances with Reserve Bank of india and other inter-bank funds		
IV. Others		
Total	....	....
	....	....

SCHEDULE 14 - OTHER INCOME

	Year ended 31.3 ... (Current year)	Year ended 31.3 ... (Previous year)
I. Commission, exchange and brokerage		
II. Profit on sale of investments		
Less : Loss on sale of investments		
III. Profit on revaluation of investments		
Less : Loss on revaluation of investments		
IV. Profit on sale of land, building and other		
assets Less: Loss on sale of land, building and other assets		
V. Profit on exchange transactions		
Less : Loss on exchange transactions		
VI. Income earned by way of dividends, etc.		
from subsidiaries / companies		
and / or Joint ventures abroad / in India		
VII. Miscellaneous Income		
Total	....	....
	....	....

Note : Under items II to V loss figures may be shown in brackets.

SCHEDULE 15 - INTEREST EXPENDED

	Year ended 31.3 ... (Current year)	Year ended 31.3 ... (Previous year)
I. Interest on deposits		
II. Interest on Reserve Bank of India /		
Inter - Bank borrowings		
III. Others		
Total	....	....
	....	....

SCHEDULE 16 - OPERATING EXPENSES

	Year ended 31.3 ... (Current year)	Year ended 31.3 ... (Previous year)
I. Payments to and provisions for employees		
II. Rent, taxes and lighting		
III. Printing and stationery		
IV. Advertisement and publicity		
V. Depreciation on bank's property		
VI. Directors fees, allowances and expenses		
VII. Auditor's fees and expenses (including branch auditors)		
VIII. Law charges		
IX. Postages, telegrams, telephones, etc.		
X. Repairs and maintenance		
XI. Insurance		
XII. Other expenditure		
Total	....	....
	....	....

2.3 Non Performing Assets (NPA)

2.3.1 Introduction :

According to the Narasimham Committee report, income from non performing assets should not be recognised on accrual basis but should be booked as income only when it is actually received. An asset accounts become non performing when it ceases to generate income for a bank. Earlier assets were declared as NPA after completion of the period for the payment of total amount of loan and 30 days grace. In present scenario assets are declared as NPA if none of the installment is paid till 180 days i.e, six months in respect of a term loan.

Non Performing Asset means a loan or an account of borrower, which has been classified by a bank or financial institution as sub-standard, doubtful or loss asset in accordance with the directions or guidelines relating to asset classification issued by RBI. With effect from March 31,2004, a non-performing asset (NPA) shall be a loan or an advance where;

    i)   Interest and / or installment of principal remain overdue for a period of more than 90 days in respect of a Term Loan,

    ii)   The account remains 'out of order' for a period of more than 90 days, in respect of an Over draft (OD) Cash Credit (CD).

    iii)   The bill remains ovderdue for a period of more than 90 days in the case of bills purchased and discounted,

    iv)   Interest and / or installment of principal remains overdue for two harvest seasons but for a period not exceeding two half years in the case of an advance granted for agricultural purpose, and

v) Any amount to be received remains overdue for a period of more than 90 days in respect of other documents.

The bank assets are classified in two categories i.e. Performing Assets and Non Performing Assets. The following diagram shows the classification of assets of banking sector.

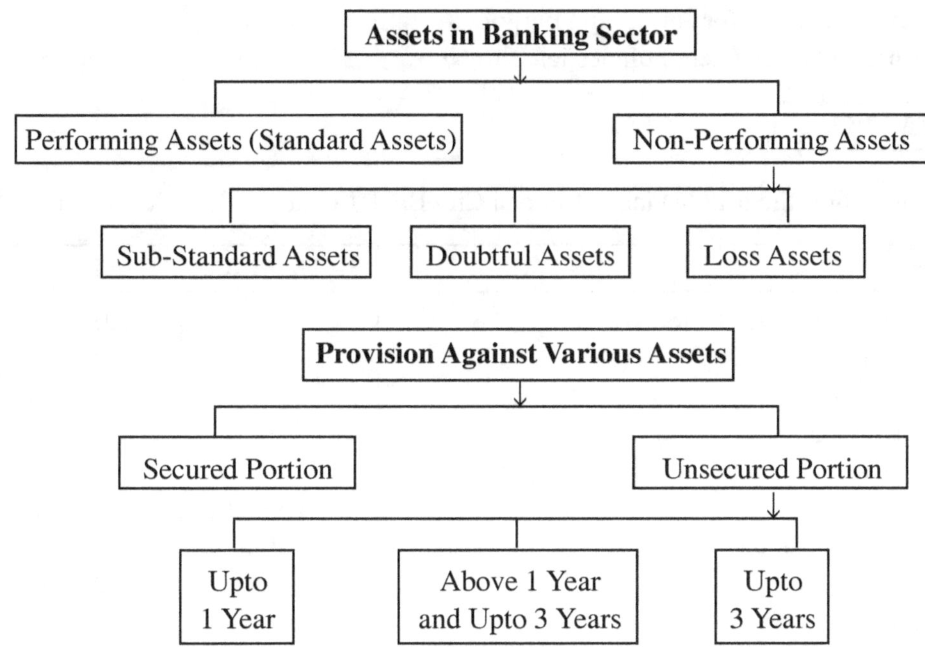

2.3.2 Type of NPA :

There are three major types of NPA :

i) Sub-Standard :

The account holder not paying three installment continuously after 90 days and upto 1 year comes under this category. For this category bank has made 10% provision of funds from their profit to meet the losses generated from NPA.

ii) Doubtful NPA :

Under doubtful NPA there are three sub categories:

1) D1 i.e. upto 1 year: 20% provision is made by the banks.

2) D2 i.e. upto 2 years : 30% provision is made by the bank.

3) D3 i.e. upto 3 years: 100% provision is made by the bank.

iii) Loss Assets :

Under this 100% provision is made. Bank may write of the account holder's account after certain period. After this assets are handed over to recovery agents for sale.

2.3.3 Reasons Behind NPA :

1) Absence of or non effective background checking of a customer before sanctioning loan.
2) Non-performance of the business or the purpose for-which the customer has taken the loan.
3) Willful defaulter.
4) Loans sanctioned for agriculture purposes.
5) Change in Government policies leads to NPA.

PROBLEM NO. 1

1) The following is the trial balance of Poona City Bank Ltd. as on 31st December 2015.

Particulars	Debit Rs.	Credit Rs.
Share Capital 3000 Shares of Rs. 10	...	3,00,000
Statutory Reserve.	...	4,00,000
Deposits - Fixed	....	2,78,000
Saving	...	4,50,000
Current	...	3,74,000
Cash in hand	2,90,000	...
Cash with Reserve Bank of India	4,20,000	...
Interest and discount	...	3,00,000
Commission and Brokerage	...	50,000
Interest on Fixed deposit	30,000	...
Interest on Saving deposit	20,000	...
Interest on Current deposit	12,500	...
Salaries (Including Rs. 12,000 to Manager)	1,31,000	...
Rent, Insurance and Taxes	4,000	...
Postage and Telegram	900	...
Printing and stationery	7,000	...
Audit Fees	4,000	...
Depreciation	3,300	...
Investment in shares	84,000	...
Loans, Cash credit and Overdraft	4,90,000	...
Bills discounted and Purchased	1,80,000	...
Government Bonds	1,60,000	...
Furniture	40,000	...
Premises	3,00,000	...
Branch Adjustment Account	...	24.700
	21,76,700	21,76,700

Additional Information :

1) Rebate on bills discounted Rs. 27,000.
2) Create Reserve for bad and doubtful debts Rs. 11,000.
3) Acceptances on behalf of customers Rs. 80,000.

   You arc required to prepare Profit and Loss Account for the year ended 31 st Decembcr 2015 and Balance Sheet as on that date.

(Pune University)

Solution :

Bank Accounts, Poona City Bank Ltd /

SCHEDULE -1 : CAPITAL

As on 31 -12-15

	Rs.
30,000 Fully paid-up shares of Rs. 10 each	3,00,000
	3,00,000

SCHEDULE - 2 : RESERVES AND SURPLUS

As on 31 -12-15

	Rs.
Statutory Reserve	
(opening balance) 4,00,000	
Additions during the year 19,860	4,19,860
Surplus i.e. Balance in the P and L Appropriation A/c	79,440
	4,99,300

SCHEDULE - 3 : DEPOSITS

As on 31-12-2015

	Rs.
(i) Demand Deposits	
(i.e. current deposits)	3,74,000
(ii) Saving Bank deposits	4,50,000
(iii) Term Deposits	
(i.e. Fixed, Recurring Deposits etc.)	2,78,000
	11,02,000

SCHEDULE - 4 : BORROWINGS

As on 31 -12 -2015

	Rs.
(i) Borrowings in India	Nil
(ii) Borrowings outside India	Nil
	Nil

SCHEDULE 5 : OTHER LIABILITIES AND PROVISIONS

As on 31 -12 - 2015

	Rs.
(i) Branch Adjustments (Credit Balance)	24,700
(ii) Rebate on Bills Discounted	27,000
	51,700

SCHEDULE - 6 : CASH AND BALANCES WITH RESERVE BANK OF INDIA

As on 31 - 12 - 2015

	Rs.
(i) Cash in hand	2,90,000
(ii) Cash with RBI	4,20,000
	710,000

SCHEDULE - 7 : BALANCES WITH BANKS AND MONEY AT CALL AND SHORT NOTICE

As on 31-12 - 2015

	Rs.
	Nil
	Nil

SCHEDULE- 8 : INVESTMENTS

As on 31 - 12 - 2015

	Rs.
(i) Govt. Bonds	1,80,000
(ii) Share	84,000
(iii) Debentures, Bonds	-
(iv) Gold	-
	2,64,000

SCHEDULE - 9 : ADVANCES

As on 31 - 12 - 2015

	Rs.
(i) Bill Purchased and Discounted	1,60,000
(ii) Cash credits. Overdrafts and Loans Repayable on demand	4,90,000
(iii) Term Loans	-
	6,50,000
Less RDD	-11,000
	6,39,000

SCHEDULE - 10 : FIXED ASSETS

As on 31-12-2015

	Rs.
(i) Premises	3,00,000
(ii) Other Fixed Assets	
Furniture	40,000
	3,40,000

SCHEDULE - 11 : OTHER ASSETS

As on 31-12-2015

	Rs.
	Nil
	Nil

SCHEDULE- 12 : CONTINGENT LIABILITIES

As on 31-12-2015

	Rs.
Acceptances on behalf of customers	80,000
	80,000

SCHEDULE - 13 : INTEREST EARNED

Year ended 31 -12 -2015

		Rs.
Interest, discount on advances, bills	3,00,000	
Less Rebate on bills discounted	- 27,000	
		2,73,000
		2,73,000

SCHEDULE - 14 : OTHER INCOME

Year ended 31 -12 - 2015

	Rs.
Commission and Brokerage	50,000
	50,000

SCHEDULE- 15 : INTEREST EXPENDED

Year ended 31 - 12 - 2015

	Rs.
Interest on :	
(i) Current Accounts	12,500
(ii) Saving Deposits	20,000
(iii) Fixed Deposits	30,000
	62,500

SCHEDULE - 16 : OPERATING EXPENSES

Year ended 31-12-15

	Rs.
Payments to and provisions for employees :	
Salaries including Rs. 12,000 / - to Manager	1,31,000
Rent, taxes and lighting	4,000
Printing and stationery	7,000
Advertisement and Publicity	-
Depreciation on bank's property	3,300
Directors' fees, allowances and expenses	-
Auditors' fees, expenses	4,000
Law charges	-
Postage, telegrams, telephone	900
Repairs and maintenance	-
Insurance	-
Other expenditure	-
	1,50,200
Provisions and Contingencies : RDD	11,000

Poona City Bank Ltd.
Profit and Loss Account

for the year ended 31 -12 - 2015

	Schedule No.	Year ended	
		31-12-2015 Rs.	**31-12-2015** Rs.
(I) INCOME			
Interest earned	13	2,73,000	
Other income	14	50,000	
Total		3,23,000	
(II) EXPENDITURE			
Interest expended	15	62,500	
Operating expenses	16	1,50,200	
Provisions and contingencies	-	11,000	
Total		2,23,700	
(III) PROFIT /LOSS			
Net profit for the year		99,300	
Profit brought forward		-	
Total		99,300	
(IV) APPROPRIATIONS			
Transfer to Statutory Reserve		19,860	
(20% of Net profit)			
Balance carried over to		79,440	
Balance Sheet	Total	99,300	

Balance Sheet of Poona City Bank Ltd.
Balance Sheet as on 31 - 12-2015

	Schedule No.	As on 31-12-2015 Current year) Rs.	As on 31-12-2015 Previous year) Rs.
Capital and Liabilities			
Capital	1	3,00,000	
Reserves and Surplus	2	4,99,300	
Deposits	3	11,02,000	
Borrowings	4	-	
Other Liabilities and Provisions	5	51,700	
Total		19,53,000	

Assets :			
Cash and Balances with RBI	6	71,0000	
Balances with Banks and Money	7	-	
at call and short notice			
Investments	8	2,64,000	
Advances	9	6,39,000	
Fixed Assets	10	3,40,000	
Other Assets	11	-	
	Total	19,53,000	
Contingent Liabilities	12	80,000	
Bills for collection	-	-	

PROBLEM NO. 2

Following is the trial balance of the Baramati Bank Ltd. as on 31st March 2015. You are required to prepare Profit and Loss A/c for the year 31 -3-2015 ended, and Balance Sheet as on above date.

Particulars	Debit Rs.	Credit Rs.
Share Capital (20,000 equity shares of Rs. 100 each, Rs. 50 paid - up)	-	10,00,000
Profit and Loss Account 1st April 2014	-	81,500
Current Deposit Accounts	-	21,44,000
Fixed Deposit Accounts	-	23,43,000
Saving Bank Accounts	-	11,07,000
Directors Fees	9,300	-
Audit Fees	8,800	-
Furniture (cost at Rs. 1,00,000)	85,900	-
Interest and Discounts	-	7,04,000
Interest paid	4,00,400	
Commission and Exchange	-	2,03,000
6 % Government Bonds	10,40,000	-
Shares in companies	8,00,000	-
Branch Adjustment Account	2,04,000	-
Postage and Printing	6,900	-
Premises (cost Rs. 18,50,000)	17,03,000	-
Salaries (Including salary of Rs. 25,000 to Manager)	67,000	-
Law charges	5,300	-
Provident Fund Contribution	11,200	-
Cash in hand	2,07,000	-
Bills discounted and Purchased	67,000	-
Unexpired insurance	2,700	-
Statutory Reserve Fund	-	85,000
Loans, Cash credit and Overdrafts	30,49,000	-
	76,67,500	76,67,500

Following Additional Information :

a) Rebate on bills discounted amounted to Rs. 7,100.

b) Provide Rs. 38,500 for doubtful debts.

c) The Bank has accepted bills worth Rs. 2,50,000 on behalf of The customers against the securities of Rs. 3,10,000 lodged with the Bank.

d) Provide depreciation on premises Rs. 73,000 and on furniture Rs. 5,900.

e) Provide for Taxation Rs. 7,500.

(Pune University)

Solution :

Bank Accounts, Baramati Bank Ltd.

P and L A/c for the year ended 31-3-2015 the Balance Sheet as on that date.

SCHEDULE.1 : CAPITAL

As on 31 - 3 - 2015

	Rs.
20.000 Equity Shares of Rs. 100 each , Rs. 50 per share paid-up	10,00,000
	10,00,000

SCHEDULE - 2 : RESERVES AND SURPLUS

As on 31 - 3 - 2015

		Rs.
Statutory Reserve Fund		
(opening balance)	85,000	
Additions during the year	53,220	1,38,220
Surplus i.e. Balance in the P and L Appropriation A/c		2,94,380
		4,32,600

SCHEDULE - 3 : DEPOSITS

As on 31 -3 - 2015

	Rs.
(i) Demand Deposits	
(i.e. current deposits)	21,44,000
(ii) Saving bank deposits	11,07,000
(iii) Term Deposits	
(i.e. Fixed, Recurring Deposits etc.)	23,43,000
	55,94,000

SCHEDULE- 4 ; BORROWINGS

As on 31-3-2015

	Rs.
(i) Borrowings in India	Nil
(ii) Borrowing outside India	Nil
	Nil

SCHEDULE- 5 : OTHER LIABILITIES AND PROVISIONS

As on 31-3-2015

	Rs.
(i) Rebate on Bills Discounted	7,100
(ii) Provision for Taxation	7,500
	14,600

SCHEDULE - 6 : CASH AND BALANCES WITH RESERVE BANK OF INDIA

As on 31-3-2015

	Rs.
(i) Cash in hand	2,07,000
	2,07,000

SCHEDULE - 7 : BALANCES WITH BANKS AND MONEY AT CALL AND SHORT NOTICE

As on 31-3-2015

	Rs.
	Nil
	Nil

SCHEDULE - 8 : INVESTMENTS

As on 31-3-2015

	Rs.
(i) 6 % Govt Bonds	10,40,000
(ii) Share in companies	8,00,000
	18,40,000

SCHEDULE - 9 : ADVANCES

As on 31-3-2015

	Rs.
(i) Bills Purchased and Discounted	67,000
(ii) Cash credils, Overdrafts and Loans repayable on demand	30,49,000
(iii) Term Loans	-
	31,16,000
Less RDD	-38,500
	30,77,500

SCHEDULE - 10 : FIXED ASSETS

As on 31-3-2015

			Rs.
(i)	Premises at cost Rs.	18,50,000	
	Less Depreciation to date	2,20,000	
	(Rs. 1,47,000 + Rs. 73,000)		16,30,000
(ii)	Other Fixed Assets :		
	Furniture at cost Rs.	1,00,000	
	Less Depreciation to date	20,000	
	(Rs. 14,100 + Rs. 5,900)		80,000
			17,10,000

SCHEDULE. 11 : OTHER ASSETS

As on 31-3-2015

	Rs.
Branch Adjustments (Dr)	2,04,000
Unexpired Insurance	2,700
(i.e. Prepaid Insurance)	
	2,06,700

SCHEDULE- 12 : CONTINGENT LIABILITIES

As on 31-3-2015

	Rs.
Acceptances, Endorsements and other obligations :	
Bills Accepted	2,50,000
(Against security of Investments of the value	
of Rs. 3,10,000 lodged with the Bank)	
	2,50,000

SCHEDULE- 13 : INTEREST EARNED

As on 31-3-2015

		Rs.
Interest, discount on advances, bills	7,04,000	
Less Rebate on bills discounted	- 7,100	
		6,96,900
		6,96,900

SCHEDULE - 14 : OTHER INCOME

As on 31-3-2015

	Rs.
Commission, Exchange Brokerage	2,03,000
	2,03,000

SCHEDULE - IS : INTEREST EXPENDED

As on 31-3-2015

	Rs.
Interest Paid	4,00,400
	4,00,400

SCHEDULE - 16 : OPERATING EXPENSES

As on 31-3-2015

		Rs.
Payments to and Provisions for employees :		
Salaries (including Rs. 25,000 / - to Manager)	67,000	
+ Provident fund contribution	11,200	
		78,200
Depreciation on Bank's Property		78,900
Directors' fees, Allowances and expenses		9,300
Auditors' fees, Expenses		8,800
Law Charges		5,300
Postage and Printing		6,900
		1,87,400
Provisions and Contingencies : RDD		38,500
Provition for taxation		7,500
		46,000

Baramati Bank Ltd.
Profit and Loss Account

for the Year ended 31 - 3 - 2015

	Schedule No.	Year ended	
		31-12-2015 **Rs.**	**31-12-2014** **Rs.**
(I) INCOME			
Interest earned	13	6,96,000	
Other income	14	2,03000	
Total		8,99,900	
(II) EXPENDITURE			
Interest expended	15	4,00,400	
Operating expenses	16	1,87,400	
Provisions and contingencies	-	46,000	
Total		6,33,800	
(III) PROFIT /LOSS			
Net profit for the year		2,66,100	
Profit brought forward		81,500	
Total		3,47,600	
(IV) APPROPRIATIONS			
Transfer to Statutory Reserve (20% of Net profit)		53,220	
Balance carried over to Balance Sheet		2,94,380	
Total		3,47,600	

Balance Sheet of Baramati Bank Ltd.
as on 31-3-2015

	Schedule No.	As on 31-12-2015 Current year) Rs.	As on 31-12-2014 Previous year) Rs.
(I) Capital and Liabilities :			
Capital	1	10,00,000	
Reserves and Surplus	2	4,32,600	
Deposits	3	55,94,000	
Borrowings	4	-	
Other Liabilities and Provisions	5	14,600	
Total		70,41,200	

(II) Assets:		Debit Rs.	
Cash and Balances with RBI	6	2,07,000	
Balances with Banks and Money at call and short notice	7	-	
Investments	8	18,40,000	
Advances	9	30,77,500	
Fixed Assets	10	17,10,000	
Other Assets	11	2,06,700	
Total		70,41,200	
Contingent Liabilities	12	2,50,000	
Bills for collection	-	-	

PROBLEM NO. 3

The following is the trial Balance of Someshwar Bank Ltd. as on 31st March, 2015 You arc required to prepare the Profit and Loss Account for the year ended and the Balance Sheet as on that date.

Particulars	Debit Rs.	Credit Rs.
Subscribed Capital		
1,00,000 equity shares of Rs. 10 each fully paid	–	10,00,000
Reserve Fund	–	5,00,000
Loans, Cash credit and overdraft	5,70,000	–
Premises	1,00,000	–
Govt -securities	8,00,000	–
Current Deposits	–	2,00,000
Fixed Deposits	–	2,50,000
Salaries	56,000	–
General expenses	54,800	–
Rent, Rates and Taxes.	4,600	–
Saving Bank Deposits	–	1,00,000
Directors fees	3,600	–
Profit and Loss Account(2014)	–	32,000
Interest and Discount	–	2,56,000
Stock of stationary	17,000	–
Bills purchased and discounted	92,000	–
Interim divided paid	34,000	–
Recurring deposits	–	40,000
Shares	1,00,000	–
Cash in hand and with RBI	3,86,000	–
Money at call and short notice	1,60,000	–
	23,78,000	23,78,000

Adjustments :

a) The Authorised share capital of the Bank is 2,00,000 equity shares of Rs. 10 each.

b) Provision for bad and doubtful debts is required to be Rs. 10,000.

c) Rebate on bills discounted amounted to Rs. 760.

d) Interim dividend declared was 4 % actual.

e) Endorsements made on behalf of customers totalled Rs. 2,30,000.

f) Rs. 20,000 were added to the premises during the year, and depreciation is allowed at 5% p. a. on the opening balance. (Pune University T. Y. B.Com)

Solution :

Bank Accounts, Sonicshwar Bank Ltd.
SCHEDULE - 1 : CAPITAL

	As on 31-3-15 (Current year) Rs.	As on 31-3-14 (Previous year) Rs.
Authorised : 2,00,000 Equity Shares of Rs. 10 each	20,00,000	
Called up : 1,00 ,000 Equity Shares of Rs. 10 each fully called up and paid up	10,00,000	
	10,00,000	

SCHEDULE - 2 : RESERVES AND SURPLUS

	As on 31-3-15 Rs.	As on 31-3-14 Rs.
Reserve Fund 5,00,000 + Profit added 24,448	5,24,448	
Surplus	89,792	
	6,14,240	

SCHEDULE - 3 : DEPOSITS

	As on 31-3-15 Rs.	As on 31-3-14 Rs.
(i) Demand Deposits (i.e. Current deposits)	2,00,000	
(ii) Saving Bank Deposits	1,00,000	
(iii) Term Deposits :		
Fixed	2,50,000	
Recurring Deposits	40,000	
	5,90,000	

SCHEDULE - 4 : BORROWINGS

	As on 31-3-2015 Rs.	As on 31-3-2014 Rs.
	Nil	
	Nil	

SCHEDULE - 5 : OTHER LIABILITIES AND PROVISIONS

		As on 31-3-15 Rs.	As on 31-3-14 Rs.
Rebate on Bills Discounted		760	
Unclaimed Interim Dividend :			
Declared	40,000		
Less Paid	34,000		
		6,000	
		6,760	

SCHEDULE - 6 : CASH AND BALANCES WITH RESERVE BANK OF INDIA

	As on 31-3-15 Rs.	As on 31-3-14 Rs.
Cash and Balance with RBI	3,86,000	
	3,86,000	

SCHEDULE - 7 : BALANCES WITH BANKS AND MONEY AT CALL AND SHORT NOTICE

	As on 31-3-15 Rs.	As on 31-3-14 Rs.
Money at call and short notice	1,60,000	
	1,60,000	

SCHEDULE - 8 INVESTMENTS

	As on 31-3-15 Rs.	As on 31-3-14 Rs.
Govt. Securities	8,00,000	
Shares	1,00,000	
	9,00,000	

SCHEDULE- 9 : ADVANCES

	As on 31-3-15 Rs.	As on 31-3-14 Rs.
Bill Purchased and Discounted	92,000	
Cash credits, Overdrafts and Loans	5,70,000	
Term Loans	-	
	6,62,000	

SCHEDULE - 10 : FIXED ASSETS

		As on 31-3-15 Rs.	As on 31-3-14 Rs.
Premises :	Rs.		
Opening Balance	80,000		
+ cost of additions			
during the year	20,000		
	1,00,000		
Less Depreciation			
@ 5 % on the Op.			
Balance	4,000		
		96,000	
		96,000	

SCHEDULE - 11 : OTHER ASSETS

	As on 31-3-15 Rs.	As on 31-3-14 Rs.
Slock of Stationery	17,000	
	17,000	

SCHEDULE - 12 : CONTINGENT LIABILITIES

	As on 31-3-15 Rs.	As on 31-3-14 Rs.
Endorsements on behalf of customers	2,30,000	
	2,30,000	

SCHEDULE- 13 : INTEREST EARNED

	For the Year ended 31-3-2015 Rs.	For the Year ended 31-3-2014 Rs.
Interest/ discount on Advances, Bills	2,56,000	
Less Rebate on Bills Discounted	760	
	2,55,240	

SCHEDULE - 14 : OTHER INCOME

	For the Year ended 31-3-2015 Rs.	For the Year ended 31-3-2014 Rs.
	Nil	
	Nil	

SCHEDULE - 15 : INTEREST EXPENDED

	For the Year ended 31-3-2015 Rs.	For the Year ended 31-3-2014 Rs.
	Nil	
	Nil	

SCHEDULE 16 : OPERATING EXPENSES

	For the Year ended 31-3-2015 Rs.	For the Year ended 31-3-2014 Rs.
Salaries	56,000	
Rent, Rates and Taxes	4,600	
Printing and stationery	-	
Advertisement and Publicity	-	
Depreciation on bank's property on Premises	4,000	
Directors' fees, Allowances and Expenses	3,600	
Auditors' fees, expenses		
Law charges	–	
Postage, Telegrams, Telephone		
Repairs and Maintenance		
Insurance		
Other Expenditure :		
General Expenses	54,800	
	1,23,000	
Provisions and Contingencies : RDD	10,000	

Someshwar Bank Ltd.
Profit and Loss Account for the Year ended 31-3 - 2015

	Schedule No.	Year ended 31-12-2015	Year ended 31-12-2014
(I) INCOME			
Interest earned	13	2,55,240	
Other Income	14	–	
Total		2,55,240	
(II) EXPENDITURE			
Interest expended	15	–	
Operating expenses	16	1,23,000	
Provisions and contingencies	-	10,000	
Total		1,33,000	
(III) PROFIT /LOSS			
Net profit for the year		1,22,240	
Profit brought forward		32,000	
Total		1,54,240	
(IV) APPROPRIATIONS			
Transfer to Statutory Reserve (20% of Net profit)		24,448	
Interim dividend declared		40,000	
Balance carried over to Balance Sheet		89,792	
Total		1,54,240	

Someshwar Bank Ltd.
Balance Sheet as on 31-3-2015

	Schedule No.	As on 31-12-2015 (Current year) Rs.	As on 31-12-2014 (Previous year) Rs.
(1) Capital and Liabilities :			
Capital	1	10,00,000	
Reserves and Surplus	2	6,14,240	
Deposits	3	5,90,000	
Borrowings	4	–	
Other liabilities and Provisions	5	6,760	
Total		22,11,000	
(II) Assets :			
Cash and Balances with RBI	6	3,86,000	
Balances with Banks and			
Money at Call and Short Notice	7	1,60,000	
Investments	8	9,00,000	
Advances	9	6,52,000	
Fixed Assets	10	96,000	
Other Assets	11	17,000	
Total		22,11,000	
Contingent Liabilities	12	2,30,000	
Bills for Collection	–	–	

PROBLEM NO. 4

From the following ledger balances of Satara Bank Ltd. as on 31st March 2015, prepare the Profit and loss Account for the year ended 31-3-2015 and Balance Sheet as on that date.

Particulars	Rs.
Share Capital (Shares of Rs. 100 each, Rs. 50 paid)	2,50,000
Reserve Fund	1,50,000
Profit and Loss Account (Cr. Balance on 1-4-2014)	1.30,000
Bills Payable	4,00,000
Unclaimed Dividend	5,000
Sundry Creditors	25,000
Bills for Collection	70,000
Acceptances on behalf of customers	1,00,000
Non-Banking Assets	1,70,000
Bills discounted	2,50,000
Cash Credit and Overdrafts	20,00,000
Term Loans	16,00,000
Interest and discount received	3,25,000
Borrowing from Banks	4,80,000
Cash in hand	1,25,000
Cash with RBI	5,00,000
Cash with other Banks	7,25,000
Premises (Original Rs. 6,50,000)	6,00,000
Dividend for (2013-2014)	25,000
Miscellaneous Expenses	10,000
Rent, Rates and Lighting	5,000
Salaries to staff	50,000
Interest on Deposits Paid	90,000
Investment in Govt. Securities	10,00,000
Investment in Shares	5,00,000
Money at call and short notice	2,90,000
Demand Deposits	35,00,000
Saving Bank Deposits	17,00,000
Term Deposits	9,75,000

Adjustmcnus :

   (a) Provide Rebate on bills discounted Rs. 5,000.

   (b) Provide Rs. 12,500 for Taxation Reserve.

   (c) Provide Rs. 10,000 for doubtful debts.

   (d) Claim against the bank not acknowledged as debts amounted to Rs. 25,000.
      [Pune University. T. Y. B. Com.]

Solution :

Bank Accounts, Satara Bank Ltd. Final Accounts for the Year ended 3l-3-2015

SCHEDULE - 1 : CAPITAL

	As on 31-3-15 (Current year) Rs.	As on 31-3-14 (Previous year) Rs.
5,000 Shares of Rs. 100 each , Rs, 50 per share paid	2,50,000	
	2,50,000	

SCHEDULE - 2 : RESERVES AND SURPLUS

	As on 31-3-15 Rs.	As on 31-3-14 Rs.
Reserve Fund 1,50,000		
Additions out of profit 28,500	1,78,500	
Surplus i.e. Balance in the P and L Appropriation A/c	2,19,000	
	3,97,500	

SCHEDULE - 3 : DEPOSITS

	As on 31-3-15 Rs.	As on 31-3-14 Rs.
(i) Demand Deposits (i.e. Current deposits)	35,00,000	
(ii) Saving Bank Deposits	17,00,000	
(iii) Term Deposits : (ie. Fixed, Recurring Deposits, Cash certificates etc.)	9,75,000	
	61,75,000	

SCHEDULE - 4 : BORROWINGS

	As on 31-3-15 Rs.	As on 31-3-14 Rs.
Borrowings : From Banks	4,80,000	
	4,80,000	

SCHEDULE - 5 : OTHER LIABILITIES ANIL PROVISIONS

	As on 31-3-15 Rs.	As on 31-3-14 Rs.
Bills Payable	4,00,000	
Unclaimed Dividend	5,000	
Sundry Creditors	25,000	
Rebate on Bills Discounted	5,000	
Provision for Taxation	12,500	
	4,47,500	

SCHEDULE- 6 : CASH AND BALANCES WITH RESERVE BANK OF INDIA

	As on 31-3-15 Rs.	As on 31-3-14 Rs.
Cash-in-hand	1,25,000	
Cash with RBI	5,00,000	
	6,25,000	

SCHEDULE - 7 : BALANCES WITH BANKS AND MONEY AT CALL AND SHORT NOTICE

	As on 31-3-15 Rs.	As on 31-3-14 Rs.
Cash with other Banks	7,25,000	
Money at call and short notice	2,90,000	
	10,15,000	

SCHEDULE - 8 : INVESTMENTS

	As on 31-3-15 Rs.	As on 31-3-14 Rs.
Govt. Securities	10,00,000	
Shares	5,00,000	
	15,00,000	

SCHKDLLK- 9 : ADVANCES

	As on 31-3-15 Rs.	As on 31-3-14 Rs.
Bill Purchased and Discounted	2,50,000	
Cash credits. Overdrafts and Loans	20,00,000	
Term Loans	16,00,000	
	38,50,000	
Less R. D. D.	– 10,000	
	38,40,000	

SCHEDULE- 10 : FIXED ASSETS

	As on 31-3-15 Rs.	As on 31-3-14 Rs.
Premises : at Original Cost	6,50,000	
Less Depreciation written of up to		
end of Previous Year.		
	50,000	
	6,00,000	

SCHEDULE - 11 : OTHER ASSETS

	As on 31-3-15 Rs.	As on 31-3-14 Rs.
Non-Banking Assets	1,70,000	
	1 ,70,000	

SCHEDULE - 12 : CONTINGENT LIABILITIES

	As on 31-3-15 Rs.	As on 31-3-14 Rs.
(i) Acceptances for customers	1,00,000	
(ii) Claims against the Bank not acknowledged as debts	25,000	
	1,25,000	
Bills for Collection	70,000	

SCHEDULE - 13 : INTEREST EARNED

	For the Year ended 31-3-2015 Rs.	For the Year ended 31-3-2014 Rs.
Interest/ discount on Advances, Bills	3,25,000	
Less Rebate on Bills Discounted	5,000	
	3,20,000	

SCHEDULK- 14 : OTHER INCOME

	For the Year ended 31-3-2015 Rs.	For the Year ended 31-3-2014 Rs.
(i) Commission Exchange, Brokerage		
(ii) Profit on Sale of Investment	–	
Less : Loss on Sale of Investments		
(iii) Profit on revaluation of Investments		
Less : Loss on Revaluation of Investments	–	
(iv) Profit on Sale of Land, Buildings and Other assets		
Less : Loss on Sale of Land, Buildings and Other assets	–	
(v) Profit on Exchange transactions		
Less : Loss on Exchange transactions	–	
(vi) Income earned by way of Dividends etc	–	
(vii) Miscellaneous Income	–	
Total	Nil	

SCHEDULE- 15 : INTEREST EXPENDED

	For the Year ended 31-3-2015 Rs.	For the Year ended 31-3-2014 Rs.
Interest paid on Deposits	90,000	
	90,000	

SCHEDULE. 16 : OPERATING EXPENSES

	For the Year ended 31-3-2015 Rs.	For the Year ended 31-3-2014 Rs.
(i) Payments to and Provisions for employees : Salaries to Staff	50,000	
(ii) Rent, taxes and lighting	5,000	
(iii) Printing and Stationery	–	
(iv) Advertisement and Publicity	–	
(v) Depreciation on Blank's property :	–	
(vi) Directors' fees, Allowances and Expenses	–	
(vii) Auditors' fees, and expenses	–	
(viii) Law charges	–	
(ix) Posiagc, Telegrams, Telephones etc.	–	
(x) Repairs and Maintenance	–	
(xi) Insurance	–	
(xii) Other Expenditure : Miscellaneous Expenses	10,000	
Total	65,000	
Provisions and Contingencies : RDD	10,000	
Provision for taxation	12,500	
	22,500	

Satara Bank Ltd.
Profit and Loss Account for the Year ended 31 - 3 -2015

	Schedule No.	Year ended 31-12-2015	Year ended 31-12-2014
(I) INCOME			
Interest earned	13	3,20,000	
Other income	14	–	
Total		3,20,000	
(II) EXPENDITURE			
Interest expended	15	90,000	
Operating expenses	16	65,000	
Provisions and Contingencies	–	22,500	
Total		1,77,500	
(III) PROFIT /LOSS			
Net Profit /Loss (-)for the year		1,42,500	
P/L (-) brought forward 1-4-2014		1,30,000	
Total		2,72,500	
(IV) APPROPRIATIONS			
Transfer to Statutory Reserve		28,500	
Dividend for (2013-2014)		25,000	
Balance carried over to		2,19,000	
Baiance Sheet	Total	2,72,500	

Satara Bank Ltd.
Balance Sheet as on 31 - 3 - 2015

	Schedule No.	As on 31-3-15 (Current year) Rs.	As on 31-3-14 (Previous year) Rs.
(I) Capital and Liabilities			
Capital	1	2,50,000	
Reserves and Surplus	2	3,97,500	
Deposits	3	61,75,000	
Borrowings	4	4,80,000	
Other Liabilities and Provisions	5	4,47,500	
Total		77,50,000	

(II) Assets :			
Cash and Balances with RBI	6	6,25,000	
Balances with banks and Money at call and short notice	7	10,15,000	
Investments	8	15,00,000	
Advances	9	38,40,000	
Fixed Assets	10	6,00,000	
Other Assets	11	1,70,000	
Total		77,50,000	
Contingent Liabilities	12	1,25,000	
Bills for collection	-	70,000	

PROBLEM NO. 5

Following is the Trial Balance of Vidya Bank Ltd. as on 31 March 2015

Trial Balance

	Debit Rs.	Credit Rs.
Premises less Depreciation	1,85,000	–
Money at call and Short notice	2,15,000	–
Furniture less Depreciation	30,000	–
Depreciation on Bank's Assets	11,000	–
Non-Banking assets acquired in settlement of claims	20,000	–
Cash in hand	3,00,000	–
Cash at Banks	2,50,000	–
Investments	3,50,000	–
Loans, Cash Credit and Overdrafts	12,65,000	–
Interest on Deposits and Borrowings	2,00,000	–
Audit Fees	4,500	–
Salaries and Allowances to Staff	40,500	–
Directors' Fees	4,000	–
Postage and Telegrams	1,350	–
Printing and Stationary	3,700	–
Other Expenditure	2,450	–
Interest and Discounts	–	3,67,500
Share Capital :		
Authorised 7,500 eq. shares Rs. 100 each		
Issued and subscribed.	–	–
6,000 equity shares of Rs. 100 each fully paid	–	6,00,000
Statutory Reserve	–	1,20,000
Deposits	–	12,50,000
Provident Funds	–	1,35,000
Borrowings from Maharaja Bank Ltd.	–	2,55,000
Unclaimed Dividend -.	–	4,000
Commission and Exchange	–	37,500
Profit on Sale of Non-Banking Assets	–	1,200
Profit and Loss Account as on 1-4-2014	–	1,12,300
	28,82,500	28,82,500

Adjustments :

1) Provide Rs. 10,000 for Bad and Doubtful Debts.
2) Bills for collection amounted to Rs. 1,05,000.
3) Acceptances, Endorsements and other Obligations amounted to Rs. 52,000.
4) Provide Rs. 1,500 for Rebate on Bills discounted.
5) Provide Rs. 10,500 for taxation.
6) Stamps of Rs. 160 and Stationery of Rs. 700 was in hand on 31-3-2015

   Prepare Profit and Loss Account for the year ended 31st March 2015 and the Balance Sheet as on that date as per Banking Regulation Act.

(Pune Uni. April 95)

Solution :

Bank Account, Vidya Bank Ltd.

SCHEDULE 1 : CAPITAL

	As on 31-3-15 (Current year) Rs.	As on 31-3-14 (Previous year) Rs.
Authorised : 7,500 Equity shares of Rs. 100 each	7,50,000	
Issued and Subscribed ; 6,000 fully paid Equity Shares of Rs. 100 each.	6,00,000	
	6,00,000	

SCHEDULE - 2 : RESERVES AND SURPLUS

		As on 31-3-15 Rs.	As on 31-3-14 Rs.
Statutory Reserve (opening balance)	1,20,000		
Added out of Profit	+ 23,512		
		1,43,512	
Surplus i.e. Balance in P and L Appropriation A/c		2,06,348	
		3,49,860	

SCHEDULE - 3 : DEPOSITS

	As on 31-3-15 Rs.	As on 31-3-14 Rs.
(i) Demand Deposits (i.e. current deposits)	–	
(ii) Saving Bank Deposits	12,50,000	
(iii) Term Deposits (i.e. Fixed, Recurring Deposits etc.)	–	
	12,50,000	

SCHEDULE- 4 : BORROWINGS

	As on 31-3-15 Rs.	As on 31-3-14 Rs.
Borrowings From Maharaja Bank	12,50,000	
	12,50,000	

SCHEDULE - 5 : OTHER LIABILITIES AND PROVISIONS

	As on 31-3-15 Rs.	As on 31-3-14 Rs.
(i) Provident Funds	1,35,000	
(ii) Unclaimed Dividend	4,000	
(iii) Rebate on Bills Discounted	1,500	
(iv) Provision for Taxation	10,500	
	1,51,000	

SCHEDULE - 6 : CASH AND BALANCES WITH RESERVE BANK OF INDIA

	As on 31-3-15 Rs.	As on 31-3-14 Rs.
Cash-in-hand	3,00,000	
	3,00,000	

SCHEDULE - 7 : BALANCES WITH BANKS AND MONEY AT CALL AND SHORT NOTICS

	As on 31-3-15 Rs.	As on 31-3-14 Rs.
Balances with Bank's	2,50,000	
Money at call and Short Notice	2,15,000	
	4,65,000	

SCHEDULE - 8 : INVESTMENTS

	As on 31-3-15 Rs.	As on 31-3-14 Rs.
Investments	3,50,000	
	3,50,000	

SCHEDULE - 9 : ADVANCES

	As on 31-3-15 Rs.	As on 31-3-14 Rs.
(i) Bills Purchased and Discounted	-	
(ii) Cash Credits, Overdrafts and Loans	12,65,000	
	12,65,000	
Less R.D.D.	– 10,000	
	12,55,000	

SCHEDULE - 10 : FIXED ASSETS

	As on 31-3-15 Rs.	As on 31-3-14 Rs.
(i) Premises Less Depreciation	1,85,000	
(ii) Furniture Less Depreciation	30,000	
	2,15,000	

SCHEDULE - 11 : OTHER ASSETS

		As on 31-3-15 Rs.	As on 31-3-14 Rs.
Non-Banking Assets		20,000	
Stock of Stationery	700		
Stock of Stationery Postage stamps	+160		
		860	
		20,860	

SCHEDULE- 12 : CONTINGENT LIABILITIES

	As on 31-3-15 Rs.	As on 31-3-14 Rs.
Acceptances, Endorsements and other obligations	52,000	
	52,000	

SCHEDULE - 13 : INTEREST EARNED

	For the Year ended 31-3-2015 Rs.	For the Year ended 31-3-2014 Rs.
Interest/ Discount on Advances / Bills Less Rebate on Bills Discounted	3,67,500 - 1,500	
	3,66,000	

SCHEDULE - 14 : OTHER INCOME

	For the Year ended 31-3-2015 Rs.	For the Year ended 31-3-2014 Rs.
(i) Commission, Exchange, Brokerage	37,500	
(ii) Profit on Sale of Investments	–	
Less : Loss on Sale of Investments		
(iii) Profit on revaluation of Investments		
Less : Loss on Revaluation of Investments	–	
*(iv) Profit on Sale of Land, Buildings and Other assets	– 1,200	
Less : Loss on Sale of Land, Buildings and Other assets	–	
(v) Profit on Exchange transactions		
Less : Loss on Exchange transactions	–	
(vi) Income earned by way of Dividends etc.	–	
(vii) Miscellaneous Income	–	
Total	38,700	

* This is profit on sale of Non-banking Assets

SCHEDULE - I5 : INTEREST EXPENDED

	For the Year ended 31-3-2015 Rs.	For the Year ended 31-3-2014 Rs.
Interest on Deposits and Borrowings	2,00,000	
	2,00,000	

SCHEDULE- 16 : OPERATING EXPENSES

		For the Year ended 31-3-2015 (Rs.)	For the Year ended 31-3-2014 (Rs.)
(i) Payments to and provisions for employees : (Salary and Allowances)		40,500	
(ii) Rent, Taxes, Lighting			
(iii) Printing and Stationery	3,700		
Less Stock	- 700	3,000	
(iv) Advertisement and Publicity		–	
(v) Depreciation on Bank's property :		11,000	
(vi) Directors' fees, Allowances and Expenses		4,000	
(vii) Auditors' fees, and expenses		4,500	
(viii) Law charges		–	
(ix) Postage, Telegrams, Telephones etc.	1,350		
Less Stock	- 160	1,190	
(x) Repairs and Maintenance		–	
(xi) Insurance		–	
(xii) Other Expenditure :		2,450	
Total		66,640	
Provisions and Contingencies : RDD		10,000	
Provision for Taxation		10,500	
		20,500	

Vidya Bank Ltd.
P and L Account for the year ended 31-3-2015

	Schedule No.	Year ended 31-12-2015	Year ended 31-12-2014
(I) INCOME			
Interest earned	13	366,000	
Other income	14	38,700	
Total		4,04,700	
(II) EXPENDITURE			
Interest expended	15	2,00,000	
Operating expenses	16	66,640	
Provisions and contingencies	–	20,500	
Total		2,87,140	
(III) PROFIT /LOSS			
Net profit/Loss (-) for the year		1,17,560	
Profit/loss (-) brought forward		1,12,300	
Total		2,29,860	
(IV) APPROPRIATIONS			
Transfer to Statutory Reserve (20% of Net profit)		23,512	
Bal. carried over to Balance Sheet		2,06,348	
Total		2,29,860	

Vidya Bank Ltd.
Balance Sheet as on 31-3-2015

	Schedule No.	As on 31-3-15 (Current year) Rs.	As on 31-3-14 (Previous year) Rs.
(1) Capital and Liabilities :		–	–
Capital	1	6,00,000	–
Reserves and Surplus	2	3,49,860	–
Deposits	3	12,50,000	–
Borrowings	4	2,55,000	–
Other liabilities and Provisions	5	1,51,000	–
Total		26,05,860	
(2) Assets :			
Cash and Balances with RBI	6	3,00,000	
Balances with banks and Money at call and short notice	7	4,65,000	
Investments	8	3,50,000	
Advances	9	12,55,000	
Fixed Assets	10	2,15,000	
Other Assets	11	20,860	
Total		26,05,860	
Contingent Liabilities	12	52,000	
Bills for collection	-	1,05,000	

PROBLEM NO. 6

The following is the Trial Balance ol Modern Bank Ltd. as at 31st March 2015

Trail Balance as on 31-3-2015

Particulars	Debit Rs.	Credit Rs.
Subscribed Capital		
75,000 equity shares of Rs. 10 each fully paid	–	7,50,000
Reserve Fund	–	3,75,000
Loans, Cash Credit and Overdraft	3,25,000	–
Premises	75,000	–
Indian Govt Securities	6,00,000	–
Current Deposits	–	1,50,000
Fixed Deposits	–	1,87,500
Saving Bank Deposits		75,000
Salaries	42,000	–
General Expenses	40,500	–
Rent, Rates and Taxes.	4,500	–
Directors fees	3,000	–
Profit and Loss Account (1-4-2014)	–	27,000
Interest and Discount received	–	1,87,500
Stock of Stationery	12,000	–
Bills purchased and discounted	69,000	–
Interim Dividend paid	26,000	–
Shares of Company	75,000	–
Cash in hand and with R.B.I.	2,85,000	–
Money at call and short notice	1,20,000	–
Interest paid	75,000	–
	17,52,000	17,52,000

Adjustments :

a) Provide rebate on Bills discounted Rs. 1,500.

b) Provide Rs. 4500 for Doubtful Debts.

c) Authorised capital was 1,20,000 Equity Shares of Rs. 10 each.

d) Provide Rs. 12,000 for Taxation Reserve.

You are required to prepare Profit and Loss Account for the year ended 31st March 2015 and the Balance Sheet as on that date as per the Banking Companies Regulation Act. (Pune University, T. Y. B.Com).

Solution :

Bank Accounts, Modern Bank Ltd.

SCHEDULE - 1 : CAPITAL

	As on 31-3-15 (Current year) Rs.	As on 31-3-14 (Previous year) Rs.
Authorised : 1 ,20,000 Equity Shares of Rs, 10 each	12,00,000	
Subscribed : 75,000 Equity Shares of Rs. 10 each fully paid-up	7,50,000	
	7,50,000	

SCHEDULE - 2 : RESERVF.S AND SURPLUS

	As on 31-3-15 Rs.	As on 31-3-14 Rs.
Reserve Fund 3,75,000 Add out of Net profit + 900	3,75,900	
Surplus i.e. Balance in P and L Appropriation A/c	4,600	
	3,80,500	

SCHEDULE - 3 : DEPOSITS

	As on 31-3-15 Rs.	As on 31-3-14 Rs.
(i) Current Deposits	1,50,000	
(ii) Saving Bank Deposits	75,000	
(iii) Fixed and Recurring Deposits	1,87,500	
	4,12,500	

SCHEDULE- 4 : BORROWINGS

	As on 31-3-15 Rs.	As on 31-3-14 Rs.
	Nil	
	Nil	

SCHEDULE - 5 : OTHER LIABILITIES AND PROVISIONS

	As on 31-3-15 Rs.	As on 31-3-14 Rs.
Rebate on Bills Discounted	1,500	
Provision for Taxation	12,000	
	13,500	

SCHEDULE - 6 : CASH AND BALANCES WITH RESERVE BANK OF INDIA

	As on 31-3-15 Rs.	As on 31-3-14 Rs.
Cash in hand and with RBl	2,85,000	
	2,85,000	

SCHEDULE- 7 : BALANCES WITH BANKS AND MONEY AT CALL AND SHORT NOTICE

	As on 31-3-15 Rs.	As on 31-3-14 Rs.
Money at call and short notice	1,20,000	
	1,20,000	

SCHEDULE - 8 : INVESTMENTS

	As on 31-3-15 Rs.	As on 31-3-14 Rs.
Indian Govt. Securities	6,00,000	
Shares of Companies	75,000	
	6,75,000	

SCHEDULE - 9 : ADVANCES

	As on 31-3-15 Rs.	As on 31-3-14 Rs.
Bill Purchased and Discounted	69,000	
Cash credits, Overdrafts and Loans	3,25,000	
	3,94,000	
- RDD	− 4,500	
	3,89,500	

SCHEDULE - 10 : FIXED ASSETS

	As on 31-3-15 Rs.	As on 31-3-14 Rs.
Premises	75,000	
	75,000	

SCHEDULE- 11 : OTHER ASSETS

	As on 31-3-15 Rs.	As on 31-3-14 Rs.
Stock of Stationery	12,000	
	12,000	

SCHEDULE- 12 : CONTINGENT LIABILITIES

	As on 31-3-15 Rs.	As on 31-3-14 Rs.
	Nil	
	Nil	

SCHEDULE - 13 : INTEREST EARNED

	For the Year ended 31-3-2015 Rs.	For the Year ended 31-3-2014 Rs.
Interest/ Discount on Advances, Bills	1,87,500	
Less Rebate on Bills Discounted	-1,500	
Total	1,86,000	

SCHEDULE - 14 : OTHER INCOME

	For the Year ended 31-3-2015 Rs.	For the Year ended 31-3-2014 Rs.
i) Commission Exchange Brokerage	–	–
ii) Profit on Sale of Investments less Loss	–	–
iii) Profit on revaluation of investments less loss on revaluation of investments	–	–
iv) Profit on Sale of Land, Buildings and other assets less Loss	–	–
v) Profit on Exchange transactions Less loss on Exchange transactions	–	–
vi) Income earned by way of Dividend etc.	–	–
vii) Miscellaneous Income	–	–
Total	Nil	Nil

SCHEDULE - 15 : INTEREST EXPENDED

	For the Year ended 31-3-2015 Rs.	For the Year ended 31-3-2014 Rs.
Interest paid	75,000	
Total	75,000	

SCHEDULE- 16 : OPERATING EXPENSES

	For the Year ended 31-3-2015 (Rs.)	For the Year ended 31-3-2014 (Rs.)
(i) Payments to and Provisions for employees : Salary	42,000	
(ii) Rent, Taxes, Lighting	4,500	
(iii) Printing and Stationery	–	
(iv) Advertisement and Publicity	–	
(v) Depreciation on Bank's property :	–	
(vi) Directors' fees, Allowances and Expenses	3,000	
(vii) Auditors' fees, and expenses	–	
(viii) Law charges	–	
(ix) Postage, Telegrams, Telephones etc.	–	
(x) Repairs and Maintenance	–	
(xi) Insurance	–	
(xii) Other Expenditure :	40,500	
Total	90,000	
Provisions and Contingencies : RDD	4,500	
Provision for taxation	12,000	
	16,500	

Modern Bank Ltd. : Profit and Loss Account for year ended 31-3-2015

	Schedule No.	Year ended 31-12-2015	Year ended 31-12-2014
(I) INCOMK			
Interest earned	13	1 ,86,000	
Other Income	14	–	
Total		1 ,86,000	
(II) EXPENDITURE			
Interest expended	15	75,000	
Operating expenses	16	90,000	
Provision and Contingencies	–	16,500	
Total		1,81,500	
(III) PROFIT /LOSS			
Net profit for the year		4,500	
Profit brought forward		27,000	
Total		31,500	
(IV) APPROPRIATIONS			
Transferred to Statutory Reserve (20% of Adjusted NP)		900	
Interim dividend declared		26,000	
Balance Carried over to Balance Sheet		4,600	
Total		31,500	

Modern Bank Ltd.
Balance Sheet as on 31 - 3 - 2015

	Schedule No.	As on 31-3-15 (Current year) Rs.	As on 31-3-14 (Previous year) Rs.
(I) Capital and Liabilities :			
Capital	1	7,50,000	
Reserves and Surplus	2	3,80,500	
Deposits	3	4,12,500	
Borrowings	4	–	
Other Liabilities and Provisions	5	13,500	
Total		15,56,500	
(II) Assets :			
Cash and Balances with RBI	6	2,85,000	
Balances with Bank and			
Money at Call and Short Notice	7	1,20,000	
Investments	8	6,75,000	
Advances	9	3,89,500	
Fixed Assets	10	75,000	
Other Assets	11	12,000	
Total		15,56,500	
Contingent Liabilities	12	Nil	
Bills for Collection		Nil	

PROBLEM NO. 7

From the following balances of Shri Shivaji Bank Ltd., Satara on 31st March, 2015 Prepare Profit and Loss Account and Balance Sheet as on that date.

Particulars	Debit Rs.	Credit Rs.
Equity Share Capital		
of Rs. 100 each Rs. 50 paid-up	–	4,00,000
Profit and Loss Account (1-4-2014)	–	1,60,000
Current Deposit A/c	–	13,64,000
Fixed Deposit A/c	–	15,60,000
Saving Bank A/c	–	10,26,000
Director's fees	18,000	–
Audit Fees	4,000	–
Furniture (Cost Rs. 4,00,000)	3,48,000	–
Interest and Discount Received	–	8,40,000
Commission and Exchange	–	4,00,000
Reserve Fund	–	1,40,000
Printing and Stationery	16,000	–
Rent and Taxes.	34,000	–
Salary	2,80,000	–
Building (Cost Rs. 12,00,000)	9,00,000	–
Law Charges	6,000	–
Cash-in-hand	64,000	–
Cash with RBI	14,00,000	–
Cash with other Bank	13,00,000	–
Investment at Cost	4,80,000	–
Loans, Cash Credit and Overdraft.	12,00,000	–
Bills Discounted and Purchased	5,60,000	–
Interest paid	6,00,000	–
Borrowing from Laxmi Bank	–	8,00,000
Branch Adjustment A/c	–	5,20,000
	72,10,000	72,10,000

Following additional information is available :

a) The Bank has accepted on behalf of the customers bills worth Rs. 6,00,000 against the securities of Rs. 7,60,000 lodged with the bank.

b) Rebate on bills discounted Rs. 22,000.

c) Provide Depreciation on building 10 % and Furniture 5 % on cost

d) Provide Rs. 6,000 for bad and doubtful debts. (Pune University T. Y. B.Com).

Solution :

Bank Accounts, Shri Shivaji Bank Ltd.

SCHEDULE - 1 : CAPITAL

	As on 31-3-15 (Current year) Rs.	As on 31-3-14 (Previous year) Rs.
Subscribed : 8,000 Equity Shares of Rs. 100 each, Rs. 50 per share paid-up	4,00,000	
	4,00,000	

SCHEDULE - 2 : RESERVES AND SURPLUS

		As on 31-3-15 Rs.	As on 31-3-14 Rs.
Reserve Fund	1,40,000		
Additions during the year	22,800	1,62,800	
Surplus i.e. Balance in			
P and L Appropriation A/c		2,51,200	
		4,14,000	

SCHEDULE - 3 : DEPOSITS

	As on 31-3-15 Rs.	As on 31-3-14 Rs.
(i) Current Deposits	13,64,000	
(ii) Saving Bank Deposits	10,26,000	
(iii) Fixed Deposits	15 60,000	
	39,50,000	

SCHEDULE - 4 : BORROWINGS

	As on 31-3-15 Rs.	As on 31-3-14 Rs.
Borrowings from Laxmi Bank Ltd.	8,00,000	
	8,00,000	

SCHEDULE - 5 : OTHER LIABILITIES AND PROVISIONS

	As on 31-3-15 Rs.	As on 31-3-14 Rs.
Branch Adjustments (Cr)	5,20,000	
Rebate on Bills Discounted	22,000	
	5,42,000	

SCHEDULE - 6 : CASH AND BALANCES WITH RESERVE BANK OF INDIA

		As on 31-3-15 Rs.	As on 31-3-14 Rs.
Cash in hand	64,000		
Cash with RBI	14,00,000		
		14,64,000	
		14,64,000	

SCHEDULE - 7 : BALANCES WITH BANKS AND MONEY AT CALL AND SHORT NOTICE

	As on 31-3-15 Rs.	As on 31-3-14 Rs.
Cash with Banks	13,00,000	
	13,00,000	

SCHEDULE - 8 : INVESTMENTS

	As on 31-3-15 Rs.	As on 31-3-14 Rs.
Investments at cost	4,80,000	
	4,80,000	

SCHEDULE - 9 : ADVANCES

	As on 31-3-15 Rs.	As on 31-3-14 Rs.
(i) Bills Purchased and Discounted	5,60,000	
(ii) Cash Credits, Overdrafts and Loans	12,00,000	
	17,60,000	
Less R.D.D.	-6,000	
	17,54,000	

SCHEDULE - 10 : FIXED ASSETS

		As on 31-3-15 Rs.	As on 31-3-14 Rs.
(i) Premises at Original Cost Less Depreciation to date	12,00,000 - 4,20,000		
		7,80,000	
(ii) Furniture at original cost Less Depreciation to date	4,00,000 - 72,000		
		3,28,000	
		11,08,000	

SCHEDULE - 11 : OTHER ASSETS

	As on 31-3-15 Rs.	As on 31-3-14 Rs.
None	Nil	
	Nil	

SCHEDULE- 12 : CONTINGENT LIABILITIES

	As on 31-3-15 Rs.	As on 31-3-14 Rs.
Acceptances (Against securities worth Rs. 7,20,000)	6,00,000	
	6,00,000	

SCHEDULE - 13 : INTEREST EARNED

	As on 31-3-15 Rs.	As on 31-3-14 Rs.
Interest/ Discount on Advances / Bills Less Rebate on Bills Discounted	8,40,000 - 22,000	
	8,18,000	

SCHEDULE- 14 : OTHER INCOME

	For the Year ended 31-3-2015 Rs.	For the Year ended 31-3-2014 Rs.
(i) Commission Exchange Brokerage	4,00,000	
(ii) Profit on Sale of Investments	–	
Less : Loss on Sale of Investments	–	
(iii) Profit on revaluation of Investments	–	
Less : Loss on Revaluation of Investments	–	
(iv) Profit on Sale of Land, Buildings and Other assets		
Less : Loss on Sale of Land, Buildings and Other assets	–	
(v) Profit on Exchange transactions		
Less : Loss on Exchange transactions	–	
(vi) Income earned by way of Dividends etc	–	
(vii) Miscellaneous Income	–	
Total	4,00,000	

SCHEDULE - I5 : INTEREST EXPENDED

	For the Year ended 31-3-2015 Rs.	For the Year ended 31-3-2014 Rs.
Interest paid	6,00,000	
	6,00,000	

SPHEDLLK - 16 : OPERATING EXPENSES

	For the Year ended 31-3-2015 Rs.	For the Year ended 31-3-2014 Rs.
(i) Payments to and Provisions for employees : Salary	2,80,000	
(ii) Rent, Taxes, Lighting	34,000	
(iii) Printing and Stationery	16,000	
(iv) Advertisement and Publicity	–	
(v) Depreciation on Bank's property :		
Premises 1,20,000		
Furniture 20,000	1,40,000	
(vi) Directors' fees. Allowances and Expenses	18,000	
(vii) Auditors' fees, and expenses	4,000	
(viii) Law charges	6,000	
(ix) Postage, Telegrams, Telephones etc	–	
(x) Repairs and Maintenance	–	
(xi) Insurance	–	
(xii) Other Expenditure :	–	
Total	4,98,000	
Provisions and Contingencies : R.D.D	6,000	
	6,000	

Shri Shivaji Bank Ltd., Satara
Profit and Loss Account for the Year ended 31-3 - 2015

	Schedule No.	Year ended 31-12-2015	Year ended 31-12-2014
(I) INCOME			
Interest earned	13	8,18,000	
Other Income	14	4,00,000	
Total		12,18,000	
(II) EXPENDITURE			
Interest expended	15	6,00,000	
Operating expenses	16	4,98,000	
Provisions and Contingencies	–	6,000	
Total		11,04,000	

(III)	**PROFIT /LOSS**			
	Net profit /Loss (-) for the year		1,14,000	
	Profit/Loss (-) brought forward		1,60,000	
		Total	2,74,000	
(IV)	**APPROPRIATIONS**			
	Transferred to Statutory Reserve (20% of Net Profit)		22,800	
	Balance carried over to Balance Sheet		2,51,200	
		Total	2,74,000	

Shri Shivaji Bank Ltd.
Balance Sheet as on 31 - 3 - 2015

	Schedule No.	As on 31-3-15 (Current year) Rs.	As on 31-3-14 (Previous year) Rs.
(I) Capital and Liabilities :			
Capital	1	4,00,000	
Reserves and Surplus	2	4,14,000	
Deposits	3	39,50,000	
Borrowings	4	8,00,000	
Other Liabilities and Provisions	5	5,42,000	
Total		61,06,000	
(II) Assets :			
Cash and Balances with RBI	6	14,64,000	
Balances with Banks and Money at Call and Short Notice	7	13,00,000	
Investments	8	4,80,000	
Advances	9	17.54,000	
Fixed Assets	10	11,08,000	
Other Assets	11	–	
Total		61,06,000	
Contingent Liabilities	12	6,00,000	
Bills for Collection	-	Nil	

PROBLEM NO. 8

Following is the trial balance of Sandhya Bank Ltd. as on 31st March 2015. You are required to prepare Profit and Loss Account for the year ended 2015. Balance Sheet as on above date.

Particulars	Debit Rs.	Credit Rs.
Share Capital		
30,000 Equity Shares of Rs. 100 each		
Rs. 50 paid up	–	15,00,000
Profit and Loss Account	–	1,22,250
(1st April 2014)		
Current Deposits Accounts	–	32,16,500
Fixed Deposits Accounts	–	35,14,500
Savings Bank Accounts	–	16,60,500
Directors Fees	13,950	–
Audii Fees	13,200	–
Furniture	1,28,850	–
Interest paid	6,00,600	–
Interest and Discount	–	10,56,000
Commission and Exchange	–	3,04,500
6 % Govt. Bonds	15,60,000	–
Shares in companies	12,00,000	–
Branch Adjustment Account	3,06,000	–
Postage and Printing	10,350	–
Premises	25,54,500	–
Salaries	1,00,500	–
Law Charges	7,950	–
Provident Fund contribution	16,800	–
Cash in hand	3,10,500	–
Bills Purchased and Discounted	1,00,500	–
Unexpired Insurance	4,050	–
Statutory Reserve Fund	–	1,27,500
Loans, Cash credit And Overdrafts	45,73,500	–
	1,15,01,250	1,15,01,250

Following additional information :

a) Rebate on bills discounted amounted to Rs. 10,650 /-

b) Provide Rs. 57,750 for Doubtful Debts.

c) The Bank has accepted bills worth Rs. 3,75,000 on behalf of the customers against the securities of Rs. 4,65,000 lodged with the Bank.

d) Provide depreciation on premises Rs. 1,09,500 and on furniture Rs. 8,850.

e) Provide for Taxation Rs. 11,250   (Pune University T. Y. B.Com).

Solution : Bank Accounts, Profit and Loss A/c and Balance Sheet of Sandhya Bank Ltd. for the year ended 31-3-2015

SCHEDUCE - 1 : CAPITAL

	As on 31-3-15 (Current year) Rs.	As on 31-3-14 (Previous year) Rs.
Subscribed : 30,000 Equity Shares of Rs. 100 each, Rs. 50 per Share paid-up	15,00,000	
	15,00,000	

SCHEDULE - 2 : RESERVES AND SURPLUS

		As on 31-3-15 Rs.	As on 31-3-14 Rs.
Statutory Reserve Fund	1,27,500		
Added 20% of N. P.	79,830	2,07,330	
Surplus i.e. Balance in			
P and L Appropriation A/c		4,41,570	
		6,48,900	

SCHEDULE - 3 DEPOSITS

	As on 31-3-15 Rs.	As on 31-3-14 Rs.
(i) Current Deposits	32,16,000	
(ii) Saving Bank Deposits	16,60,500	
(iii) Fixed Deposits	35,14,500	
	83,91,000	

SCHEDULE - 4 : BORROWINGS

	As on 31-3-15 Rs.	As on 31-3-14 Rs.
	Nil	
	Nil	

SCHEDULE - 5 : OTHER LIABILITIES AND PROVISIONS

	As on 31-3-15 Rs.	As on 31-3-14 Rs.
Rebate on Bills Discounted	10,650	
Provision for Taxation	11,250	
	21,900	

SCHEDULE - 6 : CASH AND BALANCES WITH RESERVE BANK OF INDIA

	As on 31-3-15 Rs.	As on 31-3-14 Rs.
Cash-in-hand	3,10,500	
	3,10,500	

SCHEDULE - 7 : BALANCES WITH BANKS AND MONEY AT CALL AND SHORT NOTICE

	As on 31-3-15 Rs.	As on 31-3-14 Rs.
	Nil	
	Nil	

SCHEDULE - 8 : INVESTMENTS

	As on 31-3-15 Rs.	As on 31-3-14 Rs.
6 % Govt. Bonds	15,60,000	
Share in Companies	12,00,000	
	27,60,000	

SCHEDULE - 9 : ADVANCES

	As on 31-3-15 Rs.	As on 31-3-14 Rs.
Bill Purchased and Discounted	1,00,500	
Cash Credits, Overdrafts and Loans	45,73,500	
Term Loans	–	
	46,74,000	
Less Reserve for Doubtful Debts	-57,750	
	46,16,250	

SCHEDULE - 10 : FIXED ASSETS

		As on 31-3-15 Rs.	As on 31-3-14 Rs.
Premises :	25,54,500		
Less Depreciation	1,09,500		
		24,45,000	
Furniture	1,28,850		
Less Depreciation	8,850		
		1,20,000	
		25,65,000	

SCHEDULE - 11 : OTHER ASSETS

	As on 31-3-15 Rs.	As on 31-3-14 Rs.
Branch Adjustments (Debit Balance)	3,06,000	
Unexpired Insurance	4,050	
	3,10,050	

SCHEDULE - 12 : CONTINGENT LIABILITIES

	As on 31-3-15 Rs.	As on 31-3-14 Rs.
Bills Accepted	3,75,000	
(Against securities of the value of		
Rs. 4,65,000 lodged with the Bank)		
	3,75,000	

SCHEDULE - 13 : INTEREST EARNED

	For the Year ended 31-3-2015 (Rs.)	For the Year ended 31-3-2014 (Rs.)
Interest/ Discount on Advances/Bills	10,56,000	
Less Rebate on Bills Discounted	10,650	
	10,45,350	

SCHEDULE - 14 : OTHER INCOME

	For the Year ended 31-3-2015 (Rs.)	For the Year ended 31-3-2014 (Rs.)
(i) Commission Exchange Brokerage	3,04,500	
(ii) Profit on Sale of Investments		
Less : Loss on Sale of Investments		
(iii) Profit on revaluation of Investments		
Less : Loss on Revaluation of Investments		
(iv) Profit-on Sale of Land, Buildings and Other assets		
Less. : Loss on Sale of Land, Buildings and Other assets		
(v) Profit on Exchange transactions		
Less :Loss on Exchange transactions		
(vi) Income-earned by way of Dividends etc.		
(vii) Miscellaneous Income		
Total	3,04,500	

SCHEDULE - 15 : INTEREST EXPENDED

	As on 31-3-15 Rs.	As on 31-3-14 Rs.
Interest Paid	6,00,600	
	6,00,600	

SCHEDULE - 16 : OPERATING EXPENSES

	As on 31-3-15 Rs.	As on 31-3-14 Rs.
Payments to and Provisions for employees : Salary	1,00,500	
Provident Fund Contribution	16,800	
Rent, Taxes, Lighting	–	
Postage and Printing	10,350	
Advertisement and Publicity	–	
Depreciation on Bank's property	1,18,350	
Directors' fees, Allowances and Expenses	13,950	
Auditors' fees, expenses	13,200	
Law charges	7,950	
Postage, Telegrams, Telephone etc.	–	
Repairs and Maintenance	–	
Insurance	–	
Other Expenditure :		
Total	2,81,100	
Provisions and Contingencies : RDD 57,750		
Provision for Taxation 11,250		
	69,000	

Sandhya Bank Ltd.
Profit and Loss Account for the Year ended 31 - 3 - 2015

	Schedule No.	Year ended 31-12-2015	Year ended 31-12-2014
(I) INCOME			
Interest earned	13	10,45,350	
Other Income	14	3,04,500	
Total		13,49,850	
(II) EXPENDITURE			
Interest expended	15	6,00,600	
Operating expenses	16	2,81,100	
Provisions and Contingencies	–	69,000	
Total		9,50,700	

contd...

(III) **PROFIT /LOSS**			
Net profit / Loss for the year (-)	15	3,99,150	
Profit / Loss brought forward	16	1,22,250	
	Total	5,21,400	
(IV) **APPROPRIATIONS**			
Transferred to Statutory Reserve (20% of Net Profit)		79,830	
Balance carried over to Balance Sheet		4,41,570	
	Total	5,21,400	

Sandhya Bank Ltd.
Balance Sheet as on 31 - 3 - 2015

	Schedule No.	As on 31-3-15 (Current year) Rs.	As on 31-3-14 (Previous year) Rs.
(I) Capital and Liabilities :			
Capital	1	15,00,000	
Reserves and Surplus	2	6,48,900	
Deposits	3	83,91,000	
Borrowings	4	-	
Other Liabilities and Provisions	5	21,900	
	Total	1,05,61,800	
(II) Assets :			
Cash and Balances with RBI	6	3,10,500	
Balances with Banks and Money at Call and Short Notice	7	-	
Investments	8	27,60,000	
Advances	9	46,16,250	
Fixed Assets	10	25,65,000	
Other Assets	11	3,10,050	
	Total	1,05,61,800	
Contingent Liabilities	12	3,75,000	
Bills for Collection	-	-	

PROBLEM NO. 9

Following is the Trial Balance of Cosmos Co-operative Bank Ltd. as on 31-3-2015.

Trial Balance as on 31-3-2015

Particulars	Debit Rs.	Credit Rs.
Subscribed Capital		
56,250 Equity Shares of Rs. 10 each fully paid	–	5,62,500
Reserve Fund	–	2,81,250
Loans, Cash Credit and Overdraft	2,44,125	–
Premises	56,250	–
Indian Gov. Securities	4,50,000	–
Current Deposits	–	1,12,500
Fixed Deposits	–	1,40,625
Saving BankDeposits	–	56,250
Salaries	31,500	–
General Expenses	30,375	–
Rent and Taxes.	3,375	–
Directors' Fees	2,250	–
Profit and Loss Account (1-4-2014)	–	20,250
Interest and Discount Received	–	1,40,625
Stock of Stationery	9,000	–
Bills Purchased and Discounted	51,750	–
Interim Dividend Paid	19,125	–
Shares of Company	56,250	–
Cash-in-hand with RBI	2,13,750	–
Money at Call and Short Notice	90,000	–
Interest paid	56,250	–
	13,14,000	13,14,000

Adjustments :

1) Provide rebate on bills discounted Rs. 1,125.
2) Provide Rs. 3,375 for doubtful debts.
3) Authorised capital was 1 ,20,000 Equity Shares of Rs. 10 each.
4) Provide Rs. 9,000 for taxation reserve. You are required to prepare Profit and Loss Account for the year ended 31st March, 2015 and the Balance Sheet as on that date as per Banking Companies Regulation Act with schedules.

   (T. Y. B. Com.)

Solution :

P and L A/c for the year ended 31-3-2015 and the Balance sheet as on that date for Cosmos Co-oprtative Bank Ltd.

SCHEDULE -1 : CAPITAL

	As on 31-3-15 (Current year) Rs.	As on 31-3-14 (Previous year) Rs.
Authorised : 1,20,000 Equity Shares of Rs. 10 each Subscribed : 56,250 Equity Shares of Rs. 10 each fully paid	12,00,000 5,62,500	
	5,62,500	

SCHEDULE-2 : RESERVES AND SURPLUS

		As on 31-3-15 Rs.	As on 31-3-14 Rs.
Reserve Fund	2,81,250		
Additions 20 % of			
current year's net profit	675	2,81,925	
Surplus i.e. Balance in			
P and L Appropriation A/c		3,825	
		2,85,750	

SCHEDULE - 3 : DEPOSITS

	As on 31-3-15 Rs.	As on 31-3-14 Rs.
(i) Current Deposits	1,12,500	
(ii) Saving Bank Deposits	56,250	
(iii) Fixed Deposits	1,40,625	
	3,09,375	

SCHEDULE - 4 : BORROWINGS

	As on 31-3-15 Rs.	As on 31-3-14 Rs.
	Nil	
	Nil	

SCHEDULE - 5 : OTHER LIABILITIES AND PROVISIONS

	As on 31-3-15 Rs.	As on 31-3-14 Rs.
Rebate on Bills Discounted Provision for Taxation	1,125 9,000	
	10,125	

SCHEDULE - 6 : CASH AND BALANCES WITH RESERVE BANK OF INDIA

	As on 31-3-15 Rs.	As on 31-3-14 Rs.
Cash-in-hand and with RBI	2,13,750	
	2,13,750	

SCHEDULE- 7 : BALANCES WITH BANKS AND MONEY AT CALL AND SHORT NOTICE

	As on 31-3-15 Rs.	As on 31-3-14 Rs.
Money at call and Short Notice	90,000	
	90,000	

SCHEDULE 8 : INVESTMENTS

	As on 31-3-15 Rs.	As on 31-3-14 Rs.
Indian Govt Securities Shares of Companies	4,50,000 56,250	
	5,06,250	

SCHEDULE - 9 : ADVANCES

	As on 31-3-15 Rs.	As on 31-3-14 Rs.
(i) Bills Purchased and Discounted (ii) Loans, Cash Credits, Overdrafts	51,750 2,44,125	
	2,95,875	
Less R.D.D.	− 3,375	
	2,92,500	

SCHEDULE - 10 : FIXED ASSETS

	As on 31-3-15 Rs.	As on 31-3-14 Rs.
Premises	56,250	
	56,250	

SCHEDULE - 11 : OTHER ASSETS

	As on 31-3-15 Rs.	As on 31-3-14 Rs.
Stock of Stationery	9,000	
	9,000	

SCHEDULE - 12 : CONTINGENT LIABILITIES

	As on 31-3-15 Rs.	As on 31-3-14 Rs.
None	Nil	
	Nil	

SCHEDULE - 13 : INTEREST EARNED

	For the Year ended 31-3-2015 Rs.	For the Year ended 31-3-2014 Rs.
Interest/ Discounts Advances / Bills	1,40,625	
Less Rebate on Bills Discounted	- 1,125	
	1,39,500	

SCHEDULE - 14 : OTHER INCOME

	For the Year ended 31-3-2015 Rs.	For the Year ended 31-3-2014 Rs.
(i) Commission Exchange Brokerage	–	
(ii) Profit on Sale of Investments	–	
Less : Loss on Sale of Investments		
(iii) Profit on Revaluation of Investments		
Less : Loss on Revaluation of Investments	–	
(iv) Profit on Sale of Land, Buildings and Other assets		
Less : Loss on Sale of Land, Buildings and Other assets	–	
(v) Profit on Exchange transactions		
Less : Loss on Exchange transactions	–	
(vi) Income earned by way of Dividends etc	–	
(vii) Miscellaneous Income	–	
Total	Nil	

SCHEDULE- 15 : INTEREST EXPENDED

	For the Year ended 31-3-2015 Rs.	For the Year ended 31-3-2014 Rs.
Interest paid	56,250	
	56,250	

SCHEDULE - 16 : OPERATING EXPENSES

	For the Year ended 31-3-2015 (Rs.)	For the Year ended 31-3-2014 (Rs.)
(i) Payments to and Provisions for employees : Salaries	31,500	
(ii) Rent, Taxes, Lighting	3,375	
(iii) Printing and Stationery	–	
(iv) Advertisement and Publicity	–	
(v) Depreciation on Bank's property	–	
(vi) Directors' fees Allowances and Expenses	2,250	
(vii) Auditors' fees and Expenses	–	
(viii) Law charges	–	
(ix) Postage, Telegrams, Telephones etc.	–	
(x) Repairs and Maintenance	–	
(xi) Insurance	–	
(xii) Other Expenditure : General Expenses	30,375	
Total	67,500	
Provisions and Contingencies : RDD	3,375	
Provision for Taxation	9,000	
	12,375	

Cosmos Co-operative Bank Ltd.
Profit and Loss Account for the Year ended 31-3-2015

	Schedule No.	For the Year ended 31-3-2015 (Rs.)	For the Year ended 31-3-2014 (Rs.)
(I) INCOME			
Interest earned	13	1,39,500	
Other Income	14	Nil	
Total		1,39,500	
(II) EXPENDITURE			
Interest expended	15	56,250	
Operating expenses	16	67,500	
Provisions and Contingencies		12,375	
Total		1,36,125	
(III) PROFIT / LOSS			
Net profit for the year		3,375	
Profit brought forward		20,250	
Total		23,625	
(IV) APPROPRIATIONS			
Transferred to Statutory Reserve (20% of Net Profit)		6,75	
Interim Dividend Paid		19,125	
Balance carried over to Balance Sheet		3,825	
Total		23,625	

Cosmos Co-operative Bank : Balance Sheet as on 31 - 3 - 2015

	Schedule No.	As on 31-3-15 (Current year) Rs.	As on 31-3-14 (Previous year) Rs.
(I) **(Capital and Liabilities) :** Capital	1	5,62,500	
Reserves and Surplus	2	2,85,750	
Deposits	3	3,09,375	
Borrowings	4	Nil	
Other Liabilities and Provisions	5	10,125	
Total		11,67,750	
(II) **Assets :** Cash and Balances with RBI	6	2,13,750	
Balances with Banks and Money at Call and Short Notice	7	90,000	
Investments	8	5,06,250	
Advances	9	2,92,500	
Fixed Assets	10	56,250	
Other Assets	11	9,000	
Total		11,67,750	
Contingent Liabilities	12	Nil	
Bills for Collection		Nil	

PROBLEM NO. 10

The following figures were extracted from the books of New Era Bank Ltd. as on 31-3-2015

	Rs.
Interest and Discount received	37,05,738
Interest paid on Deposits	20,37,452
Issued and Subscribed Capital	10,00,000
Salaries and Allowances	2,00,000
Directors' Fees ant,Allowances	30,000
Rent and Taxes paid	90,000
Postage and Telegrams	60,286
Statutory Reserve Fund	8,00,000
Commission, Exchange and Brokerage	1,90,000
Rent Received	65,000
Profit on Sale of Investment	2,00,000
Depreciation on Bank's properties	30,000
Stationery Expenses	40,000
Preliminary Expenses	25,000
Auditor's Fees	5,000

The following further information given :

a) A customer to whom a sum of Rs. 10 lakh has been advanced has become insolvent and it is expected that only 50% can be recovered from his estate.

b) There were also other debts for which a provision of Rs. 1,50,000 was found necessary by the auditors.

c) Rebate on Bills discounted on 31-3-2014 was Rs.12,000 and on 31-3-2015 was Rs. 16,000.

d) Provide Rs. 6,50,000 for Income Tax.

e) The director's desire to declare 10% dividend.

Prepare the Profit and Loss Account of New Era Bank Ltd. for the year ended 31-3-2015 and also show how the Profit and Loss Account will appear in the Balance Sheet if the Profit and Loss Account opening balance was Nil as on 31-3-2014

(Pune University T. Y. B.Com).

Solution :

Bank Accounts, New Era Bank Ltd.

The effect of the adjustments on the Balance Sheet i.e. where they will appear in the Balance Sheet.

New Era Bank Ltd.
Profit and Loss Account for the year ended 31-3-2015

	Schedule No.	Year ended 31-03-2015	Year ended 31-03-2014
(I) INCOME			
interest earned	13	37,01,738	
Other Income	14	4,55,000	
Total		41,56,738	
(II) EXPENDITURE			
Interest expended	15	20,37,452	
Operating expenses	16	4,80,285	
Provisions and contingencies		13,00,000	
Total		38,17,733	
(III) PROFIT /LOSS			
Net Profit /Loss (-) for the year		3,39,000	
Profit/Loss (-) brought forward from previous vcar		Nil	
Total		3,39,000	
(IV) APPROPRIATIONS			
Transferred to Statutory Reserve (20% of Net Profit)		67,800	
Proposed Div. @ 10% on the Subscribed Cap. of Rs. 10,00,000		1,00,000	
Bal. carried over to Balance Sheet		1,71,200	
Total		3,39,000	

SCHEDULE - 2 : RESERVES AND SURPLUS

		As on 31-3-15 Rs.	As on 31-3-14 Rs.
Statutory Reserve Fund	8,00,000		
Added 20% of Net Profit for			
the Current Year	67,800		
		8,67,800	
Surplus i.e. Balance in			
P and L Appropriation A/c		1,71,200	
		10,39,000	

SCHEDULE - 5 : OTHER LIABILITIES AND PROVISIONS

	As on 31-3-15 Rs.	As on 31-3-14 Rs.
Rebate on Bills Discounted	16,000	
Provision for Taxation	6,50,000	
Proposed Equity Dividend	1,00,000	
	7,66,000	

And, on the Assets Side, from the total of Advances (Schedule 9)
RDD amounting to Rs. 6,50,000 will be Subtracted.

SCHEDULE- 13 : INTEREST EARNED

	Schedule No.	Year ended 31-12-2015 (Current year) Rs.	Year ended 31-12-2014 (Previous year) Rs.
Interest, Discount on Advances/Bills		37,05,738	
Add Rebate on Bills Discounted on			
31-3.2014		12,000	
		37,17,738	
Less Rebate on Bills Discounted on			
31-3-2015		16,000	
		37,01,738	

SCHEDULE - 14 : OTHE INCOME

	Year ended 31-12-2015 Rs.	Year ended 31-12-2014 Rs.
(i) Commission Exchange Brokerage	1,90,000	
(ii) Profit on sale of Investments	2,00,000	
Less : Loss on Sale of		
Investments		2,00,000
(iii) Profit on revaluation of Investments		
Less : Loss on Revaluation		
of Investments		
(iv) Profit on Sale of Land, Buildings		
and Other Assets		
Less : Loss on Sale of Land, Buildings		
and Other Assets		
(v) Profit on Exchange transactions		
Less : Loss on Exchange transactions		
(vi) Income earned by way of dividends etc.		
(vii) Miscellaneous Income Rent Received	65,000	
Total	4,55,000	

SCHEDULE - 15 : INTEREST EXPENDED

	Year ended 31-12-2015 Rs.	Year ended 31-12-2014 Rs.
Interest paid on deposits	20,37,452	–
	20,37,452	

SCHEDULE - 16 : OPERATING EXPENSES

	Year ended 31-12-2015 Rs.	Year ended 31-12-2014 Rs.
(i) Payments to and Provisions for employees : Salaries and Allowances	2,00,000	
(ii) Rents, Taxes, Lighting -	90,000	
(iii) Printing and stationery	40,000	
(iv) Advertisement and Publicity	–	
(v) Depreciation on Bank's property	30,000	
(vi) Directors' fees, Allowances and Expenses	30,000	
(vii) Auditors' fees,, and expenses	5,000	
(viii) Law charge	–	
(ix) Postage, Telegrams, Telephones etc.	60,286	
(x) Repairs and Maintenance	–	
(xi) Insurance	–	
(xii) Other Expenditure : Preliminary Expenses	25,000	
Total	4,80,286	
Provisions and Contingencies :		
(i) RDD	6,50,000	
(ii) Provision for Taxation	6,50,000	
	13,00,000	

PROBLEM NO. 11

From the following particulars prepare the Balance Sheet of Progressive Bank Ltd. as on 31st March, 2015

Particulars	Debit Rs.	Credit Rs.
Share Capital	–	10,00,000
Reserve Fund	–	16,00,000
Fixed Deposits	–	40,00,000
Saving Bank Deposits	–	60,00,000
Current Accounts	–	2,20,00,000
Money at call and short notice in India	2,00,000	–
Bills Discounted and Purchased in India	9,00,000	–
Investment at cost :		
Central and State Govt :		
- Securities	1,00,00,000	–
- Debentures	4,00,000	–
- Bullion	24,00,000	–
Reserve for Buildings	–	10,00,000
Premises at cost	1,00,00,000	–
Addition to Premises	20,00,000	–
Depreciation Fund on Premises	–	80,00,000
Cash with R. B. I.	34,00,000	–
Cash with State Bank of India	12,00,000	–
Unclaimed Dividend	–	24,000
Unexpired Discount	–	50,000
Loans, Advances, Overdrafts and		
Cash Credits in India	1,00,00,000	–
Brunch Adjustments	57,94,000	–
Silver	2,00,000	–
Advance Payment of Tax	1,10,000	–
Interest accrued on Investments	2,60,000	–
Non-banking Assets Acquired	70,000	–
Borrowing from Bank in India	–	2,50,000
Bills Payable	–	20,00,000
Profit and Loss A/c including Rs. 2,10,000		
for the year	–	4,10,000
Dividend Fluctuation Fund	–	6,00,000
	4,69,34,000	4,69,34,000

The bank had bills for collection for its constituents Rs. 3,00,000 and acceptances Rs. 4,00,000. There was a Claim of Rs. 2,00,000 against the bank but not acknowledged as debts. The liabilities for bills rc-discountcd was Rs. 32,000. Liability for forward exchange contract was Rs. 20,00,000.

The directors decided to reserve Rs. 2,000 for unexpired discount and transfer reserve for building to depreciation fund. (Pune University T. Y. B.Com)

Solution :

Bank Accounts, Progressive Bank Ltd.

SCHEDULE - 1 : CAPITAL

	As on 31-3-15 (Current year) Rs.	As on 31-3-14 (Previous year) Rs.
Share Capital	10,00,000	
	10,00,000	

SCHEDULE - 2 : RESERVES AND SURPLUS

		As on 31-3-15 Rs.	As on 31-3-14 Rs.
(i) Reserve Fund	16,00,000		
Add 20% of NP	41,600		
		16,41,600	
(ii) Dividend Equalisation Fund		6,00,000	
(iii) Surplus i.e. Balance in			
P and L Appropriation A/c		3,66,400	
		26,08,000	

SCHEDULE - 3 : DEPOSITS

	As on 31-3-15 Rs.	As on 31-3-14 Rs.
(i) Current Deposits	2,20,00,000	
(ii) Saving Bank Deposits	60,00,000	
(iii) Fixed Deposits	40,00,000	
	3,20,00,000	

SCHEDULE - 4 : BORROWINGS

	As on 31-3-15 Rs.	As on 31-3-14 Rs.
Borrowings from Banks in India	2,50,000	
	2,50,000	

SCHEDULE - 5 : OTHER LIABILITIES AND PROVISIONS

		As on 31-3-15 Rs.	As on 31-3-14 Rs.
Unclaimed Dividend		24,000	
Unexpired Discount	50,000		
plus Additional	+ 2,000	52,000	
Bills Payable		20,00,000	
		20,76,000	

SCHEDULE - 6 : CASH AND BALANCES WITH RESERVE BANK OF INDIA

	As on 31-3-15 Rs.	As on 31-3-14 Rs.
Cash with RBI	34,00,000	
	34,00,000	

SCHEDULE - 7 : BALANCES WITH BANKS AND MONEY AT CALL AND SHORT NOTICE

	As on 31-3-15 Rs.	As on 31-3-14 Rs.
Cash with State Bank of India	12,00,000	
Money at Call and Short Notice in India	2,00,000	
	14,00,000	

SCHEDULE - 8 : INVESTMENTS

	As on 31-3-15 Rs.	As on 31-3-14 Rs.
Central and State Govt. securities	1,00,00,000	
Debentures	4,00,000	
Bullion (i. e. Gold)	24,00,000	
	1,28,00,000	

SCHEDULE - 9 : ADVANCES

	As on 31-3-15 Rs.	As on 31-3-14 Rs.
(i) Bills Purchased and Discounted (in India)	9,00,000	
(ii) Cash Credits, Overdrafts and Loans	1,00,00,000	
(iii) Term Loans	–	
	1,09,00,000	

SCHEDULE - 10 : FIXED ASSETS

	As on 31-3-15 Rs.	As on 31-3-14 Rs.
(i) Premises	1,00,00,000	
plus cost of Additions	20,00,000	
	1,20,00,000	
(ii) Less Provision for Depreciation	90,00,000	
including Reserve for Building		
	30,00,000	

SCHEDULE - 11 : OTHER ASSETS

	As on 31-3-15 Rs.	As on 31-3-14 Rs.
Branch Adjustments (Dr)	57,94,000	
Silver	20,0000	
Advance Tax paid	1,10,000	
Interest Accrued on investments	2,60,000	
Non-Banking Assets	70,000	
(acquired in satisfaction of Debts)		
	64,34,000	

SCHEDULE- 12 : CONTINGENT LIABILITIES

	As on 31-3-15 Rs.	As on 31-3-14 Rs.
Liability for Bills rediscounicd	32,000	
Acceptances	4,00,000	
Claims against bank		
not acknowledged as a debts	2,00,000	
Liabilities for		
Forward Exchange Contracts	20,00,000	
	26,32,000	

Progressive Bank Ltd.
Profit and Loss Account for the Year ended 31-3-2015

	Shedule No.	For the Year ended 31-3-2015 (Rs.)	For the Year ended 31-3-2014 (Rs.)
(I) INCOME			
Interest earned	13	–	
Other Income	14	–	
Total		Nil	
(II) EXPENDITURE			
Interest expended	15	–	
Operating expenses	16	–	
Provisions and Contingencies	-		
Total		Nil	
(III) PROFIT /LOSS			
Net profit for the year	2,10,000		
Less Unexpired Discount (additional)	- 2,000	2,08,000	
Profit brought forward		2,00,000	
Total		4,08,000	
(IV) APPROPRIATIONS			
Transferred to Statutory Reserve (20% of Adjusted NP)		41,600	
Balance carried over to Balance Sheet		3,66,400	
Total		4,08,000	

Progressive Bank Ltd. Balance Sheet on 31-3-2015

	Shedule No.	For the Year ended 31-3-2015 (Rs.)	For the Year ended 31-3-2014 (Rs.)
(I) Capital and Liabilities :			
Capital	1	10,00,000	
Reserves and Surplus	2	26,08,000	
Deposits	3	3,20,00,000	
Borrowings	4	2,50,000	
Other Liabilities and Provisions	5	20,76,000	
Total		3,79,34,000	

contd...

(II) Assets :			
Cash and Balances with RBI	6	34,00,000	
Balances with Banks and			
Money at Call and Short Notice	7	14,00,000	
Investments	8	1,28,00,000	
Advances	9	1,09,00,000	
Fixed Assets	10	30,00,000	
Other Assets	11	64,34,000	
	Total	3,79,34,000	
Contingent Liabilities	12	26,32,000	
Bills for Collection		3,00,000	

PROBLEM NO. 12

The following is the trial Balance of Dhanashri Bank Ltd. as on 31st March 2015

Particulars	Debit Rs.	Credit Rs.
Subscribed Capital		
50,000 equity Shares of Rs.10 each fully paid	–	5,00,000
Reserve Fund	–	2,50,000
Loans Cash credit and Overdraft	2,85,000	–
Premises	61,000	–
Indian Govt. Securities	4,00,000	–
Current Deposits	–	1,00,000
Fixed Deposits	–	1,25,000
Savings Bank Deposits	–	50,000
Salaries	28,000	–
General Expenses	27,400	–
Rent, Rate and Taxes	2,300	–
Director's Fees	1,800	–
Profit and Loss Account (1 - 4 - 2014)	–	16,000
Interest and Discount	–	1,28,000
Stock of Stationery	8,500	–
Bills Purchased and Discounted	46,000	–
Interim Dividend paid	17,000	–
Recurring Deposits	–	31,000
Shares in Ltd. Company	50,000	–
Cash in hand and with Reserve Bank	1,93,000	–
Money at call and Short notice	80,000	
	12,00,000	12,00,000

The following information should be considered :

1) Provision for Bad and Doubtful debts is required to be made at Rs. 5,000.
2) Interest accrued on investment was Rs. 8,000.
3) Unexpired discount amounted to Rs. 380.
4) Interim Dividend declared was 4 % actual.
5) Endorsement made on behalf of customers totalled Rs. 1,15,000.
6) Authorised capital was 80,000 Equity Shares of Rs. 10 each.
7) Rs. 10,000 were added to the premises during the year. Depreciation at 5 % on the opening balance is required.
8) Market value of India Govt. Securities was Rs. 3,90,000.

   Prepare Profit and Loss Account for the year ended 31st March, 2015 and Balance Sheet as on that date, with necessary working in the prescribed schedules.

   (Pune University, T.Y.B. Com)

Solution :

Bank Accounts, Profit and Loss A/c and Balance Sheet of Sandhya Bank Ltd. for the year ended 31-3-2015

SCHEDULE -1 : CAPITAL

	As on 31-3-15 (Current year) Rs.	As on 31-3-14 (Previous year) Rs.
Authorised : 80,000 Equity Shares of Rs. 10 each	8,00,000	
Subscribed : 50,000 Equity Shares of Rs. 10 each	5,00,000	
	5,00,000	

SCHEDULE -2 : RESERVES AND SURPLUS

	As on 31-3-15 Rs.	As on 31-3-14 Rs.
Reserve Fund 2,50,000 Added 20 %N. P. 11,714	2,61,714	
Surplus i.e. Balance in P and L Appropriation A/c	42,856	
	3,04,570	

SCHEDULE - 3 : DEPOSITS

	As on 31-3-15 Rs.	As on 31-3-14 Rs.
(i) Current Deposits	1,00,000	
(ii) Saving Bank Deposits	50,000	
(iii) Fixed and Recurring Deposits	1,56,000	
	3,06,000	

SCHEDULE- 4 : BORROW1NGS

	As on 31-3-15 Rs.	As on 31-3-14 Rs.
	Nil	
	Nil	

SCHEDULE - 5 : OTHER LIABILITIES AND PROVISIONS

	As on 31-3-15 Rs.	As on 31-3-14 Rs.

Rebate on Bills Discounted
(i.e. Unexpired Discount)
Unclaimed Interim Dividend :
      Declared   20,000
      Less paid   - 17,000
	380
	
	3,000	

	3,380	

SCHEDULE - 6 : CASH AND BALANCES WITH RESERVE BANK OF INDIA

	As on 31-3-15 Rs.	As on 31-3-14 Rs.
Cash-in-hand and with RBI	1,93,000	
	1,93,000	

SCHEDULE- 7 ; BALANCES WITH BANKS AND MONEY AT CALL AND SHORT NOTICE

	As on 31-3-15 Rs.	As on 31-3-14 Rs.
Money at call and Short Notice	80,000	
	80,000	

SCHEDULE - 8 : INVESTMENTS

	As on 31-3-15 Rs.	As on 31-3-14 Rs.
Indian Govt Securities	3,90,000	
Shares of Companies	50,000	
	4,40,000	

SCHEDULE - 9 : ADVANCES

	As on 31-3-15 Rs.	As on 31-3-14 Rs.
(i) Bill Purchased and Discounted	46,000	
(ii) Cash credits, Overdrafts and Loans	2,85,000	
(iii) Term Loans	–	
	3,31,000	
Less Reserve For Doubtful Debts	-5,000	
	3,26,000	

SCHEDULE. 10 : FIXED ASSETS

	As on 31-3-15 Rs.	As on 31-3-14 Rs.
Premises : Opening Balance	51,000	
Add : Cost of Additons	10,000	
	61,000	
Less : Depreciation @ 5 % on Op. Balance	- 2,550	
	58,450	

SCHEDULE : 11 : OTHER ASSETS

	As on 31-3-15 Rs.	As on 31-3-14 Rs.
Stock of stationery	8,500	
Interest accrued on investments	8,000	
	16,500	

SCHEDULE - 12 : CONTINGENT LIABILITIES

	As on 31-3-15 Rs.	As on 31-3-14 Rs.
Endorsements made on behalf of customers	1,15,000	
	1,15,000	

SCHEDULE - 13 : INTEREST EARNED

	As on 31-3-15 Rs.	As on 31-3-14 Rs.
Interest/ Discount on Advances/Bills	1,28,000	
Add: Interest Accrued on Investments	8,000	
	1,36,000	
Less Rebate on Bills; Discounted	380	
	1,35,620	

SCHEDULE - 14 : OTHER INCOME

	For the Year ended 31-3-2015 Rs.	For the Year ended 31-3-2014 Rs.
(i) Commission Exchange Brokerage		
(ii) Profit on Sale of Investments		
Less : Loss on Sale of Investments		
(iii) Profit on revaluation of Investments		
Less : Loss on Revaluation of Investments	(- 10,000)	
(iv) Profit on Sale of Land, Buildings and Other assets		
Less : Loss on Sale of Land, Buildings and Other assets		
(v) Profit on Exchange transactions		
Less : Loss on Exchange transactions		
(vi) Income earned by way of Dividends etc		
(vii) Miscellaneous Income		
Total	(- 10,000)	

SCHEDULE - 15 : INTEREST EXPENDED

	As on 31-3-15 Rs.	As on 31-3-14 Rs.
	Nil	
	Nil	

SCHEDULE - 16 : OPERATING EXPENSES

	For the Year ended 31-3-2015 (Rs.)	For the Year ended 31-3-2014(Rs.)
Payments to and Provisions for employees :		
Salaries	28,000	
Rent, Taxes, Lighting	2,300	
Printing and Stationery	–	
Advertisement and Publicity	–	
Depreciation on Bank's property	2,550	
Directors' fees, Allowances and Expenses	1,800	
Auditors' fees expenses		
Law charges		
Postage, Telegrams, Telephones etc.		
Repairs and Maintenance	–	
Insurance	–	
Other Expenditure : General expenses	27,400	
Total	62,050	
Provisions and Contingencies : RDD	5,000	

Dhanashri Bank Ltd.
Profit and Loss Account for the Year ended 31 - 3 - 2015

	Shedule No.	Year ended 31-3-2015	Year ended 31-3-2014
(I) INCOME			
Interest earned	13	135,620	
Other Income	14	(-10,000)	
Total		1,25,620	
(II) EXPENDITURE			
Interest expended	15	–	
Operating expenses	16	62,050	
Provisions and Contingencies	-	5,000	
Total		67,050	

contd...

(III)	PROFIT /LOSS			
	Net profit / loss (-) for the year		58,570	
	Profit/Loss brought forward		16,000	
		Total	74,570	
(IV)	APPROPRIATIONS			
	Transferred to Statutory Reserve			
	(20% of Net Profit)		11,714	
	@ 4% on Rs. 5,00,000		20,000	
	Bal. carried over to Balance Sheet		42,856	
		Total	74,570	

Dhanashri Bank Ltd.
Balance Sheet as on 31 - 3- 2015

	Shedule No.	For the Year ended 31-3-2015 Rs.	For the Year ended 31-3-2014 Rs.
(I) Capital and Liabilities :			
Capital	1	5,00,000	
Reserves and Surplus	2	3,04,750	
Deposits	3	3,06,000	
Borrowings	4	–	
Other Liabilities and Provisions	5	3,380	
Total		11,13,950	
(II) Assets :			
Cash and Balances with RBI	6	1,93,000	
Balances with Banks and			
Money at Call and Short Notice	7	80,000	
Investments	8	4,40,000	
Advances	9	3,26,000	
Fixed Assets	10	58,450	
Other Assets	11	16,500	
Total		11,13,950	
Contingent Liabilities	12	1,15,000	
Bills for Collection	–	Nil	

PROBLEM NO. 13

The following figures are extracted from the books of Saraswati Bank Ltd., as on 31-3-2015. You are required to prepare the Profit and Loss Account with necessary schedules :

Particulars	Rs.
Interest on Loans	3,10,000
Interest on Cash Credits	2,90,000
Interest on Overdrafts	2,00,000
Interest on Balances with RBI	40,000
Income on Investments	10,000
Interest on Fixed Deposits	2,60,000
Interest on Savings Accounts	80,000
Interest on Current Account	30,000
Discount on Bills Discounted	1,90,000
Interest on Borrowings from other Banks	10,000
Profit on sale of Investment	40,000
Loss on sale of Investment	5,000
Income from Joint Ventures	25,000
Profit on Revaluation of Investments	35,000
Loss on Revaluation of Investments	10,000
Dividends received from Joint Stock Companies	25,000
Salaries to Staff	65,000
Rent and Taxes	8,000
Depreciation on Bank's Assets	21,000
Sundry Income	18,000
Printing and Stationery	17,000
Repairs and Maintenance	14,000
Advertisement	6,000
Directors' Fees and Allowances	9,000
Audit Fees	6,000
Law Charges	8,000
Postage and Telephone Charges	11,000
Other Expenses	4,000
Profit on (1-4-2014)	1,20,000

Adjustments :
1) Write off Rs. 19,000 for Bad and Doubtful Debts.
2) Provide 40 % for taxation.
3) Rebate on bills discounted is to be provided for Rs. 20,000.
   (Pune University, T. Y. B. Com.)

Solution :

Preparation of P and L A/c
Someshwar Bank Ltd.
SCHEDULE - 13 : INTEREST EARNED

		For the Year ended 31-3-2015 (Rs.)	For the Year ended 31-3-2014 (Rs.)
(i) Interest/ Discount on Advances, Bills			
Interest on Loans	3,10,000		
Interest on Cash Credits	2,90,000		
Interest on Overdrafts	2,00,000		
Discount Rs. 1,90,000			
Less Rebate on bills			
discounted Rs.40,000	1,70,000		
		9,70,000	
(ii) Income (i.e. interest) on Investments		10,000	
(iii) Interest on balance with RBI		40,000	
		10,20,000	

SCHEDULE - 14 : OTHER INCOME

		For the Year ended 31-3-2015 (Rs.)	For the Year ended 31-3-2014 (Rs.)
(i) Commission, Exchange Brokerage			
(ii) Profit on Sale of Investments	40,000		
Less : Loss on Sale of			
Investments	- 5,000		
(iii) Profit on revaluation of			
Investments	35,000		
Less : Loss on Revaluation			
of Investments	-10,000		
		25,000	
(iv) Profit on Sale of Land, Buildings and Other assets			–
Less : Loss on Sale of Land, Buildings and			
Other assets		–	
(v) Profit on Exchange Transactions			
Less : Loss on Exchange Transactions		–	
(vi) Income earned by way of Dividends etc.			
form Subsidiaries / companies and Joint ventures :			
Dividends	25,000		
Income from Joint Ventures	25,000		
		50,000	
(vii) Miscellaneous Income - Sundry Income		18,000	
Total		1,28,000	

SCHEDULE- I5: INTEREST EXPENDED

	For the Year ended 31-3-2015 Rs.	For the Year ended 31-3-2014 Rs.
(i) Interest on Deposits :		
Fixed Deposits 2,60,000		
Saving Deposits 80,000		
Current Accounts 30,000		
(ii) Interest on Borrowings from other Banks 10,000		
	3,80,000	
	3,80,000	

SCHEDULE - 16 : OPERATING EXPENSES

	For the Year ended 31-3-2015 Rs.	For the Year ended 31-3-2014 Rs.
Payments to and Provisions for Employees : (Salaries to staff)	65,000	
Rent, Taxes, Lighting	8,000	
Printing and Stationery	17,000	
Advertisement and Publicity	6,000.	
Depreciation on Bank's Property	21,000	
Directors' fees, Allowances and Expenses	9,000	
Auditors' fees Expenses	6,000	
Law charges	8,000	
Postage, Telegrams, Telephone etc.	11,000	
Repairs and Maintenance	14,000	
Insurance	—	
Other Expenditure :	4,000	
Total	1,69,000	
Provisions and Contingencies : RDD	19,000	
Provision for Taxation	2,32,000	
	2,51,000	

Saraswati Bank Ltd.
Profit and Loss Account for the Year ended 31-3-2015

		Shedule No.	Year ended 31-3-2015	Year ended 31-3-2014
(I)	**INCOME**			
	Interest Earned	13	10,20,000	
	Other Income	14	1,28,000	
		Total	11,48,000	
(II)	**EXPENDITURE**			
	Interest Expended	15	3,80,000	
	Operating Expenses	16	1,69,000	
	RDD 19,000			
	Provision for Taxation 2,32,000		2,51,000	
		Total	8,00,000	
(III)	**PROFIT/ LOSS**			
	Net profit for the year		3,48,000	
	Profit vrought forward		1,20,000	
		Total	4,68,000	
(IV)	**APPROPRIATIONS**			
	Transferred to Statutory Reserve (20% of Net Profit)		69,600	
	Balance carried over to Balance Sheet		3,98,400	
		Total	4,68,000	

Note explaining how provision for taxation has been calculated. First find out the taxable income of the bank (i.e. income before tax) on which income tax is payable. It is Rs. 5,80,000 arrived at as follows:

Income : Interest Earned		10,20,000
Other Income		1,28,000
		11,48,000
Less: Total Expenditure		
Interest Expended	3,80,000	
Operating Expenses	1,69,000	
Provisions and contingencies (only R.D.D.)	19,000	
		5,68,000
		5,80,000

This is the bank's income before tax on which provision for taxation is to be made at 40% Therefore 40 %on Rs. 5,80,000 i.e. Rs. 2,32,000 is the provision for taxation required in this case. It is included in the list of Provision and Contingencies in the P and L A/c and included among "Other Liabilities and Provisions" in the Balance Sheet (Schedule No. 5)

PROBEM NO. 14

From the following balances and the additional information available from the books of A/c of Laxmi Bank Ltd. Kolhapur as on 31st december 2015. prepare Profit and Loss A/c for the year ended 31 December 2015 and Balance Sheet as on that date in the form prescribed under the Banking Companies Act. 1949.

Share capital		4,50,000	Money at call	
(in fully paid shares)			and short notice	39,850
Cash in hand and			Advance (In India)	2,15,000
Cash at Bank		69,525	Advances (outside India)	50,000
Investments in Govt.			Bills discounted and	
securities		2,91,555	Purchased	18,750
Other Investments		2,33,445	Profit and Loss A/c (Cr.)	9,750
Gold bullion		22,695		
Interest accrued on			Interest paid	11,925
Investments		36,930	Interest received and	
Balances with other			accrued	1,08,000
banks		35,000	Commission and	
Employees' Security			Brokerage	37,950
Deposits		22,500	Discounts (Cr.)	63,000
Saving bank deposits		11,130	Audit fee	7,500
Current Deposits		1,45,500	Loss on sale of furniture	1,500
Fixed Deposits		35,000	Directors fees	1,800
Premium on issue of			Salaries	31,800
shares		90,000	Postage, Telephones etc.	1,075
Statutory Reserve		2,10,000	Rent received	900
Silver bullion		3,000	Profit on sale of gold	1,800
Land and Building		97,500	Managing Director's	
Furniture and fillings		7,500	Remuneration	18,000
Borrowing from other			Miscellaneous receipts	4,050
banks			Loss on sale of investments	44,000
- In India	1,50,000		Deposits with Reserve	
- Outside India	11,270	1,61,270	Bank of India	1,12,500

(1) Rebate on bills discounted was Rs. 7,500.

(2) Provide for bonus to employees Rs. 22,500.

(3) Bills for collection were for Rs. 65,250.

(4) Acceptance and endorsements stand at Rs. 84,750.

(5) Create necessary statutory Reserve and also General Reserve of Rs. 10,000.

(6) Current deposit accounts include Rs. 37,500 for the Overdrawn Accounts.

(7) Authorised capital Rs. 6,00,000 in Rs. 100 shares.

   (Pune University. T. Y. B. Com.)

Solution :

Bank Account

SCHEDULE - 1 : CAPITAL

	As on 31-12-15 Rs.
Authorised : 6,000 shares of 　　　　　　　Rs. 100 each	6,00,000
Issued. and Subscribed : 4,500 fully 　　　　　　　　　paid Shares of 　　　　　　　　　Rs. 100 each.	4,50,000
	4,50,000

SCHEDULE -2 : RESERVES AND SURPLUS

	As on 31-12-15 Rs.
Premium on Issue of Shares(i.e. Share Premium)	90,000
Statutory Reserve 2,10,000	
Added 20 % of N. P. + 13,620	
	2,23,620
General Reserve	10,000
Surplus i.e. Balance in P and L Appropriation A/c	54,230
	3,77,850

SCHEDULE- 3 : DEPOSITS

	As on 31-12-2015 Rs.
(i) Current Deposits	1,45,500
(ii) Saving Bank Deposits	11,130
(iii) Fixed Deposits	35,000
Add back : Current Deposits reduced	
by inclusion of Bank Overdrafts in current deposits	37,500
	2,29,130

SCHEDULE - 4 : BORROWINGS

	As on 31-12-2015 Rs.
Borrowings from Banks in India	1,50,000
Outside India	11,270
	1,61,270

SCHEDULE - 5 : OTHER LIABILITIES AND PROVISIONS

	As on 31-12-2015 Rs.
Employees' Security Deposits	22,500
Rebate on Bills Discounted	7,500
Provision for Bonus to Employees	22,500
	52,500

SCHEDULE - 6 : CASH AND BALANCES WITH RESERVE BANK OF INDIA

	As on 31-12-2015 Rs.
Cash in hand and at Bank	69,525
Deposits with RBI	1,12,500
	1,82,025

SCHEDULE - 7 : BALANCES WITH BANKS AND MONEY AT CALL AND SHORT NOTICE

	As on 31-12-2015 Rs.
Balances with other banks	35,000
Money at Call and Short Notice	39,850
	74,850

SCHEDULE - 8 : INVESTMENTS

	As on 31-12-2015 Rs.
Investments in Govt. Securities	2,91,555
Other Investments	2,33,445
Gold bullion	22,695
	5,47,695

SCHEDULE - 9 : ADVANCES

	As on 31-12-2015 Rs.
Bills Discounted and Purchased	18,750
Advances (In India)	2,15,000
Advances (Outside India)	50,000
Add Bank Overdrafts (wrongly set of against current deposits)	37,500
	3,21,250

SCHEDULE - 10 : FIXED ASSETS

	As on 31-12-2015 Rs.
Land and Building	97,500
Furniture and fittings	7,500
	1,05,000

SCHEDULE- 11 : OTHER ASSETS

	As on 31-12-2015 Rs.
Interest Accrued on Investments	36,930
Silver Bullion	3,000
	39,930

SCHEDULE - 12 : CONTINGENT LIABILITIES

	As on 31-12-2015 Rs.
Acceptances Endorsements etc.	84,750
	84,750

SCHEDULE- 13 : INTEREST EARNED

	As on 31-12-2015 Rs.
Interest Received and accurcd	1,08,000
Discounts (Cr.)	63,000
	1,71,000
Less Rebate on Bills Discounted	- 7,500
	1,63,500

SCHKDULK- 14 : OTHER INCOME

		For the Year ended 31-12-2014 Rs.
(i) Commission Exchange Brokerage		37,950
(ii) Profit on Sale of Investments :		
Profit on Gold	1,800	
Less : Loss on Sale of Investments	- 44,000	
		(-42,200)
(iii) Profit on revaluation of Investments	–	
Less : Loss on Devaluation		
of Investments	–	
Profit on Sale of Land, Buildings		–
Other Assets	–	
Less : Loss on Sale of Furniture	1,500	
		(-1,500)
Rent Received		900
Miscellaneous Receipts		4,050
Total		(- 800)

SCHEDULE - 15 : INTEREST EXPENDED

	For the Year ended 31-12-2014 Rs.
Interest Paid	11,925
	11,925

SCHEDULE - 16 : OPERATING EXPENSES

		For the Year ended 31-12-2014 Rs.
Salaries	31,800	
Bonus to Employees	22,500	
Managing Director's Remuneration	18,000	
		72,300
Directors' fees		1,800
Audit fee		7,500
Postage, Telephone etc.		1,075
		82,675

Laxmi Bank Ltd.
P and L Account for the year ended 31 - 12 - 2015

	Schedule No.	Year ended 31 - 12 - 2015 Rs.
(I) INCOME		
Interest Earned	13	1,63,500
Other Income	14	(-) 800
	Total	1,62,700
(II) EXPENDITURE		
Interest Paid	15	11,925
Operating Expenses	16	82,675
Provisions and contingencies	-	-
	Total	94,600

contd....

(III)	PROFIT /LOSS		
	Net profit for the year		68,100
	Profit brought forward from last year		9,750
		Total	77,850
(IV)	APPROPRIATIONS		
	Transferred to Statutory Reserve (20% of Net profit)		13,620
	To General Reserve		10,000
	Bal. carried over to Balance Sheet		54,230
		Total	77,850

Laxmi Bank Ltd,
Balance Sheet for the year ended 31-12 - 2015

	Schedule No.	As on 31 - 12 - 2015 Rs.
(I) Capital and Liabilities :		
Capital	1	4,50,000
Reserves and Surplus	2	3,77,850
Deposits	3	2,29,130
Borrowings	4	1,61,270
Other Liabilities and Provisions	5	52,500
Total		12,70,750
(II) Assets :		
Cash and Balances with RB1	6	1,82,025
Balances with Banks and Money at call and short notice	7	74,850
Investments	8	5,47,695
Advances	9	3,21,250
Fixed Assets	10	1,05,000
Other Assets	11	39,930
Total		12,70,750
Contingent Liabilities	12	84,750
Bills for Collection		65,250

Notes :

1. Gold is included in the list of investments. So profit on sale of Gold is to be taken as 'profit on sale of investments'. (Silver is put in the schedule of other Assets.)

2. Loss on sale of furniture is to be taken as 'Loss on sale of Land, Buildings and other assets'. (Other assets will include furniture.)

3. Other income, in the case of this problem, is a minus quantity.

4. Bonus to staff or employee should be included in the schedule of operating expenses as 'it is now a compulsory payment under the payment of bonus A/c and no longer an appropriation of profit. The first item under 'operating expenses' is payments in and provisions for employees and it will cover bonus to employees also.

5. Current Accounts include overdrawn accounts (i.e. overdrafts) means, in the list of current accounts the accountant has included current accounts with positive (i.e.. plus) balances as well as overdrafts i.e. Current Account having minus or negative balances. This has reduced the total balance in current accounts having positive balances, (it has-become a mixture of plus current accounts and minus current accounts) The adjustment required is to add to current accounts an amount equal to the overdrafts previously included in them. This will correct the reduction in the total value of plus current accounts brought about by the inclusion of bank overdrafts in the list of current accounts.

   The second adjustment that is now required is to show overdrafts (after they have been removed from current accounts) at their proper place, that is to include them in the schedule of advances.

EXERCISE

1) The following is the Trial Balance of Balaji Bank Ltd., as on 31-3-2015

Particulars	Debit Rs.	Credit Rs.
Subscribed Capital : Equity Shares of Rs. 10		5,00,000
Reserve Fund		2,50,000
Loans, Cash Credit and Overdrafts	2,85,000	
Premises	50,000	
Indian Government Securities	4,00,000	
Current Deposits		1,00,000
Fixed Deposits		1,25,000
Savings Deposits		50,000
Salaries	28,000	
General Expenses	27,400	
Rent, Rates and Taxes	2,300	
Directors Fees	1,800	
Profit and Loss A/c (1-4-2014)		16,000
Interest and Discount		1,28,000
Stock of Stationery	8,500	
Bills Purchased and Discounted	46,000	
Interim Dividend paid	17,000	
Recurring Deposits		20,000
Shares	50,000	
Cash in Hand and with R.B.I.	1,93,000	
Money at Call and Short Notice	80,000	
Total	**11,89,000**	**11,89,000**

The Following information should be considered :

1. Provisions for bad and doubtful debts is required amounting to Rs. 5,000.
2. Interest accrued on investment was Rs. 8,000.
3. Un-expired discount (Rebate on bills discounted) amounts to Rs. 380.
4. Interim dividend declared was 4% actual.
5. Endorsements made on behalf of customers totalled Rs. 1,15,000.
6. Authorised capital was 80,000 Equity shares of Rs. 10 each.
7. Rs. 10,000 were added to the premises during the year. Depreciation @ 50% on the opening balance is required.
8. Market, value of Indian Government securities was Rs. 3,90,000
   Prepare Profit and Loss Account for the year ending 31.3.2010 and Balance Sheet as at that date in the prescribed form.

(Pune University)

2) Janata Bank Ltd. gives you the following particulais from their books for the year 2015 required to prepare Balance Sheet as on 31-3-2015 in the prescribed form.

Particulars	Debit Rs.	Credit Rs.
Cash in Hand	1,50,000	
Share capital		25,00,000
Investments in shares		
(Fully paid 3 lacks, partly paid 2 lacks)	5,00,000	
General Reserve		3,00,000
Statutory Reserve		6,00,000
Investment in Government Securities	5,75,000	
Interest Accrued on Investments	15,000	
Balance with R.B.I.	2,00,000	
Balance with Other Banks	1,50,000	
Borrowings from Central Bank		4,00,000
Bills payable		2,00,000
Fixed Deposits		25,00,000
Current Deposits		40,00,000
Contingency Accounts		4,00,000
Loans		50,00,000
Cash Credits	80,00,000	
Overdrafts	7,50,000	
Savings Accounts		65,00,000
Un-claimed dividends		25,000
Bills Discounted and Purchased	15,00,000	
Branch Adjustments		74,000
Profit and Loss Account (1/4/2014)		1 ,00,000
Advances	7,50,000	
Premises (Less Depreciation)	6,00,000	
Furniture (Less Depreciation)	2,00,000	
Provision for Taxation		3,91,000
Profit for (2015)		4,00,000
Total	**1,83,90,000**	**1,83,90,000**

Following further information is given :

a) Authorised Capital Rs. 1,00,00,000 (2,00,000 shares of Rs. 50 each)

b) Issued Capital is half of authorised capital. All shares are fully subscribed on which Rs. 25 per share are paid up.

c) Constitutents liability for acceptances and endorsements Rs. 5 lakhs

d) Bills for collection Rs. 3 Lakhs

e) Contingent liability for partly paid shares Rs. 2 lakhs

(Pune University)

3) Following ledger Balances have been extracted from the books of Union Bank Ltd. Show the Profit and Loss Account for the year ending 31-3-2015 and Balance Sheet as on that date in prescribed form.

Particulars	Debit Rs.	Credit Rs.
Equity Share Capital of Rs. 100 each	–	4,00,000
General Expenses	24,000	
Current Accounts	–	20,20,000
Interest Paid	23,000	
Reserve Fund (Statutory)	–	1,00,000
Fixed Deposits	–	12,80,000
Savings Bank Accounts		2,00,000
Cash in Hand	35,000	
Interest Received	–	1,60,000
Loans, Cash, Credits and Overdrafts	20,60,000	
Depreciation on premises	27,000	
Premises	4,31,000	
Silver		32,000
Bad Debts	8,000	
Cash with R.B.I.	2,00,000	
Cash with Foreign Banks	1,03,000	
Gold - Bullions	39,000	
Money at call and short notice	1 ,00,000	
Profit and Loss Account		90,000
Discount Earned		30,000
Commission		5,000
Investments in company shares etc.	9,40,000	–
Bills Discounted and Purchased	2,63,000	
Recurring Deposits		20,000
Government Bonds	20,000	
Total	**43,05,000**	**43,05,000**

The following additional information was available :

1. During the year 2013-2014 dividend of Rs. 30,000 was paid for the previous year.
2. Rebate on Bills Discounted for un-expired period Rs. 12,000 to be provided for.
3. Interest accrued on Investments was Rs. 10,000.
4. Provide Rs. 20,000 for taxation.
5. Investments shown in trial balance include Rs. 50,000 on account of partly paid shares of the limited company (shares are paid up to the extent of 50%).
6. Bills for collection being B/R and liabilities for customer's acceptances were Rs. 80,000 and Rs. 1,20,000 respectively.
7. The Profit and Loss Account shows the credit balance Rs. 1,20,000 on 1-4-2014

(Pune University)

4) Following is the trial balance of Laxmi Bank Ltd., as on 31-3-2015

Particulars	Debit Rs.	Credit Rs.
Premises Less Depreciation	1,85,000	
Money at call and short notice	2,15,000	
Furniture Less Depreciation	30,000	
Depreciation on bank assets	11,000	
Non-banking assets	20,000	
Cash in hand	3,00,000	
Cash at Bank	2,50,000	
Investment	3,50,000	
Loan, Cash-Credit and overdraft	12,65,000	
Interest on Deposit and borrowings	2,00,000	
Audit fee	4,500	
Salaries and allowances to staff	40,500	
Director fees	4,000	
Postage and Telegram	1,350	
Printing and stationery	3,700	
Other expenditure	2,450	
Interest and discount		3,67,500
Statutory reserve		1,20,000
Deposits		12,50,000
Provident fund		1,35,000
Borrowings from bank		2,55,000
Unclaimed dividend		4,000
Commission and exchange		37,500
Profit on sale of Non-banking assets		1,200
Profit and Loss A/c (1-4-2014)		1,12,300
Share Capital		
Authorised share capital 7,500		
Equity shares of Rs. 100 each		
Issued and subscribed capital		
6,000 equity shares of Rs. 100 each fully paid		6,00,000
Total	**28,82,500**	**28,82,500**

1. Provide Rs. 10,00 for bad and doubtful debts.
2. Bill for collection amount Rs. 1,05,000.
3. Acceptance, endorsement and other obligation amount Rs. 52,000.
4. Provide Rs. 1,500 for rebate on bill discount.
5. Provide,Rs. 10,500 for taxation.
6. Postage stamps of Rs. 160 and stationery Rs. 700 was in Hand on 31.3/201

(Pune University)

5) The following is the trial balance of Garware Bank Ltd., as on 31-3-2015

Particulars	Debit Rs.	Credit Rs.
Premises less depreciation	7,40,000	–
Money at call and short notice	8,60,000	–
Furniture less depreciation	1 ,20,000	–
Depreciation on bank's assets	44,000	–
Non-banking assets acquired in settlement of claims	80,000	–
Cash in hand	12,00,000	–
Cash at banks	10,00,000	–
Investments	14,00,000	–
Loans, cash credit and overdrafts	50,60,000	–
Interest on deposits and borrowings	8,00,000	–
Audit, fees	18,000	–
Salaries and allowances	1 ,62,000	–
Directors fees	16,000	–
Postage and telegrams	5,400	–
Printing and stationery	14,800	–
Other expenditure	9,800	–
Interest and discounts	–	14,70,000
Shares capital - Authorised 30,000 equity shares of Rs. 100 each issued and subscribed 24,000 equity shares of Rs. 100 each fully paid	–	24,00,000
Statutory reserve	–	4,80,000
Fixed deposits	–	12,00,000
Recurring deposits	–	10,00,000
Current deposits	–	8,00,000
Savings bank A/cs	–	20,00,000
Provident funds	–	5,40,000
Borrowings	–	10,20,000
Unclaimed dividend	–	16,000
Commission and exchange	–	1 ,50,000
Profit on sale of non-banking assets	–	4,800
Profit and Loss A/c as on 1-4-2014	–	4,49,200
Total	**1,15,30,000**	**1,15,30,000**

Adjustments :

1) Provide Rs. 40,000 for bad and doubtful debts.
2) Bills for collection amounted to Rs. 4,20,000.
3) Acceptances, endorsements and other obligations amounted to Rs. 2,08,000.
4) Provide Rs. 6,000 for rebate on bills discounted.
5) Provide Rs. 42,000 for taxation
6) Postage stamps of Rs. 640 and stationery of Rs. 28,000 was in hand on 31-3-2015

Prepare profit and loss A/c for the year ended 31-3-2015and the Balance Sheet as on that date as per the Banking Regulation Act. **(P.U. Oct., 2005)**

Objective Type Questions

1. State whether each of the following statements is "True" or "False"

   a)   The accounting year of a banking company ends on 31. March.

   b)   Provision for taxation after 1.4.1991 is shown on the debit side of the Profit and Loss Account of a banking company.

   c)   The subscribed capital of banking company must be at least one-half of its authorised capital.

   d)   A banking company cannot grant loan to any of its directors.

   e)   Profit and Loss Appropriation Accounts was prepared in case of a banking company prior to 1.4.1991.

Ans : (a) True, (b) True, (c) True, (d) True, (e) False

2. Select the most appropriate answer :

   a)   Prior to 1.4.1991 Provision for bad and doubtful debts in case of a banking company was :

      i)   Shown on the debit side of the profit and loss account.

      ii)   Shown as a deduction from the "interest and discount" income on the credit side of the profit and loss account.

      iii) No where shown in the published accounts.

   b)   Rebate on bills discounted for a banking company is:

      i) an expense

      ii) an income

      iii) a liability

   c)   Appropriations out of profits in case of a banking company are to be made after 1.4.1991 in

      i) Prof it and Loss Appropriation Account ii) Profit and Loss Account iii) Balance sheet

   d)   Paid up capital of a banking company must be one-half of:

      i)   Authorised capital

      ii)   Subscribed capital

      iii) Called up capital

Ans : (a) (iii), (b) (iii), (c) (ii), (d) (ii)]

3. Under what heading will you show the following items in the balance sheet of a banking company. Give your answers in the brackets provided:

   1.   Unclaimed dividend   (.........)

   2.   Bills discounted   (.........)

   3.   Rebate on bills discounted   (.........)

<table>
<tr><td>4.</td><td>Government of India bonds</td><td>(..........)</td></tr>
<tr><td>5.</td><td>Demand drafts</td><td>(..........)</td></tr>
<tr><td>6.</td><td>Telegraphic transfers</td><td>(..........)</td></tr>
<tr><td>7.</td><td>Letters of credit</td><td>(..........)</td></tr>
<tr><td>8.</td><td>Employee's security deposits</td><td>(..........)</td></tr>
<tr><td>9.</td><td>Building acquired in satisfaction of a claim</td><td>(..........)</td></tr>
<tr><td>10.</td><td>Interest accrued on investments</td><td>(..........)</td></tr>
</table>

4. Fill in the blanks :

1. When interest on doubtful debts is realised, the amount is debited to.......... account and credited to......... account.

2. The basis for recording bank transactions are the ......prepared by customers and sometimes bank staff.

3. Bills for collection will appear on ....of the bank's balance sheet.

4. Compulsory deposits made by tax payers are to be shown on......... of the bank's balance sheet.

5. Banks are required to transfer........of their profits to a statutory reserve.

5. Indicate the correct answer :

1. Banks prepare the accounts for
   (a) the calendar year
   (b) the financial year
   (c) the Diwali year

2. Banks show provision for income-tax under the head
   (a) Contingency account
   (b) Other liabilities
   (c) Contingent liabilities

3. The heading 'Other assets' does not include
   (a) Silver
   (b) Gold
   (c) Library books

4. Rebate on bills discounted is
   (a) an item of income
   (b) income received in advance
   (c) an asset

5. A non-banking asset is
   (a) an item of office equipment
   (b) bank premises
   (c) secured property acquired from defaulting borrowers.

Insurance Claims

3.1 Introduction

There are several different reasons by wich a business may suffer abnormal losses such as fire, theft, burglary, strike, etc. Among them, the most common which destroys or causes severe damage to the assets like stock, building, plant, machinery, furniture, etc., is fire. Normal business operations are disrupted and incures hevy losses when a fire takes place. There may arise a tremendous pressure on the working capital if the business does not possess adequate funds to replace the assets so destroyed. To cover the risk of loss from such events, a business may take on an insurance policy with an Insurance Company.

The business has to pay insurance premium at regular intervals as per the terms of the agreement - the insurance premium is charged to the Profit and Loss Account as an expense at the year-end. The insurance policy matures on the occurrence of any such mishap and the business is entitled to recover from the insurance company, the full value of the insurance policy or the actual cost of the assets lost, whichever is lower. When a business suffers a loss from an insured event, it has to notify the insurance company regarding the loss of the assets and to file a claim for compensation against those losses. Such claims are known as Insurance Claims. When a fire takes place, to file a claim with the Insurance Company for the loss of assets damaged or destroyed, a set of procedures is to be followed. Apart from the legal formalities, one of the most important problems that a business has to face is the determination of the amount of the claim to be lodged.

3.2 Types of Claims

A business takes a fire insurance policy to cover (i) the loss of assets including stock; and (ii) loss of profit (consequential loss). A business may take insurance policy for loss of cash due to theft or misappropriation.

When a fixed asset is destroyed, the computation of loss is simple. The value of such assets on the date of fire can be ascertained from the books of account of the business because most of them usually maintain proper records of the fixed assets. Fixed assets are recorded in the books of accounts at their acquisition cost, which becomes the basis for calculation of claim for the loss of fixed assets.

When a stock is destroyed the computation of loss is not so simple because the prices of different items of stock are seldom stable and are acquired at varying rates. For most of the businesses, particularly for trading concerns, stock taking is not maintained up to date. Therefore, at the time of accident no readymade value of stock is available. If the Stock Register is maintained properly, the value of stock lost by fire can be ascertained from it. However, the business may face a problem, even when the Stock Register is maintained up to date, if the books of account are also destroyed along with the stock.

A business organisation is always faced with a danger of heavy loss due to fire, and as a result the business activities are collapsed. Therefore as a safety measure against such a probable loss, the business organisation generally takes a fire insurance policy. Such policy may be in respect of :

a) Loss of stock, b) Loss of profit, c) Comprehensive policy / Package policy.

3.3 Loss of stock :

In absence of proper inventory record, the following procedure may be adopted, though it is difficult to decide the estimate. However, a reasonable estimate of loss of stock can be made by the following procedure : Or Different steps

3.3.1 Preparation of Trading Account:

Prepare Trading A/C for last financial year, immediately proceeding the date of fire and ascertain the Gross Profit of that Year. If information is available, prepare Trading A/c for each of the years proceeding the date of fire and then ascertain the Gross Profit of each of the years as under.

Dr.   **Trading A/C for the year ended on ....**   **Cr.**

Particulars	2012	2013	2014	Particulars	2012	2013	2014
To Opening stock	-	-	-	By sales		-	-
To Purchases	-	-	-	By closing stock	-	-	-
To Wages	-	-	-				
To Carriage inwards	-	-	-				
To Gross Profit (Bal. fig.)	-	-	-				
-	-	-	-	-		-	-	- -

If the stock figures given in the problem are not at cost price and are below or above cost price, it is necessary to convert them to cost price before ascertaining the percentage of Gross Profit.

Adjustment, if any, is to be made in respect of items to be taken in the Trading Account, must be made first as usual.

The goods of irregular line or slow moving or shop spoiled goods are generally disposed off at a loss and there is wide fluctuation in the rate of loss or profit of these goods. Therefore, the value of such goods included in various items must be deducted from the respective items to get the value of goods of regular line. A Trading Account is then prepared for goods of regular line only, to ascertain the percentage of gross profit.

3.3.2. Calculation of Gross Profit Rate :

The Gross Profit Rate for each year is calculated with the help of following formula:

$$\text{Gross Profit Rate} = \frac{\text{Gross Profit}}{\text{Sales}} \times 100 \text{ Sales}$$

If the Gross Profit Rate are in ascending order then take the next higher Gross Profit Rate for the fire period. If the Gross Profit Rate are in descending order then instead of taking lesser rate, take the smallest Gross Profit Rate. If the calculated Gross Profit Rate are neither in ascending order nor in descending order but are mixed then take the average Gross Profit Rate of these rates for fire period.

3.3.3 Preparation of Memorandum Trading Account :

Prepare Memorandum Trading Account up to the date of fire to ascertain the stock on the date of fire as under.

Dr. **Memorandum Trading A/c for the period ended on.** **Cr.**

Particulars	Rs.	Rs.	Particulars	Rs.	Rs.
To Opening Stock	–	–	By sales	–	–
To Purchases	–	–	By stock on the date of fire	–	–
To Gross Profit	–	–	(Bal.fig.)		
(@ - % on sales)					
	–	–		–	–

Preparing Trading Account upto the date of fire trace out the value of stock on the date of fire. If any stock is salvaged then deducted salvaged from the 'Stock on the date of fire' and remaning amount is the loss of stock due to fire' for which a claim is to be lodged with the insurance company, .provided there is no 'Average clause' in the policy.

3.3.4 Calculation of Net Loss of stock by fire :

The calculation of net loss of stock by fire as under

Particulars	Rs.
Stock on the date of fire	–
Less - stock salvaged	–
Value of stock destroyed by fire	–

3.3.5 Average Clause :

If the amount of stock on the date of fire is more than the amount of policy and it is mentioned in the policy that average clause is applicable then the stock destroyed by fire should be reduced proportionately by adopting following formula :

$$\text{Insurance claim} = \frac{\text{Value of policy}}{\text{Value of stock on the date of fire}} \times \text{Value of stock destroyed}$$

3.3.6 Loss of Stock

PROBLEM NO. 1

A fire, occurred in the business premises of Rajesh Traders on 15th Oct., 2010. From the following particulars, ascertain the loss of stock and parepare a claim for insurance :

Stock on 1-1-2009 Rs.15,300

Purchases from 1-1-2009 to 31-12-2009 - Rs. 61,000.

Sales from 1-1-2009 to 31-12-2009 Rs. 90,000

Stock on 31-12-2009 Rs. 13,500

Purchases from 1-1-2011 to 14-10-2010 - Rs. 73,500.

Sales from 1-1-2010 to 14-10-2010 - Rs. 75,000

The stock were always valued at 90% of cost. The stock saved was worth Rs. 9,000. The amount of the policy was Rs. 31,500, there was an average clause in the policy.

(P. U. Oct. 2003)

Dr.   **Trading A/c for the year ended 31-12-2009**   **Cr.**

Particulars	Rs.	Particulars	Rs.
To Stock at cost (Note - 1)	17,000	By Sales	90,000
To Purchases	61,000	By Stock	15,000
To Gross Profit (30% of sales)	27,000		
	1,05,000		**1,05,000**

$$\textbf{Step 2 : Gross Profit Rate} \;\; = \frac{\text{Gross Profit}}{\text{Sales}} \times 100$$

$$= \frac{27,000}{90,000} \times 100 = 30\%$$

Dr.   **Memorandum Trading A/c for the year ending 15-10-2010**   **Dr.**

Particulars	Rs.	Particulars	Rs.
To Stock	15,000	By Sales	75,000
To Purchases	73,500	By Stock (Bat. fig.)	36,000
To Gross profit (30% of sales)	22,500	on the date of fire	
	1,11,000		**1,11,000**

Statement of Claim :

Estimated stock on the date of fire	36,000
Less - Stock salvaged	9,000
Loss of stock (Value of stock destroyed)	27,000

Average Clause :

As there is average clause, the proportionate amount of loss to be claimed will be

$$= \frac{\text{Value of Policy}}{\text{Value of Stock on the date of fire}} \times \text{Value of Stock destroyed}$$

$$= \frac{31,500}{36,000} \times 27000 = \text{Rs. } 23,625$$

PROBLEM NO. 2

On 1th April, 2010 the godown of Panjarpol Ltd. was destroyed by fire. The records of the company revealed the following particulars :

Particulars	Rs.
Stock on 1st January, 2009	1,50,000
Stock on 31st December, 2009	1,60,000
Purchases during the year 2009	6,20,000
Sales during the year 2009	8,00,000
Purchases from 1st January, 2010 to the date of fire.	1,50,000
Sales from 1st January, 2010 to the date of fire.	2,00,000

In valuing closing stock of 2009 Rs. 10,000 were Written off whose cost was Rs. 9,600. Part of this stock was sold in 2,000 at a loss of Rs. 800 whose cost was Rs. 4,800.

Stock salvaged was Rs. 10,000. The godown was fully insured. Find out the amount of claim for loss of stock.

(P. U. April. 2001)

Solution :

In the Books of Panjarpol Ltd.

Dr.   **Trading A/c for the year ended 31-12-2009**   Cr.

Particulars	Rs.	Particulars	Rs.	
To Opening Stock	150,000	By Sales		8,00,000
To Purchases	6,20,000	By Stock	1,60,000	
To Gross Profit	2,00,000	Add - Written off	10,000	170,000
(25% on sales)				
	9,70,000			**9,70,000**

Gross profit Rate

$$= \frac{\text{Gross Profit}}{\text{Sales}} \times 100$$

$$= \frac{2,00,000}{8,00,000} \times 100$$

$$= 25\%$$

Memorndum Trading A/c

Dr.   **For 1-1-2010 to the date of fire**   Cr.

Particulars	Rs.	Rs.	Particulars	Rs.	Rs.
To Stock	1,70,000		By Sales	2,00,000	
Less : Inrregular stock	9,600	1,60,400	Less Sale of	4,000	1,96,000
To Purchase		1,50,000	Irregular Goods		
To Gross Profit		49,000	By Stock (4800-800)		1,63,400
(25% on sales)					
		3,59,400			**3,59,400**

Statement of Claim :

Estimated stock on the date of fire	1,63,400
Less Salvage	10,000
Claim	1,53,400

PROBLEM NO. 3

Fire occurred in the premises of Good-luck Ltd. on 20th July, 2010. The Company has taken out a Fire Insurance Policy of Rs. 2,00,000 covering its stock in trade and the policy was subject to average clause. From the following particulars ascertain the claim to be lodged :

Particulars	Rs.
Stock on 1st April, 2015	1,80,000
Purchases during the year 2015-2016	7,30,000
Purchases Returns during the year 2015-16	10,000
Stock on 31st March, 2016	2,52,000
Sales for the year 2015-2016	8,20,000
Sales Returns during the year 2015-2016	20,000
Purchases from 1st April, 2016 to the date of fire	1,68,000
Sales from 1st April, 2016 to the date of fire	2,06,000
Sales Returns from 1st April, 2016 to the date of fire	8,000
Value of stock saved	39,600

It was the practice of the concern to value stocks at cost less 10%

(P. U. April 2005)

Solution :

In the Books of Good-Luck Ltd.,

Dr.　　　　　**Trading A/c for the year ended 31-3-2016**　　　　　Cr.

Particulars		Rs.	Particulars		Rs.
To Opening Stock (1,80,000 × 10/9)		2,00,000	By Sales	8,20,000	
			Less Return	20,000	8,00,000
To Purchases	7,30,000		By closing sock		
To Less Return	10,000	7,20,000	(2,52,000 × 10/9)		2,80,000
To Gross profit (Bal.fig.)		1,60,000			
		10,80,000			**10,80,000**

$$2)\ \textbf{Gross Profit Rate}\ =\ \frac{\text{Gross Profit}}{\text{Sales}} \times 100$$

$$=\ \frac{1,60,000}{8,00,000} \times 100\ =\ 20\%$$

Memorandum Trading A/c

Dr.　　　　　**(1-4-2016 to 20-7-2016)**　　　　　Cr.

Particulars	Rs.	Particulars		Rs.
To Opening Stock	2,80,000	By Sales	2,06,000	
To Purchases	1,68,000	Less Return	8,000	1,98,000
To Gross profit (198000 × 20%)	39,600	By closing sock (Bal. fig.)		2,89,000
	4,87,600			**4,87,6000**

4) Statement of claim :

Stock on date of fire	2,89,600
Less - Salvages	39,600
Claim	2,50,000

PROBELM NO. 4

(Undervaluation of stock)

Fire occurred in the business premises of M/s Ramesh on 15th Oct., 2010. From the following particulars ascertain the loss of stock and prepare a claim for insurance.

	Rs.
Stock on 1-1-2009	30,600
Purchases from 1-1-2009 to 31-12-2009	1,22,000
Sales from 1-1-2009 to 31-12-2009	1,80,000
Stock on 31-12-2009	27,000
Purchased from 1-1-2010 to 14-10-2010	1,47,000
Sales from 1-1-2010 to 14-10-2010	1,50,000

The stocks were always valued at 90 percent of cost. The stock saved was worth Rs.18,000. The amount of the Policy was Rs. 63,000. There was an average clause in the policy.

(P.U.April 1994, Oct 1995)

Solution :

Dr.		Trading A/c for the year ended 31-12-2010		Cr.

Particulars	Rs.	Particulars	Rs.
To Stock at cost	34,000	By Sales	1,80,000
To Purchases	1,22,000	By stock	30,000
To Gross Profit (30% on Sales)	54,000		
	2,10,000		**2,10,000**

$$\textbf{Gross Profit Rate} \ = \ \frac{\text{Gross Profit}}{\text{Sales}} \times 100$$

$$= \frac{54,000}{1,80,000} \times 100$$

$$= 30\,\%$$

Dr.   **Trading A/c for the year ended on 15-1-2010**   **Cr.**

Particulars	Rs.	Particulars	Rs.
To Stock	30,000	By Sales	1,50,000
To Purchases	1,47,000	By stock	72,000
To Gross Profit			
(@ 30% on Sales)	45,000		–
	2,22,000		**2,22,000**

Statement of Claim :

	Rs.
Estimated Stock on the date of fire	72,000
Less Stock Salvaged	18,000
Loss of Stock	54,000

Average Clause :

As there is average clause, the proportionate amount of loss to be claimed will be,

$$\frac{63000}{72,000} \times \frac{54,000}{1} = Rs.47,250$$

PROBLEM NO. 5

(Goods purchased but not recorded)

Find out the amount of claim to be lodged with the insurance company from the following information.

Particulars	2007 Rs.	2008 Rs.	2009 Rs.	2010 to Up to the date of fire
Opening Stock	15,000	–	–	–
Purchases				
Less : Return	50,000	75,000	90,000	60,000
Sales				
Less : Return	60,000	80,000	1,30,000	84,000
Wages	3,000	5,000	6,000	4,000
Closing Stock	20,000	40,000	50,000	

During the year 2008 closing stock included goods purchased but not recorded Rs. 5,000. The salvage stock was valued at Rs. 9,000. The amount of policy was Rs. 34,000. There was ar average clause in the policy. The firm closes its books on 31st December every year.

                                                              (P.U. April 1993)

Solution :

Dr.	Trading A/c for the year ended 2007			Cr.
	Rs.			**Rs.**
To Stock	15,000	By Sales		60,000
To Purchases	50,000	By Closing Stock		20,000
To Wages	3,000			
To Gross Profit (20% on Sales)	12,000			
	80,000			**80,000**

Dr.	Trading A/c for the year ended 2008			Cr.
	Rs.			**Rs.**
To Stock	20,000	By Sales 75000 + 5000 =		80,000
To Purchases	75,000	By Closing Stock		40,000
To Wages	5,000			
To Gross Profit (25% on sales)	20,000			
	1,20,000			**1,20,000**

Dr.		Trading A/c for the year ended 2009			Cr.
	Rs.		**Rs.**		
To Stock		40,000	By Sales		1,30,000
To Purchases	90,000		By Closing Stock		50,000'
Add : Unercorded	5,000	95,000			
To Wages		6,000			
To Gross Profit (30% on sales)		39,000			
		1,80,000			**1,80,000**

∵ Average Gross Profit = 25%

Dr.	Memorandum Trading A/c upto the date of fire.			Cr.
Particulars		**Rs.**	**Particulars**	**Rs.**
To Stock		50,000	By Sales	84,000
To Purchases		60,000	By Closing Stock	51,000
To Wages		4,000	(Upto the date of fire)	
To Gross Profit				
(25% on 84,000)		21,000		-
		1,35,000		**1,35.000**

Statement of Claim :

	Rs.
Stock on the date of fire	51,000
Less : Salvage	9,000
Loss of Fire	42,000

$$\text{Average Clause} = \frac{\text{Amount of Policy}}{\text{Stock on the date of fire}} \times \text{Actual Stock destroyed by fire}$$

$$= \frac{34,000}{51,000} \times 42,000 = 28,000$$

Claim = Rs. 28,000

PROBLEM NO. 6

Average Clause

Fire occurred in the business premises of M/s Mahajan & Co. on 15th October 2010 From the following particulars ascertain the loss of stock and prepare a claim for insurance.

	Rs.
Stock on 1-1-2009	34,000
Purchases from 1-1-2009 to 31-1-2009	1,22,000
Sates from 1-1-2009 to 31-1-2009	1,80,000
Stock on 31-12-2009	30,000
Purchases from 1-1-2010 to 14-10-2010	1,47,000
Sates from 1-1-2010 to 14-10-2010	1,50,000

The stock salvaged was worth Rs. 18,000. The amount of policy was Rs. 63,000. There was an average clause in the policy.

Solution :

In the Books of M/s. Mahajan & Co.

Dr.   **Trading A/c for the year ended 2009**   Cr.

Particulars	Rs.	Particulars	Rs.
To Opening Stock	34,000	By Sales	1,80,000
To Purchases	1,22,000	By Closing stock	30,000
To Gross Profit (30% on Sales)	54,000		-
	2,10,000		**2,10,000**

$$\textbf{Gross Profit Rate} \;=\; \frac{\text{Gross Profit}}{\text{Sales}} \times 100$$

$$=\; \frac{54,000}{1,80,000} \times 100$$

$$=\; 30\,\%$$

Dr.   **Memorandum Trading A/c for the period ended 15.10.2010**   **Cr.**

Particulars	Rs.	Particulars	Rs.
To Opening Stock	30,000	By Sales	1,50,000
To Purchases	1,47,000	By Closing stock	72,000
To Gross Profit (30% on Sales)	45,000		
	2,22,000		**2,22,000**

Statement of Claim :

	Rs.
Estimated stock on the date of fire	72,000
Less : Salvaged stock	18,000
Loss of Stock	54,000

Average Clause :

$$=\; \frac{\text{Loss of Stock}}{\text{Stock on the date of fire}} \times \text{Policy Amount}$$

$$=\; \frac{54,000}{72,000} \times 63,000$$

Claim   = Rs. 47,250.

PROBLEM NO. 7

(G. P. Rate not given)

A fire broke out in the premises of XYZ Company on 1ˢᵗ July 2011 and stock of the value of Rs. 1,57,500 was salvaged and the books and records were saved. The following information was obtained :

	Rs.
Stock on 31st March, 2010	4,20,000
Stock on 31 st March 2009	4,20,000
Sales from 1st April to 30th June 2011	5,10,000
Purchases from 1st April to 30th June 2011	3,15,000
Sates for the year ended 31 st March 2011	15,00,000
Purchases for the year ended 31st March, 2011	9,00,000

Calculate the amount of claim to be submitted to the Insurance company in respect of Loss of stock.

(P.U. April 1997)

Solution :

In the Books of XYZ co.

Dr. **Trading A/c for the year ended 31-3-2011** **Cr.**

Particulars	Rs.	Particulars	Rs.
To Opening Stock	4,20,000	By Sales	15,00,000
To Purchases .	9,00,000	By Closing stock	4,20,000
To Gross Profit (40% on Sales)	6,00,000	6,00,000	
	19,20,000		**19,20,000**

Gross Profit Rate :

$$= \frac{\text{Gross Profit}}{\text{Sales}} \times 100$$

$$= \frac{6,00,000}{15,00,000} \times 100 = 40\%$$

Dr. Memorandum / Trading A/c for the period from 1-4-2011 to 30-6-2011 **Cr.**

Particulars	Rs.	Particulars	Rs.
To Opening Stock	4,20,000	By Sales	5,10,000
To Purchases	3,15,000	By stock	4,29,000
To Gross Profit (40%)	2,04,000	(as on date of fire)	-
	9,39,000		**9,39,000**

Statement of Claim :

Stock as on date of fire	4,29,000
Less : Salvaged	1,57,500
Claim for settlement	2,71,500

PROBLEM NO. 8

(Abnormal items written off)

On 15th Septmeber, 2009 the premises of ABC Ltd. were destroyed by fire and a stock of Rs. 1,500 was salvaged and retained by the insured. The business books and records were saved from which the following information was obtained :

The following information was obtained :

	Rs.
Stock on 1st January, 2008	12,500
Stock on 31st December, 2008	17,500
Purchases for the year ended 31st December 2008	1,18,500
Sales for the year ended 31st December 2008	1,50,000
Purchases from 1st January 2016 to 15th Sept. 2009	37,500
Sales from 1st January 2016 to 15th Sept. 2016	51,250

In valuing the stock as on 31st Dec. 2015 Rs. 1,000 had been written off, certain stock having cost of Rs. 2,250.

Half of these goods were sold in July, 2016 for Rs. 1,250. The balance is estimated to be worth the original cost. Subject to the above exception, gross profit had remained at the uniform rate.

On 14th September 2016 goods worth Rs. 1,000 had been received by the godown keeper but had not been entered in purchase A/c. Show the amount of the claim.

(P.U. April 1995)

Solution :

In the books of ABC Ltd.

Dr.　　　　　　**Trading A/c for the year ended 31" Dec., 2008**　　　　　　Cr.

Particulars	Rs.	Particulars		Rs.
To Opening Stock	12,500	By Sales		1,50,000
To Purchases	1,18,500	By Closing stock	17,500	
To Gross Profit		Add: Poor		
(25% on sales)	37,500	Selling Goods	1,000	18,500
	1,68,500			**1,68,500**

Gross Profit Rate :

$$= \frac{\text{Gross Profit}}{\text{Sales}} \times 100$$

$$= \frac{37,500}{1,50,000} \times 100$$

$$= 25\%$$

Memorandum Trading A/c
for the Period ended 15th Sept. 2009

Dr.   Cr.

Particulars	Rs.	Rs.	Particulars	Rs.	Rs.
To Opening Stock	18,500		By Sales	51,250	
Less : Poor Selling			**Less :** Poor Selling		
Goods	1,000	17,500	Goods	1,250	50,000
To Purchases		37,500	By Goods taken by		1,000
To Gross Profit		12,500	Store keeper		
			By Stock	16,500	
			(as on date of fire)		
		67,500			**67,500**

Statement of Claim

Stock on the date of fire	16,500
Add : Unsold Goods of Poor line sales	500
Claim for settlement	17,000

PROBLEM NO. 9

(Insurance at % of cost)

From the following particulars ascertain the value of stock on the date of fire.

Particulars	2007 Rs.	2008 Rs.	2009 Rs.	Up to the date of fire
Opening stock	15,000	?	?	?
Purchases less Returns	50,000	75,000	90,000	60,000
Sales less Returns	60,000	80,000	1,30,000	84,000
Factory Expenses	3,000	5,000	6,000	4,000
Closing Stock	20,000	40,000	50,000	?

During the year 2009 closing stock included goods purchased but not recorded Rs. 5,000. The salvage is Rs. 11,000. It is the practice of the firm to insure the goods at 90% cost.

(P.U.April 1986, Oct. 2002, April 2002)

Solution :

Trading A/c

Dr.   **for the Period ended 31-12-2009**   **Cr.**

Particulars	2007 Rs.	2008 Rs.	2009 Rs.	Particulars	2007 Rs.	2008 Rs.	2009 Rs.
To Stock	15,000	20,000	40,000	By Sales	60,000	80,000	1,30,000
To Purchases	50,000	75,000	95,000	By Stock	20,000	40,000	50,000
To Factory							
Expenses	3,000	5,000	6,000				
To Gross Profit	12,000	20,000	39,000				
	80,000	1,20,000	1,80,000		80,000	1,20,00	1,80,000

Gross Profit Rate :

Profit to sales   20%   25%   30%   Hence average percentage is 25%.

Memorandum Trading A/c from 1st January, 2016 upto the date of fire

Dr.   **Cr.**

Particulars	Rs.	Particulars	Rs.
To Stock	50,000	By Sales	84,000
To Purchases	60,000	By Stock (Balancing figure)	51,000
To Factory Expenses	4,000		
To Gross Profit			
(at 25% on Sales)	21,000		
	1,35,000		1,35,000

Statement of Claim :

Estimated stock on the date of fire	51,000
Less : Salvage	11,000
Loss of stock	40,000

Average Clause :

As the goods are insured 90% of the stock, the claim for loss of stock (according to average clause) will be Rs. 40,000 × 90%

= Rs. 36,000

(It is presumed there in an Average Clause in the Policy)

PROBLEM NO. 10

(Abnormal items written off)

On 15th September 2009 the premises of AB Ltd. were destroyed by fire and stock of Rs. 12,000 was salvaged and retained by the insured. The business books and records were saved from which the following information was obtained :

	Rs.
Stock on 1-1-2008	1,00,000
Stock on 31-12-2008	1,40,000
Purchases for the year ended 31-12-2008	9,48,000
Sales for the year ended 31-12-2008	12,00,000
Purchases from 1-1-2016 to 15-9-2009	3,00,000
Sates from 1-1-2016 to 15-9-2009	4,10,000

- In valuing the stock as on 31-12.2008 Rs. 8,000 had been written off certain stock having cost of Rs. 18,000.
- Half of these goods were sold in July 2009 for Rs. 10,000. The balance is estimated to be worth the original cost. Subject to the above exception, gross profit had remained at the uniform rate.
- On 14th September 2009 goods worth Rs. 8,000 had been received by the godown keeper but had not been entered in purchases account.
- Show the statement of the claim for loss of stock.

(P.U.Oct 1999)

In the Books of AB Ltd.

Dr.		Trading A/c for the year ended 31st Dec., 2008			Cr.

Particulars	Rs.	Rs.	Particulars	Rs.	Rs.
To Opening Stock		1,00,000	By Sales		12,00,000
To Purchases		9,48,000	By Closing stock	1,40,000	
To Gross Profit			Add: Poor		
(25%)		3,00,000	Selling Goods	8,000	1,48,000
		13,48,000			**13,48,000**

Gross Profit Rate :

$$= \frac{\text{Gross Profit}}{\text{Sales}} \times 100$$

$$= \frac{3,00,000}{12,00,000} \times 100 = 25\%$$

Memorandum Trading A/c

Dr.   for the period from 1-1-2009 to 15-9-2009   Cr.

Particulars	Rs.	Rs.	Particulars	Rs.	Rs.
To Opening Stock	1,48,000		By Sales	4,10,000	
Less : Poor Selling			Less : Poor		
Goods	8,000	1,40,000	Selling Goods	10,000	4,00,000
To Purchases	3,00,000		By stock		
Add : Unrecorded			(as oh date of fire)		1,48,000
Goods	8,000	3,08,000			
To Gross Profit					
(25%)		1,00,000			
		5,48,000			**5,48,000**

Statement of a Claim :

Stock (as on date of fire)	1,48,000
Less : Salvaged	12,000
Claim for settlement	1,36,000

PROBLEM NO. 11

(Abnormal Items)

On 1st August, 2009 the premises of Jawahar Mills Ltd. was destroyed by fire, from the saved records :

	Rs.
Stock at Cost on 1-4-2008	1,10,250
Stock valued on 31-03-2009	1,19,400
Purchase for the year ended 31-3-2009	5,97,000
Sates for the year ended 31-3-2009	7,30,500
Purchases from 1-4-2009 to 1-8-2009	2,43,000
Sales from 1-4-2009 to 1-8-2009	3,46,800

In Closing Stock as on 31-3-2009 a portion of goods purchased for Rs. 10,350 had been valued below cost by Rs. 3,450 as it was from a poor selling line. A portion of these goods were sold in June, 2016 at a loss of Rs. 2375 on its original cost of Rs. 5,175. The remaining stock of these goods was estimated at Rs. 2800. Subject to this gross profit was constant. The value of salvage was Rs. 700.

Prepare a statement showing the amount of claim.

Solution :

In the Books of Jawahar Mills Ltd.

Dr. **Trading A/c for the year ended 31-03-2009** Cr.

Particulars	Rs.	Rs.	Particulars	Rs.	Rs.
To Opening Stock		1,10,250	By Sales		7,30,500
To Purchases	59,700		By Closing stock	1,19,400	
Poor selling	10,350		Poor selling	6,900	1,12,500
To Gross Profit		5,86,650			
		1,46,100			
		8,43,000			8,43,000

Gross Profit Rate :

$$= \frac{\text{Gross Profit}}{\text{Sales}} \times 100$$

$$= \frac{68,800}{3,44,000} \times 100 = 20\ \%$$

Memorandum Trading A/c

Dr. **for the period ended 1 st August, 2009** Cr.

Particulars	Rs.	Rs.	Particulars	Rs.	Rs.
To Opening Stock		1,12,500	By Sales	3,46,800	
To Purchases		2,43,000	Less : Poor Selling		
To Gross Profit			Goods	2,800	3,44,000
(920% of 3,44,000)		68,800	By stock (as on date		
			of fire)		80,300
		4,24,300			4,24,300

Statement or Claim :

	Rs.
Stock on the date of fire	80,300
Regular Goods	2,800
Poor Selling Goods	83,100
Less: Salvage	700
Amount of Claim	82,400

PROBLEM NO. 12

(Goods taken for personal use not recorded)

From the following Information ascertain the value of stock on the date of fire.

Particulars	2007 Rs.	2008 Rs.	2009 Rs.	Up to the date of fire
Opening stock	15,000	-	-	-
Purchases	50,000	75,000	90,000	60,000
Sales	60,000	80,000	1,30,000	84,000
Factory Expenses	3,000	5,000	6,000	4,000
Closing stock	20,000	40,000	50,000	-

During the year 2016, the proprietor has withdrawn goods from business to the extent of Rs. 5,000 which are not recorded in the books and goods purchased for Rs. 10,000 are unrecoreded in the books.

(P.U. April 1989)

The Salvage is valued at Rs. 21,000.

Solution :

Trading A/c

Dr. **for the year ended 31st March.** **Cr.**

Particulars	2007 Rs.	2008 Rs.	2009 Rs.	Particulars	2007 Rs.	2008 Rs.	2009 Rs.
To Opening stock	15,000	20,000	40,000	By Sales	60,000	80,000	1,30,000
To Purchases	50,000	75,000	95,000	By Stock	20,000	40,000	50,000
To Factory Expenses	3,000	5,000	6,000				
To Gross Profit	12,000	20,000	39,000				
	80,000	1,20,000	1,80,000		80,000	1,20,00	1,80,000

Gross Profit Rate :   2014   2015   2016

% of G. P. Sales   20%   25%   30%

∴ **Average Profit**

$$= \frac{20+25+30}{3}$$

$= 25\ \%$

Memorandum Trading A/c to the date of fire

Dr.   **Cr.**

Particulars	Rs.	Particulars	Rs.
To Opening Stock	50,000	By Sales	84,000
To Purchases	60,000	By Stock	51,000
To Factory Expenses	4,000	(on the date of fire)	
To Gross Profit			
(@ 25% of 84,000)	21,000		
	1,35,000		1,35,000

i) **Statement of Claim :**

Value of stock

on the date of fire Rs.   51,000

Less : Salvage   21,000

∴ Actual Loss :   30,000

ii) **Purchases :**   90,000

Add : Unrecorded Purchases   10,000

    1,00,000

Less : for personal use

not recorded   5,000

    95,000

PROBLEM NO. 13

(Undervalution of stock)

The premises and stock of Sumedha Stores were totally destroyed by fire on 30th January, 2011 From the account books and other records that were saved the following infomation is available. The stock on hand has always been valued at 10% less than cost.

Particulars	2008	2009	2010	2011
Opening stock as valued	27,090	32,400	36,000	36,900
Purchases less returns	74,900	80,000	81,000	6,000
Sales less returns	1,20,000	1,32,000	1,40,000	12,000
Wages	17,400	19,000	20,900	2,000
Closing stock as valued	32,400	36,000	36,900	-

Prepare a statement of submission for the insurance co. in support of the claim for loss of stock.

In the Books of Sumedha Stores
TradingA/c

Dr.   **for the year ended 31 st December 2008**   Cr.

Particulars	Rs.	Particulars	Rs.
To Opening Stock $\left(27,090\times\dfrac{100}{90}\right)$	30,100	By Sales Returns	1,20,000
To Purchases less returns	74,900	By Closing Stock $\left(32,400\times\dfrac{100}{90}\right)$	36,000
To Wages	17,400		
To Gross Profit	33,600		
	1,56,000		**1,56,000**

Gross Profit Rate :

$$= \frac{\text{Gross Profit}}{\text{Sales}}\times 100$$

$$= \frac{33,600}{1,20,000}\times 100 = 28\ \%$$

Trading A/c

Dr.   **for the year ended 31st December 2009**   Cr.

Particulars	Rs.	Particulars	Rs.
To Opening Stock $\left(32,400\times\dfrac{100}{90}\right)$	36,000	By Sales less returns	1,32,000
		By Closing Stock $\left(36,000\times\dfrac{100}{90}\right)$	40,000
To Purchases less returns	80,000		
To Wages	19,000		
To Gross Profit	37,000		
	1,72,000		**1,72,000**

Gross Profit Rate :

$$= \frac{\text{Gross Profit}}{\text{Sales}}\times 100$$

$$= \frac{37,600}{1,32,000}\times 100 = 28\ \%$$

Dr.   **Trading A/c . for the year ended 31st December, 2010**   **Cr.**

Particulars	Rs.	Particulars	Rs.
To Opening Stock $\left(36,000\times\dfrac{100}{90}\right)$	40,000	By Sales less returns	1,40,000
		By Closing Stock $\left(36,900\times\dfrac{100}{90}\right)$	40,000
To Purchases less returns	81,000		
To Wages	20,900		
To Gross Profit	39,100		
	1,81,000		1,81,000

Gross Profit Rate :

$$= \frac{\text{Gross Profit}}{\text{Sales}} \times 100$$

$$= \frac{39,100}{1,40,000} \times 100 = 28\ \%$$

Average Gross Profit = Average percentage of gross profit

$$\frac{28\% + 28\% + 28\%}{3} = 28\%$$

Memorandum Trading A/c
upto 30th Jauary, 2011

Dr.   **Cr.**

Particulars	Rs.	Particulars	Rs.
To Opening Stock $\left(36,000\times\dfrac{100}{90}\right)$	41,000	By Sales less returns	12,000
		By Closing Stock	40,360
To Purchases less returns	6,000	(Balacing Figure)	
To Wages	2,000		
To Gross Profit (28% Rs. 12,000)	3,360		
	52,360		52,360

Stock worth Rs. 40,360 has been completely destroyed by fire. So claim for loss of stock to be lodged is Rs. 40,360.

PROBLEM NO. 14

Find out the amount of claim to be lodged with the insurance company from the following information.

Particulars	2013	2014	2015	2016
Opening stock	15,000	----	----	----
Purchases				
Less - Return	50,000	75,000	90,000	60,000
Sales				
Less Return	60,000	80,000	1,30,000	84,000
Wages	3,000	5,000	6,000	4,000
Closing Slock	20,000	40,000	50,000	...

During the year 2016 closing stock included goods Purchased but not recorded Rs. 5,000. The salvaged stock was valued at Rs. 9,000. The amount of policy was Rs. 34,000. There was an average clause in the policy. The firm closes its books on 31st December every year.

Solution :

Fire Claims: Loss of Stock

Trading Accounts for the years 2013, 2014 and 2015

Particulars	2013 Rs.	2014 Rs.	2015 Rs.	Particulars	2013 Rs.	2014 Rs.	2015 Rs.
To Opening Stock	15,000	20,000	40,000	By Sales	60,000	80,000	1,30,000
To Purchases				Less Returns			
Less Returns	50,000	75,000	95,000	By Closing	20,000	40,000	50,000
To Wage	3,000	5,000	6,000	Stock			
To Gross Profit	12,000	20,000	39,000				
	80,000	1,20,000	1,80,000		80,000	1,20,00	1,80,000

The Gross Profit rates for 2013, 2014 & 2015 are respectively 20 %, 25 %, and 30 %. on sales. The Average Gross Profit rate derived from the total of these three rates is :

$$\frac{75}{3} = 25\%$$

Estimated Trading A/C
for the period 1 -1 - 2016 to the date of fire in 2016

	Rs.		Rs.
To Opening Stock (on 1-1-2016)	50,000	By Sales less Returns	84,000
To Purchases less Returns	60,000	By Stock (Balancing figure)	51,000
To Wages	4,000		
To Gross Profit @ 25 % on sales	21,000		
	1,35,000		1,35,000

(I) Ascertainment of Stock destroyed by fire :

The value of stock destroyed by fire will be Rs. 42,000 determined as follows :

Total stock as disclosed by the Estimated Trading A/c:	Rs. 51,000
Less Value of salvaged stock	Rs. 9,000
Value of stock destroyed by fire	Rs. 42.000

To determine how much the Insurance Company will actually pay by way of compensation, we have to apply the Average Clause.

(II) Application of the Average Clause Formula :

$$\frac{\text{Actual Insurance}}{\text{Insurance required}} \times \frac{\text{Value of Stock}}{\text{destroyed by fire}}$$

$$\therefore \frac{\text{Rs.}34,000}{\text{Rs. }51,000} \times \frac{42,000}{1} = \text{Rs. }28,000$$

Answer : Insurance Comipany will pay by way of compensation only RS. 28,000 (though the value of slock destroyed by fire has been ascertained to be Rs. 42,000/-)

Note 1 : All goods included in the closing stotk have first to be accounted for or recorded as purchases of the year (unless they are from the opening stock.) Only the 'purchased goods' can remain in an unsold state and be pan of the closing stock. So we have to record the unrecorded purchase by adding its value (Rs. 5,000). to the value of other purchases. After this, the total purchases will be Rs. 95,000.

Note 2 : How much insurance was required in the case of stock, is decided by the total stock in the possession of the insured at the time of fire. To disclose this 'total stock' is the function of the Estimated Trading A/c. It includes stock destroyed by fire and also, stock salvaged. The need for the application of the Average Clause arises when there is under-insurance ie. the sum assured or actual insurance is less than the insurance cover required, which is equal to the value of total stock, as disclosed by the Estimated Trading Account.

PROBLEM NO. 15

On l6th May 2016 the premises of Newasa Ltd. were destroyed by the fire but sufficient records were saved from which the following information was ascertained.

Stock on 1-1-2015	76,800
Purchases during the year 2015	3,20,000
Sales during the year 2015	4,05,200
Stock on 31-12-2015	63,600
Purchase from 1-1-2016 to 16-5-2016	Rs. 1,08,000
Sales from 1-1-2016 to 16-5-2016	Rs. 1,22,800

An item of stock purchased in 2016 at cost of Rs. 20,000 was valued at Rs. 12,000 on 31-12-14. Half of this stock was sold in 2015 for Rs. 5,200, the remaining was valued at Rs. 4,800 on 31-12-2015. One-fourth of the originial stock was sold on 15th March 2016 for Rs. 2,800 and the remaining stcok was considered to be worth 60 % of the original cost. The salvaged stock was worth Rs. 24,000. The amount of policy was Rs. 60,000 and there was an average cla» se hi the policy. Find out the amount of claim.

(Pune University)

Solution :

Fire Insurance Claims : Loss of Stock ; Newasa Ltd

Trading Account for the year 2015

Particulars	Rs.	Rs.	Particulars	Rs.	Rs.
To Openin stock 1-1-2015	76,800		By Sales	4,05,200	
Less value of the abnormal item	- 12,000		Less sale- Proceeds of half of the abnormal item sold	- 5,200	
		64,800			4,00,000
To Purchases		3,20,000			
To Gross Profit		74,000	By Closing Stock 63,600 31-12-2015 Less value placed on the remaining abnormal item	- 4,800	
					58,800
		4,58,800			**4,58,800**

The rate of Gros Profit on sales is 18.5%

Estimated Trading Account for the period 1-1-2016 to 16-5-2016

(i.e. the date of fire)

	Rs.			Rs.
To Opening Stock 1-1-2016 (excluding the abnormal item)	58,800	By Sales 1,22,800 Less sale proceeds of half of the remaining abnormal item sold - 2,800		1,20,000
To Purchases	1,08,000			
To Gross Profit	22,200			
@ 18-5 % on sales of Rs. 1,20,000		By Closing Stock of normal items existing at the item of fire. (Balancing Figure)		69,000
	1,89,000			**1,89,000**

(I) Statement showing the value of stock at the time of fire

     1. Normal items   Rs.

       (as per the Estimated Trading A/c)   69,000

add : 2. Abnormal item in stock :

       60 % of Rs. 5,000   + 3,000   * See Note

                                      72,000

Less : Value of the salvage   -24,000

       Value of stock destroyed by fire   48,000

(II) The Net claim for stock destroyed by fire after application of the Average Clause. Formula :

$$\frac{\text{Actual Insurance}}{\text{Insurance required}} \times \text{Value of stock destroyed by fire}$$

$$= \frac{\text{Rs. } 60,000}{\text{Rs. } 72,000} \times \text{Rs. } 48,000$$

$$= \frac{5}{6} \times 48,000 = \text{Rs. } 40,000$$

The Insurance Company will pay by way of compensation, Rs. 40,000

Note : The total cost of the abnormal item was Rs. 20,000. Half of it was sold in 2015 Half of this half was sold on 15th Marc 2016 (i.e. 1/4 th of the original stock). This means only one-fourth of the abnormal item was in stock at the time of fire Its cost was one-fourth of Rs. 20,000 i.e. Rs. 5,000. For claim purposes we have been asked to value it @ 60 % of Rs. 5,000 i.e. 3,000.

PROBLEM NO 16

Baramati Stores closed their Books every year on 31st March, On 30th April 2016 their Premises and Stock were destroyed by fire. From books of accounts and other records the following information is obtained. The stock on hand every year has always been valued at 10% less than the cost.

Particulars	2013-2014 Rs.	2014-2015 Rs.	2015-2016 Rs.	1-4-2016 30-4-2016
Opening stock	270,900	3,24,000	3,60,000	3,69,000
Purchases less returns	7,49,000	8,00,000	8,10,000	60,000
Sales less returns	12,00,000	13,20,000	14,00,000	1,20,000
Wages	2,10,000	2,30,000	2,50,900	20,000
Closing stock as valued	3,24,000	3,60,000	3,69,000	-

They have taken Fire Insurance policy of Rs. 3,50,000 and there is an average clause in the policy. The salvaged goods amounted to Rs. 10,000.

Find out the amount of claim to be submitted to the Insurance Company .

Solution :

Fire Insurance claims: Loss of Stock, Baramati Stores. Accounting Year : April - March.

Trading Accounts for the years 2013-2014, 2014-2015 and 2015-2016

	2013-14 (1-4-2013 to 31-3-2014) Rs.	2014-15 (1-4-2014 to 31-3-2015) Rs.	2015-16 (1-4-2015 to 31-3-2016) Rs.		2013-14 (1-4-2013 to 31-3-2014) Rs.	2014-15 (1-4-2014 to 31-3-2015) Rs.	2015-16 (1-4-2015 to 31-3-2016) Rs.
To Opening Stock at cost	3,01,000	3,60,000	4,00,000	By Sales Less Returns	12,00,000	13,20,000	14,00,000
To Purchases Less Returns	7,49,000	8,00,000	8,10,000	By Closing Stock	3,60,000	4,00,000	4,10,000
To Wage	2,10,000	2,30,000	2,50,000				
To Gross Profit	3,00,000	3,30,000	3,50,000				
	15,60,000	17,20,000	18,10,000		15,60,000	17,20,000	18,10,000

(I) Gross Profit in 2013-2014 is Rs. 3,00,000. It is 1/4th of sales which are Rs. 12,00,000.

∴ G.P. rate is 25% on Sales.

Gross Profit in 2014-2015 is Rs. 3,30,000. It is 1/4th of sales which are Rs 13,20,000 ∴ G.P. rate is 25% on Sales.

Gross Profit 2015-2016 Rs. 3,50,000. It is 1/4th of sales which are Rs. 14,00,000 ∴ G.P. rate is 25% on Sales.

(II) So the Average Rate of Gross Profit is 25% on sales.

Estimated Trading A/c

	Rs.		Rs.
To Opening Stock at cost (on 1-4-2016)	4,10,000	By Sales Less Returns	1,20,000
To Purchases		By Stock at the time of fire	
Less Returns	60,000	30-4-2016	
To Wages	20,000	(Balancing figure)	4,00,000
To Gross Profit @ 25 % on sales	30,000		
	5,20,000		**5,20,000**

(I) The value of the stock held by Baramati Stores immediately before the fire on 30-4-2016   Rs. 4,00,000

Less : The value of salvaged stock   Rs. 10,000

The value of stock destroyed by fire   Rs. 3,90,000

(II) Application of the Average Clause as there is underinsurance.

Formula :

$$= \frac{\text{Sum Insured or Actual Insurance}}{\substack{\text{The value of the stock immediately before the} \\ \text{fire as shown by the Estimated Trading A/c}}} \times \text{Value of stock destroyed by fire}$$

$$= \frac{\text{Rs.3,50,000}}{\text{Rs.4,00,000}} \times \frac{\text{Rs.3,90,000}}{1} = \text{Rs. 341,250}$$

Answer : The claim - amount the Insurance Company will sanction and pay is Rs. 3,41,250

PROBLEM NO. 17

On l5th September, 2016 the premises of Lecmic Ltd were destroyed by fire and a stock of Rs 1,500 was salvaged and retained by the insured. The business books and records were saved from which the following information was obtained :

Purticulars	Rs.
Stock on lst January 2015	12,500
Stock on 31st December, 2015	17.500
Purchases for the year ended 31st Dec. 2015	1,18,500
Sales for the year ended 31st Dec. 2015	1,50,000
Purchases from 31st January 2016 to 15th Sept 2016	37,500
Sales from 31st January 2016 to 15th Sept. 2016	51,250

In valuing the stock as on 31st Dec. 2015 Rs. 1,000 had been written off certain stock having cost of Rs. 2,250.

Half of these goods were sold in July 2016 for Rs. 1, 250. The balance is estimated to be worth the original cost. Subject to the above exception, gross profit had remained at the uniform rate.

On 14th Sept 2016, goods worth Rs. 1,000 had been received by the godown-keeper but had not been entered in Purchase A/c Show the amount of the claim.

(Pune University T.Y.B.Com.)

Solution :

Fire Insurance Claims : Loss of Stock. Lecmic Ltd. Date of fire 15th Sept. 2016, Accounting Year Jan/December.

Trading A/c for the year 2015

	Rs.	Rs.		Rs.	Rs.
To Opening Stock (on 1-1-2015)		12,500	By Sales :		1,50,000
To Purchases .		1,18,500	By Closing Stock on 31-12-2015	17,500	
To Gross Profit :		37,500	Add amt, written off a certain item	1,000	
			of Stock		18,500
		1,68,500			1,68,500

Cross Profit rate is 25% on sales.

Estimated Trading A/c
for the period 1-1-2016 to 15 9-2016 i.e. the date of the fire

	Rs.	Rs.		Rs.	Rs.
To Opening Slock (on 1 - 1 -2016) Less full cost of the abnormal item	18,500 2,250		By Sales : Less sale proceeds of 1/2 of the abnormal item	51,250 1,250	
		16,250	By Stock immediately before the fire (Balancing figure)		50,000
To Purchases	37,500				17,250
Add Unrecorded Purchase at cost	1,000				
		38,500			
ToG.P. @25% on sales		12,500			
		67,250			67,250

The value of all the stock held by Lecmic Ltd immediately beforel

		Rs.
(1)	Normal items at cost us	17,250
Plus (2)	Abnormal item at cost (50% of Rs 2250)	+ 1,125
		18,375
	Less the salvage at cost	- 1,500
	The value of the stock destroyed by fire.	16,875

As the sum insured is not mentioned, we cannot apply the average clause But we can assume that it was not less than the insurance cover needed in this case i.e. there was no under-insurance.

The insurance-claim will therefore be for Rs 16,875, which is the value of the stock destroyed by fire.

PROBLEM NO. 18

A Fire occurred in the business premises of M/s Bombaywala on 15th Oct. 2016. From the following particulars ascertain the Loss of stock and prepare the claim for Insurance :

Purticulars	Rs.
Slock on 1-1-2015	15,300
Purchase from 1-1-2015 to 31-12-2015	61,100
Sales from 1-1-2015 to 31-12-2015	90,000
Stock on 31-12-2015	13,500
Purchases from 1-1-2016 to 14-10-2016	73,500
Sales from 1-1-2016 to 14-10-2016	75,000

The stock were always valued at 90% of cost. The stock saved was worth Rs. 9,000. The amount of the policy was Rs. 31,500. There was an average clause in the policy.

(Pune Uni. T.Y. B. Com.)

Solution :

Fire claims : Loss of Stock,
Mr. Bombaywala.

Special Point: Slocks valued at 90% of cost. Date of fire 15-10-2016

	Rs.		Rs.
To Opening Stock	17,000	By Sales	90,000
(on 1 -1-2015)		By Closing Stock	
To Purchases	61,000	(at cost)	15,000
To Gross Profit	27,000		
	1,05,000		1,05,000

Gross Profit is 30 % on sales. (Rs. 27,000 on Sales of Rs. 90,000)

Estimated Trading A/c Tor the period. 1-1-2016 to 15-10-2016

	Rs.		Rs.
To Opening Stock	15,000	By Sales	75,000
To Purchases	73,500	By Stock on the	
To Gross Profit	22,500	date of fire	
@ 30 % on sales		(Balancing figure)	36,000
	1,11,000		1,11,000

(I) **The value of the stock held by Mr. Bombaywala**	**Rs.**
immediately before the fire broke out	36,000
(as per Estimated Trading Account)	
Less Value of Salvage	- 9,000
Value of stock destroyed	27,000

(II) The application of the average clause

$$\text{Formula} : \frac{\text{Sum insured}}{\substack{\text{Insurance Cover required in} \\ \text{Mr. Bombaywala's case}}} \times \text{Stock Destroyed}$$

$$= \frac{\text{Rs. } 31,500}{\text{Rs. } 36,000} \times 27,000$$

$$= \frac{31,500}{4} \times 3 = \text{Rs. } 23,625$$

(III) Value of stock for claim Rs. 23,625.

Note : Valuation of stocks at 10% below their real cost will cause the normal rate of Gross Profit to .be disturbed; So, before preparing the Trading Account, Opening & Closing Stocks should be restored to their true or real Cost.

When the Op. Stock is valued at Rs. 90 → its true cost is Rs. 100 So, when it is valued at Rs. 15,300 → What is its real cost ?

$$\textbf{Ans. :} \ \frac{15300}{90} \times 100 = \text{Rs. } 17,000$$

PROBLEM NO. 19

A Fire broke out in the premises of Megha Company on 1st July 2016 and stock of the value of Rs. 1,57,500 was salvaged and the books and records were saved.

The following Information was obtained :

Stock on 31st March, 2015	4,20,000
Stock on 31st March, 2016	4,20,000
Sales from 1st April to 30th June, 2016	5,10,000
Purchases from 1st April on 30th June, 2016	3,15,000
Sales for the year ended 31st March, 2016	15,00,000
Purchases for the year ended 31st March 2016	9,00,000

Calculate the amount of claim to be submitted to the Insurance Company in respect of Loss of stock. **(Pune University)**

Solution : Fire Insurance Claims : Loss of stock owned by Megha Co. Date of fire 1-7-2016

Trading Account for the year ended 31-3-2016

	Rs.		Rs.
To Opening Stock (on 1-4-2015)	4,20,000	By Sales	15,00,000
		By Closing Stock on 31-3-2016	
To Purchases	9,00,000		4,20,000
To Gross Profit	6,00,000		
	19,20,000		**19,20,000**

Gross Profit is Rs. 6,00,000 on sales of Rs. 15,00,000

The rate of Gross Profit is 40% on Sales

Estimated Trading A/c
for the period 1-4-2016 to 1-7-2016 (Date of fire)

Rs.		Rs.	
To Opening Slock	4,20,000	By Sales	5,10,000
(on 1-4-2016)		By Stock held by	
To Purchases	3,15,000	Megha Company	
To Gross Profit	2,04,000	immediately before	
@ 40 % on sales		the occurrence of fire	
		(Balancing figure)	4,29,000
	9,39,000		**9,39,000**

	Rs.
Value of stock held by Megha Company immediately before the Fire occurred	4,29,000
Less Value of Salvaged stock	- 1,57,500
Value of stock destroyed as a result of the fire & value for claim	2,71,500

PROBLEM NO. 20

A fire occurred in the business premises of M/s Patange & Company on 15th Oct. 2016. From the following particulars ascertain the loss of stock and prepare a claim insurance.

Stock on 1-1-2015	Rs. 68,000
Purchases from 1-1-2015 to 31-2-2015	Rs. 2,44,000
Sales from1-1-2015 to 31-12-2015	Rs. Rs. 3,60,000
Stock on 31-12-2015	Rs. 60,000
Purchases from 1-1-2016 to 14-10-2016	Rs. 2,94,000
Sales from 1-1-2016 to 14-10-2016	Rs. 3,00,000

The stock salvaged was worth Rs. 36,000. The amount of policy was Rs. 1,26,000. There was an average clause in the policy.

(Pune University, T. Y. B. Com.)

Solution :

**Fire Insurance Claims : Loss of Stock in
the case of Patange & Company, Date of Fire 15-10-2016
Accounting Year, January - December.
Trading Account for the year 2015**

	Rs.		Rs.
To Opening Stock	Rs. 68,000	By Sales	Rs.3,60,000
(on 1-1-2015)		By Closing Stock	60,000
To Purchases	2,44,000		
To Gross Profit	1,08,000		
	4,20,000		**4,20,000**

Gross Profit is Rs. 1,08,000 on sales of Rs. 3,60,000.
So the rate of Gross Profit on Sales is 30%.

**Estimated Trading A/c
for the period from 1-12016 to 15-10-2016 i.e. the date of fire**

	Rs.		Rs.
To Opening Stock	Rs. 60,000	By Sales	3,00,000
(on 1-1-2016)		By Stock	
To Purchases	2,94,000	(Balancing figure)	1,44,000
To Gross Profit	90,000		
@ 30 % on sales			
	4,44,000		**4,44,000**

(I) Value of stock held by Patange & Co. immediately before the fire broke out

(as disclosed by the Estimated Trading A/c.)	1,44,000
less Value of Stock Salvaged	(–)36,000
$\therefore$ value of stock destroyed by fire	1,08,000

(II) Application of the Average Clause as there is under insurance : Formula :

$$= \frac{\text{Sum Assured}}{\text{Insurance Cover Required}} \times \text{value of stock destroyed}$$
in this particular case

$$= \frac{126000}{1,44,000} \times \frac{108000}{1} = \text{Rs. 94,500}$$

$\therefore$ Value for Insurance claim is Rs. 94,500

Note 1 : It is the value of stock held on the date of fire which determines how much insurance was required in the case under consideration.

PROBLEM NO. 21

The Premises of Ratanlal were destroyed by fire on 30-6-2016. The following figures were, however collected from available sources. Prepare statement of claim in respect of the loss of stock for submission to the Insurance Company explaining basis of your claim. The firm closes its books on 31 st December each year.

Details	2013 Rs.	2014 Rs.	2015 Rs.	2016 30-6-2016 Rs.
Opening Stock	20,000	22,000	11,800	34,020
Purchases	1,78,000	1,50,000	1,77,000	36,000
Sales	2,22,000	2,02,000	1,93,500	28,000
Purchases Returns	18,000	5,000	7,000	1,000
Sales Returns	22,000	4,000	6,000	2,000
Freight Inward	5,000	3,000	5,000	1,000
Closing Stock	22,000	11,800	34,020	-

In 2013 while valuing closing stock, a slow moving item costing Rs. 5,000 was valued at Rs. 4,000. This was sold for Rs. 4,500 in 2014. In 2014 an item costing Rs. 6,000 was wrongly valued at Rs. 7,000. This was sold for Rs. 5,500 in 2015. in 2015 slow moving item, costing Rs. 12,000 was valued at Rs. 10,000, 50 % of which was sold before 30 th June 2016 for Rs. 6,000. The value of Salvage was Rs. 8,000.

(Pune University, T. Y. B. Com.)

Solution :

Trading Account for Sona Ltd. Fire Claims: Loss of stock.
Trading Account for 2013

		Rs.			Rs.
To Opening Stock		20,000	By Sales :	2,22,000	
To Purchases	1,78,000		Less R. Inward	22,000	
Less R.Outward	- 18,000				2,00,000
		1,60,000	By Closing Stock	22,000	
To Freight Inward		5,000	Add Adjustment for		
To Gross Profit		38,000	undervaluation of		
			an item of stock	+1,000	
					23,000
		2,23,000			2,23,000

Gross Profit is Rs. 38,000 on sales of Rs. 2,00,000 which means the rate of Gross Profit is 19%

Trading Account for 2014

	Rs.			Rs.
To Opening Stock 23,000		By Sales 2,02,500		
Less full cost of the abnormal item -5,000		Less Proceeds from the sale of Abnormal item - 4,500		
	18,000		1,98,000	
To Purchases 1,50,000		Less R. Inward - 4000	1,94,000	
Less R.Outward - 5,000		By Closing Stock 11,800		
	1,45,000	Less Adjustment for overvaluation of		
To Freight Inward	3,000	an item of stock - 1,000	10,800	
To Gross Profit	38,800			
	2,04,800			**2,04,800**

The rate of Gross Profit (on Sales) is 20 %

Trading Account for 2015

	Rs.			Rs.
To Opening Stock 10,800		By Sales 1,93,500		
Less Elimination of the full cost of the abnormal item - 6,000		Less Proceeds from the sale of abnormal item -5,500		
	4,800		1,88,000	
To Purchases 1,77,000		Less R. Inward - 6000		
Less R.Outward - 7,000				
	1,70,000			1,82,000
To Freight Inward	5,000	By Closing Stock 34,020		
To Gross Profit	38,220	Add Adjustment for undervaluation of an item of stock + 2,000	36,020	
	2,18,020			**2,18,020**

The G. P. is Rs, 38,220 on sales of Rs. 1,82,000. So the G. P. rate is 21 %

The Average rate of Gross Profit is $\dfrac{19+20+21}{3} = \dfrac{60}{3} = 20\%$

Estimated Trading Account for the period 1-1-2016 to 30-6-2016
i.e. the date of fire.

	Rs.			Rs.
To Opening Stock 36,020 Less Elimination of the original cost of the abnormal item − 12,000	24,020	By Sales : 28,000 Less Proceeds from the sale of 50 % of the abnormal item − 6,000	22,000	
To Purchases 36,000 Less R.Outward − 1 ,000	35,000	Less R. Inward − 2,000	20,000	
To Freight toward	1,000	By Stock held by Mr. Ratanlal immediately		
To Gross Profit @ 20 %. on sales	4,000	before the occurrence of fire on 30-6-2016 (Normal items only)	44,020	
	64,020		**64,020**	

Stock held by the insured on 30-6-2016 immediaiely before the fire broke the fire broke out.

(i) Normal items	44,020
Plus (ii) Abnormal item	+ 6,000
	50,020
Less value of salvage	−8000
Value for Claim in respect of stock destroyed.	42,020

PROBLEM NO. 22

On 15th September, 2016 the premises of Red Ltd. were destroyed by fire and a stock of Rs. 12,000 was salvaged and retained by the insured. The business books and records were saved from which the following information was obtained.

Particulars	Rs.
Stock on 1-1-2015	1,00,000
Stock on 31-12-2015	1,40,000
Purchases for the year ended 31-12-2015	9,48,000
Sales for the year ended 31-12-2015	12,00,000
Purchases from 1-1-2016 to 15-9-2016	3,00,000
Sales from 1-1-2016 to 15-9-2016	4,10,000

In valuing the stock as on 31-12-2015 Rs. 8,000 had been written off certain stock having a cost of Rs. 18,000.

Half of these goods were sold in July 2016 for Rs. 10,000. The balance is estimated to be worth the original cost. Subject to the above exception, gross profit had remained at the uniform rate.

On 14th September 2016 goods worth Rs. 8,000 had been received by the godown-keeper but had not been entered in purchases account. Show the statement of the claim for loss of stock.

Solution :

Loss of Stock by fire in the premises of Red Ltd. on 15th Sept. 2016
Trading Account for the year 2015

	Rs.			Rs.
To Opening Stock	1,00,000	By Sales		12,00,000
(on 1-1-2015)		By Stock	1,40,000	
To Purchases	9,48,000	on31-12-2015		
To Gross Profit	3,00,000	Add the amt previously		
		written off	8,000	1,48,000
	13,48,000			**13,48,000**

The Gross Profit of Rs. 3,00,000 on sales amounting to Rs. 12,00,000 is 25% of Sales.

Estimated Trading A/c for the period 1-1-2016 to 15-9-2016

		Rs.			Rs.
To Stock on 1-1-2016	1,48,000		By Sales	4,10,000	
Less Abnormal item at			Less Proceeds from		
original cost	-18,000	1,30,000	the sale of 50% of the ab-		
			normal item	10,000	4,00,000
To Purchases	3,00,000		By Normal Stock		
Add Unrecorded			immediately before the		
Purchase at cost	+ 8,000		occurrence of fire		
		3,08,000	on 15-9-2016		
To Gross Profit @25%			(Balancing FIg.)		1,38,000
on sales of Rs.	4,00,000	1,00,000			
		5,38,000			**5,38,000**

1) Value of the stock held by Red Ltd. on the date of fire i.e. 15-9-2016

		Rs.
	(1) Normal items	1,38,000
+	(2) Abnormal item at its original cost	9,000
	(i.e. $\frac{1}{2}$ of Rs. 18000)	1,47,000

Rs. 1,47,000 was the value of all the stock (consisting of normal as well as abnormal items) held by Red Ltd. immediately before the occurrence of the fire on 15-9-2016.

2) Value of stock for insurance claim will be Rs. 1,35,000 arrived at as follows :

	Rs.
(1) Value of total stock	1,47,000
(2) Less Value of the salvaged stock	
Retained by the insured	-12,000
Value of stock destroyed by fire	1,35,000
i.e. value of stock for insurance claim	

3.4 Loss of Profit Policy

The fire not only destroys stock or assets but also causes distrurbance to the business and hence, the business concern-suffers reduction in usual profits. But to compensate such loss of profit, Insurance Co. issues a cover but before claiming the loss of profit there is a condition that you should have policy for the loss of stock and you have claimed for loss of stock. The procedure of calculation of claim is as given below.

3.4.1 Calculate Short Sales:

The short sales calculate as under

Particulars	Rs.
Estimated sales during the period of indemnity	....
Add : Increase in price (if any)	....
Less : Actual sales during the period of indemnity	
Short sales	....

- Indemnity period:

It is the period during which sales are expected to be affected due to fire, this period is mentioned in the policy.

The usual period is one year.

2. Calculate Gross Profit Rate:

The Gross profit rate calculated as under

$$\text{Gross Profit Rate} = \frac{\text{Net profit + Insured standing charges}}{\text{Annual Sales}} \times 100$$

- **Standing charges :**

These are the expenses required to be incurred irrespective of the fact whether the business activites are suspended or not. They includes wages & salary, rent, rates, taxes; insurance, directors fees, Auditors fees, depreciation, interest on loan etc.

3. Calculate Loss of Profit:

The loss of profit calculate as under

Loss of Profit = Short Sales × Gross Profit Rate

4. Calculate increase in cost of working (Working Expenses):

The increase in cost of working is calculated as under

$$= \frac{\text{Net profit + Insured standing charges}}{\text{Net profit + All standing charges}} \times \text{increased working expenses}$$

5. Average Clause :

If the amount of the policy is less than the Gross profit in the standard sales, the amount of claim is reduced in the ratio of amount of policy to Gross Profit in standard sales.

6. Insurance Claim :

The insarance claim can be calculated with the help of following fromula -

$$\text{Insurance claim} = \frac{\text{Amount of policy} \times \text{Amount of claim}}{\text{Gross Profit in standard sales}}$$

3.4.2 Important Point :

Besides insuring against loss of stocks or assets, businesses often take out loss of profit insurance to cover them against loss of profits if a fire (or other perils) interrupts their business. This insurance is designed to provide for indemnification of the insured for losses ensuing from the interruption, wholly or in part, of the normal business activities consequent upon a fire or other perils. Therefore, loss of profit insurance is an insured protection against loss of gross profit. Insuring from interruption of or interference as a result of destruction of or damage to any building or any other property of the insured premise by fire. While a fire policy covers loss of or damage to insured property, a loss of profit policy covers loss of gross profit sustained in consequence of a business interruption.

The terms of such policies vary widely, but they are usually framed to meet the requirements of the insured. A business interruption due to destruction of/ or damage to property by fire is likely to result in :

(a) the reduction in turnover during the period of indemnity and

(b) the increased cost of working incurred for the purpose of avoiding or reducing the reduction in turnover.

The claim for loss of profit insurance is granted only when the insured has a valid claim in respect of the property, the loss of or damage to which results in interruption, being admissible under a corresponding fire policy. Therefore, it is a basic condition that a business unit cannot have a loss of profit insurance policy without the presence of a fire policy covering property damage, giving rise to the loss of profit claim. The period of indemnity is the contemplated period of disorganisation for which loss of insurance policy is effected. The length of this period may vary with the nature of the business and required time to obtain new plant and machinery.

3.4.3 Some Important Terms

Gross Profit For loss of profit insurance purposes Gross Profit is the sum produced by adding the amount of the insured standing charges to the Net Profit. If there is net loss, gross profit is the amount of insured standing charges less such a proportion of any net trading loss as the amount of die insured standard charges bears to all the standing charges (insured + uninsured) of the business.

Net Profit The net trading profit (exclusive of all capital receipts and accretions and all outlay properly chargeable to Capital) resulting from the business of the insured at the premises after due provision has been made for all standing and other charges including depreciation but before the deduction of any taxation chargeable on profits.

Insured Standing Charges The insured standing charges are those charges specified in the policy which the insured desires to recover in the case of an accident. It may include the following :

   (i) Rent, rates and taxes (not related with the profit of the business);

  (ii) Interest on debentures and loans;

 (iii) Salaries of permanent staff;

 (iv) Wages of skilled workers;

  (v) Directors' fees;

 (vi) Auditor's fees;

(vii) Advertising;

(viii) Travelling; and

 (ix) Unspecified standing charges (not exceeding 5% of the amount of specified standing charges).

Turnover The money paid or payable to the insured for goods sold and delivered and for services rendered in course of the business at the premises.

Indemnity Period The period beginning with the occurrence of the damage and ending not later than 12 months thereafter during which the results of the business shall be affected in consequence of the damage.

Rate of Gross Profit The rate of Gross Profit earned on the turnover during the financial year immediately before the date of the damage.

Annual Turnover The turnover during the twelve months immediately before the date of the damage.

Standard Turnover The turnover during that period in the twelve months immediately before the date of damage which corresponds with the indemnity period

Memo 1 : If during the Indemnity Period goods shall be sold or services shall be rendered elsewhere than at the premises for the benefit of the business either by the insured or by others on his behalf the money paid or payable in respect of such sales or services shall be brought into account in arriving at the turnover during Indemnity Period.

Memo 2 : If any standing charges of the business be not insured by this policy then in computing the amount recoverable hereunder as increase in cost of working that proportion only of the additional expenditure shall brought into account which the sum of the net profit and the insured standard charges bears to the sum of net profit and all standing charges.

Example

From the following information calculate: (i) Standard Turnover; (ii) Short Sales; and (iii) Annual Turnover.

X Ltd. had taken a loss of profi policy for Rs 1,50,000 being Rs 65,000 for net profit and Rs 85,000 for standing charges. On 1st June 2016 there was a fire as a result of which sales suffered a lot for a period of 6 months. The indemnity period was 4 months

Month	2015 (Rs.)	2016 (Rs.)	Month	2015 (Rs.)	2016 (Rs.)
January	1,00,000	1,10,000	July	2,00,000	25,000
February	1,00,000	1,00,000	August	1,70,000	30,000
March	1,25,000	1,37,500	September	1,50,000	40,000
April	1,25,000	1,37,500	October	1,25,000	55,000
May	1,50,000	1,65,000	November	1,25,000	75,000
June	1,80,000	25,000	December	75,000	80,000

Solution :

Jan	Feb	Mar	Apr	May	Jun	July	Aug	Sep	Oct	Nov	Dec	Jan	Feb	Mar	Apr	May	Jun	July	Aug	Sep	Oct	Nov	Dec
				Standard Turnover Rs. 7,70,000 (Adjusted)												Indemnity Period (4 Months) Turnover Rs. 1,20,00							

Annual Turnover Rs. 18,53,500 (Adjusted)

Calculation of Standard Turnover

Particulars	Rs.
Sales from 1st June 2015 to 30th September 2015	7,00,000
Add : 10% for upward trend*	70,000
	7,70,000

* Sales from 1st January 2015 to 31st May2016 are 6,00,000; for the corresponding months of 2016, Sales is Rs. 6,60,00.

Therefore, increase in sales is 10%.

Particulars	Rs.
Standard Turnover	7,70,000
Less: Sales from 1st June 2016 to 30th September 2016	1,20,000
	6,50,000

Calculation of Annual Turnover (Adjusted)

Particulars	Rs.
Sales for 12 months immediately preceding the month of fire (i.e. 1st June, 2015 to 31st May 2016	16,85,000
Add : 10% increase for upward trend as noticed between 1-1-2016 and 31-5-2016	1,68,500
	18,53,500

3.4.4 Procedures to Ascertain Amount of Claim

The following steps are followed to arrive at the amount of a claim under loss of profit insurance :

Step 1 Calculate rate of gross profit (adjust to provide for the trend of the business, if any).

Step 2 Calculate short sales. (It is the difference between the standard sales (adjusted) and actual sales of dislocated period.

Step 3 Calculate gross profit on short sales.

Step 4 Calculate the amount of admissible additional expenses as follows :

The least of the following shall be taken as admissible additional expenses.

(i) Actual expenses incurred

(ii) Gross Profit on additional sales

(iii) Additional Expenses $\times \dfrac{\text{G.P. on Annual Turnover}}{\text{G.P. on Annual Turnover + Uninsured standing charges}}$

OR

$$\text{Additional Expenses} \times \frac{\text{Net Profit} + \text{Insured standing charges}}{\text{Net Profit} + \text{All standing charges}}$$

Step 5 Deduct from the sum of 3 and 4 any savings in insured standing charges during the period of indemnity.

Step 6 Apply average clause : $\text{Net Claim} = \text{Gross Claim} \times \dfrac{\text{Policy value}}{\text{G.P. on Annual Turnover}}$

3.4.5

PROBLEM NO. 1

From the following information, find the claims under a loss of profit policy: (all figures in rupees)

Sales in 2012	1,00,000	Policy value	50,000
Sales in 2013	1,20,000	Date of dislocation by fire	1-1-2016
Sales in 2014	1,44,000	Period of dislocation	3 months
Sales in 2015	1,72,800	Indemnity period	9 months
Standing charges		Sales from	
(all Insured) in 2015	7,280	1-1-2015 to 31-3-2015	43,200
Net prof it in 2015	10,000	Sales from	
		1-1-2016 to 31-3-2016	11,840

There was no reduction in standing charges during the dislocation period, nor were there any additional costs.

Solution :

(1) Grots Profit Ratio

Net Profit in 2015	10,000	Rate if Gross Profit	$= \dfrac{\text{Gross Profit}}{\text{Sales}} \times 100$
Insured standing charges	7,280		$= \dfrac{\text{Rs.}\,17,280}{\text{Rs.}\,1,72,800} \times 100$
Grots Profit	17,280		$= 10\%$

(2) Short Sales

(a) Standard Sate (adjusted)	Rs.	(b) Actual Sales of dislocated period = Rs 11,840
Sales from 1-1-2015 to 31-3-2015	43,200	Short Sales = Standard Sales - Actual Sales
Add : 20% increase	8,640	= Rs. 51,840 - Rs. 11,840 = Rs. 40,000
	51,840	
Sales figures of 2012 to 2015 clearly indicate 20% in year. So standard sales are to be adjusted accordingly		(3) Amount of Claim = Short Sales x Gross Profit ratio = Rs 40,000 x 10% = Rs 4,000 (The claim is payable in full, since the policy is adequate)

PROBLEM NO. 2

Bright Ltd. has a 'loss of profit' insurance policy of Rs 12,60,000. The period of indemnity is three months. A fire occured on 31st March 2016.

The following information is available (all figures in rupees):

Sales for the year ended 31st December 2015	42,00,000	Standing charges for 2015	9,60,000
Sales for the period from 1st April 2015 to 31st Mar.2016	18,00,000	Profit for 2015	3,00,000
Sales for the period from 1st April 2015 to 31st June.2016	10,80,000	Saving in standing charges because of fire	30,000
Sales for the period from 1st April 2016 to 31st June.2016	72,000	Additional expenses to reduce loss of turnover	60,000

Assuming no adjustment has to be made for the upward trend in turnover, compute the claim to be made on the insurance company.

Solution :

(1) Gross Profit Ratio

Net Profit in 2015	3,00,000	Rate if Gross Profit	$= \dfrac{\text{Gross Profit}}{\text{Sales}} \times 100$
Insured standing charges	9,60,000		$= \dfrac{\text{Rs. } 12,60,000}{\text{Rs. } 42,00,000} \times 100$
Gross Profit	12,60,000		$= 30\%$

(2) Short Sales

(a) Standard Sales (adjusted) Sales for the corresponding period in the preceding year, i.e., 1-4-2015 to 30-6-2015	Rs. 10,80,000	(b) Actual Sales of dislocated period = Rs 72,000 Short Sales = Standard Sales - Actual Sales = Rs 10,80,000 - Rs 72,000 = Rs. 10,08,000

(3) Loss of Gross Profit = Short Sales × Gross Profit ratio = Rs 10,08,000 × 30% = Rs. 3,02,400.

(4) Admissible increased working cost :

Lower of the following:

(a) Actual additional expenses to reduce loss of turnover = Rs 60,000.

(b) Gross profit on additional sales = Rs 72,000 X 30% = Rs 21,600.

(5) Statement of Claim

Particulars	Rs.
Loss of Gross Profit (Note 3)	3,24,000
Admissible increased working cost (Note 4)	21,600
	3,24,000
Less: Saving in insured standing charges	30,000
Gross Claim	2,94,000

(6) Application of Average Clause

$$\text{Net Claim} = \text{Gross Claim} \times \frac{\text{Policy Value}}{\text{G.P. on Annual Sales}}$$

$$= \text{Rs. } 2,94,000 \times \frac{\text{Rs. } 12,60,000}{30\% \text{ of Rs. } 48,00,000} = \text{Rs. } 2,57,250$$

Therefore, amount of claim under the policy = Rs 2,57,250.

Assumptions :

(1) All standing charges are insured; and

(2) All sales during indemnity period have been effected by incurring additional expenses.

PROBLEM NO. 3

A businessman took out a 'loss of profit policy' for Rs 40,000 with an indemnity period of 6 months. The financial year of the business ended on 30th June. Gross profit for the last financial year was Rs 50,000 and turnover for that period was Rs 2,00,000. Turnover for the 12 months immediately preceding the fire was Rs 2,20,000. A fire occured on 3 1 st March, 2016. Turnover for 6 months immediately following the fire, compared with the turnover of corresponding months in the previous year was :

	April	May	June	July	August	September
2015 (Rs.)	16,000	17,000	18,000	16,000	17,000	19,000
2016 (Rs.)	-	6,000	9,000	14,000	16,000	18,000

Rs 1,000 was spent on putting the fire out. During the indemnity period, increase in the cost of working directly attributable to sales amounted to Rs 8,050. All standing charges of the business were insured and paid.

From the above particulars, you are required to assess the loss and the amount payable by the insurance company as claim under the policy.

Solution :

$$1) \text{ Gross Profit Ratio} = \frac{\text{Gross Profit}}{\text{Sales}} \times 100 = \frac{\text{Rs. } 50,000}{\text{Rs. } 2,00,000} \times 100 = 25\%$$

2) Short Sales

(a) Standard Sales (adjusted)	**Rs.**	(b) Actual Sales from April to Sept 2016
Sales from 1-4-2015 to	1,03,000	= Rs. 63,000 Short Sales = Standard Sales
30-9-2015	10,300	- Actual Sales = Rs. 1,13,300 - Rs. 63,000
Add : 10% increase (Note 1)		= Rs. 50,300
	1,13,300	

3) Loss of Gross Profit = Short sales × Gross Profit ratio = 50,300 × 25% = Rs 12,575.

4) Admissible increased working cost

Lower of the following:

(a) Gross Profit on additional sales = 25% of Rs 63,000 = Rs 15,750.

$$\text{(b) Additional Expenses} \times \frac{\text{G.P. on Annual Turnover (Adjusted)}}{\text{G.P. on Annual Turnover (Adjusted)} + \text{Uninsured standard charges}}$$

$$= \text{Rs. } 8,050 \times \frac{\text{Rs. } 55,000}{\text{Rs. } 55,000 + \text{nil}} = \text{Rs } 8,050$$

5) Statement of Claim

Particulars	Rs
Loss of Gross Profit (Note 3)	12,575
Admissible insured working cost (Note 4)	8,050
Gross Claim	20,625

6) Application of Average Clause

$$\text{Net Claim} = \text{Gross Claim} \times \frac{\text{Policy Value}}{\text{G.P. on Annual Sales}}$$

$$= \text{Rs. } 20,625 \times \frac{\text{Rs. } 40,000}{\text{Rs. } 55,000} = \text{Rs. } 15,000$$

7) Total Claim

Amount of claim under policy	Rs. 15,000
Expenses for putting off fire	Rs. 1,000
	Rs. 16,000

Tutorial Note : Insurance company is liable to pay all expenses for putting off fire.

Working Note :

(1) Calculation of Upward Trend in Turnover

Turnover for the 12 months immediately preceding fire was Rs 2,20,000 and Sales of the previous accounting period were Rs 2,00,000. Increase in Sales Rs 20,000. Therefore, % of increase = 20,000 / 2,00,000 × 100 =10%.

PROBLEM NO. 4

A fire occured on 1st February 2016 in the Premises of Pioneer Ltd., a retail store, and business was partially disorganised up to 30th June 2007. The company was insured under a 'loss of profit' for Rs 1,25,000 with a six months period indemnity. From the following information, compute the amount of claim under the loss of Profit policy (all figures in rupee)

Actual turnover from 1st Feb. to 30th June 2016	80,000	Turnover from 1st February to 30th June 2015	2,00,000
Turnover from 1st Feb. 2015 to 31st January 2016	4,50,000	Net Profit for last financial year	70,000
Insured standing charges for last financial year	56,000	Total standing charges for last financial year	64,000
Turnover for the last financial year	4,20,000		

The company incurred additional expenses amounting to Rs 6,700 which reduced the loss in turnover. There was also a saving during the indemnity period of Rs 2,450 in the insured standing charges as a result of the fire.

There had been a considerable increase in trade since the date of the last annual accounts and it has been agreed that an adjustment of 15% be made in respect of the upward trend in turnover.

Solution :

(1) Gross Profit. Ratio

	Rs		
Net Profit for last financial year	70,000	Rate if Gross Profit =	$\dfrac{\text{Gross Profit}}{\text{Sales}} \times 100$
Insured standing charges	56,000	=	$\dfrac{\text{Rs.} 1,26,000}{\text{Rs.} 4,20,000} \times 100$
Grots Profit	1,26,000		= 30%

2) Short Sales

(a) Standard Sales (adjusted)	**Rs.**	(b) Actual Sales of disorganised period = 80,000
Sales from 1-2-2015 to	2,00,000	Short Sales = Standard Sales- Actual Sales
30-6-2015	30,000	= Rs. 2,30,000 - Rs. 80,000 = **1,50,000**
Add : 10% increase (expected)	2,30,300	

(3) Loss of Gross Profit = Short Sales × Gross Profit ratio = Rs 1,50,000 × 30%
= Rs. 45,000.

(4) Annual Turnover

Particulars	Rs
Turnover for 12 months immediately preceding the month of fire i.e. from 1-2-2015 to 31-01-2016	4,50,000
Add : 15% expected increase	67,500
	5,17,500
Gross Profit on Annual Turnover = 30% of 5,17,500	1,55,250

(5) Admissible increased working cost :

Lower of the following:

(a) Gross Profit on additional Sales = 30% of Rs. 80,000 = Rs. 24,000.

(b) Additional Expenses $\times \dfrac{\text{G.P. on Annual Turnover}}{\text{G.P. on Annual Turnover + Uninsured Standing Charges}}$

$= \text{Rs. } 6,700 \times \dfrac{\text{Rs. } 1,55,250 \text{ (Note 4)}}{\text{Rs. } 1,55,250 + \text{Rs. } 8,000^*} = \text{Rs. } 6,372$

*(Total standing charges - Insured standing charges)

(6) Statement of Claim

Particulars	Rs
Loss of Gross Profit (Note 3)	45,000
Admissible increased working cost (Note 5)	6,372
	51,372
Less : Saving in insured standing charges	2,450
Gross claim	48,922

(7) Application of Average Clause

$$\text{Net Claim} = \text{Gross Claim} \times \frac{\text{Policy Value}}{\text{Gross Profit on Annual Turnover}}$$

$$= \text{Rs. } 48,922 \times \frac{1,25,000}{1,55,250} = \text{Rs. } 39,390$$

Amount of claim under the policy = Rs 39,390.

Assumption : (1) All sales during indemnity period have been effected by increasing additional expenses only.

PROBLEM NO. 5

From the following information, you are required to work out the claim under the 'loss of profit' insurance policy.

(1) Cover - Gross profit Rs 1,00,000.

(2) Indemnity period - Six months.

(3) Damage - due to a fire accident on 28th December, accounting year ends on 31 st December.

(4) Net profit plus all standing charges in the prior accounting year - Rs 1,30,000.

(5) Standing charges uninsured - Rs. 25,000.

(6) Turnover of the last accounting year was Rs 5,00,000, the rate of gross profit being 25%.

(7) The annual turnover - namely the turnover for 12 months immediately preceding the fire - Rs. 5,20,000.

(8) As a consequence of fire, there was a reduction in certain insured standing charges at the rate of Rs 25,000 per annum.

(9) The standard turnover was Rs 2,60,000.

(10) Increased costs of working during the period of indemnity were Rs 20,000.

(11) Turnover during the period of indemnity was Rs 1,00,000 and out of this, turnover of Rs 80,000 was maintained due to increased costs of working.

Solution :

1) Gross Profit Ratio = 25% (given).

2) Short Sales = Standard Sales - Actual Sales = (Rs 2,60,000 (given) - Rs 1,00,000) = Rs 1,60,000.

3) Loss of Gross Profit = Short Sales × Gross Profit Ratio = Rs 1,60,000 × 25% = Rs 40,000.

4) Annual Turnover = Rs 5,20,000. Gross Profit on Annual Turnover = Rs 5,20,000 × 25 % = Rs 1,30,000.

5) Admissible Increased Working Cost:

Lower of the following:

(a) Gross Profit on additional Sales = 25% of Rs 80,000 = Rs 20,000.

$$\text{(b) Additional Exp.} \times \frac{\text{G.P. on Annual Turnover (Adjusted)}}{\text{G.P. on Annual Turnover (Adjusted)} + \text{Uninsured standard charges}}$$

$$= \text{Rs } 20,000 \times \frac{\text{Rs. } 1,30,000}{\text{Rs. } 1,30,000 + \text{Rs.}25,000} = \text{Rs } 16,774$$

6) Statement of Claim

Particulars	Rs
Loss of Gross Profit (Note 3)	40,000
Add: Admissible Increased Working Cost (Note 5)	16,774
	56,774
Less: Saving in Standing Charges (6 months)	12,500
Gross Claim	44,274

(7) Application of Average Clause

$$\text{Net Claim} = \text{Gross Claim} \times \frac{\text{Policy Value}}{\text{G.P. on Annual Sales}}$$

$$= \text{Rs. } 44,274 \times \frac{\text{Rs. } 1,00,000}{\text{Rs. } 1,30,000} = \text{Rs. } 34,057$$

Assumption : (1) Annual Turnover and Standard Turnover as given in the problem have already been adjusted for upward trend.

PROBLEM NO. 6

The premises of a company was partly destroyed by fire on 1 st March 2016; as a result of which the business was disorganised from 1st March to 31st July, 2016. Accounts are closed on 31st December every year. The Company is insured under a 'loss of profit' policy for Rs 7,50,000. The period of indemnity specified in the policy is 6 months. From the following information, you are required to compute the amount of claim under the loss of profit policy, (all figures in Rs)

Turnover for the year 2015,	40,00,000	Standard turnover for the	
Net profit for the year 2015	2,40,000	corresponding period in the	20,00,000
Insured standing charges	4,80,000	preceding year i.e. from	
Uninsured standing charges	80,000	1-3-2015 to 31-7-2015	
Turnover during the period of disloc.		Annual turnover for the year	
i.e. from 1-3-2016 to 31-7-2016	8,00,000	immediately preceding the	
Savings in insured standing charges	30,000	fire i.e. from 1-3-2015 to	
		28-2-2016	44,00,000
		Increased cost of working	1,50,000
		Reduction in turnover	
		avoided through increase in	
		working cost	400,000

Owing to reasons acceptable to the insurer, the "Special circumstances clause" stipulates for: (a) Increase of turnover (standard and annual) by 10% and (b) Increase of rate of gross profit by 2%.

Solution :

(1) Gross Profit Ratio

	Rs		
Net Profit in 2015	2,40,000	Rate if Gross Profit	$= \dfrac{\text{Gross Profit}}{\text{Sales}} \times 100$
Insured standing charges	4,80,000		$= \dfrac{\text{Rs. } 7,20,000}{\text{Rs. } 40,00,000} \times 100$
Grots Profit	7,20,000		$= 18\%$
		Revised Rate of G.P. = 18% + 2% increase = 20%.	

(2) Short Sate

(a) Standard Sales (adjusted)	Rs.	(b) Actual Sales of dislocated period
Sales from 1-3-2015 to	20,00,000	= Rs. 8,00,000 Short Sales = Standard Sales
31-7-2015	2,00,000	- Actual Sales = Rs. 22,00,000 - Rs. 8,00,000
Add : 10% increase (agreed)	22,00,000	= Rs.14,00,000

(3) Loss of Gross Profit

= Short Sales × Gross Profit Ratio = Rs 14,00,000 × 20% = Rs 2,80,000.

(4) Annual Turnover

Particulars	Rs.
Turnover for 12 months immediately preceding the month of fire, i.e. from 1-3-2015 to 28-2-2016	44,00,000
Add : 10% increase (agreed)	4,40,000
	48,40,000
Gross Profit on Annual turnover = 20% of Rs. 48,80,000 = Rs. 9,68,000	

(5) Admissible Increased Working Cost :

Lower of the following:

(a) Gross Profit on additional Sales = 20% of Rs 4,00,000 = Rs 80,000.

$$\text{(b) Additional Exp.} \times \frac{\text{G.P. on Annual Turnover}}{\text{G.P. on Annual Turnover + Uninsured standard charges}}$$

$$= \text{Rs } 1,50,000 \times \frac{\text{Rs. } 9,68,000}{\text{Rs. } 9,68,000 + \text{Rs. } 80,000} = \text{Rs. } 1,38,550$$

(6) Statement of Claim

Particulars	Rs
Loss of Gross Profit (Note 3)	2,80,000
Add: Admissible Increased Working Cost (Note 5) being lower	80,000
	3,60,000
Less: Saving in Insured standing charges Gross Claim	30,000
	3,30,000

(7) Application of Average Clause

$$\text{Net Claim} = \text{Gross Claim} \times \frac{\text{Policy Value}}{\text{G.P. on Annual Sales}}$$

$$= \text{Rs } 3,30,000 \times \frac{\text{Rs. } 7,50,000}{\text{Rs. } 9,68,000} = \text{Rs. } 2,55,682$$

PROBLEM NO. 7

A fire occured in the premises of a businessman on 31st January 2016, which destroyed stock. However, stock worth Rs 5,940 was salvaged. The company's insurance policy covers the following :

Stock - Rs 6,00,000; Loss of profit (including standing charges) - Rs. 3,75,000; and Period of indemnity - 6 months.

The summarised Profit and Loss Account for the year ended 31 st December 2015 is as follows: (all figures in rupees)

Dr. **Profit and Loss Account forthe year ended 3 1 st December 2015** **Cr.**

Particulars	Rs	Particulars	Rs
To Opening Stock	6,18,750	By Sales	30,00,000
To Purchases	27,18,750	By Closing Stock	7,87,500
To Standing charges	2,51,250		
To Variable expenses	1,20,000		
To Net Profit	78,750		
	37,87,500		**37,87,500**

The transactions for the month of January, 2016 were :

(i) Turnover - Rs. 1,50,000; and

(ii) Payment to creditors - Rs. 1,60,020.Trade Creditors : 1st January, 2016 - Rs. 26,000; 31st January, 2016 - Rs. 2,30,980.

The company's business was disrupted until 30th April, (2016) during which period the reduction in the turnover amounted to Rs 2,70,000 as compared with the corresponding turnover of same period in the previous year.

You are required to submit the claim for insurance for loss of stock and loss of profit.

Solution :

Loss of Stock

Dr. **Memorandum Trading Account for the period** **Cr.**
1st January to 31st January -2016

Particulars	Rs	Particulars	Rs.
To Opening Stock	7,87,500	By Sales	1,50,000
To Purchases (Note 3)	1,65,000	By Closing Stock	8,25,000
To Gross Profit @ 15% on		(Balancing figure)	
Sales (Note 2)	22,500		
	9,75,000		**9,75,000**

Statement of Claim for Loss of Stock as on 31st January, 2016

Particulars	Rs.
Book value of Stock	8,25,000
Less : Salvaged	5,940
Loss of Slock	**8,19,060**

The insurance policy for loss of stock was taken for Rs 6,00,000 but the value of stock on the date of fire was Rs 8,25,000. Therefore, the average clause is applicable.

$$\textbf{Net claim} = \text{Loss of stock} \times \frac{\text{Policy Value}}{\text{Value of stock on the date of fire}}$$

$$= \text{Rs. } 8{,}25{,}000 \times \frac{\text{Rs. } 6{,}00{,}000}{\text{Rs. } 8{,}25{,}000} = \text{Rs. } 5{,}95{,}680$$

Working Notes :

Dr.　　　　(1) **Trading Account for the year ended 31 st December 2015**　　　　Cr.

Particulars	Rs	Particulars	Rs.
To Opening Stock	6,18,750	By Sales	30,00,000
To Purchases	27,18,750	By Closing Stock	7,87,500
To Gross Profit	4,50,000		
	37,87,500		**37,87,500**

(2) Rate of Gross Profit = Rs 4,50,000 / Rs 30,00,000 × 100 = 15%.

Dr.　　　　　　(3) **Trade Creditors Account**　　　　　　Cr.

Particulars	Rs	Particulars	Rs.
To BankA/c	1,60,020	By Balance b/d	2,26,000
To Balance c/d	2,30,980	By Purchases (credit)	1,65,000
	3,91,000		**3,91,000**

Loss of Profit

(1) **Gross Proflt Ratio**

	Rs	
Net Profit in 2015	78,750	Rate of Gross Profit $= \dfrac{\text{Gross Profit}}{\text{Sales}} \times 100$
Insured standing charges	2,51,250	$= \dfrac{\text{Rs. } 3{,}30{,}000}{\text{Rs. } 30{,}00{,}000} \times 100$
Grots Profit	3,30,000	$= 11\%$

(2) Short Sales = Rs 2,70,000 (given).

(3) Amount of Claim = Short Sales × Gross Profit Ratio = Rs 2,70,000 × 11 % = Rs 29,700. (The claim is payable in full, since the policy is adequate).

Total claim = Rs 5,95,680 (Stock) + Rs 29,700 (Profit) = Rs 6,25,380.

PROBLEM NO. 8

A "loss of profit" policy was taken for Rs 80,000. Fire occured on 15th March, 2016 Indemnity period was for three months. Net profit for 2015 year ending on 31st December was Rs 56,000 and standing charges (all insured) amounted to Rs. 49,600. Determine insurance claims from the following details available from quarterly sales tax returns :

Sales	2013 (Rs)	2014 (Rs)	2015 (Rs)	2016 (Rs)
From 1 st January to 31st March	1,20,000	1,30,000	1,42,000	1,30,000
From 1st April to 30th June	80,000	90,000	1,00,000	40,000
From 1st July to 30th September	1,00,000	1,10,000	1,20,000	1,00,000
From 1 st October to 31 st December	1,36,000	1,50,000	1,66,000	1,60,000

Sales from 16-3-2015 to 31-3-2015 were Rs. 28,000.
Sales from 16-3-2016 to 31-3-2016 were Rs. Nil.
Sales from 16-6-2015 to 30-6-2015 were Rs 24,000.
Sales from 16-6-2016 to 31-6-2016 were Rs 6,000.

Solution :

(1) Gross Profit Ratio

	Rs.	
Net Profit in 2015	56,000	Rate of Gross Profit $= \dfrac{\text{Gross Profit}}{\text{Sales}} \times 100$
Insured standing charges	49,600	$= \dfrac{\text{Rs. } 1,05,600}{\text{Rs. } 5,28,000} \times 100$
Grots Profit	1,05,600	$= 20\%$

*(Rs 1,42,000 + Rs 1,00,000 + Rs 1,20,000 + Rs 1,66,000)

(2) Short Sales

(a) Standard Sales (adjusted)	
Indemnity period : 16-3-2016 to 15-6-2015 Standard sales are to be calculated on the basis of sales of corresponding period of the previous year, i.e., 16-3-2015 to 15-6-2015 in this problem, however, sales value for this period has not been given directly. Therefore, it is to be calculated part by part from the given information :	
(i) Sales for the period 16-3-2015 to 31-3-2015 (given)	28,000
(ii) Sales for the period 1-4-2015 to 15-6-2015	76,000
	1,04,000
Add : Upward trend in Sales 10% (Note 2)	10,400
	1,14,400

	Rs.
(b) Actual Sales of disorganised period	
Sales value from 16-3-2016 to 15-6-2016 has not been given directly.	
So it is also to be calculated part by part from the given information :	
(i) Sales for the period 16-3-2016 to 31-3-2016	Nill
(ii) Sales for the period 1-4-2016 to 15-6-2016 (Note. 3)	34,000
	34,000
Short Sales = Standard Sales - Actual Sales	
= Rs 1,44,400 - Rs 34,000 = Rs 80,400	

(3) Loss of Gross Profit = Short Sales × Gross Profit Ratio = Rs 80,400 × 20% = Rs 16,080.

(4) Application of Average Clause

$$\text{Net Claim} = \text{Gross Claim} \times \frac{\text{Policy Value}}{\text{Gross Profit on Annual Turnover}}$$

$$= \text{Rs } 16,080 \times \frac{\text{Rs.80,000}}{\text{Rs.1,19,680}} = \text{Rs } 10,749 \text{ (Approx.)}$$

Amount of claim under the policy = Rs 10,749.

Working Notes :

(1) Sales for the period 1-4-2015 to 30-6-2015	1,00,000
Less : Sales for the period 16-6-2015 to 30-6-2015 (given)	24,000
Sales for the period 1-4-2016 to 15-6-2016	76,000

(2) Calculation of Upward Trend in Sales

(a) Total Sales of 2014 = Rs. 4,80,000 less total sales of 2013
   = Rs. 4,36,000. Increase of Sales in 2014 over 2013
   = Rs 44,000. Therefore, % of increase = Rs. 44,000 /
   Rs. 4,36,000 × 100 = 10.09%.

(b) Total Sales of 2015 = Rs 5,28,000 less total Sales of 2014
   = Rs 4,80,000. Increase of Sales in 2015 over 2014
   = Rs 48,000. Therefore, % of increase = Rs 48,000 /
   Rs 4,80,000 × 100 = 10%.

Average Percentage of increase = (10.09% +10%) / 2 = 10% (Approx.)

PROBLEM NO. 9

From the following details, ascertain the value of a claim under a Loss of Profits policy :

Indemnity period 6 months; Value of Policy Rs. 50,000.

Date of fire - 1-10-2015. Dislocation up to 29-2-2016

Sales for 2014 accounting year	Rs. 2,40,000
Net Profit for 2014	26,000
Standing charges for 2014 (all covered)	34,000
Sales from 1-10-2014 to 30-9-2015	3,00,000
Sales from 1-10-2015 to 29-2-2016	15,000
Sales from 1-10-2014 to 29-2-2015	60,000

There was a clear 10% upward trend in business.

(ICWA Final, June, 1988)

Solution :

Period of indemnity   5 months

$$\text{Gross Profit Ratio for 2014} = \frac{\text{Net Profit + Insured Standing Charges}}{\text{Sales}} \times 100$$

$$= \frac{26,000 + 34,000}{2,40,00} \times 100$$

$$= \frac{60,000}{2,40,000} \times 100$$

$$= 25\%$$

Computation of Short Sales

	Rs.
Standard Turnover during period of indemnity	66,000
(60,000+10% of 60,000)	(–)
Actual Turnover	15,000
Short sales	51,000

Computation of Amount of Claim

	Rs.
Loss of Profit on Short Sales: 51,000 × 25%	12,750
Amount for which policy should have been taken	
(3,30,000 × 25/100)	82,500
Amount of Policy	50,000

$$\text{Amount of Claim after applying the average clause} = \frac{12,750 \times 50,000}{82,500} = 7,727$$

PROBLEM NO. 10

From the following details, determine the amount of claim under a loss of profit policy:

Indemnity period	-	4 months
Date of fire	-	1-4-1994
Dislocation continued upto	-	1-4-1994

		Rs.
Sum insured	-	60,000
Sales for the last accounting year	-	2,40,000
Net Profit for the last accounting year	-	34,000
Standing charges for the last accounting year all insured	-	26,000
Sales for the year dislocation period, i.e. 1-4-1994 to 1-8-1994	-	30,000
Sales for the year 1-4-1993 to 31-3-1994	-	3,20,000
Sales for the corresponding period in the preceding year i.e. 1-4-1993 to 1-8-1993		1,00,000

The policy contains 'special circumstances clause which stipulates for increase of turnover (standard and annual) by 10% as there is an upward trend in the business.

(CS Inter June, 1995)

Solution :

COMPUTATION OF CLAIM AMOUNT

(1) Dislocation period of 4 months is completely covered by the policy.

(2) Short Sales   Rs.

Standard Turnover for the corresponding period in the preceding year i.e. 1-4-1993 to 1-8-1994	1,00,000
Add : Allowed increase of 10% for Upward Trend	10,000
Adjusted Standard Turnover	1,10,000
Less : Actual Turnover in the dislocation period	30,000
Short Sales	80,000

(3) Gross Profit Ratio (based on trading results for 1993)

$$\text{Gross Profit Ratio} = \frac{\text{Net Profit} + \text{Insured Standing Charges}}{\text{Turnover}} \times 100$$

$$= \frac{34,000 + 26,000}{2,40,000} \times 100$$

$$= \frac{60,000}{2,40,000} \times 100 = 25\%$$

(4) Loss of Gross Profit on Short Sales   =   Short Sales × Gross Profit Ratio

                       =   Rs. 80,000 × 25/100 = Rs. 20,000

(5) Application of Average Clause :

Annual Turnover preceding the date of fire	3,20,000
Add: Allowed increase of 10% for upward trend	32,000
Adjusted Annual Turnover	3,52,000

Insurable amount for the Loss of Profit :

$$\frac{25 \times Rs.3,52,000}{100} = Rs.\ 88,000$$

Applying Average Clause:

$$\text{Sum Insured Amount of Net Claim} = \text{Loss of Profit} \times \frac{\text{Sum Insured}}{\text{Actual Insurable Value}}$$

$$= \frac{Rs.20,000 \times Rs.60,000}{Rs.88,000} = Rs.\ 13,636$$

PROBLEM NO. 11

A fire occurred on 1-2-1995 in the premises of Unfortunate Ltd. and business was partially disorganised upto 30-6-1995

From the books of accounts, the following information was extracted :

		Rs.
(a) Actual turnover from	1-2-1995 to 30-6-1995	75,000
(b) Turnover from	1-2-1994 ti 30-6-1994	2,10,000
(c) Turnover from	1-2-1994 to 31-1-1995	4,50,000
(d) Net profit for last financial year		70,000
(e) Insured standing charges for the last financial year		56,000
(f) Total standing charges for the year		64,000
(g) Turnover for the last financial year		4,20,000

The company incurred additional expenses amounting to Rs. 6,700 which reduced the loss in turnover. There was also a saving during the indemnity period of Rs. 2,450 in the insured standing charges as a result of the fire.

The Company holds a "Loss of Profit" Policy for Rs. 1,24,200 having an indemnity of 6 months.

There has been a considerable increase in trade since the date of the last annual accounts and it had been agreed that an adjustment of 15% be made in respect of the upward trend in turnover.

Compute the Claim under the policy.

(C.A. Inter May, 1994)

Solution : (i)

COMPUTATION OF SHORT SALES

Particulars	Rs.
Turnover from 1-2-1994 to 30-6-1994	2,10,000
Add : 15% Upward trend in turnover	31,500
Expected Turnover	2,41,500
Less : Actual Turnover from 1-1-1995 to 30-6-1995	(–)75,000
Short Sales	
	1,66,500

(ii) Rate of Gross Profit:

$$= \frac{\text{Net Profit for Last Financial year + Insured Standing Charges}}{\text{Turnover for the Last Financial Year}} \times 100$$

$$= \frac{\text{Rs. } 70,000 + \text{Rs.} 56,000}{\text{Rs.} 4,20,000} \times 100 = 30\ \%$$

(iii) Amount of Gross claim :

	Rs.
Gross Profit on Short Sales (30% of Rs. 1,66,500)	49,950
Add : Admissible Additional Expenses (WN1)	6,300
	56,250
Less : Saving in Insured Standing Charges	2,450
	53,800

(iv) Application of Average Clause :

	Rs.
Anual Turnover, i.e. Turnover from 1-2-1994 to 31-1-1995	4,50,000
Add : 15% Upward trend (WN 2)	67,500
Adjusted Annual Turnover	5,17,500
Gross Profit on Adjusted Annual Turnover (at 30%)	1,55,250
Amount for which policy have been taken	1,24,200

The actual policy amount is less than gross profit on adjusted annual turnover, the average clause is applicable.

$$\text{Hence, the amount of Claim is} \quad = \frac{\text{Rs.} 1,24,200}{\text{Rs.} 1,55,250} \times \text{Rs. } 53,800$$

$$= \text{Rs } 43,040$$

Working Notes :

1. Admissible Additional Expenses : The additional expenses admissible is limited to the lower of the following:

   (i) Gross Profit earned on sales during disturbed period arising from additional expenses
   = 30% of Rs. 75,000 = Rs. 22,500

   (ii) Additional Expenses $\times \dfrac{\text{Net Profit} + \text{Insured Standing Charges}}{\text{Net Profit} + \text{All Standing Charges}}$

   $$\text{Rs. } 6,700 \times \frac{70,000 + 56,000}{70,000 + 64,000} = \frac{6,700 \times 1,26,000}{1,34,000}$$

   $$= \text{Rs, } 6,300$$

2. In the absence of information, it has been assumed that 15% upward trend is applicable to entire annual turnover.

PROBLEM NO. 12

Hirro Idnani effected a policy of insurance covering loss of Profits and Standing Charges to the extent of Rs. 46,000 (based on the previous year's profits) plus an allowance of Rs. 8,000 for Profits and Standing charges expected to accrue from increased turnover, the period of indemnity being three months. The turnover for the previous year ended 28th Feb. was Rs 1,12,500 and for the ensuring year was estimated at Rs 1,35,000. A fire occurred on 1st October. The following relative figures have been ascertained :

Month	Sales Previous year Rs.	Sales Budget Rs (Current Year) (Previous Year + 20%)	Actual Sales Rs.
October	9,750	11,700	Nil
November	10,500	12,600	Nil
December	9,000	10,800	2,100

Upon investigation, it was found that the increased sales for the past seven months were over-estimated by 50% and that the ratio of expense was consistent with such reduction.

The additional expenses of carrying on the business during the partial disablement amounted to Rs 850.

Prepare Statement of Claim against the insurance company and show workings.

(CS Inter NS, December 1977)

Solution :

Computation of Short Sales

The sales for the past seven months of the current year are only 10% above the preceding period's sales, hence the standard sales in the indemnity period of 3 months are :

	Rs.				Rs.		Rs.		Rs.
October	9,750	+	10%	=	9,750	+	975	+	10,725
November	10,500	+	10%	=	10,500	+	1,050	+	11,550
December	9,000	+	10%	+	9,000	+	900	=	9,900
									32,175

$$\text{Short Sales} = \text{Standard Sales - Actual Sales}$$
$$= 32,175 - 2,100$$
$$= \text{Rs. } 30,075$$

Adjusted Insured Gross Profit Ratio

$$= \frac{46,000 + 4,000 \text{ (for increases*)}}{1,12,500 + 11,250 \text{ (for increases*)}} = \frac{50,000}{1,23,750} = 40.4\% \text{ approx.}$$

*See working note

Computation of Permissible Additional Expenses

Permissible increased working cost is subject to the ceiling of amount derived from the application on adjusted Gross Profit Ratio to die avoidance of reduction in sales (assumed to be equal to the actual sales of Rs 2,100) in the interruption period:

$$40.4\% \times \text{Rs } 2,100 = \text{Rs } 848$$

Amount of Claim = Loss of Profit on Short Sales + Increased Cost of Workings
$$= \text{Rs } 12,150 + \text{Rs. } 848$$
$$= \text{Rs } 12,998 \text{ or Rs } 13,000 \text{ approx.}$$

Working Note :

Rs 8,000 was insured as an extra allowance for expenses on account of increased turnover. It was expected that turnover would increase by 20% in the ensuring year. However, as stated in the question, that there was an over-estimation by 50%. In other words the increase in sales would be only 10% and not 20%. Moreover, the ratio of expenses was also consistent with such reduction. The increased expenses have therefore been taken only as Rs 4,000 in place of Rs 8,000 for computing adjusted Gross Profit Ratio.

Loss of Profit = Short Sales × Adjusted G.P. Ratio
$$= \text{Rs. } 30,075 \times 40.4\% \text{ Rs. } 12,150$$

PROBLEM NO. 13

A fire occurred in the premises of Bala Shoe Co. Ltd. on 1st May, 1995. The company had a loss of profit policy for Rs 1.20 lakhs. Sale from 1st May 1994 30ᵗʰ April, 1995 were Rs. 10 lakhs from 1st May 1994 August, 1994 being Rs 3 lakh. During the indemnity period which lasted four months sales amounted to only Rs 40,000. The company made up its accounts on 31ˢᵗ December. The Profit and Loss Account for 1994 given below:

PROFIT & LOSS ACCOUNT
For the year 1994

Particulars	Rs	Particulars	Rs
Opening Stock	1,00,000	Sales	9,50,000
Purchases	6,00,000	Closing Stockg	50,000
Manufacturing Expenses	67,000		
Variable Selling Expenses	90,500		
Fixed Expenses	72,500		
Net Profit	70,000		
	10,00,000		**10,00,000**

Comparing the sales of first four months of 1994 those of 1994, it was found that sales were 20% higher in 2016. Ascertain the loss of profit.

(CS Inter, June, 1989)

Solution :

	Rs.
Computation of Short Sales :	
Sales from 1st May 1994 to 31st August, 1994	3,00,000
Add : 20% increase observed in 1994 over 1994	60,000
	3,60,000
Less : Sales from 1st May, 1995 to 31st August, 1995	40,000
Short Sales	3,20,000

PROBLEM NO. 14

From the following information, find out the claims under a Loss of Profits Policy :

	Rs.
Sales in 1991	1,00,000
Sales in 1992	1,20,000
Sales in 1993	1,44,000
Sales in 1994	1,72,800
Net Profit in 1994	10,000
Standing Charges (all insured) in 1994	7,280
Date of dislocation by fire	1-1-2016
Period of dislocation	3 months
Sales from 1-1-1994 to 31-3-1994	43,200
Sales from 1-1-1995 to 31-3-1995	11,840
Indemnity Period	9 months
Policy Value	50,000

There was no reduction in standing charges during the dislocation period nor were there any additional costs.

(CA Inter. N.S., Nov., 1975, adapted)

Solution :

Computation of Claim for Loss of Profits

1. Computation of Gross Profit Ratio :

	Rs.
Net Profit in 1994	10,000
Insured Standing Charges	7,280
Gross Profit	17,280

$$\text{Gross Profit Ratio} = \frac{\text{GrossProfit}}{\text{Sales}} \times 100$$

$$= \frac{17,280}{1,72,800} \times 100$$

2. Computation of Short Sales :

	Rs
Sales from Jan. 1994 March, 31, 1994	43,200
Add : 20% increase (on the basis of past figures of sales)	8,640
Standard Sales	51,840
Sales from Jan.1, 1995 to March 31, 1995,	11,840
Short Sales	40,000

3. Amount of Claim : 10% on Rs 40,000 — 4,000

PROBLEM NO. 15

A fire occurred on 1st July 1992 in the premises of Arolite Ltd. and business was practically disorganised up to 30th November, 1992 From the books of account, the following information was extracted :

(1)	Actual turnover from 1st July 1991 to 30th Nov. 1992	60,000
(2)	Turnover from 30-11-1991	2,00,000
(3)	Net Profit for the last financial year	90,000
(4)	Insured Standing Charges for the last financial year	60,000
(5)	Turnover for the last financial year	5,00,000
(6)	Turnover for the year ending 30th June 1992	5,50,000
(7)	Total Standing Charges for the year	72,000

The company incurred additional expenses amounting to Rs. 9,000 which reduced the loss in turnover. There was also a saving during the indemnity period of Rs 2,486.

The company holds a "Loss of Profit" policy for Rs 165,000 having an indemnity period for 6 months. There has been a considerable increase in trade and it had been agreed that an adjustment of 20% be made in respect of upward trend in turnover.

Compute claim under "Loss of Profit Insurance".

(CA Inter. NS, Nov. 1981, adapted)

Solution :

Claim for Loss of Profit

	Rs
Short Sales :	
Standard Turnover : Sales from 1-7-1991 to 30-11-1991	2,00,000
Add : 20% for increase in sales	40,000
Standard sales to form 1-7-1992 to 30-1-1992	2,40,000
Less : Sales during the indemnity period, 1-7-1992 to 30-11-1992	60,000
Short-Sales	1,80,000
Gross Pro/if on Short Sales @ 30%	54,000

Additional Expenses will be allowed lowest of the following:

(i) Actual $= 9,000$

(ii) Gross Profit on additional sales 30% of 60,000 $= 18,000$

(iii) Additional Expenses $\times \dfrac{\text{Net Profit + Insured Standing Charges}}{\text{Net Profit + All Standing Charges}}$

$$90,000 \times \dfrac{90,000 + 60,000}{90,000 + 72,000} \qquad\qquad 8,333$$

62,333

Less : Saving in Expenses
Claim subject to average clause
Application of Average Clause:

$$\text{Net Claim} = \text{Amount of Claim} \times \frac{\text{Sum Assured}}{\text{Gross Profit on Annual Turnover (Adjusted)}}$$

= 59,847 × 1,65,000 / 1,98,000* = Rs 49,872

*30% of Rs 6,60,000 (ie., Rs 5,50,000 + 20%)

Working Notes :

	Rates of Gross Profit	Rs
(i)	Sales in the last financial year	5,00,000
(ii)	Net Profit (+) insured standing charges of last financial year	1,50,000
(iii)	Rate of Gross Profit 30%	

PROBLEM NO. 16

The premises of a company were partly destroyed by fire which took place on 1st March, 1992 and as a result of which the business was disorganised from 1st March to 31st July 1992. Accounts are closed on 31st December every year. The company is insured under a Loss of Profits policy for 7,50,000. The period of indemnity specified in the policy is 6 months. From the following information, you are required to compute the amount of claim under the Loss or Profits policy :

	Rs
Turnover for the year 1991	40,00,000
Net Profits for the year 1991	2,40,000
Insured standing charges	4,80,000
Uninsured standing charges	80,000
Turnover during the period of dislocation i.e., from 1-3-1992 to 31-7-1992	8,00,000
Standard turnover for the year immediately preceding the fire i.e., from 1-3-1991 to 29-2-1992	44,00,000
Increased cost of working	1,50,000
Savings in insured standing charges	30,000
Reduction in turnover avoided through increase in working cost	4,00,000

Owing to reasons acceptable to the insurer, the "special circumstances clause" stipulates for :

(a) Increase of turnover (Standard and annual) by 10% and

(b) Increase of rate of gross profit by 2%.

(CA Inter, May,1983 adapted)

Solution :

Computation of Amount of Claim for the Loss of Profit

(i) Computation of Short Sales :

Turnover for the corresponding period in the preceding year i.e., from 1st March, 1991 to 31st July 1991		20,00,000
Add :	Agreed increase for upward trend @ 10%	2,00,000
	Standard Turnover	22,00,000
Less :	Actual turnover in the dislocation period	8,00,000
	Short Sales	14,00,000
	Gross Profit on short sales® 20%	2,80,000
Add :	Increased cost of working, limited to the Gross Profit on Sales resulting from the increased cost	80,000
		3,60,000
Less :	Saving in Insured Standing Charges	30,000
	Gross Claim	3,30,000

Application of Average Clause :

$$\text{Gross Claim} \times \frac{\text{Amount of Policy}}{\text{G.P. on Annual (Adjusted) Turnover}}$$

$$3,30,000 \times (7,50,000/9,68,000) = \text{Rs } 2,55,680$$

Working Notes :

(i) Period of Claim : Dislocation period (being less than indemnity period) i.e. 5 months from 1st March, 1992 to 31st July, 1992

(ii) Gross Profit Ratio based on the trading results of the last accounting year i.e.1991 has been ascertained as follows:

$$\text{G.. P. Ratio} = \frac{\text{Net Profit} + \text{Insured Standing Charges}}{\text{Sales}} \times 100$$

$$= \frac{2,40,000 + 4,80,000}{40,00,000} \times 100 = 18\%$$

Adjusted Gross Profit Ratio = 18% + Agreed Increase by 2% = 20%

(iii) Increased Cost of Working: The amount restricted to the minimum of the following :

(a) Saving in the liability of Insurer

20% on Rs. 4,00,000   Rs 80,000

(b) $$\frac{\text{Increased cost of Working} \times \text{Net Profit} + \text{Insured Standing Charges}}{\text{Net Profit} + \text{All Insurable Standing Charges}}$$

$$= 1,50,000 \times 2,40,000 + 4,80,000 / 2,40,000 + 5,60,000$$

$$= 1,50,000 \times 7,20,000 / 8,00,000$$

$$= \text{Rs. } 1,35,000$$

(c) The amount of gross profit on short sales plus increased working expenses should not exceed the amount of gross profit on standard turnover i.e. $22,00,000 \times (20/100) = \text{Rs. } 4,40,000$.

The amount of the claim for increased cost of working will, therefore be restricted to Rs.80,000.

(d) Annual adjusted turnover

		Rs
	Sales for 12 months immediately preceding the date of fire	44,00,000
Add :	Increase in turnover as agreed 10%	4,40,000
		48,40,000
	Gross Profit on Annual adjusted turnover $48,40,000 \times 20/100 =$	Rs. 9,68,000

PROBLEM NO. 17

A fire occurred on 1st February 1995 in premises of Pioneer Ltd., a retail store and business was partially disorganised up to 30th June 1995. The company was insured under a loss of profits for Rs. 1,25,000 with a six months period indemnity. From the following information, compute the amount of claim under the loss of profit policy.

	Rs.
Actual turnover from 1 st February to 30th June 1995	80,000
Turnover from 1st February to 30th June 1994	2,00,000
Turnover from 1st February to 1994 to 31st January 1995	4,50,000
Net Profit for last financial year	70,000
Insured standing charges for last financial year	56,000
Total standing charges for last financial year	64,000
Turnover for the last financial year	4,20,000

The Company incurred additional expenses amounting to Rs 6,700 which reduced the loss in turnover. There was also a saving during the indemnity period of Rs 2,450 in the insured standing charges as a result of the fire.

There had been a considerable increase in trade since the date of the last annual accounts and it has been agreed that an adjustment of 15% be made in respect of the upward trend in turnover.

(CA Inter, May 1988)

Solution :

Computation of Amount of Claim for Loss of Profit

	Rs.
Loss of Sales :	
Turnover from 1st Feb.1994 to 30th June 1994	2,00,000
Add : 15%expected increase	30,000
	2,30,000
Less : Actual turnover from 1st Feb 1995 to 30th June 1995	80,000
Shot Sales	1,50,000
Gross Profit on Short Sales	45,000
@ 30% on Rs. 1,50,000 (see Working Note 1)	
Add : Additional Expenses:	
(1) Actual	Rs 6,700

(2) $$\frac{\text{Additional Expenses} \times \text{Net Profit} + \text{Insured Standing Charges}}{\text{Net Profit} + \text{All Standing Charges}}$$

$6,700 \times 70,000 + 56,000/70,000 + 64,000 = 6,300$	6,300
(lower of the two)	51,300
Less : Savings in Insured Standing Charges	2,450
Amount of claim before application of Average Clause	48,850

Insurance Claims

Application of Average Clause:

$$= \frac{\text{Amount of Policy}}{\text{Amt. for which policy should have been taken}} \times \text{Amount of Claim}$$

$$= \frac{1,25,000}{1,55,250} \times 48,850 \times \text{Rs } 39,332$$

Amount of claim under the policy = Rs. 39,332

Working Notes :

(i) Rate of Gross Profit for the last financial year

$$= \frac{\text{Net Profit} + \text{Insured Standing Charges}}{\text{Sales}} \times 100$$

$$= \frac{70,000 + 56,000}{4,20,000} \times 100$$

$$= \frac{12,600}{42,000} \times 100 = 30\%$$

(ii) Annual Turnover :

Turnover from 1st Feb, 1994 to 31st January, 1995	4,50,000
Add : 15% expected increase	67,500
	5,17,500
Amount for which policy should have been taken - Rs 5,17,500 @ 30%	1,55,250

PRPBLEM NO. 18

M/s Amar Traders are insured under a loss of profit policy for Rs. 1,26,000. Their books of A/cs are closed on 31st December each year. The fire occurred in the premises of the business on 1-7-1998

The recods saved disclosed the following information :	**Rs.**
Turnover during the year ended 30-6-1998	14,40,000
Turnover during the ended 31-12-1997	12,00,000
Turnover from 1-7-1998 to 30-9-1998	60,000
Turnover in the corresponding period of 1997	3,60,000
Standing charges for the year ending 31-12-1997	72,000
Net Profit during the year ending 31-12-1997	48,000

It has been ascertained that the business has consistently shown an increase of 25% in turnover in the months preceding the fire over corresponding period of the previous year.

Caluculate the amount of the claim.

(Pune Univ. T.Y.B.Com. April 1999)

Solution :

Insurance Policy taken by Amar Traders for Rs. 1,26,000

Basic Data : Last Accounting Year 1997

Current Accounting Year 1998

Date of fire 1-7-1998

Period of Indemnity or Dislocation 1-7-1998 to 30-9-1998

i.e. 3 months.

1. **Short Sales :** Standard Tunover	3,60,000
Add : 25% increase that was expected in the sales of the indemnity period	+ 90,000
	4,50,000
Less : Actual Turnover in the Indemnity period (or period of dislocation)	−60,000
Shortage in turnover	3,90,000

2. Gross Profit Rate :
Formula :

$$= \frac{\text{Net profit in the Last Accounting Year (i.e. 2015)} + \text{Insured standing charges in the Last Accounting Year}}{\text{Sales in the Last Accouning Year (i.e. 2015)}} \times 100$$

$$= \frac{\text{Rs.}48,000 + \text{Rs.}72,000}{\text{Rs.}12,00,000} \times 100 = \frac{1,20,000}{12,00,000} \times 100 = 10\%$$

= Gross Profit Rate is 10% on sales

3. Loss of Profit : 10 % of short sales = 10% of Rs. 3,90,000

$$= \text{Rs. } 39,000$$

Gross claim before application of the Average Clause is Rs. 39,000

4. Application of the Average Clause :

Formula : $\dfrac{\text{Actual Insurance}}{\text{Insurance Cover required}} \times \text{Gross Claim}$

How much insurance was required in a particular case is determined by applying the Gross Profn Rate to the Annual Turnover adjusted for any upward or downward trend in sales. Annual Turnover means the Turnover achieved in the twelve months immediately preceding the dale of fire - in this case in the twelve months ending on 30-6-1998

Annual Turnover in the year ending on 30-6-1998	<u>14,40,000</u>
+ Plus Adjustment for an upward trend of 25% in sales	3,60,000
Adjusted Annual Turnover	18,00,000

By applying the G. P. Rate to the' adjusted annual turnover we can arrive at the figure of the exact insurance cover that was required in this case :

10 % of Rs 18,00,000 = Rs. 1,80,000. Actual insurance is only Rs. 1,26,000 which means there is underinsurance.

$$= \frac{\text{Actual Insurance}}{\text{Insurance required}} \times \text{Gross Claim}$$

$$= \frac{1,26,000}{1,80,000} \times 39,000 = \text{Rs. } 27,300$$

Net claim for Loss of profit Rs. 27,300

PROBLEM NO. 19

In the dislocation period (four months) covered by a Consequential Loss Policy (Rs. 30.000/-), a sale of Rs. 20,000/- was obtained out of which Rs. 8.000/- sale was received from another premises,hired for this period at a rent of Rs. 200/- per month on temporary basis. However, there was saving in Insured Standing Charges during this period @ Rs. 1.200/-per annum.

Sale in the same period last year amounted to Rs. 60.000/- and an upward trend of 10% in the business was expected in the current year. Sales in the 12 months immediately preceding fire were Rs. 2,00,000/-. The following information is available from the last year's Profit and Loss Account.

- Sales   -   Rs. 1,80,000/-
- Net profit   -   Rs. 20,000/-
- Standing Charges   -   Rs. 20,000/- (Out of which Rs. 4,000/- uninsured)
   Calculate the claim

Solution :

Loss of Profit Insurance

1. **Short Sales**	Rs.	Rs.
Standard turnover	60,000	
Add Adjustment for an expected upward trend in sales @ 10%	+ 6,000	
		66,000
Less actual turnover in the dislocation Period of 4 months		20,000
Short Sales		46,000

2. Gross Profit Ratio :

Formula :

$$= \frac{\text{Net Profit in the Previous Acounting Year} + \text{Insured standing charges (LAY)}}{\text{Sales in the Previous Accounting Year}} \times 100$$

$$= \frac{\text{Rs.} 20,000 + \text{Rs.} 16,000}{\text{Rs.} 1,80,000} \times 100$$

$$= \text{i.e.} \frac{36,000}{1,80,000} \times 100 = 20\%$$

3. Loss of Profit :

Determined by applying G. P. rate to short sales

∴ 20% on Rs. 46,000   Rs. 9,200.

4. Add Extra Compensation for Extra Expenses :

(incurred to get Extra Sales): Extra Costs incurred Rs. 800

(subject to a maximum of Rs. 1,600 i.e. 20% of Extra

Sale obtained i.e. Rs. 8,000)

Formula :

$$= \frac{\text{N.P. in the Last Accouming Year + Insured standing charges in the Last Accounting Year}}{\text{N.P. in the Last Accounting Year +All standing charges}} \times \text{Extra Costs incurred}$$

$$= \frac{\text{Rs.20,000 + Rs.16,000}}{\text{Rs.20,000 + Rs. 20,000}} \times 800$$

$$= \frac{36,000}{40,000} \times 800 = \frac{9}{10} \times 800 \qquad\qquad = \frac{720}{9,920} \quad \text{i.e. } 9,200 + 720$$

Less : $\dfrac{\text{Saving in insured standing charges - 400}}{\text{(@Rs. 1,200 per annum for 4 months) Gross Claim Rs. 9,520}}$

5. Average Clause : Formula :

$$= \frac{\text{Sum Insured}}{\text{Insurance Cover required in the case under consideration}} \times \text{Gross claim}$$

$$= \frac{\text{Rs. 30,000}}{\text{Rs. 44,000}} \times \text{Rs. 9,520} = \frac{15}{22} \times 9,520$$

$$= \frac{71,400}{11} = \text{Rs. 6,491 approx.}$$

6. Net Claim : After application of the Average Clause Rs. 6,491.

Notes :

1. For solving problems of this type I have followed the method used by Prof. Pickles and the Institute of Chartered Accoutants of India.

2. To encourage the insured to obtain sales; even during the period of dislocation, the insurance companies agree to; pay a suitable compensation for any extra costs incurred by the insured to get additional sales. These costs are described as "the extra costs" incurred to mitigate (i.e. lessen) the loss.

   If the extra sales obtained in the indemnity / dislocation period as a result of extra costs are not separately mentioned in the problem we have to assume that all the sales obtained in that period are additional sales .

A reduction is made in the compensation payable for additional costs incurred to get extra sales, if all the insurable standing charges were not insured by the insured, that is, there was under-insurance in respect of the fixed or standing charges.

3. Prof. Pickles uses the G. P. rate to ascertain the loss of profit and at the last stage applies the Average Clause, in case there is underinsurance.

PROBLEM NO. 20

M/s. Sudarshan Traders is insured under a loss of profit policy for Rs. 12,400. The books of accounts are closed on 31st December each year. The fire occurred on 1-7-2009.

The records saved disclosed the following information :

Particulars	Rs.
i) Turnover during the year ended 30-6-2009	1,44,000
ii) Turnover during the year ended 31-12-2008	1,20,000
iii) Turnover from 1-7-2009 to 30-9-2009	6,000
iv) Turnover from 1-7-2009 to 30-9-2009	36,000
v) Standing charges for the year ending 31-12-2008	7,200
vi) Net profit during the year ending 31-12-2008	4,800
vii) It has been ascertained that the business has consistently shown an increase of 25% in turnover in the months preceding the fire over corresponding period of the previous year. Calculate the amount of claim.	

(P. U. April 2004) (P. U. Oct 2004)

Solution :

In the books of M/s. Sudarshan Traders

A) Calculation of Short Sales   **Rs.**

Turnover from 1-7-2008 to 30-9-2008	36,000
Add : 25% increase	9,000
Estimated turnover	45,000
Less : Actual turnover from 1-7-2009 to 30-9-2009	6,000
Short Sales	39,000

B) Calculation of Gross profit Rate.
Gross Profit Rate :

$$= \frac{\text{Net Profit + Insured Standing Charges}}{\text{Sales for the last acounting year}} \times 100$$

$$= \frac{4800 + 7200}{1,20,000} \times 100 = 10\%$$

C) Indemnity Ratio

$$= \frac{\text{Sum Insured}}{\text{Adjusted Sales for twelve months immediately preceding the date of fire}} \times 100$$

$$= \frac{12,400}{144000 + 36,000} \times 100$$

$$= \frac{12,400}{1,80,000} \times 100$$

$$= 6.9\,\%$$

$$= \text{i.e. } 7\,\%$$

D) Calculation of claim :

Claim- for loss profit = Short Sales × Lower of the two percentages

$$= \frac{39,000}{100} \times 7$$

$$= \text{Rs. } 2,730$$

PROBLEM NO. 21

From the following particulars, find out the amount of claim for loss of profit

Date of Fire : 30-6-2010

Period of indemnity : Six months

Amount of policy : Rs. 40,000

Net profit for the accounting year 31st March 2009 Rs. 12,500

Sales for the year ended 30-6-2009 Rs. 2,00,000

Standing charges for the accounting year 31-3-2009 : Rs. 28,500.

Turnover for the year ending 31-3-2009 : Rs. 1,98,000

Turnover for the indemnity period from 1-7-2009 to 31-12-2009 Rs. 56,000

Turnover for the period from 1-7-2008 to 31-12-2008 Rs. 1,10,000

The turnover for the year 2009-2010 had shown a tendency of increase of 10% over the turnover of the preceding year   (P. U. Oct, 2001)

Solution :

A) Calculation of Short Sales	Rs.
Turnover from 1-7-2008 to 30-9-2008	1,10,000
Add - 10% increase	11,000
Estimated turnover	1,21,000
Less Actual turnover from 1-7-2009 to 31-12-2009	56,000
Short Sales	65,000

B) Calculation of Gross profit Rate.

Gross Profit Rate :

$$= \frac{\text{Net Profit + Insured Standing Charges}}{\text{Sales for the last acounting year}} \times 100$$

$$= \frac{12500 + 28500}{1,98,000} \times 100$$

$$= 20.7\%$$

C) Loss of Profit (Calculation of claim)

= Short sales × Gross profit role

= 65,000 × 20.7%

= Rs. 13,455

D) Application of Average Clause.

i)	Loss of Prom		Rs. 13,455
ii)	Amount of policy		Rs. 40,000
iii)	Standard sales	2,00,000	
	Add - 10% increase	20,000	2,20,000
iv)	Gross profit rate		20,7%
v)	Profit on Adjusted standard sales		

$$= \frac{2,20,000}{100} \times \frac{20.7}{1}$$

= Rs. 45540

Being the policy amount is less than the profit as adjusted standard sales, there is an average clause

$$\text{Insurance Claim} \ = \ \frac{\text{Loss of Profit} \times \text{Amount of Insurance Policy}}{\text{Profit on Adjusted standard Sales}}$$

$$= \frac{13.455}{45.540} \times 40000$$

= 11,818

PROBLEM NO. 22

From the following details find out the claim under a loss of profit policy :
Indemnity period 6 months
Date of fire 1-7-2016
Dislocation upto 1-11-2016
Policy value

Sales for the year 2015-2016 (Accounting year)	Rs. 30,000
Net Profit for 2015-2016 (Accounting year)	Rs. 1,20,000
Insured Standing charges for 2015-2016 (Accounting year)	Rs. 13,000
Sales from 1-7-2015 to 30-6-2016	Rs. 17,000
Sales from 1-7-2015 to 1-11-2016	Rs. 1,60,000
Sales from 1-7-2015 to 1-11-2016	Rs. 15,000
There is a clear 10% upward trend in the business	Rs. 50,000

(P. U. April)

Solution :

A) Calculation of Short Sales

Turnover from 1-7-2015 to 1-11-2015	50,000
Add - 10% increase	5,000
Estimated turnover	55,000
Less Actual turnover from 1-7-2016 to 1-1-2016	15,000
Short Sales	40,000

B) Calculation of Gross Profit Rate.
Gross Profit Rate :

$$= \frac{\text{Net Profit} + \text{Insured Standing Charges}}{\text{Sales for the last acounting year}} \times 100$$

$$= \frac{13,000 + 17,000}{1,20,000} \times 100 = 25\%$$

C) Calculation of Claim :

= Short Sales × Gross Profit Rate

= 40,000 × 25% = Rs. 10,000

3) Application of Average Claus.

i) Loss of Profit		Rs. 1,00,000
ii) Amount of policy		Rs. 30,000
iii) Standard Sales	1,60,000	
Add : 10% increase	16,000	1,76,000
iv) Gross profit Rate		25%

v) Profit on Adjusted standard sales

= 17,6000 × 25% = Rs. 44,000

Being the policy amount is less than the profit on adjusted standard sales, there is an average clause

$$\text{Insurance Claim} = \frac{\text{Loss of Profit} \times \text{Amount of Insurance Policy}}{\text{Profit on Adjusted standard Sales}}$$

$$= \frac{10,000 \times 30000}{44,000} = \text{Rs. } 6,818$$

PRACTICAL PROBLEM

A) Loss of stock

1) A fire occurred in the premises of a Good Luck Ltd on 18th September, 2015 and a considerable part of the stock was destroyed. The value of the stock saved wasRs. 8,200. The books disclosed that on 1st April, 2015, the stock was valued at Rs. 65,850 the purchases to the date of fire amounted to Rs. 1,85,000 and the sales to Rs. 2,82,500. Goods costing Rs. 500 were taken for personal use and goods sold for Rs. 2,500 were returned to the merchant. On investigation it is found that during the past five years the average gross profit on the cost was 25%.

You are required to prepare a statement showing the amount the merchant should claim from the insurance company in respect of stock destroyed by fire.

(Ans. Rs. 19,150)

2) Fire occurred in the premises of Bright Ltd. on 20th February, 2015. The company has taken out a fire insurance policy of Rs. 1,00,000 covering its stock in trade and the policy was subject to average clause. From the following particulars ascertain the claim to be lodged.

Particulars	Rs.
Stock on 1st January, 2014	90,000
Purchase during the year 2014	3,65,000
Purchases Returns during the year 2014	5,000
Stock on 31st December, 2014	1,26,000
Sales for the year 2014	4,10,000
Sales Returns during the year 2014	10,000
Purchases from 1.1.2015 to date of fire	84,000
Sales from 1-1-2015 to date of fire	1,03,000
Sales Returns from 1-1-2015 to date of fire	4,000
Value of stock saved	19,800
It was the practice of the concern to value stocks at cost less 10%	

(Ans. Rs. 86,326)

3) On 30th September, 2015, the stock of Sunrise Ltd. was lost in a'fire accident, From the available records, the following information is made available to you to enable you to prepare a statement of claim on the insures.

Particulars	Rs.
Stock on 1-4-2014	37,500
Stock at cost on 31-3-2015	52,000
Purchases less returns for the year ended 31-3-2015	2,53,750
Sales less returns for the year ended 31-3-2015	3,15,000
Purchases less returns upto 30-9-2015	1,45,000
Sales less returns upto 30-9-2015	1,84,050

In valuing stock on 31-3-2015 due to obsolescence 50% of the value of the stock which originally cost Rs. 6,000 had been written off. In May, 2015 three-fourths of this stock had been sold at 90% of the original cost and it is now expected that the balance of the obsolete stock would also realise the same price. Subject to the above, gross profit had remained uniform throughout.

Stock to the value of Rs. 7,200 was salvaged.

(Ans.: Amount of claim to be lodged = Rs. 53,150)

4) Fire occurred in the premises of Royal India Co. on 1st September, 2015 and stock of the value of Rs. 1,01,000 was salvaged and the business books and records were saved. The following information was 'obtained :

Particulars	Rs.
Purchases for the year ended 31st March, 2015	6,80,000
Sales for the year ended 31st March, 2015	11,00,000
Purchases from the 1st April, 2015 to 1st September, 2015	2,50,000
Sales from 1st April, 2015 to 1st September, 2015	3,60,000
Stock on 31st March, 2014	3,00,000
Stock on 31st March, 2015	3,40,000

Further information is also given that the stock on 31" March 2015 was over valued Rs. 20,000. Calculate the amount of the claim to be presented to the insurance company in respect of the loss. In April, 2015 selling price was lowered by 10%.

(Ans : Claim Rs. 2,29,000)

5) Raj General Stores closed their books every year on 31st March. On 30st April, 2015 their premises and stock were totally destroyed by fire. From the books of account and other records that were saved, the following information is available. The stock on hand has always been valued at 10% less than cost.

	2012-13	2013-14	2014-15	1-4-2015 to 30-4-2015
	Rs.	Rs.	Rs.	Rs.
Opening Stock as valued	2,70,900	3,24,000	3,60,000	3,69,000
Purchases less Returns	7,49,000	8,00,000	8,10,000	60,000
Sales less Returns	12,00,000	13,20,000	14,000	1,20,000
Wages	1,74,000	1,90,000	2,09,000	20,000
Closing Stock as valued	3,24,000	3,60,000	3,69,000	

Prepare a statement for submission to the Insurance Company in support of the. claim for loss of stock

(Ans : Claim Rs. 4,03,600)

B) Loss of Profit Policy

11) The account of Surat Textile Mills Ltd., ended on 30th September each year. On 28-2-2015 its premises were destroyed by fire. The Company had effected a loss of profit insurance for Rs. 7,50,000

    The profit for the year, 30th September, 2014 was Rs. 4,50,000 after debiting standing charges Rs. 1,50,000 and the turnover for the year was Rs. 90,00,000.

    The turnover for the year ending 28th February, 2015 was Rs. 93,745,000 (of which Rs. 37,50,000 related to last six months) and that of six months ending 31th August, 2015 was Rs. 18,75,000

    The period of indemnity is 6 months after fire.

    Calculate the amount recoverable from Insurance co. against Loss of profit Policy.

    (Ans. Claim Rs. 2,50,000)

12) Mr. Advani is insured under a loss of profit policy for Rs. 42,000. He closes his books of accounts on 31" December every year. A considerable damage was' caused to his premises on 1st July, 2015. The following further information is available to you from his records.

Particulars	Rs.
Turnover from 1-7-2009 to 30-9-2015	20,000
Turnover in the corresponding period of 2015	1,20,000
Turnover during the year ending 31-12-2014	4,00,000
Turnover during the year ending 30th June, 2015	4,80,000
Standing charges during the year ending 31-12-2014	24,000
Net Profit during the year ending 31-12-2014	16,000

It is been ascertained that the business of Mr. Advani has consistently shown an increase of 25% in the turnover in the months preceding the fire over the corresponding period of the previous year.. Show amount of claim.

(Ans. Claim Rs. 9,100)

13) From the following particulars find out claim under the loss of profit policy.
    1. Date of fire - 1st April, 2015
    2. Policy Value - Rs. 40,000
    3. Indemnity period - Four months
    4. Dislocation period upto 30-9-2015
    5. Sales for 2014 accounting year Rs. 1,20,000. Net Profit for 2015 Rs. 13,000
       Standing Charges (All insured) Rs. 1,60,000
    6. Sales from 1-4-2014 to 31-3-2014 - Rs. 1,60,000
    7. Sales from 1-4-2015 to 1-8-2015 - Rs. 20,000
    8. Sales from 1-4-2015 to 1-8-2015 - Rs. 15,000
    9. Sales from 1-4-2014 to 30-9-2014 - Rs. 35,000
    10. Sales from 1-4-2014 to 1-8-2014 - Rs. 50,000
       There is clear upward trend of 10% in the business. (Ans.: Claim Rs. 9,091)

14) Mr. Lord holds a loss of profit policy. From the following prepare a claim for consequential loss.
    a) The accounts are prepared annually to 31th December. The net profit plus insured standing charges for the year ended 31th December, 2014 amounted to Rs. 2,00,000.
    b) A fire occurred on 30th April 2015. The period of indemnity is six months.
    c) The sales for the year ended 30th April, 2015 were Rs. 5,24,000 and for the year ended 31thDecember, 2014 were Rs. 5,00,000.
    d) The sales during the period of dislocation were Rs. 80,000 and for corresponding period in preceding year were Rs. 1,80,000.
    e) The expenses incurred to mitigate loss were Rs. 8,000.
    f) The saving on insured standing charges due to fire amounted to Rs. 2,000.
    g) The amount insured was Rs. 1,57,200. (Ans. Claim Rs. 34,000)

15) From the following details find out the claim under a loss of profit policy : Indemnity period 6 months. Policy value Rs. 30,000 Date of fire 1-4-2015. Dislocation upto 1-8-2015.

Particulars	Rs.
Sales for 2014 accounting year	1,20,000
Net Profit for 2014 accounting year	13,000
Standing charges for 2014 accounting year (all insured)	17,000
Sales from 1-4-2014 to 31-3-2015	1,60,000
Sales from 1-4-2015 to 1-8-2015	15,000
Sales from 1-4-2014 to 1-8-2014	50,000

There is a clear 10% upward trend in the business.
(Ans. Claim Rs. 6,818)

Objective Type Questions

I. State whether the following statements are True' or 'False'.

1. Under a contract of fire insurance, the insurer may indemnify either by paying cash or by replacing or reinstating the subject-matter insured.

2. When stock in trade is destroyed by fire, for the same quantity of goods a retailer can claim more amount than a manufacturer.

3. A standard fire policy also covers loss by theft during or after the occurrence of a fire.

4. Where the property insured is of a value greater than the sum insured, then the insured is considered as being his own insurer for the difference and in the event of any loss, must share a proportionate loss.

5. The object of both fire and profits insurance is to indemnify the revenue losses arising due to fire.

6. Annual turnover is the turnover during the twelve months immediately before the damage. 2.32

7. Under a profits insurance policy, loss of profits is measured with reference to budgeted profit.

8. Whatever be the amount of the policy, the loss incurred is to be totally indemnified by the insurer.

Ans : 1) True,   2) True,   3) True,   4) True,   5) False,   6) True,   7) False,   8) False.

II) Fill in the blanks :

1. The difference between standard turnover and actual turnover during the indemnity period is........ .

2. The maximum period for which indemnity is granted by the insurer is......... years for a consequential loss policy.

3. The average clause in a policy discourages...........

4. If the standard turnover is Rs. 72,000 actual turnover Rs. 15,000 and the rate of gross profit Rs, $33^{1/3}$ % on cost, the claim for loss of profits will be...........

5. The minimum period for which indemnity is to be sought by the insured is.........in the case of a consequential loss policy.

6. For the preparation of claim for loss of stock, the difference between the value of stock on the date of fire and....... is considered.

Ans : 1) Short sales,   2) three,   3) under Insurance,   4) Rs. 19,000,

    5) three months, 6) stock salvaged.

III) Indicate the correct answer:

1. Consequential loss policy indemnifies

   a) Capital losses.

   b) Revenue losses.

   c) Budgeted losses.

2. Fire insurance provides cover for

   a) Tangible assets.

   b) Intangible assets.

   c) Fictitious assets.

3. With the opening stock at Rs. 13,500. purchases at Rs. 82,500 sales at Rs. 1,20,000 and stock salvaged at Rs. 1,260 the rate of gross profit being 50% on cost, the stock destroyed in fire will be

   a) Rs. 14,740.

   b) Rs.24,740.

   c) Rs. 36,000.

4. The average clause in a loss of profits policy protects the

   a) Insured.

   b) Insurer.

   c) Workers.

5. If indemnity period is six months, standard turnover Rs. 20,000 annual turnover Rs. 50,000 tunover during indemnity period Rs. 8,000 short sales will amount to

   a) Rs. 30,000.

   b) Rs. 12,000.

   c) Rs. 42,000.

6. A fore insurance policy is taken up to indemnify

   a) Capital losses to tangible property.

   b) Revenue losses to tangible property.

   c) Capital losses to intangible property.

Ans. : 1) b,   2) a,   3) a,   4) b,   5) b,   6) a

4

Final Accounts of Co-operative Societies

4.1 Introduction :

Co-operative means "coming and working together for a common purpose". This working together is quiet common among men and women. Co-operative societies are organisations formed to take the benefits of co-operation. The co-operative societies are democratic self-governing institutions. They are raised and managed by members on the basis of equality. 'One man one vote' is the principle adopted by the co-operative societies. Co-operative societies are formed with an object of promoting economic and moral conditions of the weaker section of the community. The success of the society depends upon their members loyalty and active participation. The member of the co-operative societies are expected to be alert, vigilant and must participate in the working of the society.

Each co-operative society has to be registered under the Co-operative Societies Act of the concerned state. Co-operation is the state subject. So every state is required to do co-operative societies Act for their state. In Maharashtra, co-operative societies are formed and registered under the Maharashtra Co-operative Societies Act, 1960. Each co-operative Society must have its rules and regulations which are known as Bye-laws. While registering the society these bye-laws need to be approved by the concerned authority.

There are different kinds of societies, namely; Consumers' Co-operative Society, Credit Co-operative Society, Housing Co-operative Society and the like. The exact nature and scope of accounting would, therefore, depend on the nature of its business.

Co-operative Account Keeping : Co-operative Account Keeping is an indigenous system of account keeping based on the idea that each transaction involves either 'receipt' or 'payment' of money. Transaction involve either receipt of money or payment of money. These receipt and payment aspects of transactions are recorded in the books of original entry known as 'Day-Book' (or Cash Book). This system, therefore, is described as 'Receipts and Payments System of Account Keeping.'

4.2 Books of Accounts :

Every co-operative society should keep a regular account of :

a) all sums of money received and expended by the society and of matters in respect of which the receipt or expenditure takes place;

b) all sales and purchases of goods by the society;

c) the assets and liabilities of the society.

List of Books of Accounts for Common Co-operative Societies :

1) Cash book
2) Cash sales subsidiary book
3) Credit sales register
4) Purchase book
5) Stock register
6) Bin-cards for itemwise up-to-date quantity records.
7) Register of excesses and shortages
8) General ledger
9) Debtor's ledger and creditor's ledger
10) Journal proper
11) Register of tenders
12) List of approved suppliers and register of market rates.

List of Books of Accoutns for Co-operative Credit Societies :

1) Day books
2) Payment book for loans and advances
3) Sundry payment book
4) Receipts and payment book for F.D.receipts
5) Sundry receipt book
6) Dividend payment book
7) Members register

8) Share ledger form
9) Fixed deposit personal ledger
10) Balance book F.D.R.
11) Due Register for F.D.R.
12) Unpaid dividend register
13) Recoveries register for advances.
14) F.D.R. interest due register
15) Suspense register
16) Sundry creditors' ledger
17) Surety deposit account book
18) Surety liability register
19) Journal
20) Bank reconciliation book
21) Trial balance book
22) Demand and time liability register
23) Yearly balance book for loans and shares
24) Head office and branches- loan application register
25) Sanction register for loans for membership, for share refund
26) Register of cheques, drafts, P.O. Inward.
27) Inward register
28) Register of postage stamps and franking machine

Under the Maharashtra Co-operative Societies Rules, 1968 and under Rule 61 the managing committee of every society should prepare annual statements of accounts, within 42 days of the closure of the co-operative year showing :

i) Receipts and Disbursements during the previous co-operative year;
ii) The Profit and Loss Account of the year, and
iii) The Balance Sheet as at the close of the year.

The co-operative year begins on 1st April and ends on 31st March every year (Section 2 (10 a iii).

4.3 Preparation of Receipts and Payments Statements :

This statement is a summary of totals of general ledger accounts for a period. It is prepared monthly in the Register of Receipts and Payments. At the end of the year, the annual statement of Recipts and Payments is prepared. This statement contains two sides i.e. Receipts Side (left hand side) and Payment Side (right hand side). The totals of receipts columns of various accounts in the general ledger are listed on the receipt side of a statement in a particular order. The totals of payments column of various acounts are listed on the payments side of the statement. The opening Cash Balance is added on the receipt side and closing cash balance to the payment side. The total of receipt side will agree with the total of payment side. This statement serves as a means for checking the arithmatical accuracy of the accounts. It also forms as a basis for preparation of Profit and Loss A/c and Balance Sheet.

4.4 (1) Preparation of Final Accounts of Co-operative from the Receipt and Payment Statement or Statement of Balances :

In order to prepare the Final Accounts i.e. Trading and Profit and Loss Account and Balance Sheet, we have to consider the information given in
   a) Previous year's Balance Sheet
   b) Statement of Receipts and Payments
   c) Other adjustments

1) Preparation of Trading Account : If the society is engaged in trading activities, is required to prepare Trading Account. There is no separate form provided for Trading Account. It can be prepared as usual.

2) Profit and Loss Account and Balance Sheet : According to section 65 of the Maharashtra Co-operative Societies Act, 1960 read with the Rule 62 (1) of the Maharashtra Co-operative Societies Rule 1961, the Balance Sheet and the Profit and Loss Account of the Society shall be prepared in form 'N'.

Expenses are listed on left-hand side and Incomes on the right-hand side of the Profit and Loss A/c. The amount of expenditure relating to the period is arrived at as under :-

		Rs.
(1)	**Amount of Expenditure paid during the years**	....
	(as shown in Receipt and Payment A/c).	
	Add : Amount due (outstanding) at the end of the year	....
	(as per adjustment).	
	Total	....
	Less : Expenditure due at the end of the previous year	....
	(as shown in previous Balance Sheet).	
	Current years's Expenditure	....
		Rs.
(2)	**Amount of Income is arrived at as under :**	
	Income received during the year	....
	(As shown in Receipt and Payment A/c)	
	Add : Income accrued at the end of the year	....
	(as per adjustment)	
	Total	....
	Less : Income accrued at the end of the previous	
	(Last) year.	....
	Current Year's Income	....

Balance Sheet is a statement of Assets and Liabilities on a particular date. It is not an account. These assets and liabilities are to be listed in a **definite order** in the Balance Sheet.

The form of Profit and Loss Account and Balance Sheet is given under rule 62 (i) Form 'N' of Maharashtra Co-operative Societies rule 1961. Under Rule 62 it is stated that the Balance Sheet and Profit and Loss A/c to be laid before the A.G.M. of a society by the managing committee shall ordinarily be in the form 'N'. **The amounts of assets** (other than cash on hand) on the last date of the Balance Sheet are ascertained as under :

	Rs.
Opening Balance of Assets	....
(as shown in previous year's Balance Sheet)	
Add : Addition (purchase) to the assets during the year	....
(as per payment side of R and P Account)	
Less : Assets sold during the year	
(as per Receipt side of the R and P Account)	....
Balance of Assets as on date of Balance Sheet.	....

The amount of liabilities on the last date of year are ascertained as under :

	Rs.
Opening Balance of Liability	....
(as shown in previous year's balance sheet)	
Add : Addition to liabilities or Amount received in respect	....
of the liability	
(as shown on receipt side of R and P Account)	
Total	....
Less : Amount paid in respect of liability during the year	....
(as shown on payment side of R and P Account)	
Amount of liability on the date of Balance Sheet	....

(2) Preparation of Final Accounts when Trial Balance or Statement of Debit and Credit Balances are given :

When in the problem, trial balance or statement of debit and credit balances are given then prepare Final Accounts **as usual in the prescribed form** after considering adjustments given. The specimen form of Profit and Loss Account and Balance Sheet in the form 'N' under Rule 62 (i) given as under :

From - 'N'
Profit and Loss Account for the year ended..............

Last Year figures	Expenditue	This Year figures	Last Year figures	Income	This Year figures
	1. **Interest : -** a. Paid - b. Payable 2. Bank charge 3. Salaries and Allowances of staff 4. Contribution to Staff Proivident Fund. 5. Salary and Allowances of Managing Director 6. Attendance fees and travelling expenses of Directors and Committee member 7. Travelling expenes of Staff 8. Rent, Rates and Taxes 9. Postage, Telegrams and Telephone charges 10. Printing and Stationery 11. Audit Fees 12. General Expenses (Contingencies) 13. Bad Debts written off or provision made for Bad Debts. 14. Depreciaton on Fixed Asets 15. Land Income and Expenditure A/c 16. Other Items 17. Net Profit carried to Balance Sheet			1. **Interest Received :** a.On Loans and Adv. b.On Investment 2. Dividend received on shares 3. Commission 4. Miscellaneous Income : a. Share Transfer Fees b. Rent c. Rebate in Interest d. Sale of forms e. Other Items 5. Land Income and Expenditure A/c	

Note : In the case of marketing societies, consumer's societies and similar other societies which have undertaken trading activities, the profit and Loss Account shall be devided into two parts showing separately the trading account and the profit and Loss Account. In case of product societies, processing societies / forest labourer's societes and other societies which have undertaken production activities, the manufacturing account shall also be prepared in addition.

From - 'N' [See rule 62(1)]
Balance Sheet of
as on ....

Figures for the Previous year	Liabilities	Figures for the Current year	Figures for the Previous year	Assets	Figures for the Current year
	I. Share Capital Authorised..... shares of Rs. ....each Subscribed...... shares of Rs...... each. Less : Call in arrears - Add Calls in Advance **II. Reserve Fund and Other Funds :** Statutory Reserve Fund Building Funds Special Development, Fund Bad & Doubtful Debts Reserve Investment Depreciation Fund Dividend Equalisation Fund Bonus Equ.Fund Reserve for overdue interest Other Funds **III. Staff Provident Fund** **IV. Secured Loans :** Debentures Loans, Overdrafts & Cash credit from Banks, Loan from Govt. Other Secured Loans **V. Unsecured Loans :** Loans cash credit & overdraft from Central Banks.			**I. Cash/ Bank Balances** Cash on hand Cash in Banks : i. Current A/c ii. Savings A/c iii. Call Deposits iv. Call Deposits on Banks **II. Investments :** Govt. Securities Other Trustee Securities Non-Trustee Securities Shares of other Co-op. Societies Shares, Debentures or Bonds of companies registered under Co. Act. Fixed Deposits **III. Staff Provi. Funds** Investment of staff provident funds Advance against staff provident fund **IV. Loans & Advances :** **Loans** Overdrafts Cash Credit Loans due by Managing Committee Members Rs.... Loans due by secretary & other employees Rs...	

Figures for the Previous year	Liabilities	Figures for the Current year	Figures for the Previous year	Assets	Figures for the Current year
	From Govt. From others Bills payable **VI. Deposits :** Fixed Deposits Recurring Deposits Thrift or Saving Deposits Current Deposits Deposits at call Other Deposits Credit balance in cash : credit & overdraft A/cs **VII. Current Liabilities & Provisions :** Sundry creditors Outstanding creditors : i. for purchases ii. for expenses including salary of staff, rent, taxes etc. Advance recoveries, unexpired subscription premium, commission etc. **VIII Unpaid Dividends** **IX. Interest accrued due but not paid** **X. Other Liabilities (to be specified)** **XI. Proft & Loss A/c :** Profit for the Last Year - Less : Appropriations - Add: Current profit - **Foot Note :** Contingent Liability			**V. Sundry Debtors :** Credit sales Advances Others. **VI. Current Assets :** Stores & Spare parts Loose tools Stock in trade Work in progress **VII. Fixed Assets :** Land & Buildings Leaseholds Railway siding Plant & Machinery Loose tools & Others equipments. Dead Stock Furniture & Fittings Live Stock Vehicles etc. **VIII Miscellaneous Exp. & Losses** Goodwill Preliminary Expenses Expenses connected with the issue of shares & debentures including under writing charges brokerage etc. Deferred revenue expenditure **IX Other Items :** Prepaid expenses Interest accrued but not due Other items (to be specified) **X Profit & Loss A/c** Accumulated Loss not written of. **XI. Current Losses**	

Explanation of Items in Balance Sheets :

A. Asset Side

I. Cash and Bank Balance : Fixed deposits and call deposits with Central Banks and other approved bankers should be shown under the heading "Investments" and not under the heading "cash and bank balances".

II. Investments : The value of each investment and the mode of valuation (cost or market value) should be mentioned. If, the book value of any security is less than the market value, a remark to that effect should be made against each item.

III. Investment of Staff Provident Fund : Quoted and un-quoted securities should be shown separately.

IV. Loans and Advances : In case of central Banks and other federal societies, Loans due by societies and individual members should be shown separately.

V. Current Assets : Mode of valuation and stock shall be stated and the amount in respect of raw-materials, partly finished and finished goods and stores required for consumption should be stated seperately. Mode of valuation of work in progress shall be stated.

VI. Fixed Assets : Under each head the original cost and the additions there to and deductions therefrom made during the year and the total depreciation written off or provided up to the end of the year should be stated.

B. Liability Side

I. Share Capital : Share capital contributed by Govt. and by Co-operative societies and different classes of individual members should be shown separately. Terms of redemption or conversion of any redeemable preference shares should be mentioned.

II. Reserve Fund and Other Funds :
a) Statutory Reserve Fund and other reserves and funds should be shown separately.
b) Additions and deductions since last balance sheet are to be shown under each of the specified head.
c) Funds in the nature of reserves and funds created out of any profits for specific purposes should be shown separately.

III. Staff Provident Fund : Staff Provident funds and any other insurance or Bonus Funds maintained for the benefit of the employees should be shown separately.

IV. Secured Loans : The nature of security should be specified in each case. Where Loans have been guaranteed by Government or state Co-operative or Central Banks, a mention thereof should also be made together with the maximum amount of such guarantee. Loans from Government, state Co-operative Bank or Central Bank or State Bank of India and other banks should be shown separately.

V. Deposits : Deposits from societies and individuals should be shown separately.

Contingent Liabilities which have not been provided for should also be mentioned in the Balance Sheet by way of a foot note.

4.5 Allocation of profit as per Maharashtra Co-operative Societies Act :

After Profit and loss account and Balance Sheet are prepared they are required to be approved by the members in the Annual General Meeting. The appropriation / Allocation of profit as recommended by the managing committee also needed to be approved in the A.G..M. as the A.G.M. is held only after finalising the accounts, the effects of these appropriotions are given in the accounts for the next year. This is shown in item No. XI of the liability side. It shows the profit for the last year. **Less** appropriations then **added** with current year profit. The various appropriations are as under :

I. Reserve Fund

Section 65 (2) provides that a society may appropriate its net profit to the reserve fund or any other fund for payment of divident to members on their shares. It further provides that no part of the profit shall be appropriated except with the approval of the General Body.

According to section 66 every society has to carry at least one-fourth of the net profits i.e. 25% of net profit of each year to the reserve fund.The reserve fund so created can be used by the society for:

a) the business of the society or

b) invested as provided under section 70, or

c) be used in part for some public purpose, with the prior approval of the State Government or

d) for some such purpose of the state or of local interest.

The Reserve Fund cannot be utilised for payment of divident or bonus :

Since this fund is required to be maintained statutorily, it is also termed as "Statutory Fund"

II. Dividend

According to section 67 of the Act, no society can pay dividend to its members at a rate exceeding 12% on the paid-up share capital, except with the prior sanction of the State Government. This rate can be increased maximum upto 15% with the prior sanction of the State Govt. The co-operative societies are not allowed to pay dividend otherwise than out of profit.

III. Dividend Equalisation Fund

This fund is created in order to enable the Society to pay dividend at a certain rate every year. A co-operative society may credit a sum not exceeding 2 percent of the paid-up share capital in any year, until the total fund amounts to 9% of the paid-up share capital. The law provides that dividend is to be paid only from net profit of that year or from the Dividend Equalisation Fund. Therefore, when the profits are not adequate in a particular year, this fund can be utilised for payment of dividend at a certain rate.

IV. Bonus Equalisation Fund

A Co-operative society may create a Bonus Equalisation Fund out of its net profits for payment of bonus to persons other than its paid employees, who are not its members.

V. Guarantee Fund

A Co-operative Society may raise debenture capital or loan which is guaranted by the State Government. Therefore, a society may require to contribute a portion of its profits towards 'guarantee fund'.

VI. Education Fund

According to Section 68, every society is required to contribute annually towards the education fund of the State Federal Society. Such a contribution is to be made at prescribed rates. Presently, a Primary Consumers Society has to contribute 2 paise per Rs.100 of the working capital subject to a maximum of Rs.1000. For Credit Co-operative Societies these rates are : Rs.10 in case of those societies who have suffered loss in the last year. And for the Credit Co-operative Societies which have earned profits, the contribution is 10 percent of their working capital subject to a maximum of Rs.500.

VII. Writing off Bad Debts

Rule 49 provides that all loans including interest and recovery changes which are found irrecoverable and are certified as Bad Debts by the auditor can be written off against the Reserve for Bad Debts and the balance of bad debts will be debited ro Profit and Loss Account or may be written off against the Reserve Fund.

VIII. Share Capital Redemption Fund

There may be some shares purchased by the Government which are to be redeemed after a certain period. For this purpose, share capital redemption fund may be created out of the net profits of the society.

IX. Investment of Funds

Section 70 provides that a Co-operative Society can invest or deposit its funds in one or more of the following :

a) a Central Bank or the State co-operative Bank
b) in any of the securities specified under section 20 of the Indian Trust Act.
c) in the shares or securities of any other registered society with limited liability.
d) in any other Co-operative bank or banking company approved for this purpose by the Registrar. or
e) any other mode permitted by the rules or special order of the State Government.

X. Building Fund :

For the purpose of construction or purchase of building for the business of the society this fund may be created.

XI. Common Good Fund or Charity Fund :

Co-operative Societies are permitted to set aside a sum not execuding 20% of their net profits towards a common good fund and to utilise it for charitable or public purpose. (Charitable purpose includes relief for the poor, education, medical relief or any other public utility but does not include religious teaching or workship. Societies are also permitted to donate or contiribute to charitable purpose with the approval of their general body.

4.6 Important Tips for Preparation of Final Accounts of Co-operative Society :

1) Prepare Final Accounts under Rule 62(i) of the Maharashtra Co-operative Societies Rule, 1961 i.e. in the Form "N"

2) While Solving the Problem, First Prepare Blank Proforma of Profit and Loss Account and Balance Sheet in the Form "N".

3) Put down Current year's Expenditure/ losses on the debit side of P and L Account against that particular Item.

4) Put down Current Year's incomes/gains on the credit side of P and L Account against that particular item.

5) Calculate Current year's Expenditure and Current years Income as explained earlier, when Receipt and Payment account and last year's Balance Sheet are given. If Trial Balance or Statement of debit and Credit balances is given, then take directly revenue expenditures and revenue incomes on the debit side and credit side respectively.

6) Make Adjustments for depreciation, Bad debts, Closing Stock etc. in the usual manner.

7) Make Adjustments for outstanding incomes and expenses at the end of the year in the usual way.

8) Make Appropriations as given by considering ceiling etc. if any,

9) Transfer 25% of the net profit of the year to a Reserve Fund whether it is clearly given or not in the problem.

10) If there are no Specific items of expenditure or incomes and Assets or liabilites, then put down-(dash) or write down as "Nil" against that particular item in P and L Account and Balance Sheet.

11) Separate Profit and Loss Appropriation Account may be prepared, though it is not compulsory.

12) Final Account as well as the appropriation of profit as recommended by the Managing Committee need to be approved in the A.G..M. Since the A.G.M. is held only after finalising the account the effects of the appropriations should be given in the accounts for the next year. It shows in item No. XI of the liability side.

It shows the profit for last year less appropriations then added with the current profit.

4.7 Illustrations :

4.7.1 illustrations of Final Accounts of Co-operative Credit Societies

ILLUSTRATION 1

From the following Trial Balance of Omkar Credit Co-operative Society, Pune. Prepare final accounts for the year ended 31st March, 2015

Trial Balance

Particulars	Debit Rs.	Credit Rs.
Share Capital	–	4,00,000
Reserve fund	–	36,000
Members deposit	–	10,80,000
Unpaid dividend	–	800
Staff providend fund	–	9,600
Profit and Loss A/c 2014-15	–	14,000
Interest	–	1,72,000
Renewal fees	–	1,600
Sundry income	–	1,280
Development fund	–	8,000
Education fund	–	2,400
Cash in hand	8,720	–
Cash at bank	61,160	–
Loans to members	14,00,000	–
Contribution to providend fund	960	–
Insurance	2,080	–
Travelling expenses	6,840	–
Printing and stationery	1,920	–
Manager's salary	24,000	–
Staff salary	54,400	–
Interest on loans	3,840	–
Interest on deposits	38,400	–
Furniture	3,360	–
Fixed deposits	1,20,000	–
	17,25,680	17,25,680

Adjustments :

a) Salary due Rs. 2,400.

b) Audit fees due Rs. 1,600.

c) Interest due on members deposits Rs. 4,000.

d) Interest due but not received Rs. 9,600.

e) Depreciate furniture by 5%.

f) Directors propose to pay dividend of 5% on paidup capital.

g) Transfer Rs. 100 to Education Fund and Rs. 5,000 to dividend equalisation fund.

Solution :

Omkar Credit Co-operative Society, Pune
Profit and Loss A/c
for the year ended 31 st March 2015

Particulars		Amount	Particulars		Amount
To Interest on deposits	38,400		By Interest	1,72,000	
Add : Payable	4,000		Add : Due	9,600	1,81,600
Add : Interest on loan	3,840	46,240	By Miscellaneous		
To staff Salaries	54,400		Incomes :		
Add : Outstanding	2,400	56,800	Renewal fees		1,600
To Managers salary		24,000	Sundry income		1,280
To Contribution to					
provident fund		960			
To Travelling exp.		6,840			
To Printing and stationery		1,920			
To Audit fees		1,600			
To Depreciation on furniture		168			
To Insurance		2080			
To Education fund		100			
To Net Profit c/d		43,772			
		1,84,480			**1,84,480**

Dr. **Memorandum Profit and Loss Appropriation A/c** **Cr.**

Particulars	Amount	Particulars	Amount
To Reserve fund	10,943	By Balance b/d	14,000
(25% Of 43,772)		By Current years net profit	43,772
To Proposed dividend	20,000		
To Dividend equalisation fund	5,000		
To Balance c/d	21,829		
	57,772		**57,772**

Omkar Credit Co-operative Society, Pune
Balance Sheet as on 31st March, 2015

Liabilities		Amount	Assets		Amount
1) Share capital		4,00,000	**1) Cash and bank balance**		
2) Reserve fund and other funds			Cash in hand		8,720
Reserve fund		36,000	Cast at bank		61,160
Development fund		8,000	**2) Investments**		
Education fund		2,500	Fixed deposits		1,20,000
3) Staff providend fund		9,600	**3) Investment of staft P.F.**		-
4) Secured loans		–	**4) Loans and advances**		
5) Unsecured loans		–	Loans to members		14,00,000
6) Deposits - Members		10,80,000	**5) Sundry debtors**		–
7) Current liabilities			**6) Current assets**		–
Salary outstanding		2,400	**7) Fixed assets**		
Audit fees outstanding		1,600	Furniture	3,360	
8) Unpaid dividend		800	Less: Dep 5%	168	3,192
9) Interest accrued			**8) Miscellaneous Exp.**		–
but not paid		4,000	**and losses**		
10) Other liabilities			**9) Other items**		
11) Profit and Losses A/c			Interest accrued		
Profit last year	14,000		but not received		9,600
Add : Net Profit	43,772	57,772	**10) Profit and loss A/c**		-
			11) Current Losses		-
		16,02,672			**16,02,672**

ILLUSTRATION 2

From the following Trial Balance of Ram Co-operative Credit Society, Pune prepare Profit and Loss account and Balance Sheet as on 31st March, 2015 after considering the information given below :

Trial Balance

Particulars	Debit Rs.	Credit Rs.
Share Capital :		
Authorised share capital	–	25,00,000
Paidup share capital	–	15,00,000
Cash credit (P.D.C.C. Bank)	–	3,37,500
Interest on loan	–	3,00,000
Sale of loan forms	–	500
Dividend on shares	–	10,000
Interests on fixed deposits	–	17,500
Dividend equalisation fund	–	25,000

Particulars	Debit Rs.	Credit Rs.
Reserve fund	–	2,37,500
Profit and Loss A/c on 1-4-2014	–	8,000
Building fund	–	50,000
Cash at bank	37,500	–
Cash in hand	500	–
Loans to members	20,75,000	–
Investment of reserve fund	2,00,000	–
Investment in shares of P.D.C.C.	1,00,000	–
Interest on cash credit	40,000	–
Printing and stationery	3,750	–
Salary to manager	10,000	–
Annual General meeting expenses	4,500	–
Postage and telegrams	250	–
Audit fees	2,000	–
Travelling expenses	1,000	–
Education fund	1,250	–
Furniture	7,500	–
Advertisement	1,250	–
General expenses	1,500	–
	24,86,000	**24,86,000**

Additional Information :

1) Depreciate furniture @ 10%.
2) Interest accrued on investment Rs. 2,500.
3) Manager's salary payable Rs. 1,000.
4) Stock of stationery on 31st March, 2015 Rs. 1,250.
5) Provide reserve for bad and doubtful debts Rs. 1,250.

Solution :

Ram Co-operative Credit Society, Pune
Profit and Loss A/c

Cr.   **for the year ended 31st March, 2015**   Dr.

Particulars		Amount	Particulars		Amount
To Interest on cash credit		40,000,	By Interest received		
To Salary to manager	10,000		on loans		3,00,000
Add : Outstanding	1,000	11,000	By Interest on		
To Travelling expenses		1,000	investment	17,500	
To Postage and telegrams		250	**Add :** O/s. interest	2,500	20,000

Particulars		Amount	Particulars	Amount
To Printing and stationery	3,750		By Dividend on shares	10,000
Less : Stock	1,250	2,500	By Sale of loan forms	500
To Audit fees		2.000		
To General expenses		1,500		
To R.D.D.		1,250		
To Advertisements		1,250		
To Annual general meetings exp.		4,500		
To Education fund		1,250		
To Dep. on furniture		750		
To Net Profit		2,63,250		
		3,30,500		**3,30,500**

Education fund is to be paid as per the statutory requirement, hence it is shown as an expenditure.

Ram Co-operative Credit Society, Pune
Balance Sheet as on 31st March 2015

Liabilities		Amount	Assets		Amount
1) Share Capital			**1) Cash and bank**		
Authorised sh. cap.		25,00,000	Cash in hand		500
Issued and paid-up sh. cap.		15,00,000	Cash at bank		37,500
2) Reserve fund and other fund			**2) Investments**		
Reserve fund		2,37,500	a) Fixed deposits		2,00,000
Dividend equalisation fund		25,000	b) Investment in shares		1,00,000
Building fund		50,000	**3) Staff providend fund**		
Reserve for doubtful debts		1,250	**4) Loans and advances**		
3) Staff providend fund		–	Loans to members		20,75,000
4) Secured loans		–	**5) Sundry Debtors**		
5) Unsecured loans			**6) Current assets**		
a) Cash credit		3,37,500	Stock of stationary		1,250
6) Deposits		–	**7) Fixed assets**		
7) Current liabilities and provisions			Furniture	7,500	
Outstanding managers salary			**Less :** Depreciation 10% 750		6,750
8) Unpaid dividend		1,000	**8) Misc.expenses and losses**		
9) Interest accrued		–	**9) Other items**		
10) Other liabilities			Interest due on investment		2,500
11) Profit and Loss A/c			10) Profit and loss A/c		–
Last year	8,000		11) Current losses		–
Add : N/P of current year	2,63,250	2,71,250			
		24,23,500			24,23,500

ILLUSTRATION 3

You are required to prepare Profit and Loss Account for the year ended 31th March 2015 and Balance Sheet as on that date from the following Trial Balance of Uday Co-operative Credit Society as on 31st March 2015 and other information given.

Trial Balance

	Dr. Rs.		Cr. Rs.
Cash in hand	350	Share Capital	3,75,000
Cash at Bank	7,000	Reserve Fund	25,000
Fixed Deposit with Maha		Member's Deposits	11,23,875
State Co-op Bank	77,500	Unpaid Dividend	1,050
Furniture	3,500	Dividend Equalisation	9,000
Interest on Deposits	40,000	Reserve	
Interest due on Loans	4,000	Staff Provident Fund	10,000
Salaries	15,000	Profit and Loss Appropriation	
Office Rent	2,500	A/c Balance	15,500
Printing and Stationery	200	Interest	89,000
Travelling Expenses	300	Renewal Fees	2,000
Insurance Premium	500	Miscellaneous Income	150
Contribution to Provident	1,000	Co-operative Develop	1,025
Fund		ment Fund	
Loan due from Members	15,00,000	Education Fund	250
	16,51,850		**16,51,850**

Additional Information :
a) Interest accrued on members deposit Rs.2,500.
b) Interest accrued due but not received Rs.1,000.
c) Addition to Furniture during the year Rs.500.
d) Provide depreciation @ 10% on closing balance of furniture.
e) Oustanding salary Rs.150.
f) Advance Salary Rs.250
g) Audit Fees due Rs.1,500.
h) Authorised capital : 50,000 shares of Rs.10 each.
i) Directors have recommended the following appropriations for the current year.
   i) Dividend to sharholders at 5%.
   ii) Required amount to Reserve Fund.
   iii) Transfer to Co-operative Development Fund at 5% of net profit after contributing to Reserve Fund.
   iv) Transfer to Dividend Equalisation Reserve Rs.1000.
   v) Addition to Building Fund Rs.5,000.

Solution :

Uday Co-operative Credit Society Ltd.
Profit and Loss Account for the year ended 31st March 2015

Expenditure		Rs.	Income		Rs.
1) Interest Paid on Deposits	40,000		1) Interest received :	89,000	
Add : Interest due	2,500	42,500	Add Interest account		
2) Bank Charges		–	due	1,000	90,000
3) Salaries	15,000		2) Dividend Received		–
Less : Advance	250		3) Commission		–
	14,750		4) Miscellaneous Income :		–
Add Outstanding	150	14,900	Renewal Fees		2,000
4) Contribution to P.F.		1,000	Miscellaneous Income		150
5) Salaries and Allowances to M.D.		–	5) Land Income and		
6) Attendance fees		–	Expenditure		–
7) Travelling Exp.		300			
8) Rent, Rates and Taxes :					
9) Office Rent		2,500			
10) Postage, Telegram and		–			
Telephone					
11) Printing and Stationery		200			
11) Audit fee due		1,500			
12) General Exp.		–			
13) Bad Debts and R.D.D.		–			
14) Depreciation on Furniture		350			
15) Land Income and Exp. A/c		–			
16) Other Items-Insurance					
Premium		500			
17) Net Profit c/d		28,400			
		92,150			92,150

Memorandum P and L Appropriation A/c

To Reserve Fund (25% of of Rs.28,400)	7,100	By Bal. b/d	15,500
To Dividend (5% of Rs.3,75,000)	18,750	By N.P. of the year	28,400
To Co-operative Development Fund	1,065		
(5% of Rs.21,300) (28400-7100)			
To Dividend Equilisation Reserve	1,000		
To Building Fund	5,000		
To Balance c/d to B/S.	10,985		
	43,900		43,900

Balance Sheet of Uday Co-op. Credit Society
(as on 31st March 2015)

Liabilities	Rs.	Assets		Rs.
1) Share Capitals :		**1) Cash and Bank Balances:**		
Authorised : 50,000 shares of		Cash		350
Rs. 10 each.	5,00,000	Bank		7,000
2) Issued and Subscribed :		**2) Investments :**		
37,500 shares of Rs.10 each	3,75,000	Fixed Deposit		77,500
Reserve Fund	25,000	**3) Investment of Staff P.F.**		–
Dividend Equilisation Reserve	9,000	**4) Loans and Advances :**		
Co-operation Development	1,025	Due from members		15,00,000
Fund		**5) Sundry Debtors**		
Education Fund	250	For Advance Salary		250
3) Staff P.F.	10,000	**6) Current Assets**		–
4) Secured Loans	–	**7) Fixed Assets :**		–
5) Unsecured Loans	–	Furniture	3,000	
6) Deposits :		**Add :** Purchase	500	
Members Deposits	11,23,875		3500	
7) Current Liabilities and		**Less :** Depreciation	350	3,150
Provisions :		**8) Miscellaneous Expenditure**		
Outstanding Audit Fee	1,500	and Losses		–
Outstanding Salary	150	**9) Other Items :**		
8) Unpaid Dividend	1,050	Interesnt due on		
9) Interest accrued due	2,500	Investment	1,000	
10) Other Liabilities		Interest due on		
11) Profit and Loss A/c Bal. :		Loan	4,000	5,000
Opening Balance 15,500		**10) Profit & loss A/c**		–
+ Current Year Profit 28,400	43,900	**11) Current losses**		–
	15,93,250			**15,93,250**

Note :

The Directors have recommended the appropriations out of the current year's profit. But as these appropriations are needed to be approved by the A.G.M., it is to be shown as an memorandum profit and loss appropriation A/c. Hence, it has not placed in profit and loss account and balance sheet of the society for the year ended 31st March, 2015.

ILLUSTRATION 4

**The Trial Balance of Shruti Co-operative Credit Society,
Dhule as on 31-03-2015 is as follows :
Trial Balance as on 31-03-2015**

Particulars		Debit	Credit
Cash in hand		5,400	–
Cash with D.D.C.C. Bank		20,000	–
Balance with Canara Bank		19,800	–
Investments		3,10,000	–
Loan due from Members		60,00,000	–
Office Furniture		20,000	–
Share Capital		–	15,00,000
Reserve Fund		–	70,000
Dividend Equilisaton Reserve		–	40,000
Staff Provident Fund		–	40,000
Deposits from Members		–	44,96,000
Dividend		62,000	–
Profit and Loss Account :			–
i) Balance as on 1-4-2013	4,600		–
ii) Profits for the year 2013-2014	1,20,000		1,66,000
Interest on Investment and Loan		–	3,50,000
Renewal Fees		–	8,000
Sundry Income		–	4,600
Salaries and allowances of staff		59,400	–
Establishment charges for an executive office		10,000	–
Printing and Stationery		800	–
Travelling Expenses of Staff		1200	–
Insurance Premium		2,000	–
Contribution to Provident Fund		4,000	–
Interest paid on Deposits		1,60,000	–
		66,74,600	**66,74,600**

Adjustments :

1) Interest payable on member's deposits amounted to Rs.10,000.
2) Interest receivable on member's loan Rs.16,000 and on Investments Rs.4,000.
3) Outstanding expenses were as follows : Salaried - Rs.600; Audit fees Rs.6000
4) Dividend declared at 5% on share capital on Rs. 14,00,000 on 31-3-2014 out of profits of 2013-14.
5) Transfer 25% of profit of 2013-14 to Reserve Fund. Prepare profit and loss A/c for the year ended 31-03-2015 and a Balance sheet as on that date.

Solution :

In the Books of Shruti Co-operative Credit Society
Profit and Loss Account for the year ended 31-03-2015

Expenditure		Rs.	Income		Rs.
1. Interest paid and payable :			**1.** Interest received :		
On Deposits	1,60,00		On Loans and Advances		
Interest payable	10,000	1,70,000	and Investments	3,50,000	
2. Bank Charges		–	Add Interest receivable		
3. Salaries and Allowances			on Loans	16,000	
to staff	59,400		Add Interest receivable		
Add Payable	600	60,000	on Investments	4000	3,70,000
4. Contribution of Staff P.F.		4,000	**2.** Dividend received		–
5. Salaries and Allowances			on shares		
to M.D.		–	**3.** Commission		–
6. Allowance fees and Travelling					
Exp. of Directors		–			
7. Travellign Expensess of Staff		1,200	**4.** Miscellaneous Incomes :		
8. Rent, rates and Taxes		–	Renewal Fees		8,000
9. Postage, Telegram and			Sundry Income		4,600
Telephone Exp.		–	**5.** Land Income and		
10. Printing and Stationery		–	Expenditure A/c		–
11. Audit fee outstanding		800			
12. General Exp.		6,000			
13. Bad debts and R.D.D.		–			
14. Depreciation on Fixed Assets		–			
15. Land Income and Expendiure					
A/c		–			
16. Other Items :		–			
Establishment charges					
Insurance premium		10,000			
17. Net profit c/d		2,000			
		1,28,600			
		3,82,600			**3,82,600**

**Balance Sheet of Shruti Co-operative Credit Society
as on 31-03-2015**

Liabilities		Rs.	Assets	Rs.
1. Share Capital :			**1. Cash and Bank Balances :**	
Authorised Issued and subscribed		15,00,000	Cash in hand	5,400
2. Reserve fund and other funds			Cash with D.D.C.C. Bank	20,000
i) Reseve Fund	70,000		Balance with Canara Bank	19,800
Add 25% transfer	30,000	1,00,000	**2. Investments:**	
ii) Dividend Equilisation Reserve			Investments	3,10,000
3. Staff Provident Fund		40,000	**3. Investments of staff P.F.**	–
4. Secured Loan		40,000	**4. Loan and Advances :**	
5. Unseured Loans		–	loan due form members	60,00,000
6. Deposits :		–	**5. Sundry Debtors**	–
Deposits from Member			**6. Current Assets**	–
7. Current liabilities and Prov.		44,96,000	**7. Fixed Assets :**	
Outstanding Salaries			Furniture	20,000
Outstanding Audit Fees		600	**8. Miscellaneons**	–
8. Unpaid Dividends :		6,000	**Exp. and Losses**	
Provision	70,000		**9. Other Items :**	
Less Paid	62000		Interest receivable on	16,000
9. Interest Accured due but		8,000	members loan Interest	4,000
not paid : Interest payable			receivable on Investment	
members Deposits			**10. Profit and Loss A/c**	–
10. Other Liabilities		10,000	**11. Current Losses**	–
11. Profit and Loss Account :		–		
P and L A/c Balance as on				
1-4-2013	46000			
Add : Profits for the				
year 2013-2014	1,20,000			
	1,66,000			
Less Dividend 5% on				
14,00,000	70,000			
Less 25% transfer				
R.F.	30,000			
	66,000			
Add Profit for	1,28,600			
2014-2015		1,94,600		
		63,95,200		63,95,200

ILLUSTRATION 5

From the following statement of Balance of Shri Amrut Co-op Credit Society, prepare the Profit and Loss Account and Balane sheet as on 31st March 2015 after considering the adjustments given below :

Statement of Balances
as on 31st March 2015

Receipts Balances	Rs.	Payment Balances		Rs.
1. Share capital :	10,00,000	1. Loans to members :		
Authorised Paid up	6,00,000	a. Medium term	8,20,000	
2. Cash Credit (P.D.C.C.Bank)	1,35,000	b. Emergencey	10,000	8,30,000
3. Interest on Loan	1,20,000	2. Investment of Reserve		
4. Sale of Loan forms	200	Fund in Fixed Deposits		80,000
5. Dividend on shares	4,000	3. Investment in shares of		
6. Interest on Fixed Deposits	7,000	P. D. C. C. Bank		40,000
7. Dividend Equ. Fund	10,000	4. Interest on Cash Credit		16,000
8. Reserve Fund :	80,000	5. Hon. to Secretary		4,000
9. Common Good Fund	15,000	6. Printing and Stationery		1,500
10. Balance of Profit for last		7. Annual General meeting		1,800
year	3,200	expenses		
11. Building Fund	20,000	8. Postage and Telegrams		100
		9. Audit Fees		800
		10. Travelling Expenses		400
		11. Education Fund		500
		12. Furniture		3,000
		13. Advertisement		500
		14. General Expenses		600
		15. Cl. Cash at Bank		15,000
		16. Cl. cash in hand		200
	9,94,400			**9,94,400**

Adjustments :

1) Depreciate Furniture at 10%.
2) Interest accrued on Investment Rs.1,000.
3) Honararium payable to Secretary Rs.400.
4) Stock of stationery (30-6-2015) Rs.500.
5) Provide Reserve for Bad and Doubtful Debts Rs.500.

Solution :

Profit and Loss Account of Amrut Co-operative Society
for the year ended 31st March 2015

Expenditure		Rs.	Income		Rs.
1. Interest on Cash Credit		16,000	1. Interest received :		
2. Bank Charges		–	a) On Loans	1,20,000	
3. Hon. to Secretary	4000		b) On Investments	7,000	
Add Payable	400	4400		1,27,000	
4. Contribution to Stall P.F.		–	Add Interest allowance	1000	1,28,000
5. Salaries and Allowances		–	2. Dividend on shares		4,000
of M.D.			3. Commission		–
6. Attendans Fee		–	4. Miscellaneous Income :		
7. Travelling Exp.		400	Sale of Loose forms		200
8. Rent, rates and Taxes		–	5. Land Income and Exp. A/c		–
9. Postage and Telegram		100			
10. Printing and Stationery	1500				
Less Stock of Stationery	500	1000			
11. Audit Fees		800			
12. General Exp.		600			
13. Bad Debts and R.D.D.		500			
14. Depreciation on Furniture					
at 10%		300			
15. Land Income and					
Expenditure A/c		–			
16. Other items :					
Advertisement		500			
Annual General Meeting Exp.		1800			
Education Fund		500			
17. Net Profit c/d		1,05,300			
		1,32,200			1,32,200

Balance Sheet of Amrut Co-op.Credit Society
as on 31-03-2015

Liabilities		Rs.	Assets		Rs.
1. Share Capital :			**1. Cash and Bank Balances**		
Authorised		10,00,000	Cash in hand		200
Issued and Paid		6,00,000	Cash at Bank		15,000
2. Reserve Fund and			**2. Investments :**		
Other funds			a) Fixed Deposits		80,000
Reserve Fund	80,000		b) Shares		40,000
Add 25% transfer	800	80,800	**3. Staff P.F.**		–
Dividend Equilisation fund		10,000	**4. Loans and Allowances :**		
Common Good Fund		15,000	Loan to Members :		
Building Fund		20,000	a) Medium	8,20,000	
R.D.D.		500	b) Emergency	10,000	8,30,000
3. Staff P.F.		–	**5. Sundry Debtors**		–
4. Secured loans		–	**6. Current Assets :**		500
5. Unseured loans :			Stock of Stationery		
Cash credit (P.D. C.C.Bank)		1,35,000	**7. Fixed Assets :**		
6. Deposits			Furniture	3,000	
7. Current Liabilities and		400	Less Dep.	300	2,700
Provisions - Hon to			**8. Miscellaneous Exp. ....**		
Secretary due			**9. Other Items :**		
8. Unpaid Dividend			Interest accrued on		
9. Interest Account due			Investment		1,000
but not paid			**10. Profit and Loss A/c**		
10. Other Liabilities :			**11. Current Losses**		
Profit of the last year	3200				
Less : 25% Transfer	800				
	2400				
Add Current year's Profit					
	105300	1,07,700			
		9,69,400			9,69,400

ILLUSTRATION 6

Following is the trial balance of Maharashtra High School employee's Co-operative Credit Society, Pune as on 31 March 2015.

Particulars	Debit	Credit
Share Capital	–	7,50,000
Reserve Fund	–	70,000
Dividend Equalisation Fund	–	20,000
Building Fund	–	30,000
Fixed Deposits	–	50,000
Loans and Overdrafts	–	14,70,000
Profit and Loss A/c	–	42,000
Dividend Received	–	5,000
Commission Received	–	9,000
Interest Received	–	4,52,000
Buildings	70,000	–
Furniture	20,000	–
Office Equipments	30,000	–
Investments	10,000	–
Interest on Loans and Deposits	2,02,000	–
Salaries and Allowances	62,000	–
Travelling Expenses	14,000	–
Printing and Stationery	12,000	–
Advertisement	10,000	–
Postage, Telegram and Telephone	15,000	–
Loans to Members	23,50,000	–
Audit Fees	3,000	–
Honorarium to Secretary	5,000	–
Office Expenses	10,000	–
Cash in hand	7,000	–
Cash at Bank	78,000	–
	28,98,000	28,98,000

Prepare Profit and Loss Account for the year ended 31th March, 2015 and a Balance Sheet as on that date after taking into consideration following adjustments :

1) Depreciate Building by 5% and Furniture and Office Equipment by 10%.
2) Salaries outstanding amounted to Rs.7,000.
3) Transfer the required amount of Reserve Fund and Education Fund.

Solution :

Profit and Loss Account of
Maharashtra High School employees Co-operative credit Society
for the year ended 31st March 2015

	Rs.	Rs.		Rs.	Rs.
1. Interest Paid and Payable		2,02,000	1. Interest on Loan		4,52,000
2. Bank Charges			2.Interest on		
3. Salaries and Allowances	62,000		Investments		1,200
Add Outstanding	7,000	69,000	3.Dividend on		5,000
4. Contribution to			shares		
5. Staff P.F.			Commission		9,000
6. Salaries and Allowance		–	Msc. Income		–
7. Travelling Expenses		14,000	4. Land Income		–
8. Rent, Rates and Taxes		–	and Expenditrue		
9. Postage		15,000			
10. Printing and Stationery		12,000			
11. Audit Fees		3,000			
12. Office xpenses		10,000			
13. R.D.D.		–			
14. Depreciation on					
Building	3,500				
Furniture	2,000				
Office Equipment					
and Exp. A/c	3,000	8,500			
15. Land Income and					
expenditure					
16. Other Items					
Advance 10,000		15,000			
Hon.to Secretary 5,000					
17. Net Profit		1,18,700			
		4,67,200			4,67,200

Maharashtra High School Employees Co-operative Credit Society Limited, Pune
Balance Sheet as at 31st March 2015

Liabilities	Rs.	Rs.	Assets	Rs.	Rs.
1) **Share Capital**		7,50,000	1. **Cash and Bank**		
2) **Reserve Fund and**			**Balances :**		
Other Reserves			Cash in hand	7,000	
Reserve Fund	70,000		Cash in bank	78,000	85,000
Add 25% transfer	10,500	80,500	2) **Investments**		10,000
Dividend Equalisation		20,000	3) **Investments**		
Fund			of P.F.		
Building Fund		1,30,000	4) **Loans and Advances**		
Education Fund			Loans		23,50,000
3) **Staff P.F.**		500	5) **Sundry Debtors**		–
4) **Secured Loans :**			6) **Current Assets**		–
Loans		14,70,000	7) **Fixed Assets**		
5) **Unsecured Loans**			Building 70,000		
6) **Deposit**		50,000	Dep. 3,500	66,500	
7) **Current liabilities**			Furniture 20,000		
and Provisions			Dep. 2,000	18,000	
Salaries Outstanding		7,000	Office Equipments		
8) **Unpaid Dividend**			30,000		
9) **Interest Accrued due**			Dep. 3,000	27,000	1,11,500
and unpaid			8) **Misc. Expenses**		
10) **Other liabilities**			**and Losses.**		
11) **Profit and Loss Account :**			9) **Interest Accured**		1200
Balance Last year	42,000		10) **Profit and Loss A/c**		–
Less 25% transfer to R.F.			11) **Current Losses**		–
	10,500				
Less Education Fund	500				
	31,000				
Add Current year					
profit	1,18,700				
		1,49,700			
		25,57,700			**25,57,700**

ILLUSTRATION 7

From the following Trial Balance of Kartiki Credit Co-operative Society Ltd., Pune Prepare final Accounts for the year ended 31st March 2015 in the prescribed form.

Debit Balances	Rs.	Credit Balances	Rs.
Loans to Members	3,50,000	Share Capital	1,00,000
Contribution to staff Provident Fund	240	Reserve Fund	9,000
Insurance Premium	520	Members Deposits	70,000
Travelling & Conveyance	1,710	Unpaid Dividend	200
Printing & Stationery	480	Staff Provident Fund	2,400
Salary of Managing Director	6,000	P & L A/c (1-04-2014)	3,500
Salaries to Staff	13,600	Interest	43,000
Interest on Loan	960	Renewal fees	400
Interest on Deposit	9,600	Sundry Income	320
Office Furniture	840	Co-op Development Fund	2,000
Fixed Deposit with Co-op Bank		Education Fund	600
Cash in hand	30,000		
Cash at Bank	2,180		
	15,290		
	4,31,420		**2,31,420**

Adjustments :

1) Interest due on members Deposit Rs.1,000.
2) Interest due but not received Rs.2,400
3) Salary outstanding on 31st March 2015 Rs.600.
4) Audit fees unpaid Rs.400.
5) Authorised Capital - 10,000 Shares of Rs.20 each.
6) Directors propose to pay Dividend 2%.
7) Depreciate Furniture by 5%.

Solution :

Kartiki Credit Co-op. Society Ltd.,
Profit and Loss Account for the year ended 31st March 2015

	Rs.		Rs.
To Interest		By Interest	
Paid	9,600	Received 43,000	
Payable	1,960	Add Outstanding 2,400	45,400
To Bank Charges		By Dividented on Shares	–
To Salaries & Allowances of		By Commission	–
Staff	14,200	By Miscellanceous	
To Contribution to Staff Provident Fund		Income	–
	240	Renewal Fees	400
To Salaries & Allowance to Menaging Director		Sundry Income	320
	6,000	Land Income & Exp. A/c	–
To Attendance Fees and Travelling Exp. of Directors			
To Travelling Exp. of Staff	–		
To Rent, Rates & Taxes	1,710		
To Postage & Telegram & Tele-phone Charges			
To Printing and Stationery	–		
To Audit Fees	480		
to General Expenses	400		
To Bad Debts Written off and Bad Debts Provision			
To Depreciation Furniture	–		
To Land Income & Exp. A/c.	42		
Insurance & Premium			
To Net Profit	520		
	10,968		
	46,120		**46,120**

Kartiki Credit Co-op. Society Ltd.,
Balance Shet as on 31st March 2015

Liabilities	Rs.	Assets	Rs.
I Share Capital :		**I Cash & Bank**	
Authorised 10000 shares		Balance :	
of Rs.20 each	2,00,000	Cash in Hand	2,180
Issued & Subscribed	1,00,000		
5000 Shares of Rs.20		Cash at Bank	15,290
Each Fully Paid.		**II Investments :**	
II Reserve Fund &		Fixed Deposit with	
Others Funds		Bank	30,000
Reserve Fund 9000			
Add : 25% transfer 875	9,875	**III Investment of Staff**	–
Co-op Development Fund	2,000	Provident Fund	–
Education Fund 600			
Add transfer 500	1,100	**IV Loans & Advances :**	–
III Staff Provident Fund	2,400	Loans to Members	3,50,000
IV Secured Loans	-	**V Sundry Debtors**	–
V Unsecured Loans	-	**VI Current Assets**	–
VI Deposits :			
Members Deposit	2,70,000	**VII Fixed Assets :**	
VII Current Liabilities		Office Furniture 840	
& Provisions :		**Less :** Depreciation 42	798
Salaries Outstanding	600		
Audit Fees Payable	400	**VII Miscellaneous**	–
VII Unpaid Dividend	200	Expenses & Losses	
IX Interest Accrued		**IX Other Items**	
due but not paid	1,000	Interest accrued	
X Other Liabilities		but not received	2,400
XI Profit and Loss A/c		**X Profit and Loss A/c**	–
Profit for the Last Year		**XI Current Losses**	–
3,500			
Less transfer 25% - 875			
Less Education Fund 500			
2,125			
Add Profit of the year 10,968	13,093		
	4,00,668		**4,00,668**

4.7.2 Final Account of Consumers Co-operative Society

ILLUSTRATION 1

From the following Trial Balance of Sudarshan Co-operative Purchases and Sales Society Ltd. as on 31st March 2015, prepare Trading, Profit and Loss Account for the year ended 31st March, 2015 and Balance Sheet as on that date after considering the adjustment given thereafter.

Trial Balance as on 31ˢᵗ March 2015

Particulars	Debit Rs.	Credit Rs.
Share capital	–	3,36,000
Reserve fund	–	60,000
Creditors	–	40,000
Profit and loss A/c 1-4-2014	–	1,76,000
Opening stock	3.92,000	–
Furniture and equipments	1,24,000	–
Container deposits	32,000	–
Salaries	3,00.000	–
Sundry debtors	60,000	–
Commission	88,000	–
Rent and taxes	60,000	–
Postage	8,000	–
Travelling expenses	18,000	–
Printing and stationery	14,000	–
Admission fee	–	2,000
Purchases	63,40,000	–
Carriage inwards	1,60,000	–
Investments	2,40,000	–
Sales	–	76,20,000
Cash in hand	6,000	–
Cast at bank	4,00,000	–
Development fund	–	8,000
	82,42,000	**82,42,000**

Adjustments :

1) Closing stock valued at Rs. 4,40,000.
2) Outstanding rent Rs. 4,000 and commission payable Rs. 20,000.
3) Rs. 8,000 salary was paid in advance.
4) Accrued income on investment Rs. 20,000.
5) Provide 10% depreciation on furniture and equipments

Solution :

Sudarshan Co-operative Purchases and Sales Society

Dr.　　　　**Trading Account for the year ended 31st March 2015**　　　　**Cr.**

Particulars	Amount	Particulars	Amount
To Opening Stock	3,92,000	By Sales	76,20,000
To Purchases	63,40,000	By Closing Stock	4,40.000
To Carriage Inwards	1,60,000		
To Gross Profit transferred to			
Profit and Loss A/c	11,68,000		
	80,60,000		**80,60,000**

Profit and Loss A/c

Dr.　　　　**for the year ended 31st March 2015**　　　　**Cr.**

Particulars		Amount	Particulars	Amount
To Salaries	3,00,000		By Gross Profit b/d	11,68,000
Less : Prepaid	8,000	2,92,000	By Interest on Investment	
To Commission	88,000		accrued	20,000
Add : Commission			By Admission fee	2,000
payable	20,000	1,08,000		
To Rent and taxes	60,000			
Add : Outstanding Rent	4,000	64,000		
To Postage		8,000		
To Travelling expenses		18,000		
To Printing and stationery		14,000		
To Depreciation on furniture		12,400		
To Net profit carried to the				
Balance sheet		6,73,600		
		11,90,000		**11,90,000**

Balance Sheet as on 31st March 2015

Liabilities		Amount	Assets		Amount
Share capital		3,36,000	**Cash and bank balances**		
Reserve fund and other Reserve			Cash in hand		6,000
Reserve fund		60,000	Cash at bank		4,00,000
Development fund		8,000	**Investments**		2,40,000
Current liabilities			**Sundry debtors**		60,000
Creditors		40,000	**Current assets**		
Commission payable		20,000	Closing stock		4,40,000
Outstanding rent		4,000	**Fixed assets**		
Profit and Loss A/c			Furniture and equipment	1,24,000	
Profit on 1.4.2014	1,76,000		Less : Dep. 10%	12,400	1,11,600
Add : Profit of			**Other Items**		
current year	6,73,600	8,49,600	Prepaid salary		8,000
			Container deposit		32,000
			Interest accrued		20,000
		13,17,600			**13,17,600**

ILLUSTRATION 2

From the following Trial Balance of Sukanya Consumer's Co-operative Society, Pune as on 31st March 2015

Trial Balance

Particulars	Debit Rs.	Credit Rs.
Share capital	–	80,000
Deposit from members	–	50,000
Sales	–	12,50,000
Purchases returns	–	5,000
Suppliers	–	10,000
Interest on investments	–	12,000
Rebate received	–	3,000
Common good fund	–	4,000
Price fluctuation fund	–	8,000
Reserve fund	–	20,000
Cash in hand	400	–
Cash at bank	86,000	–
Furniture	6,000	–
Purchases	10,05,000	–
Customers	30,000	–
Carriage inward	5,000	–
Sales return	2,000	–
Rent	10,000	–
Audit fees	2.000	–
Sales tax	3,000	–
Staff salary	50,000	–
Printing and stationery	10,000	–
Investment	2,00,000	–
Stock in trade (1-4-2014)	30,000	–
Interest paid	2,600	–
Total	**14,42,000**	**14,42,000**

Adjustments :

1) Closing stock on 31st March, 2015 was Rs. 60,000.
2) Depreciation on furniture @ 10% p.a.
3) Interest accrued on deposits Rs. 1,500 and interest accrued on investments Rs. 6,000.
4) Outstanding salary of Rs. 3,000.
5) Outstanding sales tax of Rs. 1,000.

You are required to prepare Trading, Profit and Loss Account and Balance Sheet as on 31 st March 2015.

(Pune university)

Solution :

Sukanya Consumer's Co-operative Society
Trading, Profit and Loss Account
for the year ended 31 st March, 2015

Particulars		Amount	Particulars		Amount
To Opening stock		30,000	By Sales	12,50,000	
To Purchases	10,05,000		Less : Return inwards	2,000	12,48,000
Less : Return outwards	5,000	10,00,000	By Closing Stock		60,000
To Carriage inwards		5,000			
To Gross Profit transferred to					
Profit and Loss A/c		2,73,000			
		13,08,000			**13,08,000**
To Interest paid	2,600		By Gross profit b/d		2,73,000
Add : Accrued	1,500	4,100	By Interest on		
To Salary	50,000		investments	12,000	
Add : Outstanding	3,000	53,000	**Add :** Accrued	6,000	18,000
To Rent		10,000	By Rebate received		3,000
To Printing and stationery		10,000			
To Audit fees		2,000			
To Sales tax	3,000				
Add : Outstanding	1,000	4,000			
To Education fund		100			
To Depreciation on furniture		600			
To Net profit trans. to B/Sheet		2,10,200			
		2,94,000			**2,94,000**

Memorandum Profit and Loss Appropriation A/c

| Dr. | | for the year ended 31st March, 2015 | | Cr. |

Particulars	Amount	Particulars	Amount
To Reserve fund (25% on N.P.)	52,550	By Net profit	2,10,200
To Balance transferred			
to B/Sheet	1,57,650		
	2,10,200		**2,10,200**

- Current year's appropriation can't be adjusted in the final A/c of that year as they are required to be sanctioned in the Annual General Meeting.

Sukanya Consumer's Co-operative Society
Balance Sheet as on 31st I

Liabilities	Amount	Assets		Amount
Share Capital	80,000	**Cash and Bank**		
Reserve fund and-Other funds		Cash in hand		400
Reserve fund	20,000	Cash at bank		86,000
Common good fund	4,000	**Investments**		2,00,000
Price fluctuation fund	8,000	**Sundry debtors**		30,000
Education fund	100	**Current Assets**		
Deposits		Closing stock		60,000
Deposit from members	50,000	**Fixed Assets**		
Current Liabilities		Furniture	6,000	
Creditors	10,000	Less : Dep. 10%	600	5,400
Outstanding exp.		**Other items**		
Salary	3,000	Interest accrued on		
Sales tax	1,000 4,000	investments		6,000
Interest accrued on deposits	1,500			
Profit and Loss A/c	2,10,200			
	3,87,800			**3,87,800**

ILLUSTRATION 3

Following is the Trial Balances of Harshal Co-operative consumer's Co-operative society for the year ended 31st March 2008. Prepare Trading Account, Profit and Loss Account and Balance Sheet.

Particulars	Debit	Credit
Opening Stock of Goods	12,000	–
Purchases	3,27,000	–
Carriage Inward	4,000	–
Sales		
Sale of empty bags	–	3,44,000
Return Outward	–	14,000
Salaries	12,000	5,000
Sundry expenses		
Interest on Govt. Loan	720	–
General Exp.	150	–
Printing & Stationery	1,420	–
Cash in hand	4,840	–
Cash Bank	6,000	–
National Saving Certificate	500	–
Electricity	320	–
Advances	850	–
Debtors	5,600	–
Dead Stock	800	–
Reserve Fund	–	10,000
Government Loans	–	6,000
Educational Fund	–	1,000
Building	60,000	–
Share Capital	–	50,000
Creditors	–	6,200
	4,36,200	4,36,200

Adjustments -

1) Closing Stock was valued at Rs.18,000.

2) Audit fees payable Rs.500

3) Charge Depreciation @ 10% on Dead stock and 5% on Building.

4) Make provision for Bad Debts Rs.200.

5) Authorised capital is Rs.1,00,000 divided into shares of Rs.20 each.

Solution :

Harshal Consumers Co-operative Society
Trading Account for the year ended 31st March 2015

	Rs.		Rs.
To Opening Stock of Goods	12,000	By Sales	3,44,000
To Purchases 3,27,000		By Sale of empty	
Returns 5,000	3,22,000	Bags	14,000
To Carriage inward	4,000	By Stock	18,000
To Gross profit c/d	38,000		
Total	3,76,000	Total	3,76,000

Profit and Loss Account for the
Year ended 31st March 2015

	Rs.		Rs.
To Interest on Govt. Loan	720	By Gross Profit	
To Bank Charges	-	From Trading A/c	38,000
To Salaries & allowances	12,000	By Dividend Received	-
To Contribution to P.F.	-	By Commission	-
To Salaries & Allowances of	-	By Miscellaneous	-
Managing Director		Income	
To Attendance Fees	-	By Land Income &	
Travelling		Expenditure A/c	-
Exp. of Director			
To Travelling Exp.	-		
of Staff			
To Rent Rates Taxes	-		
To Postage Telephone	-		
To Printing & Stationery	1,420		
To Audit Fees	500		
To General Expenses	150		
To Bad Debts Provision	200		
To Deprciation			
Building 3,000			
Dead Stock 80	3,080		
To Land Income & Exp. A/c	-		
To Other items			
Electricity	320		
To net Profit	19,610		
	38,000		38,000

Harshal Consumers Co-operative Society Ltd
Balance Sheet as on 31st March 2015

Liabilities		Rs.	Assets		Rs.
I	**Share Capital**		I	**Cash & Bank**	
(i)	Authorised 50,000 shares of Rs. 20 each.	1,00,000		Balance : Cash in Hand	4,840
(ii)	Subscribed 2500 shares of Rs.20 each fully Paid.	50,000		Cash at Bank	6,000
II	**Reserve Funds & Other Funds**		II	**Investments :**	
	Reserve Fund	10,000		National Saving Certificate	500
	Education Fund	1,000	III	**Investment of Staff**	
	Bad Debts Reserve	200		**P.F.**	
III	**Staff P.F.**	-	IV	**Loans & Advances**	
IV	**Secured Loans**	-		Advances	850
V	**Unsecured Loans**	-	V	**Sundry Debtors**	5,600
	Government Loan	6,000	VI	**Current Assets**	
VI	**Deposits**	-		Stock of Goods	18,000
VII	**Current Liabilities & Provisions**		VII	**Fixed Assets**	
	Creditors	6,200		Building 60,000	
	Audit Fees Payable	500		Depreciation 3,000	57,000
VIII	**Unpaid Dividend**	-		Dead Stock 800	
IX	**Interest Accrued but not paid**	-		Depreciation 80	720
X	**Other Liabilities**	-	VIII	**Miscellanceous Expenditure**	
XI	**Profit & Loss A/c**	19,610	IX	**Other Items**	-
			X	**Profit & Loss A/c**	-
			XI	**Current Losses.**	-
		93,510			93,510

N.B. :

There is no tranfer to Reserve Fund (25% as required) during the year as this appropriation is needed to be approved in Annual General Meeting which is to be hold within 42 days after completion of Final Accounts.

ILLUSTRATION 4

You are required to Prepare Trading and profit and loss. Account for the year ended 31st March 2015 and a Balance Sheet as on that date from the Trial Balance for the year ended 31st March 2015 and adjustments given in respect of Usha Consumers Co-operative Society, Pune 2015

Trial Balance

Particulars	Debit	Credit
Share Capital	-	50,000
Calls in arrears	5,000	-
Reserve Fund	-	7,500
Co-operative Development Fund	-	2,500
Opening Stock of Consumer's Goods	55,000	-
Furniture	24,000	-
Education Fund	-	4,000
Creditors for Purchases	-	10,000
Sundry Debtors	15,000	-
Commission Payable	-	2,000
Salaries	35,500	-
Commission	8,700	-
Rent & Taxes	10,000	-
Postage	1,350	-
Travellings & Conveyance	1,200	-
Printing & Stationery	1,500	-
Contribution to Staff P.F.	4,500	-
Audit Fees	2,000	-
Interest on Investment	-	5,000
Profit & Loss Appropriation A/c Balance	-	30,000
Equipments	10,000	250
Admission Fee	-	-
Purchases	8,00,000	-
Carriage & Coolie Charges	20,000	-
Investments	50,000	-
Sales	-	10,30,000
Cash in hand	12,500	-
Cash at Bank	85,000	-
	11,41,250	11,41,250

Adjustments :

1. Outstanding Rent payable on 31st March 2015 was Rs.500.
2. Outstanding salary payable on 31st March 2015 was Rs.1,000.
3. Of the salaries paid Rs.1,500 was as an advance to employee on 31st March 2015.
4. Interest accrued on investments Rs.1,000.
5. Directors recommend 10% Dividend to its shareholders and transfer of Rs.500 to Development Fund out of the profit of Last Year.
6. Charge 5% Depreciation on furniture.
7. Closing stock of consumers goods is valued at cost Rs.70,000.

Solution :

Trading Account of Usha Consumer's Co-operative Society for the year ended 31st March 2015.

	Current years figures Rs.		Current years figures Rs.
To Opening Stock of Consumers' Goods	55,000	By Sales	10,30,000
To Purchase of Goods	8,00,000	By Closing Stock of consumer's Goods	70,000
To Carriage and Collie Charges			
To Gross Profit transferred to Profit & Loss A/c	20,000		
	2,25,000		
	11,00,000		11,00,000

Profit and Loss Account
for the year ended 31-03-2015

		Rs.			Rs.
To Interest Paid and Payable		–	By Gross Profit		2,25,000
To Bank Charges		–	By Interest on Invest	5000	
To Salaries and Allow.	35,500		Add: Interest Accumed	1000	6,000
Add : Outstanding	1,000		By Dividend received		–
	36,500		By Commission		–
Less : Advance	1,500	35,000	By Miscellaneous Income :		
To Contribution to Staff P.F.		4,500	Admission Fee		250
To Salaries and Allowances to			By Land Income and		–
Managing Director		–	Expenditure A/c		
To Attendance Fees		–			
To Travelling and Allowances		1,200			
To Rent Rates Taxes	10,000				
Add : Outstanding	500	10,500			
To Postage		1,350			
To Printing and Stationery		1,500			
To Audit Fees		2,000			
To General Expenses		–			
To Bad Debts and R.D.D.		–			
To Deprciation on Furniture		1,200			
To Land Income					
and Expenditure		–			
To Other items :					
Commission Paid		8,700			
To Net Profit		1,65,300			
		2,31,250			2,31,250

**Balance Sheet of Usha Co-op Credit Society
as on 31-03-2015**

Liabilities		Rs.	Assets		Rs.
1) **Share Capitals**			1) **Cash and Bank Balances :**		
Share Captial	50,000		Cash in hand		12,500
Less Calls in Arrers	5,000	45,000	Cash at bank		85,000
2) **Reserve Fund and Other Fund**			2) **Investments**		50,000
Resere Fund :	7,500		3) **Investments of Staff P.F.**		–
Add 25%	7,500	15,000			
1) **Development Fund**	2,500		4) **Loans and Advances :**		
Add : transfer during			Salary Advance		1500
the year	500	3,000	5) **Sundry Debtors**		15,000
2) **Education Fund**		4,000	6) **Current Assets :**		
3) **Staff P.F.**		–	Closing Stock		70,000
4) **Secured loans**		–	7) **Fixed Assets :**		
5) **Unsecured loans**		–	Furniture	24000	
6) **Deposits**		–	Less : Dep.	1200	22,800
7) **Current liabilities and**			Equipments		10,000
Provisions :			8) **Miscellaneous**		
Sundry Creditors :		10,000	Expenditure and Losses		
Outstanding Expenses :			9) **Other Items :**		1,000
Rent	500		Interest Accured		
Dividend Proposal	4,500		10) **Profit and Loss A/c**		–
Salary	1,000	6,000	11) **Current Losses**		–
8) **Unpaid Dividend**		–			
9) **Interest Accrued**		–			
10) **Other Liabilities :**					
Commission Payable		2,000			
11) **Profit and Loss A/c**					
Balance as on 1-4-14	30,000				
Less : 25% transfer	7,500				
Less : Development	500				
Less Dividend	4,500				
Add Profit of the	17,500				
Current year	1,65,300	1,82,800			
		2,67,800			**2,67,800**

ILLUSTRATION 5

From the following Trial Balance and the adjustments given in respect of Kunda consumers Co-operative Society, Pune, Prepare the final Accounts for the year ended 31st March 2015.

Trial Balance
as on 31st March 2015

Particulars	Debit	Credit
Opening Stock of Fertilisers and Machinery	10,000	–
Share Capital	–	75,000
Deposits from Members	–	90,000
Printing and Stationery	3,000	–
Investment in Shares of District Co-operative Bank	60,000	–
Investment in Shares of Co-operative Purchases and Sales Society	36,000	–
Loan from Bank (Unsecured)	–	92,000
Loan to Members	1,35,000	–
Interest earned on Loan given to Member	–	45,000
Purchases of fertilisers and Machinery	3,70,000	–
Sales of fertilisers and Machinery	-	4,50,000
Office Equipments	25,000	–
Office Rent	5,000	–
Salaries	25,000	–
Travelling Expesnses	5,000	–
Carriage Inward	3,500	–
Freight	1,500	–
Interest paid	8,000	–
Reserve Fund	–	86,000
P and L A/c as on 1-4-2014	–	1,00,000
Cash in hand	51,000	–
Cash at Bank	2,00,000	–
	9,38,000	**9,38,000**

Adjustments :

1) Closing Stock of Fertilisers and Machinery as on 31st march 2015 was Rs.70,000.
2) Outstanding office rent Rs.1,000.
3) Office Equipments are to be depreciated @ 5%.
4) Create Reserve for Bad and Doubtful Debt of Rs.4,500.
5) Audit Fees are to be paid of Rs.2,000.
6) Directors declared a Dividend to Members @ 1% on paid up capital on 1-4-2014.

Solution :

**Trading Account for the year
ended 31st March 2015**

Expenditure	Current years figures Rs.	Income	Current years figures Rs.
To Opening Stock	10,000	By Sales	4,50,000
Purchases	3,70,000	By Closing Stock	70,000
To Carriage Inward	3,500		
To Freight	1,500		
ToGross Profit			
transferred to			
To P and L A/c	1,35,000		
	5,20,000		**5,20,000**

**Profit and Loss Account
for the year ended 31st March 2015**

		Rs.		Rs.
To Interest Paid		8000	By Gross Profit b/d	1,35,000
To Bank Charges		–	By Interest earned on loan	45,000
To Salaries and Allow.			given to Memebrs	
to Staff		25,000	By Dividend received	–
To Salaries and Allow.			By Commission received	–
to M.D.		–	By Miscellaneous Income	–
Attendance Fees etc.		–	By Land Income and Ex. A/c	–
Travelling Expenses		5,000		
Rent, Rates and Taxes	5,000			
Add : Outstanding	1,000	6,000		
Postage and Telegram		–		
Printing and Stationery		3,000		
Outstanding Audit Fees		2,000		
General Exp.		–		
Bad debts and R.D.D.		4,500		
Dep. on office Equipments		1,250		
Land Income and Exp. A/c		–		–
Other Item		–		–
Net Profit c/d		1,25,250		–
		1,80,000		**1,80,000**

**Balance Sheet of Kunda Consumer Co-op Society
as on 31-03-2015**

Liabilities		Rs.	Assets		Rs.
1) **Share Capital**		75,000	1) **Cash and Bank Balances :**		
2) **Reserve Fund and Other Fund**			Cash in hand		51,000
Reserve Fund	86,000		Cash at Bank		2,00,000
Add : 25% transfer	25,000	1,11,000	2) **Investments :**		
R.D.D.		4,500	Shares of D.C.C. Bank		60,000
3) **Staff P.F.**		–	Shares of Co-op purchase		36,000
4) **Secured loans**		–	and sales society.		
5) **Unseured loan (from Bank)**		92,000	3) **Investment of Staff P.F.**		–
6) **Deposits :**			4) **Loans and Advances :**		
Deposits from Members		90,000	Loans to Members		1,35,000
7) **Current Liabilities and Prov.**			5) **Sundry Debtors**		
Outstanding Office Rent		1,000	6) Current Assets :		
Outstanding and it fees		2,000	Closing Stock		70,000
8) **Proposed Dividend**		7,500	7) **Fixed Assets :**		
9) **Interest Accrued but not due**		–	Office Equip.	25000	
10) **Other Liabilities**		–	Less Dep.	1250	23,750
11) **Profit and Loss A/c :**			8) **Mis. Expenditure**		
Balance as on 1-4-14	1,00,000		**and Losses**		–
Less 25% transfer	25,000		9) **Other Items :**		–
Less Proposed Dividend	7,500		10) **P and L A/c**		–
	67,500		11) **Current Losses**		
Add : Profit of the year	1,25,250	1,92,750			
		5,75,750			**5,75,750**

ILLUSTRATION 6

From the following Trial Balance for the year ended 31st march 2015 and the adjustments in respect of Tejas Consumer's Co-Op.Society, Prepare the final Accounts for the year ended 31st March 2015.

Particulars	Debit Rs.	Credit Rs.
Share Capital	–	8,00,000
Reserve Fund	–	2,00,000
Purchases	12,00,000	–
Stock on 1-04-2014	2,00,000	–
Carriage Inward	10,000	–
Salaries and Allowances to Staff	1,40,000	
Building Fund	–	1,40,000
Share Capital Redemption fund	–	25,000
Contribution to Staff Provident Fund	10,000	–
Staff Providend Fund	–	34,000
Sales	–	16,00,000
Bad Debts	8,000	–
Reserve for Bad and Doubtful Debts	–	20,000
Postage	6,000	–
Machinery (at Cost)	28,000	–
Travelling Expenses	10,000	–
Bonus to Employees	10,000	–
Printing and Stationery	3,500	–
Insurance	11,000	–
Building (at cost)	6,00,000	–
Furniture (at cost)	1,00,000	–
Depreciation Fund	–	90,000
Sundry Debtors	2,00,000	–
Sundry Creditors	–	25,000
Investment in Shares of Co-op. Societies	1,20,000	–
Staff Provident Fund		
Investment	34,000	–
Fixed Deposit with District Central Co-op Bank	1,60,000	–
Sundry Expenses	10,000	–
Repairs to Building	20,000	–
Interest on Fixed Deposit	–	16,000
Dividend received on shares	–	12,000
Transfer Fees	–	5,000
Profit and Loss Appropriation A/c balance of last year	–	20,000
Cash at Bank	1,00,000	
Cash in hand	6,500	
	29,87,000	**29,87,000**

Adjustments :

1) Closing Stock on 31st March 2015 was Rs.3,20,000
2) Salaries unpaid on 31-03-2015 was Rs.8,000
3) Prepaid Insurance is Rs.1,500.
4) Provide Reserve for Bad and Doubtful Debts @ 5%.
5) Provide Depreciation for the year as shown below :

    On Building   Rs.   30,000

    On Furniture   Rs.   10,000

    On Machinery   Rs.   2,800

6) Transfer to Education Fund Rs.100
7) Audit Fees are outstanding for the year Rs.5,000.
8) Provide for Share Capital Redemption Fund Rs.3,000.
9) Directors declared dividend to Members @ 10%. out of profit.

Solution :

In the Book of Consumer co-op society Ltd.
Trading Account
For the year ended 31 March 2015

	Rs.		Rs.
To Opening Stock	2,00,000	By Sales	16,00,000
To Purchases	12,00,000	By Closing Stock	3,20,000
To Carriage Inward	10,000		
To Gross Profit			
Transferred to P and L A/c	5,10,000		
	19,20,000		19,20,000

Profit and Loss Account
for the year ended 31st March 2015

	Rs.		Rs.
To Interest Paid	–	By Gross Profit b/d	5,10,000
To Bank Charges	–	By Interest received	16,000
To Salaries and Allow.		By Dividend received	12,000
to Staff 1,40,000		By Commission received	–
Add : outstanding salary 8,000	1,48,000	By Miscellanceous Income :	
To Contribution to staff P.F.	10,000	Transfer Fees	5,000
To Salaries and Allow.		Old R.D.D.	20,000
to M.D.	–	Less : Bad debts 8000	
To Attendance Fees etc.	–	Less : New Reserve 10,000	18,000
To Travelling Expenses	10,000		2,000
To Rent, Rates and Taxes	–	By Land Income and Exp. A/c	–
ToPostage and Telegram	6,000		
ToPrinting and Stationery	3,500		
ToOutstanding Audit Fees	5,000		
To General Expenses			
(Sundry Exp)	10,000		
Bad debts and R.D.D. 18,000			
Less : as per Contra 18,000	–		
Depreciation on Fixed Assets:			
On Building 30,000			
On Machinery 2,800			
On Furniture 10,000	42,800		
Land Income and Exp A/c	–		
Other Items :			
Bonus to employee	10,000		
Insurance 11,000			
Less : Prepaid 1,500	9,500		
Repairs to buildings	20,000		
Net Profit c/d	2,70,200		
	5,45,000		**5,45,000**

Balance Sheet of Tejas Counsumer Co-op Society
for the year ended 31st March 2015

Liabilities		Rs.	Assets	Rs.
1) **Share Capital**		8,00,000	1) **Cash and Bank Balances :**	
2) **Reserve Fund and Other Fund**			Cash in hand	6,500
Reserve Fund	2,00,000		Cash at Bank	1,00,000
Add : 25% transfer	5,000	2,05,000	2) **Investments :**	
Building Fund		1,40,000	Shares of co-op society	1,20,000
Shares Cap.redemption		–	Fixed Deposit with	1,60,000
Fund	25,000	–	D.C.C. Bank	
Add Transfer during			3) **Investment of Staff P.F.**	34,000
the year	3,000	28,000	4) **Loans and Advances :**	–
R.D.D. (New)		10,000	5) **Sundry Debtors**	2,00,000
Education Fund		100	6) **Current Assets :**	
Depreciation Fund	90,000		Closing stock	3,20,000
Add : Addition during			7) **Fixed Assets at Cost :**	
the year	42,800	1,32,800	Building	6,00,000
3) **Staff P.F.**		34,000	Furniture	1,00,000
4) **Secured loans**		–	Machinery	28,000
5) **Unsecured loans**		–	8) **Mis. Expenditure and**	–
6) **Deposits**		–	**Losses**	
7) **Current Liabilitiess Prov.**			9) **Other Items :**	
S.Creditors		25,000	Prepaid Insurance	1,500
Outstanding Salary		8,000	10) **P and L A/c**	–
Outstanding audit fees		5,000	11) **Current Losses**	–
proposed Divided		2,000		
8) **Unpaid Dividend**				
9) **Interest Accured but not paid**				
10) **Other Liabilities**				
11) **Profit and Loss Account**				
balance as on 1-4-2014	20,000			
Less : 25% transfer	5,000			
Less : transfer to share				
capital rel.fund	3,000			
Less: transfer to				
Education	100			
Less : proposed dividend	2,000			
	9,900			
Add: Current year's	2,70,200	2,80,100		
Profit		16,70,000		16,70,000

ILLUSTRATION 7

From the following Trial Balance is on 31st March 2015 and the information given thereafter of Ramesh Consumer's Co-operative Society Ltd, prepare Trading A/c and Profit and Loss A/c for the year ended 31.3.2015 and a Balance Sheet as on that date.

Trial Balance as on 31-03-2015

Particulars	Debit Rs.	Credit Rs.
Share Capital as on 1-4-2014	–	10,000
Reserve Fund	–	1,500
Co-operative Development Fund	–	500
Stock of Consumer's Goods as on 1-4-2014	11,250	–
Office Furniture	5,300	–
Price Fluctuation Fund	–	800
Sundry Creditors for purchases	–	2,000
Sundry Debtors for sales	3,000	–
Salaries	7,500	–
Commission	2,700	–
Commission payable	–	500
Rent and Taxes	2,600	–
Postage	1,250	–
Travelling and conveyance.	200	–
Printing and Stationery	400	–
Calls in arrears as on 1.4.2014	600	–
Dividend for 2013-2014	470	–
Audit Fees	400	–
Interest on Investment	–	1,100
Profits for the year 2013-2014	–	5,000
Equipments	1,800	–
Admission Fees	–	50
Purchases	1,58,500	–
Carriage and Cartage	4,000	–
Investments	10,000	–
Sales	–	2,05,000
Cash in hand	1,480	–
Cash at bank	15,000	–
	2,26,450	2,26,450

Additional Information :

1) Closing Stock of consumer's Goods as on 31.3.2015 is valued at cost price Rs.12,500 and at market price Rs.14,000.

2) Outstanding expenses on 31.3.2015 were as follows :

   (i) Rent Rs.100

   (ii) Salary Rs.200

3) Salary Prepaid amounted to Rs.300.

4) Interest accrued on investments was Rs.200.

5) Charge 5% depreciation on office furniture.

6) The Society declared 10% dividend on its paid up capital as on 31.3.2015. The society also transferred 25% of their profits for the year ended 31.3.2015 to Reserve Fund and transferred Rs.310 to Co-operative Development Fund is approved in the Annual General Meeting held on 31.7.2014.

Solution :

In the Books of Ramesh Consumer's Co-operative Society Ltd.

Trading A/c for the year ended 31st March 2015

Expenditure	Rs.	Income	Rs.
Stock of Consumer's Goods as on 1-4-2014	11,250	Sales 2,05,000	2,05,000
Purchases 1,58,500		Less Sales Returns Nil	
Less Returns Outward Nil	1,58,500		
Carriage and Freight	4,000	Closing Stock of Consumer's	
Gross Profit transferred to		Goods as on 31.3.2015	12,500
Profit and Loss A/c	43,750		
	2,17,500		2,17,500

Profit and Loss A/c for the year ended 31st March 2015

Expenditure	Rs.	Income	
1. Interest - (a) Paid (b) Payable		1. Interest received : (a) On Loans and Advances (b) On Investment 1,100 Add interest accrued on investment 200	1,300
2. Bank Charges -			
3. Salaries and Allowances of staff Salares 7,500 (+) Outstanding Salary 200 7,700 Less Salary Prepaid 300	7,400		
4. Contributin to Staff Provident Fund -	–	2. Dividend Received on shares	–
5. Salaries and allowances of Managing Director.	–		
6. Attendance fees and Travelling expenses of directors :	–	3. Commission	–
7. Travelling expenses of Directors : Travelling and Conveyance	– 200	4. Miscellaneous Income : Admission Fees	50
8. Rent Rates and Taxes : Rent and Taxes 2,600 Add outstanding rent 100	2,700	5. Land Income and Expenditure A/c	–
9. Postage, Telegram and Telephone charges : Postage	1250	Gross Profit B/D	43,750
10. Printing and Stationery	400		
11. Audit Fees : Audit fees	400		
12. General xpenses			
13. Bad debts or provision for bad debts.			
14. Dep. on Fixed Assets : Office Furniture @ 5% p.a.	265		
15. Land Income and Expenditrue A/c :			
16. Other Items : Commission	2,700		
17. Net Profit carried to Balance Sheet.	29,785		
	45,100		45,100

Balance Sheet as on 31st March 2015

Liabilities	Rs.	Rs.	Assets	Rs.	
1. Share Capital			**1. Cash and Bank Bal.**		
(a) Authorised Capital			Cash in hand		1,480
(b) Issued and Subscribed			Cash at Bank		15,000
Capital	10,000				
Less calls in arrears	-600	9,400	**2. Investments**		–
2. Reserve Fund and			Investments		
other funds. :			**3. Investments of**		10,000
Reserve Fund	1,500		**Staff provident**		
(+) 25% transfer	+1,250	2,750	**Fund :**		
Co-operative	500		**4. Loans and**		–
Development Fund			**Advances**		
(+) Transfer	+310	810	**5. Sundry Debtors :**		
Price Fluctuation Fund		800	Sundry Debtors		
3. Staff Provident Fund :		–	for sales		3,000
4. Secured Loans :		–	**6. Current Assets :**		
5. Unsecured Loans :		–	Closing Stock of		
6. Deposits :		–	Consumer's Goods		12,500
7. Current Liabilities and Prov.		–	**7. Fixed Assets :**		
Sundry creditors for		2,000	Office Furniture	5,300	
purchases Commission		500	Less : Dep. @ 5% p.a.	-265	5,035
payable		100	Equipments		
Outstanding Rent		200	**8. Miscellaneous**		1,800
Outstanding Salary		470	**expenses and Losses:**		
8. Unpaid Dividentds :		–	**9. Other Items :**		
(Provision - Paid)			Salary Prepaid :		
Rs. 940 - Rs.470			Interest accrued on		300
9. Interest Accrued Due		–	Investments		
but not paid .			**10. Profit and Loss A/c**		200
10. Other Liabilities :		–	**11. Current Losses :**		–
11. Profit and Loss A/c	5,000				
Profit for the year 2013-14	-940				
Less Dividend	4,060				
(10% on Rs.9400)					
Less 25% profits trans-					
ferred to Reserve Fund	1,250				
(25% of Rs.5,000)					
Less transferred to Co-	2,810				
operative Development	310				
Fund					
(+) Profits for the year2014-15	2,500				
Contingent Liability	29,785	32,285			
		49,315			49,315

4.8 Exercises

Theory Questions

1) Distinguish between double entry accounting and co-operative accounting.
2) Explain the procedure involved in the preparation of final accounts of Consumers Co-operative Stores.
3) State the various steps in the preparation of final accounts of Co-operative credit Society.
4) Give the specimen form under Type 'N' of
   a) Profit and Loss A/c
   b) Balance Sheet.
5) What are the books of accounts to be kept by the co-operative society? Explain in brief.
6) Write Notes on
   a) Co-operative year.
   b) Member
   c) Co-operative Credit Society.
   d) Co-operative consumer's Society.

Objective Type

A. State whether the following statements are True of False.

1) Co-operation means working together for common purpose.
2) One share one vote is the principle which is followed by co-op.society.
3) Each co-op.society has to be registered under the co-operative society Act of the concerned state.
4) Final Accounts of the co-op society shall be prepared in form 'M' as per Rule 62(1) of Maharashtra Co-op. society Rules, 1961.
5) Co-operative Society are democratic and self governing bodies.
6) Every Co-operative Society is required to maintain books of registers as per Rule 65 of the co-operative Society Act 1960 and their Rules, 1961.

Ans. : 1) True   2) False   3) True   4) False   5) True   6) True

B) Fill in the Blanks :

1) According to Section 66 every co-op society has to carry at least --------------- of the net profit of the year to the reserve Fund (1/3,1/4,1/5)
2) According to Section 66 of Act the society cannot pay dividend to its members more that ---------- of on the paid up capital. (10%,12%,15%)
3) Final Accounts of the Co-op.society is prepared in form --------------- (M, N,B)
4) According to section ---------- every society is required to contribute annully towards the education fund. (67,68,69)
5) To Pay dividend at certain rate every year --------- is created. (Bonus Equilisation Fund, Dividend Equlisation Fund, Reserve Fund)
6) Co-operative Year ends on ----------- every Year. (31st December,30th June,31st March)

7) Maharashtra state co-operative society are registered under -------- Act (1970,1904, 1960)
8) The final Accounts of the co-operative society are to be prepared within -----------days of the close of the accounting year.(90,45,42).

Ans. : 1) 25% 1/4   2) 12%   3) N   4) 68   5) Dividend Equilisation Fund
   6) 31st March   7) 1960   8) 42

EXERCISES

1) From the following Trial balance of Shri Shivaji Co-operative consumer society Dist Pune and other details prepare final accounts for the year ended 31.03.2015.

Trial Balance

Particulars	Debit Rs.	Credit Rs.
Share Capital	–	45,000
Deposit from members	–	90,000
Furniture	21,000	–
Printing and Stationery	3,000	–
Investment in shares of P.D.C.C. Bank	1,11,000	–
Loan from Bank	–	93000
Loan to members	1,35,000	–
Interest received on loans	–	45,000
Purchased of fartilizers and Machinery	3,60,000	
Sale of fertilizers and machinery	–	4,50,000
Office Rent	27,000	–
Office Salaries	24,000	–
Travelling expenses	4,500	–
Carriage	3,900	–
Freight	5,700	–
Cash at Bank	1,36,800	–
Interest Paid	24,900	–
Reserve Fund	–	1,77,000
Cash in hand	13,200	–
Bank Current A/c	30,000	–
	9,00,000	**9,00,000**

Additional Information :

1) Stock of fertilizer and machinery as on 31-03-2015 was Rs.60,000.
2) Outstanding office Rent was Rs.90,000 on 31-03-2015.
3) Depriciate Furniture @ 10%.
4) Provide for Audit Fee Rs.1,800.
5) Reserve for Bad and doubtful debts against loan to members is required at Rs.4,500.

2) Followings is the trial balance of Vivek Anand Co-op. Society. for the year ended 31st March 2015 prepare Trading Accounts, Profit and Loss A/c and Balance Sheet.

Trial Balance

Particulars	Debit Rs.	Credit Rs.
Share Capital	–	4,50,000
Call in arrears	4,500	–
Common Goods fund	–	15,000
Opening stock of consumer goods	1,80,000	–
Furniture	1,40,000	–
Educational Fund	–	6,000
Creditors	–	36,000
Debtors	35,000	–
Commission payable	–	10,000
Salaries	1,10,000	–
Commission	15,000	–
Rent, Rates and Taxes	18,000	–
Postage	4,700	–
Land	1,10,000	–
Interest on investments	–	6,000
Office Equipment's	80,000	–
Purchases	16,00,000	–
Investments	1,50,000	–
Sales	–	20,00,000
Cash in Hand	25,000	–
Cash at Bank	50,800	–
	25,23,000	25,23,000

Adjustments :

1) Closing stock was valued at Rs.2,20,000.
2) Prepaid Rent is 1,900.
3) Contribution to common goods fund Rs.10,000.
4) Salary is outstanding at Rs.1,500.
5) On Investments interest is receivable @ 8%.
6) Depricate Land and Equipments @ 5%.

3) From the following Trial Balance of Maharashtra Co-Op credit society Ltd. as on 31-03-2015 and the information there under profit and loss A/c for the year ended 31-03-15 and Balance Sheet as on that date.

Trial Balance

Dr. Balance	Rs.	Cr.Balance	Rs.
Cash in hand	6,000	Share Capital	6,00,000
Cash with Bank	30,000	Reserve Fund	1,00,000
Fixed Deposit	1,50,000	Members deposit	8,47,000
Office Furniture	20,000	Unclaimed dividend	6,000
Interest on Deposit	75,000	Dividend equilisation	10,000
Interest on Loans	15,000	Reserve	
Salary	50,000	Staff providend fund	40,000
Printing and stationery	3,000	Interest	2,50,000
Travelling xpenses	4,000	Share transfer fees	2,000
Insurance	3,500	Sundry Income	3,000
Contributing to providend fund	8,000	Development fund	4,000
Loan to members	3,00,000	Education Fund	2,500
Building	12,00,000		
	18,64,500		18,64,500

Adjustments :

1) On members deposit Rs. 4,000 interest is still payable as on 31-03-2015.

2) Interest accrued but not received on fixed deposit is Rs. 3,000.

3) Depriciate Building @ 2% p.a.

4) Insurance is paid for one year ending 30-09-2015.

5) Directors propesed the following approprications.

    a) dividend to share holders.

    b) Necessary transfer to reserve fund.

    c) 5% of next profit be transfered to Developments fund after setting aside an amount for Reserve Fund.

4) From the following Trial Balance of Kaveri Credit Co-op society Ltd. prepare final accoutns for year ended 31-03-2015.

Trial Balance

Dr. Balance	Rs.	Cr.Balance	Rs.
Cash in hand	2,000	Share Capital	20,000
Cash with Bank	4,000	Reserve Fund	5,000
Salary	6,000	P and L appropriation A/c	3,000
Establishment for	2,000	Interest Received	21,000
executive officers		Share transfer fees	1,000
Loan given to members	40,000	Education Fund	700
Providend Fund	2,700	Development fund	3,000
Contribution		Unpaid dividend	5,000
Printing and stationery	1,200	Deposit from members	38,400
Interest on Deposit	13,000	Sundry income	300
Interest on loans	2,000		
Fixed deposit	15,000		
Office Furniture	700		
Travelling	1,000		
Insurance	1,500		
	97,400		**97,400**

Adjustments :

1) The Authorised share capital of the society is 5000 equity shares of Rs.10 each.
2) On Loan to members interest still receivable Rs.1300 and deposit to members interest of Rs.700 is still payable as on 31.03.15
3) Depriciate furniture @ 10% p.a.
4) Insurance is paid for one year up to 30.06.2015.
5) Salary is paid in advance Rs.400.
6) Directors proposed 10% dividend on share capital.

5) From the following Trial Balance of New Pune Consumers Co-operative Society, prepare the final accounts of the society for the year ended 31st March 2015.

Particulars	Debit Rs.	Credit Rs.
Stock on 1-4-2014	15,000	–
Purchases	6,25,000	–
Carriage	3,700	–
Coolie Charges	1,500	–
Sales	–	6,50,000
Sale of Empty Bags	–	18,000
Return outwards	–	1,500
Salaries	8,400	–
Sundry Expenses	950	–
Interest on Government Loan	160	–
Legal Fees	120	–
Printing and Stationery	1,100	–
National Saving Certificates	10,000	–
Deposit with Government	100	–
Electricity charges	330	–
Advances	650	–
Sundry Debtors	4,500	–
Dead Stock	500	–
Consumers Federation Deposit	8,900	–
Reserve Fund	–	8,500
Special Reserve Fund	–	4,500
Government Loans	–	1,200
Government Grants	–	800
Education Fund	–	1,000
Creditors	–	6,500
Buillding Fund	–	21,000
Investments in shares	20,000	–
Cash in hand	7,510	–
Cash at Bank	19,580	–
Fixed Deposits with Bank	25,000	–
Share Capital (Shares of Rs.10 each)	–	40,000
	7,53,000	**7,53,000**

Adjustments :
1) Closing stock was valued at Rs.4000.
2) Audit Fees Payable Rs.500.
3) Charge depreciation on Dead Stock at 10%.
4) Make provision for Bad Debts Rs.500.

(**Ans :** GP Rs. 10,300 M.P. Rs. 16,990 B/S Rs.1,00,690).

6) From the following Trial Balances of Bharati Medical College Employee's Credit Society. Pune you are required to prepare Profot and Loss Account for the year ended 31st March 2015 and Balance Sheet as on that date.

Particulars	Dr. Rs.	Cr. Rs.
Share Capital	–	2,00,000
General Reserve	–	28,800
Dividend Equalisation Fund	–	2,000
Welfare Fund	–	2,500
Deposits from Members	–	75,000
Fixed Deposit with Bank	25,000	
Cash Credit from Bank	–	6,22,500
Int. Payable on Fixed Deposit	–	12,500
Dividend Payable	–	26,000
Profit and Loss Account 1-4-2014	–	550
Loans	9,00,000	–
Furniture	47,500	–
Cash at Bank	35,000	–
Interest received on Deposits	–	1,800
Dividend received	–	3,700
Interest received on Loans	–	1,74,000
Commission	–	500
Other receipts	–	700
Interest paid on Loans	1,28,000	–
Interest paid on Deposits	1,150	–
Salaries	8,000	–
Printing and Stationery	2,400	–
Meeting Expenses	500	–
Cash in hand	1,600	–
Postage and Telephone	1,000	–
Other Expenditure	400	–
	11,50,550	**11,50,550**

Other information

1) Authorised Capital of the Society is Rs.5,00,000.divided into shares of Rs.10 each.
2) Charge depreciation on Furnitrue Rs.1,000.
3) Audit Fees are to be provided Rs.500.
4) Transfer Rs.500 to Education Fund and Rs.500 to Employee's provident Fund.)

(**Ans :** NP Rs.37,250 B/S Total Rs.10,81,000).

7) Following is the trial balance of Shri Siddhivinayak co-operative credit society ltd. on 31-03-2015 prepare final accounts for the year ended 31th March 2015 after taking into consideration additional information.

Dr. Balance	Rs.	Cr. Balance	Rs.
Loans Due	3,70,000	Share Capital	1,00,000
Contribution to Provident fund	300	Reserve Fund	10,000
Insurance	200	Deposit from Members	2,70,000
Travelling Expenses	250	Dividend payable	300
Printing and Stationery	100	Dividend Equalisation Fund	4,000
Salaries	5,000	Staff Provident Fund	3,000
Interest due on bonus	1,000	P and L Appropriation A/c	4,500
Interest on Deposits	9,000	Interest	25,000
Furniture	900	Co-operative Development	500
Fixed Deposit with Saraswat		Fund	
Cooperative Bank	29,150	Education Fund	100
Cash with Bank	2,000	Miscellaneous Income	700
Cash	200		
	4,18,100		**4,18,100**

Additional Information :

i) Interest due on member's deposits Rs.1,000.

ii) Interest due but not received Rs.400.

iii) Outstanding salary Rs.200.

iv) Unpaid audit fees Rs.450.

v) Authorised capital : 10,000 shares of Rs.10 each.

vi) Directors propose to recommend dividend at 25%.

8) From the following Trial Balance of Bharat Co-op credit society as on 31ˢᵗ March 2015 and the information there under prepare profit and loss A/c for the year ended 31st March 2015. and Balance sheet as on that.

Trial Balance

Dr. Balance	Rs.	Cr.Balance	Rs.
Cash in hand	1,000	Share Capital	6,70,000
Cash with Bank	20,000	Reserve Fund	65,000
Fixed Deposit	1,84,000	Members deposit	27,00,000
Office Furniture	10,000	Unclaimed dividend	3,000
Interest on deposit	70,000	Dividend utilisation	25,000
Interest due on loan	10,000	Fund	
Salary	40,000	Staff providend fund	30,000
Printing and Stationery	1,000	Profit and Loss A/c	40,000
Travelling expenses	1,000	Interest	3,00,000
Insurance	2,000	Share transfer fees	5,000
Contribution to P.F.	5,000	Sundry income	1,000
Loan to members	25,00,000	Development fund	3,000
Building	10,00,000	Education Fund	2,000
	38,44,000		**38,44,000**

Adjustments :

1) Interest outstanding on members deposit Rs.2700.
2) Interest Accrued but not received Rs.8000.
3) Charge depriciation on building @ 2 ½ p.a.
4) Audit fee Rs.5000 still unpaid on 30-06-2015.
5) Directors proposed the following appropriations for the current year.
    i)   Dividend to share holders @ 8%.
    ii) Necessary Transfer to reserve Fund.
    iii) 5% of net profit before transferrering to reserve fund to development fund

5

Computerized Accounting Practices

5.1 Introduction
5.2 Value Added Tax (VAT) : VAT Reporting and Central Vlaue added tax
5.3 Service Tax
5.4 TDS (Income Tax)

5.1 INTRODUCTION :

The Value Added tax (VAT) is a type of indirect tax and is one of major source of revenue to the state. The VAT system was introduced in India by replacing the General Sales Tax Laws of each state. The administration of VAT system was undertaken by the commercial taxes department of each state along with the Excise and other indirect taxes. For assessing the VAT liability of dealers, each state has introduced the system of filing returns for different tax periods.

5.2 VALUE ADDED TAX

VAT is charged on the 'increase in value' of goods and services at each stage of production and circulation. It is also chargeable on the value of all imported goods. It is charged by registered VAT businesses/persons/taxpayers. VAT has replaced a number of other taxes and its introduction has not resulted in either increased prices to final consumers or reduced profitability of business. VAT is levied on the difference between the sale price of the goods produced or the services rendered, and the cost thereof that is, the difference between the output and the input.

5.2.1 FEATURES OF VAT:

1. Tax levied and collected at every point of sale.
2. Tax collected at every point of sale and the tax already paid by the dealer at the time of purchase of goods will be deducted from the amount of tax paid at the next sale.
3. Dealers reselling tax paid goods will have to collect VAT and file returns and pay VAT at every stage of sale (value addition)
4. It is transparent and easier.

5. VAT dispenses with such forms and sets off all tax paid at the time of purchase from the amount of tax payable on sale.
6. The returns and the challans are filed together in a simple format after self assessment done by the dealer himself.
7. Very few forms are required.
8. Tax on goods and services both.
9. Self assessments by dealers.
10. Penalties will be stricter.

5.2.3 CALCULATION A VAT

VAT is calculated by deducting tax credit from tax collected during the payment period

Example 1 : (Rate of Tax is assumed at 10%)

Purchase Price	Rs. 100
Tax paid during purchase	Rs. 10 (input tax)
Selling Price	Rs. 150
Tax collected during resale	Rs. 15 (output tax)
Input tax credit (tax paid during purchase)	Rs. 10
VAT payable (output tax – input tax)	Rs.5
Total tax collected by government	Rs.10
At the time of purchase by the dealer	Rs.5
At the time of resale by the dealer	Rs. (10+5) =
Total tax :	**Rs.15**

5.2.4 GENERAL REQUIREMENTS FOR VAT SYSTEM

1. Compulsory issue of tax invoice and retail invoice : Tax invoice is issued to a dealer/consumer who has to take input VAT Credit whereas retail invoice is meant for inter-state sales or sale to a consumer who does not require input credit of VAT.

2. Registration : There is a compulsory registration of the dealer if the aggregate turnover exceeds a certain specified limit. (Five lakhs in a financial fear starting from 1st April to 31st March)

3. Composition scheme : A small dealer whose turnover does not exceed a specified limit (say in Delhi Rs. 50 lakhs) can opt for composition scheme where he shall have to pay tax himself at a small percentage of gross turnover and in this case buyer of goods will not get input VAT Credit.

4. Tax payer identification Number (TIN) : There will be a taxpayer's identification number of 11 digits numerical which will be unique to each dealer.

5. Simplified returns of VAT are to be filed monthly or quarterly as specified by each state.

6. Self assessment by dealers.

7. Audit under VAT has been made compulsory by various States.

8. No requirement of any declaration form as bill will be raised for each sale and VAT shall be levied.

9. Comprehensive coverage as only few commodities have been exempted from VAT.

5.2.5 ADVANTAGES OF VAT

VAT being a broad based tax levied at multiple stages is generally perceived as an explicit replacement of State sales tax for raising additional revenue for the Government. The purpose of a tax system is to bring in revenues to the Government. Tax revenues can be raised in many ways. However, the main characteristic of good tax system should be –

1. The tax system should be fair or equitable.

2. It should cause the least possible harmful effects to the economy and to the extent possible it should promote growth to the economy.

3. It should be simple both for its compliance by the payer and for its administration by the Government.

4. It should be income elastic.

Keeping in view the above objectives, VAT is being implemented in various states in place of the local sales tax payable by the seller. VAT is also expected to be more effective and efficient for every person including Government, manufactures, traders and consumers and hold the following advantages:

1. Easy to Administer & Transparent
2. Less Litigation
3. Tax Credit on purchase of Capital Goods
4. Abolition of Statutory Forms
5. Self Assessment
6. Deterrent against Tax Avoidance
7. No Cascading Effect
8. Effective Audit & Enforcement Strategies
9. Minimum Exemptions
10. Removal of Anomaly of First Point Taxation

5.2.6 General Terminologies of VAT

- **Input Tax** This is the tax paid on purchases
- **Output Tax** This is the tax charged on sales
- **Input Credit** The excess amount of Input tax over output tax for the current period which is permitted to be set off against Output tax of subsequent periods is termed as **Input Credit**.
- **TIN Tax Identification Number (TIN)** is the Registration Number given by the department to the dealer at the time of Registration. This needs to be quoted at all required places where the registration details are to be provided.
- **Tax Invoice** This is the Sales invoice format issued by one Registered Dealer to another. Based on this Invoice, ITC can be claimed by the purchasing dealer.
- **Retail Invoice** The Sales invoice format used for invoicing the Exempted Sales and the Sales made to unregistered dealers is termed as Retail Invoice.
- **Registered Dealer** This term is used to identify a dealer who is registered either under Voluntary Registration or Compulsory Registration under the VAT Act. Such dealer can

issue tax invoice and also claim the tax paid on purchases made from other registered dealers as Input tax credit.

- **Unregistered Dealer** Dealers who are not registered under the VAT Act are called as Unregistered Dealers (URD). Such dealers cannot issue tax invoice. They can neither Charge Tax nor Claim Input Tax Credit.
- **Purchase Tax** The Tax paid on goods purchased from unregistered dealers is liable to Purchase Tax. The purchase tax is treated as **Output VAT** payable by the dealer as it is a liability. It has to be paid while making the payment towards VAT liability. Based on the Rules and Regulations, the Input Tax Credit can be claimed on the payment made towards Purchase Tax.
- **Reversal of Tax Credit** It refers to the reversal of input tax credit already claimed and availed.

5.2.7 Features of VAT in Tally.ERP 9

The salient features provided for VAT in Tally.ERP 9 are as follows :

- Quick, easy to setup and use.
- Pre-defined VAT/Tax Classifications for Purchase and Sale of goods
- Facility to create separate VAT ledgers with VAT/Tax Classifications for input as well as out-put VAT
- Facility to print tax invoice
- Complete tracking of each transaction till generation of returns
- Better VAT-returns management
- Generating of VAT Computation report with details pertaining to :
  a) The value of transactions recorded using the classifications available for VAT
  b) Increase/decrease in input/output VAT on account of adjustment entries made using the VAT Adjustments available on using the voucher class created for journal voucher.
  c) VAT Payable or refundable
- Generating of "VAT Classification Vouchers" report for each of the VAT/Tax classifications
- Facility to Drill-down the various VAT classifications from VAT Computation report till the last level of voucher entry
- Generating VAT Returns and Annexure
- Greater tax compliance

5.2.8 Enabling VAT in Tally.ERP 9

Following are the important step for enabling VAT in tally.ERP9

Go to **Gateway of Tally > F11: Features > F3 : Statutory & Taxation**

In the **F3: Statutory & Taxation features,**

1. Set **Enable Value Added Tax (VAT)** to **Yes**
2. Set **Set / Alter VAT Details** to **Yes**
3. The Company VAT Details screen will be displayed.

4. In the Company VAT Details screen, select the State where the business of the dealer is registered. Here select the State as Maharashtra. Select the Type of Dealer as Regular and enter the Date in Regular VAT Applicable from field.

5. Under Additional Information section, new fields have been introduced to specify the details pertaining to Assessment Circle, Division, Area Code, Import Export Code, Authorized by, Authorized person, Status/Designation and Place. The details entered in these fields will be captured in the Print Report screen of Return Form and Annexure as per requirement.

6. Specify the details in VAT TIN (Regular), Inter-state Sales Tax Number and PAN / Income - Tax Number.

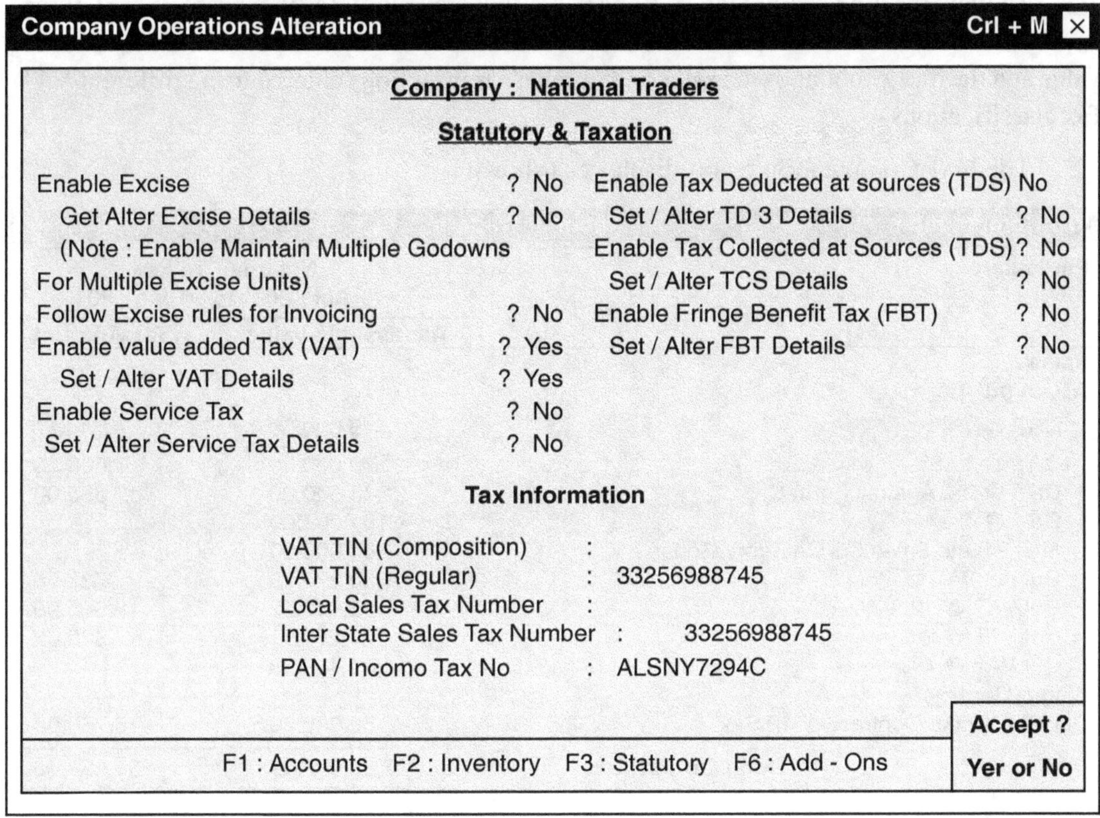

7. Press **Enter/Y** to accept and save.

5.2.9 Processing Purchases & Sales Entries

A VAT registered dealer, while purchasing goods within the state pays Input VAT and charges Output VAT at the time of sales on the assessable value of taxable goods. At the end of each month they are required to compute Input VAT paid on purchases made during the month and Output VAT payable on sales during the month. If the VAT payable is more than the Input VAT paid on purchases, the difference is payable to the government or in case where the Input

VAT paid on purchases is in excess of Output VAT payable during the month, the excess VAT paid is carried forward to the next month.

5.2.10 VAT Reports

The VAT system is based on self-assessment and transparency at every stage of transaction. Hence, accurate record maintenance is of critical importance. In Tally.ERP 9, you can generate statutory returns as prescribed in the statues. In this lesson, we will discuss about the books of accounts, reports and registers that assists you in managing your business and compliance with VAT.

5.2.10.1 VAT Computation Report

To view the VAT Computation Report, Go to Gateway of Tally > Display > Statutory Reports > VAT > VAT Computation The VAT Computation reports provide the Assessable Value and the Tax Amount of the sales and purchase transactions entered using different VAT/ Tax classifications.

The VAT Computation report displays as shown :

VAT Computation	National Traders	Ctrl + M ✕

Particulars	National Traders 1 - Apr - 2011 to 30 Jan - 2011	
	Assessable Value	**Tax Amount**
Sales **A. Out put Tax**		
CST @ 1%	45,000.00	
CST @ 12.5%	70,000.00	7,600.00
CST @ 2% Against Form C	1,44,500.00	2,890.00
CST @ 4%	15,000.000	
Inter - State Sales Spl Category Goods	64,000.00	
Out put VAT @ 1%	1,30,277.78	787.78
Out VAT @ 12.50%	1,32,847.22	16.605.90
Out VAT @ 2%	53,261.11	323.78
Out VAT @ 4%	71,113.89	
Works Contract		
Out VAT Works Contract @ 12.5%	60,000.00	3,750.00
Total Output Tax	**7,86,000.00**	**31.957.46**
Purchases **C. Input Tax**		
Excess Input Credit Brought Fonward		
Input VAT @ 1%	1,00,133.53	1,001.34
Input VAT @ 12.5%	60,118.69	7,514.84
Input VAT @ 12.5 % (Job Work)	35,000.00	2,187.50
Input VAT @ 2%	22,623.89	452.48
Input VAT @ 4%	90,773.89	3,630.96
Input VAT @ 4% (Industrial Input)	3,250.00	130.00
Purchase From URDs Taxable Goods @ 1%	40,400.00	
		4 more...
VAT Payable		**17,040,34**

The above screen displays the total of VAT payable on sales and input tax credit available on purchases made during the specified period. The essence of VAT is the offsetting of Input VAT against Output VAT. The VAT computation report shown above precisely indicates the value of VAT Payable after offsetting the input VAT against the output VAT along with CST liability if any.

Assessable Value : The Assessable Value is the sum of total value of goods at which they are purchased and sold. This assessable value is the value on which VAT is calculated.

Tax Amount : The total Tax Amount calculated on Assessable value using the respective Tax percentage is the Tax Amount

Show All VAT Classifications

From the VAT Computation screen, click on **F12 : Configure** and set **Show All VAT Classifications to Yes.**

Configuration	
Show All VAT Classifications	**? Yes**
Show CST Details	? No
Show VAT Analysis	? No

The VAT Computation screen displays as shown:

VAT Computation National Traders Ctrl + M ☒		
Particulars	**National Traders** 1 - Apr - 2011 to 30 Jan - 2011	
	Assessable Value	**Tax Amount**
Sales		
A. Out put Tax		
CST @ 1%	45,000.00	
CST @ 12.5%	70,000.00	7,600.00
CST @ 2% Against Form C	1,44,500.00	2,890.00
CST @ 4%	15,000.000	
Inter - State Sales Spl Category Goods	64,000.00	
Out put VAT @ 1%	1,30,277.78	787.78
Out VAT @ 12.50%	1,32,847.22	16.605.90
Out VAT @ 2%	53,261.11	323.78
Out VAT @ 4%	71,113.89	
Others (VAT Not Applicable)		
Consignment / Branch Transfer Outward	7,800.00	
Exports	1,57,440.00	
Sales - Exempt	34,000.00	
Works Contract		
Output VAT - Works Contract @ 12.5%	60,000.00	3,750.00
Total Output Tax	**9,85,240.00**	**31,957.46**
Purchases		
C. Input Tax		
Excess Input Credit Brought Forward		
Input VAT @ 1%	1,00,133.53	1,001.34
Input VAT @ 12.50%	60,118.69	7,514.84
VAT Payable		**17,040.34**

VAT Computation	National Traders		Ctrl + M ☒
Particulars		**National Traders**	
		1 - Apr - 2011 to 30 Jan - 2011	
		Assessable Value	**Tax Amount**
... 15 more			
Works Contract			
Output VAT Works Contract @ 12.5%		60,000.00	3,750.00
Total Output Tax		**9,85,240.000**	**31,957.46**
Purchases			
C. Input Tax			
Excess Input Credit Brought Forward			
Input VAT @ 1 %		1,00,133.53	1,001.34
Input VAT @ 12.5%		60,118.69	7,514.84
Input VAT @ 12.5% - (Job Work)		35,000.000	2,187.50
Input VAT @ 2%		22,623.89	452.48
Input VAT @ 4%		90,773.89	3,630.96
Input VAT @ 4% - (Industrial Input)		3,250.00	130.00
Purchase From URDs - Taxable Goods @ 1%		40,400.00	
Purchase From URDs - Taxable Goods @ 12.5%		50,625.00	
Purchase From URDs - Taxable Goods @ 4% 1,664.00			
Purchase - Capital Goods @ 4%		1,50,000.00	
Others (VAT Not Applicable)			
Imports			78,300.00
Interstate Purchases @ 1%		40,400.00	
Interstate Purchases @ 12.5%		33,750.00	
Interstate Purchases @ 2% Against From C		3,82,500.00	
Interstate Purchases @ 4%		9,984.00	
Purchases Exempt		30,000.00	
Total Input Credit		**11,29,523.00**	**14,917.12**
VAT Payable			**17,040.34**

Click on **Alt + F1 :** Detailed button to view the detailed VAT Computation report. A part of the detailed report displays as shown :

VAT Computation	National Traders		Ctrl + M ✕
Particulars			**National Traders** 1 - Apr - 2011 to 30 Jan - 2011
			Assessable Value	**Tax Amount**
Sales				
A. Output Tax				
CST @ 1%			45,000.00	
Gross Value	45,000.00	450.00		
Advance Tax paid		(-)450.00		
CST @ 12.5%	70,000.00	7,600.00		
Gross Value	70,000.00	8,750.00		
Advance Tax Paid		(-) 1,150.00		
CST @ 2% Against From C			1,44,500.00	2,890.00
CST @ 4%			15,000.00	
Gross Value	15,000.00	600.00		
Advance Tax Paid		(-) 600.00		
Inter - State Sales - Spl Category Goods			64,000.00	
Gross Value	64,000.00	1,280.00		
Adjustment Towards Entry Tax paid		(-) 980.00		
Advance Tax Paid		(-)300.00		
Output VAT @ 1%			1,32,847.22	16,605.90
Gross Value	87,847.72	10,980.90		
Tax on URD Purchase	45,000.00	5,625.00		
Output VAT @ 2%			53,261.11	323.78
Gross Value	59,261,11	1,119.22		
Adjustment Towards Entry Tax Paid		(-) 675.44		
Goods Sold Returned	(-) 600.00	(-) 120.00		
				74 more...
VAT Payable				**17,040,34**

The report also provides drill down facility for each VAT classification listed in the report. To drill down, select the required classification and press Enter.

VAT Classification Vouchers : To view the VAT Classification vouchers, select any one the VAT Classifications from the VAT Computation report and press Enter.

The VAT Classification Vouchers report is displayed as shown :

VAT Computation		National Traders					Ctrl + M ☒
VAT Classification	Input VAT @ 12.5%					1-Apr-2011 to 30 - Apr - 2011	
Voucher Date	Particulars	VAT TIN	Voucher Type	Vouchers Number	Supplier Inv/ Ref No.	Assessable Value	VAT Amount
1-4-2011	Excel Traders	33589845121	Purchase	1	01	1,20,118,69	15,014,84
13-4-2011	Refund Claimed on Zero Rated Sales	33025485652	Journal	2		(-)30,000.00	(-)3,750.00
20-4-2011	Swasthik Associates	33254785521	Purchase	9	09	12,500.00	1,562.50
20-4-2011	Reverse Credit Purchase of Automabiles Spare Parts		Journal	6		(-)12,500.00	(-) 1,562.50
21-1-2011	Dewpoint Traders	33250025850	Purchase	10	10	50,000.00	6,250.00
21-4-2011	Reverse Credit - Purchase of Air Conditioners		Journal	7		(-) 50,000.00	(-) 6,250.00
27-4-2011	Reverse Credit Interstate Sate Without C Form		Journal	14		(-) 30,000.00	(-) 3,750.00
	Grand Total					**60,118.69**	**7,514.84**

5.3 Service tax :

Introduction

Service tax is an indirect tax levied on certain category of service provided by a person, firm, agency, etc. The government of India has marked a set of taxable items under the service tax structure. The seller provides a services and the responsibility of paying the service tax to the government rests with the seller.

Service Tax is a destination based consumption tax in the form of Value Added Tax. It is imposed on specified services (taxable services) provided by a service provider (Company, Individual, Firm etc.). Service Tax was first brought into force with effect from 1 July 1994. All service providers in India, except those in the state of Jammu and Kashmir, are required to pay a Service Tax in India. Initially only three services were brought under the net of Service Tax and the tax rate was 5% 2015-16. Gradually more services came under the ambit of Service Tax. In accordance with the Annual Budget the current Service tax rate has been increased from 12.36% to 14%.

5.3.1 FEATURES OF SERVICE TAX

The salient features of levy of service tax are:

1. Scope : It is leviable on taxable services 'provided' or 'to be provided' by a service provider. The services 'to be provided' in future are taxed only if payment in its respect is received in advance.

Two separate persons required Payment to employees not covered : For charge of service tax, it is necessary that the service provider and service recipient should be two separate persons acting on 'principal to principal basis'. Services provided by an employee to his employer are not covered service tax and, therefore, salaries or allowances paid to them cannot be charged to service tax.

(S.Maruthappan v. CCEx. [2007] 8 STR 228 (Tri Chennai)).

2. Rate : It is leviable @ 12% of the value of taxable services. Education Cess @ 2% and Secondary and Higher Education Cess @ 1 % are chargeable on the amount of service tax, thus, making the effective rate of service tax at 12.36% of the value of taxable service. The rate of Service Tax is increased from 12.36% to 14% from 2015-16.

3. Taxable services : Service tax is leviable only on the taxable services. Taxable services mean the services taxable under section 65(105) of the Finance Act, 1994. The taxable services with their scope, inclusions/ exclusions and specific exemptions are discussed in the next chapter.

4. Value : For the levy of the service tax, the value shall be computed in accordance with section 67 read with Service Tax (Determination of Value) Rules, 2006.

5. Free services not taxable : No service tax is leviable upon the services provided free of cost.

6. Payment of service tax : The person providing the service (i.e. the service provider) has to pay service tax in such manner and within such period as is prescribed in the Service Tax Rules, 1994. The service tax is to be paid only on the receipt of payment towards the value of taxable services.

7. Procedures : Provisions have been made for registration, assessment including self assessment, rectifications, revisions, appeals and penalties on the service provider.

8. CENVAT credit : The credit of service tax and excise duty across goods and services is allowable in accordance with the CENVAT Credit Rules, 2004. Accordingly, output service provider (i.e. provider of any taxable service) can avail credit not only of the service tax paid on any input service consumed for rendering any output service but also of the excise duty paid on any inputs and capital goods used for rendering output service. CENVAT credit so availed can be utilized for payment of service tax on taxable output service.

9. Services provided by an unincorporated association/body to its members also taxable

[Explanation to Sec. 65] : 'Taxable service' includes any taxable service provided or to be provided by any unincorporated association or body of persons to a member thereof, for cash, deferred payment or any other valuable consideration. Hence, the services (falling under any category of taxable service) provided or to be provided by any unincorporated association/ body to member thereof shall be liable to service tax.

This provision is an exception to the 'principle of mutuality'.

10. Performance of statutory activities/duties, not 'service': An activity performed by a sovereign /public authority under provisions of law does not constitute provision of taxable service to a person and, therefore, no service tax is leviable on such entities.

11. Import/Export of services : While import of services is chargeable to tax u/s 66A, the export of services has been made exempt from tax. Import/export provisions are discussed separately.

5.3.3. Applicability of service tax :

Service Tax is applicable on taxable services :

1. Provided and taxable in the hands of service provider

2. Received and taxable in the hands of service receiver : Generally it is the service provider who is liable to collect Service Tax from his customer/client and pay the same to the Government. But section 68(2) empowers the Government to notify the services with regard to which the service receiver would be held liable to pay Service Tax to the Government. For the below mentioned services the service receiver is liable to pay Service Tax (as per Notification 36/2004 ST dated 31.12.2004 as amended from time to time)

- Goods Transport Agency service
- Business auxiliary service of distribution of mutual fund by a mutual fund distributor or agent
- Sponsorship service provided to anybody corporate/firm
- Taxable services received by any person in India from abroad
- Insurance auxiliary service by an insurance agent

With effect from 1 July 2012, Negative list-based System of Tax on Services was introduced which provides,

- A list of services which will not be subject to Service Tax (Negative List)
- All services, other than those mentioned in the Negative List, will fall under the purview of Taxable services

The definition of taxable service is different for each class of services, e.g. in case of Stock Broker agency, any service provided to an investor by buy or sell securities listed on a recognized stock exchange will be a Taxable service.

5.3.4 Features of service tax in Tally.ERP 9 :

Service tax integrated in Tally takes care of your service tax transactions. It eliminates error-prone information, incorrect remittance, penalties, interests, compliance issues, etc. service tax in Tally needs a one-time configuration for service tax features to be activated.

- Tally tracks bill-wise (bill-by-bill) detail and automatically calculated service tax payable and input credit with the flexibility to make adjustment later.
- Service tax is part of a regular transaction. Information on service tax is maintained and produced category-wise, which is mandatory in service tax returns.

- Adjusts input credit towards service tax payable
- Accounts for abatement and expenses
- Provision for exemption notification details
- Built-in assessable value feature on which service tax is calculated
- Transfer earlier pending service tax payable and available service tax input credit in to Tally.ERP 9
- Reports are generated as per government suggested format. Print and file reports: TR6 Challans, Input Credit Form, ST3 Report and ST3-A Report.
- Management Information Services (MIS) reports: Service tax payable report and input credit form.

5.3.5 Enabling Service Tax in Tally.ERP 9

It is one time configuration for Service Tax features to be enabled in Tally.ERP 9. Follow the steps given below to configure Service Tax for a new company Crystal Services (P) Ltd.

1. Create Company
2. Enable Service Tax

Crystal Services (P) Ltd., is a company engaged in providing multiple services to their clients. The services provided by Crystal Services (P) Ltd., fall within the ambit of tax net and are taxable@ **12.36%.**

Enable Service Tax feature in F11: Features Go to Gateway of Tally > F11: Features > Statutory & Taxation

- Set Enable Service Tax to Yes
- Enable Set/Alter Service Tax Details to Yes

<table>
<tr><td colspan="4" align="center"><u>Company - Crystal Sercvices (P) Ltd</u></td></tr>
<tr><td colspan="4" align="center"><u>Statutory & Taxation</u></td></tr>
<tr><td>Enable Excise</td><td>? No</td><td>Enable Tax Deductec at Source (TDS)</td><td>? No</td></tr>
<tr><td>Set / Alter Excise Details</td><td>? No</td><td>Set / Alter TDS Details</td><td>? No</td></tr>
<tr><td>(Note : Enable Maintain Multiple</td><td></td><td>Enable Tax Collected at Sources (TCS)</td><td>? No</td></tr>
<tr><td>Godown's For Multiple Excise Units)</td><td></td><td>Set / Alter TCS Details</td><td>? No</td></tr>
<tr><td>Follow Excise rules for Invoicing</td><td>? No</td><td>Enable Fringe Benefit Tax (FBT)</td><td>? No</td></tr>
<tr><td>Enable Value Added Tax (VAT)</td><td>? No</td><td>Set / Alter FBT Details</td><td>? No</td></tr>
<tr><td>Set / Alter VAT Details</td><td>? No</td><td>Enable MCA Reports</td><td>? No</td></tr>
<tr><td>Enable Sercvice Tax</td><td>? Yes</td><td></td><td></td></tr>
<tr><td>Set / Alter Service Tax Details</td><td>? yes</td><td></td><td></td></tr>
<tr><td colspan="4" align="center"><u>Tax Information</u></td></tr>
<tr><td colspan="4">Local Sales Tax Number   :</td></tr>
<tr><td colspan="4">Inter State Sales Tax Number   :</td></tr>
<tr><td colspan="4">PAN Income - Tax No   :</td></tr>
<tr><td colspan="4" align="center">F1 Accounts   F2 : Inventcry   F6 Add - Ons</td></tr>
</table>

The Company Service Tax Details sub-form appears as shown

Company Service Tax Details

Service Tax Registration No	: ███████	Assesseee Code	:
Date of Registration	:	Premises Code No	:
Type Of Organisation	:	Is Large Tax Payer	**? No**
Enable Service Tax Round off	: **Yes**	Large Tax Payer Unit	:

Range

Code :

Name :

Division

Code :

Name :

Commissionerate

Code :

Name :

(Note : All the Above details will be used in Challan, Foms & Retums)

After filling all the necessary details the completed **Company Service Tax Details** screen will appears as shown below

Company Service Tax Details

Service Tax Registration	: **ASDCE1588PST001**	Assesseee Code	: **ASDCE1588PST001**
Date of Registration	: **15 Mar - 2002**	Premises Code No	: **SC0500012**
Type Of Organisation	: **Registered Private Ltd Company**	Is Large Tax Payer **? No** Large Tax Payer Unit	
Enable Service Tax Round off	: **No**		

Range

Code : **06**

Name : **Bommanahalli**

Division

Code : **02**

Name : **Division II**

Commissionerate

Code : **09**

Name : **Bangalore I_**

(Note : All the Above details will be used in Challan, Foms & Retums)

Service Tax Reports

Payables, Input Credit - Summary, Input Credit - Reversal Details and ST3 at the end of the month or half yearly, as prescribed under the Act. To view the **Service Tax Reports.** Go to **Gateway of Tally > Display > Statutory Reports > Service Tax Reports**

```
          Gateway of Tally .......
          Display Menu ......
          Statutory Reports ........
       ┌──────────────────────────┐
       │   Service Tax Reports    │
       ├──────────────────────────┤
       │   Computation            │
       │   Service Tax Payables   │
       │   Input Credit           │
       │   ST3                    │
       │   Exception Reports      │
       │   Quit                   │
       └──────────────────────────┘
```

5.3.5.1 Computation

Service Tax Computation report displays information about Service Tax transactions. This report gives information of Input Credit, Service Tax Payable, Service Tax Payments/ Credit Adjustments, Balance Service Tax Payable, Balance Available Credit & Other Payments like Arrears, Interest etc. for the period specified.

To view the computation report Go to Gateway of Tally > Display > Statutory Reports > Service Tax Reports > Computation

Service Tax Computation	Crystal Services (P) Ltd.		Ctrl + M ✕
Particulars	Crystal Services (P) Ltd. 1 - Apr - 2012 to 31 Oct- 2012		
	Total Amount	Assessable Value	Tax Amount
A. Input Credit	**11,47,129.80**	**9,97,128.70**	**1,09,001.10**
Current Period	11,47,129.80	9,97,128.70	1.08.001.10
B. Service Tax Payable			
Current Period	46,88,776.00	36,69,049.49	4,53,494.51
Previous Period	46,88,776.00	36,69,049.49	4,53,494.51
C. Service Tax Payments / Credit Adjustments			**1,29,091.55**
G. A. R. 7 Payaments			90.234.16
Service Tax Credit Adjustment			7,416.00
CENVAT Credit Adjustment			18,540.00
Adjustment Towards Advance Tax Paid			7,951.23
Other Adjustment			4,950.16
D. Balance Service Tax Payable (B-D)			**3,24,402.96**
E. Refund of Service Tax Input Credit			
F. Balance Available Credit			
Advance Tax Paid			1,07,633.87
Service Tax Credit			7,048.77
G. Service Tax Adjusted Towards Excise Payable			
H. Other Payments			**5,800.00**
Arrears			5,000.00
Interest			800.00

5.3.5.2 Service Tax Payables

Service Tax Payables report displays the Total Service Tax Payables as on a specified date. In Tally.ERP 9 Service Tax Payables can be viewed based on sales Bill Date, Receipt Date and for tax payable on services received like GTA and Imports.

To view Service Tax Payables report Go to Gateway of Tally > Display > Statutory Reports > Service Tax Reports > Service Tax Payables

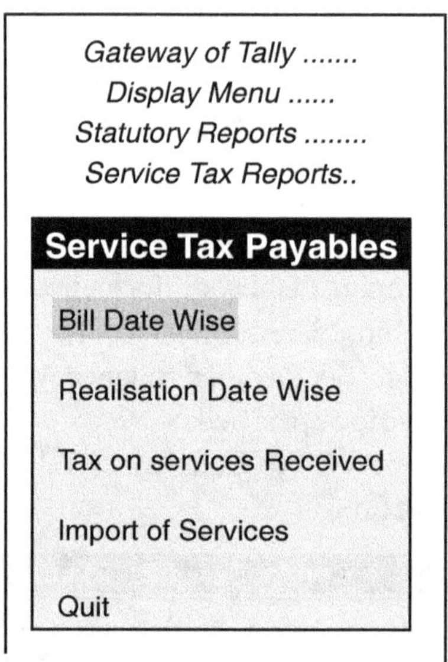

Service Tax Payables report can be viewed

- Bill Date-wise
- Realisation Date-wise
- Tax on Services Received
- Import of Services

5.3.5.3 ST3

The ST3 Report is a statutory report. This report displays the ST3 Form in the Government prescribed format that is used to file Half yearly Service Tax returns to the Commissionerate of Service Tax. Both physical and electronic formats are supported in Tally.ERP 9.

ST3 Report

- In Period For field, select the period for which ST3 Report to be printed.
- Specify the Place and Date for Printing ST3 Report. To print physical form of ST3 report, Go to Gateway of Tally > Display > Statutory Reports > Service Tax Reports > ST3 > Report Use the Alt+P key or click on Print option to print your report. This will display the Form ST-3.

Printing

Printer	: NP19F3EB3	**Paper Type :**	Letter
	(Hp Laser Jet P4015 (Ne 02)		
No. of Copies	: 1		
Print Language	: English		*(Printing Dimensions)*
Method	: Neat Mode	**Paper Size**	: (8.50 × 10.98) Or
			(216 mm × 279 mm)
Page Range	: All	**Print Area**	: (8.03 × 10.71) Or
			(204 mm × 272 mm)

Report Titles

Form ST - 3

(With Print Preview)
Without Company Phone No.

ST - 3 Preiod

Priod For : **(April - September)**

Place : **Bangalore**

Date : **10-10-2012**

Print ?
Yes or **No**

- **Press Enter/yes** to view Print Preview of From **ST 3**

The **Print Preview of Form ST-3** appears as shown

From ST - 3

(Return under section 70 of the Finance Act 1994)

[ORIGINAL / REVISED RETURN]

Financial year | 2012-13 |

For the period

[✓] **April - September**   [ ] **October - March**

1A.   Has the assessee opted to operate as large Taxpayer | No |

(As Defined under Rule 2 (ea) of the Central Excise Rules, 2002 read with rule 2 (1) (000)
 of the Service Tax Rules, 1994)

1B.   If reply to column 1A is yes name of large taxpayer Unit (LTU) opted for | |

2A.   Name of the assessee   Crysial Services (P) Ltd

2B.   Name of the assessee   ASDCE1588PST001

2C.   Premises Code No.   SCO50012

2D.   Constitution of assesses

i)   Individual / Proprietary   [ ]

ii)   Patnership   [ ]

iii)   Registered public Ltd Company   [ ]

iv)   Registered private Ltd Company   [✓]

v)   Registered Trust   [ ]

vi)   Society Co - op Society   [ ]

vii)   Other   [ ]

3. **Computation of Service Tax**
A1. **Name of Taxable service**
<u>Exempted Service</u>
A2. **Assessee is liable to pay Service Tax on this taxable service as.**
(i) a service provider, or   `Yes`
(ii) a service receiver liable to make payment of Service Tax   `No`
B. **Sub clause No. of clause (105) of section 65**   `[  ]`
C1. **Has the assessee availed benefit of any exemption notification (Y/N)**   `No`
C2. **If reply to column 'C1' is 'Yes', please furnish notification nos.**
D. **If abatement is claimed as per notification no. 1/2006-ST, please furnish**
   Sr. No. in the notification under which such abatement is clamied
E1. **Whether provisionally assessed ('Y/N')** `[  ]` **E2. Prov.assessment order No. ('if any')** `[  ]`
F. **Value of taxable service, service tax payable and gross amount charged.**

	Month / Quarter (1)	April (2)	May (3)	June (4)	July (5)	august (6)	September (7)
(I)	**Services Tax Payable**						
(a)	Gross Amount received / (Paid) in money						
	i) Against Service Provided					5,00,000.00	
	ii) In advance for service to be provided						
(b)	Money equivalent of considerations received / (Paid) in a form other than money						
(c)	Value on which service Tax is exempt not Payable						
	i) Amount received against export of service						
	ii) Amount eceived /(paid) towards exempted service Other than export of service i.e i) above					5,00,000.00	
	iii) Amount received as (Paid to) Pure Agent						
(d)	Abatement b/a mount amoutn claimed						
(e)	Taxable value = (a + b) Minus (c + d)						
(f)	Service Tax rate wise break up of taxable value = (e)						
	i) Value on which service Tax is payable @ 5%						
	ii) Value on which service Tax is payable ('@ 8%						
	iii) Value on which service Tax is payable @ 10 %						
	iv) Value on which service Tax is payable @ 12%						
	v) Other rate, if any						
(g)	Service Tax Payable = (5% of f (i) + 8% of (ii) 10% of f (iii) + 12% of f (iv) + f (v) x other rate						
(h)	Education cess payable = @ 2% of Service Tax						
(i)	Secondary and Higher Education Cess Payable = (@ 1% of Service Tax)						
(II)	**Taxable amount charged**						
(l)	Gross amount for which bills / invoices / Challans are issued relating to service provided / to be provided including export of service and exempted service)					5,00,000.00	
(k)	Money equivalent of other consideration charged, if any, in a form other than money						
(l)	Amount charged for Exported service provided / to be provided						
(m)	Amount Charged for Exempted service provided to be provided Other than export of service given at (l) above					5,00,000.00	
(n)	Amount Charged as pure agent						
(n)	Amount Claimed as Abatement						
(P)	Net Taxable Amount Charged = (i + k) Minus (l + m + n + o)						

3. Computation of Service Tax

A1. Name of Taxable service

<u>Taxable Service</u>

A2. Assessee is liable to pay Service Tax on this taxable service as -

(i) a service provider, or → Yes

(ii) a service receiver liable to make payment of Service Tax → No

B. Sub clause No. of clause (105) of section 65

C1. Has the assessee availed benefit of any exemption notification (Y/N) → No.

C2. If reply to column 'C1' is 'Yes', please furnish notification nos.

D. If abatement is claimed as per notification no. 1/2006-ST, please furnish Sr. No. in the notification under which such abatement is clamied

E1. Whether provisionally assessed ('Y/N') [ ] **E2. Prov.assessment order No. ('if any')** [ ]

F. Value of taxable service, service tax payable and gross amount charged.

	Month / Quarter (1)	April (2)	May (3)	June (4)	July (5)	august (6)	September (7)
(I)	**Services Tax Payable**						
(a)	Gross Amount received (Paid) in money						
	i) Against Service Provided					7,70,000.00	10,41,260.24
	ii) In advance for service to be provided						62,789.25
(b)	Money equivalent of considerations received / (Paid) in a form other than money						
(c)	Value on which service Tax is exempt not Payable						
	i) Amount received against export of service						
	ii) Amount eceived /(paid) towards exempted service Other than export of service i.e i) above						1,50,000.00
	iii) Amount received as (Paid to) Pure Agent						
(d)	Abatement b/a mount claimed						
(e)	Taxable value = (a + b) Minus (c + d)					7,50,000.00	9,54,049.49
(f)	Service Tax rate wise break up of taxable value = (e)						
	i) Value on which service Tax is payable @ 5%						
	ii) Value on which service Tax is payable @ 8%						
	iii) Value on which service Tax is payable @ 10 %						
	iv) Value on which service Tax is payable @ 12%					7,50,000.00	9,39.049.49
	v) Other rate, if any						
(g)	Service Tax Payable = (5% of f (i) + 8% of (ii) 10% of f (iii) + 12% of f (iv) + f (v) x other rate					90,000.00	1,12,695.94
(h)	Education cess payable = @ 2% of Service Tax					1,800.00	2,253.71
(i)	Secondary and Higher Education Cess Payable						
	= (@ 1% of Service Tax)					900.00	1,126.86
(II)	**Taxable amount charged**						
(I)	Gross amount for which bills / invoices / Challans are issued relating to service provided / to be provided including export of service and exempted service)					7,50,000.000	10,63,994.66
(k)	Money equivalent of other consideration charged, if any, in a form other than money						
(I)	Amount charged for Exported service provided / to be provided						1,50,000.00
(m)	Amount Charged for Exempted service provided / to be provided Other than export of service given at (I) above						
(n)	Amount Charged as pure agent						15,000.00
(n)	Amount Claimed as Abatement						
(P)	Net Taxable Amount Charged = (i + k) Minus (I + m + n + o)					7,50,000.00	8,99,999.65

4. Amount of service tax paid in advance under sub rule (1A) of rule 6.

	Month / Quarter (1)	April (2)	May (3)	June (4)	July (5)	august (6)	September (7)
(a)	Ammount Deposited in advance						15,000.00
(b)	Challan Nos.						4,56,847
(c)	Challan Dates						3-oct-2012

4A. Service Tax, Education cess and other amounts paid

	Month / Quarter (1)	April (2)	May (3)	June (4)	July (5)	august (6)	September (7)
(II)	Service Tax, Education Cess, Secondary and Higher Education Cess Paid						
(a)	Service Tax paid						
	(i) In Cash					82,800.00	4,805.98
	(ii) by CENVAT Credit						7,200.00
(iia)	by adjustment or amount earlier paid in advance and adjusted in this period under rule 5 (1A)						7,951.23
(iii)	by adjustment of excess amount paid earlier and adjusted in this period under Rule 5 (3) Of ST Rules						4,805.98
(iv)	by adjustment of excess amount paid earlier and adjusted in this period under Rule 5 (4A) of ST Rules						
(d)	Education cess paid						
(i)	In Cash					1,555.00	96.12
(ii)	by CENVAT Credit					144.00	
(iia)	by adjustment or amount earlier paid in advance and adjusted in this period under rule 5 (1A)						
(iii)	by adjustment of excess amount paid earlier and adjusted in this period under Rule 5 (3) Of ST Rules						96.12
(iv)	by adjustment of excess amount paid earlier and adjusted in this period under Rule 5 (4A) of ST Rules						
(c)	Second and Higher Education Cess Paid						
(i)	In Cash					828.00	48.06
(ii)	by CENVAT Credit					72.00	
(iia)	by adjustment or amount earlier paid in advance and adjusted in this period under rule 5 (1A)						
(iii)	by adjustment of excess amount paid earlier and adjusted in this period under Rule 5 (3) Of ST Rules						48.06
(iv)	by adjustment of excess amount paid earlier and adjusted in this period under Rule 5 (4A) of ST Rules						
(d)	Other Amounts Paid						
(i)	Arrears of revenue paid in Cash						5,000.00
(ii)	Arrears of revenue paid in credit						
(iii)	Arrears of Education Cess Paid in Cash						
(iv)	Arrears of Education Cess paid in Credit						
(v)	Arrears of Sec & Higher Edu Cess paid in Cash						
(vi)	Arrears of Sec & Higher Edu Cess Paid in Credit						
(vii)	Interest Paid						800.00
(viii)	Penalty paid						
(ix)	Section 734 amount paid						
(x)	Any other amount						

(II) Details of challan [Vide which service Tax, Education Cess, Secondary and Higher Education Cess and Other Amounts Paid in cash]

(a)	Challan Nos							6,58,274	5,69,874
		i)							
		ii)							8,52,745
		iii)							4,56,847
		iv)							

(b)	Challans Date							4-sep-2012	30-sep-2012
		i)							
		ii)							30-sep-2012
		iii)							30-oct-2012
		iv)							

4B. Source documents details for entries at column 4A (I) (a), (iii), 4A(I)a (iv), 4A (I) (b) (iii), 4A (I) (b) (iv), 4A(I) (C) (iii), 4A (I) (C) (iv), 4A (I) (d) (i) to (vii)

Entry in table 4A above		Source documents, No / Period	Source documents date
St. No.	Month / Quarter		

4C. Details of Amount of Service Tax Payable but not paid as on the last day of the period for which return is filed ....

5. Details of input stage CENVAT Credit

5A) Whether the assessee providing exempted non taxable service or exempted goods.

	(1)	(2)
(a)	Whether providing any exempted or non taxable service (Y / N)	
(b)	Whether manufacturing any exempted goods (Y / N)	
(c)	If any one of the above is yes, whether maintainin separate account for receipt or consumption of input service and input goods (refer to rule 6 (2) of CENVAT credit rule, 2004	
(d)	If any one of the (a) and (b) is 'yes' and (c) is 'no' which option is being availed under rule 6 (3) of the Cenvat Credit Rules, 2004	
	(i) Opted to pay an amount equal to 10% of the value of exempted goods and 8 % of the value of exempted service (Y / N) or	
	(ii) Opted to pay an amount equivalent to CENVAT Credit attributable to inputs and input services used in or in relation to manufacture of exempted goods or provision of exempted.	

5.AA Amount payable under rule 6 (3) of the Cenvat Credit Rules, 2004

	Month / Quarter (1)	April (2)	May (3)	June (4)	July (5)	august (6)	September (7)
(a)	Value of exempted goods cleared						
(b)	Value of exempted services provided						
(c)	Amount paid under rule 6 (3) OF Cenvat Credit Rules, 2004, by Cenvat Credit						
(d)	Amount paid under rule 6 (3) of Cenvat Credit Rules, 2004 by cash						
(e)	Total Amount paid = (c) + (d)						
(f)	Challan Nos, Vide which amount mentioned in (d) is paid						
(g)	Challan Dates						

5B.   Cenvat Credit Taken and Utilized

Month / Quarter (1)	April (2)	May (3)	June (4)	July (5)	August (6)	September (7)
(I) CENVAT Credit of Service Tax and Central Excise Duty						
(a) Opening Balance						(-)7,200.00
b) Credit Taken						
(i) On Inputs						
(ii) On Capital Goods						
(iii) On Input Services received directly						66,877.57
(iv) As received from input service distributor						
(v) From inter unit transfer by a LTU						
Total Credit Taken = (i + ii + iii + v)						66,877.57
c) Credit Utilized						
i) For Payment of Service Tax						7,200.00
ii) For Payament of Education Cess or Taxable Service						
iii) For payament of Excise or any other Duty						
iv) Towards clearance of Input Goods and Capital Goods removed as such						
v) Towards inter unit transfer of LTU						
vi) For payment under rule 6 (3) of the cenvat credit Rules 2004						
Total Credit Taken = (i + ii + iii + v)					7,200.00	
(d) Closing Blance of CENVAT Credit = (a + b - c)					(-) 7,200.00	59,677.57
(II) CENVAT Credit of Education Cess and Secondary and Higher Education Cess						
(a) Opening Balance						(-)216.00
(b) Credit of Education Cess and secondary and Higher Education Cess Taken						
(i) On Inputs						
(ii) On Capital Goods						
(iii) On Input Services received directly						2,006.33
(iv) As received from input service distributor						
(v) From inter unit transfer by a LTU						
Total Credit of Education Cess and Secondary and Higher Education Cess Taken = (i + ii + iii + iv)						2,006.33
c) Credit of Education Cess and Secondary and Higher Education cess Utilized						
(i) For Payment of Education cess and Secondary and Higher Education Cess on services					216.00	
(ii) For Payament of Education Cess and Secondary and Higher Education Cess on goods.						
(iii) Towards payament of Education Cess and Secondary and Higher Education Cess on clearance of Input Goods and Capital Goods removed as such						
(iv) Towards inter unit transfer of LTU Total Credit of Education Cess and Secondary and Higher Education Cess Utilized = (i + ii + iii + iv)					216.00	
(d) Clossing Balance of Education Cess and Secondary and Higher Education Cess = (a + b - c)					(-)216.00	1,790.33

6. Credit details for input service distributor

	Month / Quarter (1)	April (2)	May (3)	June (4)	July (5)	August (6)	September (7)
(I)	**CENVAT Credit of Service Tax and Central Excise Duty**						
(a)	Opening Balance of CENVAT Credit						
(b)	Credit taken (for distribution) On Input Service						
(c)	Credit Distributed						
(d)	Credit not eligible for distribution (rule 7 (b) of CENVAT Credit Rules, 2004)						
e)	Closing Balance						
(II)	**CENVAT Credit of Education Cess and Secondary and Higher Education Cess Credit**						
(a)	Opening Balance of Education Cess and Secondary and Higher Education Cess Credit						
(b)	Credit of Education Cess and Secondary and Higher Education Cess taken (for Distribution) On Input Service						
(c)	Credit of Education Cess and Secondary and Higher Education Cess distribued						
(d)	Credit of Education Cess and Secondary and Higher Education Cess not eligible for distribution (rule 7 (b) of CENVAT Credit Rules, 2004)						
(e)	Closing Balance						

7. Self Assessment memorandum

a) I/we declare that the above particulars are in accordance with the records and books maintained by me / us and are correctly stated.

b) I / we have assessed and paid the service Tax and / or availed and distributed CENVAT credit correctly as per the provisions of the Finance Act, 1994 and the rules made thereunder.

c) I / We have paid duty within the specified time limit and in case of delay, I / We have deposited the interest leviable thereon.

8. If the return has been prepared by a Service Tax Return Preparer (STRP), furnish further details as below :

a) Identification No. of STRP

(Signature of Service Tax Return Preparer)

Place : Bangalore
Date : 10 Oct 2012

(Name and Signature of Assessee or Authorised Signatory)

> ### Acknowledgement
>
> Date : 10 - oct - 2012
>
> Place : Bangalore
>
>
> I hereby acknowledge the receipt of your ST - 3 return for the period April 2012 - September 2012
>
>
> (Signature of the officer of Centreal Excise & Service Tax)
>
> (With Name & Official Seal)

5.3.5.4 Service tax E-filing (ST3)

As per the latest rule, ST3 Electronic filing is mandatory with effect from1st October, 2011. Every Service Tax Assessee is required to file Half-yearly returns electronically irrespective of Service Tax paid.

To file returns electronically, CBEC has provided the Excel Format where assessee can enter the values manually, generate the file in XML format and upload the same in ACES website. In Tally.ERP 9, to facilitate the users to fill the details in Excel format, ST3 E-filing Format has been provided.

To view ST3 E-filing,

Go to Gateway of Tally > Display > Statutory Reports > Service Tax Reports > ST3 > E-filing In Form ST3 E-filing screen

In Period For field, select the period for which ST3 Report to be printed. ST3 Form is half yearly return hence, the application displays Two Period option:

- April - September
- October – March

5.4 Tax deducted at source (TDS) :

TDS means Tax Deducted at Source. The concept of TDS was introduced in the Income Tax Act, 1961, with the objective of deducting the tax on an income, at the source of income. It is one of the methods of collecting Income Tax, which ensures regular flow of income to the Government.

5.4.1 Scope & Applicability

5.4.1.1 Scope

Tax deduction at source means the tax required to be paid by the assessee, is deducted by the person paying the income to him. Thus, the tax is deducted at the source of income itself. The income tax act enjoins on the payer of such income to deduct the given percentage of income as income tax and pay the balance amount to the recipient of such income. The tax so deducted at source by the payer is to be deposited in the income tax department account. The tax so deducted from the income of the recipient is deemed payment of income tax by the recipient at the time of his assessment.

Example : Person responsible for paying any income which is chargeable to tax under the head 'Salaries' is required to compute the tax liability in respect of such income and deduct tax at source at the time of payment. If the employee has any other income, he needs to inform the employer so that employer can take that income into consideration while computing his tax liability but he will not take into account losses except loss from house property. Similarly, person responsible for paying any income by way of 'interest on securities' or any other interests are required to deduct tax at source at the prescribed rates at the time of credit of such income to the account of the payee or at the time of payment, whichever is earlier.

5.4.1.2 Applicability

Tax will be deducted at source based on the rate defined in the Act, only on the fulfillment of the below mentioned conditions.

- The Assessees (includes individual & HUF as covered U/S 44AB) carrying on business is deducting the tax at the Time of Payment or Credit, (whichever is earlier) against following type of Recipient (Deductee)
- Individual
- Hindu undivided Family (HUF)
- Body of Individual (BOI)
- Association of person (AOP)
- Co-Operative society
- Local Authority
- Partnership firm
- Domestic company (Indian company)
- Foreign company
- Artificial Judicial Person

5.4.2 TDS Process

- A seller (Deductee) provides services to the buyer (Deductor).
- The buyer deducts the Tax at the time of payment of advances or while accounting the Bills received.
- The buyer deposits the deducted amount to the designated branches of the authorized bank
- The buyer issues Form No.16A to the Deductee
- The buyer files annual returns electronically to the Income Tax department.
- The seller files returns, along with Form 16A claiming the credit of the Tax deducted at source.

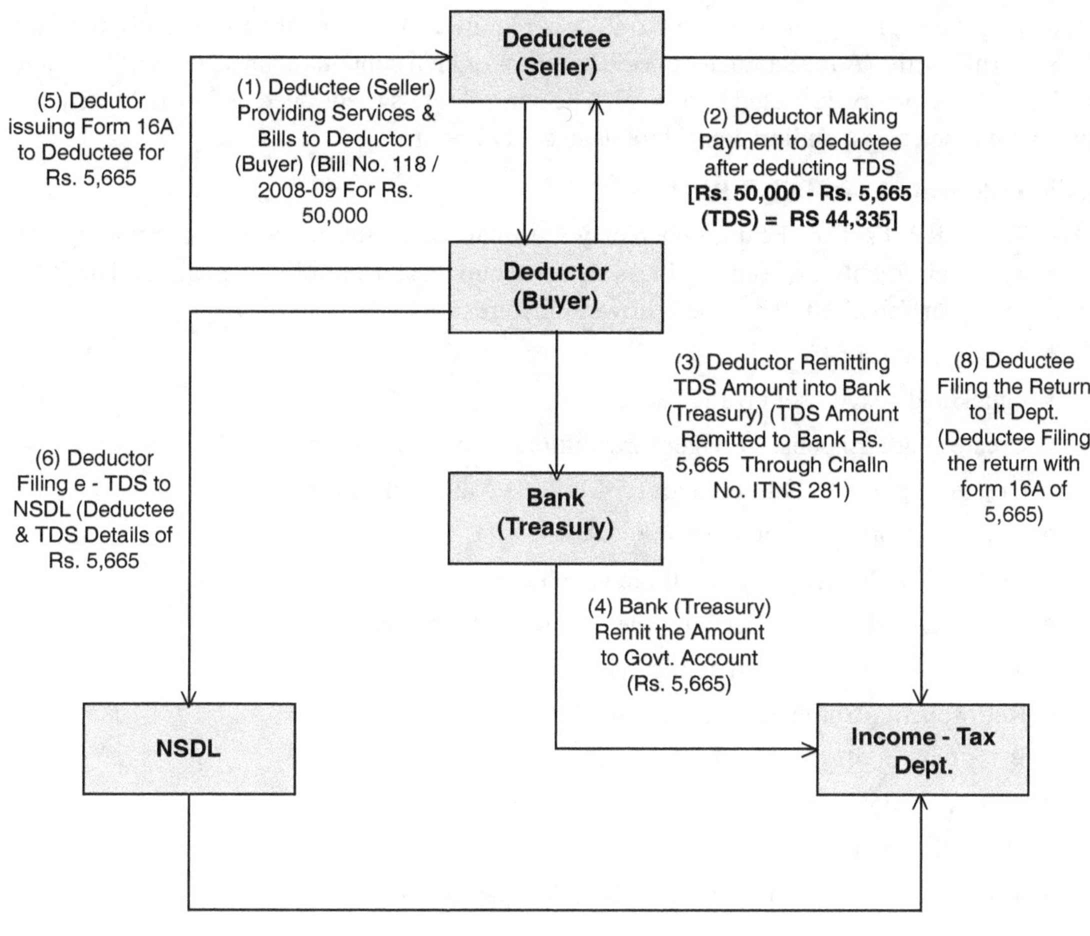

5.4.3 E-TDS Returns

The Income Tax department has now notified 'Electronic Filing of Returns of Tax Deducted at Source Scheme, 2003'. It is applicable to all deductors furnishing their TDS return in electronic form. As per this scheme,

- It is mandatory for corporate deductors to furnish their TDS returns in electronic form (e- TDS return) with effect from June 1, 2003.
- For government deductors it is mandatory to furnish their TDS returns in electronic form (e-TDS return) from financial year 2004-2005 onwards.
- Deductors (other than government and corporates) may file TDS return in electronic or physical form.

Deductors furnishing TDS returns in electronic form (e-TDS) have to furnish Form 27A. Form 27A is a control chart to be furnished in physical form along with CD/ Floppy containing the e-TDS returns. Form No 27A is required to be furnished separately for each TDS return. Form 27A is a summary of e-TDS returns which contains control totals of 'Amount paid' and 'Income tax deducted at source'. The control totals mentioned on Form 27A should match with the corresponding control totals in e-TDS returns.

5.4.5 TDS Features in Tally.ERP 9

Tally.ERP 9's TDS Feature enables you to handle all the functional, accounting and statutory requirements of your business in an accurate and simplified manner. The TDS functionality in Tally.ERP 9 has the following features :

- Simple and user-friendly
- Quick and easy to set up and use
- Create single Expenses Ledger for Multiple Nature of Payment
- Create single TDS Duty Ledger for Multiple Nature of Payment
- Book & Deduct TDS in the same voucher
- Single TDS deduction for multiple vouchers
- Single TDS deduction for Multiple Nature of Payments
- TDS deduction on partial applicable value
- Retrospective Surcharge Deduction
- Party wise configuration for Lower / Zero rate
- Party wise configuration to Ignore IT / Surcharge exemption Limit
- Deduction of TDS on advance payments
- TDS deduction on Non-Resident (Sec.195) payments
- Reversal of TDS
- Print TDS Challan (ITNS 281)
- Print Form 16A
- Generate E-TDS Returns
- Print Form 27A
- Print Form 26, 26Q, 27, 27Q with Annexure(s)
- TDS Computation Report
- Generate TDS Outstanding and TDS Exception Reports

Branch Accounts

6.1 Introduction
6.2 Definition
6.3 Objectives / Need of Branch Accounting
6.4 Types of Branches
6.5 Accounting System for dependent Brandes
6.6 Problems

6.1 Introduction

The main aim of every business organisation is to earn maximum profits. As such a business can not achieve this aim by setting up business establishment at one place only. Therefore, business opens its branches at various places in the same city or in different parts of the country or even in foreign countries according to the nature of its products demand for the product and size of production and also the capacity of the business.

The main or parent establishment is known as Head office and the other subsidiary establishments are known as branches. According to william pickles 'Branch is a section of a business segregated physically from the main section. Main section means the Head Office.

6.2 Definition

A Branch may be defined as a section of an enterprise, geographically separated from the rest of the business, controlled by a Head Office, and generally carrying on the same activities as of the enterprise. As business grows, it may open up branches in different towns and cities in order to market its products services over a large territory and thus increase its profits.

The manufacturers who produce good on large scale in anticipation of demand, would like to sell them over a wide area and for this purpose a wide chain of distribution can be created by opening branches at distant places. Chain stores and multiple shops are quite common now a days for promoting sales.

A business with branches spread over a wide area is interested in knowing the profit or loss and financial result of each branch. And for that accoutns of each branch must be separately kept by the Head Office. If the result of each branch is konwn to the management, then corrective actions can be taken immediately. If a particular branch is incurring losses, then either that branch can be closed down or some improvements in its working can be made. Ulimately, the aim of starting new branches is to maximise the profits and if this purpose is not served then, it is better to close down the branch.

6.3 Objectives : Need of Branch Accounting

In order to ascertain the trading results i.e profit or loss of each branch, separate branch accounts are maintained for each branch to record its transactions. The main objectives of maintaining separate Branch Accounts can be stated in brief as under

1) To ascertain the profit or loss of each branch.
2) To enable the Head Office to as certain the commission payable to branch manager, if it is based on certain percentage of profit earned by the branch.
3) To know the financial position of each branch.
4) To keep control over working of each branch.
5) To findout whether a branch is working efficiently or otherwise. And to take steps to improve the working of the branch, if found necessary.
6) To as certain and to meet the requirements of goods and cash of each branch.
7) To meet the requirements of special Acts.
8) To take decision whether to continue the branch or to close down.

6.4 Types of Branches :

The branches are classified mainy into three types i.e.
i) Dependent Agency Branches   ii) independent Branches and
iii) Foreign Branches

The Various types of Branches are shown in following chart

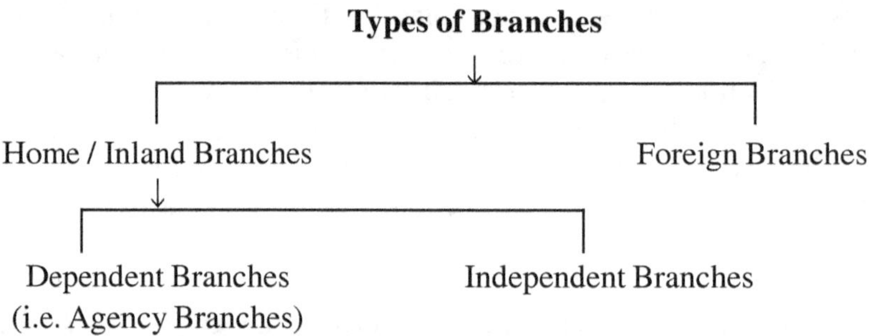

Dependent Branches are those branches which do not maintain a complete record of its transactions. The Head Office may maintain the accounts of such branches according to any of the following methods.

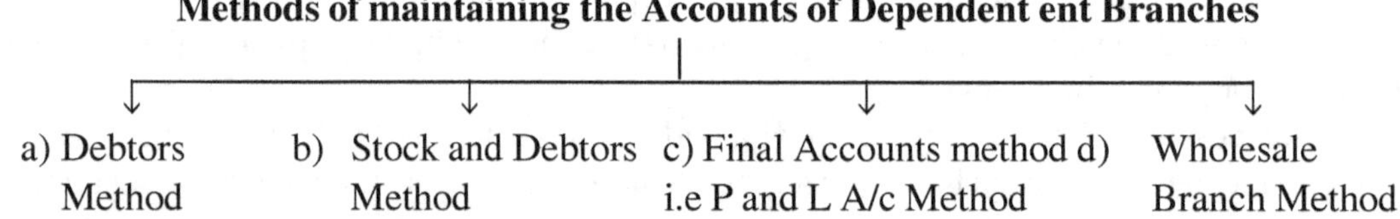

Dependent Branches may be classified as follows :

1) A branch selling for cash only the goods supplied by Head Office at cost.
2) A branch selling for cash and on credit the goods supplied by Head Office at cost.
3) A Branch sellinzg for cash and on credit the goods supplied by Head Office at inflated price, at cost pluscertain percentage or at selling price.

The following are the characteristics of all the three types of dependent branches Mentioned above -

1) These branches sell only those goods which are supplied by the Head Office. They are not allowed to make purchases in the open market.
2) The Branch expenses are usually met by the Head Office.
3) The Branch promptly remits the proceeds of cash sales and collection from Debtors to the Head Office.
4) Some petty expenses are paid by the branch manager out of petty cash balance. Petty cash account at the branch is generally Maintained on an imprest system.
5) These branches enjoy very little powers and are mostly dependent on head office for supply of goods and for expenses. They do not keep any account and as such entire accounting work of a dependent branch is performed at the Head Office. Branches keep only some memorandun records like Stock Register, Sales ledger (in case of credit sales) and petty cash book And periodical statements are sent by the branch to the Head Office.

6.5 Accounting system for Dependent Branches :

The system of Branch Accounting varies with the nature and the status of the branch i.e. type of the branch -

In the Case of Dependent Branches.

a) In the Head office books the following accounts are maintained.
   i) Only Branch A/c or
   ii) Branch A/c and Branch Adjustment A/c. (Goods are supplied at above cost.)
   iii) Branch A/c and or Branch Trading and Profit and Loss A/c
   iv) Branch Stock A/c, Branch, Adjustment A/c, Branch Debtors A/c, Branch Expenses A/c, Branch Cash A/c, and Branch Profit and Loss A/c
   (This method is called branch stock and Debtors method.)
b) in the Branch Books :
   Only Cash Book or cash and Destors A/c's are maintained

The accounting system that will be followed by the Head in case of dependent branches will depend on the size of such branches, the number of branches, Frequency of transactions with such branches, degree of control required etc. Mainly, there are three methods of maintaining accounts for dependent branches -

1) Debtors system Synthetic Method :

Under this system, each branch is treated as a debtor of the Head office and a separate account for each branch is opened. All transactions with the branch are synthetically recorded in one Branch A/c Which also serves the purpose of profit and loss A/c.

2) Stock and Debtors system Analytical method :

In this system, elaborate records are maintained regarding the debtors and stock of the branch and several Accounts are opened like Branch stock A/c, Branch Debtors A/c, Branch Expenses A/c, Branch Assets A/c, Branch profit and loss A/c) (When goods are sent at cost price or Branch Adjustment A/c (When Goods are sent at inflated price.)

3) Branch Trading and profit and loss A/c Method :

Under this method the Head Office prepares in its books Branch. Trading and profit and Loss A/c to as certain the trading results i.e. net profit or loss of the Branch. Trading and Profit and loss A/c is prepared in the same manner as an ordinary Trading and profit and Loss A/c. Even if the goods are sent to the Branch by the Head Office at above cost, opening stock, closing stock, Goods sent to Branch, Goods returned by the branch etc. are recorded invariably.

Stock and Debtors system Analytical Method :

Debtor's System we have studied in preceeding part is inadequate when numerou branch transactions, especially credit sales takes place and the Head Office wants detailed information regarding Stock and Debtors. Information regarding Opening Balance, Closing Balance of debtors and cash collected from debtors is only available from Branch A/c, Where as it fails to give information regarding credit sales, Discount Allowed, Bad Debts, Returns from customers. Regarding stock also, details only on opening stock, closing stock and goods sent and returned are available from Branch A/c. But it fails to give detaied picture of Stock. ins and wastages, spoilage etc.

In order to remove in dequacy of the 'Debtors System' and to have detaile records of stock and Debtors, Branch accounting in the Head Office books is done by stock and debtors system or Analytical Method in which serveral A/c, such as Branch stock A/c, Branch Debtors A/c, Brach expenses A/c, Branch petty cash A/c, Branch profit and Loss A/c, Branch Adjustment A/c are prepared instead of one solitary Branch Account.

We will study this system under two cases -

A)   Where goods are sent to Branch at cost price.

B)   Where goods are invoiced at inflated price are selling price.

A) Where Goods are sent to the Branch at cost price

Under 'Stock and Debtors System' the Head Office Maintains the following accounts relating to the Branch.

1)   Branch Stock A/c : On the Debit side, opening stock, Goods Sent to Branch, Returns from customers are recorded. on the credit side sales, cash as well as credit returns to Head Office from the Branch and closing stock are recorded. The differnece between the two sides will show Gross Profit or Gross loss will be transferred to Branch profit and loss A/c.

2)   Branch Debtors A/c : This accounts will be prepared in the usual manner i.e the debitside we record Opening Balance, credit sales and on the creditside we recor cash received, cheques received, returns from customers, Bad Dbts. Discount allowed and closing Balance.

3) Branch Expenses A/c : All expenses of the Branch are debited to this account and the Balance of this account is transferred to Branch profit and loss A/c.

4) Branch profit and loss A/c : Gross profit or Gross Loss shown by Branch stock A/c is transferred to this account, Branch expenses are transperred to this account, and the balance of this account frepresents net result of the Branch which will be transferred to General Profit and loss A/c.

Besides these Branch Petty cash A/c and Branch Assets A/c are also opened.

Proforma Journal Entries (Head Office Books)

1) When Goods are sent to the branch
   Branch Stock A/c .... Dr.
   To Goods sent to Branch A/c.
2) When Good are returned by the Branch to Head Office.
   Goods sent to Branch A/c .... Dr.
   To Branch Stock A/c.
3) When Branch sells goods for cash or on credit
   Cash A/c OR Branch Debtors A/c .... Dr.
   To Branch Stock A/c.
4) When cash or cheque is collected from Branch Debtors
   Cash / Bank A/c .... Dr.
   To Branch Debtors A/c.
5) When goods are returned by customers
   Branch stock A/c .... Dr.
   To Branch Debtors A/c.
6) For Amount Allowed, Bad Debts, Allowances to Debtors etc.
   Branch Expenses A/c .... Dr.
   To Branch Debtors A/c.
7) When expenses are paid for the branch.
   Branch expenses A/c .... Dr.
   To cash A/c.
8) Opening Stock will be put on the credit side of Branch stock A/c and the balance in Branch stock A/c will represent Gross Profit or Gross loss which will be transferred to Branch profit and loss A/c.
   For Gross Profit :   Branch Stock A/c .... Dr.
             To Branch profit and Loss A/c
   For Gross Loss   :   Reverse entry will be passed i.e.
             Branch profit and Loss A/c ....Dr.
             To Branch Stock A/c.
9) Branch Expenses A/c Will be closed by transferring its balance to Branch Profit and Loss A/c.
   Branch profit and loss A/c .... Dr.
   To Branch Expenses A/c.

Now, the Balance on the Branch profit and Loss A/c Representing Branch profit and loss which will be transferred to General profit and Loss A/c.

B) Where Goods are invoiced at selling price or Inflated price :

Stock and Debtors system is best suited to the operations of a Branch to which goods are sent at selling price which the Branch is not authorised to vary. In this case, the Head Office will prepare Branch Stock A/c at invoice or selling price and when all transactions relating to goods are recorded at invoice or selling price and when closing stock is placed on the credit side of Branch Stock A/c Should agree. Branch stock A/c does not reveal the Gross result as in the case of a branch to which goods are sent at cost.

Adjustment must be made of the differences between the selling prices and cost prices of Goods sent, opening and closing stock, Returns by branches (Which are recorded in Branch Stock A/c at selling or inflated price) through Branch Adjustment A/c as follows -

1) For excess of selling price over cost cahrgeds on Goods sent to Branch.
   Goods sent to Branch A/c .... Dr.
   To Branch Adjustment A/c
2) For loading on returns by the branch
   Branch Adjustment A/c .... Dr.
   To Goods Sent to Branch A/c
3) For loading in closing stock.
   Branch Adjustment A/c .... Dr.
   To Stock Reserve A/c.

This Stock Reserve A/c will be Carried to the next year and it will be taken to the credit of Branch Adjustment A/c. It means that for loading in the opening stock (Closing stock of the previous year). Branch Adjustment A/c will be Credited and stock Reserve A/c will be debited.

When Branch expenses and other charges are debited to Branch Adjustment A/c, it will show the net result, and there is no necessity to open Branch profit and loss A/c.

The proforma Branch Adjustment A/c will be as follows

Dr.   **Branch Adjustment Account**   **Cr.**

Praticulars	Rs.	Particulars	Rs.
To Goods sent to Branch A/c. (Adjustment of loading in Goods Returned by branch)	...	By Stock Reserve A/c (Adjustment of loading in opening stock)	...
To Branch Stock A/c (Leakage, Spoilage, shortage)	...	By Goods sent to Branch A/c (Adjustment of loading in Goods sent)	...
To stock Reserve A/c (Adjustment of loading in closing stock)	...	By Branch Stock A/c (Surplus in stock)	...
To Branch Expenses A/c	...	By General profit and Loss A/c (Loss)	...
To General profit and Loss A/c (Profit)			
	...		...

Branch Adjustment A/c can be splitted into two parts. First Part will show Gross Profit or Gross loss. Adjustment on Goods sent, Returned opening and closing stock will be made in the first part and Branch Expenses will be taken to second part. The result of the first part (Gross profit / Loss) Will be transferred to the second part and the result of the second part will represent net result of the branch which will be transferred to profit and loss A/c.

Sometimes, in the problem, Branch Adjustment A/c and Branch Profit and Loss A/c both these accounts are to be prepared. Then the second part of Branch Adjustment A/c as explained in the previous paragraph Will be be named as Branch Profit and Loss A/c and the first Part will be treated as Branch Adjustment A/c as usual.

The other Accounts will be prepared as prepared in the preceeding case.

Treatment of leakages, Surplus of stock in stock and Debtors System.

When the Branch Stock A/c is maintained at invoice price (which is the same as selling price) and if there is no discrepancy or pilferage the Branch stock A/c must tally. But if it does not tally, then the difference may be cased dueto shortage, leakage, piuferage or surplus in stock. The difference in the selling price and cost price of shortage or surplus will be transferred to Branch Adjustment A/c and the cost price will be transferred to Branch profit and loss A/c. The corresponding debitor credit will be given to branch stock A/c. Sometimes invoice price does not coincide with the selling price and as such, Branch Stock A/c does not tally due to difference between invoice price and the selling price. The difference should be transferred to Branch Adjustment A/c as apparent. Profit or Apparent loss.

If there is no Branch Profit and Loss A/c the entrie Amount of Shortage or surplus will be tansferred to Branch Adjustment A/c. The corresp Sonding debit or Credit will be given to Branch stock A/c.

The entry for shortage of stock (When there is no Branch Profit and

Loss A/c) -   Branch Adjustment A/c .... Dr.

　　　　　To Branch Stock A/c.

The entry for surplus of stock When there is no Branch profit and (Loss A/c)

　　　　　Branch Stock A/c .... Dr.

　　　　　To Branch Adjustment A/c.

STOCK AND DEBTORS SYSTEM

PROBLEM NO. 1

Rahul Bros. have two retail sales branches selling goods supplied to them by the firm's central warehouse. All such supplies of goods are charged at the fixed selling price of cost plus 50 percent.

Sales are mainly for cash but in approved cases limited credit sales are authorised. The whole book-keeping work is centralized at the Head Office.

From the following particulars in respect of the transactions of the branch at Underhill,

Delhi, for the period of 3 months ending on 31ˢᵗ March, 1992, you are required to record-them in ledger accounts in the Head Office books showing clearly how any balances thereon are dealt with (i.e., prepare Branch Stock account, Branch Debtors Account, Branch Adjustment Account, Branch Profit and Loss Account, and Goods sent to Branch Account.)

Stock (at selling price) January 1, 1992	26,700
Debtors, January 1, 1992	1,400
Cash sales	72,940
Cash remitted to Head Office by customers	2,800
Goods returned : by Branch to Head Office	1,170
by credit customers to Branch	570
by credit customers to Head Office	120
Goods transferred by the Branch to Low Hill Branch	4,500
Goods issued to Branch by head office (at selling price)	78,300
Bad debts written off	150

The amount due by credit customers on March 31, 1992 was Rs. 960. Goods (at a sales value of Rs. 660) lost in transit from Head Office to the Branch, the actual stock on that date was in agreement with the book figures. A claim was made on the carrier in respect of the lost stock and the sum of Rs. 500 accepted in full settlement.

(Gross Profit Rs. 25,150; Net Profit Rs. 25060; Stock at the end at selling price Rs. 23,100)

Hints :

1. For calculating Gross Profit :
   Branch Adjustment Account will be debited by Rs. 220 for the adjustment of goods lost in transit; The actual loss of stock Rs. 440 will be taken to P. and L. A/c debit side. Claim of Rs. 500 will be credited to P. and L. Account. Goods returned by the branch debtors to Head Office are treated at par with goods returned by Branch to Head Office. In both cases it is not sale and must be adjusted to calculate gross profit.
2. For calculating Net Profit :
   Profit on settlement of transactions with the carrier Rs. 60 will be taken to the credit side of Profit and Loss Account.

Solution :

<table>
<tr><td>Dr.</td><td colspan="3" align="center">Branch Stock Account (At Selling Price)</td><td>Cr.</td></tr>
<tr><td>Particulars</td><td>Amount Rs.</td><td>Particulars</td><td>Amount Rs.</td></tr>
<tr><td>Opening balance</td><td>26,700</td><td>Cash sales</td><td>72,940</td></tr>
<tr><td>Goods sent to branch</td><td>78,300</td><td>Credit sales*</td><td>3,200</td></tr>
<tr><td>Sales returns (from debtors</td><td></td><td>Goods returned to H.O.</td><td>1,170</td></tr>
<tr><td> to branch)</td><td>570</td><td>Goods transferred to</td><td></td></tr>
<tr><td>Sales returns from debtors</td><td></td><td> Low Hill Branch</td><td>4,500</td></tr>
<tr><td> to head office</td><td>120</td><td>Returns to H.O. (goods</td><td></td></tr>
<tr><td></td><td></td><td>returned by debtors to H.O.)</td><td>120</td></tr>
<tr><td></td><td></td><td>Loss in transit</td><td>660</td></tr>
<tr><td></td><td></td><td>Balance (balancing figure)</td><td>23,100</td></tr>
<tr><td></td><td>1,05,690</td><td></td><td>1,05,690</td></tr>
</table>

<table>
<tr><td>Dr.</td><td colspan="3" align="center">Branch Debtors</td><td>Cr.</td></tr>
<tr><td>Particulars</td><td>Amount Rs.</td><td>Particulars</td><td>Amount Rs.</td></tr>
<tr><td>Opening balance</td><td>1,400</td><td>Remittances</td><td>2,800</td></tr>
<tr><td>*Credit sales</td><td>3,200</td><td>Returns to B.O.</td><td>570</td></tr>
<tr><td> (balancing figure)</td><td></td><td>Returns direct to H.O.</td><td>120</td></tr>
<tr><td></td><td></td><td>Bad debts</td><td>150</td></tr>
<tr><td></td><td></td><td>Closing balance</td><td>960</td></tr>
<tr><td></td><td>4,600</td><td></td><td>4,600</td></tr>
</table>

<table>
<tr><td>Dr.</td><td colspan="3" align="center">Branch Adjustment</td><td>Cr.</td></tr>
<tr><td>Particulars</td><td>Amount Rs.</td><td>Particulars</td><td>Amount Rs.</td></tr>
<tr><td>Sales returns</td><td>390</td><td>Stock reserve (adjustment</td><td></td></tr>
<tr><td>Goods returned (direct to H.O.)</td><td>40</td><td> of opening stock)</td><td>8,900</td></tr>
<tr><td>Adjustment of goods transferred</td><td>1,500</td><td>Goods sent</td><td>26,100</td></tr>
<tr><td>Adjustment of goods lost in</td><td></td><td></td><td></td></tr>
<tr><td> transit</td><td>220</td><td></td><td></td></tr>
<tr><td>Stock reserve (adjustment of</td><td></td><td></td><td></td></tr>
<tr><td>closing stock)</td><td>7,700</td><td></td><td></td></tr>
<tr><td>Gross profit</td><td>25,150</td><td></td><td></td></tr>
<tr><td></td><td>35,000</td><td></td><td>35,000</td></tr>
<tr><td>Loss in transit (at cost)</td><td>440</td><td>Gross profit</td><td>25,150</td></tr>
<tr><td>Bad debts</td><td>150</td><td>Claim for loss of stock</td><td>500</td></tr>
<tr><td>Net profit</td><td>25,060</td><td></td><td></td></tr>
<tr><td></td><td>25,650</td><td></td><td>25,650</td></tr>
</table>

PROBLEM NO. 2

The Kota Doria Ltd. with its head office at Kota opened a branch at Ajmer on 1ˢᵗ January, 1996. Goods are invoiced to the branch at cost plus 25%. From the following particulars calculate gross profit and net profit or loss at Ajmer Branch (by Stock and Debtors system) and open all necessary accounts.

	Rs.
Goods sent to Ajmer branch at invoice price	45,000
Expenses paid by head office	7,200
Discount allowed to debtors	50
Bad debts written off	80
Sales : Cash 21,000	
Credit 12,000	33,000
Stock on December 31 (invoice price)	11,800
Goods returned by branch (Invoice price)	600
Goods returned by debtors	500
Cash remitted to head office	30,500
Cash in hand on December 31	300

(Gross profit Rs. 6,500: Net loss Rs. 910; Debtors at the end Rs. 1,570)

Solution :

Dr.		Branch Stock		Cr.
Particulars	**Amount Rs.**	**Particulars**		**Amount Rs.**
Goods sent to branch	45,000	Sales (cash)		21,000
Branch debtors (sales returns)	500	Sales (Credit)		12,000
		Returns of goods		600
		Shortage (balancing figure)		100
		Balance		11,800
	45,500			**45,500**

Dr.		Branch Debtors		Cr.
Particulars	**Amount Rs.**	**Particulars**		**Amount Rs.**
Sales	12,000	Branch cash		9,800
		Discount		50
		Bad debts		80
		Branch stock (returns)		500
		Balance (balancing figure)		1,570
	12,000			**12,000**

Dr.   **Branch Cash**   **Cr.**

Particulars	Amount Rs.	Particulars	Amount Rs.
Cash sales	21,000	Cash (cash remitted)	30,500
Bank (for expenses)	7,200	Branch adjustment account	
Branch debtors, being cash		(expenses)	7,200
received from debtors		Closing balance	300
(balancing figure)	9,800		
	38,000		**38,000**

Dr.   **Branch Adjustment**   **Cr.**

Particulars	Amount Rs.	Particulars	Amount Rs.
Return of goods (adjustment)	120	Goods sent to branch	
Shortage (adjustment)	20	(adjustment)	
Stock reserve (adjustment of			
closing balance of stock)	2,360		
Gross profit	6,500		
	9,000		9,000
Shortage (Rs. 100 - Rs. 20)	80	Gross profit	6,500
Discount	50	Net loss	910
Bad debts	80		
Expenses	7,200		
	7,410		**7,410**

PROBLEM NO. 3

Messrs Eastern Traders, Delhi, have opened a branch at Jaipur on 1-7-1998. The goods were sent by the Head Office to the branch and invoiced at selling price of the branch whichwas 125% of the cost price of the head office. The following are the particulars relating to the transactions of Jaipur branch :

		Rs.
Goods sent to branch (at cost to Head Office)		2,80,800
Sales : Cash		1,25,000
Credit		1,75,000
Cash collected from debtors		1,56,000
Discount allowed		4,000
Cash sent to branch for:		
Wages	3,000	
Freight	11,000	
Other expenses including godown rent	6,000	20,000
Spoiled coth in bales written off at invoice price		500
Stock on June 30, 1999 at invoice price		55,500

Ascertain the gross profit and net profit for the Jaipur Branch for the year ended 30 -6 - 1999 after preparing Branch Stock Account and Branch Debtors Account.

(Gross profit Rs. 59,000: Net profit Rs. 34,600)

[Hints: Calculate the missing figure in respect of sales returns which will be Rs. 5,000 and debtors at the end which will be Rs. 10,000.]

Solution :

Dr.	Branch Stock (at invoice price)		Cr.
Particulars	**Amount Rs.**	**Particulars**	**Amount Rs.**
Goods sent to branch at invoice price (2)	3,51,000	Cash account, cash sales	1,25,000
		Branch debtors, credit sales	1,75,000
Branch debtors, sales returns (balancing figure) (1)	5,000	Branch adjustment account Spoilage	500
		Balance (given)	55,500
	3,56,000		**3,56,000**

See Branch Cash Account

Dr.	Branch Debtors		Cr.
Particulars	**Amount Rs.**	**Particulars**	**Amount Rs.**
Branch stock, credit sales	1,75,000	Branch cash	1,56,000
		Branch stock, returns	5,000
		Branch expenses, discount	4,000
		Balance (balancing figure)	10,000
	1,75,000		**1,75,000**

Dr.	Branch Adjustment		Cr.
Particulars	**Amount Rs.**	**Particulars**	**Amount Rs.**
Branch stock, adjustment of spoilage ($\frac{1}{5}$ × Rs. 500).	100	Goods sent to branch ($\frac{1}{5}$ × Rs. 3,51,000)	70,200
Stock reserve ($\frac{1}{5}$ × Rs. 55,500)	11,100		
Gross profit	59,000		
	70,200		70,200
Branch expenses	24,000	Gross profit	59,000
Branch stock, spoilage at cost (Rs. 500 - Rs. 100)	400		
Net profit	34,600		
	59,000		**59,000**

Notes :

1. The difference in branch stock account has been assumed as returns from customers. Since branch has been opened, the difference cannot be taken as balance of stock in hand in the beginning. The only possible assumption could be to take it as returns from customers.

2. Invoice price of goods sent has been calculated as under :

Let   Rs. 125 be the invoice price

                 100 be the cost price to head office

$\therefore$ 25 is the profit.

Thus,

(i) Rate of profit on cost $\dfrac{25}{100} = \dfrac{1}{4}$

(ii) Rate of profit on invoice price $\dfrac{25}{125} = \dfrac{1}{5}$

With these rates calculation can be done as under :

	Rs.
Cost price of goods sent	2,80,800
Add Profit $\frac{1}{4}$ on cost	70,200
Invoice price of goods sent	3,51,000

PROBLEM NO. 4

The Mangi Bros. of Dadwara have a branch at Rohtak. Goods are sent to the branch at cost price plus $\dfrac{1}{2}$ of cost price. From the following particulars, prepare necessary accounts on Stock and Debtors system and calculate gross profit and net profit for the branch :

	Rs.
Stock in the beginning (at invoice price)	3,900
Goods sent to branch	30,000
Goods returned by the branch	3,000
Credit sales by the branch	15,000
Cash remitted by the branch	31,000
Debtors balance in the beginning	4,000
Cash received by the branch from the debtors	16,000
Cash received by the head office direct from the branch debtors	2,000
Bad debts	100
Cash discount on cash payment	20
Shortage at the branch	120
Recurring expenses paid by the head office	1,600
Non-recurring expenses paid by the head office	200

(Gross profit Rs. 9,800; Net profit Rs. 8,000)

Hints :

1. Difference between cash remitted and cash received will be treated as cash.
2. Non-recurring expenses is a term used for direct expense. Hence, non-recurring expenses have been taken to adjustment account for calculating gross profit.
3. Recurring expenses, being indirect expenses, have been taken to branch Profit and loss account.
4. Shortage has been divided into two parts. The adjustment portion of shortage is considered for calculating gross profit and rest of the portion for net profit.

Solution :

BOOKS OF MANGI BROS.

Dr.   **Branch Stock**   **Cr.**

Particulars	Amount Rs.	Particulars	Amount Rs.
Opening balance	3,900	Branch debtors (credit sales)	15,000
Goods sent to branch	30,000	Branch cash (cash sales)	15,000
		Goods returned by branch	3,000
		Branch adjustment (shortage)	40
		Branch profit and loss (shortage)	80
		Closing balance (balancing figure)	780
	33,900		**33,900**

Dr.   **Branch Debtors**   **Cr.**

Particulars	Amount Rs.	Particulars	Amount Rs.
Opening balance	4,000	Branch cash	16,000
Branch stock	15,000	Cash (cash received by the	
(credit sales)		head office)	2,000
		Branch profit and loss (bad debts)	100
		Branch profit and loss (discount)	20
		Closing balance (balancing figure)	880
	19,000		**19,000**

Receipts   **Branch Cash**   **Payments**

Particulars	Amount Rs.	Particulars	Amount Rs.
Branch debtors	16,000	Cash (cash remitted)	31,000
Cash (cash received		Branch profit and loss (expenses	
from head office)	1,600	met out of the cash received	
Cash (cash received		from H.O.)	1,600
from head office)	200	Branch adjustment (expenses	
Cash sales	15,000	met out of the cash received	
(balancing figure)		from H.O.)	200
	32,800		**32,800**

Dr.		Branch Adjustment		Cr.
Particulars	**Amount Rs.**	**Particulars**		**Amount Rs.**
Goods returned (adjustment)	1,000	Stock reserve		1,300
Branch stock (shortage)	40	Goods sent to branch		10,000
Stock reserve (adjustment of		(adjustment)		
closing stock)	260			
Branch cash (non-recurring				
expenses)	200			
Gross profit	9,800			
	Rs. 11,300			**Rs. 11,300**

Dr.		Branch Profit and Loss		Cr.
Particulars	**Amount Rs.**	**Particulars**		**Amount Rs**
Branch stock (shortage)	80	Gross profit		9,800
Branch cash (recurring expenses)	1,600			
Branch debtors (bad debts)	100			
Branch debtors (discount)	20			
Net profit	8,000			
	9,800			**9,800**

PROBLEM NO. 5

Dara Stores Ltd., with its head office at Delhi, invoiced goods to its branch at Ghaziabad at 20% less than the list price which is cost plus 100% with instructions that cash sales were to be made at invoice price and credit sales at catalogue price (i.e. list price).

From the following particulars available from the branch, prepare branch stock account, branch adjustment account, branch profit and loss account and branch debtors account for the year ending December 31, 19..... You are also required to verify the gross profit so calculated by preparing branch trading account.

		Rs.
Stock on 1st January 19..... (invoice price)		6,000
Debtors on January 1, 19...		5,000
Goods received from head office (invoice price)		66,000
Sales : Cash	23,000	
Credit	50,000	
		73,000
Cash received from debtors		42,817
Expenses at branch		8,683
Remittances to head office		60,000
Debtors on December 31, 19....		12,183
Stock on December 31, 19....(invoice price)		8,800

(Gross profit Rs. 33,625; Net profit Rs. 24,817)

Solution :

	Rs.
If cost price is	100
List price is cost plus 100%, i.e.	200
Invoice price is 20% less than list price, i.e. (Rs. 200 - Rs. 40)	160

Dr.   **Branch Stock Account**   **Cr.**

Particulars	Amount Rs.	Particulars	Amount Rs.
Balance b/d (invoice price)	6,000	Sales at invoice price :	
Goods from head office	66,000	Cash sales at invoice price	23,000
(invoice price)		Credit sale at list price	50,000
		Less 20% thereof	10,000
		Credit sale at invoice price	40,000
		Balance c/d (invoice price)	8,800
		Shortage (invoice price)	
		(balancing figure)	200
	72,000		**72,000**

Dr.   **Branch Adjustment Account**   **Cr.**

Particulars	Amount Rs.	Particulars	Amount Rs.
Shortage $\left(\dfrac{60}{160}\times Rs.200\right)$	75	Stock reserve $\left(\dfrac{60}{160}\times Rs.6,000\right)$	2,250
Stock reserve $\left(\dfrac{60}{160}\times Rs.8,800\right)$	3,300	Goods from the head office	
Gross profit transferred to		$\left(\dfrac{60}{160}\times Rs.66,000\right)$	24,750
branch profit and loss account	33,625	Branch stock account (excess of list price over invoice price in credit sale)	10,000
	37,000		**37,000**

Dr.   **Branch Profit and Loss Account**   **Cr.**

Particulars	Amount Rs.	Particulars	Amount Rs.
Expenses	8,683	Gross profit	33,625
Shortage at cost (Rs. 200 - Rs. 75)	125		
Net profit transfer to general profit and loss account	24,817		
	33,625		**33,625**

Dr.   **Branch Debtors Account**   **Cr.**

Particulars	Amount Rs.	Particulars	Amount Rs.
Balance b/d	5,000	Cash	42,817
Sales (credit)	50,000	Balance c/d	12,183
	55,000		**55,000**

Note : Gross profit calculated branch adjustment account may be verified by preparing simple trading account as preparing simple trading account and putting stocks and goods sent at cost price.

This is as follows :

Dr.   **Trading Account**   **Cr.**

Particulars	Amount Rs.	Particulars		Amount Rs.
Stock at cost $\left(\dfrac{100 \times Rs.6,000}{160}\right)$	3,750	Sales - Cash	23,000	
		Credit	50,000	73,000
Goods sent at cost		Stock at the end at cost		
$\left(\dfrac{100 \times Rs.66,000}{160}\right)$	41,250	$\left(\dfrac{100 \times Rs.8,800}{160}\right)$		5,500
Gross profit	33,625	Shortage at cost		
		$\left(\dfrac{100 \times Rs.200}{160}\right)$		125
	78,625			78,625

PROBLEM NO. 6

The Grand Tails of Ratlam operates a retail branch at Do Batti. All purchases are made by the head office and goods are charged out to branch at selling price which is cost plus 50 percent.

Cash received from sales by the branch is remitted to head office and branch expenses are paid out of an imprest account which is reimbursed by the head office monthly.

All branch transactions are recorded in the books at Head Office of which details are as follows :   **Rs.**

Stock (at selling price) January 1,1991	24,780
Debtors (January 1, 1991)	6,840
Cash sales	62,300
Credit sales (less Returns)	44,600
Goods received from head office at (selling price)	1,03,800

Goods returned to head office at selling price	1,620
Cash received from debtors	46,830
Discounts allowed to debtors	1,070
Bad debts written off	370
Expenses of branch	15,180
Stock (December 31, 1991) at selling price	19,800

You are required to write up the branch stock account, branch debtors account, branch adjustment account and branch profit and loss account.

Also prepare branch trading account and see that you get the same gross profit as you got from branch adjustment account.

[Normal gross profit Rs. 35,633; Net profit Rs. 18,880;
Shortage of stock Rs. 260 (at selling price)]

[**Hints :** Trading account will be credited by abnormal loss of stock Rs. 173 at cost price and same amount will be debited to profit and loss account.]

Solution :

Dr.		Branch Stock		Cr.

Particulars	Amount Rs.	Particulars	Amount Rs.
Opening balance	24,780	Branch cash (sales)	62,300
Goods sent to branch	1,03,800	Branch debtors (credit sales)	44,600
		Goods returned	1,620
		Shortage (balancing figure)	260
		Closing balance	19,800
	1,28,580		**1,28,580**

Dr.		Branch Debtors		Cr.

Particulars	Amount Rs.	Particulars	Amount Rs.
Opening balance	6,840	Cash	46,830
Sales (credit)	44,600	Discounts	1,070
		Bad debts	370
		Balances (balancing figure)	3,170
	51,440		**51,440**

Dr.   **Branch Adjustment**   **Cr.**

Particulars	Amount Rs.	Particulars	Amount Rs.
Returns	540	Stock reserve	8,260
Shortage ($\frac{1}{3}$ × Rs. 260)	87	Goods sent to branch	34,600
Stock reserve	6,600		
Gross profit	35,633		
	42,860		42,860
Shortage (Rs. 260 - 87)	173	Gross profit	35,633
Discount	1,070		
Bad debts	370		
Expenses	15,140		
Net profit	18,880		
	35,633		**35,633**

Dr.   **Branch Trading and Profit and Loss Account**   **Cr.**

Particulars	Amount Rs.	Particulars Rs.		Amount Rs.
Stock at cost		Sales : Cash	62,300	
(Rs. 24,780 - Rs. 8,260)	16,520	Credit	44,600	
Goods sent to branch:				1,06,900
At selling price 1,03,800		Stock at cost		
Less Returns 1,620		(Rs. 19,800 - Rs 6,600)		13,200
1,02,180		Shortage (abnormal loss)		
Less Profit 34,060		at cost (Rs. 260 - Rs. 87)		173
Goods at cost	68,120			
Gross profit	35,633			
	1,20,273			1,20,273
		Gross profit		35,633
Bad debts	370			
Discount	1,070			
Expenses	15,140			
Shortage (abnormal loss)	173			
Net profit	18,880			
	35,633			**35,633**

PROBLEM NO. 7

A head office at Mumbai has a branch at chennai in charge of a manager. The ratio of gross profit on turnover at branch was 25 percent constant throughout the year.

The branch manager is entitled to a commission of ten percent of the profit earned by the branch calculated before charging his commission, but subject to a deduction from such commission a sum equal to 50 percent of any as certained deficiency of branch stock. All goods were supplied to the branch by Head Office.

From the following figures extracted from the branch books, calculate the commission due to the manager for the year ended 31st December, 1994.

	Rs.		Rs.
Stock on 1-1-1994 at cost	31,210	Establishmentexpenses	22,550
Goods received from head		Drawings by manager	
Office at cost	1,08,700	against commission	1,000
Sales	1,46,400	Stock on 31-12-94	
		at selling price	39,880

Solution :

**Calculation of the Value of the Stock
on 31st December, 1994**

Particulars	Amount Rs.	Total Rs.
Stock on 1-1-1994	31,210	
Add Goods received from head office at cost	1,08,700	
Add Gross profit being 25% of sales	36,600	1,76,510
Less Sales for 1994		1,46,400
Actual value of stock on 31-12-94		30,110
Stock on 31-12-1994 at selling price is		39,880
Less Inflated price being 25% of the stock		9,970
Stock actually in hand on 31-12-1994		29,910

Deficiency of Branch stock

Actual value of Stock on 31-12-1994	30,110
Less Stock actually in hand on 31-12-1994	29,910
Deficiency of stock	200

Calculation of Manager's commission		**Rs.**
Gross Profit		36,600
Less Establishment expenses	22,550	
Deficiency of stock	200	
		22,750
Net profit before charging Manager's commission		13,850

Manager is entitled to get 10% commission on net
profit before charging his commission.

Therefore, his commission will be Rs. 1,385

	Rs.
Commission of the Manager	1,385
Less 50% of the Stock deficiency	100
Actual commission of the Manager	1,285
Less Drawings by Manager against commission	1,000
Amount to be paid to the Manager	285

PROBLEM NO. 8

Stock and Debtors System

Gama Stores of Delhi operates a retail branch at Madras. The head office makes all the purchases and the branch is charged at cost price plus 50%. All cash received by the Madras branch is remitted to Delhi. Branch expenses are paid by the branch out of an imprest account which is reimbursed by Delhi H.O. monthly.

The branch keeps a sales ledger and certain essential subsidiary books, but otherwise all branch transactions are recorded at Delhi. On 1st January 1993 stock in trade at the branch at selling price amounted to Rs. 6,000 and debtors' balances were Rs. 4,000.

During the year ended 31st December, 1993 the following branch transactions were made.

Goods received from Delhi at selling price	15,000
Cash Sales	6,900
Goods returned to Delhi at selling price	300
Credit Sales (less returns)	6,300
Authorised reductions in selling price of goods sold	150
Cash received from debtors	4,800
Debtors written off as irrecoverable	200
Cash discounts allowed to debtors	150

A consignment of goods despatched to the branch on 28th December 1993 with a selling price of Rs. 180 was not received until 5th January 1994 and had not been included in stock figure, which at selling price was Rs. 7,290.

The expenses relating to the branch for the year ended 31th December 1993 amounted to Rs. 1,800.

You are required

    (a)   to write up the Branch stock account and branch debtors account maintained at Delhi with a view to control stock and debtors, and

    (b)   to prepare the trading and profit and loss account of the branch for the year ended 31th Dec., 1993.

    Note : Any stock unaccounted for is to be regarded as normal wastage and pilferage.

[Delhi B.Com. (Hons.)]

Solution :

(a)   **Ledger of Gama Stores**

Dr.   **(i) BRANCH STOCK ACCOUNT**   Cr.

	Rs.		Rs.
To Balance b/d	6,000	By Cash Sales	6,900
To Goods received from H.O.	15,000	By Return to H.O.	300
To Goods from H.O. in transit	180	By Branch debtors - sales	5,300
		By Branch adjust A/c	
		reduction in S.P	150
		By Goods in transit c/d	180
		By Balance c/d	7,290
		By Branch adjust A/c	
		normal difference	60
	21,180		21,180
To Goods in transit b/d	180		
To Stock b/d	7,290		

Dr.   **(ii) BRANCH DEBTORS ACCOUNT**   Cr.

Rs.			Rs.
To Balance b/d	4,000	By Cash	4,800
To Branch Stock A/c	6,300	By P and L A/c - bad debts	200
Credit sales		By P and L A/c - discounts	150
		By Balance c/d	5,150
	10,300		10,300

Dr. **BRANCH ADJUSTMENT A/C** **Cr.**

	Rs.		Rs.
To Branch Stock A/c		By Balance b/f	
To Mark-up on returns		(1/3 of Rs. 6,000)	2,000
to H.O. (1/3 of Rs. 300)	100	By Branch Stock A/c	
To Reduction in Selling Price	150	(1/3 of Rs. 15,000)	5,000
To Normal shortage	60	By Mark-up on goods	
To Balance c/d (1/3 of Rs. 7,290 + 180)	2,490	in-transit (1/3 of Rs. 180)	60
To Profit and Loss A/c- difference	4,260		
	7,060		**7,060**

Dr. **BRANCH PROFIT AND LOSS A/C** **Cr.**

		Rs.		Rs.
To Branch expenses		1,800	By Branch Adjustment A/c	4,260
Branch debtors A/c				
Bad debts	200			
discounts	150	350		
Net Profit		2,110		
		4,260		**4,260**

(b) MEMORANDUM BRANCH TRADING AND PROFIT AND LOSS A/C
for the year ending 31st December 1993

	Rs.			Rs.
To Opening stock		By Sales :		
(2/3 of 6,000)	4,000	Cash :	6,900	
To Purchase less return	9,920	Credit	6,300	13,200
To Gross profit c/d	4,260	By Closing stock		
		(2/3 of Rs. 7,470)		4,980
	18,180			18,180
To Sundry expenses	1,800	By Gross Profit b/d		4,260
To Bad debts	200			
To Discounts allowed	150			
To Net Profit	2,110			
	4,260			**4,260**

Goodsfrom H.O.	15,000
Goods In transit -	180
	15,180
Less Return to H.O.	300
	14,880
2/3rds of Rs. 14,880	= Rs. 9,920

PROBLEM NO. 9

Multichain Stores Ltd., Delhi has its branches at Lucknow and Madras. It charges goods to its branches at cost plus 25%. Following information in available of the transactions of the Lucknow branch for the year ended on 31st March 1995.

Balances on 1-4-94	
Stock	30,000
Debtors	10,000
Petty Cash	50
Transactions during 1994-95 (Lucknow branch)	
Goods sent to Lucknow Branch at Invoice price	3,25,000
Goods returned to Head Office at invoice price	10,000
Cash Sales	1,00,000
Credit Sales	1,75,000
Goods pilfered (Invoice price)	2,000
Goods lost in fire (Invoice Price)	5,000
Insurance Co. paid to H.O. for loss by fire at Lucknow	3,000
Cash sent for Petty Expenses	34,000
Bad debts at Branch	500
Goods transferred to Madras	
Branch under H.O. advice	15,000
Insurance charges paid by H.O.	500
Goods returned by Debtors	500
Balance on 31-3-95	
Petty Cash	230
Debtors	14,000

Goods worth Rs. 15,000 (included above) sent by Lucknow Branch to Madras Branch was in transit on 31-3-95.

Show the following accounts in the books of Multichain Stores Ltd.

[ICWA Inter]

Solution :

In the books of Multichain Stores Ltd.

Dr.		LUCKNOW BRANCH STOCK ACCOUNT			Cr.

		Rs.			Rs.
To Balance b/f		30,000	By Goods sent to branch A/c		
To Goods sent to Branch A/c		3,25,000	Goods returned		10,000
To Branch Debtors A/c		500	By Cash - Cash Sales		1,00,000
Goods returned			By Branch Debtors A/c		
			Credit sales		1,75,000
			By Goods pilfered	Rs.	
			Loading	400	
			Cost	1,600	2,000
			By Goods lost in Fire	Rs.	
			Loading	1,000	
			Cost	4,000	5,000
			By Goods in Transit A/c		
			Sent to Madras Branch		15,000
			By Balance c/d		48,500
		3,55,500			**3,55,500**

Dr.		LUCKNOW BRANCH DEBTORS ACCOUNT		Cr.

	Rs.		Rs.
To Balance b/f	10,000	By Branch Stock A/c	
		By Goods returned	500
To Branch Stock A/c		By Bad Debts	
Credit Sales	1,75,000	transferred to	
		Branch P and L A/c	500
		By Cash - Collected	
		(Balancing figure)	1,70,000
		By Balance c/d	14,000
	1,85,000		1,85,000

Dr.	GOODS SENT TO LUCKNOW BRANCH ACCOUNT		Cr.

		Rs.		Rs.
To Branch Adjustment A/c			By Branch Stock A/c	
Load on goods sent	65,000		Goods sent	3,25,000
To Branch Stock A/c	10,000		By Branch Adjustment A/c -	
returned			Load on goods returned	2,000
To General Trading A/c	2,52,000			
	3,27,000			3,27,000

Dr.		GOODS IN TRANSIT ACCOUNT	Cr.
	Rs.		**Rs.**
To Branch Stock A/c Sent to Madras Branch	15,000	By Branch Adjustment A/c Loading BY Balance c/f	3,000 12,000
	15,000		15,000

Dr.		LUCKNOW BRANCH PETTY CASH A/C	Cr.
	Rs.		**Rs.**

To Balance b/f	50	By Petty Expenses
		   - transferred to Branch
		   P and L A/c (Balancing figure)
			33,820

To Cash Sent	34,000	By Balance c/d	230
	34,050		34,050

Dr.		LUCKNOW BRANCH ADJUSTMENT A/C	Cr.
	Rs.		**Rs.**
To Goods pilfered - load	400		
To Goods lost In fire load	1,000	By Stock Reserve A/c - opening	6,000
To Goods sent to Branch A/c - Load	2,000	By Goods sent to Branch A/c	65,000
To Stock Reserve - closing	9,700	- Load	
To Goods inTransit -Load	3,000		
To Branch P and L A/c - Gross Profit	54,900		
	71,000		**71,000**

Dr.		LUCKNOW BRANCH P and L A/C	Cr.
	Rs.		**Rs.**
To Goods Pilfered - Cost	1,600	By Branch Adjustment A/c	
To goods lost in Fire - Cost	4,000	- Gross profit	54,900
To Bad Debts	500	By Cash Recovered from	
To Cash - Insurance Charges	500	Insurance Co.	3,000
To Petty Expenses	33,820		
To General P and L A/c - Net Profit	17.480		
	57,900		**57,900**

Working Notes :

25% on cost work out to 20% on sales.

PROBLEM NO. 10

Messrs.AmitTraders,Khandwa, opened a Branch at Delhi on 1st July, 1999. The goods were sent by the Head Office to the Branch and invoiced at selling price of the Branch which was 125% of the cost price of the Head Office.

The following are the particulars relating to the transactions of Delhi Branch:

Goods sent to branch (at cost to Head Office)		2,80,800
Sales :		
Cash		1,25,000
Credit		1,75,000
Cash collected from Debtors		1,56,000
Discounts allowed		4,000
Returns from debtors		5,000
Cash sent to branch for :		
Wages	Rs. 3,000	
Freight	Rs. 11,000	
Other Expenses	Rs. 6,000	20,000
Spoiled cloth in bales written off at Invoice price		500
Stock on 30th June, 2000 at Invoice price		55,500

Ascertain the profit or loss for the Delhi Branch for the year ended 30th June 2000 after preparing Branch Stock Account and Branch Debtors Account.

[(Delhi B. Com., (Hons.).]

Solution :

Dr. **Branch Stock A/c** **Cr.**

Particulars	Amount Rs.	Particulars	Amount Rs.
To Goods Sent to Branch A/c		By Branch Debtors A/c	
(IP)	3,51,000	Cash	1,25,000
Branch Debtors A/c		Credit	1,75,000
- Returns	5,000	By Branch Adj. A/c	100
		By Branch Profit and Loss A/c (spoiled cloth)	400
		By Balance c/d	55,500
	3,56,000		3,56,000

Dr.   **BRANCH DEBTORS A/C**   **Cr.**

Particulars	Amount Rs.	Particulars	Amount Rs.
To Branch Stock A/c (Cr. sales)	1,75,000	By Cash A/c	1,56,000
		By Discounts A/c	4,000
		By Branch Stock A/c (Returns)	5,000
		By Balance c/d	10,000
	1,75,000		1,75,000

Dr.   **BRANCH ADJUSTMENT A/C**   **Cr.**

Particulars	Amount Rs.	Particulars	Amount Rs.
To Branch Stock A/c Loading	100	By Goods sent to Branch A/c - Loading	70,200
To Wages[1]	3,000		
To Freight[1]	11,000		
To Stock Reserve A/c	11,100		
To Gross Profit - tr. to Branch P andL A/c	45,000		
	70,200		70,200

Dr.   **BRANCH P and L A/C**   **Cr.**

Particulars	Amount Rs.	Particulars	Amount Rs.
To Expenses	6,000	By Gross Profit	45,000
To Discounts	4,000		
To Branch Stock A/c (CP) (Spoiled cloth)*[2]	400		
To P and L A/C (Net Profit)	34,600		
	45,000		45,000

Note*:

1. Wages and freight have been treated as direct expenses and debited to Branch adjustment A/c.

2. Spoiled cloth is considered as abnormal loss.

PROBLEM NO. 11

Delhi head - office supplies goods to its branch at Kanpur at Invoice price Which is cost plus 50%. All cash received by the branch is remitted to Delhi and all branch expenses are paid by the head office. From the following particulars related to Kanpur branch for the year 1998, prepare -

(i) branch account, and

(ii) Branch Stock account, branch Debtors account, branch Expenses account and Branch Adjustment account in the books of the head office so as to find out the gross profit and net profit made by the branch:

	Rs.
Stock with Branch on 1-1-98 (at Invoice Price)	60,000
Branch Debtors on 1-1-98	12,000
Petty Cash Balance on 1 -1 -98	100
Goods received from Head-Office (at invoice Price)	1,86,000
Goods Returned to Head Office	3,000
Credit Sales less returns	84,000
Allowance to Customer off Selling Price (already adjusted while invoicing)	2000
Cash received from Debtors	90,000
Discount allowed to Debtors	2,400

Expenses (Cash paid by Head Office):

	Rs.	
Rent	Rs. 2,400	
Salaries	24,000	
Petty cash	1,000	
Cash Sales		27,400
Stock with branch on 31-12-98 (at Invoice Price)		1,04,000
Petty Cash Balance on 31-12-98		54,000
		100

[Delhi B.Com. (Hons).]

Solution:

Dr.		BRANCH PETTY CASH A/C		Cr.
Particulars	**Amount Rs.**	**Particulars**		**Amount Rs.**
To Balance b/d	100	By Petty cash expenses - Bal. figure		1,000
To H.O. A/c - Petty cash received	1,000	By Balance c/d		100
	1,100			1,100

Dr.   **BRANCH DEBTORS A/C**   **Cr.**

Particulars	Amount Rs.	Particulars	Amount Rs.
To Balance b/d	12,000	By Cash A/c	90,000
To Branch Stock A/c	84,000	By Branch Expenses A/c	
(Credit Sales)		(Discount)	2,400
		By Balance c/d	3,600
		(Balancing figure)	
	96,000		96,000

Dr.   **BRANCH STOCK A/C**   **Cr.**

Particulars	Amount Rs.	Particulars	Amount Rs.
To Balance b/d	60,000	By Goods sent to Branch A/c	
To Goods sent to Branch A/c	1,86,000	(Returns)	3,000
To Branch Adjustment A/c[3]	1,000	By Br. Debtors A/c	
		(Credit Sales)	84,000
		By Br. Adjustment A/c	
		(Allowance)	2,000
		By Br. Cash A/c	
		(Cash Sales)	1,04,000
		By Balance c/f	54,000
	2,47,000		**2,47,000**

Dr.   **BRANCH EXPENSES A/C**   **Cr.**

Particulars	Amount Rs.	Particulars	Amount Rs.
To Branch Debtors A/c		By Branch Adj. A/c	29,800
(Discount)	2,400		
To Rent	2,400		
To Salaries	24,000		
To Petty Expenses	1,000		
	29,800		**29,800**

Dr.   BRANCH ADJUSTMENT A/C   Cr.

Particulars	Amount Rs.	Particulars	Amount Rs.
To Goods Sent to Branch A/c (Loading)	1,000	By Branch Stock Reserve A/c	20,000
To Branch Stock A/c (Allowance)	2,000	Goods sent to Branch A/c[1] Loading	62,000
To Branch Stock Reserve A/c	18,000	Branch Stock A/c[2]	1,000
To Gross Profits	62,000		
	83,000		83,000
To Br. Expenses A/c	29,800	By Gross Profit	62,000
To Net Profit	32,200		
	62,000		**62,000**

Notes :

1. Invoice Price (IP) = Cost Price + Margin. IP = CP + Margin = 100 + 50 = 150
2. Branch Petty Expenses Rs. 1,000 is Balancing Figure of Branch Petty Cash A/c.
3. Rs. 1,000 is extra price charged over I.P. It is not surplus stock.

PROBLEM NO. 12

Web and Co. is a retail organisation with a number of branch shops. All accounts are kept at the head office, and goods sent to branches are recorded at cost plus the expected mark-up of $33\frac{1}{3}$ percent. The accounting system is designed to give the head office as much control as possible over the branch stocks.

At the Hull branch at 1st February 1998, goods costing Rs. 1,200 were in stock, but some of these costing Rs. 150, had been reduced in selling price of Rs. 160. The balances of the Hull debtors accounts totalled Rs. 920 at the same date.

The following information relates to the Hull branch for the year to 31st January 1999 or at the end of that year.

	Rs.
Goods sent to branch (cost)	18,600
Cash sales (including all the goods marked down at the beginning of the year and others costing Rs. 1,800 sold for half of the normal selling price)	16,060
Cash received from debtors	6,280
Goods returned by branch debtors direct to head office (selling price)	80
Bad debts written off	30
Closing stock of goods at selling price	2,400
Closing total of debtors' balances	830

You are required to :

    (a) Prepare the relevant accounts for the Hull branch and calculate the branch profit for the year.

    (b) Comment briefly on whether you think the management would need to investigate any aspect of the position revealed by the accounts.   **[ACCA, Accounting 3]**

Solution :

    (a)   **Webb and Co. Hull Branch Records**

Dr.   **BRANCH STOCK A/C**   **Cr.**

	Rs.		Rs.
To Balance b/d	1,560	By Cash sales	16,060
To Goods sent to branch a/c	24,800	By Credit sales	6,300
		By Branch adjustment a/c	1,200
		(mark-down on goods)	
		By Branch adjustment a/c	
		loading on stock discrepancy	100
		By Branch P and L a/c	300
		Cost of stock loss	
		Balance c/d	2,400
	26,360		**26,360**

Dr.   **GOODS SENT TO BRANCH A/C**   **Cr.**

	Rs.		Rs.
To Branch debtors - return	80	By Branch stock a/c	24,800
To Branch A/c - loading	6,200	By Branch adjustment a/c	
To Purchases A/c	18,540	- loading on return	20
	24,820		**24,820**

Dr.   **BRANCH ADJUSTMENT A/C**   **Cr.**

		Rs.		Rs.
To Branch stock a/c		1,200	By Stock reserve	
(Mark-down on abnormal items)			(opening stock)	360
To Stock reserve:			By Goods sent to branch	6,200
Returns	20		(loading)	
Closing stock	600	620		
To Branch stock a/c		100		
(deficiency)				
To Gross profit c/d		4,640		
		6,560		**6,560**

Dr.	BRANCH PROFIT AND LOSS A/C		Cr.
	Rs.		**Rs.**
To Branch debtors bad debts	30	By Gross profit b/d	4,640
To Branch stock a/c			
loading on stock loss	300		
To Profit and loss a/c			
- Net profit transferred	4,310		
	4,640		**4,640**

Dr.	BRANCH DEBTORS A/C		Cr.
	Rs.		**Rs.**
To Balance b/d	920	By Cash received	6,280
To Credit sales	6,300	By Returns (direct to H.O.)	80
(balancing figure)		By Bad debts	30
		By Balance c/d	830
	7,220		7,220

Tutorial Notes :

                                                                                Rs.

(1)   Calculation of opening stock :

	Rs.
Opening stock at cost	1,200
Less: Cost price of abnormal Item	150
Cost price of normal item	1,050
Add : Mark-up of $33\frac{1}{3}$ %	350
	1,400
Add : Sale price of abnormal items	160
	1,560

(2)   Mark-down on goods debited to adjustment a/c :

	Rs.
Cost price items sold at below normal price	1,800
Add : Mark-up @$33\frac{1}{3}$ %	600
Sale price of the item	2,400
Sold @ 50% - sale proceeds	1,200
Loss debited to branch adjustment	1,200

(b) There are two aspects that deserve attention. The first aspect is about stock deficiency. The management must ensure that it is within reasonable limits by making inter-firm and Inter-period comparisons. The second aspect is about selling the goods below the usual price. The H.O. must make sure that such a sale was effected under justifiable circumstances.

PROBLEM NO. 13

Dara Stores Ltd., with their head office at Delhi, invoiced goods to its branch at Ghaziabad at 20% less than the list price which is cost plus 100% with instructions that cash sales were to be made at invoice price and credit sales at catalogue price (i.e. list price).

From the following particulars available "from the branch, prepare branch stock account, branch adjustment account, branch profit and loss account and branch debtors account for the year ending 31st December, 19...

	Rs.		Rs.
Stock on 1st January 19...		Cash received from debtors	42,817
(invoice price)	6,000	Expenses at branch	8,683
Debtors on 1st January, 19...	5,000	Remittances to head office	60,000
Goods received from head office	66,000	Debtors on 31st December, 19...	12,183
(invoice price)		Stock on 31st December, 19...	
Sales - Cash 23,000		(invoice price)	8,800
Credit 50,000	73,000		

[Adapted from C.A.; Inter. B. Com. (Hons.) Delhi, B.Sc. Madras]

[I.C.W.A. (F) June 1996]

Solution :

If cost price is	Rs. 100
List price is cost plus 100%, i.e.,	200
Invoice price is 20% less than list price i.e. (Rs. 200 - Rs. 40)	160

Dr.   **BRANCH STOCK ACCOUNT**   **Cr:**

	Rs.		Rs.
To Balance b/d (invoice price)	6,000	By Sales (invoice price):	
To Goods from head office		Cash sales at invoice	
(invoice price)	66,000	price	23,000
To Branch adjustment account		Credit sales at list price	50,000
sale proceeds in excess of		By Shortage (invoice price)	
invoice price 10,000		(balancing figure)	200
		By Balance c/d (invoice price)	8,800
	82,000		**82,000**

Dr. BRANCH ADJUSTMENT ACCOUNT **Cr.**

	Rs.		Rs.
To Stock reserve: $\left(\dfrac{60}{160}\times Rs.8,800\right)$	3,300	By Stock reserve: $\left(\dfrac{60}{160}\times Rs.6,000\right)$	2,250
To Shortage $\left(\dfrac{60}{160}\times Rs.200\right)$	75	By Goods from the head office - $\left(\dfrac{60}{160}\times Rs.66,000\right)$	24,750
To Gross profit c/d	33,625	By Branch stock account (excess of list price over invoice price in credit sales)	10,000
	37,000		37,000
To Expenses	8,683	By Gross profit b/d	33,625
To Shortage at cost (Rs. 200 - Rs. 75)	125		
To Net profit to general profit and loss account	24,817		
	33,625		**33,625**

Dr. BRANCH DEBTORS ACCOUNT **Cr.**

	Rs.		Rs.
To Balance b/d	Rs. 5,000	By Cash	Rs. 42,817
To Sales (credit)	50,000	By Balance c/d	12,183
	Rs. 55,000		Rs. 55,000

Note : Gross profit calculated as per branch adjustment account can be verified by preparing simple Trading Account putting stocks and goods sent at cost price. This is as follows:

Dr. TRADING ACCOUNT **Cr.**

	Rs.			Rs.
To Stock at cost, $\dfrac{100\times Rs.6,000}{160}$	3,750	By Sales - Cash	23,000	
To Goods sent at cost, $\dfrac{100\times Rs.66,000}{160}$	41,250	Credit	50,000	73,000
To Gross Profit	33,625	By Stock at the end, $\dfrac{100\times Rs.8,800}{160}$		5,500
		By Shortage at cost, $\dfrac{100\times Rs.200}{160}$		125
	78,625			78,625

PROBLEM NO. 14

The Jhaveris of Bombay have a branch at Delhi to which goods are sent at cost price to be sold for cash and credit. Transactions during the year were as under :

Branch stock at cost as on 1.1.94	Rs. 9,000
Branch debtors as on 1.1.94	3,000
Branch Bank balance as on 1.1.94	2,800
Transactions during 1994:	
Goods sent to branch at cost	18,000
Goods returned by branch (at cost to H.O.)	360
Cash sales paid Into bank	4,800
Credit sales	24,000
Goods returned by customers at selling price	180
Cheques received from credit customers	22,000
Discount allowed to customers	440
Bad debts written off	260
Cash remitted to H.O. by branch	25,000
Expenses paid by branch :	
Wages and salaries	400
Miscellaneous expenses	200
Rent, rates and insurance paid by H.O.	500
Balance as on 31.12.94 :	
Branch stock (at cost to H.O.)	6,420
Branch debtors	?
Branch bank	?

Required : Compute the profit made by the branch under stock and debtors system after opening the necessary accounts.

Solution :

Dr.	BRANCH STOCK ACCOUNT					Cr.
1994		Rs.		1994		Rs.
Jan. 1	To Balance b/d	9,000	Dec. 31	By Goods Sent to branch		360
Dec. 31	To Goods sent to branch	18,000		By branch bank Cash sales		4,800
	To Branch debtors (returns)	180		By Branch debtors By Credit sales		24,000
	To Branch Profit and loss a/c G. P. transferred	8,400		Balance c/d		6,420
		35,580				35,580
1995						
Jan. 1	To Balance b/d	6,420				

Dr.　　　　　　　　　　**GOODS SENT TO BRANCH**　　　　　　　　　**Cr.**

1994		Rs.	1994		Rs.
Dec. 31	To Branch stock	360	Dec. 31	By Branch Stock	18,000
	To H.O. purchases	17.640			
		18,000			18,000

Dr.　　　　　　　　　　　**BRANCH DEBTORS**　　　　　　　　　　**Cr.**

1994		Rs.	1994		Rs.
Jan. 1	To Balance b/d	3,000	Dec. 31	By Branch bank	22,000
Dec. 31	To Branch Stock -	24,000		By Branch expenses:	
	credit sales			By Bad debts 260	
				Discounts 440	700
				By Branch stock -	
				returns	180
				By Balance c/d	4,120
		27,000			27,000

Dr.　　　　　　　　　　　**BRANCH EXPENSES**　　　　　　　　　　**Cr.**

1994		Rs.	Rs.	1994		Rs.
Dec. 31	To Branch debtors			Dec. 31	By Branch profit	
	Discounts	440			and loss a/c	
	Bad debts	260	700		transfer	1,800
	To Branch cash					
	Wages and salaries	400				
	Misc. expenses	200	600			
	To Bank - Rent, rates					
	and insurance		500			
			1,800			1,800

Dr.　　　　　　　**BRANCH PROFIT AND LOSS A/C**　　　　　　**Cr.**

	Rs.		Rs.
To Branch expenses	1,800	By Branch Stock	8,400
To General profit			
and loss a/c — transfer			
of branch net profit	6,600		
	8,400		8,400

Dr.   BRANCH BANK A/C   Cr.

1994	Particulars	Rs.	1994	Particulars	Rs.	Rs.
Jan. 1	To Balance b/d	2,800	Jan. 1	to		
Jan. 1	to		Dec. 31	By Branch expenses:		
Dec. 31	To Branch stock	4,800		Wages and salaries	400	
	To Branch debtors	22,000		Misc. expenses	200	600
				By H.O. Bank a/c		25,000
			Dec. 31	By Balance c/d		4,000
		29,600				29,600
1995						
Jan. 1	To Balance b/d	4,000				

PROBLEM NO. 15

Abdullah and Sons of Madras have a branch at Calcutta to which goods are sent at 25% above cost. The branch makes both cash and credit sales. Branch expenses are met from branch cash and the balance money remitted to the Head Office. All the necessary accounts are maintained by H.O. under stock and debtors system. From the particulars given below calculate the profit or loss made by the branch for the year ending 31st December 2000 :

Opening stock at invoice price	25,000
Cost price of goods sent to branch	50,000
Goods received by branch till 31st December 2000 at invoice price	60,000
Credit sales for the year	64,000
Branch debtors as on 1st January 2000	12,500
Branch debtors as on 31st December 2000	15,000
Bad debts and discounts written off	500
Cash remitted to Head Office	60,000
Branch cash balance as on 1-1-2000	3,000
Branch cash balance as on 31 -12-2000	2,000
Cash remitted by H.O. to branch	3,000
Branch stock at close - invoice price	20,000
Branch expenses paid by branch	12,000

Solution :

Books of Abdullah and Sons

Dr.		BRANCH DEBTORS ACCOUNT		Cr.
	Rs.			**Rs.**
To Balance b/d	12,500	By Bad debts and discount		
To Credit sales	64,000	written off		500
		By Branch cash		
		Collection from debtors		
		(balancing figure)		61,000
		By Balance c/d		15,000
	76,500			76,500
To Balance b/d	15,000			

Dr.		BRANCH CASH ACCOUNT		Cr.
	Rs.			**Rs.**
To Balance b/d	3,000	By Branch expenses		12,000
To Bank - remittance from		By Bank - remittance from		
H.O.	3,000	branch		60,000
To Branch debtors	61,000	By Balance c/d		2,000
To Branch stock - cash sales				
(balancing figure)	7,000			
	74,000			74,000
To Balance b/d	2,000			

Dr.		BRANCH STOCK ACCOUNT		Cr.
	Rs.			**Rs.**
To Balance b/d	25,000	By Branch cash account		
To Goods sent to branch		cash sales		7,000
account $\dfrac{125}{100}$ x 50,000	62,500	By Branch debtors account		
To Branch adjustment account -		credit sales		64,000
Excess of sale proceeds over		By Balance c/d:		
Invoice price	6,000	Goods in transit*		2,500
		Stock at branch		20,000
	93,500			93,500

* Goods sent to branch - Goods received by branch, ie., Rs. 62,500 - Rs. 60,000 = Rs. 2,500.

Dr.   **BRANCH ADJUSTMENT ACCOUNT**   **Cr.**

	Rs.		Rs.
To Stock reserve on closing stock	4,500	By Stock reserve - opening	5,000
To Gross profit c/d	19,000	By Goods sent to branch account	12,500
		By Branch stock account	6,000
	23,500	excess of sale proceeds	23,500
To Branch expenses	12,500	By Gross profit b/d	19,000
To Branch debtors	500		
To General profit and loss account	6,500		
	19,000		19,000

Dr.   **GOODS SENT TO BRANCH ACCOUNT**   **Cr.**

	Rs.		Rs.
To Branch adjustment account	12,500	By Branch stock account	62,500
To Purchases account - Transfer	60,000		
	62,500		62,500

PROBLEM NO. 16

A Ltd. has a branch at Pune, goods are invoiced at cost + 50%. Branch remits all cash received to the head office and all expenses are met by the head office. The following particulars are available.

Particulars	Rs.
Stock - 1-4-2009 (Invoice price)	37,200
Debtors on 1-4-2009	27,200
Goods invoiced to branch (Invoice price)	2,12,400
Sales at Branch :	
Cash sales	1,00,040
Credit Sales	1,24,000
Goods returned by debtors	4,800
Cash collected from debtors	1,21,600
Goods returned by branch to head office (invoice price)	6,000
Discount allowed to customers	800
Expenses at Branch :	
Salary	12,000
Rent	8,000
Office expenses	1,600
Sundry expenses	2,000

You are required to prepare Pune Branch Account, Branch Stock A/c, Branch Debtors Account in the books of head office.

(P. U. April 2005)

Solution :

In the Books of A Ltd.
Pune Branch Stock A/c

Dr.   Cr.

Particulars	Rs.	Particulars	Rs.
To Balance b/d (Invoice price)	37,200	By Goods sent to branch (Invoice price)	6,000
To Goods sent to Branch A/c (Invoice price)	2,12,400	By Bank A/c (Cash Sales)	1,00,040
To Branch Debtors A/c (Return Inward)	4,800	By Branch Debtors A/c	1,24,000
		By Balance c/d. (Bal. Fig.)	24,360
	2,54,400		**2,54,400**

Branch Debtors A/c

Dr.   Cr.

Particulars	Rs.	Particulars	Rs.
To Balance b/d	27,200	By Bank	1,21,600
To Branch Stock A/c (Credit sale)	1,24,000	By Branch Stock A/c (Return)	4,800
		By Branch Expenses A/c (Discount)	800
		By Balance c/d (Bd. fig.)	24,000
	1,51,200		**1,51,200**

Branches Expenses A/C

Dr.   Cr.

Particulars		Rs.	Particulars	Rs.
To Bank A/c			By Branch P/L A/c (Bal. Fig.)	24,400
Salary	12,000			
Rent	8,000			
Office Exp.	1,600			
Sundry Exp.	2,000	23,600		
To Branch Debtors A/c (Discount)		800		
		24,400		**24,400**

Dr. **Branch Adjustment A/c** **Cr.**

Particulars	Rs.	Particulars	Rs.
To Stock Reserve A/c (Loading)	8,120	By Stock Reserve A/c	
To Goods sent to Branch		(loading)	12,400
(loading)	2,000	By Goods sent to Branch	
To Branch Stock A/c (loading)	1,000	(loading)	70,800
To Gross Profit			
(transfer to P and L A/c)	73,080		
	83,200		**83,200**

Dr. **Branch Profit and Loss A/c** **Cr.**

Particulars	Rs.	Particulars	Rs.
To Branch Expenses A/c	24,400	By Branch Adjustment A/c	73,080
To Net Profit	48,680		
	73,080		**73,080**

Working Note :

Loading = Cost + 50% = Invoice Price

= 100 + 50 = 150

= 50/50 = 1/3

i) Loading on opening stock = 37,200 × 1/3 = 12,400

ii) Loading on Goods sent to Branch = 2,12,400 × 1/3 = 70,800

iii) Loading on Goods sent to Head Office = 6000 × 1/3 = 2000

iv) Loading on closing stock = 24360 × 1/3 = 8120

PROBLEM NO. 17

Star Products Limited, Pune has its branch at Goa. It charges goods to its branch at cost plus 25%. Following information is available of the transaction of the Goa Branch for the year ended on 31st March, 2010.

Particulars	Rs.
Balances on 1-4-2009	
Stock (at Invoice Price)	30,000
Debtors	10,000
Petty Cash	50
Transactions during 2009-2010	
Goods sent to Branch (at cost price)	2,60,000
Goods return to Head Office (at Invoice Price)	10,000
Cash Sales	1,00,000
Credit Sales	1,75,000
Goods pilfered (at Invoice Price)	2,000
Goods lost in fire (at invoice Price)	5,000
Insurance Co. paid to head office for loss by fire	3,000
Cash sent for Petty Expenses	34,000
Bad Debts at Branch	500
Goods transferred to Pune Branch under Head Office advice	
(at Invoice Price)	15,000
Insurance charges paid by Head Office	500
Goods returned by Debtors	500
Balances on 31-3-2010	
Petty Cash	230
Debtors	14,000

Goods worth Rs. 15,000 (included above) sent by Goa Branch to Pune Branch were lost in transit on 31st March, 2010.

Prepare Branch Stock A/c. Branch Debtors A/c, Branch Adjustment A/c, Branch Profit and Loss A/c, Stock Reserve A/c and Goods sent to Branch A/c. **(I.C.W.A.)**

Solution :

1) Goods sent to Branch at cost price   2,60,000

   + Loading @ 25% on cost price   65,000

   Invoice Price of Goods   3,25,000

2) Loading   = Cost Price + 25% = Invoice Price

           = 100 + 25 = 125

           = 25/125 i.e. = 1/5

In the Books of Star Product Ltd.

Dr.		Goa Branch Stock A/c		Cr.
Particulars	**Rs.**	**Particulars**		**Rs.**
To Balance b/d (I.P.)	30,000	By Goods sent to branch (I.P.)		10,000
To Goods sent to Branch A/c (I.P)	3,25,000	By Bank A/c (Cash Sales)		1,00,000
To Branch Debtors A/c (R / I)	500	By Branch Debtors A/c		1,75,000
		(Credit Sales)		
		By Branch Adjustment A/c		
		(Pilferage - loading)		400
		By Profit and Loss A/c		
		(Pilferage cost)		1,600
		By Loss by fire		5,000
		By Goods in Transit A/c		
		(Sent to Pune Branch)		15,000
		By Balance c/d (Bal. Fig.)		48,500
	3,55,000			3,55,000

Dr.		Branch Debtors A/c		Cr.
Particulars	**Rs.**	**Particulars**		**Rs.**
To Balance B/d	10,000	By Bank A/c		1,70,000
To Bank Stock A/c	1,75,000	(Collection from Debtors)		
(Credit Sales)		By Branch Stock A/c		
		(R/Inward)		
		By Branch Expenses A/c		500
		Bad Debts		500
		By Balance c/d		14,000
	1,85,000			**1,85,000**

Dr.		Branch Petty cash A/c		Cr.
Particulars	**Rs.**	**Particulars**		**Rs.**
To Balance B/d	50	By Branch expenses		
To Bank A/c	34,000	(Balance Figure)		33,820
		By Balance c/d		230
	34,050			**34,050**

Dr. Branch Expenses A/c **Cr.**

Particulars	Rs.	Particulars	Rs.
To Bank A/c (Insured)	500	By Profit and Loss A/c	
To Branch Debtors A/c	500	(Balance Figure)	34,820
(Bad Debts)			
To Branch Petty Cash A/c	33,820		
	34,820		**34,820**

Dr. Branch Adjustment A/c **Cr.**

Particulars	Rs.	Particulars	Rs.
To Branch Stock A/c (loading)	400	By Stock Reserve A/c	
To Loss by fire A/c	1,000	(Loading)	6,000
To Stock Reserve A/c (Loading)	9,700	By Goods sent to Branch	63,000
To Goods in Transit A/c (Loading)	3,000	(Loading)	
To Gross Profit (transfer to Profit			
and Loss A/c)	54,900		
	69,000		**69,000**

Dr. Branch Profit and Loss A/c **Cr.**

Particulars	Rs.	Particulars	Rs.
To Branch Stock A/c (Pilfered)	1,600	By Branch Adjustment A/c	
To Loss by fire A/c	1,000	(Gross Profit)	54,900
To Branch Expenses A/c	34,820		
To Net Profit			
(transferte General P and L A/c)	17,480		
	54,900		**54,900**

Dr. Goods Sent to Branch A/c **Cr.**

Particulars	Rs.	Particulars	Rs.
To Branch Adjustment A/c		By Branch Stock A/c	3,25,000
(loading)	63,000		
To Branch Stock A/c	10,000		
To Purchase A/c			
(transfer to Trading A/c)	2,52,000		
	3,25,000		**3,25,000**

Dr.		Stock Reserve A/c		Cr.
Particulars	Rs.	Particulars		Rs.
To Branch Adjustment A/c	6,000	By Balance b/d		6,000
To Balance c/d	9,700	By Branch Adjustment A/c		9,700
	15,700			**15,700**

Dr.		Loss by Fire A/c		Cr.
Particulars	Rs.	Particulars		Rs.
To Branch Stock A/c	5,000	By Branch Adjustment A/c		1,000
		By Cash		3,000
		By Branch Profit and Loss A/c		1,000
	5,000			**5,000**

Dr.		Goods in Transit A/c		Cr.
Particulars	Rs.	Particulars		Rs.
To Branch Stock A/c	15,000	By Branch Adjustment A/c (Loading)		3,000
		By Balance c/d		12,000
	15,000			**15,000**

PROBLEM NO. 18

Prachi Ltd., Poona has a branch at Nashik to which goods are sent at invoice price which is fixed at a profit of 20% on sales, under the instructions of selling goods only at Invoice price. The following are the particulars about the branch transactions :

	Rs.
Stock (at invoice price) on 1st April, 2008	5,000
Branch Debtors on 1st April, 2008	2,000
Goods sent to Branch	40,000
Total sales	43,600
Cash sales	32,000
Cash received from debtors	8,400
Goods returned by debtors	600
Cheques sent to Branch for :	
Rent	1,200
Salaries	3,600
Sundry Expenses	300

Discount allowed to debtors	150
Bad debts	250
Stock (at Invoice price) on 3Jst March, 2009	2,100

Calculate profit made by the Branch. Accounts are to be opened on "Stock and Debtors" system.

(PUP oct. 2009)

Solution :

In the Books of Head Office under stock and Debtors System

Dr.   **Branch Stock A/C**   **Cr.**

Particulars	Rs.	Particulars	Rs.
To Bal. b/d.	5000	By Br. Debtors. A/c	11,600
To Goods sent	40,000	(Cr. Sales)	
To Br. Debtors	600	By Cash A/c	32000
To Br. Adj. A/c (Surplas)	100	By Bal. c/d	2,100
	45,700		**45,700**

Dr.   **Br. Debtors A/c**   **Cr.**

Particulars	Rs.	Particulars	Rs.
To Bal. b/d	2000	By Cash A/c	8,400
To Br. Stock	11,600	By Br. Stock A/C (Returns)	600
(Cr. Sales)		By Expenses A/C	
		Discount	150
		Bad debts	250
		By Bal. c/d	4,200
	13,600		**13,600**

Dr.   **Stock Reseme A/c**   **Cr.**

Particulars	Rs.	Particulars	Rs.
To Br. Adj. A/c	1000	By Bal b/d	1000
To Bal c/d	420	By Br. Adj. A/c	420
	1420		**1420**

Dr.   **Br. Expenses A/c**   **Cr.**

Particulars	Rs.	Particulars	Rs.
To Bank A/C		By Branch	
Rent	1200	Adjustments A/c	5500
Salaries	36,00		
S. Expe.	300		
To Br. Drs. A/c			
Discount	150		
Bud debts	250		
	5500		**5500**

Dr.   **Goods Sent to Branch A/c**   **Cr.**

Particulars	Rs.	Particulars	Rs.
To Br. Adj A/c	8000	By Branch	
To Trading A/c	32000	Stock A/c	40,000
	40,000		40,000

Dr.   **Branch Adjustment A/c**   **Cr.**

Particulars	Rs.	Particulars	Rs.
To Stock Reser.	420	By stock Res. A/c	1000
To G/P	8,600	By Goods sent to Br.	8000
		By Br. stock A/c	
		(loading in surplus)	20
	9020		9020
To Br. Expenses A/c	5500	By Gross Profit	8600
To Net profit		By Br. stock A/c	80
tr. to P and C A/c	3180	(cost of surplus)	
	8680		**8680**

Scheme of Marking Marks

Br. Stock A/c	= 2
Br. Debtos A/c	= 3
Stock Res. A/c	= 2
Goods sent to pro. A/c	= 2
Br. Expe. A/c	= 2
Br. Adjument A/c	= 4
Marks	= 15

PROBLEM NO. 19

Deluxe Corporation of Bangalore supplies goods to its branch at Mysore at cost. Mysore Branch sells goods for cash and on credit and remits cash to the head office promptly. All branch expenses are paid by the head office by cheques :

From the following particulars for the year ended 31ˢᵗ March, 2013, prepare accounts in the books of Deluxe Corporation of Bangalore :

	Rs.
Stock at Branch (1ˢᵗ April 2012)	12,000
Branch Debtors (1ˢᵗ April 2012)	16,000
Goods send to Branch during the year (2012-2013)	90,000
Cash sales at Branch	44,000
Credit sales at Branch	1,14,000
Returns from customers	8,000
Collection from Debtors	84,000
Discount Allowed	7,000
Bad debts written off	5,000
Cheques sent by Head, office for expenses	

	Rs.	
Salaries	10,000	
Rent	5,000	
Petty Expenses	1,000	16,000
Stock at Branch (31-3-2013)		18,000

Solution :

In The Books of Deluxe Corporation

Mysore Branch Account

Dr.   Cr.

Particulars		Rs.	Particulars		Rs.
To bal b/d			By Cash		
Stock	12,000		Cash Sales	44,000	
Debtors	16,000		Collection from	84,000	
		28,000	Debtors		1,28,000
To Goods sent to Brach A/c		90,000			
To Bank - Expenses			By Balance c/d		
Salaries	10,000		Stock	18,000	
Rent	5,000		Debtors	26,000	
Petly expenses	1,000	16,000			44,000
To Profit and loss A/c		38,000			
(Profit)					
		1,72,000			**1,72,000**

Dr. **Branch Stock A/c** **Cr.**

	Rs.		Rs.
1-4 To bal b/d	12000	1-4 By Mysore Branch A/c	12000
31-3 To Mysore Branch A/c	18,000	31-3 By Balance c/d	18000
1-4 To balance b/d	18000		

Dr. **Branch Debtors A/c** **Cr.**

	Rs.		Rs.
1-4 To bal b/d	16000	1-4 Mysore Branch A/c	16000
31-3 To Mysore Branch A/c	26000	31-3 By bal c/d	26,000
1-4 To bal b/d	26,000		

Dr. **Goods sent to Branch A/c** **Cr.**

	Rs.		Rs.
31-3 To Purchases A/c	90,000	1-4 By Mysore Branch	90,000
	90,000		**90,000**

7

Single Entry System

7.1 Introduction
7.2 Methods of Ascertaining Profit
7.3 Problems
7.4 Exercise

Introduction :

Under double entry systetm two fold effect of each transaction is recorded i.e. one account is debited and the other account is credited which in turn means every debit has a corresponding credit. Thus, this system enables the business concern to prepare a Trial Balance and final accounts. The final Accounts indicate the correct profit or loss for the period and the true and fair position of the business as on a particular date.

As against the above system, the other system followed is known as single Entry system. under this method each business transaction is recorded only once in the leger. A single entry system is thus a method employed for rearding of transactions which ignores the two fold aspect and conseqently fails to provide business with information neccessary for him to be able to ascertan his position.

However, it is not a pure single entry system, as under this system double entry is effected with respect of transaction involving personal accounts and cash accounts. Hence it is called single entry in the popular sense. In this method, cash account is maintained perfectly. Accounts of Debtors and Creditors are also kept to know the amount receivable and amount payable.

Under this sysetem a cash Book and personal accounts are maintained but other real or Nominal Accounts are not maintained.

Therefore, inrespect of transactions involving Real Accounts (Except Cash) and Nominal accounts only one aspect is recorded i.e either cash or personal Account is debited or credited as the casemay be. Thus, if the transaction is cash paid to manohar its double effect is recorded i.e Manohar's A/c is debited and cash A/c is credited of the transaction is 'Paid wages' or purchased machinery for cash or on credit. only cash A/c, or personal A/c in case of credit purchase) is credited & wages A/c or machinery A/c is not debited as these accounts are not Maintained at all so far as maintenance of Subsidiary books are concerned they are Practically the same as there is no journal. The only items those are posted from the subsidiary books in to the leger are there which affect personal accounts of debtors and creditors.

Disadvantages of single Entry System :

1) Trial Balance can not be perpared and thus arithmatic accuracy of books can not be checked.
2) Frauds can not be detected
3) Trading are profit loss Account and Balance sheet can not be prepared as real Accounts of assets and nominal Accounts of income and expenses are not maintained.
4) Proper Valuation of Good will is not possible.
5) Values of assets and liablilities are written as an estimation Inspite of the above disadvantages many businessman adopt this system as it is time and money saving.

7.2 Methods of Ascertaining profit.

1) Statement of Affairs method.
2) Conversion of single Entry into Dobule Entry Method.

1) Statement of Affairs Method (or net worth method. i.e. capital comparison method)

Profit or loss under single entry system can be found out by comparison method i.e. the profit or loss made during the period is arrived at by comparing the balance of capital as at the end of the period with that at the beginning of the year. If the capital at the end is more than the capital at the beginning, the difference is the profit earned during the period and if the capital at the beginning is more the difference is loss. But before arriving at profit or loss in this manner it is neccessary to ascertain that the change in capital at the end is due to business transactions i.e. additional capital brought in or drawings made during the year. Hence, effect of such personal transactions must be removed i.e additional capital brought in is to be deducted from and drawings to be added of the capital at the end of the period.

If there are any adjustments to be made on the profit or loss arrived as above, depreciation, interest on capital, reserve for doubtful debts etc. they are to be made and then the resulting figure is net profit or net loss as the case may be.

Example

Mr. X Started his business with Rs. 10,000 and at the end of the year his capital is Rs. 15,000 then Rs. 5000 (i.e the difference between two capitals) is his profit. Now suppose he has introduced Rs. 2000 during the year as capital then the profit is not Rs. 5000 but Rs. 3000 only because increase of Rs. 2000 is due to fresh capital intrduced Mr. X withdraw Rs. 1200 from his personal use, then his profit Will be increased to that extent because had he not withdrawn the amount for personal use, his closing capital would be higher to that extent.

Thus, Profit under single entry system is ascertained as follows.

Statement of profit or loss :

	Rs.
Closing capital Balance	....
+ Drawings during the year	....
+ Interest on Drawings	....
	....
Less : Fresh capital introduced during the year	....
Less : Interest on capital	....
Less : Opening capital Balance	....
Gross profit made during the year	....
Less : (of profit) Add (of Loss) the following items.	
Expenses Losses to the adjusted depreciation	....
R. D.D. etc	....
Net profit Loss for the year ended	....

If there are certian adjustments to be made the profit before such adjustments will be called as Gross Profit. It is only after adjustment have been given effect to that the profit will be known as net profit. In case of no adjustments to be made, the profit will naturally be net profit. The adjustments may be pertaining to

1) Outstanding expenses or incomes.
2) Prepaid expenses
3) Income received in advance
4) Depreciation on Assets or
5) Interest on capital or Drawings

The Closing statements of Affairs (B/s) can be drawn up after making the necessary adjustments given in the problem.

Important :

Closing capital is found out by preparing the closing Balance Sheet Which is known as Statement of Affairs in single entry

Closing capital = Closing Assets - Closing Liabilities of opening capital is not given then opening statement of Affairs is prepared and

Opening Capital : Opening Assets - Opening Liabilities

Statements of Affairs :

A Statments of Affairs is a statements of Assets and liablilities on a particular date. The information regards assets and liabilities is obtained partly from the ledger accounts (Personal Accounts and Cash book) and partly from other sources of information. the statment is prepared on the lines of Balance sheet. i.e on the left hand side liabilities are shown and on the right hand side assets are shown.

2) Conversions of Single Entry into Double Entry System :

Information given in the single entry can be converted into Double Entry system for the preparation of the Trading and profit & Loss A/c and the Balance sheet.

Steps :

1) To open all Real and Nomial Accounts.

2) From the subsidiary Books including cash Book and personal Account posting is made to respective accounts.

For this conversion the following steps are essential :

1) Opening statement of Affairs.

This Statement is prepared to find out opening capital balance. Opening capital is the difference between the opening assets and opening liabilities. This opening capital is to be transferred to the liability side of the closing Balance sheet.

2) Cash Book :

The cash Book is the be prepared and the information from the cash book will be transferred as follows.

a) **Opening Cash and Bank Balance :** Which are to be transferred to the asset side of the opening Balance Sheet.

b) **New Capital introduced :** Which is to be added in the capital Account in the closing Balance Sheet.

c) **Cash Sales :** Which is to be transferred to the credit side of trading Account.

d) **Amounts Received from Debtors and Bills Recivables :** Which are to be transferred to the credit side of Debtors or Bills Receivables Account

e) **Sale of Assets :** Which are to be deducted from Assets in Closing Balance Sheet.

f) **Nominal Accounts of Incomes :** Which are to be transferred to the credit side ot the profit and loss Accounts.

The credit side of the cash book gives the information of :

a) **Closing Cash and Bank Balances :** Which are to be transferred on asset side of the closing Balance sheet.

b) **Drawings :** Which are to be deducted from capital Account in the closing Balance Sheet

c) **Cash Purchase :** Which are to be transferred to Trading Account debit side.

d) **Amounts paid to creditors & Bill payable :** Which are to be transferred to the debit side of creditors and Bills payable Account.

e) **Purchase of an Asset :** Which is to be added in the asset in the closing Balance Sheet.

f) **Nominal Accounts of Expenses :** Which are to be transferred either to the debit side of the Tranding Account or debit side of the profit and loss Account.

3) Total Debtors Accounts.

This Account is prepared to find out credit sales. Suppose the opening Balance of Debtors is Rs. 15,000 Closing Balance Rs. 17,000 and Cash recevied from the debtors is say Rs. 25,000 then Credit. Sales = 17,000 + 25,000 - 15,000 = Rs. 27,000

Dr.	Total Debtors Account		Cr.
Particulars	**Rs.**	**Particulars**	**Rs.**
To opening Balance	....	By Cash Received	....
To B/R Dishonoured	....	By B/R Received	....
To Credit sales	....	By Returns Inward	....
(Balancing figure)		By Bad Debts	....
		By Discount & Allowances	....
		By Closing Balance	....
	....		....

(**Note :** R.D.D. Bad Debts Reserve, Reserve for Discount on Debtors not taken into Account. Opening Balance before deduction of R.D.D. is taken)

4) Total Creditors Account :

This Account is prepared to find out credit purchases suppose opening balance of creditors Account is Rs. 12,000 Closing Balance is Rs. 15,000 and During the year cash paid to creditors is Rs. 13,000 then credit purchases = 15,000 + 13,000 = 12,000 = Rs. 16,000

Dr.	Total Creditors Account		Cr.
Particulars	**Rs.**	**Particulars**	**Rs.**
To Cash paid	....	By Opening Balance	....
To B/P Issued	....	By B/P Dishonoured	....
To Discount & Allowance Recd	....	By Credit Purchases	....
To Returns outwards	....	(Bal Figure)	
To B/R (Endorsed)	....		
To Closing Balance	....		
	....		....

(**Note :** Reserve for Discount on creditors is not to be taken in the above account.)

5) Bills Receivable Account.

This Account is prepared to find out the Bills Receivable Received from Debtors and it will appear as follows.

<table>
<tr><td colspan="4">Dr.   Bill Receivable Account   Cr.</td></tr>
</table>

Particulars	Rs.	Particulars	Rs.
To opening Bal B/d	....	By Cash Received	....
To B/R Received From	....	By B/R Dishonoured (Destors)	....
Debtors (Bal Figure)		By B/R Endorsed (S. Creditors)	....
		By Closing Balance c/d	....
	....		....

6) Bills Payable Account :

This Account is prepared to find out Bills payable issued during the year and it will appear as follows.

<table>
<tr><td colspan="4">Dr.   Bill Payable Account   Cr.</td></tr>
</table>

Particulars	Rs.	Particulars	Rs.
To Cash paid		By Opening Balance	
To B/p Dishnoured (Creditors)		By bills payable to Creditors	
To Closing Balance		(Bal figure)	
	....		....

Note :

1) The difference between the totals of the two sides of the above accounts indicates the missing items such as cerdit sales / Purshcases opening and Closing Blance etc.

2) If bills receivable received during the year are not given first prepare B/R A/c to trace out that figure and the prepare total Debtors A/c

Similary, if Bills Payable Accepted during the year, are not given first prepare Bills payable A/c and then the total creditors A/c.

After preparing all these accounts the missing items will be found out and then Trading & P & L A/c And Balance sheet can be prepared.

PROBLEM NO. 1

Shri Rajendra keeps his books under single entry system and the following information is supplied by him for the year ending 31st March, 2007

Particulars of Account

Summary of Cash Book :		Rs.
Bank Balance (1-4-2006)		2,400
Cash Balance (1-4-2006)		100
Drawings		4,500
Wages		4,200
Salaries		5,400
Sundry Expenses		7,950
Paid to Creditors (Including payment for B.P. Rs. 2,400)		
Received from Debtors (Including Receipts		22,800
on B.R. Rs. 2,800)		32,184
Cash Sales		9,486
Bank Overdraft (31-3-2007)		

Other Assets and Liabilities :	on 1-4-06	31-3-07
Stock	11,880	15,000
Furniture	720	720
Buildings	12,000	12,000
Creditors	13,200	4,200
Debtors	15,000	11,610
Bills Payable	1,800	Nil
Bills Receivable	3,000	4,200

Interest on capitals as on 1-4-2006 to be charged Rs. 1,500. Depreciation on Buildings and Furniture is to be written off at 5% and 10% respectively. Reserve of Rs. 300 is to be created for doubtful debts.

Prepare the Trading and Profit and Loss A/c for the year ended 31-3-2007 and Profit and Loss A/c for the year Balance Sheet as on that date. **(April 2007 PUP)**

Solution :

Statement of Affiars as on 31st March 2006

Particulars	Rs.	Particulars	Rs.
Creditors	13,200	Stock	11,880
Bills Payable	1800	Furniture	720
Capital	30,000	Building	12,000
(Bal. Fig)		Debtors	15,000
		Bills Receivable	
		Cash in hand	1,00
		Cash at bank	2,400
	45,100		45,100

Cash Book

Particulars	Rs.	Particulars	Rs.
To balance b/d :		By wages	4,200
Cash in hand	100	By salaries	5400
Cash at bank	2400	By sundry exps.	7950
To Bills Receivable	2800	By creditors	20,400
To Debtors	29,384	By Bills payable	2,400
To Sales	9,486	By Drawings	4,500
To Bank Balance (O.D)	900	By Balance cash (Bal Fig)	220
	45,070		**45,070**

Total Debtors A/c

Particulars	Rs.	Particulars	Rs.
To Balance b/d	15,000	By Cash A/c	29384
To Credit salss	29,994	By Bills Receivable A/c	4,000
(Bal fig)		By Balance c/d	11,610
	44,994		**44,994**

Bills Reveivable A/c

Particulars	Rs.	Particulars	Rs.
To Balance b/d	3,000	By cash A/c	2800
To Sundry Debtors A/c	4,000	By Balance c/d	4200
(Bal. Fig)			
	7,000		**7,000**

Total Creditors A/c

Particulars	Rs.	Particulars	Rs.
To Cash A/c	20,400	By Balance b/d	13,200
To Bills Payable	600	By credit purchases	12,000
To Balance c/d	4,200	(Bal. fig)	
	25,200		**25,200**

Bills Payable A/c

Particulars	Rs.	Particulars	Rs.
To cash A/c	2,400	By Balance b/d	1800
To Balance c/d	-	By Sundry creditors	600
		(Bal. fig)	
	2,400		**2,400**

Trading and Profit & Loss Account
for the year ened 31st March 2007

Praticulars		Rs.	Particulars		Rs.
To Stock		11,880	By Sales :		
To Purchases		12,000	Cash	9486	
To Wages		4,200	Credit	29994	39480
To Gross profit c/d		26,400	By stock		15,000
		54,480			54,480
To Salaries		5,400	By Gross profit b/d		26,400
To Sundry Expereses		7,950			
To Int. on capital		1,500			
To R.D.D.		300			
To Depriciation :					
Building	600				
Furniture	72	672			
To Net profit		10,578			
		26,400			**26,400**

Balance Sheet as on 31-3-2007

Liabilities		Rs.	Assets		Rs.
Creditors		4,200	Cash		220
Bank over Draft		900	Stock		15,000
Capital	30,100		Debtors	11610	
Int.	1500		Less R.D.D.	300	11310
N.D.	10578				
	42178		Bills Receivable		4200
Less Drawing	4500	37678	Furniture	720	
			Less Dep.	72	648
			Buildings	12000	
			Less Dep.	600	11,400
		42,778			**42,778**

PROBLEM NO. 2

The items given ahead are extracted from the books of Shri Sunil who keeps his books of account under single entry system. You are required to prepare Trading and Profit & Loss Account for the year ending 31-3-2006 and the Balance Sheet as on that date :

Receipts and Payments Account
for the year ending 31-03-2006

Receipts	Rs.	Payments	Rs.
To Balance b/d	3,000	By Creditors	40,500
To Sales	17,000	By Salary	2,250
To Debtors	62,500	By Rent	1,000
		By Wages	7,000
		By Sundry Expenses	4,000
		By Purchases	3,000
		By Drawings	7,500
		By Balance c/d	17,250
Total	**82,500**	**Total**	**82,500**

The assets and liabilities were as follows :

Assets and Liabilities	As on 1-4-2005	As on 31-3-2006
Stock	12,500	18,000
Creditors	6,500	7,000
Debtors	13,500	16,000
Furniture	6,000	6,000
Machinery	20,000	20,000

Additional Information :

(a) Provide for depreciation on Furniture at 5% and on Machinery at 10% p.a.

(b) Make provision for doubtful debts at 5% on Debtors. [15]

(PUP Oct 2007)

Solution :

Dr.		Trading A/c for the 31-3-2006	Cr.
Particulars	**Rs.**	**Particulars**	**Rs.**
To Op. stock	12,500	By cash sales	17,000
To cash Purchase	3000	By credit sales	65,000
To credit purchase	41,000	By Cl. stock	48,000
To wages	7,000		
To Gross profit (Bal. Fig.)	36,500		
	100,000		100,000

Dr.   **Cr.**

P & C A/c or the year ending 31-03-2014

Particulars	Rs.	Particulars	Rs.
To Salary	2,250	By G/P b/d	36,500
To Rent	1,000		
To sundry exp.	4,000		
To Dep on Machinery	1,000		
To R. D. D.	8,00		
To Net profit	27,150		
	36,500		**36,500**

Dr.   **Balance sheet as on 31-3-2006**   **Cr**

Liabilities		Rs.	Assets		Rs.
Capital	48,500		Furniture	6,000	
Drawing	7,500		Dep. 5%	3,00	5,700
	41,000		Machinery	2,000	
+ Net p.	27,150	68,150	Dep 10%	1,000	19,000
Creditors		7,000	Cash in hand		17,250
			Cl. stock		18,000
			Debtors	16,000	
			R.D.D.	8,000	1,52,000
Total		**75,150**	**Total**		**75,150**

Op. Balance sheet as on 2005

Liabilities	Rs.	Assets	Rs.
Creditors	6,500	Cash	3,000
Capital	48,500	Stock	12,500
(Bal. fig.)		Debtors	1,35,000
		Furniture	6,000
		Machinery	20,000
	55,000		**55,000**

Total Debtors A/c

Particulars	Rs.	Particulars	Rs.
To Bal b/d	13,500	By cash	62,500
To credit sales (Bal. fig.)	65,000	By Bal c/d	16,000
	78,500		**78,500**

Total Creditors A/c

Particulars	Rs.	Particulars	Rs.
To cash A/c	40,500	By Bal b/d	6,500
To Bal c/d	7,000	By credit purchases (Bal fig)	41,000
	47,500		**47,500**

PROBLEM NO. 3

The following information is supplied from which you are required to prepare the Profit and Loss Account for the year ended 31st March, 2008 and Balance Sheet as on that date :

(I) Assets and Liabilities	1-4-2007 (Rs.)	31-3-2008 (Rs.)
Sundry Assets	36,000	40,000
Stock	28,000	38,000
Cash in hand	16,400	9,600
Debtors	?	52,000
Cash at Bank	4,400	16,000
Creditors	24,000	19,600
Miscellaneous expenses outstanding	2,000	1,200

(II) Details relating to the year's transactions are	Rs.
Receipts in the year and discount credited to debtors accounts	4,90,000
Returns from debtors	12,000
Bad debts	2,000
Sales - cash and credit	6,00,000
Returns to creditors	6,000
Payment to creditors by cheque	4,72,400
Receipts from debtors deposited into bank	4,86,000
Cash purchases	20,000
Salaries and wages paid out of bank	36,000
Miscellaneous expenses paid by cash	10,000
Drawing by cash	18,800
Purchases of Sundry assets by cheque	4,000
Cash withdrawn from bank	42,000
Cash Sales deposited in bank	?
Discount allowed by creditors	8,000

(PUP April 2008)

Solution :

b)

Cash Book

Particulars	Cash Rs.	Bank Rs.	Particulars.	Cash Rs.	Bank Rs.
To Balance b/d	16,400	4,400	By Sundry creditors	-	4,72,400
To Sundry Debtors	-	48,6,000	By Purchases	20,000	-
To Bank A/c (C)	42,000	-	By salary / wages	-	36,000
To cash sales		30,000	By Misc. Exps	10,000	-
(Bal figure)			By Drawings	18,800	
			By Sundry Assets	-	4,000
			By Cash A/c (c)	-	42,000
			By Balance c/d	9,600	16,000
	58,400	**5,70,400**		**58,400**	**5,70,400**

Sundry Debtors Account

Particulars		Rs.	Particulars	Rs.
To Balance b/d		36,000	By Cash received	4,86,000
(Bal. Fig)			By Discount Allowed	4,000
To Credit Sales			By Bad debts	2,000
Total sales	6,00,000		By Sales Returns	12,000
Less cash sale	80,000	5,20,000	By Balance c/d	52,000
		5,56,000		**5,56,000**

Sundry Creditors Account

Particulars	Rs.	Particulars	Rs.
To cash paid	4,72,400	By Balance b/d	24,000
To Discount received	8,000	By Crdit purchases	4,82,000
To Return out wards	6,000	(Bal. fig.)	
To Balance c/d	19,600		
	5,06,000		**5,06,000**

Balance Sheet as on 1-4-2007

Liabilties	Rs.	Assets	Rs.
Misc. Exps outstanding	2,000	cash in hand	16,400
Sundry creditors	24,000	Cash at bank	4,400
Capital	94,800	Sundry Debtors	36,000
(Bal. Fig)		Stock	28,000
		Sundry Assets.	36,000
	1,20,800		**1,20,800**

Trading & Profit and Loss Account
for the year ended 31st March 2008

Particulars		Rs.	Particulars		Rs.
To opening stock		28,000	By sales -		
To purchases			cash	80,000	
Cash	20,000		credit	5,20,000	
Credit	4,82,000			6,00,000	
	5,02,000				
Less Pur Ret.	6,000	4,96,000	Less Sales Retn.	12,000	5,88,000
To Gross Profit		1,02,000	By closing stock	38,000	
		6,26,000			6,26,000
To salaries & wages		36,000	By Gross Profit		1,02,000
To Misc. Expenses -	10,000		By Discount received		8,000
Add out at the end	1,200				
	11,200				
Less out at the begining	2,000	9,200			
To Disecout Allowed		4,000			
To Bad dets		2,000			
To Net profit		58,800			
		1,10,000			1,10,000

Balance Sheet as on 31st March, 2008

Liabilties		Rs.	Assets	Rs.
Misc. Exps outstanding		1,200	Cash in hand	9,600
Sundry creditors		19,600	Cash at bank	16,000
Capital	94,800		Sundry Debtors	52,000
Less Drawings	18800		Stock	38,000
	76,000		Sundry Assets.	40,000
Add Net Profit	58,800	1,34,800		
		1,55,600		1,55,600

PROBLEM NO. 4

Mr. Suhas Shinde maintains his books on single entry system. From the following particulars, prepare the Tracing & Profit and Loss Account for the year ended 31-3-2007 and the Balance Sheet as on that date :

Summary of Cash Book

Particulars	Amount Rs.	Particulars	Amount Rs.
To Balance b/d	15,900	By Creditors	59,100
To Debtors	65,100	By Bills Payable	45,900
To Bills Receivable	39,900	By Wages	22,470
To Cash Sales	43,500	By Carriage inward	330
To Interest	5,100	By Salaries	13,200
		By Printing	1,590
		By Postage	1,410
		By Insurance	1,500
		By Drawings	12,600
		By Balance c/d	11,400
	1,69,500		**1,69,500**

Particulars of Assets and Liabilities :

Particulars	1 - 4 - 2006	31-3-2007
Investments	30,000	30,000
Debtors	75,000	87,000
Bills Receivable	30,000	27,000
Creditors	59,100	53,700
Bills Payable	12,300	4,200
Stock	42,300	34,200
Plant and Machinery	90,000	90,000
Loan from Ashok Karve	45,000	45,000

Adjustments :

(1) Interest on loan from Ashok Karve was outstanding for the year at 10% per annum.

(2) Outstanding wages were Rs. 420 and outstanding printing bill was Rs. 630.

(3) Postage stamps of Rs. 90 were in hand on 31-3-2007

(4) Insurance was Prepaid the extent of Rs. 360

(5) Depreciate plant and machinery at 10% and maintain reserve for doubtful debts on debtors at 5%.

(PUP Oct. 2008)

Solution :

Statement of Affairs as on 31-3-2007

Liabilities	Rs.	Assets	As.
Creditors	59,100	Investments	30,000
Bills Payable	12,300	Debtors	75,000
Loan from Ashok Karve	45,000	Bills Receivables	30,000
		Stock	42,300
Capital	1,66,800	Plant & machinery	50,000
(Balancing Figure)		Cash	15,900
	2,83,200		**2,83,200**

Dr. **Total Debtors Account** **Cr.**

Particulars	Rs.	Particulars	Rs.
To Bal b/d	75,000	By cash a/c	65,100
To credit Sales	1,14,000	By Bills Receivable	36,900
(Bal figure)		By Bal c/d	87,000
	1,89,000		**1,89,000**

Dr. **Total Creditors Account** **Cr.**

Particulars	Rs.	Particulars	Rs.
To Cash Paid	59100	By Bal b/d	59,100
To Bills Payable	37800	By Purchases	91500
To Bal c/d	53,700		
	1,50,600		**1,50,600**

Dr. **Bills Receivable Account** **Cr.**

Particulars	Rs.	Particulars	Rs.
To Bal b/d	30,000	By cash a/c	39,900
To Debtors a/c	36,900	By Bal c/d	27,000
	66,900		**66,900**

Dr. **Bills Payable Account** **Cr.**

Particulars	Rs.	Particulars	Rs.
To Cash Paid	45,900	By Bal b/d	12,300
To Bal c/d	4,200	By Creditors (Bal. Fig.)	37,800
	50,100		**50,100**

Trading and Profit and Loss Accounts
for the year ended 31st March 2007

Dr.   Cr.

Particulars		Rs.	Particulars		Rs.
To opening stock		42,300	By sales		
To purchases		91,500	Cash sales	43,500	
To wages	22,470		+ Credit sales	1,14,000	1,57,500
+ o/s wages	4,20	22,890			
To Carriage inward		3,30	By closing stock		34,200
To Gross Profit		34,680			
		1,91,700			1,91,700
To Salaries		13,200	By Gross Profit b/d		34,680
To Printing	1,590		By Int.		5,100
+ o/s bill	6,30	2,220			
To Postage	1,410				
Less closing stock	90	1,320			
To Insurance	1,500				
Less Prepaid	3,60	1,140			
To o/s Int on Loan		4,500			
To Dep on plant of Machinery		9,000			
To R.D.D.		4,350			
To Net Profit		4,050			
		39,780			**39,780**

Balance Sheet
as on 31st March 2007

Liabilities		Rs.	Assets		Rs.
Capital	1,66,800		Plant & Machinery	90,000	
+ Net Profit	4,050		Less Depreciation	9,000	81,000
	1,70,850		Inverstment		30,000
Less Drawings	12,600	1,58,250	Debtors	87,000	
Creditors		53,700	Less R.D.D.	4,350	82,650
Bills Payable		4,200	Bills Receivables		27,000
Loan from As			Prepaid Insurance		360
Karve	45,000		Postage Stamp		90
+ o/s Int.	4,500	49,500	Closing stock		34,200
o/s Wages		4,20	cash		11,400
o/s Printing Bill		6,30			
		2,66,700			**2,66,700**

PROBLEM NO. 5

Shri Pradhan, who maintains his books of accounts on single entry system, supplies you the following information :

Particulars of Accounts	as on 31-12-2007	ason31-12-2008
Sundry Creditors	10,000	12,500
Bills payable	2,000	4,500
Stock	15,000	14,000
Machinery	25,000	35,000
Furniture	4,000	4,000
Sundry Debtors	16,500	19,300
Bills Receivable	1,500	2,200
Salary outstanding	500	—

Summary of Cash Transaction during 2008

Particulars	Rs.	Particulars	Rs.
To Balance on 1-1-08	500	By Payment to	
To Cash sales	6,000	creditors (including	
		(bills payable)	37,000
To Receipts from		By Wages	11,000
Debtors (including Bills		By Salaries	12,500
Receivable)	77,100	By Office Expenses	8,000
To Miscellaneous		By Drawings	7,000
Receipts	300	By Fixed Deposit	5,000
To Loan from Amir	10,000	By Machinery (1-10-2008)	10,000
		By Balance c/d	3,400
	93,900		**93,900**

Discount allowed were Rs. 900 and discount received during the year Rs. 500. You are required to prepare Trading and Profit and Loss Account for the year ending 31st December, 2008) after taking into
consideration the following adjustments :

(1)   Office expenses included insurance at Rs. 500 per annum paid upto 31st March, 2009.

(2)   Wages Rs. 2,000 are due on 31-12-2008

(3)   Of the sundry debtors Rs. 800 are to be written off as bad debts.

(4)   Depreciation is to be provided on furniture at 5% p.a. and on machinery at 10% p.a.

(5)   During the year Shri Pradhan had taken goods of Rs. 500 for his own use. No entry is made in the books.

(PUP April 2009)

Solution :

Statement of Affairs as on 1st Jan 2008

Liabilities	Rs.	Assets	As.
S. creditiors	10,000	Cash	500
Bills Payable	2000	Stock	15,000
Salaries outstanding	500	Debters	16,500
		B.R.	1,500
Capital	50,000	Funrniture	4,000
(Balancing Figure)		Machinery	25,000
	62,500		**62,500**

Total Debtors A/C (Including B.R.)

Particulars	Rs.	Particulars	Rs.
To Balance b/d			
Debtors	16,500	By Cash	77,100
B.R.	1,500	By Discount	900
To credit sales	81,500	By Balance c/d -	
(Bal. Fig)		Debtors	19,300
		B.R.	2,200
	99,500		**99,500**

Total Creditors A/c (Including B.P.)

Particulars	Rs.	Particulars	Rs.
To Cash	37,000	By Balance b/d -	
To Discount	500	Creditors	10,000
To Balance c/d		B/p	2000
Creditors	12,500	By credit purchases	42,500
B/p	4,500	(Bal. fig)	
	54,500		**54,500**

Trading and Profit and Loss Accounts

Dr.   for the year ended 31st March 2008   Cr.

Particulars		Rs.	Particulars		Rs.
To opening stock		15,000	By sales		
To purchases	42,500		Cash	6,000	
Less Drawings	5,00	42,000	Credit	81,500	87,500
To wages	11,000		By stock		14,000
Add. O/S	2,000	13,000			
To Gross Profit c/d		31,500			
		1,01,500			1,01,500
To salaries	12,500		By Gross Profit b/d		31,500
Less for 2007	500	12,000	By Misce. Receipts		300
To office Expenses	8,000		By Discount		500
Less prepaid	1,25	7,875	By Discount		500
To Discount		9,00			
To Bad Debts.		8,00			
To Depreciation					
Furniture		2,00			
Machinery		2,750			
To N. P. transfered		7,775			
		32,300			32,300

Balance Sheet
as at 31st Dec. 2008

Liabilities		Rs.	Assets		Rs.
Creditors		12,500	Cash		3,400
Bills Payable		4,500	Fixed Deposits		5,000
Loan		10,000	Debtors	19,300	
O/S wages		2,000	Less Bad Debts	800	18,500
Capital	50,000		Stock		14,000
Add	7,775		Bills Receivable		2,200
	57,775		Prepaid Insurance		125
Less Drawings	7,500	50,275	Furniture	4,000	
			Less Dep.	200	3,800
			Machinery	25,000	
			Addition	10,000	
				35,000	
			Less Dep.	2,750	32,250
		79,275			79,275

PROBLEM NO. 6

Mr. Avinash maintains his books by single Entry System. His Cash Book for the year ended 31st March, 2010 was as follows :

Summary of Cash Book

Receipts	Rs.	Payments	Rs.
To Blance B/d	12,300	By Investments	2,000
To Cash Sales	8,700	By Avinash's Drawings	6,500
To Debtors	35,700	By Purchases	7,300
To Bills Receivable	15,300	By Creditors	28,900
To Interest	1,500	By Bills Payable	7,500
To Avinash's Capital Account	10,000	By Wages	17,300
To Balance c/d	3,730	By Carriage Inwards	1,350
		By Postage	550
		By Salaries	12,000
		By Rent and Taxes	930
		By Insurance	700
		By Printing and Stationery	2,200
	87,230		**87,230**

Particulars of Assets and Liabilities were as follows :

Particulars	1-4-2009	31-3-2010
Investments	15,000	17,000
Stock	13,700	29,300
Debtors	21,000	25,000
Bills Receivable	14,000	18,000
Creditors	31,000	29,000
Bills Payable	7,000	9,000
Plant and Machinery	45,000	42,500
Furniture	3,500	3,100

Adjustments :

(i)   A provision of Rs. 1,250 was necessary on Debtors for doubtful debts. .

(ii)   Outstanding wages were Rs. 1,500 and outstanding salary was Rs. 700.

(iii)   Insurance was paid for one year ending 30th September, 2010

(iv)   An advertising bill was payable amounting to Rs. 400.

Prepare Trading and Profit & Loss Account for the year ended 31st March, 2010 and the Balance Sheet as on that date.

(PUP April 2010)

Solution :

Statement of Affairs as on 1st April 2009

Liabilities	Rs.	Assets	Rs.
Creditiors	31,000	Cash at Bank	12,300
Bills Payable	7,000	Debtors	21,000
Debters	86,500	B.R.	14,000
(Balancing Figure)		Stock	13,700
		Investments	15,000
		Plant & Machinery	45,000
	1,24,500		**1,24,500**

Total Debtors A/C

Particulars	Rs.	Particulars	Rs.
To Balance b/d	21,000	By Cash	35,700
To Credit sales	59,000	By B. R.	19,300
(Bal. Fig)		By Bal c/d	25,000
	80,000		**80,000**

Total Creditors A/c

Particulars	Rs.	Particulars	Rs.
To Cash	28,900	By Balance b/d -	31,000
To B.P.	9,500	By Credit Purchases	36,400
To Bal c/d	29,000		
	67,400		**67,400**

Bills Receivable A/C

Particulars	Rs.	Particulars	Rs.
To Balance B/d	14,000	By Cash	15,300
To Debtors A/c	19,300	By Bal c/d	18,000
(Bal. Fig)			
	33,300		**33,300**

Bills Payable A/c

Particulars Rs.		Particulars	Rs.
To Cash	7,500	By Balance b/d -	7000
To Bal c/d	9,000	By Creditors A/c	9,5000
	16,500		**16,500**

Trading and Profit and Loss Accounts
for the year ended 31st March 2010

Dr.   Cr.

Particulars		Rs.	Particulars		Rs.
To opening stock		13,700	By sales		
To purchases					
Cash		7,300	Cash		8,700
Credit		36,400	Credit		59,000
To wages	17,300		By Closing stock		29,300
Add. out	1500	18,800			
To Carriage Inward		1350			
To Gross Profit c/d		19,450			
		97,000			97,000
To Postage		550	By Gross Profit b/d		19,450
To salaries	12,000		By Interest		1,500
Add O/s	700	12,700	By Net Loss		3,30
To Rent & Taxes		930			
To Insurance	700				
Less Pre-paid	350	350			
To Printing & stationery		2,200			
To Dep. on p & m		2,500			
To Dep on Furniture		4,00			
To R. D. D.		1,250			
To O/s-Advertising Bill		400			
		21,280			21,280

Balance sheet as on 31st March, 2010

Liabilities		Rs.	Assets		Rs.
Bank Overdraft		3,730	Debtors	25,000	
Creditors		29,000	Less R.D.D.	1,250	23,750
Bills Payable		9,000	Bills Receivable		18,000
O/s Exps -			Stock		29,300
Wages		1,500	Prepaid Insurance		350
Salary		700	Investments	15000	
Advertising		400	+ New pur	2000	17,000
Capital A/c	86,500		Furniture	3500	
+ New Cap.	10,000				
	95,500		Less Dep.	400	3,100
Less Drawing	6,500		Plant & machinery	45,000	
Less Net Loss	300	89,670	Less Dep.	2500	42,500
		1,34,000			1,34,000

PROBLEM NO. 7

Mr. Joshi Maintains his books by single entry system. His cash book for the year ended 31st March, 2013 was as follows :

Receipts	Rs.	Payments	Rs.
To Balanced b/d	12,300	By Investment	2,000
To Sales	8,700	By Joshi's drawings	6,500
To Debtors	35,700	By Purchases	7,300
To Bills Receivable	15,300	By Creditors	28,900
To Interest	1,500	By Bills Payable	7,500
To Joshi's Capital Account	10,000	By Wages	17,300
To Balance c/d	3,730	By Carriage Inwards	1,350
		By Postage	550
		By Salaries	12,000
		By Rent and Taxes	930
		By Insurance	700
		By Printing and Stationery	2,200
Total	**87,230**	**Total**	**87,230**

Particulars of Assets and Liabilities were as follow :

Particulars	1-4-2012 (Rs.)	31-3-13 (Rs.)
Investments	15,000	17,000
Stock	13,700	29,300
Debtors	21,000	25,000
Bills Receivable	14,000	18,000
Creditors	31,000	29,000
Bills Payable	7,000	9,000
Plant and Machinery	45,000	42,500
Furniture	3,500	3,100

Other Informations :

   (i)   Credit Sales - Rs. 59,000

  (ii)   Bills receivable from Debtors -Rs. 19,300

 (iii)   Credit Purchases - Rs. 36,400

 (iv)   Bills Payable issued to Creditors - Rs. 9,500

  (v)   Capital balance as on 1-4-2013 Rs. 86,500

Adjustments :

   (i)   A provision of Rs. 1,250 was necessary on debtors for doubtful debts.

   (ii)   Outstanding wages were Rs. 1,500 and outstanding salary was Rs. 700.

   (iii)   Insurance was paid for one year ending 30th September, 2013

   (iv)   An advertising bill was payable amounting to Rs. 400.

      Prepare Trading and Profit & Loss Account for the year ended 31st March, 2013 and the Balance Sheet as on that date of Mr. Joshi.

(PUP April 2013)

Solution :

Single Entry Mr. Joshi's

Dr.	Trading A/c For the year ended 31-3-13			Cr.
Particulars		**Rs.**	**Particulars**	**Rs.**
To Opening stock		13,700	By Sales cash	8,700
To Purchases - Cash		7,300	By Sales credit	59,000
To Purchases - Credit		36,400	By closing stock	29,300
To Wages	17,300			
+ outstanding	+ 1,500	18,800		
To carriage in ward		1,350		
To Gross Profit		19,450		
		97,000		**97,000**

Dr.	Profit & Loss A/c 31-3-13			Cr.
Particulars		**Rs.**	**Particulars**	**Rs.**
To Postage		550	By Gross profit	19,450
To Salaries	12,000		By Interest	1500
+ outstanding	+700	12,700	By Net Loss	330
To Rent & Taxes		930		
To Insurance	700			
- prepaid	-350	350		
To Printing and stationery		2,200		
To Dep. on Plant & Machinery		2,500		
To Dep. on Furniture		400		
To R. D. D.		1,250		
To o/s Advt Bill		400		
		21,280		**21280**

Balance sheet as on 31-3-2013

Liabilities		Rs.	Assets		Rs.
Bank Overdraft		3,730	Debtors	25,000	
Creditors		29,000	Less R.D.D.	-1250	23,750
Bills Payable		9000	Bills Receivable		18,000
o/s Wages		1,500	Stock		29,300
o/s Salary		700	Prepaid Insurance		350
o/s Advt		400	Investments	15000	
Capital A/c	86,500		+ Additions	+ 2000	17,000
+ New Cap.	10,000		Furniture	3500	
	96,500		- Dep.	400	3,100
Less Drawing	6,500		Plant & machinery	45,000	
	90,000		- Dep.	2500	42,500
Less Net Loss	-300	89,670			
		1,34,000			**1,34,000**

PROBLEM NO. 8

Shankar keeps his books under single entry system. He gives you the following information relating to the year ending 31st March 2013,

Summary of Bank Transactions

Dr.   **Cr.**

Particulars	Rs.	Particulars	Rs.
To Balance at Bank	4,350	By Drawings	7,520
To Sundry Debtors	38,400	By Trade Creditors	27,100
To Bills Receivable Realised	12,000	By Bills payable	9,300
To Commission Received	1,500	By wages	12,000
To Cash sales	8,600	By Salaries	6,500
To Balance c/d	3,350	By Rent and Taxes	4,400
		By Insurance	800
		By Carriage inward	250
		By Advertising	330
	68,200		**68,200**
		By Balance b/d	3,350

Particulars of Other Assets and Liabilities	31-3-12	31-3-13
Stock on hand	18,700	23,400
Debtors	12,000	14,000
Creditors	9,000	1,500
Bills Payable	1,000	200
Outstanding salaries	600	1,200
Office Furniture	600	600
Office Building	12,000	12,000
Bills Receivable	4,000	5,000

A provision of Rs. 1,450 is required for doubtful debts on debtors and depreciation at 5% is to be charged on furniture and building. There are outstanding wages Rs. 3,000. Insurance has been prepaid to the extent of Rs. 250. Legal expenses are outstanding to the extent of Rs. 700.

You are required to prepare Total Debtors A/c, Total Creditors A/c, Total Bills receivable A/c, Total Bills Payable A/c, Trading, Profit and Loss Account for the year ending 31st March, 2013 and Balance Sheet as on that date.

(PUP Oct. 2013)

Solution :

Bills Receivable A/C

Particulars	Rs.	Particulars	Rs.
To Balance B/d	4,000	By Cash	12,000
To Debtors A/c	13,000	By Balance c/d	5,000
(Balancing Figure)			
	17,000		**17,000**

Total Debtors A/c

Particulars	Rs.	Particulars	Rs.
To Balance B/d	12,000	By Bank	38,400
To Sales (Bal. Fig)	53,400	By Bills Receivable	13,000
		By Bal. c/d	14,000
	65,400		**65,400**

Total Payable A/c

Particulars	Rs.	Particulars	Rs.
To Bank	9,300	By Balance b/d -	1,000
To Bal c/d	200	By Creditors (Bal. fig)	8,500
	9,500		**9,500**

Total Creditors A/c

Particulars	Rs.	Particulars	Rs.
To Bank	27,100	By Balance b/d -	9000
To Bills Payable	8,500	By Purchases	28,100
To Bal c/d	1,500		
	37,100		**37,100**

Opening Balance Sheet on 1-1-2012

Liabilities	Rs.	Assets	Rs.
Creditors	9,000	Bank Bal	4,350
B/P	1,000	Stock	18,700
O/s Salary	600	Debtors	12,000
Capital	41,050	B/R	4,000
(Bal. fig)		Office Furniture	600
		Office Building	12,000
	51,650		**51,650**

Shri. Shankar Trading and Profit and Loss Accounts
Dr.   for the year ended 31st March 2013   **Cr.**

Particulars		Rs.	Particulars		Rs.
To opening stock		18,700	By sales		
To purchases		28,100	Cash sales	8,600	
To Carriage Inward		250	Credit sles	53,400	62,000
To wages	12,000				
o/s	3000	15,000	By Closing stock		23,400
To Gross Profit c/d		23,350			
		85,400			**85,400**
To salaries	6,500		By Gross Profit b/d		23,350
Less : for 2012	600		By Commission		1,500
	5,900				
O/s for 2013	1,200	7,100			
To Rent & Taxes		4,400			
To Insurance	800				
Less Prepaid	250	550			
To Legal Exp.		700			
To R. D. D.		1,450			
To Advertisement		330			
To Dep.					
Furniture	30				
Building	600	630			
To N. P. Transferred to capital		9,690			
		24,850			**24,850**

Balance sheet as on 31st March, 2013

Liabilities		Rs.	Assets		Rs.
Sundry Creditors		1,500	Stock on hand		23,400
Bills Payable		200	Debtors	14,000	
Bank Overdraft		3,350	Less R.D.D.	1,450	12,550
Outstanding Expenses					
Wages	3,000		Bills Receivable		5,000
Salaries	1,200		Prepaid Insurance		250
Legal Exp.	700	4900	Furniture	600	
Capital Balance	41,050		Less Dep.	30	570
Add N.P.	9,690		Building	12,000	
	50,740		Less Dep.	600	11,400
Less : Drawings	7,520	43,220			
		53,170			**53170**

PROBLEM NO. 9

The items given ahead are extracted from the books of Shri Sunil, who keeps his books of account under Single Entry system. You are required to prepare Trading and Profit and Loss Account for the year ending 31-3-2014 that date :

Receipt and Payment Account
for the year ending 31st March, 2014

Receipts	Rs.	Payments	Rs.
To Balance b/d	3,000	By Creditors	40,500
To Sales	17,000	By Salary	2,250
To Debtors	62,500	By Rent	1,000
		By Wages	7,000
		By Sundry Expenses	4,000
		By Purchases	3,000
		By Drawings	7,500
		By Balance c/d	17,250
	82,500		**82,500**

The Assets and Liabilities were as follows :

Assets and Liabilities	As on 1 -4-2013	As on 31-3-2014
Stock	12,500	18,000
Creditors	6,500	7,000
Debtors	13,500	16,000
Furniture	6,000	6,000
Machinery	20,000	20,000

Additional Information :

(a) Provide for depreciation on Furniture at 5%, and on Machinery at 10% p.a.
(b) Make provision for Doubtful Debts at 5% on Debtors.

(PUP oct 2014)

Opening Balance Sheet on 1-4-2015

Liabilities	Rs.	Assets	Rs.
Creditors	6,500	Stock	12,500
Capital	48,500	Debtors	13,500
(Bal. figurs)		Furniture	6,000
		Machninary	20,000
		Cash	3,000
	55,000		**55,000**

Total Debtors A/C

Particulars	Rs.	Particulars	Rs.
To Balance b/d	13,500	By Cash	62,500
To Credit sales	65,000	By clossing Bal c/d	16,000
(Bal. Fig)			
	78,500		**78,500**

Total Creditors A/c

Particulars	Rs.	Particulars	Rs.
To Cash A/c	40,500	By Balance b/d -	6,500
		By Credit Purchases	41,000
To Bal c/d	7,000	(Bal. fig)	
	47,500		**47,500**

Dr. **Trading A/c For the year ended 31-3-14** **Cr.**

Particulars	Rs.	Particulars	Rs.
To Opening stock	12,500	By cash sales	17,000
To Cash Purchases	3,000	By credit sales	65,000
To Credit Purchases	41,000	By closing stock	18,000
To Wages	7,000		
To Gross Profit	36,500		
	1,00,000		**1,00,000**

Dr. **Profit & Loss A/c 31-3-14** **Cr.**

Particulars	Rs.	Particulars	Rs.
To Salary	2,250	By Gross profit	36,500
To Rent	1,000		
To Sundry Exp	4,000		
To Dep. on Furniture	300		
To Dep. on Machinery	2,000		
To R. D. D.	800		
To profit	26,150		
	36,500		**36,500**

Balance sheet as on 31-3-2014

Liabilities		Rs.	Assets		Rs.
Capital	48,500		Furniture	6000	
Drawing	7,500		Less Dep. 5%	300	5700
	41,000		Machinary	20,000	
+ N/P	+26,150	67,150	- Dep 10%	2000	18,000
Creditors		7000	Cash		17,250
			Closing Stock		18,000
			Drs	16,000	
			- R.D.D. 5%	800	15,000
		74,150			**74,150**

PROBLEM NO. 10

(a) The Balance Sheet of Shubham, Pravaranagar as on 1-4-2013

(b) The summary of Cash Transactions for the year 2013-2014

(c) The remaining transactions and

(d) Adjustments.

(a) **Balance Sheet as on 1-4-2013**

Liabilities	Rs.	Assets	Rs.
Capital	1,20,600	Land & Building	80,000
Creditors	69,800	Machinery	50,000
Bills Payable	29,000	Patents	20,000
Loans	30,600	Fixtures.	15,000
General Reserve	20,000	Stock	44,600
Outstanding Wages	2,680	Debtors	49,400
Bank overdraft	4,000	Bills Receivable	14,600
		Cash in hand	3,080
	2,76,680		**2,76,680**

(b) **Cash-book for the year ended 31-3-2013**

Receipts	Rs.	Payments	Rs.
To Balance b/d	3,080	By Bank overdraft	4,000
To Debtors	45,980	By Wages	15,280
To Bills Receivables	11,400	By Loan paid	10,600
To Capital	15,000	By Creditors	41,000
To Sales (Cash)	35,820	By Bills Payable	21,800
To Commission	5,000	By Salaries	23,400
To Rent	22,000	By Sundry Expenses	1,460
		By Interest on Loan	2,000
		By Drawing	8,940
		By 6% Investments	
		(Purchased on 1-10-2013)	8,000
		By Balance c/d	
		Cash	1,580
		Bank	220
	1,38,280		**1,38,280**

(c)   **The remaining transactions :**

	(Rs.)
Credit Sales	76,000
Credit Purchases	70,000
Bills Receivable Received	21,400
Stock on 31-3-2014	59,000
Discount to Customers	1,020
Discount from Suppliers	740
Bills Payable issued	19,400
Bills Receivable dishonoured	3,000

(d) Adjustments :

(i) Provide 5% for Doubtful Debts on Debtors and Bills Receivable.

(ii) Depreciate Machinery by 5% and Land and Building by $2\frac{1}{2}\%$ and Patents and Fixtures by 10%.

(iii) Outstanding wages are Rs. 1,820 and salary outstanding amounted to Rs. 1,080.

(iv) Transfer Rs. 10,000 to General Reserve.

Prepare Trading and Profit and Loss A/c for the year ended 31-3-2014, and Balance Sheet as on that date.

(PUP Oct. 97, May 2001, April 2014)

Solution :

In the Books of Shubham
Sundry Debtors A/C

Particulars	Rs.	Particulars	Rs.
To Balance b/d	49,400	By Cash	45,980
To Credit sales	76,000	By Bills Receivable	21,400
To Bills Receivable	3,000	(B/R received)	
(B/R Dishonoured)		By Discount to customers	1,020
		By Bal. c/d (Bal. fig)	60,000
	1,28,400		**1,28,400**

Bills Receivable A/C

Particulars	Rs.	Particulars	Rs.
To Balance B/d	14,600	By Cash	11,400
To Sundry Debtors		By Sundry Debtors	3,000
(B/R Received)	21,400	(B/R Dishonoured)	
		By Bal C/D	21,600
	36,000		**36,000**

Sundry Creditors

Particulars	Rs.	Particulars	Rs.
To Cash	41,000	By Balance b/d -	69,800
To Discount from	740	By Credit Purchases	70,000
Suppliers			
To Bills Payable			
(B/P issued)	19,400		
To Balance c/d	78,660		
(Bal. fig)			
	1,39,800		**1,39,800**

Bill Payable A/c

Particulars	Rs.	Particulars	Rs.
To Cash	21,800	By Bal b/d -	29,000
To Bal c/d	26,600	By Sundry crs.	
(Bal. fig.)		(Bills Payable issued)	19,400
	48,400		**48,400**

Trading A/c For the year ended 31-3-14

Particulars		Rs.	Particulars	Rs.	
To Opening stock		44,600	By Sales		
To Purchases			Cash	35,820	
Cash		-	Credit	76,000	1,11,820
Credit		70,000	By Closing Stock		59,000
To Wages	15,280				
Less out standing	2,680				
	12,600				
Add out standing	1820	14,420			
To Gross Profit		41,800			
		1,70,820			**1,70,820**

Profit and Loss A/c for the year ended 31-3-2014

Particulars		Rs.	Particulars	Rs.
To Salaries	23,400		By G. P.	41,800
Add. o/s	1,080	24,480	By commission	5,000
To Sundry Exp.		1,460	By Rent	22,000
To Interest on Loan		2,000	By o/s Int. on	
To Discount to customers		1,020	6% investment	240
To R.D.D. @ 5%		3,000	By Discount for suppliers	740
To Pror. @ 5% on B/R		1,080		
To Dep.				
Machinary 5%		2,500		
Land & Building		2,000		
Patents		2,000		
Fixtures		1,500		
To Transfer to Gen. Res.		10,000		
To Net Profit Tr. to B/s		18,740		
		69,780		**69,780**

Balance sheet as on 31-3-2014

Liabilities		Rs.	Assets		Rs.
Capital	1,20,600		Land & Buildings	80,000	
Add. Additions	15,000		Less Dep.	2,000	78,000
Add. Net Profit	18,740		Machinery	50,000	
	1,54,340		Less Dep.	2,500	47,500
Les Drawings	- 8940	1,45,400	Patents	20,000	
Loans	30,600		Less dep.	2,000	18,000
Less Loans Paid	10,600	20,000	Fixtures	15,000	
Gen. Reserve	20,000		Less Dep	1,500	13,500'
Add. Transfer	10,000	30,000	6% Investment		8,000
Sundry crs.		78,660	outstanding Int.		240
Bills Payable		26,600	Cash		1,580
Out standing wages		1,820	Bank		220
Salary outstanding		1,080	Colsing stock		59,000
			Debtors	60,000	
			Less R.D.D.	3,000	57,000
			Bills Receivable	21,600	
			Less Prov.	1,080	20,520
		3,03,560			**3,03,560**

PROBLEM NO. 11

Shri Patil keepsTiis books on single entry system. From the following particulars, prepare Trading and Profit and Loss Account for the year ended 31st March 2011 and Balance Sheet as on that date:

Particulars	1-4-2010 (Rs.)	31-3-2011 (Rs.)
Stock	4,500	6,000
Sundry Debtors	24,000	27,000
Sundry Creditors	15,000	12,500
Furniture	6,000	8,000
Machinery	30,000	30,000
Bills Receivable	20,000	21,000
Bills Payable	16,500	14,500
Bank Overdraft	6,000	-

Cash Book

Particulars	Rs.	Particulars	Rs.
To Sundry Debtors	68,000	By Bank Overdraft	6,000
To Cash Sales	24,400	By Sundry Creditors	40,000
To Bills Receivable.	7,800	By Cash Purchases	16,000
		By Interest	500
		By Salary	8,000
		By Insurance	2,500
		By Sundry Expenses	2,500
		By Rent and Taxes	1,000
		By Drawings	4,000
		By Wages	4,000
		By Furniture	2,000
		By Bills Payable	12,000
		By Balance c/d	1,700
	1,00,200		**1,00,200**

Adjustments :

1) Interest on capital is to be allowed at 5% p.a.

2) Depreciate Machinery at 5% and Furniture at 10% on opening balance.

3) He had allowed Rs. 450 as discount and earned Rs. 300 as discount.

4) Provide Reserve for Bad and Doubtful Debts of Rs. 400

(P. U. Oct. 2001)

Solution :

In the books of Patil
Trading and Profit and Loss A/c
for the year year ended 31-3-2015

Dr.   Cr.

Particulars	Rs.	Particulars	Rs.
To Stock	4,500	By Sales	1,04,650
To Purchases	63,800	By Stock	6,000
To Wages	4,000		
To Gross Profit	38,350		
	1,10,650		**1,10,650**
To Salary	8,000	By Gross Profit	38,350
To Interest	500	By Discount	300
To Insurance	2,500		
To Sundry Expenses	2,500		
To Rent & Taxes	1,000		
To Discount	450		
To R. D. D.	400		
To Depreciation			
Machinery 1,500			
Furniture 600	2,100		
To Interest on Capital	2,350		
To Net Profit	18,850		
	38,650		**38,650**

Balance Sheet as on 31-3-2011

Liabilities	Rs.	Rs.	Assets	Rs.	Rs.
Sundry Creditors		12,500	Cash at Bank		1,700
Bills payable		14,500	Stock		6,000
Capital			Debtors	27,000	
Balance	47,000		Less : R.D.D.	400	26,600
Add : Interest	2,350		Furniture	8,000	
Add : Net Profit	18,850		Less : Depreciation	600	7,400
	68,200		Machinery	30,000	
Less : Drawings	4,000	64,200	Less : Depreciation	1,500	28,500
			Bills Receivable		21,000
		91,200			**91,200**

Dr.			Bills Receivable A/c.		Cr.

Particulars	Rs.	Particulars	Rs.
To Balance b/d	20,000	By Cash	7,800
To Debtors	8,800	By Balance c/d (Bal. fig.)	21,000
	28,800		**28,800**

Dr.			Total Debtors A/c.		Cr.

Particulars	Rs.	Particulars	Rs.
To Balance b/d	24,000	By Cash	68,000
To Sales	80,250	By Bill Receivable	8,800
		By Discount	450
		By Balance c/d (Bal. fig.)	27,000
	1,04,250		**1,04,250**

Dr.			Bills Payable A/c.		Cr.

Particulars	Rs.	Particulars	Rs.
To Cash	12,000	By Bal. b/d	16,500
To Balance c/d (Bal. fig.)	14,500	By Creditors	10,000
	26,500		**26,500**

Dr.	Total Creditors A/c.		Dr.
Particulars	**Rs.**	**Particulars**	**Rs.**
To Cash	40,000	By Balance b/d	15,000
To Discount	300	By Purchases	47,800
To Bills Payable	10,000		
To Balance c/d (Bal. Fig.)	12,500		
	62,800		**62,800**

Statement of Affairs as on 1-4-2010

Liabilities	Rs.	Assets	Rs.
Creditors	15,000	Stock	4,500
Bills Payable	16,500	Debtors	24,000
Bank c/d	6,000	Furniture	6,000
Capital	47,000	Machinery	30,000
(Balancing Figure)		Bills Receivable	20,000
	84,500		**84,500**

PROBLEM NO. 12

Shri Sachin Tendulkar who maintains his books of account on single entry, supplies you the following information.

Particulars	31-12-2014 (Rs.)	31-1 2-2015 (Rs.)
Sundry Creditors	20,000	25,000
Bills Payable	4,000	9,000
Stock	30,000	28,000
Machinery	50,000	50,000
Furniture	8,000	8,000
Sundry Debtors	33,000	38,600
Bills Receivable	3,000	4,400
Salaries Outstanding	1,000	—

Summary of Cash Transactions during the year 2015

Receipts	Rs.	Payments	Rs.
To Balance on 1-1-2013	1,000	By Payment to Creditors	74,000
To Cash Sales	12,000	(Including Bills Payable)	
To Receipts from Debtors	1,54,200	By Wages	22,000
(Including Bills Receivable)		By Salaries	25,000
To Miscellaneous Receipts	600	By Office Expenses	16,000
To Loan from	20,000	By Drawings	14,000
Kuber @ 10%		By Fixed Deposits	10,000
		By Machinery (1-10-2015)	20,000
		By Balance c/d.	6,800
	1,87,800		**1,87,800**

Discount allowed were Rs. 1,800 and discount received during the year Rs. 1,000.

You are required to prepare the trading A/c and Profit and Loss A/c for the year ended 31st Dec. 2015

After taking into consideration the following adjustments. :

1) Office expenses included insurance at Rs. 1,000 per annum paid up to 31st March. 2016

2) Wages Rs. 4,000 are due on 31-12-2016

3) Of Sundry Debtors Rs. 1,600 are to be written off as reserve for bad and doubtful debts.

4) Depreciation is to be provided on furniture at 5% p.a. and on machinery at 10% p.a.

5) During the year Shri. Tendulkar had taken goods of Rs. 1,000 for his own use. No entry is made in the books.

(P.U. April, 1996, April 2002)

Solution :

In the Books of Mr. Sachin Tendulkar
Statement of Affairs as on 31-12-2014

Liabilities	Rs.	Assets	Rs.
Sundry Creditors	20,000	Stock	30,000
Bills Payable	4,000	Machinery	50,000
Outstanding Salary	1,000	Furniture	8,000
Capital (Balance Fig.)	1,00,000	Debtors	33,000
		Bills Receivable	3,000
		Cash	1,000
	1,25,000		**1,25,000**

Dr.   **Total Debtors A/c (including B/R A/c).**   **Cr.**

Particulars	Rs.	Particulars	Rs.
To Balance b/d	33,000	By Cash	1,54,200
To Bills Receivable (Op. Bal.)	3,000	By Discount Allowed	1,800
To Credit Sales (Bal. fig.)	1,63,000	By Bills Receivable (Cl. Bal.)	4,400
		By Balance c/d	38,600
	1,99,000		**1,99,000**

Dr.   **Total Creditors A/c (Including B/P A/c).**   **Cr.**

Particulars	Rs.	Particulars	Rs.
To Cash	74,000	By Balance b/d	20,000
To Discount Received	1,000	By Bills payable (Op. Bal.)	4,000
To Bills Payable (Cl. Bal.)	9,000	By Credit Purchases	
To Balance c/d	25,000	(Bal. fig.)	85,000
	1,09,000		**1,09,000**

Trading'and Profit and Loss A/c

Dr.   **for the year ended 31-12-2015**   **Cr.**

Particulars	Rs.	Rs.	Particulars	Rs.	Rs.
To Opening Stock		30,000	By Sales		
To Purchases		85,000	Cash	12,000	
To Wages	22,000		Credit	1,63,000	1,75,000
Add : Outstanding	4,000	26,000	By Drawings (Goods)		1,000
To Gross Profit		63,000	By Closing Stock		28,000
		2,04,000			**2,04,000**
To Salaries	25,000		By Gross Profit b/d		63,000
Less : Outstanding	1,000	24,000	By Miscellaneous		
To Insurance	1,000		Receipts		600
Less : Prepaid	250	750	By Discount		1,000
To Office Expenses	16,000		Received		
Less : Insurance	1,000	15,000			
To Discount Allowed		1,800			
To R. D. D.		1,600			
To Depreciation on					
Furniture	400				
Machinery	5,500	5,900			
To Net Profit		15,550			
		64,600			**64,600**

Balance Sheet as on 31-12-2015

Liabilities	Rs.	Rs.	Assets	Rs.	Rs.
Creditors		25,000	Cash		6,800
Bills Payable		9,000	Fixed Deposits		10,000
Loan from Bank		20,000	Debtors	38,600	
Outstandng Wages		4,000	Less : R. D.D.	1,600	37,000
Capital	1,00,000		Stock		28,000
Add : Net Profit	15,550		Bills Receivable		4,400
	1,15,550		Prepaid Insurance		250
Less : Drawings			Furniture	8,000	
Cash 14,000			Less : Depreciation	400	7,600
Goods 1,000	15,000	1,00,550	Machinery	50,000	
			Add : Purchased	20,000	
				70,000	
			Less : Depreciation	5,500	64,500
		1,58,550			1,58,550

PROBLEM NO. 13

Mr. Ganesh does not know how to keep the accounts. He submits the data as under :

Summary of Bank Trasactions

Particulars	Rs.	Particulars	Rs.
To Balance at Bank	4,350	By Drawings	7,520
To Sundry Debtors	38,400	By Trade creditors	27,100
To Bills Receivable	12,000	By Bills Payable	9,300
To Commission received	1,500	By Wages	12,000
To Cash Sales	8,600	By Salaries	6,500
To Balance c/d	3,350	By Rent and Taxes	4,400
		By Insurance	800
		By Carriage Inward	250
		By Advertising	330
	68,200		68,200
		By Balance b/d	3,350

Particulars of other assets and Liabilities

Particulars	31-12-2014 (Rs.)	31-1 2-2014 (Rs.)
Stock on hand	18,700	23,400
Debtors	12,000	14,000
Creditors	9,000	1,500
Bills Receivable	4,000	5,000
Bills Payable	1,000	200
Outstanding Salaries	600	1,200
Office Furniture	600	600
Office Building	12,000	12,000

A Provision of Rs. 1,450 is required for doubtful debts on Debtors and depreciation @ 5% is to be charged on Furnitures and Building. There are outstanding wages Rs. 3,000 insurance has been prepaid to the extent of Rs. 250. Legal expenses are outstanding to the extent of Rs. 700.

You are required to prepare Total Debtors A/c, Total Creditors A/c, Total Bills Receivable A/c, Total Bills Payable A/c, Trading Profit and Loss Account for the year ending 31-12-2015 Balance Sheet on that date.

(P. U. April 1986, Oct. 2002)

Solution :

Dr.   **In the books of Mr. Ganesh**   **Cr.**

Bills Receivable A/c.

Particulars	Rs.	Particulars	Rs.
To Balance b/d	4,000	By Bank	12,000
To Debtors A/c		By Balance c/d	5,000
(Balancing figure)	13,000		
	17,000		**17,000**

Dr.   **Total Debtors A/c.**   **Cr.**

Particulars	Rs.	Particulars	Rs.
To Balance b/d	12,000	By Bank	38,400
To Sales (Balancing figure)	53,400	By Bills Receivable	13,000
		By Balance c/d	14,000
	65,400		**65,400**

Dr.   **Bills payable A/c.**   **Cr.**

Particulars	Rs.	Particulars	Rs.
To Bank	9,300	By Balance b/d	1,000
To Balance c/d	200	By Creditors	
		(Balancing Figure)	8,500
	9,500		**9,500**

Dr.   **Total Creditors A/c.**   **Cr.**

Particulars	Rs.	Particulars	Rs.
To Bank	27,100	By Balance b/d	9,00
To Bills Payable	8,500	By Purchases	
To Balance c/d	1,500	(Balancing Figure)	28,100
	37,100		**37,100**

Shri. Ganesh Trading and Profit and Loss A/c

Dr.   **for the year ended 31-12-2015**   **Cr.**

Particulars	Rs.	Rs.	Particulars	Rs.	Rs.
To Opening Stock		18,700	By Sales		
To Purchases		28,100	Cash Sales	8,600	
To Carriage Inward		250	Credit Sales	53,400	62,000
To Wages	12,000		By Closing Stock		23,400
Add : Outstanding	3,000	15,000			
To Gross Profit		23,350			
		85,400			**85,400**
To Salaries	6,500		By Gross Profit		23,350
Less : o/s for 2012	600		By Commission		1,500
	5,900				
Add : o/s for 2013	1,200	7,100			
To Rent and Taxes		4,400			
To Insurance	800				
Less : Prepaid	250	550			
To Legal Expenses		700			
To R. D. D.		1,450			
To Advertisement		330			
To Depreciation					
Furniture	30				
Building	600	630			
To Net Profit		9,690			
		24,850			**24,850**

Balance Sheet
as on 31-12-2015

Liabilities	Rs.	Rs.	Assets	Rs.	Rs.
Sundry Creditors		1,500	Stock on hand		23,400
Bills Payable		200	Debtors	14,000	
Bank Overdraft		3,350	Less : R.D.D.	1,450	12,550
Outstanding Expenses			Bills Receivable		5,000
Wages	3,000		Prepaid Insurance		250
Salaries	1,200		Furniture	600	
Legal expenses	700	4,900	Less : Depreciation	30	
Capital	41,050		Building	12,000	
Add : Net Profit	9,690		Less : Depreciation	600	11,400
	50,740				
Less : Drawings	7,520	43,220			
		53,170			**53,170**

PROBLEM NO. 14

You are given :   a)   The Balance Sheet of Mr. Prashant as on 1st January 2015
                 b)   The summary of cash transactions during the year 2015
                 c)   The remaining transactions

Balance Sheet As on 1-1-2015

Liabilities	Rs.	Assets	Rs.
Capital Account	60,300	Land and Building	40,000
Creditors	34,900	Plant & Machinery	25,000
Bills Payable	14,500	Patents	10,000
Loans	15,300	Fixtures	7,500
General Reserve	10,000	Stock	22,300
Outstanding Wages	1,340	Debtors	24,700
Bank overdraft	2,000	Bills Receivables	7,300
		Cash in hand	1,540
	1,38,440		**1,38,440**

Cash Book for the year ended 31-12-2015

Particulars	Rs.	Particulars	Rs.
To Balance b/d	1,540	By Bank overdraft	2,000
To Debtors	22,990	By Wages	7,640
To Bills Receivables	5,700	By Loans paid	5,300
To Capital	7,500	By Creditors	20,500
To Cash Sales	17,910	By Bills payables	10,900
To Commission	2,500	By Salaries	11,700
To Rent	11,000	By Sundry Expenses	730
		By Interest on loans	1,000
		By Drawings	4,470
		By 6% Investment purchased on 1st July 2015	4,000
		By Cash Balance	790
		By Bank balance	110
	69,140		**69,140**

Other Information

Credit Sales	38,000	Discount to Customers	510
Credit Purchases	35,000	Discount from suppliers	370
Bills Receivables (Received)	10,700	Bills Payable (Issued)	9,700
Stock on 31-12-2014	29,500	Bills Receivables (dishonoured)	1,500

Adjustments :

1) Provide 5% for doutful debts on Debtors & Bills Receivables.

2) Depreciate, Plant and Machinery 5% Land & Building by $2\frac{1}{2}$ %, Patents & Fixtures by 10%

3) Outstanding wages for 2015 amounted to Rs. 910 & Salary outstanding for 2010 amounted to Rs. 540.

4) Transfer Rs. 5,000 to General Reserve.

   Prepare Trading & Profit & Loss Account for the year ended 31-12-2015 and the Balance Sheet as on that date.

Solution :

In the books of Mr. Prashant

Dr.   **Total Debtors Account**   **Cr.**

Particulars	Rs.	Particulars	Rs.
To Balance b/d	24,700	To Cash A/c	22,990
To Bills Receivables disho.	1,500	By Discount to Customers	510
To Credit Sales	38,000	By Bills Receivables A/c	10,700
		By Balance c/d	30,000
		(Balancing figure)	
	64,200		**64,200**

Dr.   **Bills Receivable Account**   **Cr.**

Particulars	Rs.	Particulars	Rs.
To Balance B/d	7,300	By Cash A/c	5,700
To Debtors A/c	10,700	By Debtors A/c	1,500
		By Balance c/d	10,800
		(Balancing figure)	
	18,000		**18,000**

Dr.   **Total Creditors Account**   **Cr.**

Particulars	Rs.	Particulars	Rs.
To Cash A/c	20,500	By Balance B/d	34,900
To Discount from suppliers	370	By Credit Purchases	35,000
To Bills Payable A/c	9,700		
To Balance c/d (Balancing figure)	39,330		
	69,900		**69,900**

Dr.   **Bills Payable Account.**   **Cr.**

Particulars	Rs.	Particulars	Rs.
To Cash A/c.	10,900	By Balance B/d	14,500
To Balance C/d (Balancing Figure)	13,300	By Creditors A/c	9,700
	24,200		**24,200**

Trading & Profit & Loss Account for the year Ended 31-12-2015

Particulars	Rs.		Particulars	Rs.
To Opening Stock		22,300	By Cash Sales	17,910
To Credit Purchases		35,000	By Credit Sales	38,000
To Wages	7,640		By Closing Stock	29,500
Less : Outstanding	1,340			
for last year	6,300			
Add : Outstanding	910			
for current year		7,210		
To Gross Profit		20,900		
		85,410		**85,410**
To Salaries	11,700		By Gross Profit	20,900
Add : Outstanding	540	12,240	By Commission	2,500
To Sundry Expenses		730	By Rent	11,000
To Interest on Loans		1,000	By Outstanding	120
To Discount to Customers		510	Interest on Investments	
To R. D. D. on Debtors		1,500	By Discount from suppliers	370
To R. D. D. on Bill Receivables		540		
To Depreciation on				
Plant & Machinery		1,250		
Land & Building		1,000		
Patents		1,000		
Fixtures		750		
To General Reserve		5,000		
To Net Profit		9,370		
		34,890		**34,890**

Balance Sheet As on 31-12-2015

Liabilities		Rs.	Assets		Rs.
Capital A/c	60,300		Land & Building	40,000	
Add : Additions	7,500		**Less :** Depreciation	1,000	39,000
Less : Drawinas	4,470				
	63,330		Plant & Machinery	25,000	
Add : Net Profit	9,370	72,700	**Less :** Depreciation	1,250	23,750
Loans	15,300				
Less : Paid	5,300	10,000	Patents	10,000	
			Less : Depreciation	1,000	9,000
General Reserve	10,000		Fixtures	7,500	
Add : Additions	5,000	15,000	**Less :** Depreciation	750	6,750
Creditors		39,330	Investments		4,000
Bills Payable		13,300	Stock		29,500
Outstanding Wages		910	Debtors	30,000	
Outstanding Salaries		540	Less R. D.D.	1,500	28,500
			Bills Receivable	10,800	
			Less : R. D. D.	540	10,260
			Outstanding Interest		120
			on Investments		
			Cash in Hand		790
			Cast at Bank		110
		1,51,780			**1,51,780**

PROBLEM NO. 15

Shri Ramrao keeps his books on single entry system. From the following information required to prepare his Trading and Profit and Loss Account for the year ended 31st March, 2011 Balance Sheet as on that date :

(A) **Balance Sheet**
(As on 31st March 2010)

Liabilities	Rs.	Assets	Rs.
Sundry Creditors	3,000	Cash	2,250
Bills Payable	6,000	Bills receivable	3,000
Outstanding wages	150	Sundry Debtors	3,750
Capital	14,850	Stock	3,000
		Furniture	1,500
		Plant and Machinery	10,500
	24,000		**24,000**

(B) Cash Account for the year ended 31st March, 2011

Receipts	Rs.	Payments	Rs.
To Balance b/d	2250	By Wages	3,000
To Cash Sales	5,250	By Drawings	1,800
To Debtors	12,000	By Payment to creditors	5,250
To Bills receivable	11,250	By Bills payable	9,000
		By Sundry expenses	4,500
		By Rent, rates & taxes	3,000
		By Balance C/d	4,200
	30,750		**30,750**

(C) Additional Information :

	Rs.
Sundry Creditors 31-3-2011	3,750
Sundry debtors 31-3-2011	6,000
Bills receivable 31-3-2011	6,750
Bills Payable 31-3-2011	7,500
Stock 31-3-2011	4,500
Bills receivable dishonoured during the year	750
Bills Payable dishonoured	300
Discount allowed	375
Bills receivable endorsed	2,250
Bills receivable endorsed dishonoured	300
Discount received	975

(P. U. April 2005)

Solution :

In the books of Shri Ramrao

Dr.		Total Debtors Account.		Cr.

Particulars	Rs.	Particulars	Rs.
To Balance b/d	3,750	To Cash A/c	12,000
To Biffs Receivables dishonour	750	By Discount Allowed	375
To Sundry Creditors	300	By Bills Receivables	18,000
To Credit Sales (Bal. fig.)	31,575	By Balance c/d	6,000
	36,375		**36,375**

Dr.   **Bills Receivable Account.**   **Cr.**

Particulars	Rs.	Particulars	Rs.
To Balance B/d	3,000	By Cash	11,250
To Sundry Debtors (Bal. fig.)	18,000	By Sundry Creditors	2,250
		By Sundry Debtors.	750
		By Balance c/d	6,750
	21,000		**21,000**

Dr.   **Total Creditors Account**   **Cr.**

Particulars	Rs.	Particulars	Rs.
To Cash	5,250	By Balance b/d	3,000
To Bills Receivable	2,250	By Bills Payable	300
To Discount received	975	By Sundry Creditors	300
To Bills Payable issued	10,800	By Credit Purchase	19,425
To Balance c/d	3,750	(Bal. fig.)	
	23,025		**23,025**

Dr.   **Bills Payable Account.**   **Cr.**

Particulars	Rs.	Particulars	Rs.
To Cash	9,000	By Balance b/d	6,000
To Sundry Creditors	300	By Sundry creditors	10,800
To Balance c/d	7,500	(Bal. fig.)	
	16,800		**16,800**

Dr.   **Trading Account for the year ended 31-3-2011**   **Cr.**

Particulars		Rs.	Particulars		Rs.
To Opening Stock		3,000	By Sales		
To Purchases			i) Cash	5,250	
i) Cash			ii) Credit	31,575	36,825
ii) Credit	19,425	19,425	By Closing Stock		4,500
To Wages	3,000				
Less : O/s	150	2,850			
To Gross Profit		16,050			
		41,325			**41,325**

Profit & Loss Account

| Dr. | | for the year ended 31-3-2015 | | Cr. |

Particulars	Rs.	Particulars	Rs.
To Sundry Expenses	4,500	By Gross Profit	16,050
To Rent, Rates & Taxes	3,000	By Discount Received	975
To Discount Allowed	375		
To Net Profit	9,150		
	17,025		**17,025**

Balance Sheet as on 31-3-2015

Liabilities		Rs.	Assets	Rs.
Capital A/c			Cash	4,200
Opening balance	14,850		Sundry Debtors	6,000
Less : Drawings	1,800		Bill Receivable	6,750
	13,050		Stock	4,500
Add : Net Profit	9,150	22,200	Furniture	1,500
			Plant & Machinery	10,500
Sundry Creditors		3,750		
Bills Payable		7,500		
		33,450		**33,450**

Conversion Method

EXERCISES

1) Mr. Pravin keeps his books by single entry system. He keeps the records of his cash transactions and assets and lliabilities.

His Assets and liabilities on 1st January 2009.

Cash Rs. 4.350, Stock on hand Rs. - 15,500, Debtors Rs. 13,200, Furniture Rs. 2,600, Building Rs. 12,000 and creditors Rs. 8,500

His Cash book shows Receipts and Payments as follows :

Receipts	Rs.	Payments	Rs.
Received from Trade debtors	46,900	Paid to Trade Creditors	37,300
Commission Received	1,600	Drawing	7,200
Cash Sales	22,600	Wages	8,000
		Furniture Purchased	4,000
		Salaries	6,200
		Rent, Taxes	4,200
		Insurance	200
		Carriage	300
		Sundry Expenses	3,700
	71,100		**71,100**

He valued his assets and liabilities on 31st December, 2009 as cash Rs. 7,700, Stock on hand Rs. 12,450, Debtors Rs. 18,400, Furniture Rs. 6,000, Building Rs. 12,000 and Creditors Rs. 6,500

He wants to create 5% reserve for bad and doubtful debts and charge depreciation at $2\frac{1}{2}$% on Building, Rs. 2,500 are outstanding for salaries and Rs. 800 are outstanding for wages, Insurance is paid for the year ending 31st March, 2010. He has to pay legal charges of Rs. 500

Prepare his Trading and Profit and Loss Account for the year ended 31st December, 2009 and the Balance £heet as on that date.

(P. U. April 1990)

2) Mr.(Patil Maintains his books on single entry system. From the following particulars, prepare the Trading and Profit and Loss A/c for the year ended 31-3-2009 and the Balance Sheet as on that date.

Summary of Cash Bank

Particulars	Rs.	Particulars	Rs.
To Balance b/d	15,900	By Creditors	59,100
To Debtors	65,100	By Bills Payable	45,900
To Bills Receivables	39,900	By Wages	22,470
To Sales	43,500	By Carriage Inward	330
To Interest	5,100	By Salaries	13,200
		By Printing	1,590
		By Postage	1,410
		By Insurance	1,500
		By Drawings	12,600
		By Balance c/d	11,400
	1,69,500		**1,69,500**

Particulars of Asset and Liabilities.

Particulars	1-1-202008 (Rs.)	31-12-2009 (Rs.)
Investments	30,000	30,000
Debtors	75,000	87,000
Bills Receivables	30,000	27,000
Creditors	59,100	53,700
Bills Payables	12,300	4,200
Stock	42,300	34,200
Plant and Machinery	90,000	90,000
Bank Loan	45,000	45,000

Adjustments :

a) Interest on Bank Loan was outstanding for the year at 10% p.a.

b) Outstanding wages were Rs. 420 and outstanding printing Bill was Rs. 630.

c) Postage stamps of Rs. 90 were in hand on 31-3-2009.

d) Insurance was prepaid to the extent of Rs. 360.

e) Depreciate Plant and Machinery at 5% and maintain reserve for doubtful debts on debtors at 5%.

(**Ans.:** Capital on 1-4-2008, Rs. 1,66,800, Purchase Rs. 91,500, Sales - Rs. 11,400, G P. Rs. 34,680, N. P. Rs. 8,550. B/s Total Rs. 2,71,200)

3) Mr. Prem maintains his books on single entry system. From the following particulars prepare the Trading and Profit and Loss Account for the year ended 31st March, 2009 and the Balance Sheet as on that date :

Summary of Cash Book

Particulars	Rs.	Particulars	Rs.
To Balance b/d	6,600	By Creditors	21,700
To Debtors	21,700	By Bills Payable	13,300
To Bills Receivables	12,000	By Wages	6,500
To Sales	14,500	By Carriage Inward	100
To Rent	1,700	By Salaries	5,400
To Interest	900	By Printing and Stationery	500
		By Postage and Telegram	500
		By Insurance	1,500
		By Drawings	4,200
		By Taxes	900
		By Balance c/d	2,800
	57,400		**57,400**

Particulars of Assets and Liabilties.

Particulars	1-4-2008 (Rs.)	31-3-2009 (Rs.)
Investments	20,000	20,000
Debtors	50,000	58,000
Bills Receivables	20,000	18,000
Creditors	39,400	35,800
Bills Payables	8,200	2,800
Stock	28,200	22,800
Plant and Machinery	60,000	60,000
Loan from Bank	30,000	30,000

Adjustments:

a) Interest on Loan from Bank was outstanding for the year at 10% p.a.

b) Outstanding wages were Rs. 280 and Outstanding printing and stationery bill was Rs. 420

c) Postage stamps of Rs. 60 were in hand on 31-3-2009

d) Insurance was prepaid to the extent of Rs. 240.

e) Depreciate Plant and Machinery at 5% and Maintain Reserve for doubtful debts on debtors at 5%.

(P. U. April 97)

(**Ans:** G P. Rs. 15,920, N. P. Rs. 700, B/s. Total Rs. 1,76,000 credit purchases Rs. 26,000, Credit Sales Rs. 39,700. opening capital Rs. 1,07,200, Bills Receivables drawn Rs. 10,000, Bills Payble accepted Rs. 7,900)

4) You are given :

a) The Balance Sheet of Mr. Z as on 1-4-2008.

b) The summary of cash transaction for the year 2008-2009.

c) The remaining transaction.

d) Adjustments.

Balance Sheet as on 1-4-2008

Liabilities	Rs.	Assets	Rs.
Capital A/c	1,20,600	Land and Building	80,000
Creditors	69,800	Machinery	50,000
Bills Payable	29,000	Patents	20,000
Loans	30,600	Fixture	15,000
General Reserve	20,000	Stock	44,600
Outstanding Wages	2,680	Debtors	49,400
Bank Overdraft	4,000	Bills Receivable	14,600
		Cash in hand	3,080
	2,76,680		**2,76,680**

Cash Book for the year ended 31-3-2009

Particulars	Rs.	Particulars	Rs.
To Balance b/d	3,080	By Bank Overdraft	4,000
To Debtors	45,980	By Wages	15,280
To Bills Receivable	11,400	By Loan paid	10,600
To Capital	15,000	By Creditors	41,000
To Cash Sales	35,820	By Bills Payable	21,800

Particulars	Rs.	Particulars	Rs.
To Commission	5,000	By Salaries	23,400
To Rent	22,000	By Sundry Expenses	1,460
		By Interest on loan	2,000
		By Drawings	8,940
		By 6% Investment	
		(Purchased on 1-10-2009)	8,000
		By Cash Balance	1,580
		By Bank Balance	220
	1,38,280		**1,38,280**

c) The remaining transactions :

Credit Sales	76,000
Credit Purchases	70,000
Bills Receivable Received	21,400
Stock on 31-3-2009	59,000
Discount to Customers	1,020
Discount from Suppliers	740
Bills Payable Issued	19,400
Bills Receivable Dishonoured	3,000

d) Adjustment :

i) Provide 5% for doubtful debts on Debtors and Bills Receivable.

ii) Depreciate machinery by 5% and Land and Building by $2\frac{1}{2}$ %. Patents and Fixtures by 10%.

iii) Outstanding wages are Rs. 1,820 and salary outstanding amounted to Rs. 1,080.

iv) Transfer Rs. 10,000 to General Reserve.

Prepare Trading and Profit and Loss Account for the year ended 31-3-2009 and the Balance Sheet as on that date.

(P. U. October, 1997)

(**Ans :** G. P. Rs. 41,800, N. P. Rs. 18,740. B/s Total Rs. 3,03,560 Debtors balance Rs. 60,000. Bills Receivable balance Rs. 21,600 creditors balance Rs. 78,660, Bills Payable balance Rs. 26,600)

5) You are given below :

a) The Balance Sheet of Mr. Sunit on 1st April, 2008.

b) The Cash transactions for 12 months to 31st March, 2009.

c) A summary of remaining transactions for the year.

a)   **Balance Sheet of Mr. Sunit as on 1-4-2008**

Liabilities	Rs.	Assets	Rs.
Bank Overdraft	5,000	Cash in hand	700
Sundry Creditors	36,000	Bills Receivable	25,000
Bills Payable	16,000	Sundry Debtors	39,000
Capital	2,00,000	Machinery	47,000
		Stock in Trade	75,300
		Buildings	70,000
	2,57,000		**2,57,000**

b)   **Cash Book**

Particulars	Rs.	Particulars	Rs.
To Balance b/d	700	By Bank Overdraft	5,000
To Receipts from Debtors	2,90,000	By Salaries	12,000
To Bills Realised	1,00,000	By Wages	15,800
		By Bills Payable paid	1,43,000
		By Paid to Creditors	1,47,000
		By Office expenses	8,000
		By Drawings	45,000
		By Balance c/d	
		Cash in hand	2,400
		Cash in Bank	12,500
	3,90,700		**3,90,700**

c) **The remaining transactions :**	Rs.
Sales	4,07,000
Discount allowed	2,000
Purchases	3,00,000
Discount Received	1,000
Bills Receivable received during the year	1,09,000
Bills Payable issued during the year	1,50,000
Stock of goods on 31-3-2009	53,000

Provide a 5% reserve for doubtful debts and write off depreciation on Machinery at 5% and Building at $2\frac{1}{2}\%$.

From the above particulars prepare a Trading and Profit and Loss Account for the year ended 31-3-2009 and a Balance Sheet as on that date.   (P. U. April, 98)

(**Ans :** G. P. Rs. 68,900, N. P. 41,550, B/s. Total Rs. 2,57,550, debtors balance Rs. 45,000 creditors balance Rs. 38,000, bills Receivable balance Rs. 34,000, Bills payable balance Rs. 23,000)

6) Mr. Sharad Keeps his books of accounts on Single Entry System. His books reveal the following :

Particulars of Assets and Liabilities

Particulars	1st July 2008 (Rs.)	30st July 2008 (Rs.)
Stock	20,000	17,300
Debtors	16,000	14,800
Bills Receivable	6,200	4,800
Bills payable	5,000	5,600
Sundry Creditors	10,000	9,300
Cash at Bank	2,500	1,800
Furniture and Fittings	10,000	12,000

Summary of Cash Transactions

Receipts	Rs.	Payments	Rs.
To Opening Balance b/d	2,500	By Payments to Creditors	20,000
To Received from Debtors	35,000	By Payment against Bills	15,000
To Received against	15,600	Payable	
Bills Receivable		By Office Expenses	6,000
To Cash Sales	10,900	By Domestic Expenses	13,100
To Miscellaneous	500	By Investments	6,600
		By Furniture purchased	2,000
		By Balance c/d	1,800
	64,500		**64,500**

i) Investments consisted of 5% Government Bonds of the face value of Rs. 8,000 which were purchased on 1st January, 2009.

ii) A provision of 5% of the Sundry Debtors is necessary. Write off depreciation on furniture and Fittings at 5%.

iii) Interest on Capital is to be allowed at 5% p.a. office expenses owing on Rs. 810.

iv) Manager is entitled to a Commission of Rs. 665.

Prepare Trading Profit and Loss A/c for the year ended 31st June, 2009 and Balance Sheet as on that date.

(**Ans. :** OP Capital 39,700, Cr. Sales 48,000, Cr. purchases 34,900, Bills Receivable drawn 14,200, Bills Payble accepted 15,600 Gross Profit 21,300, Net Profit 11,200 B/s Total 56,160).

7) Mr. Kalam maintains his books on Single Entry Systems from his following particulars prepare Trading and Profit and Loss A/c for the year ended 31-3-2009 and Balance Sheet as on that date.Summary of Cash Book.

Particulars	Rs.	Particulars	Rs.
To Balance b/d	15.900	By Creditors	59,100
To Debtors	65,100	By Bills payable	45,900
To Bills Receivable	39,900	By Wages	22,470
To Sales	43,500	By Carriage Inward	330
To Interest	5,100	By Salaries	13,200
		By Printing	1,590
		By Postage	1,410
		By Insurance	1,500
		By Drawings	12,600
		By Balance c/d	11,400
	1,69,500		**1,69,500**

Particulars of other Assets and Liabilities

Particulars	1-4-2008 (Rs.)	31-3-2009 (Rs.)
Investments	30,000	30,000
Debtors	75,000	87,000
Bills Receivable	30,000	27,000
Creditors	59,000	53,700
Bills payable	12,300	4,200
Stock	42,300	34,200
Plant and Machinery	90,000	90,000
Loan from Mr. Pawar	45,000	45,000

Adjustment :

1) Interest on loan from Mr. Pawar was outstanding for the year at 10% per annum.

2) Outstanding Wages were Rs. 420 & Outstanding Printing bill was Rs. 630.

3) Postage stamps of Rs. 90 were in hand on 31-3-2009.

4) Insurance was prepaid to the extent of Rs. 360.

5) Depreciation Plant and Machinery at 5% and maintain reserve for doubtful debts on debtors at 5%.

(P.U. April, 1995)

8) Rukmini keeps her books by single entry. On 1-4-2010 her capital was Rs. 69,000. Analysis of her cash book for the year 2010-11 gives the following particulars :

Debit side	Rs.	
Received from sundry debtors		60,000
Paid into Capital A/c		5,000
Credit side :		
Due to bank on 1-4-2010		7,400
Payment to sundry creditor		25,000
General expenses of business		10,000
Salaries paid		15,500
Drawings		3,000
Balance at Bank on 31-3-2011		4,000
Cash in hand		100

Assets and Liabilities Were

Particulars	1-4-2008 (Rs.)	31-3-2009 (Rs.)
Debtors	53,000	88,000
Creditors	15,000	19,500
Stock	17,000	19,000
Plant & machinery	20,000	20,000
Furniture	1,400	1,400

From the above information prepare Trading and Profit & Loss A/c for the year ended 31-3-2011 and Balance Sheet as on that date. You are also required to prepare Total Debtors A/c and Total Creditors A/c after providing 5% interest on opening capital balance, 10% depreciation on plant and machinery, 5% depreciation on furniture and reserve of 5% on sundry debtors.

(PUP April 2011)

8

Analysis of Financial Statements

8.1 Introduction
8.2 Limitations of Financial statements
8.3 Analysis
8.4 Problems

8.1 Introduction

Financial Statements contain a wealth of information if properly analysed and interpreted provide valuable insights into firms performance and position.

Accounting involve recording classifying and summarising the business transactions which ultimately aims at preparing financial statements financial Statments are the out come of summarising process of accounting. Financial statements primarily Comprise two basic Statements 1) the Balance sheet or the financial position statement and ii) the profit & Loss Account or the income statement.

Preparation of financial statements has been made compulsory by law directly or indirectly. Apart from the management there are many other parties who are interested in the financial statements of business organisations such as share holders, debentureholders, creditors, Government authorities research scholars, Financing institutes and banks etc.

8.2 Limitations of Financial statements :

The financial Statements are of great use to the various persons and institutes as mentioned above but these statements suffer from a number of limitations. Some of the limitations are stated below.

1) Historical Data : The financial Statement are prepared after the completion of the accounting year, hence, They provide the historical data. As far as decision making is concerned with this historical data provided by the financial statements, proves to be of less importance as it does not talk about future. one can assess the performance and financial position of the organisation during the year or at the and of the year.

2) Fulfilment of legal Requirements : The Financial Statements are prepared for the purpose of fulfilment of statutory requirements. Hence the fact and figures provided by these statements do not speak much about solvency, profitability, liquidity etc. of the business organisation.

3) Emphasis on merely quantitative Information : The financial Statements record and present only those transactions which are expressed in monetary terms. The transactions or the elements which can not be expressed interms of money are not considered by the Financial Statements e.g Quality of product, labour relations, efficiency of managerial personal, efficiency of employees, loyalty of empolyee's etc.

4) Interim Reports : Financial Statements are prepared at the financial year, hence they are necessarily interim reports and not final. These statements can provide us the results of financial year only. To get the final profit or loss of the business organisation. The business will have to be wound up.

5) Misleading Reports : While preparing the balance sheet the assets and liabilities are shown at their historical prices and not at their market values, as per ther principle of good concern. This may affect income statements i.e Profit Loss Account, as incorrect provision will be made for depreciation on fixed assets. Hence the financial position shown in these reports may not be true in real sense and may prove to be misleading as far as decision making is concened.

6) Impact of personal judgements : Accounting procedure provides number of occasions where the incharge personnel can take decision on personal judgement which detinitely affects the figures of financial statements. For example decisions regarding depreciation policy, Valuation of inventory, Valuations of fictitous assets etc.

Due to the above limitations the Financial Statement, though carefully and correctly prepared do not convery exact message regarding the true financial position of the business organisation. Hence they must be examined analysed and interpreted carefully. and Definition

Meaning and Definition of financial analysis and interpretation :

The Financial Statements prepared in absolute manner are of very little significance to the management. The figures in the financial statments standing alone, convery no meaning to the managment. The Management wants to know the financial strength of the business, The liqudity and solvency position of the business, the earning capacity trends and future prospects to serve this purpose the figures recorded in the financial Statements are required to be re arranged and analysed in such a manner that they become easily inteligible to the managment personnel, Who may not be experts in accountancy.

The figures provided by the financial statements can be made more meaningful throughth the process called "Analysis and interpretation." Analysis of financial Statements is an analysis which highlights important relationship in the financial Statements. It is useful to find out the financial and operational strengths and weakchesse of the business organisation.

Analysis is the process of critically examining in detail accounting information given in the financial staments. The Analysis and interpretation of Financial Statements are an attempt to determine the significace and meaning of the financial data contained in the Financial Statement. These financial statments are not an end in it self they are only vehicles of communication. The technique of financial anlaysis is typically devoted to evaluate the past present and projected performance of a business firm. A Chief Finance officer or an accountant has to evaluate the past performance, present Financial position, liquidity, enquire into the profitability of the firm and to forecast and Plan for future operations. Financial Analysis is an analysis which highlights important relationships in the financial statements. It is an important means of assessing past perfermance and in forecasting and planning future performace Understanding the past is a pre requisite for anticipating the future.

8.3 Analysis Meaning :

It refers to proper arrangement and rearrangment, grouping and regrouping of the financial and operational data into their distinct and different component parts. Regrouping of the data becomes inevitable because the financial statements comparise of a number of varied and diverse accounting information.

8.3.1 Definition information :

1) "Financial Analysis is a process of evaluating the realationship between component parts of a financial statement to obtain a better understanding of a firms position and performance.

2) According to Foster G. "Financial Analysis is the process of indentifying the financial Strengths and weaknesses of the firm by properly establishing relationships between the items of the Balance sheet and the profit and loss Account."

3) According to Meigs W. B. and others, Financial Analysis is the process of selection relations and evaluation."

8.3.2 Meaning of Interpretation :

If refers to the process of drawing inference regarding earning capacity, liquidity, Profitability, Solvency, efficiency etc. of the business unit by comparing various components and examining their contents.

Interpretations is the drawing of inference and stating what the figures in the financial Statements really mean. Interpretation is not an easy job. Interpreter must have experience understanding and intelligence to draw correct and reliable conclusions from the analysis of data. Interpretation is not possible without analysis and analysis has no value with out interpretation. In short "Analysis" is the simplification of the data incorporated in the financial statements where as, "Interpretation" is explaining the meaning of and significance of the data simplified.

Interpretation means bringing out the meaning of the financial statements with the help of the analysis. In other words. Interpretation means to present an explaination of financial data with the help of analysis.

In short the analysis is the pre requisite to interpretation.

Thus, analysis and interpretation both assist the management in measuring and maintaining efficiency of various levels.

The analysis consists of breaking down a complete set of facts or figures into simple elements and arranging them in such manner that they can be easily understood.

The analysis of the profit and loss Account consists of breaking it down into various elements as under -

Gross sales, Net sales, cost of Goods sold, Gross Margin operating expenses, operating Net profit Non eperating Income expenses Net profit before Tax and Net Profit after tax.

The Main elements of Balance Sheet may be as under proprietors funds or owners equity, other Debts, total funds employed fixed Assets Current Assets, Current liabilities and working capital.

Operating Incomes and Expenses :

These are the incomes and the expenses which result from the normal conduct or operation of the business Such incomes are earned and expenses are incurred in the routine operation of the business. Such expenses are required to be incurred to run the business smoothly and efficiently.

Operating expenses are classified as

1) Administative or office expenses, such as office staff salaries officer Rent, Printing and stationery, depreciation of office assets etc. Which related to administration.

2) Finance Expenses, Such as interest an debentures or on loans or deposits cash discount allowed, bad debts etc. Which related to raising of finance.

3) Selling and Distribution expenses, such as salaries and commission of salesman, advertisement, packing charges, delivery van expenses etc. Which are incurred to secure, maintain and increase sales and to deliver or distribute the goods there after.

Non Operating Incomes and Expenses :

Such income or expenses are not related to the business operations but they are of accidental and non - recuring nature. e.g Profit on sale of fixed assets interest, received from non Trading investments, loss on sale of fixed assets penalty or fine for illegal act etc.

8.3.3 Objectives and purpose of financial Analaysis & Interpretations :

The main Objective of financial Statement analysis is the provide valuable information to its users about the financial position i.e short term and long term solvency, Liquidity, profitability etc. of the business organisations. The user of this information may be a creditor or investor can take proper and depend able decision on the basis of this information whether to invest in the business organisation or not. There are various parties which are interested in the financial statement analysis such as shareholders, investors, creditors, debenture financial institutions, holder, banks managments, employee and trade unions, Government authorities etc. These all persons and institutes have different objectives with different purpose for financial statement analysis. For example the object of short Term creditors like trade creditors is primarily to confirm the short term solvency whereas the financial insitutions will be interested to know about the long term solvency of the business organisation. In the same way the management is intersted to know the results of the financial statement analysis for evaluating the operational and financial efficiency of the enterprise. Financial Statement Analysis is used by the various persons and institutes for the following objectives :

1) Comparison of past performace with current performance : The past performance of any organisation regarding production sales, profit expenses net incone etc. work as an indicator of trend of the success of the business organisation. It also indicates the previous rate of return on the previous investments. Similarly, the current performance of the organisation expresses the current position of the organisation. The investor can take decisions regarding the investments in the organisation. In short such comparison explains the capacity of the organisation for repaying the loans and interest thereon.

2) Prediction of Earning capacity and Growth Rate : The Financial Statement analysis helps the investors in predicting the earning capacity and it also indicates the probable growth rate of the organisation. Hence, with the help of financial statement analysis the investor can take the proper investment decision by comparing the various alternatives. The Financial Statement anlaysis explains the risk or uncertainty associated with the expected return. It also explains the future trend of earning and growth rate of the business organisation.

3) Prediction of Insolvency : Finacial Statement analysis proves to be very useful to predict the probable business failure or the insolvency of the business organisation. The management can take remedial and preventive measures to stop such probable failure and investor can also take proper investment decision on the basis of such analysis.

4) Useful for taking lending Decisions : Financial Statement analysis is also used by the money lenders, banks and financial institutions. It helps them to assess borrower's borrowing capacity, repaying capacity, credit worthiness etc. Banks and financial institutions can have detailed investigation of the financial position of the business organisation, on the basis of the financial statement analysis and accordingly if any loan is Sanctioned they can determine the credit risk terms and canditions of loans, interest rate etc.

5) **Assessement of financial position and performance and operating performance of the firm :**

6) To make a comparative study of the firm with other industrial units :

8.3.4 Steps of financial Analysis :

The following steps will have to be taken by any analyst or the investigator or the user of the financial statements.

1) Deciding upon the scope of analysis : First of all, the depth, object and extent of analysis will have to be determined This will help to determine the scope of analysis, tool of analysis and the quantity and the quality of the date required.

2) Understanding the basic principles, form, concepts, fundamentals of financial statements :

3) Collection of necessary information : The analyst should collect other allied necessary information from the management and other sources like SEBI, Stock Exchange, Icome Tax and sales tax authorities generally not revealed by the published finacial Statements.

4) Rearrangement of financial Data : Analysis consist of breaking down a complete set of facts & figures into simple elements. The analyst must rearrange these dissected simple elements in a tabular, vertical and any other form so asto increase its reliability the approximation figures reclassification or consolidation of items in homogenous groups, rearranging Income statement and Balance sheet in a vertical form suitable for analysis will have to be undertaken by analyst to obtain accurate results.

5) Analysis : Once the financial Data are rearranged, tabulated approximated, now the actual analysis is made with the various techniques like, comparative statements, Trend Analysis, Ratio Analysis etc.

6) Interpretation and presentation : Once the analysis is done, the interpretation is made and the inferences are drawn and presented in the form of reports to the management etc. Interpretation consists in explaining the real significance of these statements. Interpretation means finding the correct meaning of financial data for future forecasting regarding the liquidity, solvency, profitability and overall performance of the business enterprise. Analysis is prerequisite to interpretation. Interpretation is thus drawing of inference and stating what the figures in the financial statements really mean. The interpreter must have knowlege, understanding, intelligence, and experience to draw correct conclusion from the analysed data. Interpretation is normally different from individual to individual. It is always subjective.

7) Taking necessary corrective and Remedial action :

8. 3. 5 Types of Financial Analysis :

It is important to distinguish between different types of analysis because the techniques fo analysis and interpretation differ according to the type of analysis.

1) External Analysis : It is done by banks, creditors, general public who do not have access to the detailed accounting records and who depend entirely on published statements and reports.

2) Inernal Analysis : Such analysis is done by the finance and Accounts department to help the top management. These people have direct approach to the relevant financial records and they narrate the inside story. Such analysis emphasises on the perfomance, appraisal and assessment of the profitability of different activities.

3) Short Term Analysis : It is mainly concerned with the working capital analysis. Activity analysis etc. Hence in short term analysis, the current assets and current liabilities are analysed and the liquidity Short term solvency of the concern is determined.

4) Long term Analysis : In long term analysis the stress is on the long term solvency solid foundation of the business and earning potentiality of the firm. In long term analysis, the fixed assets structure, leaverage analysis, capital structure are analysed.

5) Vertical and static Analysis : Analysis is made of one set of annual statements to gauge the finacial health as on particular date. This correlates different components of the same set but fails to review the preiodic changes.

6) Horizontal Analysis : Analysis may be made of several such statements to examine the trend of its affairs over a period of years. It is also known as dynamic analysis, coordinates several years data to review the periodic progress of the enterprise It is useful for long term planning as it involves the trend study of financial data.

8. 3. 6 Methods of Analysis : (i.e. Tools of Analysis / Techniques of Analysis) :

Analysis of financial Statements can be made by the following different methods according to the purpose. These methods are

1) Comparative statements.
2) Common size statements.
3) Trend percentages
4) Ratio Analysis
5) Fund Flow / Cash Flow analysis :

All these methods are discussed below in detail :

1) Comparative Financial Statements : (i.e Horizontal Analysis)

Comparative financial statements provide a base for comparison of the finacial position of different periods of time. These statements i.e Income statement and a Balance sheet, both are prepared by providing various columns to them, such as the preceeding year's amount column, current year's amount colume etc. Alongwith these columns for percentage, increase in figures as well as percentage decrease in figures are also provided in these statements. Hence these statements speak much about the Financial position of the business organisation at a glance as it gives an idea about the trend of performance regarding various aspects of the organisation. One can draw sound inferences regarding the financial position of the business organisation on the basis of comparative financial statements.

Comparative Income statement :

A Comparative Income statement shows the absolute figures for two or more periods, the absolute change from one period to another. The change may, if necessary, be expressed in percentages instead of an absolute figures, However, the items of incomes and expenses should be considered together wile interpreting the increases or decreases.

Comparative Balance Sheet :

Balance sheet as on two or more different dates are compared to ascertain changes in the assets and liablities i.e decrease or increase in the assets and liabilities comparison is useful in studying the trends in an enterprise.

Particulars	31 Dec 2000 Rs.	31-12-01 Rs.	Amt of increase or Decrease in 2001	% of increase or Decrease in 2001
Asset : Current Asset	....	....		
Fixed Asset	....	....		
Liabilities :	....	....		
Current liabilities	....	....		
Fixed liabilities	....	....		
Capital : Equity	....	....		
Preference	....	....		

Form of comparative Income statement
For the year ended 31-12-00 & 2001

Particulars	31 Dec 2000 Rs.	31-12-01 Rs.	Amt of increase or Decrease in 2001	% of increase or Decrease in 2001
Net Sales	....	....	....	
Less - Cost of goods Sold	....	....	....	
Gross Profit	....	....	....	
i.e. mi exp, selling exp	....	....	....	
Finance exp.	....	....	....	
Operating profit	....	....	....	
+ Other expenses	....	....	....	
- Other expenses	....	....	....	
Income / Net Profit before tax	....	....	....	
- Income Tax	....	....	....	
= Net profit after Tax	....	....	....	

2) Common size statements (i.e. vertical Analysis) :

Financial Statements when read with absolute figures are not easily understandable and the conclusions drawn there from may be incorrect. The absolute figures provided in the financial statements are not easily understandable. One can not draw any correct conclusion on the basis of mere figures. Even the amount of sales, profits, losses capital, Assets, liablities etc, Changes from year to year. Hence, One can not comment on the basis of mere figures, about the performance of two or more companies for example study the following details and comment:

Particulars	**ABC company**	**XYZ company**
Sales	Rs. 4,000,000	Rs. 2,00,000
Profit	Rs. 4,00,000	Rs. 40,000

If it is assuned that both the companies mentioned above were engaged in simlilar business one may draw conclusions that ABC co is more profitable than xyz company. But this may be misleading Conclusion. Because of the other factors like the capital employed by these two companies on which this profit is earned is not considered here from the above information. we can not decide which company is really more profitable. Hence, we have to use a common size according to which sales is taken as equal to 100 and the profit is expressed as a percentage of sales revenue :

$$\text{profit as percentage of sales} = \frac{\text{profit}}{\text{sales}} \times 100$$

Hence, profit percentage of sales of ABC company's as follows.

$$\frac{40,000}{40,00,000} \times 100 \ = \underline{\underline{10\%}}$$

Profit percentage of sales Revenue for XYZ company

$$\frac{40,000}{20,000} \times 100 \ = \underline{\underline{20\%}}$$

Interpretation :

It is abserved from the above calculations that XYZ company has earned 20% profit and ABC company has earned only 10% margin. Hence, it is clear that XYZ company is more profitable than ABC company.

Therefore for determination of trends and to have correct picture, the figures in the financial statements should be converted into percentage to some common base. This common base is 'Sales' in respect of 'income statements and 'Toal Assets' or 'Total liablities' in case of the Balance sheet. The sales figure is assuned to be 100 and all items in the income statements are expressed as percentage of sales. Similarly, the total of Assets, Liabilities is assumed to be 100 and all the items in the Balance sheet are expressed as percentage of total asset, liabilities. Thus, all the figures in the financial statements Are converted into common size i.e, percentage and related to a common base i.e 100. These Statements are called common size statements or 100% statements. Thus the relationship of the items in the Income statement is established with sales and that of items in the Balance sheet with total Asset, liabilities vertically. Therefore, this type of Analysis is called 'vertical analysis. This type of statement facilitates comparison between the amounts in the same statements and also between the amounts in the successive statements.

The Common size statements do not show variations in respective items from period to period. They do not give information about the trend of individual items, but they only indicate trend of their relationship to total.

3) Trend percentages or Analysis Trend Ratio : (Horizontal Analysis) :

Trend Analysis is also an important and useful technique in finacial anlaysis. Financial Statements for a number of years may be analysed to study the trend of the data given in these statements.

For the purpose of comparative study of financial Statements over a number of years trend percentages or ratios are very useful.

out of the periods under study any one year is taken as base year and each item in this year is taken as 100 percentage of the same item in each of the remaining years is calculated.

Trend percentages disclose changes in the financial and operating data between two specific periods and make it possible for the analysis to judge whether the changes that have taken place have been favourable or otherwise. The trend analysis shows the direction of progress up ward or down ward. This trend anlaysis is generally used for some of the important parameters like, sales, profit, working capital, Debt, Equity Relationship, Reserves position etc. Which can be logically connected with each other.

Under this method while comparing information of various years, one particular year, generally a beginning year is taken as a base year and comparison is made according to that base year. The financial analyst can observe the trend percentage and can draw inferences regarding various aspects of the business organisation.

For example - The figures of sales of ABC company Ltd. are given below for five years i.e from 1996 to 2000 Assuning 1996 as a base year.

Year	Sales (Rs)
1996	100
1997	110
1998	120
1999	115
2000	125

It is observed from the above information that the sale in all years as compared to 1996 is really more. It has shown upward trend except the year 1999, When sales are less than the preceeding year i.e 1998. It is also observed that as compared to sales in year 1996 there is an increase of 10% sale in 1997, 20% in 1998, 15% in 1999 and 25% in the year 2000. It is further observed that though there is an increase in sales every year, till stable growth rate is not observed secondly these figures speak about the sales only but if anlayst desirs to go for further investigation he will have to compare the figure of sales with cost of goods, sold sales to profit, Capital employed to sales etc.

4) Fund flow and cash flow Analysis :

Fund flow statements :

A Balance sheet is a static, Showing the financial position of a business on a particular day, it does not throw any light on the changes in the items that have taken place over a certain period. For this purpase, it is necessary to compare the two Balance sheet as on two dates viz as at the date of commencement of the period i.e an opening Balance Sheet and at the end of the period i.e. Closing Balance sheet. The comparisen of the two Balance Sheet indicates the changes in the items, whereas the fund flow statement discloses the reasons of such changes. For example if there is an increase in the value of machinery by Rs. 50,000 and there is also corresponding increase in the amount of debentures during the period, it can be concluded that the funds made available by issue of debentures are used for purchase of machinery. The change in the financial position does result from operating profit. The success or the failure of any business depends upon the availability of funds and their better utilisation. The fund flow statement reveals the sources from which the funds are made available and how they are utilised or applied. In other words, the fund flow statement explains in brief the changes occurred in the items in two Balance Sheets.

In the Words of Anthony, The Fund Flow statement describes the sources from which daditional funds were derived and the use to which these funds were put.

Foulke defines the fund flow statement as statement of sources and Application of funds is a technical device designsed to analyse the changes in the financial condition of a business enterprise between two dates. This statement is also known as "Funds Received and Disbursed Statement" "Statement of fund supplied and Applied." "Where got where gone statement" etc.

Cash flow statement : Cash flow statement as its name suggests takes into consideration only cash transaction which affect the cash position of the concern. The fund flow statement indicates movement of funds or changes in working capital. But the cash flow statement shows the movement of cash only i.e changes in cash position.

When all transactions such as sales, purchases, incomes and expenses are cash transactions, net profit is equivalent to net cash from operation.

In actual practice, We never come across the position as stated above. Most of the transactions of the business are on credit basis and hence the net profit can not be equal to net cash from operations. Profit and loss A/c of a firm may be showing larger net profits but at the same time the firm may not have sufficient cash to meet if day to day requirements the points will be dear if we take a simple example that the goods costing Rs. 10,000 are sold For Rs. 11,000. It means the firm earned a profit of Rs. 1000

Therefore, While preparing a cash flow statement we are required to take into consideration only cash receipts and cash payments into account alike the preparation of Receipts and payaments A/c from Income & Expenditure A/c, Balance Sheet and allied informations.

The cash flow statement consist of two parts i) Inflow of cash and ii) out flow of cash.

Cash flow Analysis is useful to the management in following ways

1) Helps in efficient management of cash.
2) Helps in internal financial management
3) Discloses the movement of cash.
4) Discloses success or failure of cash planning
5) Helps in control of cash expenditure.

5) Ratio Analysis :

Interoduction : The Financial Statements of a business organisation. are very much useful to different parties concerned such as Management, Share holders, Creditors, Investors, Banks, Finacial institutions, Goverment authorities etc. Trading A/c discloses the Gross profit or Gross loss of the firm and the profit and loss A/c discloses net profit or net loss of the business organisation. The Balance sheet discloses its true and fair financial position. i.e position of assets and liablities as on particular date. The information Provided in the finacial statement serves no purpose unless it is analysed and interpreted in some comparable terms.

An absolute figure does not convery much meaning. It therfore, becomes necessary to study a certain figure in relations to Some other relelant figure to arrive at certain conclusion. For example, if we are given the figure of only gross profit earned by a certain firm, We can not say, Whether the gross profit is heavy, reasonable or insufficient For this purpose we must take into consideration the figure of sales. Thus, the gross profit is required to be studied in relation to the sales to decide the percentage gross profit to sales. on the basis of this percentage we can conclude whether the gross profit earned in is reasonable or otherwise. Thus relationship between the figures expressed mathematically is called a ratio. According to Robert Anthony, "Ratio is one number exppessed in terms of another"

However, the two figures, must be interrelated. If the two figures are not at all connected with each other, their ratio will serve no useful purpose.

The ratio is calculated by dividing one figure by the other figure. It may be expressed in any of the three ways, Times "Proportion" or "percentage". According to the convenience or suitability. When one value is divided by the other, the quotient obtained indicates "Times" If quotient is multiplied by 100 we get the "percentage". If we take proportion between the two figures, we get the proportion or ratio. Suppose the current assets are of Rs. 50,000 and current liabilities are of Rs. 12,500 The relation between these two items can be expressed as under -

i) $\dfrac{50,000}{12,500} = 4$ Times i.e current assets 4 times the current liabilities

ii) $\dfrac{50,000}{12,500} \times 100 = 400\%$ Current assets are 400% of current labilities.

iii) $\dfrac{50,000}{12,500} = \dfrac{4}{1} = 4$ Proportion or ratio of current assets to current liabilities.

An Accounting ratio is an arithmatical relatioship between two figures in statement of account stated either as proportion (i. e. ratio) rate (i.e times) or percentage, e.g percentage of net profit to capital, ratio of current Assets and Current liabilities. Stock turnover ratio. indicating number of times the stock is replaced during the year.

Nature of Ratio Analysis :

Ratio Analysis is one of the most powerful and useful tool of financial analysis. A ratio is used as a yardstick for examining the financial position of any business organisation. As compared to other tools of financial anlaysis, the ratio analysis provides very useful conclusions about various aspects of an enterprise like financial position, solvency, stability, liquidity, profitability capital structure of an enterprise.

Ratio anlaysis is the process of identifying the financial strength and weaknesses of the firm by properly establishing relationships between the items of the Balance Sheet and the profit and loss account. The figures recorded in the financial statements are anlaysed interrelated and the they are interpreted i.e then conclusions are drawn. Ratio analysis is considered to be a very valuable tool of mangement control. Th ratio anlaysis helps the managment in discharging its functions like forecasting, planning, co - ordination, communication control etc.

Objectives of Ratio Analaysis :

Various ratios can be calculated for different purposes. The differnt objectives for which various ratios' are calculated prove the importance and utility of each and every ratio. Various objectives of ratio Analysis are as follows.

1) To Reveal the financial position : It is very difficult to draw any conclusion on the basis of information provided in finacial statement. Calculation of accounting ratios helps to reveal the true financial position of the business organisation. The financial institutions banks, creditors and suppliers can take the decision regarding sanctioning the loans to the organisation. It helps the shareholders and depositors to know the profitability of the organisation and accordingly to take the decisions regarding investment in the organisation.

2) Inter firm and Intra firm Comparison : Ratio Analysis provides inter firm comparison. It means that the firms ratio's, so calculated can be compared with its competitive firms. Such comparison explains the firms relative position with its competitors. A firm can take immmediate action to improve the performance. If ratio's shows negative results as compared to competitive firms. Such Comparison also to judge the probable industrial sickness and enables to take remedial measures earliest. Intra firm comparison is also necessary to know companys performance over period of years.

3) Trend Analysis : Ratio Analysis facilities management to know the firms financial position, whether it is improving rapidly or declining or remaining stable, by setting a trend with the help of ratio. A trend can be established by calculating the ratios for number of years. The trend analysis helps the mangement to plan, forecast and control the future activities of the organisation.

Advantages of Ratio Analysis :

Following are the principal Advantages of the ratio analysis :
1) Ratios are simply the comprehension of financial statements. They tell the whole story as a heap of Financial data is condensed in them. They indicate the changes in the financial condition of the business.
2) Ratio Analsysis provides data for interfirm or intra firm comparison.
3) They act as an index of the efficiency of the enterprise. As such they serve as an instrument of management control. The efficiency of the various individual units similary situated can be judged through inter firm comparison. It is an instrument for dignosis of the financial health of an enterprise.
4) The ratio analysis can be of invaluable aid to management in the discharge of its basic functions of forecasting, planning, co-ordination, communication and control. Past ratios indicate trends in cost sales profit and other relevant facts.

5) Investment decisions can at times be based on the conditions revealed by certain rations.

6) They make it possible to estimate the other figure when one figure is known.

Thus, the ratio analysis points out the financial condition of business whether it is very strong, good, questinable or poor and enables the management to take necessary steps.

Limitations of Ratio Analysis :

1) The benefits of ratio analysis depends to a great extent upon the correct interpretation. This interpretation may be based on a single ratio, but single ratio in itself is meaning - less as it does not provide complete picture of a company's financial position there - fore it is necessary to compute number of ratios's.

2) Reliability of Ratio's depends upon the reliablitiey of data.

3) While comparing ratios of two firms it must seen that both of them follow the same accounting plans or bases, other wise the comparison has no meaning.

4) Changes in prices distort the comparison over a period of years.

5) Ratio's sometimes gives misleading picture. It would, therefore be proper to study absolute figures alongwith ratios. Ratio analysis gives just a fractions of information needed for decision making. Therefore, one should not depend on information obtained from ratio's only.

6) Ratio's and percentages have little significance unless they can be compared with or matched against appropriate standards. Unless there are available measuring devices or standards, the analyst will not be able to determine whether the ratios indicate favourable or unfavourable conditions.

7) If there is "without dressing" the ratio's calculated will fail to give the correct picture and will prove to be misleading.

Types / Classfication of Ratios :

Classification of ratios is done in two ways viz 1) According to nature of items and ii) According to purpose or functions.

A) According to Nature of items:

i) Balance Sheet Ratios : The ratios exhibiting the relationship between two items or group of items in the balance sheet e.g. relation between current assets and current liabilities.

ii) Revenue Statement or profit and loss Accounts Ratios : The ratios disclosing the ralationship between two items or groups of items in the profit and loss account e.g relationship between sales and gross profit or net prfit.

iii) Composite ratio : The ratios indicating the relationship of certain items in the Balance Sheet with some figures in the revenue statements e.g net profit and capital or sales and fixed assets etc.

B) Functional Classification :

1) Liquidity Ratios : These ratios measure the liquid position of the esterprise e.g Whether the current assets are sufficient to pay of current liablities as and when they mature. Thus, these ratios indicate short term solvency.

2) Leverage Ratios : They indicate the relative use of debt and equity in financing the assets of the firm. The extent to which the practice of trading on equity can be carried on safely, can be known through these ratio's.

3) Activity Ratios : These ratios measure the efficiency in the employment of funds in the business operations. They reflect the company's level of activities in relation to its turnover.

4) Profit labilities Ratios : These ratio's measure overall performance and profit earning capacity of the business. They reveal the total effect of the business transactions on the profit position of the enterpirse.

Some Important Terms :

1) Capital employed : This term is used in different meanings by different accountant as given below.

a) Sum total of all assets : i.e fixed and current assets, excluding profit and loss A/c Balance, Preliminary expenses, brokerage, underwriting commission, discount and debenture or shares etc.

b) It can also be stated as share capital Reserves and surplus long term or short term liabilities.

c) Sum total of fixed asset only.

d) Sum total of long term fund i.e (Share capital Reserves and Surplus)
Long term loans) - (Non business assets and fictitious Assets.

2) Operating profit : It means gross profit less operating expenses. In other words, it means profit before charging interest on long term loans, such as debentures and tax, similarly, non trading incomes such as interest on Government securities, amount received or profit earned on sale of fixed assets. etc. are to be excluded or profit earned on sale of fixed assets etc. are to be excluded. Non. Trading losses and expenses such as loss on sale of fixed asset, loss on account of fire etc. are also to be excluded.

3) Current Assets : These assets include those assets which will either be used up or converted into cash within 12 months or normal operating cycle of the business. They thus include cash and Bank, Balance, Marketable securities other short term high quality investements, bills receivable, prepaid expenses, advance payament of tax, work in progress, sundry Debtors and inventories i.e stocks.

Investment in subsidiaries debtors outstanding for more than 6 months and loose tools are not to be included in current assets.

4) Current liabilities : These are the liabilities to be paid within 12 months from the date of Balance sheet. On the basis of this concept, the debentures the preference shares and the instalment of long term loans which are repayable during the 12 months and included in current liabilities. How ever, if the debentures are to be repaid during the year from the cash and Bank Balance available they are to be treated as current liabilities.

The current liablities generally include sundry creditors, bills payable, outstanding expenses, short term borrowings, proposed dividend, unclaimed dividend, provision for taxation bank over draft etc.

5) Liquid Assets or quick Assets : Current assets excluding stock and prepaid expenses.

6) Liquid liabilities : Current liabilities excluding bank over draft and accrued expenses, outstanding Expenses.

7) Equity net worth or properietor's or Shareholders funds : Preference Share capital, Equity share capital, Reserves and surplus less losses and ficitious Assets.

8) Common Equity Share : Equity Share capital Reserves and surplus + Share premium less losses.

Chart Showing the Important Ratios :

	Name of Ratio	Formula	Type of Ratio	According to
1)	Current Ratio Or 2:1 Ratio	$\dfrac{\text{Current Assets}}{\text{Current Liabilities}}$	**Nature** Balance Sheet	**Function** Liquidity : short term solvency
2)	Acid Test Ratio Or Quick Ratio or liquid ratio	$\dfrac{\text{Quick liquid Asset}}{\text{Quick liquid liabilities}}$	Balance Sheet	Liquidity short term
3)	Inventory Tunover Ratio (i. e. Stock)	$\dfrac{\text{Cost of Goods Sold}}{\text{Average Inventory}}$	Composite	Activity
4)	Gross Profit Ratio	$\dfrac{\text{Gross Profit}}{\text{Net Sales}} \times 100$	Revenue	Profitablity
5)	Net Profit Ratio	$\dfrac{\text{Net Profit(after tax)}}{\text{Net Sales}} \times 100$	Revenue	Profitability
6)	Operating Ratio	$\dfrac{\text{Cost of Goods sold + operating expenses}}{\text{Net Sales}} \times 100$	Revenue	Profitability
7)	Debt Equity Ratio	$\dfrac{\text{Debt}}{\text{Net worth}}$ or $= \dfrac{\text{Total Loan Term Debts}}{\text{Total Share Holders fund}}$		
8)	Debtors Turnover Ratio $=$	$\dfrac{\text{Net credits sales}}{\text{Debtors B/R}}$		

The Explaination of above Eight Ratio's has been given as under which is included is syllabus.

1) Current Ratio or Working capital Ratio or 2:1 Ratio :

It is a ratio of current assets to current liabilities. The ratio is calculated by dividing the current assets by the current liabilities

$$\text{Current Ratio} = \frac{\text{Current Assets}}{\text{Current Liabilities}}$$

Include :

Current Assets include sundry debtors, Bills Receivables, inventories, marketable securities, cash in hand and at Bank, Working progress prepaid expenses, short term loans and advances given to others, other short term high quality investments.

Current liabilities include sundry creditors, bills payable, bank overdraft, cash credit, outstanding expenses, proposed dividend, income tax payable etc.

Significance :

Current Ratio is also known as 'Solvency Ratio' as it indicates solvency position of the firm. It is also known as 'Working capital Ratio' as it represents working capital. This ratio indicates the solvency of the business i.e an ability to meet the current obligations as and when they fall due for payament. It is expected that the current ratio should be 2:1 means the current assets should be at least twice the current liabilities.

Precautions :

Current Ratio indicates the sources available to meet the current obligations. Hence, it is expected that ratio should be higher. A current ratio. of 2:1 is supposed to be ideal or standoard. However actual current ratio of the firm should not be compared with standard blindly High current ratio may indicate sound financial position but at the same time it may also indicate that there is an unnecessary huge investment in current asset which may affect the overal profitablity of the firm.

2) Liquid Ratio or Acid Test Ratio or Quick Ratio :

It is a tool of judging the immediate ability of the firm to make the payment of its curent obligations. Liquid Ratio is calculated by dividing quick current assets by liquid or quick liabilities.

$$\text{Liqud Ratio} = \frac{\text{Quick Assets}}{\text{Quick Liabilities}}$$

Generally a quick ratio of 1:1 is considered adequate A low ratio may be an indication of bad liquidity position.

The Quick Ratio indicaties the relations of quick assets With Quick liablties.

Include : Quick or liquid assets include all current assets except stock and prepaid expenses where as liquid liabilities include all current liablties except Bank overdraft and accured expenses. If this ratio is 1:1, it is considered that all claims will be met when they arise.

3) Inventory Turnover Ratio :

This is also Known as stock turnover ratio. The term Inventory turnover refers to the number of times in a year inventories are sold and replaced this ratio is computed as under -

i) Inventory Turnover Ratio $= \dfrac{\text{Cost of goods sold}}{\text{Average Inventory}}$

OR

ii) Inventory Turnover Ratio $= \dfrac{\text{Net Sales}}{\text{Average Inventory at selling price}}$

OR

iii) Inventory Turnover Ratio $= \dfrac{\text{Cost of Goods sold}}{\text{Closing Investory}}$

Where, cost of goods sold is not given in the example, net sales are taken and the second formula is used.

Average investory / Stock $= \dfrac{\text{Opening Stock} + \text{Closing Stock}}{2}$

(If opening stock is not available, Closing stock is to be taken as average stock.)

This ratio explains the rate of turnover of the inventory. It means, It gives the number of times, the investory is replaced during the accounting period. A High inventory turnover ratio indicates that maximum sales turnover is obtained by investing minimum possible funds in the inventory which is a sign of better Performance of the organisation. A low inventory tumover ratio indicates slow moving inventory. In other words it also inoicates that over investment in inventory and accumulation of unsalleable stock.

4) Gross Profit Ratio : This ratio is calculated as under

Gross Profit Ratio $= \dfrac{\text{Gross Profit}}{\text{Sales}} \times 100$

This ratio indicates the efficiency of the production as well as pricing. Gross profit is the differnece between net sales and cost of Goods Sold. The gross profit ratio exhibits the relationship between gross profit and sales. A high gross profit ratio means sufficient margin to cover the expenses other than cost of good sold. A higher gross profit ratio will be dssirable, because it indicates that the business organisation is either producing or purchasing the goods and commodities at lowest cost. On the contrary a low gross profit rato may indicate unfavourable purchasing as well as inability of the management to group the sales.

It is the ratio Which is most commonly employed by accountants for comparing the earnings of business for one period with those of the other or earnings of one concern with those of another in the same industry.

The reasons for increase or decrease of gross Profit ercentage may be any of the following.

The reasons for increase :

i) Increase in sale price without any change in production cost.

ii) Lower cost price of goods, Sales price renain constant.

iii) Increase in sales price and reduction in production cost.

iv) Reduction in the parchases upto certain extent.

v) Change in the method of valuation of stock resulting overvaluation of stock in trade.

vi) Goods sold but not delivered might have been included in closing stock.

The reasons for decrease -

i) Under valuation of closing stock & pilferage of stock.

ii) Increase in cost price, sales price remaining same.

iii) Reduction in sales price, cost price remaning unchanged.

iv) Entry recorded more than once of any purchases.

v) Goods Purchased but not included in closing stock.

5) Net profit Ratio :

Net profit is that proportion of net sales which remains to the owner or the shareholders costs, Chagnes and expenses including income tax, have been deducted. It is Calculated as under -

$$\text{Net Profit Ratio} = \frac{\text{Net Profit (after taxes)}}{\text{Net sales}} \times 100$$

Net Profit is that amount of net sales which belongs to the owner or shareholders, after deducting all cost and expenses, other eperating or non operating. A high net profit ratio exhibits higher profitabiliy of the business organisation.

The net profit ratio is used to measure overall probitability of the business organisation. This ratio also indicates the firms ability to face adverse, economic situations such as decrease in demand, cut throat competition etc. Higher net profit ratio indicates better profitablity and lower net profit ratio indicates poor profitability of the business organisation.

6) Operating Ratio :

$$\text{Operating Ratio} = \frac{\text{Cost of Goods sold} + \text{Operating expenses}}{\text{Net sales}} \times 100$$

Operating expense include -

i) Factory expenses like factory rent wages, factory insurance etc.

ii) Administrative expenses like rent, insurance, office staff salaries, printing & Stationery etc.

iii)   Selling and distribution expenses like salesmans salaries, advertising, travelling expenses, delivery van expanses etc.

The ratio shows the percentage of net sales that is absorbed by the cost of good sold and operating expenses. Naturally, higher the ratio the less favourable it is, because it will leave a small margin to meet interest, dividends and any other corporate needs.

The ratio is an index of the operating efficiency of the enterprise. It is advisable to study the ratio over a number of years so as to view the direction of the operating efficiency. Operating ratio establishes the relationship of the cost of Goods sold plus operating expenses on the one hand and sales on the other. As this is the cost ratio, lower the ratio better the position / profitablity and vice versa.

7) Debt Equity Ratio :

The DE Ratio is the most common measure of Studying the indebtedness of the firm. This ratio indicates the relationship between the long term funds provided by creditors and funds provided by owners / Sharholder. The dobt equity ratio is calculated by copmaring the long term debts with total shareholders funds as follows.

$$\text{Debt Equity Ratio} = \frac{\text{Debt}}{\text{Equity}} = \frac{\text{Debt}}{\text{Net worth}}$$

$$\text{OR} = \frac{\text{Total long term debts}}{\text{Total shareholders fund}}$$

Where the long term debts include -

The long Term loan, borrowings and debentures and the term share holders fund include the equity share capital the preference share capital and all accumulated reserves and undistributed profit, capital reserve (Less all accumulated losses and miscellaneous expenses not written off) Standard Ratio is 1:1

8) Debtors Turnover Ratio :

The liquidity position of the firm depends upon the quality of debtors (and B/R) to a great extent. This ratio shows the time lag between the sales and the collection from debtors. It shows the normal average period for which sundry debtors are outstanding. It shows how fast the debts are being collected.

$$\text{Debttors Turnover Ratio} = \frac{\text{Net credit sales}}{\text{Debtors} + \text{B/R}}$$

The debtors turnover indicates the number of times on the average that debtors turnover each year. Generally higher the value of debtors turnover the more efficient is the mangement of credit. It indicates shorter time span between credit sales and cash collection.

8.4 Problems :

PROBLEM NO. 1

You have been furnished with the financial information of Aditya Mills Limited as under.

Balance Sheet as on 31st December 2014

Liabilities	Rs	Assets		Rs
Equity Share Capital	10,00,000	Plant and equipment		6,40,000
(Rs. 100 each)		Land and Building		80,000
Retained Earnings	3,68,000	Cash		1,60,000
Sundry Creditors	1,04,000	Sundry Debtors	3,60,000	
Bills payable	2,00,000	Less : Allowances	40,000	3,20,000
Other Current liabilities	20,000	Stock		4,80,000
		Prepaid insurance		12,000
	16,92,000			**16,92,000**

Statement of Profit for the year ended 31st December 2014

Sales	40,00,000
Less : Cost of Goods Sold	30,80,000
Gross Profit	**9,20,000**
Less : Operating expenses	6,80,000
Net Profit	**2,40,000**
Less : Taxes @ 50%	1,20,000
Net Profit After Taxes	**1,20,000**

Sundry debtors and Stock at the beginning of the year were Rs, 3,00,000 and Rs. 4,00,000 respectively.

Determine the following ratios of Aditya Mills Ltd :

a)   Current ratio   b) Acid test Ratio

c)   Stock turnover ratio   d) Debtors turnover

e)   Gross Profit ratio   f) Net profit ratio

g)   Operating ratio

Solution :

a) **Current Ratio** $= \dfrac{\text{Current Assets}}{\text{Current Liabilities}}$

$= \dfrac{\text{Cash + Debtors + Stock + Prepaid Insurance}}{\text{Creditors + Bills Payable + Other Current liabilities}}$

$= \dfrac{\text{Rs. } 1,60,000 + \text{Rs. } 3,20,000 + \text{Rs. } 4,80,000 + \text{Rs. } 12,000}{\text{Rs. } 1,04,000 + \text{Rs. } 2,00,000 + \text{Rs. } 20,000}$

$= \dfrac{\text{Rs. } 9,72,000}{\text{Rs. } 3,24,000}$

$= \textbf{3:1}$

b) **Acid test ratio** $= \dfrac{\text{Liquid Assets}}{\text{Current Liabilties}}$

$= \dfrac{\text{Current Assets - Stock - Prepaid insurance}}{\text{Current liabilities}}$

$= \dfrac{\text{Rs.} 9,72,000 - \text{Rs.} 4,80,000 - \text{Rs. } 12,000}{\text{Rs. } 3,24,000}$

$= \dfrac{\text{Rs. } 4,80,000}{\text{Rs. } 3,24,000}$

$= \textbf{1.48 : 1}$

c) **Stock Turnover ratio** $= \dfrac{\text{Cost of goods sold}}{\text{Average stock}}$

$= \dfrac{\text{Rs. } 30,80,000}{\text{Rs. } 4,40,000}$

$= \textbf{7:1}$

d) **Debtors turnover ratio** $= \dfrac{\text{Credit Sales}}{\text{Average debtors}}$

$= \dfrac{\text{Rs. } 40,00,000}{\text{Rs. } 3,30,000}$

$= \textbf{12.12 : 1}$

e) **Gross Profit ratio** $= \dfrac{\text{Gross Profit}}{\text{Sales}} \times 100 = \dfrac{\text{Rs. } 9,20,000}{\text{Rs. } 40,00,000} \times 100 = \textbf{23\%}$

f) **Net profit ratio** $= \dfrac{\text{Net profit}}{\text{Sales}} \times 100$

$\qquad = \dfrac{\text{Rs. } 1,20,000}{\text{Rs. } 40,00,000} \times 100$

$\qquad = 3\%$

g) **Operating ratio** $= \dfrac{\text{Cost of goods sold} + \text{Operating expenses}}{\text{Sales}} \times 100$

$\qquad = \dfrac{\text{Rs. } 30,80,000 + \text{Rs. } 6,80,000}{\text{Rs. } 40,00,000} \times 100$

$\qquad = 94\%$

PROBLEM NO. 2

The following is the Balance Sheet of PVC Limited, Pune

Balance Sheet
(as at 31-2-2014)

Liabilities	Amount	Assets	Amount
Share Capital :		Fixed Assets :	
Equity Shares of		At cost 30,00,000	
Rs. 10 each	5,00,000	Less Dep. 4,50,000	25,50,000
Reserve fund	3,50,000	Stock	5,00,000
Profit and Loss Account	5,50,000	Debtors	4,00,000
Long term loans	17,50,000	Cash	1,00,000
Creditors	2,50,000	Other Current Liabilities	1,50,000
	35,50,000		**35,50,000**

Additional information :

1) Profit earned during the year was Rs. 4,00,000
2) The company has declared 25% dividend.
3) Market price of share is Rs. 560
4) Lgnore Provisions regarding taxation.

Calculate Following ratios :

a) Debt Equity Ratio
b) Current Ratio
c) Acid Test Ratio

Solution :

a)   **Debt Equity Ratio** $\quad = \dfrac{\text{External Liabilities}}{\text{Net worth}}$

$$= \dfrac{21,50,000}{14,00,000}$$

$$= \mathbf{1.536}$$

b)   **Current Ratio** $\quad = \dfrac{\text{Current Assets}}{\text{Current Liabilities}}$

$$= \dfrac{10,00,000}{4,00,000}$$

$$= \mathbf{2.5}$$

c)   **Acide Test Ratio** $\quad = \dfrac{\text{Liquid Asset}}{\text{Current Liabilities}}$

$$= \dfrac{10,00,000-5,00,000}{4,00,000} = \dfrac{5,00,000}{4,50,000}$$

$$= \mathbf{1.25}$$

PROBLEM NO. 3

X Company Ltd. has submitted the Trading and Profit and Loss A/c for the year ended 31st December, 2014 as follows.

Calculate : i) Gross Profit Ratio,   ii) Net profit and iii) Operating Ratio.

Trading profit & Loss A/c
For the year ended 31st December 2014

Particulars	Rs.	Particulars	Rs.
To Opening Stock	60,000	By Sales	3,50,000
To Purchases	1,60,000	By Closing Stock	80,000
To Wages	40,000		
To Factory Light Bill	44,000		
To Gross Profit c/d	1,26,000		
	4,30,000		**4,30,000**
To Office & Administration	45,000	By Gross Profit b/d	1,26,000
Expenses		By Profit on sale	
To Sales & Dist. Expenses	10,000	of Furniture	10,000
To Loss on Sale of Land	4,000		
To Net profit	77,000		
	1,36,000		**1,36,000**

Solution :

i) **Gross Profit Ratio** $= \dfrac{\text{Gross Profit}}{\text{Sales}} \times 100$

$\qquad\qquad = \dfrac{1,26,000}{3,50,000} \times 100 = 36\%$

ii) **Net Profit Ratio** $= \dfrac{\text{Net profit}}{\text{Sales}} \times 100$

$\qquad\qquad = \dfrac{77,000}{3,50,000} \times 100 = \mathbf{22\%}$

iii) **Operating Ratio** $= \dfrac{\text{Cost of Goods Sold + Operating Expenses}}{\text{Sales}}$

$\qquad\qquad = \dfrac{2,24,000+55,000}{3,50,000} = \mathbf{79.71\%}$

PROBLEM NO. 4

Alpha Manufacturing Co. has drawn up the following profit and loss Account for the year ended 31st March 2015

Dr.   **Cr.**

Particulars	Rs.	Particulars	Rs.
To Opening Stock	26,000	By Sales	1,60,000
To Purchases	80,000	By Closing Stock	38,000
To Wages	24,000		
To Manufacturing Expenses	16,000		
To Gross Profit c/d	52,000		
	1,98,000		**1,98,000**
To Sales & Dist. Expenses	4,000	By Gross Profit b/d	52,000
To Administrative expenses	22,800	By Compensation for	4,800
To General Expenses	1,200	acquisition of land	
To Value of Furniture lost by fire	800		
To Net Profit	28,000		
	56,800		**56,800**

You are required to find out the :

    i)   Gross Profit Ratio,   ii)   Net Profit Ratio,

   iii)   Opearating Ratio, and   iv)   Operating Profit Ratio.

Solution :

i) **Gross Profit Ratio** $= \dfrac{\text{Gross Profit}}{\text{Net Sales}} \times 100 = \left[\dfrac{52,000}{1,60,000}\right] \times 100$

$= 32.5\%$

ii) **Net Profit Ratio** $= \dfrac{\text{Net Profit}}{\text{Net Sales}} \times 100 = \dfrac{28,000}{1,60,000} \times 100$

$= 17.5\%$

iii) **Opearating Ratio** $= \dfrac{\text{Cost of Goods Sold + All Operating Expenses}}{\text{Sales}} \times 100$

$= \dfrac{1,08,000 + 28,000}{1,60,000} \times 100$

$= \dfrac{1,36,000}{1,60,000} \times 100$

$= 85\%$

iv) **Operating Profit Ratio** $= \dfrac{\text{Operating Profit}}{\text{Sales}} \times 100$

Where Operating Profit

= Net Profit + Non - Operating Expenses - Non Operating Income

= 28,000 + 800 - 4,800 = 24,000

$\therefore$ Operating Profit Ratio $= \dfrac{24,000}{1,60,000} \times 100$

$= 15\%$

PROBLEM NO. 5

X Ltd Presents you the following information. Calculate the rate of return on owner's net capital and Debt Equity Ratio

Liabilities	Rs	Assets	Rs
Share Capital	1,00,000	**Fixed Assets :**	
Fixed Liabilities :		Plant	1,80,000
6% Development Loan	60,000	Land and Building	70,000
7% Mortgage	5000	Furniture and Fixtures	20,000
Current Liabilities	1,56,000	**Current Assets :**	
Capital Reserves	8,500	Stock	20,000

Liabilities		Rs	Assets	Rs
Profit & Loss A/c :			Debtors	40,000
			Cash in hand and at	
Balance	5,800		Bank	15,000
for the year	13,200			
	19,000			
Less : Provision	1,000			
For tax	18,000			
Less : Dividend	2,500	15,500		
		3,45,000		**3,45,000**

Solution :

i) **Rate of Return on Owner's net Capital or Shareholder's Fund**

$$= \frac{\text{Net Profit after tax and interest on fixed interest bearing securities}}{\text{Shareholder's Funds}}$$

$$= \frac{13,200\text{-}1,000}{1,00,000\text{+}8,500\text{+}15,500}$$

$$= \frac{12,200}{1,24,000} \times 100$$

$$= \mathbf{9.84\%}$$

ii) **Debt Equity Ratio** $= \dfrac{\text{Long Term Debt}}{\text{Shareholder's Fund}}$

$$= \frac{65,000}{1,24,000} = \mathbf{0.52\text{:}1}$$

OR

$$= \frac{\text{Long Term Debt}}{\text{Shareholder's Fund \& Long Term Debts}}$$

$$= \frac{65,000}{1,24,000 + 65,000}$$

$$= \mathbf{0.34\text{:}1}$$

PROBLEM NO. 6

The following are the financial Statements of AB Ltd For the year 2014

Balance sheet as on 31ˢᵗ Dec 2014

Liabilities	Rs	Rs	Assets	Rs	Rs
Owners Equity :			**Fixed Assets :**		
7% Preference			Buildings	6,00,000	
Share Capital	2,00,000		Plant & Machinery	4,00,00	
Equity Share Capital	8,00,000		Furniture	2,00,000	
General Reseves	9,00,000		Patents	50,000	12,50,000
Retained Earnings	25,000	19,25,000			
Debt Equities :			**Current Assets :**		
6 % Debentures	1,00,000		Cash	2,20,000	
Loan (Long Term)	80,000		Bank	1,30,000	
8 % Bonds	20,000	2,00,000	Investments		
Current Liabilities :			(Government	1,80,000	
			Securities)		
Creditors	60,000		Sundry Debtors	1,15,000	
Bills Payable	20,000		Bills Receivables	80,000	
Bank Overdraft	20,000		Stock	3,00,000	
Outstanding Expenses	20,000		Prepaid Expenses	20,000	10,45,000
Proposed Dividend	50,000	1,70,000			
		22,95,000			**22,95,000**

Profit & Loss Alc

For the year ended 31-12-2014

Dr.   **Cr**

Particulars	Rs.
Sales	24,00,000
Less : Cost of Goods Sold	16,00,000
Gross Profit	**8,00,000**
Less : Expenses	7,00,000
Net Profit	**1,00,000**

You are required to compute the following ratios :

i) Current Ratio,	ii) Acid Test Ratio,
iii) Gross Profit Ratio	iv) Debt to Equity Ratio
v) Net Profit Ratio	vi) Operating Ratio

Solution :

i)   **Current Ratio** $= \dfrac{\text{Current Assets}}{\text{Current Liabilities}} = \dfrac{10,45,000}{1,70,000}$

$$= 6.15 : 1$$

ii)   **Acid Test Ratio** $= \dfrac{\text{Liquid Assets}}{\text{Liquid Liabilities}} = \dfrac{7,25,000}{1,50,000}$

$$= 4.83 : 1 \text{ (Approx.)}$$

iii)   **Gross Profit Ratio** $= \dfrac{\text{Gross Profit}}{\text{Sales}} \times 100 = \dfrac{8,00,000}{24,00,000}$

$$= 33.33\%$$

iv)   **Debt to Equity Ratio** $= \dfrac{\text{Total Debts}}{\text{Net Worth}} \times 100 = \dfrac{3,70,000}{19,25,000}$

$$= 19.22\%$$

v)   **Net profit Ratio** $= \dfrac{\text{Net Profit}}{\text{Net Sale}} \times 100 = \dfrac{1,00,000}{24,00,000} = 4.17\%$

vi)   **Operating Ratio** $= \dfrac{\text{Cost of Goods Sold} + \text{Operating Expenses}}{\text{Net Sales}} \times 100$

$$= \dfrac{23,00,000}{24,00,000} \times 100 = 95.83\%$$

PROBLEM NO. 7

Following are the financial statements of Sun Ltd, Mumbai for the year 2013 and 2014

Balance Sheet

As on 31-12-2013 & 31-12-2014

Liabilities	31-12-2014	31-12-2013	Assets Rs.	31-12-2014	31-12-2013
Equity Share :			**Fixed Assets :**	15,00,000	12,50,000
Capital in Rs. 10			**Current Assets :**		
Shares	10,00,000	10,00,000	Stock in Hand	4,25,000	3,50,000
General Reserve	9,00,000	9,00,000	Sundry Debtors	1,90,000	1,80,000
Profit & Loss A/c	75,000	25,000	Cash at Bank	6,10,000	5,15,000
6 % Debentures	3,00,000	2,00,000			
Sundry Creditors	3,50,000	1,20,000			
Proposed Dividend	1,00,000	50,000			
	27,25,000	22,95,000		27,25,000	22,95,000

Dr.   Profit & Loss A/c   Cr.
For the years ended 31-12-2014 & 31-12-2013

Particulars	31-12-2014	31-12-2013	Particulars	31-12-2014	31-12-2013
To Cost of Goods Sold	18,00,000	16,00,000	By Sales	30,00,000	24,00,000
To Gross Profit	12,00,000	8,00,000			
	30,00,000	24,00,000		30,00,000	24,00,000
To Overhead Expenses	10,00,000	7,00,000	By Gross Profit	12,00,000	8,00,000
To Net Profit	2,00,000	1,00,000			
	12,00,000	8,00,000		12,00,000	8,00,000

You are required to compute the following ratios and give possible reasons for changes in each case.

Solution :

i) **Current Ratio :**

$$= \frac{\text{Current Assets}}{\text{Current Liabilties}}$$

$$2013 = \frac{10,45,000}{1,70,000} = \mathbf{6.15 : 1}$$

$$2014 = \frac{12,25,000}{4,50,000} = \mathbf{2.72 : 1}$$

The Current ratio is reduced considerably in 2014 as compared to 2013. The main reason is considerable increase in current liabilties in 2014. Current assets have been increased by Rs. 1,80,000 Only, Whereas the current liabilties have been increased by Rs. 2,80,000 over the respective figures of 2013.

ii) **Gross Profit Ratio :**

$$= \frac{\text{Gross Profit}}{\text{Net Sales}} \times 100$$

$$2013 = \frac{8,00,000}{24,00,000} \times 100 = \mathbf{33.33\%}$$

$$2014 = \frac{2,00,000}{30,00,000} \times 100 = \mathbf{40\%}$$

As Compared to increase in cost of goods sold in 2009, the sales have been increased Considerably. Hence, the increase in Gross Profit Percentage in 2014 over to that 2013.

iii) Net Profit Ratio =

$$= \frac{\text{Net Profit}}{\text{Sales}} \times 100$$

$$2013 \ = \frac{1,00,000}{24,00,000} \times 100 = \textbf{4.1\%}$$

$$2014 \ = \frac{2,00,000}{30,00,000} \times 100 = \textbf{6.67\%}$$

As Compared to increase in gross profit in 2014, overhead expenses have not been increased in that proportion. Hence the Net Profit percentage is more than that in 2013.

PROBLEM NO. 8

The following are the figures extracted from the books XYZ Ltd. as at 31.12.2014

Particulars	Amount (Rs)
Net Sales	24,00,000
Less : Operating Expenses	18,00,000
Gross Profit	6,00,000
Less : Non - Operating Expenses	2,40,000
Net Profit	3,60,000

Liabilities	Rs.	Assets	Rs.
Net Worth	15,00,000	Current Assets	7,60,00
Debt	9,00,000	Inventories	8,00,000
Current Liabilities	6,00,000	Fixed Assets	14,40,000
Total Liabilities	30,00,000	Total Assets	30,00,000

Calculate :

i) Gross Profit Ratio,   ii) Net profit Ratio,

iii) Return on Assets;   iv) Inventory turnover.

Solution :

i) Gross Profit Ratio $= \dfrac{\text{Gross Profit}}{\text{Sales}}$

$$= \frac{6,00,000}{24,00,000} = \textbf{25\%}$$

ii) **Net Profit Ratio** $= \dfrac{\text{Net Profit}}{\text{Sales}}$

$= \dfrac{3,60,000}{24,00,000} = \mathbf{15\%}$

iii) **Inventory Turnover** $= \dfrac{\text{Net Sales}}{\text{Inventory}}$

$= \dfrac{24,00,000}{8,00,000} = \mathbf{3\ times}$

PROBLEM NO. 9

The Following is the Balance sheet of Z limited company on March 2014

Liabilities	Rs.	Assets	Rs.
Share Capital	2,00,000	Land & Buildings	1,40,000
Profit & Loss Account	30,000	Plant & Machinery	3,50,000
General Reserve	40,000	Stock in trade	2,00,000
12% Debentures	4,20,000	Sundry Debtors	1,00,000
Sundry Creditors	1,00,000	Bills Receivable	10,000
Bills Payable	50,000	Cash at Bank	40,000
	8,40,000		8,40,000

Calculate :

   i)   Current Ratio   ii) Quick Ratio,

   iii)   Inventory to working Capital,   iv) Debt to Equity Ratio

Solution :

i) **Current Ratio** $= \dfrac{\text{Current Assets}}{\text{Current liabilities}} = \dfrac{3,50,000}{1,50,000} = \mathbf{2.33 : 1}$

ii) **Quick Ratio** $= \dfrac{\text{Liquid Assets}}{\text{Current Liabilities}} = \dfrac{1,50,000}{1,50,000} = \mathbf{1{:}1}$

iii) **Inventory to working Capital** $= \dfrac{\text{Inventory}}{\text{Working Capital}} = \dfrac{2,00,000}{2,00,000} = \mathbf{1{:}1}$

Working Capital $=$ Current Assets - Current Liabilties

$= 3,50,000 - 1,50,000$

$= 2,00,000$

iii)   **Debt to Equity Ratio** $= \dfrac{\text{Long Term Debts}}{\text{Shareholder's Fund}} = \dfrac{4,20,000}{2,70,000} = 1.56 : 1$

OR

$= \dfrac{\text{Long Term Debts}}{\text{Shareholder's Fund} + \text{Long term Debts}} =$

$= \dfrac{4,20,000}{2,70,000 + 4,20,000}$

$= \dfrac{4,20,000}{6,90,000} = 0.61 : 1$

PROBLEM NO. 10

Following are the summarised profit and loss Account and Balance Sheet to Taj Ltd. For the year ended 31st December 2010 :

Profit and Loss Account for the year
ended on 31-12-2010

Particulars	Rs.	Particulars		Rs.
To Opening Stock	1,99,000	By Sales :		
To purchases	10,90,000	Credit	15,00,000	
To Carriage Inward	31,000	Cash	4,00,000	19,00,000
To Gross Profit C/d	8,80,000	By Closing Stock		3,00,000
	22,00,000			22,00,000
To operating Expenses	4,00,000	By Gross Profit b/d		8,80,000
To Non - operating expenses	80,000	By Non - Operating		
To Net Profit	5,20,000	income		1,20,000
	10,00,000			10,00,000

Balance sheet as on 31-12-2010

Liabilties	Rs.	Assets	Rs
Capital	4,00,000	Land & Buildings	3,00,000
(40,000 E. Shares of Rs. 10 each)		Plant & Machinery	3,60,000
Reserve	4,00,000	Stock in Trade	1,00,000
Profit and Loss	1,20,000	Debtors	90,000
Other Current Liabiltieis	1,80,000	Cash and Bank	1,20,000
Bills Payable	80,000	Bills Receivable	2,10,000
	11,80,000		**11,80,000**

Calculate :

a) Gross Profit Ratio   b) Net Profit Ratio
c) Operating Ratio   d) Stock Turnover Ratio
e) Debtors Turnover Ratio   f) Debts to Equity Ratio

(PUP oct 2011)

a)   Gross Profit Ratio

$$= \frac{\text{Gross Profit}}{\text{Sales}} \times 100$$

$$= \frac{8,80,000}{19,00,000} \times 100 = \mathbf{46.32\%}$$

b)   Net Profit Ratio

$$= \frac{\text{Net Profit}}{\text{Sales}} \times 100$$

$$= \frac{5,20,000}{19,00,000} \times 100 = \mathbf{27.37\%}$$

c)   Operating Ratio

$$= \frac{\text{Cost of Goods Sold} + \text{Operating Exps}}{\text{Sales}} \times 100$$

$$= \frac{10,20,000 + 4,00,000}{19,00,000} \times 100$$

$$= \mathbf{74.47\%}$$

d)   Stock Turnover Ratio

$$= \frac{\text{Cost of Goods Sold}}{\text{Average stock}}$$

$$= \frac{10,20,000}{2,49,500} \times 100 = \mathbf{4.09\ times}$$

e)   Debtors Turnover Ratio

$$= \frac{\text{Trade Debtors} + \text{BR}}{\text{Net Credit Sales}} \times 360$$

$$= \frac{90,000 + 2,10,000}{15,00,000} \times 360$$

$$= \mathbf{72\ days}$$

f)   Debt - Equity Ratio

Debts Equity

$$= \frac{\text{Total Liabilities}}{\text{Proprietors Fund}}$$

$$= \frac{2,60,000}{9,20,000} = \mathbf{0.28\!:\!1}$$

PROBLEM NO. 11

The following Summarised Trading and Profit and Loss A/c of Shah Ltd. For the year ended 31st March, 2011 and the Balance Sheet as on that date :

Dr.   **Trading Account**   **Cr.**

Particulars	Rs.	Particulars	Rs.
To Opening Stock	1,00,000	By Sales	8,50,000
To Purchases	5,60,000	By Closing Stock	1,50,000
To Gross Profit	3,40,000		
	10,00,000		**10,00,000**

Dr   **Profit and Loss Account**   **Cr.**

Particulars	Rs.	Particulars	Rs.
To Operating Expenses :		By Gross Profit b/d	3,40,000
Selling & Distribution	30,000	**By Non - Operating**	
Administrative Expenses	1,50,000	**Income :**	
Finance Charges	15,000	Interest	3,000
To Non operating Expenses :		Profit on sale	
Loss on sale of Assets	5,000	of Shares	7,000
To Net Profit c/d	1,50,000		
	3,50,000		**3,50,000**

Balance Sheet
as on 31-3-2011

Liabilities	Rs.	Assets	Rs.
Issued Capital		Land and Building	1,50,000
2000 Equity Shares of		Plant and Machinery	80,000
Rs. 100 each	2,00,000	Stock	1,50,000
Reserves	90,000	Debtors	70,000
Profit and Loss A/c	60,000	Bank Balance	30,000
Sundry Creditors	1,20,000		
Bank Overdraft	10,000		
	4,80,000		**4,80,000**

From the above statements you are required to calculate the following ratios :

1) Current Ratio
2) Liquid Ratio
3) Operating Ratio
4) Stock Turnover Ratio
5) Net Profit Ratio
6) Gross Profit Ratio

(PUP oct 2012)

Solution :

1) **Current Ratio**

$$= \frac{\text{C. Assets}}{\text{C. Liabilities}}$$

$$= \frac{\text{Drs + Stock + Bank}}{\text{Crs + Bo/d}}$$

$$= \frac{2,50,000}{1,30,000}$$

$$= \mathbf{1.92{:}1}$$

2) **Liquid Ratio**

$$= \frac{\text{Liquid Assets}}{\text{Liquid Liabilities}}$$

$$= \frac{\text{Dr + Bank}}{\text{S. Crs}}$$

$$= \frac{1,00,000}{1,20,000}$$

$$= \mathbf{0.83{:}1}$$

3) **Operating Ratio**

$$= \frac{\text{Cost of Goods Sold + Op. Exp}}{\text{Sales}} \times 100$$

$$= \text{Cost of Goods Sold} = \text{Sales - G.P.}$$

$$= \frac{5,10,000}{8,50,000} \times 100$$

$$= \mathbf{82.94\%}$$

4) **Stock Turnover Ratio**

$$= \frac{3,00,000}{\left(\dfrac{75,000 + 98,500}{2}\right)} = \frac{5,10,000}{1,25,000} = \textbf{4.08 Times}$$

5) **Net Profit Ratio**

$$= \frac{NP}{Sales} \times 100 = \frac{1,50,000}{8,50,000} \times 100 = \textbf{17.65\%}$$

6) **Gross Prof Ratio**

$$= \frac{GP}{Sales} \times 100 = \frac{3,40,000}{8,50,000} \times 100 = \textbf{40\%}$$

PROBLEM NO. 12

From the following Summarized Profit and Loss Account and Balance Sheet, Calculate:

a) Gross Profit Ratio
b) Net Profit Ratio
c) Current Ratio
d) Acid Test Ratio
e) Operating Ratio
f) Stock Turnover Ratio

Profit and Loss Account

For the year ended 31st March, 2014

Dr.   Cr

Particulars	Rs.	Particulars	Rs.
To Opening Stock	9,950	By Sales	85,000
To purchases	54,525	By Closing Stock	14,900
To Wages	1,425		
To Gross Profit c/d	34,000		
	99,900		99,900
To Operating Expenses:		By Gross Profit b/d	34,000
Selling and Distribution	3000	By Non Operating Income :	
ADministrative	15,000	Interest (Bank) 300	
Financial	1,500	Profit on Sale of Shares 600	900
To Non - Operating Expenses			
Loss on Sale of Plant			
and Machinery	400		
To Net Profit c/d	15,000		
	34,900		34,900

Balance Sheet as on 31-3-2014

Liabilities	Rs.	Assets	Rs.
Share Capital (200 Shares of Rs. 10 each)	20,000	Land & Building	15,000
		Plant & Machinery	8000
Reserve	9,000	Stock in Trade	14,900
Current Liabilities		Sundry Debtors	7,100
B/p	3000	Cash and Bank	3,000
S. Creditors	10,000		
P & L A/c	6000		
	48,000		**48,000**

(PUP oct 2012)

a) Gross Profit Ratio =

$$= \text{G/p Ratio} = \frac{\text{G/P}}{\text{Sales}} \times 100$$

$$= \frac{34,000}{85,000} \times 100 = \mathbf{40\%}$$

b) Net Profit Ratio =

$$\frac{\text{N/P}}{\text{Sales}} \times 100 = \frac{15,000}{85,000} \times 100 = \mathbf{17.65\%}$$

c) Current Ratio = $\dfrac{\text{Current Assets}}{\text{Current Liab}}$

$$= \frac{\text{Stock + Dr. Cash}}{\text{B/p + Creditors}} = \frac{14,000 + 7100 + 3000}{3000 + 10,000} = \frac{25,000}{13,000}$$

$$= \mathbf{1.92{:}1}$$

d) Acid Test Ratio

$$= \frac{\text{Liquid Assets}}{\text{Liquid Liab}} = \frac{10,100}{13,000} = \mathbf{0.77{:}1}$$

e) Operating Ratio

$$= \frac{\text{Cost of Goods Solds + Operating Exep}}{\text{Net Sales}} \times 100$$

$$= \text{Cost of Goods Sold} = \text{Sales - G.P}$$

$$= \frac{51,000 + 19,500}{85,000} \times 100$$

$$= 85,000 - 34,000 = \mathbf{51,000}$$

$$= \frac{70,500}{85,000} \times 100 = \mathbf{82.94\%}$$

Cost of Goods Sold = Sales - G.P.

= Sales - G. P

= 85000 - 34000

= **51,000**

f) Stock Turnover Ratio

$$= \frac{\text{Cost of Goods Sold}}{\text{Average Stock}}$$

$$= \frac{51,000}{12,425}$$

= **4.10 times**

Avarage Stock = Opening Stock + Closing Stock

$$= \frac{9950 + 14900}{2} = \frac{24850}{2}$$

= **12, 425**

PROBLEM NO. 13

The following are the finacial Statements of Sudarshan Ltd. for the year ended 31.3.2001

Liabilities	Rs	Assets	Rs
Equity Capital	4,00,000	Buildings	3,00,000
7% Preference Capital	1,00,000	Plant & Machinery	2,00,000
General Reserve	4,50,000	Furniture	1,00,000
Retained Earnings	12,500	Patents	25,000
6% Debentures	50,000	Cash	1,10,000
5% Long Term loan	40,000	Bank	65,000
8% Bonds	10,000	Investments (Marketable)	90,000
Creditors	30,000		
Bills Payable	10,000	Sundry Debrors	57,500
Bank overedrafts	10,000	Bills Receivable	40,000
Outstanding Exps.	10,000	By Stock	1,50,000
Proposed Divided	25,000	Prepaid Exps.	10,000
	11,47,500		**11,47,500**

Income Statement for the year ended 31-3-2011

Particulars	Rs.
Sales	12,00,000
Less Cost of goods sold	8,00,000
Gross Profit	4,00,000

Analysis and Interpretation of Financial Statements - II

Indirect Expenses	2,50,000
Operating Profit	1,50,000

Tax is payable @ 60%

You are required to Computer the following ratios.

1) Current Ratio
2) Acid Test Ratio
3) Gross Profit Ratio
4) Debts to Equity Ratio
5) Net Profit Ratio

Solution :

1) Current Ratio

$$= \frac{\text{Current Assets}}{\text{Current Liabilities}} = \frac{5,22,500}{85,000} = \mathbf{6.15:1}$$

2) Acid Test

$$= \frac{\text{Liquid Assets}}{\text{Liquid Liabilities}} = \frac{\text{Current Assets - Stock - Pref. Exps.}}{\text{Current Liabilties - Bank Overdraft}}$$

$$= \frac{5,22,500 - 1,50,000 - 10,000}{85,000 - 10,000}$$

$$= \frac{3,62,500}{75,000} = \mathbf{4.8}$$

3) Gross Profit Ratio

$$= \frac{\text{Gross Profit}}{\text{Sales}} \times 100 = \frac{4,00,000}{12,00,000} \times 100 = \mathbf{33.3\%}$$

4) Debts - Equity Ratio $= \dfrac{\text{Debt}}{\text{Debt + Equity}}$

i) Total Debts = 1,00,000

ii) Debt + Equity = 1,00,000 + 9,62,500

$$\text{Debt Equity ratio} = \frac{1,00,000}{10,62,500} \times 100 = \mathbf{9.4\%}$$

5) Net Profit Ratio $= \dfrac{\text{Net profit after Interest \& Tax}}{\text{Sales}} \times 100$

$$= \frac{57,680}{12,00,000} \times 100 = \mathbf{4.8\%}$$

PROBLEM NO. 14

The following is the Trading and Profit & Loss A/c of Asian Electronics Ltd. for the year ended on 31st March 2001.

Profit and Loss A/c (Year ended 31-3-2001)

Particulars		Rs.	Particulars		Rs.
To Stock		75,000	By Sales	5,50,000	
To Purchases		3,16,500	Less Return	50,000	5,00,000
To Carriage & Freight		2,000	By Stock		98,500
To Wages		5,000			
To Gross Profit		2,00,000			
		5,98,500			5,98,5000
To Administration Exps.		1,01,000	By Gross profit		2,00,000
To Finance Exps.			By Non-operating Inc.		
Interest	1,200		Interest on Security		1,500
Discount	2,400		Dividend on Shares		3,750
Bad debts	3,400	7,000	Profit on sale of shares		750
To Selling &					
Distribution Exps.		12,000			
To Non-operating Exps.					
Loss on sale of securities		350			
Provisions for legal suit		1,650			
To Net profit		84,000			
		2,06,000			**2,06,000**

Calculate : i) Expenses ratio ii) Gross Profit ratio iii) Net profit ratio iv) Operating ratio v) Operating Net profit ratio vi) Stock turnover ratio.

Solution :

1) Expenses Ratio

a) Administrative Exps. Ratio $= \dfrac{\text{Administrative Exps.}}{\text{Sales}} \times 100$

$= \dfrac{1,01,000}{5,00,000} \times 100 = \mathbf{20.2\%}$

b) Selling Distribution Exps. Ratio

$= \dfrac{\text{Selling \& Distribution Exps.}}{\text{Sales}} \times 100$

$= \dfrac{12,000}{5,00,000} \times 100 = \mathbf{2.4\%}$

c) Financial Exps. Ratio $= \dfrac{\text{Financial Exps.}}{\text{Sales}} \times 100$

$= \dfrac{7,000}{5,00,000} \times 100 = \mathbf{1.4\%}$

d) Non-operating Exps. Ratio $= \dfrac{\text{Non-Operating Exps.}}{\text{Sales}} \times 100$

$= \dfrac{2,000}{5,00,000} \times 100 = \mathbf{0.4\%}$

2) Gross Profit Ratio $= \dfrac{\text{G.P.}}{\text{Sales}} \times 100$

$= \dfrac{2,00,000}{5,00,000} \times 100 = \mathbf{40\%}$

3) Net Profit Ratio $= \dfrac{\text{Net Profit}}{\text{Sales}} \times 100$

$= \dfrac{84,000}{5,00,000} \times 100 = \mathbf{16.8\%}$

4) Net Operating Profit

$= \dfrac{\text{N.P + Non-Op. Exps. - Non - Op. Income}}{\text{Sales}} \times 100$

$= \dfrac{84,000 + 2,000 - 6,000}{5,00,000} \times 100 = \mathbf{16\%}$

5) **Operating Ratio**

$$\frac{\text{Cost of good sold} + \text{Operating Exps.}}{\text{Sales}} \times 100$$

Cost of goods sold = Sales - G. P. = 3,00,000

Operating Exps.   = 1,01,000 + 7,000 + 12,000 = 1,20,000

$$\text{Operating Ration} = \frac{3,00,000 + 1,20,000}{5,00,000} \times 100 = \textbf{84\%}$$

6) **Stock Turnover Ratio**

$$\frac{\text{Cost of Goods sold}}{\text{Average Inventory}} = 3,00,000$$

$$= \left(\frac{3,00,000}{\frac{75,000 + 98,500}{2}} \right) \text{ i.e. } \frac{3,00,000}{86,750} = \textbf{3.4 times}$$

PROBLEM NO. 15

From The following summarised Profit & Loss A/c and Balance Sheet Calculate :

1) Gross Profit Ratio   2) Net Profit Ratio
3) Current Ratio   4) Operating Ratio
5) Stock Turnover Ratio   6) Liquid Ratio

Profit & Loss A/c

For the year ended 31st March 2009

Dr.   Cr

Particulars	Rs.	Particulars	Rs
To Opening Stock	9,950	By Sales	85,000
To Purchases	54,525	By Closing Stock	14,900
To Wages	1,425		
To Gross Profit c/d	34,000		
	99,900		**99,900**
To Operating Expenses :		By Gross Profit b/d	34,000
Selling & Distribution	3000	By Non Operating Income	
Administrative	15,000		
Financial	1500	Interest (Bank) 300	
To Non - Operating Expenses :		Profit On Sale of	
Loss On Sale of plant M/C	400	Shares 600	900
To Net Profit c/d	15,000		
	34,900		**34,900**

Balance Sheet as on 31 st March 2014

Liabilities	Rs.	Assets	Rs
Share Capital		Land & Building	15,000
(2000 Shares or Rs. 10)	20,000	Plant & Machinery	8,000
Reserves	9,000	Stock in Trade	14,900
Current Liabilities		Sundry Debtors	7,100
Bills Payable	3,000	Cash & Bank	3,000
Sundry Creditors	10,000		
Profit & Loss A/c	6,000		
	48,000		**48,000**

(PUP oct 2009)

Solution :

A) i) Current Ratio $= \dfrac{\text{Current Assets}}{\text{Current Liabilities}}$

$$= \dfrac{\text{Stock + Drs. + Cash}}{\text{B/P + Creditors}}$$

$$= \dfrac{14,900 + 7,100 + 3,000}{3,000 + 10,000} = \dfrac{25,000}{13,000} = \textbf{1.92:1}$$

ii) Operating Ratio $= \dfrac{\text{Cost of Goods Sold + Operating Expenses}}{\text{Net Sales}} \times 100$

$$= \dfrac{51,000 + 19,500}{85,000} \times 100$$

$$= \dfrac{70,500}{85,000} \times 100 = \textbf{82.94\%}$$

Cost of Goods Sold $=$ Sales - G.P

$$= 85,000 - 34,000$$

$$= 51,000$$

iii) Stock Turnover Ratio $= \dfrac{\text{Cost of Goods Sold}}{\text{Average Stock}}$

$$= \dfrac{51,000}{12,425}$$

$$= \textbf{4.09 Times}$$

$$\text{Average Stock} = \frac{\text{Opening Stock} + \text{closing Stock}}{2}$$

$$= \frac{9,950 + 14,900}{2} = \frac{24,850}{2} = \mathbf{12,425}$$

v) **GP Ratio** $= \dfrac{\text{GP}}{\text{Sales}} \times 100$

$$= \frac{34,000}{85,000} \times 100 = \mathbf{40\%}$$

vi) **NP Ratio** $= \dfrac{\text{NP}}{\text{Sales}} \times 100$

$$= \frac{15000}{85000} \times 100 = \mathbf{17.64\%}$$

PROBLEM NO. 16

From the given profit & loss Account and Balance Sheet of a Company, Calculate the following ratios :

1) Current Ratio
2) Operating Ratio
3) Stock Turnover Ratio
4) Liquidity ratio
5) Net Profit Ratio

Profit & Loss Account
for the year ended on 31st March 2009

Particulars	Rs.	Particulars	Rs
To Opening Stock	10,00,000	By Sales	90,00,000
To Purchases	60,00,000	By Closing Stock	12,00,000
To Carriage Inwards	2,00,000		
To Gross Profit	30,00,000		
	1,02,00,000		1,02,00,000
To Administrative Exps.	14,00,000	By G.P. b/d	30,00,000
To Selling and Distribution exps.	2,50,000	By Sundry Income	1,00,000
To Non - Operating Exps.	50,000		
To Net Profit	14,00,000		
	31,00,000		31,00,000

Balance Sheet
as on 31st March 2009

Liabilities	Rs.	Assets	Rs.
Capital	20,00,000	Land & Building	10,00,000
Reserve & Surplus	17,00,000	Plant & Machinery	12,00,000
Sundry Creditors	10,00,000	Stock	12,00,000
Provision for Tax	2,00,000	Debtors	12,00,000
Bills Payable	3,00,000	Cash at Bank	6,00,000
	52,00,000		**52,00,000**

2) Operating Ratio

$$= \frac{\text{Cost of Goods Sold} + \text{Operating Exps}}{\text{Net Sales}} \times 100$$

$$= \frac{60,00,000 + 16,50,000}{90,00,000} \times 100$$

$$= \textbf{85\%}$$

3) Stock Turnover Ratio

$$= \frac{\text{Cost Of Goods Sold}}{\text{Average Inventory}} = \frac{60,00,000}{11,00,000}$$

$$= \textbf{5.45 times (Approx)}$$

4) Liquidity Ratio

$$= \frac{\text{Liquid Assets}}{\text{Liquid Liabilities}} = \frac{18,00,000}{15,00,000}$$

$$= \textbf{1.2:1}$$

5) Net Profit Ratio

$$= \frac{\text{Net Profit}}{\text{Sales}} \times 100 = \frac{14,00,000}{90,00,000} \times 100$$

$$= \textbf{15.56\% (Approx)}$$

PROBLEM NO. 17

The Following are the summarised Trading and Profit & Loss Accounts for the year ended 31-3-2010 and Balance Sheets as on 31-3-2010 of Ajay Ltd and Vijay Ltd.

Trading and Profit & Loss Account
(For the year ended 31-3-2010)

Particulars	Ajay Ltd (Rs.)	Vijay Ltd (Rs.)	Particulars	Ajay Ltd (Rs.)	Vijay Ltd (Rs.)
To Opening Stock	4,80,000	80,000	By Sales	36,00,000	36,00,000
To Purchases	33,19,000	33,40,000	By Closing		
To Gross Profit	3,21,000	3,00,000	Stock	5,20,000	1,20,000
	41,20,000	**37,20,000**		**41,20,000**	**37,20,000**
To Operating Expenses : Office			By Gross Profit	3,21,000	3,00,000
& Administration	1,00,000	50,000			
Selling And Distribution	62,000	26,000			
To Net Profit	1,59,000	2,24,000			
	3,21,000	**3,00,000**		**3,21,000**	**3,00,000**

Balance Sheets
(as on 31-3-2010)

Liabilities	Ajay Ltd (Rs)	Vijay Ltd (Rs)	Assets	Ajay Ltd (Rs)	Vijay Ltd (Rs)
Share Capital	10,00,000	12,00,000	Fixed Assets	12,80,000	10,75,000
Reserves	6,00,000	4,00,000	Stock	5,20,000	5,25,000
Profit & Loss A/c	1,00,000	80,000	Debtors	4,00,000	3,00,000
Creditors	5,50,000	3,20,000	Cash	30,000	30,000
Bank Overdraft	2,00,000	60,000	Bank	2,20,000	1,30,000
	24,50,000	**20,60,000**		**24,50,000**	**20,60,000**

You are required to compute the following ratios of the above companies.

i) Current Ratio

ii) Liquid Ratio

iii) Gross Profit Ratio

iv) Stock Turnover Ratio

(PUP April 2010)

Solution :

	Ratio	Aajy Ltd	Vijay Ltd
i)	Current Ratio $= \dfrac{\text{Current Assets}}{\text{Current Liabilities}}$	$= \dfrac{11{,}70{,}000}{7{,}50{,}000}$ $= 1.56 : 1$	$= \dfrac{9{,}85{,}000}{3{,}80{,}000}$ $= 2.59 : 1$
ii)	Liquid Ratio $= \dfrac{\text{Liquid Assets}}{\text{Liquid Liabilities}}$	$= \dfrac{6{,}50{,}000}{5{,}50{,}000}$ $= 1.18 : 1$	$= \dfrac{4{,}60{,}000}{3{,}20{,}000}$ $1.43 : 1$
iii)	Gross Profit Ratio $= \dfrac{\text{Gross Profit}}{\text{Sales}} \times 100$	$= \dfrac{3{,}21{,}000}{36{,}00{,}000} \times 100$ $= 8.91\%$	$= \dfrac{3{,}00{,}000}{36{,}00{,}000} \times 100$ $= 8.33\%$
iv)	Stock Turnover Ratio $= \dfrac{\text{Cost of Goods Sold}}{\text{Average Stock}}$	$= \dfrac{32{,}79{,}000}{5{,}00{,}000}$ $= 6.55 \text{ times}$	$= \dfrac{33{,}00{,}000}{1{,}00{,}000}$ $= 33 \text{ times}$

<u>REFERENCES</u>

1. M.C. Shukla & S.P. Grewal - Advanced Accounts (S.Chand & Co. Ltd.)

2. S.P. Jain & K.N. Narang - Advanced Accountancy (Kalyani Publishers)

3. R.L.Gupta & M. Radhaswamy - Advanced Accountancy (Sultan Chand & Sons)

4. Paul Sr. - Advanced Accounts

5. Prof. Suresh Bhirud, Prof. Bhaskar Naphade - Advanced Accountanting (Diamond Publications.)

6. Institute of Chartered Accountants of India - Accounting Standards

7. website - www.icwai.org.

* 9 7 8 8 1 8 4 8 3 6 2 0 2 *